Elmer Left.

Elmer Left.

Kate Leibfried

ISBN-13: 978 - 1475277968

Cover Design by Jacob Riggle

My first novel is lovingly dedicated to my brother, Joshua,
who was the first one to find out what I was up to.
-Sister

Chapter 1

At the age of seventy-eight, Elmer Heartland packed up his things, kissed his sleeping wife on the forehead, and left. For good.

With the soft click of the door and the crunch of gravel under his feet, Elmer headed west under a moonless night sky. He walked quietly, stepping softly down the driveway with a small black leather duffel bag clutched tightly in one hand and a cane in the other.

Elmer sneered at the cane. *I despise you.* The cane stared blankly back.

Elmer grunted and kept his head bent, his eyes focused on the ground in front of him, as he and his cane turned right and plowed determinedly through four blocks of still night air. By the time Elmer arrived at the faded wooden bench on the corner, he was out of breath and quaking. He paused, steadied himself, and glanced at his wristwatch. He was early, but only by a little bit.

Exactly as I planned.

Elmer grasped his cane as he lowered his hips onto the wooden seat. Bones and bench creaked in cadence as he squirmed and shifted, attempting to make himself comfortable. He quickly gave up. Elmer leaned back, sighed, and let his eyes drift to the stars overhead. They were bright tonight—bright and showy, like the tulips Elmer's wife planted every spring. As his eyes roved across the Big Dipper and Cassiopeia and Pleiades, Elmer wondered if people planted tulips in the place he was going. He hoped not. He never much cared for their too-sleek petals, their bold heads. They drowned out the quieter, less intrusive flowers in the garden patch. They spoke loudly without having much to say. Yes, he could do without tulips.

Elmer jumped slightly as twin lights leapt onto his face. He looked down the road. The white synthetic eyes of a taxi stared into his bright green ones. He squinted and crinkled his nose, but beneath his outward annoyance, his heart was pounding wildly in his chest. This was it.

The taxi rolled to a stop in front of the bench. Elmer waited for the young, dark-skinned man to jump out and help him up. He did. Elmer groaned as he straightened his rusty knees. He waited for the man to assist him with his bag. The man did. Elmer waited for the small-framed man to skitter around him, open the door, and help him inside the taxi. The man did. Elmer smiled to himself. *Three for three. Good man.*

As soon as Elmer was seated stiffly in the back seat, the taxi driver took off heading west, away from Here. They drove for twenty minutes in silence. Just the way Elmer liked it. He stared out the window into the dim landscape. He could barely make out the flat hay fields, stiff churches, and old wooden barns, but he knew they were there. He knew what he was leaving and he was not sad. He might have even been happy, but happiness was not a familiar emotion to Elmer, so he couldn't be sure.

He stared at the back of the driver's beige cotton seat and tried to remember the last time he was truly happy or, more importantly, the last time he was truly free. He couldn't recall. It must have been long ago—when he was a boy, probably. Since then, everything became couched in practicalities and there was no room for silly emotions like happiness. Elmer lived in a premeditated, scheduled, efficient world. Everything down to the daily six o'clock dinner hour was calculated. The cogs turned smoothly. The machine hummed uneventfully along.

No one appreciated the effort that went into making the machine hum and the cogs turn. Not one person in Elmer's life—not his children, not his wife, not his "friends" or co-workers—noticed the painstaking effort that went into the flawless machine that Elmer had engineered for the sake of everyone else's well-being. His invisible hand oiled and mended and polished and prodded the machine so that it purred softly and serenely.

Then, at age seventy-eight, Elmer left.

POP-BANG-WHIR-SCREECH-MOAN-CLICK-CLACK-BUZZ-GROAN. Stop.

After decades of mechanized perfection, Elmer mused at the chaos he created by leaving.

Then, with a jolt, the taxi stopped and Elmer snapped to attention. They arrived at the train station.

Chapter 2

Irene didn't know it, but a storm had been brewing inside Elmer's brain for years. It rattled his thoughts and swirled around his emotions. It beat-beat-beat against the walls of his skull. For over six decades, the storm raged and Irene never knew, never suspected its presence. Elmer maintained his composure, his absolute calm, and appeared to be as tranquil and content as an old dairy cow sent out to pasture.

"Good ol' Elmer, you're the only one who's ever on time for these damn meetings. The first one here as usual, Spud." Elmer despised his nickname, but nodded stiffly and politely in the direction of the voice that uttered it. Arnold Johnson spoke in a low gurgle—a sound that always made Elmer gag slightly, a sound reminiscent of a huge wad of phlegm in the back of one's throat.

Arnold continued. "Spud, we've got a pert' good guest speaker tonight. Jim's cousin from up north is coming down to share some fly fishing secrets and he's even volunteered to give out a guided fishing tour for this fall's raffle."

Twice in one minute. I hate that goddamn nickname. "Well, by gawd, that's great Arnie. That'd be a good one to win, for sure."

"That's for damn sure. Now don't go riggin' the box like last year when you won three times in a row! Ya lucky bastard."

"It was your wife that was drawing the names, Arnie! Guess you'd better talk to her."

"Ha! Looks like I'd better ask her if she's sweet on ol' Spud. I knew she always liked a good baked potato, but I can't imagine why she'd like an ol' turnip like you!" Arnold added a highly exaggerated wink. Elmer decided to respond with a silly grin.

Petty small talk—Elmer had mastered it. He knew exactly when to insert a slightly off-color joke. He knew exactly when to guffaw and when to nod gravely. He knew how to hold his arms and tilt his head to show he was listening intently. He knew precisely when to insert a "damn" or a "hell" and when to refrain from swearing all together. He even learned how to laugh along when his nickname was the butt of a joke.

That goddamn nickname.

Nicknames were forever around Here. Once you had one, you couldn't shake it. "Spud" followed Elmer clear off his father's potato farm, into the schoolyard, onto the high school football field, and eventually across town to his little yellow split-level house. Today, it followed him to his monthly Lions Club meeting.

The Lions Club was part of the calculation. Elmer was an active (but not too active) member of the club and had served as treasurer for fifteen years. This gear neatly clicked into place in Elmer's machine and Elmer applauded himself for its normalcy. It fit in perfectly amidst the wife, two kids, lower-management blue-collar job, family picnics, and weekly salvation at St. Anthony's.

Elmer was a study in ordinary. He felt like a fucking fraud.

"Arnie, you're too much!" he chuckled.

"You know I'm just joshing you. Ol' Spud has never cheated in his life, let alone for the Lions Club raffle. A more honest man there never was!"

Elmer nodded stiffly.

* * *

At age seventy-eight, the storm raged now, but the maelstrom hadn't always been so fierce. In the early years, after he and Irene were tossed together in marriage, it started out as a whisper—a tickle of wind that skated across the water and licked his ears. With each passing year, it became more violent, more demanding of his attention. Larger, fiercer, faster it grew. It became harder to contain, always whirring, spinning, beating against his skull. Elmer tried to distract himself from his internal monsoon. He worked long hours; he played golf; he attended church raffles and bingo nights and suppers; he avoided driving past his father's potato farm; he avoided visiting the river where he and Daisy shared their first kiss.

Despite his best efforts, the pressure kept building, the storm kept growing. It fed off Elmer's discontent and restlessness. It refused to be ignored. The beast grew so violent in his mid-seventies that Elmer was certain one day his head would explode and a tornado would rip out of his skull.

And Irene Heartland was none the wiser.

Irene had been married to Elmer for sixty-one years and she had never noticed the occasional flashes in his eyes or the sudden jerks of his head that marked the presence of his storm.

Oh, no. During those sixty-one years, Irene was busy simply being Irene.

* * *

"Chat chat chitter chat," said Irene on the night before Elmer's departure. "And chatter chat chat," she added. "Elmer? Elmer! Are you listening?"

"Huh? Yes. I mean, I didn't catch the last part."

"I said, don't you agree this is a much better neighborhood than the one we used to live in?"

Irene had asked the same question dozens of times. They had moved nearly three decades ago, but Irene still considered it their "new home" and loved comparing it with their old one. Now, Irene was scooping a pale spoonful of green bean casserole onto Elmer's plate and chattering about the *new* neighborhood (far superior to the old one—just think of how ill-behaved the *other* children were compared to these).

Irene's casserole stared mournfully at Elmer from his brown and orange-flowered plate. The plate was part of a kitchen set the Heartlands bought when they moved into their new home. Irene was proud of her dishes. Not one plate from the set had been broken.

"The only downside, really," Irene continued, "is that now I'm clear across town from Katherine and she always insists that we hold Book Club at *her* house, but I suppose that's a small cross to bear when you think about it. And really, Katherine does nothing but complain about the neighbor kids peeing on her rose bushes and throwing rocks at Suzie when she's out of the kennel and the Williams *never* mow their lawn until a complaint has been filed and, honestly, I don't even want to *think* about what is lingering beneath all that grass, I mean they have *seven* animals and they have to relieve themselves somewhere! And I tell you Elmer, I'm just thankful we live next to good, clean Christians in *this* neighborhood."

Elmer stared at the pastel green curtains in the kitchen. He had always hated those curtains.

* * *

Now, Elmer stared at a set of shabby red and white striped curtains framing the train station ticket booth. The curtains were probably nice at one time, but now they were coated in a dingy film and the red stripes had faded to dusty pink. Elmer glanced at his watch. 3:25 a.m. He would catch the 4:00 a.m. train bound for There. Elmer had no compelling reason for going to There, except it wasn't Here. It also happened that the train bound for There left at 4:00 a.m.—a conveniently late and unobtrusive hour. Besides that, his destination was far away and unlikely—unlikely because it wasn't Here or within a fifty-mile radius of Here. It was safe to say that no one would dream of looking for him in There. He had no family, friends, or acquaintances outside of Here, so There was just as good a destination as any.

Elmer stepped up to the counter, bought his one-way ticket, and paid in cash. From the first month he worked at Gorsheim Dairy, he began squirreling away money in a rusty tackle box in his garage. The notion struck him as romantic: hiding cash under lures and bobbers he used as a child so that he might have a great adventure some day. Although, he had expected the adventure to come sooner.

The cashier barely looked at Elmer as she slid him his ticket and change. "Thanks," she murmured. "You're welcome," he said. She went back to reading her magazine, absentmindedly twisting a brunette strand of hair around her index finger as she read. Elmer smiled. He knew she wouldn't remember him. Just a typical old person's face that blended into the elderly herds she saw every day. Old people were everywhere. In the supermarket, on the bus, in the parks, at the clinic, in church. Glasses. Wrinkles. Hearing aids. Walkers. White hair sprouting thinly from scalps, ears, noses, chins. They complained and haggled for deals and bitched about their arthritis and played bingo. They took up space.

Elmer glanced at the cashier once more. Her lips moved slightly as she read her magazine page. Her finger still twisted the strand of hair. She wouldn't remember Elmer. She wouldn't give his sparse, neatly-combed hair, his cane, the pouches under his eyes a second thought. She wouldn't wonder if he was discontent or lonely or confused about his place in the world. She wouldn't wonder if he regretted his past. All she would do that night was play with her hair, sell a few tickets, and fret about her date the next evening. She wouldn't wonder if her elderly customer also fretted about dates at one time.

Elmer neatly folded his ticket, put it inside his worn leather wallet, and slowly walked to a row of stiff, blue plastic chairs. He lowered himself onto one of the seats and sighed deeply. He could still turn back. He could still call a cab and return home. He could crawl into bed next to Irene and wake up the next morning and live for another day and then fall asleep and then wake up again and again and again and again and again. He could. But he wouldn't. His yearning for a second chance was too strong.

Elmer set his cane across his lap, adjusted his sneakers, tugged at his sleeves. He removed his glasses, breathed on the lenses, polished them on the sleeve of his sweater, and slid them back on his face. He wished the train would hurry up and arrive. Didn't it realize how important this morning was? Didn't it care? Elmer looked up at the enormous wall clock overhead. He watched the second-hand move—Tick—an inch at a time—Tick—it was long and red—Tick—he could faintly hear the tick-tocking although his hearing wasn't what it used to be—Tick—he had to look away. Looking was torture.

Elmer fiddled with his cane, polished his glasses a second time, and took turns watching the two families that accompanied him in the station. He didn't quite approve of either family. One was brown-skinned and speaking a language he did not understand; the other was Amish. They were different; they didn't fit in with the nice, normal people of Here. Elmer sneered at the families, but it was a half-hearted sneer. In his gut he knew that he despised the normalcy of Here just as much as these strange families, but his was a quiet rebellion, an internal rebellion. Elmer glanced first at one family, then at the other. He kept the half-sneer on his face. It was hard to lose.

Elmer's thoughts were interrupted by the faint tinny whistle of a train. He stiffened and grasped the head of his cane. His hand was quivering, but his back felt strong, his knees supple. He bent down and lifted his duffel bag without noticing the arthritis in his wrist. The whistle grew louder; he could hear the mammoth engine churning. Elmer stood. Lightness—exquisite, delicate lightness—captured his body and washed through his limbs. He floated towards the tracks.

The next few minutes smeared themselves across Elmer's memory in a surreal blur. He tip-toed to the waiting train, watched as the passenger doors slid open, and shielded his eyes as bright light flooded from the waiting cabin. Elmer approached, wide-eyed, vaguely wondering if he was sleep-walking towards the doors. He gingerly placed one foot at a time on the rusty metal steps and climbed aboard, barely noticing the burly ticket-taker as he passed through the doors. The ticket-taker stretched out his arm, plucked the ticket from Elmer's shaking hand, and hardly glanced at it as he muttered a "welcome aboard" through his shaggy beard. Elmer nodded and scanned his eyes over the interior of the train, hardly breathing for fear he might wake up from this wonderful dream.

The guts of the passenger car were warm and welcoming. Carpeting lined the floor and ran halfway up the walls, coating the interior with its purply-maroon shag. Soft lighting lazily illuminated the rows of bench seats and tiny tables that accompanied each pair of seats. As Elmer stepped into the warmth of the cabin, a wave of joy pumped through his heart. Liquid, molten joy. Elmer clutched his chest, shocked by the warm jolt seizing his heart. He hadn't known this particular emotion for a very, very long time—since the potato farm, probably. Since the days his feet turned hard and calloused from constantly running around barefoot. Slowly, Elmer released his chest and, marveling at the sensation that gripped his entire body, stretched his lips into a wide smile.

Freedom.

Elmer sat down in one of the many vacant booths, unfolded the waiting blanket, and spread it primly across his lap. "All aboard for There!" the conductor shouted. It was an unnecessary shout. He knew everyone was onboard. With a slight jerk, the train eased out of the station. Elmer glanced at his watch. 4:06 a.m. He was on his way. Gears churned. Engine roared. The train steadily gained speed and Elmer imagined the ground passing under his feet. He was leaving his past. Churches and barns and schools and fields fell behind him, one by one, like so many dominoes.

Elmer closed his eyes. The jolt of joy had passed, rolling out of his body like a wave from a stormy sea. Except, no water lapped up to fill the void. The old man felt empty, hollow, like a corn husk that had just been separated from a heavy, rotten ear of corn. He felt paper-thin and naked, but vaguely happy that he had somehow shucked away the rottenness. With this vacant feeling came a profound quiet. A hush. Elmer imagined if he listened closely enough, he could hear his organs working—his bowels churning, his heart pumping, his lungs inflating. He didn't know what to make of this feeling. There was something eerie about the new hollowness, but it was much better than the heavy, pounding squall that used to rage inside him. Finally, the storm had subsided.

Elmer wiped away the fog on the window and gazed at his reflection. He wondered what would fill the calm after the storm.

Chapter 3

4:45 a.m. Irene Heartland rolls over and finds Elmer's side of the bed vacant and cold. He's probably outside walking the dog. Nothing out of the ordinary.

Sleep, Irene. Sleep.

* * *

Sleep, Elmer. Sleep.

Elmer can't sleep. He is a child on Christmas Eve. He is a young groom before his wedding day. He is eight years old and sweating as he waits for the priest to call him into the confessional booth. Everyone else on the train is zombified, lulled to sleep or into a quiet stupor by the chug-chug-chugging of the train and the constant churn of gears.

The bench seats face each other—perfect for a perfect family of four.

Dark. That is what the outside world is doing. It is doing darkness very well. A few lights flick by as the train passes lamp posts near a small town. Then back to darkness.

* * *

Elmer mused to himself in the darkness. Many things could be happening out there in the black. People could be making love, raccoons could be rummaging through trash cans, gigantic barred owls could be silently stalking prey from the tree tops, murderers could be wiping bloody knives against their thighs as they prepared to skip town. Maybe a young woman was giving birth. Maybe an old person was dying. Maybe a young person was dying. Maybe an old musician was giving birth to a song.

Sleep. That's what most people on the train were doing. That's what most people off the train were also doing.

The youngest child in the foreign family was sleeping in her mother's arms while the other two children were sprawled out on their own bench seats. The little boy had passed out with headphones clinging to his ears, music blaring. The girl, clearly the oldest of the bunch, was curled up on her side in the fetal position, a delicate string of drool trailing down her chin.

Elmer looked at her—vulnerable, peaceful in her embryonic pose—and felt small and bare. He looked away.

A college-aged boy sat with a mountaineering backpack next to his seat. His sandals looked well-worn and well-loved. Elmer wondered where he had traveled in his short life. Many more places than he had ever been, he was sure. Was he going home? Was he going on another adventure? Was he reuniting with his friend or lover or family?

Elmer glanced down at his thin, wrinkled hands. *I am late.*

Two seats down, the Amish parents were asleep. Their children were quietly playing Uno.

One day, that young boy will have a beard and a wife and children of his own. And he will remember playing cards with his sister on the train.

Elmer looked at his hands again and turned his arthritic wrists in a slow, painful circle. *I'm so very late, but at least I'm here. I'm here.*

* * *

Irene was Here. She was still Here.

She stretched and sat up. Things were amiss. Awry. Askew. Abnormal. She sensed it.

Irene stumbled into her slippers and padded softly to the kitchen. She opened the refrigerator, took out a pitcher of orange juice, and poured herself a glass.

Why was she feeling so strange? The pit of her stomach was balled into a tight knot and her head was pounding. She raised the glass of orange juice to her lips and suddenly spotted the note out of the corner of her eye. Irene froze. She picked up the note as the glass of orange juice fell, crashing to the floor.

> Irene,
>
> Don't worry about me.
>
> I have gone to a better place.
>
> -Elmer

It was the first glass in the set to break.

Chapter 4

In the distance, There waited. Its skyscrapers stretched lazily upwards towards a dull, grey sky. Light rain pitter-pattered on crumbling sidewalks and stray cats and the heads of bicyclists. It was mid-day and the cafés were bustling and the roads were groaning under the weight of crawling traffic. The pungent fragrance of coffee and cigarette smoke filled the cafés. The toxic fragrance of exhaust filled the roads.

Elmer was wide awake and wide-eyed.

And There still waited. It didn't bother to change its daily routine. The cafés still bustled. The roads still creaked. The bums slept in parks, their lives neatly packed into nearby shopping carts. There was nothing for them to do during the day, so they slept and drank and casually asked passersby for spare change. Some hookers were cooking breakfast together. They were just getting up, still tired and bleary-eyed from work. There was nothing for them to do during the day, so they lounged and sipped coffee and did the daily crossword. They savored afternoon—a time when they could wear sweatpants and no makeup. Night always came too soon and they would pack themselves into tiny lingerie and grudgingly smear their eyes with eyeliner, their cheeks with rouge.

The bums sleeping and the hookers cooking breakfast were part of the daily goings-on of There, but for Elmer, these activities were couched in an entirely different world. These were things that happened occasionally on his television set. In Elmer's world, the parks were filled with children and Labrador Retrievers and the kitchens were filled with housewives and egg beaters. Needless to say, he had never seen a hooker do the daily crossword.

Elmer's train chugged at a steady, methodical clip towards There. In half an hour, the city would receive its newcomer with an indifferent shrug and the daily routine would plod on, like the consistent up-down, up-down of the pistons that ran the train. In a half an hour, Elmer would step shakily onto the platform of the train station and gaze at the skyscrapers that filled the station's windows. He would wonder how such huge structures could look bored and monstrous at the same time.

But that was in half an hour.

For now, Elmer was still on the train. He was still on the train and his brain was still racing, trying desperately to fill the cavernous space in his head that the storm had left in its wake. The thoughts spun and whirred. Elmer's mind jumped from Here to There to Daisy to the Lions Club to his Papa to his children to the train itself and briefly to Irene. He didn't dare to pause for more than a few seconds to focus on Irene. These thoughts only evoked confusion and guilt. He much preferred thinking about There.

How does it smell? What do the people look like? How do they talk? Where will I eat? What can a seventy-eight year old possibly do there? I wonder if there is a Lions Club. (But you hated that club). *It was something to do, at least.*

In the train, the littlest child was crying. Her brother had taken her fair-skinned dolly and refused to give it back. "Alfredo! Dámelo!" said the mother. "Alfredo! Comportate!" said the father. Alfredo crossed his arms, stuck out his lower lip, and glared out the window.

The young backpacker was also looking—but not glaring—out the window. His eyes were wide and bright, his lips curled up in a small, content grin, and his dimples showed for the first time since he'd stepped onto the train. He sat watching the river wend its way through the mountains, always staying to the left of the train, like a well-trained dog heeling by his master's side. The mountains reflected in the glass and in his wet, blue eyes. He was going home.

Elmer looked away from the backpacker. He was slightly embarrassed to witness the bliss that consumed the young man. He tried to remember the last time he had felt that way in his stagnant, meticulously-planned life.

Elmer's father, the potato farmer, ran on a budget and ran on a schedule. He had come to this country in search of a better life and he did not intend to squander his opportunity. He ran a militant operation, comprised of more sticks than carrots. Elmer was careful to heed his every command or be punished with the leather strap and endless, painful lectures. Papa (as Elmer called his father) was not a physically harsh man—he spent little time with the leather strap compared to most fathers in Here at the time—but he did know how to make a person feel guilty. It wasn't the strap, but his father's words that stung little Elmer and left welts on his conscience.

Words. They broke things worse than bones. Caused more damage than sticks and stones. The words spun sharply from Papa's mouth and seared the tender flesh of his son's heart. They were iron pellets raining down. They were coated in shards of guilt. They branded themselves in Papa's son's memory—the *good for nothing*s mixed with the *lazy*s and the *imbecile*s.

Papa would remind his son over and over again how he arrived in this country with nothing but the clothes on his back and seven dollars (or twelve or three or five) in his pocket. He would recount the details of his work in The City meatpacking district for two (or three or seven or four) long years, sweating and fly-ridden in the summers and hypothermic in the winters, before he was able to save up enough money to buy a few acres in the country for himself and his young bride. The first crop of potatoes failed, but they clung on like ticks to a stray dog and somehow made it through winter. They had been through thick and thin, Papa would say, and they had done it all through hard work, dedication, and a little help from our Lord Jesus. And now, *now some good for nothing child has the tenacity, the nerve, to go fishing in the creek when he is supposed to be milking the cows! Does he think that they'll stand there and milk themselves? Does he think he's so much better than the rest of us that he doesn't have to use his two hands and his pair of legs to put in an honest day's work? Huh? Answer me boy! Do you think you're doing us a blessed bit of good by lollygagging around, your head in the goddamn clouds? Do you? Do you think food magically appears on the table? Your mother and I work hard, day-in, day-out to keep a roof over your head and food in your belly and do we ask for much? Do we? Answer me boy!*

The boy answered and continued answering until his seventy-eighth year. The boy became a model of industry and efficiency and diligence. He was afraid of the lectures and iron-pellet words and so he avoided them. He avoided them through careful calculations and painstaking effort.

On the train, Elmer shook his head and blinked. The specter of Papa had followed him his entire life. Perhaps There would help him exorcise the spirit.

There. The half hour was nearly up. How many half-hours Elmer had spent on the train, he did not know. Perhaps it had been days, perhaps only a few hours. The train had been an odd kind of purgatory where time mattered very little. The old man sat rigidly in anticipation, just as he had done for the entire course of the trip. He looked around him. The backpacker still stared. The children clamored. The tired parents gathered their belongings. Even the train seemed to plunge forward with renewed purpose and willpower. They chug-a-chugged on, minute by minute, tasting the electric excitement that filled the air. And then the train rounded a bend and there, stretching grey and angular and proud across the horizon, was There.

Elmer squealed.

One of the Amish children turned around and giggled. Elmer didn't care. He locked eyes with the city and didn't let his gaze falter. He was secretly afraid that the oasis in the distance would waver and disappear at any moment. But the city did not disappear and the train barreled onward and soon, instead of mountains and fields and rivers, Elmer saw roads and buildings and Volvos. And then the train was slowing down. And then it was stopping. The gears ground, the steam whistled, and the brakes whined in protest. With a final lurch, the train gave a shudder and became eerily still and docile on the tracks, purring like a kitten.

Elmer pressed his cheek against the glass and exhaled. The window immediately fogged over with the heat of his breath. Elmer smiled, stretched, and shakily got up from his seat. He picked up his duffel bag and turned to leave, but something stopped him in mid-stride. He returned to his seat and, glancing over his shoulder to make sure no one was watching, Elmer stretched out his finger towards the fogged-up glass.

Later, Elmer would think of the *E.H.* he had carved into vapor on the window and smile. His breath, clinging to the glass like a footprint in the mud, reminded him he was not dead yet. No—he had just been born.

Chapter 5

Elmer inhaled. *Coffee and cinnamon-raisin bagels, new asphalt, fish frying, cigarette smoke, marijuana smoke, freshly trimmed grass, the sweet liquid aroma of a river, salty-sweaty skin…*

The kaleidoscope of smells was the first thing he noticed when he stepped onto the sidewalk and into the city. The air was heavy with the perfume of There. It wafted lazily into his nostrils and Elmer stood for a while, breathing in, breathing out, inhaling, exhaling. Letting the stew of aromas permeate his skin and bubble along his veins. He felt new and fresh. The world stretched out at his feet and Elmer turned left.

He meandered along the sidewalks, following his feet and his whims. He poked his head inside a doughnut shop, looked around, inhaled deeply, and kept walking. He picked a single leaf off a nearby hedge and turned it over and over in his hand, examining the veins. Any observer would immediately assume he was just another batty old man, wandering the city and telling old army tales to the trees and the pigeons.

But that observer would be mistaken. That day, Elmer was more like an infant than a crotchety old man. He saw the world with a fresh set of eyes. He was a child on Papa's farm with a fishing rod and a can of worms, sneaking away before the sun rose and the chores began. He hardly noticed his cane as he ambled along the city sidewalks, glancing this way and that, all five senses alert and inundated with new stimulants. At one point, Elmer stopped in front of a storefront window in the Chinese district of the city and stared at his reflection in the dingy glass. There, etched across the deep creases and folds of skin that hung on his face, was a smile.

Amazing. I hardly recognize myself. He peered over his glasses, scrutinizing the face in the window, taking in the crow's feet, the deep creases around his mouth, the multiple purplish spots. He sighed. *When exactly did I become an old man?*

Elmer shrugged and moved on. He spent the rest of the day wandering around There. He kept few solid thoughts in his head and flitted around like a nervous butterfly, attracted to whatever nectar he stumbled upon. He found himself poking at parked bicycles and turning into open restaurant doors. He meandered through a bookstore, a taquería, a billiards bar, a gas station and ran his fingers along the spines, salsa packets, chalk, and jugs of oil as he went. Everything he touched felt new and different. Even the jugs of oil excited him.

Elmer spent most of the day living from tiny new discovery to tiny new discovery. For someone accustomed to open fields and a town comprised of one main street, it helped to have a bit of tunnel vision. He focused on the small treasures of There and ignored most of the general hubbub around him. He reveled in polished chrome hubcaps and the smell of freshly brewed coffee and the tiny heads of spring flowers struggling through the dirt. At the end of the day he was exhausted.

Elmer gripped his cane and led his thin legs to a park across the street. He collapsed onto one of the rubber-coated benches and let his body rest against the backrest. The sun dipped low in the sky and Elmer tried to guess the time. *Six-fifteen, maybe. Judging by the sun.* He glanced at his watch. Six-eighteen. He smiled to himself.

The park was a block wide and quiet. Elmer closed his eyes momentarily and enjoyed the hush around him. He let his mind settle like a butterfly roosting in a tree; it hung serenely, comfortably. Elmer took a deep breath and wondered if he had breathed at all that day. If he had, he hadn't noticed. Now, in the quiet park, breathing seemed important. He inhaled and exhaled, tasting the odor of newly cut grass on his tongue. He thought about his first day in There and realized he had spent most of the day distracting himself. He had run around manically, smelling and seeing, touching and tasting, avoiding thoughts about the past or future. However, the past and future refused to be ignored for long. In the still air of the park, Elmer could hear his repressed demons creeping up on him, felt their hot breath on his neck. He shivered.

He tried to beat them away—thoughts of Irene and his two children and the neat rows of Here homes—but they nipped at his ankles and whistled in his ears. "Stop it! Enough!" he said. The thoughts continued to pester him. "Oh for the love of Pete!" Elmer shouted and leapt to his feet. He hobbled away from the little park and towards the commotion of downtown There. He walked frantically, desperately, attempting to elude the banished thoughts that caught up with him in the park. Every once in a while he would stop and shake a leg or an arm as if shooing away the pesky thoughts and then continue shuffling down the bustling sidewalk.

At one point, Elmer looked up. Buildings crowded around him, leaning over him, jeering at his troubles. They were a thousand feet tall, a million feet tall. They were ready to crumble, to crush his body, to squeeze the life out of his buried lungs. Elmer looked down. He walked determinedly to the nearest street corner and stuck out his arm. This is how they do it in the movies, he thought. This is how city folks hail a cab.

Elmer stood there for several minutes: thin arm jutting towards the street, head bent away from the lurking buildings, feeling vulnerable and miserable. He didn't wait long. A green and white taxicab rolled up to the curb; the driver lowered his window.

"Where you off to?" he demanded.

Elmer paused, considered. "I don't know—a hotel, I suppose."

"You suppose?" the driver sneered, tossing a handful of sunflower seeds past his thin lips. "What does that mean?"

Elmer opened the cab door and got in. "It means take me to a hotel, damn it! Any hotel will do."

The driver chewed thoughtfully on his sunflower seeds and spat the discarded shells into a waiting plastic bottle. "You in some kind of trouble old man?" He paused, examined his hunched, bespectacled passenger. "You know, don't answer that. I don't wanna know. Now let's get you to that hotel. You looking for luxury or budget?"

In a few minutes, the green and white taxicab pulled up to the entrance of the Something-or-other Inn & Suites. Elmer was too tired to care about the hotel's name. He stumbled out of the cab, paid the thin-lipped driver, and rushed into the hotel lobby, anxious to jump into a neatly-made bed and fall fast asleep. The hotel clerk greeted Elmer with bored eyes and a too-wide smile. Their interaction was short and to the point: Would you like a room—Yes (of course, dumbass)—How many—One—How will you be paying—Cash—How many nights—One for now; could be more—Ok, here's your key. Take the elevator to the fifth floor, turn to the left, your room is the third on the right. Do you need help with your bag—No, I've got it.

The clerk slid Elmer's room key across the fake granite countertop and Elmer snatched it away without a thank you. He was not in the mood for thank yous. Room 505 was waiting. It waited coyly on the fifth floor, vacant and lonely, anxious for Elmer to fill its bed, to watch its TV, to bask in its shower. It sighed deeply when Elmer swiped his room key, stepped inside, removed his shoes. Elmer glanced around briefly and sniffed the lilac-scented air. He walked over to the double bed and gave it a loving pat. It looked like a forest green and mauve heaven.

The elderly man sat down, removed one sock and then the other. He tugged on the sleeves of his sweater and slid out of it. He removed his trousers, folded them neatly, placed them on a chair. Once he was naked, Elmer slowly made his way to the bathroom. His knees and back ached. His right wrist was sore from clutching his cane—his detestable crutch—all day. He needed to rest, but he could feel the noxious layer of dirt-grime-exhaust-cigarette smoke-pollution that had accumulated on his skin and he was anxious to wash it away.

Elmer scrubbed his skin vigorously in the shower, rubbing the tiny bar of hotel soap over every piece of flesh he could reach. He felt the grey, heavy filth pour off his skin, pool by his feet, and swirl down the drain. If only his mind was as easy to clean as his skin. If only he could reach into his head and expunge his nagging memories, wipe away his feelings of guilt.

Elmer turned off the shower and stepped out of the tub. He wrapped a towel around his clean, raw skin and walked out of the bathroom, keeping his eyes trained straight ahead, avoiding the mirror. He didn't feel like seeing himself at the moment. He didn't feel like confronting his face. Instead, Elmer focused on the little patch of forest green and mauve. Bed. That's what he needed at the moment. He needed blankets and a pillow and a long, deep sleep. He stumbled towards the bed like a man in a trance and peeled back its layers one at a time: the green and mauve comforter, the beige blanket, the crisp white sheet. He crawled in naked and pulled the layers up to his chin. He was a hibernating bear; he was a caterpillar in a cocoon. He was a fetus, unsure about the cold world outside the womb.

As he drifted to sleep, Elmer felt his heart beating slowly, rhythmically inside his narrow chest. It was as steady as the tick of a clock. *There is still time*, Elmer whispered as his thoughts thickened like molasses and his breathing grew heavy. *I am late, but there is still time yet.*

Under the covers, the old man's heart pumped blood into his tired tissues, his knotted muscles. His body mended and stretched, preparing itself for another day.

Chapter 6

Elmer's second day in the city of There was not as new and delicious as his first. He tried to keep himself preoccupied with the tiny wonders and little beauties of the city, but from the moment he left his hotel room, things seemed different. More ordinary. Less fascinating. More bleak.

As Elmer stepped over broken glass on the sidewalk and evaded groups of tattooed/pierced teenagers/adults, he caught himself wondering what the hell he was doing here. He was a thousand miles away from home. A thousand miles away from Here. But when he recalled the Lions Club and the tedious smiles and the long, dragging hours in church and the even longer, dragging hours with Irene, he remembered. He remembered the anxious knots he felt in his stomach when he woke up every morning. He remembered feeling so stifled it was hard to breathe. He remembered the storm in his brain. Elmer straightened his shoulders and kept walking. Dodging sketchy people and glass was not half as bad as sitting through mass or listening to Irene's opinions about the "much-too-dry-not-sure-how-a-person-can-suck-the-moisture-out-of-a-muffin-like-that" baked goods at her latest book club meeting.

Elmer wandered. He looked. He observed. All around him, people moved. They hustled from Point A to Point B, carrying their large cups of coffee and sucking down cigarettes, always anxious and often perturbed. Even when they stood in groups, they fidgeted. Their feet and eyes shifted, their cigarette hands scrambled to their mouths. Elmer stood on the sidewalk like a rock in a stream, feeling the tide of people eddy around him. At one point, a group of over fifty children passed by, bubbly and laughing, excited about their class field trip. Elmer didn't notice their matching red jackets and smart khaki trousers; he didn't notice how they split apart and swirled around his still, hunched body. The only thing he observed was how quickly they moved: their feet, their mouths, their small, fidgety hands. He shuddered as the crimson stream engulfed him and spit him out again. None of them seemed to notice the lone rock left in the wake of their monochromatic river.

Elmer watched the children glide down the sidewalk, round a bend, and disappear. He stood, blinking after them for a moment and then scuttled away from the sidewalk and towards a soup and sandwich shop across the street. He needed to sit down for a moment. The persistent movement of There was making him nauseous.

Tucked inside Josephine's Soup Shoppe, Elmer took comfort in his bowl of chicken dumpling soup and the pane of glass that separated himself from the movement of There. He observed the city from a distance, watching the people skitter around like spiders seeking flies. He was a part of that skittering yesterday. He hadn't realized it, but he had been swept into its current; he had kept pace with its movement. Today he was tired. Today he felt aimless.

Elmer dipped his spoon into his bowl of soup and poked at a dumpling. He wasn't hungry, but the soup kept his insides warm, made him feel oddly grounded. As he harassed the dumpling, Elmer felt his mind dipping a toe into the pool of memories past and he jumped slightly at its touch. He closed his eyes and forced his thoughts into the present, into There. He opened his eyes and looked out the window.

The kaleidoscope of sidewalk goers made him dizzy. Colors and shapes whirred past. Different heights and weights and levels of shabbiness. Long and short hair—colored brown, green, turquoise. Skin stained with ink. It reminded him of a carnival. A fast-paced, fleeting carnival. Where were they going? Did they have a destination in mind? Or were they just running to run, to feel the sidewalk pass beneath their feet as if they were headed somewhere important.

As Elmer watched the sidewalk goers, he wondered if anyone actually lived in There or if they were just passing through on their way to something else, something greater. He wondered if he was just passing through as well.

Elmer spent three hours inside Josephine's Soup Shoppe, watching passersby, thinking about his place in There, avoiding swimming in memory's deep water. When the leftover soup formed a crust at the bottom of his bowl and the wait staff grew tired of refilling his water glass, Elmer decided to leave. He paid his bill and stepped outside into the thickening night air. He inhaled a mixture of feeble, lingering sun rays and darkening sky and headed east.

His feet led him past several cafés, a book store, and a group of people playing bongo drums and tambourines. He walked past a dog park and a computer store and two men making out and a Vietnamese restaurant and several beggars and a man selling balloons he molded into poodles and turtles and bicycles. His feet led him on and on, past strange people and things that Elmer had never encountered in Here. His feet didn't pause. They moved forward with purpose and drive until they stopped. Elmer looked around.

He was in the park. The same park he found yesterday, the park that lent him comfort and serenity for a few luxurious moments. Elmer looked around. His feet had carried him to the center of the park, to the heart of the serenity and, as luck or fate should have it, to the same rubber-coated bench his behind had graced yesterday. Elmer sat down. He felt the park's peace wash over and through him. He closed his eyes and breathed. The city of There was a question to Elmer—a nagging, pestering question. The park was the answer.

He drank in the park like medicine. Then he left.

Elmer flagged down a taxi and ordered the driver to take him back to his hotel. As Elmer slipped into a coma-like sleep he wondered again what the hell he was doing. But then his eyelids closed and his mind turned the color of a blank chalkboard. He would figure out what the hell he was doing tomorrow.

* * *

Tomorrow came. Tomorrow left. Then day four, day five. By day six, Elmer was accustomed to his routine. He would wake up late—nine or ten o'clock, eat a free breakfast of cornflakes, yogurt, and a cinnamon roll in the hotel, and then take the shuttle bus to There. In There, he would pace the sidewalks, no particular destination in mind. He tried again and again to regain the magic of his first day in the big city, to remember the gleam of chrome hubcaps and the smell of fresh flower beds, but all he saw now were spiky-haired teenagers and vomit on the street corner and hulking dogs on short leashes and men dressed in women's heels and countless, endless bums.

The bums bothered him the most. Growing up, Papa taught little Elmer that a man's character is defined by three things: his faith, his family, and his occupation. If a man lost his occupation, he lost a third of himself. Period. "I didn't come to this country to end up homeless on the street," Papa said. "I came to this country because of its opportunities. I came to this country because nobody and I mean *nobody* need go hungry or homeless or jobless. Any man who says he can't find work just isn't looking hard enough." Little Elmer nodded and agreed.

Big Elmer still nodded; he still agreed. Elmer thought of his beloved park on the outskirts of downtown There. He thought of the soft sound the wind made in its trees; he thought of its crisp air that filled his lungs. Even his tiny sanctuary was not sacred; even *that* was blemished by vagrants. Elmer hadn't noticed them at first; the park had seemed as pure and smooth and unspoiled as a young woman's skin. But when he examined it a little closer, Elmer became aware of the scars and scabs of the quiet park. He noticed the grungy, stocking cap-wearing, cardboard sign-holding man at the entrance. He noticed another long-haired, drum-wielding man along the path. Once he even stepped around a woman who had passed out near the bushes. Tonight, as his feet led him eastward, Elmer bristled at the thought of encountering these disgraceful people in the park.

He went anyway. He was powerless to the park's allure.

Somehow, his nightly rendezvous with the block of green space felt right, comfortable. He looked forward to it all day as he killed time wandering about, people watching and sitting in cafés, libraries, restaurants. When he walked the streets of There, he felt as if he was walking in circles, as if his wheels were turning, spinning, straining and going nowhere. In the park, he felt progress. He felt as if he was inching towards an answer, as if he was on the brink of something, on the cusp of a brilliant discovery.

As he approached the park, Elmer spotted the man with the cardboard sign at its entrance. Today's sign read ALL YOU NEED IS LOVE. Irritation struck him. A nauseating wave of it.

All you need is love? All you need is a goddamn job! All you need is to get up off the ground and do something! Parasites, all of you. Great ugly ticks sucking on the lifeblood of society…

Elmer neared the entrance of the park. The man with the cardboard sign held out his hand. Elmer paused for a moment, stepped back, examined the man sitting on the ground. The man did not make eye contact, but continued holding out his hand, silently hoping for a handout. He was a grungy-looking man—matted hair hung in clumps under his green stocking cap and bits of dirt clung to his cheeks and forehead. His red t-shirt was ripped down the side and covered in as much dirt as his face. Over the red t-shirt, a battered rosary hung limply over his chest. Elmer sneered at the rosary. He bent towards the man.

"No!" he shouted towards the silent beggar. "No, I will not give you cash! Go find yourself a job."

The man said nothing, just held his sign and sat.

Elmer stormed off, muttering to himself as he sought his park bench. His outburst had not made him feel better. In fact, he felt worse.

That uppity bum! Why did he have to look away like that? Why did he have to keep silent? Why didn't he fight back?

Elmer didn't stay long in the park that night. His feathers were ruffled from his encounter with the cardboard sign-bearing man and he felt angry and exhausted. After a few minutes he got up, walked across the park, stuck out his arm, and waited for a cab. His jaw jutted angrily; his white, bristly eyebrows were furrowed. People on the sidewalk skirted around him nervously, giving his little, hunched body a wide berth. After a few minutes, a cab heeded his call and pulled up to the curb.

As Elmer clambered into the backseat, a thought fleeted through his mind and pricked at his conscience before he scoffed at it and dismissed it. For a brief moment he wondered if he was truly mad at the homeless man in the park or if he was simply upset that the man had agitated Papa's ghost.

Chapter 7

Irene was Here, wringing her hands and choking out little sobs.

Arnie was Here too. And all the boys from the Lions Club.

The children were in the back. One on either side of Irene, supporting their mother with their arms.

The crowd hummed and swayed together. Back and forth. Back and forth. As if in trances, as if waiting for someone to give them a cue to do something else. Back and forth, they swayed. Back and forth. They stared straight ahead. They wore black—a dark sea of rocking flesh.

A priest dressed in long black robes stepped into the middle of the hypnotized throng and began shouting. He spoke of hellfire and brimstone. He spoke of betrayal and negligence. He spoke of laziness and stupidity. He spoke of turning one's back on the Lord and spitting on the Son of Man's cross. "To hell you will go!" he shouted. "If you do these things—if you sin—to hell you will go!"

The crowd nodded a collective agreement, swaying, swaying.

The priest gained momentum. "The Lord doesn't stray. He doesn't abandon. We may ask, 'My God, oh my God. Why have you abandoned me?' But He has not. He will not. Only humans abandon and stray. Only self-serving, flawed, sinful humans. Only humans that will burn on judgment day!"

A crowd of chins rose and fell at the same time. "We agree! We agree!" they murmured.

"The sinners will pay!" the priest screamed. "They will burn!"

"Burn the sinners!" The crowd shouted. "Burn the sinners!"

"Now," said the priest, lowering his voice to a near whisper. The sea of faces leaned in. "Let us bring in an example of sin, so that we may know its face. Let us bring in one of our brothers, fallen from grace, so that we may send him away to his judgment." The holy man's voice rose and quickened. "Let us learn from his flaws! Let us learn that if you live by the way of the fire, to the fire you will go! Let him feel God's wrath! Bring him in! Bring in the sinner!"

The sea parted, a black lidded box emerged, bobbing up and down as it was passed from hand to hand. Finally, it reached the front of the crowd and was slammed down. The top sprang open. Elmer Heartland looked up at the masses, his eyes wild with fear, his arms and legs strapped down with thick, leather belts. He squirmed and wriggled like a worm on a hook, but the straps held tight. The crowd glared down at him.

"Lazy and worthless!" screamed the priest. Elmer looked up at the towering form of the holy man. He was now wearing overalls and a sweat-stained t-shirt, smirking as he glared down at Elmer. Bits of dirt clung madly to his hair.

Elmer tried to shout, but no words came. His mouth opened and closed like a fish.

The priest narrowed his eyes and continued to fix them on the elderly man in the black box. "Let's put this sinner where he belongs!"

"Thy will be done," murmured the crowd and stepped back. A large hole appeared at their feet. And then Elmer was moving, bobbing and swaying inside his black, wooden box.

"No! Help!" he cried mutely.

The priest began chanting, "Judg-Ment Day! Judg-Ment Day!"

The crowd joined in, "Judgment day! Judgment day!"

Their voices crescendoed. They lowered Elmer into the hole. "Judgment day! Judgment day!"

Elmer scratched at the sides of the box, writhing desperately under the leather straps. Terror was etched on his face.

"Judgment day! Judgment day!" The crowd shouted louder and louder. They clawed at the ground, digging up clods of black earth. One-by-one they hurled the dirt down at Elmer, chanting and swaying, chanting and swaying.

Elmer watched the expressionless faces of the crowd as they took turns throwing dirt. Soon, his legs were buried, then his torso, then his chest. The weight of the dirt crushed his lungs and he gasped for air. "Stop! Stop!" he tried to shout. "Judgment day! Judgment day!" they chanted. Irene's face appeared above the hole. Eyes unblinking, mouth moving slightly, she pitched her clod of dirt and struck Elmer in the neck.

The dirt crushed Elmer's windpipe. "No! Stop!" he silently pleaded. "What's wrong with you people!?"

The face of the priest hovered over Elmer. He drew closer and closer until his lips brushed against Elmer's ear. His whisper slithered like a snake, "I always knew you were good-for-nothing."

Elmer opened his eyes wide, locking them with the priest's. They were the same shade of green. Elmer gasped and tried to struggle, but the mound of dirt pressed him down. The priest arose; the crowd throbbed around him with its steady chant. The man with Elmer's green eyes smiled maniacally. He scooped up a huge mound of dirt and flung it into the hole, covering Elmer's face.

Elmer saw black. He heard the crowd's voices rise and fall in perfect cadence. The heaping pile of dirt pressed down, crushing, squeezing Elmer's chest. He gasped for air and was rewarded with a mouthful of dirt. Coughing, sputtering, choking, Elmer tried to spit it out, but more dirt rushed in.

NO! Let me dig myself out! Please! No!

The ground became heavier and heavier. Elmer thrashed against its weight, kicking and flailing his arms. The ground was winning. The crowd and the priest were winning. He was sinking further and further underneath the dirt.

Elmer's eyes snapped open. He was tangled up in a mass of white, beige, green, and mauve.

Chapter 8

It took Elmer a long time to shake the eerie feeling of his dream. He paced back and forth in his hotel room, glancing around nervously. His head throbbed with the echo of chanting voices and reprimands from the priest. He could still taste the bitter black dirt in his mouth. Finally, he peered out the window at the bustling life below him and decided to join it.

Elmer hastily packed his life into the black duffle bag and caught the elevator downstairs. He felt it sink from the fifth to the fourth-third-second-first floor and grind-jerk-bump to a stop. He hopped out of the elevator, past the continental breakfast, into the faux lilac-scented lobby, and thrust his room key and a stack of bills towards the chubby-cheeked receptionist. He didn't wait for her to smile or thank him or give him his change. He walked quickly away, pushing his way out the revolving door and stepping into the late morning sunshine.

Elmer paused and let out a deep sigh. His chest and mind opened like a flower; he felt his lungs gasp for air. He couldn't wait for the shuttle bus today. He didn't have time. Waiting meant doing nothing and doing nothing meant thinking about his terrifying dream. He felt Irene and Papa and the swaying people in black breathing down the back of his neck. He grasped the handle of his cane and took off.

Elmer walked to There. He walked quickly. He walked for two long hours. Occasionally he would pause, stretch the fingers of his right hand, rub his stiff wrist, straighten his back, adjust the duffle bag's strap, glance at his watch, and move on. He needed to keep moving; he needed to keep walking. The past was hot on his trail and he could sense it stirring in the bushes; he could sense it licking its chops and crouching low. The past was hungry. The past was going for the kill.

Elmer shivered and moved on. Down the dusty, hot sidewalk that paralleled a busy street. Past the huge cement plant that churned out steam and fine, lung-tickling dust. Down the sycamore-lined neighborhood on the outskirts of There. Eventually he saw the city rise up and the buildings grow around him. They stood over him, but he didn't feel sheltered. He felt like prey tossed into the middle of a group of ravenous jackals. He headed towards his sanctuary. He headed towards the park.

The jackals fell away; the horizon opened slightly. Elmer let out a squeal when he sighted his beloved park. He hobbled quickly towards it, ignoring the pain in his ankles, knees, wrist, back, neck. As he approached, he spotted the man with the cardboard sign. Today he was accompanied by a long-haired companion—one that Elmer had previously seen lurking around the park—who was pounding drumsticks against overturned plastic buckets. A small crowd gathered around them and they were shouting, stamping their feet, and clapping to the rhythm.

"Good grief," Elmer said as he paused and glared at the crowd. They were mostly young and slovenly dressed, many bearing tattoos and dyed hair. He spied girls with studded belts and bracelets, a man with skull and cross-bone tights, a woman with bells around her ankles and feathers entwined in her long, dreadlocked hair. They swayed and stomped and began to sing. More and more gathered. Soon, the crowd was immense—a huge pulsating wave of humanity. They continued dancing and stomping, singing and swaying.

Elmer was annoyed. This was *his* park. They had no right polluting it with all that racket, all that dancing and brazen displays of sexuality. As he stomped across the street towards the noisy crowd, he glowered at the cardboard sign held by the grungy man in the stocking cap. Today's sign read WE SHALL INHERIT THE EARTH. "How unfortunate," he muttered and attempted to walk past them, winding his way past the moving, swaying bodies. As he elbowed his way through the crowd, Elmer felt himself become entangled in the throng, trapped between the dancing bodies. He panicked.

He felt the, swaying, swaying, swaying. Elmer choked. He stared at the crowd. The swaying. The voices in cadence. He was once again in a black wooden box, looking desperately up at the expressionless faces looming above him. He shoved his way through the crowd like a mad bull.

"Let me out!" he screamed, pushing towards the open green space. "Please! Let me out!"

Elmer stumbled through the dancing crowd and hobbled towards his favorite bench. He coughed and wheezed, attempting to keep his feet, legs, torso steady. He didn't make it to the bench. He stopped and leaned against a tree.

He could feel the cold clods of dirt sliding down his throat. He could feel the icy eyes of the crowd. The priest's whisper hissed in his ear. *Good for nothing...*

He could taste the black dirt, weighing down his stomach with its leaden judgment. Gasping desperately for air, Elmer doubled over and puked on the ground. It tasted like mud.

* * *

Elmer felt weak by the time he reached his rubber-coated bench. His legs shook as he slowly lowered himself onto the seat and leaned heavily against the backrest. The excitement of the day—the dream, the long walk, the group of swaying dancers, the whispers from the past—had left him completely drained. He shut his eyes and rested a while, waited for his breathing to slow and his heart to stop pounding maniacally against his chest. He rubbed an arthritic wrist. He gently cupped a quivering knee cap. He arched his back like an old tom cat. The sun shifted, poked through the leaves, and fell across his face. He dared to smile.

"Elmer, my boy," he said to himself, "you are getting too old for this kind of activity. One day that old ticker of yours is going to explode." He rested a hand across his chest. The pulsations mixed with the rhythm of the bucket drums. THUB-BAM-BEAT. He counted his heartbeats for a while and wondered how many he had left. Then the drumming stopped and Elmer looked up, startled.

"Thank goodness," he muttered. "It's not me. My beat is still going. It's just the drummer. The drummer has stopped. Maybe now I'll have time to think and rest and clear my head."

Elmer tried to relax. He let his head droop and his shoulders sag; he tried to nap. He tried to stretch out his legs and stop their insistent quivering. He tried to ignore the sharp pains in his wrist. But his body refused to stay calm. Elmer twisted and wriggled and turned, trying to shake off his edginess, but his body rebelled. His chest seized up; his legs and arms grew tense. Calm would not come to him when the tendrils of the past were slowly working their way through his ear canal and into the maze of his brain.

Elmer tried to shake away the tendrils, but they clung like stubborn vines. Images popped into his head—Irene baking apple pie, the Lions Club meeting room, rows of potato plants, ugly pastel green curtains, a girl tossing her yellow hair.

Goddamn it! I've been good all my life! Will you just leave me alone? Will you just leave an old man in peace?

The past did not leave the old man in peace. It hung around like a stray dog, scratching at the door of his thoughts, begging for attention.

I'm just an old man! I'm asking you, leave me alone! I've lived a good life. I was a family man. I never strayed—I kept my nose to the grindstone, stayed disciplined, kept up appearances. I worked and volunteered and attended school concerts and sports games. I knew how to be a decent man, to always act happy and content. I knew the formula and I never strayed. I never fucking strayed! Never!

Tears welled up in Elmer's eyes and he brushed them away with his shaky, withered hand.

I didn't dare stray. I planned my life meticulously. I knew exactly how to behave. I knew how to make everyone around me happy. I knew these things. I calculated these things. I never strayed. I was the perfect citizen: husband, father, breadwinner. Church-goer, volunteer, son, friend. Always a pleasant smile on my face—for your sake, not for mine. Never for mine. Feigned happiness for you—never for me. Never!

I never strayed.

Elmer's stooped shoulders shook. He closed his eyes tightly and felt warm rivulets stream down his face. He couldn't remember the last time he had cried.

Year in, year out. I never strayed. I was faithful and reliable—a rock, a giant oak tree.

Elmer looked up towards the sky. His tears dribbled down his chin and pooled on his cardigan. His eyes were red, but he continued gazing upward, squinting at the sun. His emotions bellowed and tumbled inside his thin chest. He wanted to shout, but instead he spoke in a whisper, barely audible above the din of There.

I'm sorry. Papa, I'm sorry. I held out for over seventy years. I couldn't do it a day longer. Maybe you were a better man than I was; maybe you never had a storm in your head like I did. Whatever the case might be, you win. Deep down, I'm still your good-for-nothing son who loathes the idea of getting up and milking the cows. I'm still your insolent brat who will never shine, who will never succeed, who is a ne'er-do-well to the very core. I'm still him. At least he was happy. At least he wanted to get up in the morning and start a new day.

Elmer clenched his fists as tightly as his arthritis would allow and glared at the sky.

Maybe you've won. Maybe you've proven your point. But I'd rather be that little boy any day of the week than the manufactured being I've become. I'd rather smile and fish and love life than exist in a plastic fantasy world, created to benefit everyone else. Created to please those who are watching. Judging. Scrutinizing the façade. Checking my carefully built levy for cracks. Ha! There are no cracks—it's made of plastic.

Elmer smirked. One of his psychiatrist friends had once told him about something called *sand castle syndrome.* "If you watch children making sand castles on the beach," he had said in a dry, know-it-all tone, "you can learn some valuable insight into human behavior. Many children put a lot of effort into building their castle. They pay attention to details—the towers, the moat, the decorations they make out of shells and seaweed. However, when the construction process is complete, we see distinct differences in behavior. Some children, usually the ones who are more nurturing, savor their castle. They play with it, love it, and are sad when they have to leave the beach for the day. Some children, however, destroy their castles as soon as they are built. They love the process of create-and-destroy. They love to feel powerful. They revel in the chaos."

The psychiatrist paused for dramatic effect and lowered his voice. Elmer rolled his eyes. "Some of these children outgrow this kind of behavior and learn how to nurture and care, but most never rid themselves of their deeply-rooted inclination to destroy. These are the divorcees, the alcoholics, the people who are unable to hold a steady job. These are the mothers who abandon their children and the men who earn a fat Christmas bonus and blow it playing poker."

These are the people who tried very hard to live in their castle made of sand, but felt the water rushing beneath their feet. These are the people who decided to get out before the sand and bits of shell crushed them in their sleep.

"These are the unstable, manic-depressives of society."

These are the people with itchy feet, who have trouble figuring out their place in this world, who are never truly comfortable with their lives.

The emotions tumbled. The eyes cried. Elmer had never reflected on his life like this. He had been too busy struggling through it. Seventy-odd years had piled up behind the plastic levy and, when the dam finally broke and the water rushed through, it was almost too much for his frail body to handle.

Elmer clutched his sides, letting his cane fall to the ground. His shoulders and torso shook violently. He shouted at the sky. He didn't pay attention to the strange looks he was attracting. "I'm not a bad person! I was faithful! I never, ever strayed! NEVER! Well, almost never," his voice quavered slightly. "Not since Daisy, anyway. Not since her. I haven't done one thing for myself in years and years and years. It was all for you. Never for me. I lost myself trying to please you!"

He dropped his gaze and his voice. Staring at the grass he whispered. *I'm not a bad person. It's just that…I was slowly dying. I was being crushed under the piles of routine and structure. I was being crushed under the pressure of judgment and expectation. I left because I would have perished under its weight. Sorry Irene. Sorry Papa. The life I've led was never for me. Please forgive me. Please let me have the last few years of my life to truly live. Please. Believe me, everything was for you. I never strayed. I never dared to stray. Never…*

Elmer's eyes rolled back. His head began to float and his body became stiff and calm. Silently, he slipped off the bench and tumbled forward onto the soft, manicured grass.

Before he fainted, a thought fleeted through Elmer's head. *Perhaps it is only at the end that we can truly see.*

Chapter 9

He was flying.

At first he didn't realize he was flying. The motion was smooth and silent, lulling him to sleep. But then he saw the wings and the ground below and he jolted with a start. He was hundreds of feet above the ground, balanced on the back of a large bird. *I'm surely dead. Or dreaming, maybe.*

Elmer pinched himself, but the image of the bird and the ground and his dangling feet still remained. *So, I'm dead. I didn't expect giant birds in heaven.*

Elmer stretched his arms upward, feeling the cool resistance of the air around him. He decided to enjoy the flight since he clearly could not die twice. He had never been a fan of heights, but on the sturdy back of the giant (and rather ugly) black bird, he felt secure and peaceful. At times, the bird dove and Elmer threw his arms around its neck, feeling its soft feathers flapping gently across his cheek. Then, the bird would rise again and the temperature would drop and cool breezes would tickle his face.

Elmer rode on the giant bird for what seemed like hours upon hours. They were flying away from the sun and towards a range of gigantic mountains. The sky darkened; the peaks loomed. And then they were amongst the mountains, dodging the rocky faces, swooping through the valleys that plunged between them. Elmer had never seen such mountains. They were huge and craggy with steep sides that plummeted towards the earth. There was no sign of life on these jagged peaks, only snow and great grey rock and clouds swirling between them. Elmer's jaw hung open; his eyes were wide and bright.

I've never seen such beauty, such majesty. I'm surely in heaven.

The air was cool and thin, but Elmer wasn't cold. His lungs weren't gasping for air. He felt light and free and maybe even happy. He closed his eyes to savor this feeling. Then the bird dove. Sharp and fast. Elmer's eyes snapped open. The bird's neck stretched out stiffly, pointing steeply downward. Some black feathers flew off its back and the wind whipped them away. Elmer's eyes watered; he was forced to squint against the rushing air. And then…

Oh my god.

...a gigantic mountain rose menacingly out of the ground ahead of them. They were barreling straight towards it.

I'm already dead, I'm already dead.

But Elmer wasn't convinced. At that moment, he felt very alive and very scared. The mountain wall loomed closer and closer. Elmer could see its sheer granite face grinning at him. He could see the sharp outcroppings taunting him from below. It was massive and powerful—a titan watching over the smaller peaks. Less than a hundred feet until impact. Seventy. Fifty. Elmer closed his eyes tightly.

But the impact never came. There was no CRASH-SCRAPE-THUB. There was no crunch of broken bones. There was no splat of brain matter against battered skulls. The flesh and blood stayed exactly where it was supposed to stay and did not end up dripping and smeared on the cold, jagged rocks. None of these things happened. Instead, the bird slowed down and started to glide. Elmer felt himself floating gently downward, like a fall leaf. He looked below his feet and discovered their destination.

Carved into the face of the rock was a gigantic grey temple. A long string of stairs led up to the massive building that was entirely encased by the mountain. As they dipped closer, Elmer began to make out the details of the gargantuan structure. The façade of the temple was made up of giant granite pillars, reminiscent of ancient Greece or Rome. The pillars formed neat rows that stretched inward towards the heart of the mountain as far as the eye could see. In front of the pillars, on the outside of the temple, stood a row of enormous chairs. Or thrones? It was hard to tell. They were plainly decorated and glaringly vacant. The emptiness of the place was unsettling.

With a soft bump, the black bird landed at the top of the steep rocky stairs. Elmer glanced backwards for a moment and couldn't see the ground—only row after row of stairs carved into the rock. His stomach flip-flopped and his palms started sweating. He quickly looked forward. The bird turned its head and started nibbling on Elmer's pant leg.

"Hey! Hey, cut it out you nasty bird! Stop it."

Elmer shook his leg and dismounted from his odd steed. The bird immediately turned away from Elmer, launched itself into the air, and flew upward several feet to the top of one of the gigantic thrones. There it perched and remained almost motionless, only moving its bald head slightly as if tracing Elmer's movements.

Chills rippled through Elmer's spine. He walked gingerly forward, eyeing the bird as he went. He was on a large rock platform at the foot of the thrones. He crept forward, walking underneath one of the large seats. Behind the thrones loomed the rows of massive granite pillars and long, cavernous hallways that went on without end. Elmer approached the first row of pillars and noticed for the first time that each one was elaborately decorated with unusual carvings. He ran his hand across one of the designs. A fish. It wrapped all the way around the column and looked as if it was doomed to forever chase its own tail. The carving was simple, but it was well executed and tasteful and seemed to belong in its rocky home. Elmer's eyes scanned upward. Above the fish carving, a field of wheat was etched into the pillar. Above that, a large cat. Above that, an owl. Above that, a man in long robes. Elmer squinted above the rims of his glasses. The carvings extended all the way up the massive columns, but he was unable to make out any more details.

Elmer walked from pillar to pillar, awed by what he saw. Each column of rock was a piece of art—unique and exquisite. There was a turtle. Here was a lamb. There was an eagle and a fountain and a lizard. Here was a horse and a palm frond and a human skull. At first, he tried to decipher the meaning behind the carvings, but he quickly gave up. He could find no rhyme or reason in the arrangement of these symbols and decided that he would rather just look at them than try to figure them out. For some reason, the carvings instilled in Elmer a profound feeling of calm and tranquility. They were simple and natural. They fit in perfectly with the mountain. Elmer would not have been surprised if they had been born from the earth itself.

Elmer walked deeper into the giant halls, his way lit by torches, each five feet long, their handles made of solid steel. They flickered and cast thick shadows that wavered with the flames. The little old man stopped and looked around him. He felt very small. Elmer glanced backwards. He was now fifty yards into the giant hall and the opening of the temple glimmered in the distance, contrasting sharply with the dark shadows that surrounded him. A cool breeze whispered across his neck and he shivered. Perhaps he should turn back.

Just as he spun around towards the entrance, Elmer spied movement out of the corner of his right eye. He snapped his neck towards the figure, but it darted into the shadows. Palms sweating, lips quivering, Elmer broke into a lopsided trot. He realized that his cane was no longer with him and he hobbled as quickly as he could, eyes darting this way and that, lungs wheezing and gasping for air.

I'm already dead. I'm already dead!

If he was already dead, why did he hurt so much?

Just a little further…

Elmer could feel himself being trailed by the thing in the shadows. He heard it softly loping behind him, switching to the left and then the right as if it was hunting a lone deer that had strayed too far from the herd. Elmer limped along pathetically.

The creature is taunting me. It should have caught me by now. I wish it would just get it over with!

Elmer stumbled into the sunlight and spun around to face the creature. His breath came and went in shallow spurts; his head felt light and dizzy. He started coughing and doubled over from the force of it. Holding his sides and steadying himself against a nearby rock, Elmer lifted his head towards the entrance of the temple, waiting to see his hunter.

He didn't have to wait long. Out of the darkness stepped the biggest, most powerful-looking cat he had ever seen. Elmer stopped coughing and stared nervously at the enormous animal, his eyes fixated on the large haunches, the wide, muscular shoulders, the legs like tree trunks. The cat stared back. Its dark eyes shone from a sleek, greyish-beige face that matched the rest of its short-haired body. The cat walked slowly, almost daintily towards Elmer, never taking his large unblinking eyes away from the small green ones of the man who was shaking violently in front of him.

Elmer backed away slowly, his shoulders stooped and quivering.

"Don't hurt me," he whispered lamely. "Just stay there. Leave me alone! I promise I'll go away from here."

What am I doing? Talking to a monstrous cat as if it can hear me…

Elmer kept talking anyway. "Please! Stay right there! I didn't mean to intrude. I didn't mean to trespass. Forgive me!"

Deliver me from this evil…

The cat stared mutely.

Elmer continued to back away, his frail body continued shaking. Then, his foot slipped and he found himself falling backwards into a wide, shallow pit. Elmer closed his eyes and braced himself for the hard rocky impact, but instead of stone, his body crashed against something soft and fleshy. Or rather, several soft, fleshy somethings. Underneath him, writhing and squirming in the shallow pit, were hundreds of snakes.

Elmer screamed.

He flailed his arms and kicked his legs. The snakes slithered around his limbs, through his clothing, and around his neck. They formed a thick, moving cushion between his body and the ground, but Elmer wished he would have struck bare rock rather than this deadly, writhing mass of scales and fangs and vertebrae. Elmer assessed his situation bitterly.

I think I'd rather be eaten by the cat.

The frail old man felt his body toss this way and that as the sea of snakes wriggled around him. He didn't know what to do. There was no way he could fight against the hundreds of bodies that were slowing wrapping themselves around him and bringing him further into the pit.

Elmer closed his eyes. He let his body relax.

If there is anyone—anything—out there that's listening, help me. Deliver me from this evil.

The snakes squirmed and writhed and stopped. They stopped. Just like that. Suddenly, smoothly, completely. Elmer opened his eyes and gazed incredulously at the still bodies that lay sprawled around him. They appeared to be in a coma or else in a deep, still slumber. Elmer cautiously stood up, his joints popping, his back stiff and sore from the strain it had taken that day. He stepped tentatively out of the shallow pit, leaving the reptilian danger and stepping to face the feline one. But the great cat also appeared to be sleeping. It sprawled lazily on its side, eyes closed, tongue lolling out the side of its gaping mouth. Elmer tip-toed around the animal. It was a beautiful creature and he paused to admire its sleek coat and powerful body.

You're a lovely thing, but I much prefer you this way.

He continued walking softly around the cat and found himself facing the row of thrones. He stopped in his tracks. Something wasn't right; the landscape had changed drastically. Elmer stared, wide-eyed. The plain, grey seats were now a myriad of colors. They glowed softly and playfully against their rocky backdrop, the colors dancing amongst the rocks like light emitted from a hanging crystal prism. They reminded Elmer of the stained glass windows in his childhood church, aglow with the afternoon sun. He stared, mesmerized by the purples and deep blues, the corals and bright oranges, skating across the rocks. He couldn't help walking towards them, drawn to the bright glowing hues like a moth to the flame. Slowly, Elmer reached out his hand and touched one of the chairs. The rainbow colors danced on his sagging, speckled skin. Elmer waved his arms around, this way and that, up and down, showering his body with colors. He darted after the greens and tried to lick the purples. He laughed like a schoolboy as he scampered around, immersed in a rainbow sea. He forgot about his limp, forgot about his aching bones and arthritic joints. A smile spread across Elmer's wrinkled face. He was happy.

"Elmer." A deep voice stopped him mid-twirl.

"Elmer. Right here. Look up."

Elmer obeyed, but he couldn't see a thing. The colors danced in his eyes and he squinted to see where the voice was coming from.

"Take a step backward. We're right here."

Again, Elmer did as he was told. The voice was clear and confident. It was a voice to be obeyed. For some reason, Elmer was not scared.

"Who are you? Where are you?" Elmer called. He didn't need a reply. Hovering above the chairs, was a row of eyes. Elmer gasped. A set of eyes gazed down at him from the top of each throne. They floated at about the same height, but they were different sizes, shapes, and colors. The eyes stared. Elmer stared back.

"Who are you? Where am I? What's going on? Am I dead?" The string of questions tumbled out of Elmer's mouth without pause. The eyes continued to stare. Elmer realized that he still was not scared. Why was that? Here he was, in the middle of who-knows-where, on the side of a gigantic mountain, looking up at several sets of large, bodiless eyes, and he wasn't afraid. There was something about the way that the eyes were watching him. They simply did what eyes were supposed to do—they looked. They didn't judge or critique. They didn't glare. There was nothing sinister about them. They weren't hiding anything. They merely looked.

The deep voice began speaking again. Elmer turned towards a set of round greyish eyes in the middle. "You have a lot of questions, Elmer, but you're not asking the right ones."

"Sorry—sir—I mean—I don't know, I've had a very strange day. I guess I'm just not sure what the right questions could be."

"No need to be sorry. You're right, you have had a strange day."

"That's right—"

"You felt joy."

"I—" Elmer paused. He thought his day had been strange because he rode on the back of a giant bird, ran away from a lion-sized cat, and fell into a pit of snakes, but despite all the absurd happenings of the day, the deep-voiced stranger was right. Feeling joy was just as strange to Elmer as being hunted by a cat with legs the size of tree trunks. Elmer stared at his loafers.

"You're right," he murmured. "It has been a strange day. I thought I buried that particular emotion long ago."

"You tried. But joy is resilient. It wasn't dead—it only hibernated for a while."

Another voice chimed in. This one was soft and feminine; it nibbled at Elmer's ears. "Joy isn't the only thing you've buried, Elmer. You've been burying bits of yourself for years."

Elmer looked up from his shoes. His eyes met the narrow brown ones of the speaker, but this time they were not floating. A moon-shaped face had formed around the eyes, held up by a willowy neck, attached to a slim body which was clothed in a long purple robe. The woman smiled warmly at the little, wizened man and Elmer felt his heart flutter and his insides melt.

"It's time you start digging yourself out."

Elmer nodded and thought of his recent dream. He saw himself looking up from the ground as the black-robed people flung bits of cold dirt at his helpless body. He didn't dwell on the dream for long. He was mercifully distracted by the sudden materialization of six other figures on the colossal thrones.

Each set of eyes now had a fleshy backdrop to support them as they continued to stare down at Elmer. The old man looked at each gigantic figure, one-by-one. An odd array of beings had appeared before him. On Elmer's far left sat the woman with the moon-shaped face, her violet robes shimmering just like the smile etched across her face. To her left, Elmer's right, sat a thin-framed man with an equally thin, white beard. He wore loose-fitting, indigo robes that covered his feet and nestled around the base of his chair. He nodded stiffly at Elmer and Elmer nodded back. Next in line were the familiar grey eyes belonging to the deep-voiced man. The eyes had attached themselves to a dark-skinned, shaggy face. The man's wild beard and long mane draped across his shoulders and down his bright, cyan-blue cloak. He beamed at Elmer through his thick facial hair and glanced to his left at the next figure in the row. Elmer gazed in wonder at the next set of eyes. He hadn't really looked at them before and now he noticed that they constantly changed color. They shimmered as they morphed from light blue to lilac to deep green. The woman peered down at him from a very old, very wrinkled face. Her skin creased around her mouth and neck, deep crow's feet framed her mesmerizing eyes. Her thin, veiny hands rested comfortably on the arms of her chair and her bare feet dangled from underneath a long, moss-green dress. Although she had clearly seen many seasons pass and many years go by, she still clung to some of her former beauty. Her nose was slightly curved and elegant, her neck long and thin. She sat tall and proud, her head erect and her back straight. A long, white braid fell down her back and Elmer noticed several small flowers and a feather entwined in the locks. He smiled shyly at her; he could feel warm, raw energy radiating from her wrinkled skin. Elmer blushed and turned his head towards the next seated figure.

His body jerked in shock as his watery green eyes locked with the piercing yellow ones of a hawk-like bird. Or, rather, the head of a hawk-like bird. From the shoulders down, the creature appeared to be completely human and its odd juxtaposition of feathers and flesh startled Elmer tremendously. The part-bird, part-man stared benignly at Elmer with its luminous eyes. It too wore a long robe—this one a bright shade of yellow. Elmer nodded quickly at the creature, uncertain of what to make of it. Its gaze was not unkind, but its alien appearance made him uneasy. He turned awkwardly to face the sixth being and was not at all surprised to see it draped in the next color on the spectrum: orange. A tangerine-colored tunic criss-crossed over the broad shoulders of a beautiful, olive-skinned man. The man sat cross-legged in his throne, each hand resting across a thigh. His face was relaxed, almost sleepy, and Elmer couldn't help the enormous yawn that slipped out as he watched him.

"Ex—excuse me," Elmer stammered. He knew these beings were important and he felt as if he had violated some sort of protocol.

But the handsome man laughed lightly and said in a voice that reminded Elmer of flowing water, "It's alright, Elmer. You've had a long day. Do not be embarrassed by your body's reaction; it is behaving exactly how it should."

The words were odd, but comforting. Elmer smiled gratefully at the man, looking into his deep, chocolate-colored eyes. Kindness stared back at him. Elmer took a deep breath and briefly closed his heavy lids, suddenly aware of his tired body. He steadied himself and prepared to meet the last figure. He opened his eyes and turned to the right, meeting the startling lime-colored eyes of a large, coal-black woman. She wore a red scarf on her head that matched her long, flowing dress. Unlike the others, she was not seated, but was standing upright, stretching her arms to either side and rotating her shoulders left and right, up and down. Her hips moved as well in graceful, subtle undulations. Elmer's grogginess suddenly faded. He felt like dancing again amongst the colors, chasing them as they soared through the air like the iridescent dragonflies from home. The woman continued moving, nodding her head and tapping her large, flat foot to some inaudible rhythm that coursed through her body. She wore several gold bracelets on her wrists and around her ankles and they jangled in harmony with her movement. She kept her eyes focused on Elmer, who watched her intently and tapped his foot in time with hers. She seemed to be inviting him to be a part of her dance.

For the second time that day, Elmer lost himself in a thick wave of joy that flooded his consciousness. He spun and reeled. He wiggled his hips. He pranced around like a fool, all the while hearing the steady rhythm of drums in the back of his head. BOOM-BOOM-BOOM-batta-BOOM-BOOM BOOM. The beat never wavered and Elmer continued to dance drunkenly to the percussive sounds that echoed through his brain and filled his body with energy and life. Again, he forgot to limp.

The beat changed. Instead of drums, words started coursing through Elmer's head. DIG-DIG-DIG-yourself out-FEEL-FEEL-FEEL-your joy-DIG-DIG-DIG.

Elmer stopped. He shook his head as if clearing away an intense dream. Sheepishly, he looked up at the seven. Their eyes still looked. Their eyes didn't judge. Elmer stood awkwardly before them, shifting his weight from side to side. He felt naked. And foolish.

"No need to stop on our account," said the deep voice of the shaggy man in blue. "It is nice to see you enjoying yourself for a change."

"No, no. Quite alright. An old man like me shouldn't dance around like that. I'm liable to break a hip." Elmer rubbed his hands nervously. He wasn't sure what had come over him. He decided to change the subject.

"It's—uh—nice to meet you all. I mean, you all seem very kind. But, I guess I haven't really met you at all. I still don't know a thing about any of you. Who are you exactly? I don't mean to be rude, it's just that—"

"No need to be nervous, Elmer," a new voice said. Elmer looked over at the grey-haired man in indigo. "We know how hard—even painful—it can be to release joy that has been stifled for countless years. You're doing just fine." The man smiled warmly at Elmer and continued. "As for who we are, that's something you already know."

Elmer gaped at the man, "I—I already know? No I don't. Of course I don't. I wouldn't have asked otherwise. I don't know your names or anything..."

"Oh, but you do," the man continued. "Besides, names aren't important. We go by many different names and people know us, relate to us, in different ways. A woman may be known as a daughter or a friend or a lover or a stranger on the subway. Who's to decide which is right? Or which is best?"

"But I don't know how to relate to you...people...beings," he glanced over at the half-man, half-bird.

"Elmer," continued the indigo man patiently, "a child doesn't question how it is supposed to relate to its mother. It simply feels her tender arms, listens to her loving voice, and knows. It knows this person will keep it safe and warm and well-fed. It trusts in the love it feels. It doesn't need words to decipher this relationship."

Elmer blinked. He thought about what the grey-bearded man said. *Child-like. That's how I feel right now—as small and naïve as a child.*

He looked up at his rainbow-clad "mothers." Their bodies glowed against the dull rocky backdrop. A thought suddenly struck him.

"Is—is this some sort of test? Am I dead right now? Am I being judged?" His voice began to quiver. "You're judges, aren't you? I'm sorry! I really am. I did the best I could. I only left them when I knew they could take care of themselves. I only left them when I was at the end of my rope! I'm sorry!" *I really am. I'm sorry...*

"You're ok, little one. You're ok," the woman in the shimmery purple robes spoke again. "Do you really think we are judging you?"

Elmer lifted his head to look at her. She leaned forward as she spoke, her shiny black hair framing her lovely, round face. He looked at her unassuming eyes. "No," he answered shakily, "No, I don't think you are judging me." *Your eyes show nothing but kindness.*

"Elmer, listen to me," she said softly, "You don't have to be sorry. We're sorry you've been lost so long. Now is the time to find yourself again."

Her words wrapped around Elmer like a blanket.

"You asked us who we are," she continued, "but, like my friend in blue told you earlier, you're asking the wrong questions. The question you really need to ask is—"

"Who am I," Elmer finished.

She smiled. "Precisely."

"A straightforward, simple task that *will be,"* he thought wryly.

"You're right," the man draped in orange spoke in his light, crisp voice. "It's not going to be easy. It's going to require a lot of hard work and sacrifice on your part. You have a lot of re-learning to do. But I believe in you—we all do. After all, hard work and sacrifice are not new concepts for you." The man paused and a new voice jumped in.

"But you can't waste any more time." Elmer turned towards the brown and white feathered head of the speaker. "You need to start your re-learning immediately."

"But I—I don't know where to begin," stammered Elmer, tears welling up in his eyes. "I've been living the same way for years upon years."

"You've already begun," answered the same calm, deep voice. "You left your old life in the dust."

"I'm really, very sorry—" Elmer began.

"It's ok, Elmer. We understand. You were desperate and aching and didn't know what else to do. But running away doesn't solve things. It may distract you for a while, but your problems still dwell within you. If you ignore them, they will swell up again and beat against your brain just like before."

"So, I should go back to Here?"

"Why the *hell* would you want to do that?" snapped the hawk-man. Elmer jumped at the sharp response. "You've already chosen your path. The wheels have already been set in motion. Seek yourself in new places. Learn. Grow. Be. Follow your intuition; when the time is right, move on.

You have to trust yourself, Elmer. That, above everything else, is the most important lesson we can teach you. When you feel like dancing," he glanced over at the woman in red, "dance."

Elmer soaked in the words. *Trust myself. When I feel like dancing, dance.* The old man was suddenly very tired. He leaned heavily on a nearby rock and closed his eyes.

Something gently nudged his side. Elmer turned to face the giant cat. For a moment, Elmer's body seized up in fear. The cat's shoulder stood level with his and its enormous head looked down at him. But this time, Elmer's fear subsided. He knew he was safe with the seven. He knew they would protect him. Besides, the big cat was purring.

Elmer gazed in amazement as the feline's silky coat brushed up against him and its beach ball-sized head nuzzled against his hands. Tentatively, he reached up and stroked its fur, feeling the deep vibrations of its purring. Elmer smiled and glanced towards the thrones. The seven smiled back.

"You've had a long day, my son," said the woman in purple. "Go with Tierra and rest. She'll show you the way."

Elmer nodded. He rested one arm on the flaxen-colored back of the cat and slowly walked with her towards the entrance of the great hall. Inside, a mattress waited on the floor and Elmer gratefully sank into it. Tierra curled up by his side like a tiny kitten.

The last thing Elmer saw before closing his eyes was a smear of colors painted across the horizon, dancing and glittering in the fading sun. The last thing he felt were the tremors of the purring cat mixed with the steady beat of drums.

Chapter 10

Drums. Pounding, throbbing, echoing through the caverns of his brain.

BOOM-BOOM-BOOM-batta-BOOM. BOOM-BOOM-BOOM.

The volume rose and fell. The tempo stayed constant.

BOOM-batta-BOOM-batta-BOOM-BOOM-BOOM.

Different sounds mixed in with the percussion. A metallic clang. A wooden THUB. Elmer found himself moving to the rhythms. Was the woman in red dancing too?

Elmer opened his eyes and rubbed away the sleep. He blinked in the bright sunlight. It had all disappeared. Gone was the mountain. Gone were the rows of pillars and endless hall. Gone were the thrones and their colorful occupants. Elmer sat up quickly, his head reeling and spinning, unable to focus.

But the drums…

BOOM-BOOM-BOOM-batta-BOOM-BOOM-BOOM.

The drums continued and Elmer spun around, finally able to grasp his surroundings. He was back in the park. A few feet away, the thin black man with long, straight dreadlocks was pounding away on a few over-turned five-gallon buckets. He was drumming again.

What the devil? What's going on?

Elmer was seated on a park bench, underneath a ratty grey blanket. On one side was a balled-up sweatshirt that he had been using as a pillow. The spindly drummer sat on the ground to his right; the man with the cardboard sign sat to his left. The sun was shining brightly overhead and a large crowd was gathered around the drummer. They were clapping and cheering. Some were stomping their feet to the rhythm. BOOM-batta-BOOM-batta-BOOM-BOOM-BOOM. The man pumped his arms up and down, crashing the buckets with each downward stroke. Every once in a while he would mix up the beat or throw in the metallic resonance of a trashcan lid or click-click-click his wooden drum sticks together. The crowd cheered. Some of them threw money into an overturned baseball cap. To thank them the drummer spun his sticks, threw them into the air, caught them, and continued playing.

Elmer was impressed, but hated to admit it. The whole idea of people living as street bums still annoyed him. He turned to his left; the man with the cardboard sign was looking at him. Today's sign read FEEL THE RHYTHM OF LIFE. Elmer scoffed. What did a lazy bum know about the rhythm of life? All he knew was cheap wine and begging for quarters.

Elmer was about to turn away, but the man began to speak. "You've bin out cold for almost a day now."

What? "Excuse me? Are you joking?"

"No sir, not jokin'. It's bin about a day that you've bin snorin' away on that thar bench."

Elmer cringed at the man's gravelly voice and poor grammar. The man didn't seem to notice. "Yeah, me an' Zach over thar," he nodded towards the drummer, "have bin takin' turns keepin' watch over ya. Ya know, making sure you ain't cold or nuthin.' Makin' sure no one robs ya."

Elmer blinked incredulously at the man. He wore the same hole-ridden jeans and grimy red t-shirt. His tan cheeks were still dirty and unshaven. The faded green stocking cap was perched on his head even though the sun was shining and the weather was mild. The man grinned. Elmer spied two missing teeth.

"Seems ter me you've bin havin' sum crazy dreams or sumthin'. You kept on tossin' an' turnin', cryin' out about snakes and sich. You started wrigglin' like hell when ol' Zach started playin' the drums last night. He cut his act short 'cause he didn't wanna wake you."

"I—uh—yes. I did have some vivid dreams. Now, will you kindly explain what happened to me? How long have I been out exactly? And who are you?"

"My name's Levi, sir. Levi Axton. I seen you fall off that bench over thar and knock yer head yesterday. Me an' Zach—that's short for Zacchaeus—went over ter help, but thar weren't much we could do besides set yeh down on this here bench and cover ya up. We were afeerd to call an ambulance or the police. Ya see, neither of us like the authorities much and besides, we figured you'd come 'round eventually."

"I see," Elmer said stiffly. "So you decided to leave a seventy-eight year old man lying outside on a park bench all night. You thought you could take better care of me than a hospital, did you?"

"Well—I—we," the man turned red and stumbled to find his words. "You see," he said hesitantly, "Zach went to med school back in the day and he figured you'd be alright. I dunno. You was breathing ok and e'rything."

"Oh, very good," said Elmer, raising his voice. "I feel *much* better about being left out in the cold since *Zach* went to med school. And you, I suppose, have a degree in nuclear physics?"

"I ain't lyin', I swear. Listen mister, we was just tryin' ter help. Honest."

"Don't talk to me about honesty!" Elmer snapped. "You've never worked an honest day in your life!"

The man stared, slack-jawed at the withered, old man. He hadn't expected this. Yesterday afternoon he and Zach felt like heroes, carrying the helpless elderly stranger to safety.

Elmer paused, his chest rising and falling rapidly, his breath coming in short, wheezy spurts. "I have to go," he muttered, more to himself than to Levi. Slowly, painfully, Elmer arose and stretched his limbs. They popped and crackled. He let the ratty blanket unceremoniously fall to the ground, snatched up his cane, and started shuffling away.

"Wait! Mister!" Levi shouted behind him.

Elmer ignored him.

"Mister!" The sound of Levi's footsteps made Elmer turn around. "Here." Levi extended his arm towards the elderly man. Clutched in his hand was the black duffle bag containing the few possessions Elmer had in the world.

Elmer sighed. "Thanks," he murmured as he took the bag. He almost felt bad about his rash behavior, but he had too much on his mind to think about the hurt feelings of a bum.

"No problem. Take care of yerself, mister."

Elmer turned and continued his slow shuffle. He needed to get the hell away so he could clear his head. He paused and heard the voice of the hawk-man ringing in his head. "Seek yourself in new places. Follow your intuition; when the time is right, move on. You have to trust yourself, Elmer."

Elmer looked at the duffle bag on his shoulder. He glanced at his cane. "Ok, birdman. Time to trust myself. Time to move on." As soon as he uttered the words, Elmer knew he was right. It *was* time to move on. This is not a city of permanence. It is a city of transition. It is a city people move *through*, not *to*. Elmer had sensed it from the beginning. He sensed it in the nervous cigarette hands, the twitchy mouths, the way people rushed around like water flowing towards the ocean.

It was time to move on; it was time to begin. It was time to start digging himself out.

As Elmer rushed stiffly towards the bus station, the afternoon sun congratulated him. It shone on his shoulders and down his neck. It made him think of possibilities. It made him think of fresh starts. And, as the sun danced through a group of prisms hanging in a shop window and split apart into seven pieces, it made him think of the robed figures.

Elmer didn't know what to make of them. He didn't know whether they were real or an elaborate piece of fiction cooked up by his brain. At the moment, he didn't care. He was getting the hell out of dodge.

He arrived at the central bus station and scrambled into the ticket office. Lines of people stretched around roped-off aisles. He got into the shortest line and tapped his foot impatiently, waiting for the serpentine of people to move forward. As the line inched, Elmer reflected.

Was I really out for a day? I must have been. That dream lasted forever.

But was that really all it was? A dream? It was so vivid, so detailed. Their eyes—they were so real. That cat—I could feel its silky fur, its hot breath. I could taste the cool mountain air. I could feel the jagged carvings in the pillars. Everything was so precise, so realistic…

But was it realistic? I danced amongst shimmering colors and giant thrones. I fell into a pit of snakes and came out unscathed. I stood before giant people (if you could even call them that!) and listened to their wisdom. I slept next to an enormous cat…

But still. Still, they knew so much about me. They pinpointed exactly what I need to do with my life. They offered me guidance and comfort. I felt joy. I felt it in my bones, in my very core. There were drums…

Those were just the plastic buckets of a street bum. My subconscious heard them while I was asleep. That's all it was! The lousy plastic buckets of a street bum.

The woman in red. I could see her soul dancing. I could feel her movements. Her movements were mine.

Don't be ridiculous! It was just a dream.

It was so much more than a dream…

The woman behind the ticket counter interrupted Elmer's thoughts with a light cough. "Ahem. Excuse me sir. What is your destination?"

"I—uh—sorry. It's—" Elmer paused, froze. He stared at the woman behind the counter. Her eyes beamed, her moon-shaped face smiled politely at the elderly man. She adjusted one sleeve of her purple robe and spoke again.

"Your destination? Sir?"

"It—it's you!" Elmer said back. "What are you doing here?"

"Helping you reach your destination," the voice remained calm and kind. "Now will you please decide sir?"

"Uh—yes. It's just—it's just, I don't know which one to choose."

The woman laughed. It sounded like church bells. "Of course you do."

"I do?" said Elmer incredulously. "Ok then." His eyes scanned the destination board in front of him. "Uh miss, can I ask you a question?"

"Of course."

"Which city on that board is the most boring? I mean, which one is the most average, the most…normal? I think I'd like to be in that kind of city for a while. I've had enough of strange haircuts and street urchins for a while. I'd like to be around people more like me."

"I see," the woman replied, her knowing eyes boring into Elmer's soul. Elmer's cheeks reddened. "Better be this one then," she pointed to the destination board. "It's as *normal* as they come," she cast Elmer an impish smile. Elmer looked back at her curiously.

"Ok, miss. If you say so." He stared at her dancing eyes and shimmering purple robe. She didn't fit in with the dusty backdrop of the bus station or the shabby walls of the ticket booth.

"Excellent, sir. You won't regret it." The woman took a few dollars from Elmer's shaking hand, printed off his ticket, gave him a wink, and said, "Alright sir. You're all set for your journey. Good luck."

"Thanks," Elmer said, taking the money stiffly, still reeling from seeing the moon-faced woman in the ticket booth. He started walking away, but turned back. "What if I chose wrong?" he cried. A somber-eyed man stared back at him, whiskers sprouting from his wobbly chin.

"What the devil are you talking about old man? Did we print your ticket correctly?"

"I—um," Elmer paused. "Yes. Yes, you did."

"Alright. Move along then. There are folks waiting and those seats ain't going to sell themselves."

* * *

The bus to City A was crowded, but not uncomfortable. Elmer sat by a window, his hands folded primly in his lap, his head turned towards the outdoors, vaguely taking in the passing fields and hills. There was not much topography near Here. Here was flatter, more open. The passing landscape was bumpier with more trees. But Elmer didn't think much about his surroundings. His thoughts drifted further away, to a place filled with gigantic, rocky mountains.

"Was it really just a dream?" he asked himself for the thousandth time that day.

It was so realistic. I could feel the smooth scales of the writhing snakes; I could taste the clean mountain air. Damn. It was so realistic.

Elmer's head throbbed against his skull. His insides twirled and spun and turned themselves into knots. He wanted desperately to believe in his dream-like experience. He wanted to believe in the wise seven and their guidance. But Elmer had not believed in anything quite so god-like in ages.

I might be going mad. This may all be an elaborate, schizophrenic creation, but I want to believe. I really want to believe.

The sun was beginning to sink in the sky and it cast dark patterns across the hilly landscape. Elmer watched the last beams of light struggle through tree branches and skip across the edges of a pond. The outside world basked in the worn-out light of dusk and waited for darkness to cradle it in its arms and rock it to sleep. As Elmer watched the shadows stretch eastward, a few tears worked their way into his eyes and he hastily brushed them away. He felt lost and small and more than a little afraid. But amidst his internal anguish, one phrase repeated over and over in his head.

It's time you start digging yourself out.

The shadows grew longer, darker.

It's time you start digging yourself out.

It was good advice, even if it was only from a dream. It was exactly what Elmer needed to hear.

It's time…

It was time. It was high time. Time was, in fact, running out.

you…

Yes, no one else could do it. He had to do it himself. This was his lonely path to travel. The path, as the hawk-headed man had said, that he had already chosen. Seek yourself. Learn. Grow. Be.

start digging…

He had miles to go.

start digging yourself out. Out. Out!

He longed to be free. He longed to find the bits of himself he buried a long time ago. Elmer looked out the window. Across a long field, a gigantic black bird soared. It rose up, skirted across the tops of a few ancient oak trees and dove, its feathers plastered back from the air's force. Elmer's heart leapt as he watched the bird; his skin prickled with excitement. He made a resolution.

I will believe.

The practical side of his brain screamed in protest. Elmer ignored it.

I will believe. I may be a crazy. I may be a delusional old man, but at this point I really don't care. I haven't believed in anything for decades, maybe it's about time I started. Besides…

Elmer watched the bird rise up again slightly and begin to fly low to the ground, its feathers almost touching the wheat tops it sailed across.

I felt joy. I felt pure, utter, ridiculous joy. If nothing else, I believe in that. I believe in the joy I experienced, the joy that made me dance. Yes! I believe that emotions can come back from the dead.

Elmer watched the black bird parallel the bus. Its neck stretched outward; its nose reminded him of the cone of a jet plane. The bird rose and dipped again; it soared and then swooped sharply downward. Elmer closed his eyes. All the irritation from the day melted away. All the doubt and unease crumbled and blew away behind the bus. He whispered to himself as the world gathered darkness and the huge bird melted into its black.

I will believe. I will believe. I will believe because it feels right. I will believe because I miss believing in something. I will believe.

Elmer opened his eyes and looked out the bus window. He couldn't see a thing except bluish-black shapes against a bluish-black backdrop. And his own reflection. He could see his reflection staring back at him from the dark world. Elmer studied his face, traced the contours of the wrinkles surrounding his eyes and mouth. He locked eyes with the reflection.

Hello old man. Are you ready to start digging? Are you ready to start believing again?

Elmer gave his reflection a little half-smile and nestled into the bus seat. He closed his eyes and imagined the road passing quickly under his feet. As he drifted to sleep, Elmer felt his heart beating slowly, rhythmically inside his narrow chest. The corners of his mouth twitched upward. There was still time to dig.

Chapter 11

The bus screeched to a stop and knocked Elmer out of his dreams. He blinked and rubbed his eyes, squinting through the early morning haze at City A. The streets were calm and quiet; a few lights shone through kitchen windows. A few car engines turned. City A was getting ready to start its day. Excited, Elmer propelled himself out of his bus seat and rushed out the door. He stepped into the city.

City. It was hardly that. More like a biggish town or a stand-alone suburb. There were no freeways or skyscrapers cutting across town. There were no subways or metro stations. There were not throngs of people crowding the sidewalks, just a light smattering—walking to work, out for a morning jog, exercising their poodles and cocker spaniels and yellow labs. Elmer sighed and breathed in the young air of a new day. He was going to like it here. He was certain.

He stepped down the sidewalk, cane in hand, and began another day of wandering.

Elmer spent the morning and most of the afternoon admiring the normalcy of City A. As he walked down perfect sidewalks and alongside well-groomed lawns, he congratulated himself on his decision to leave the chaos and never-ending movement of There. He congratulated himself for leaving the dirt and pollution and excess of vagabonds. He needed repose. He needed a quiet place to mull things over and grow and think and chip away at the layers of muck he had packed on top of his life. He was confident he had found that quiet place.

When afternoon rolled around, Elmer was tired. He had spent most of the day walking—meandering through parks, wandering through school yards, ambling alongside neat rows of houses. He trekked from one end of the city to the other and, even though City A was not nearly as immense as There, he still put several miles on his tan loafers. By the time Elmer reached City A's main plaza on the north side of town, he decided it was time to rest.

He grabbed a bagel from a nearby shop and sat outside, nibbling absentmindedly on its edges, as he watched the wind play lightly over the decorative pond in the middle of the plaza. Elmer admired the pond and the elegant fountain in its center and the red brick walkway that surrounded both pond and fountain. He wrapped up the rest of his bagel, squirreled it away in his duffel bag, and walked to the water's edge.

Elmer leaned over the short iron fence that surrounded the pond. Wind skipped off the water and brushed across his face, leaving its damp kiss on his cheek. Elmer touched his hand to his face. He looked at the fountain again. Water spit out its top and spilled over its three tiers, splashing quietly into the clear pond water below. The fountain was a clean, sparkling white. It stood unblemished in the afternoon sun, showing off for the watching old man. Elmer wondered why it didn't look right. He wondered why it looked lonely.

A thought struck him. Elmer dug his hand into his pocket and retrieved a penny. He looked at its dull face and then flicked his eyes back towards the fountain. It stood tall, a solitary tower jutting out of the flat. Elmer turned his attention back to the penny. He breathed on it, rubbed it against the leg of his pants, and scrutinized it to make sure it was sufficiently clean. When he determined it was, Elmer flicked it towards the fountain whispering, "Here's to new beginnings."

He watched the penny arch over the water and land on the lip of the fountain's upper tier. The water gurgled with pleasure. Elmer smiled. He plunged his hand into his pocket and emerged with a handful of change. He cleaned the coins, one at a time, and lobbed them towards the fountain.

"Here's to remembering who I am."

"Here's to lost love."

"Here's to regaining faith."

"Here's to old dreams."

"Here's to following my intuition."

"Here's to finding me."

Elmer leaned against the fence that surrounded the pond and watched the pennies, dimes, nickels, quarters gleaming in the sun. Glimmering wishes. He watched them until the sun went down.

* * *

The next day, Elmer found himself in the late afternoon, watching the residents of City A as they finished work and made their way home. He paused his wandering, planted himself on a bench, and observed as they bustled along the sidewalks, pedaled down streets, and motored past in neatly washed and waxed cars. They patiently made their way towards their husbands and wives and pets and 2.3 children. Elmer watched the workforce of City A and smiled. They were exquisitely normal. They sported normal haircuts and wore normal clothing. They were courteous and patient. They carried themselves with style and grace. They nodded politely at Elmer as they passed by and elderly visitor nodded politely back.

Elmer appreciated their humble cars and practical footwear. He applauded their beige and cream and tan-colored houses and neatly manicured lawns. These were responsible people. These were people with a strong moral code and an equally strong work ethic. There were no miscreants or rebels or homeless folks. Just ordinary people immersed in their ordinary lives. Elmer sighed. He could taste the city's averageness.

Elmer walked down the street, still observing the city's returning workforce. Papa would surely approve of City A. Elmer paused. He hadn't meant to drag Papa along to City A, but somehow he had. "Go on," Elmer muttered. "Leave me alone now. You're not welcome here." He walked a little faster, as if he could leave Papa's memory buried in the daffodil bed behind him.

He muttered to himself as he fled Papa's ghost. "I'm here for myself, not for you," he said. "I'm starting over in City A because *I* like it. *I* want to be here. It is comfortable for me; it meets *my* expectations, not yours." A voice tickled the back of his brain.

You know Papa and Irene and the others would approve of this place. You know they appreciate tedium and normalcy.

"But so do I!" Elmer replied. "I like those things too. I just needed a change of scenery. I needed to get out of Here, that's all. I never intended to settle down amongst thieves and beggars and drunks. City A is *my* kind of city! I came here for me!"

"If you say so," the voice replied.

"I do say so! City A is safe. This is surely where I will find myself. This is where I will start to dig."

Agitated, Elmer leapt to his feet and hobbled down the sidewalk. He enjoyed the comfort of City A. He did! And no nagging voice in the back of his head was going to tell him otherwise.

Elmer followed his feet westward through downtown City A, past quaint brick storefronts and down the oak-lined street of a quiet neighborhood on the outskirts of the city. At the end of the oak-lined street he came to a tee in the road. He paused a moment and turned right, heading north. Late afternoon shadows played on his face and he felt the city slip away, replaced by trees and open air. He found himself in a park.

Elmer smiled to himself. He felt his shoulders relax and the acidity in his stomach calm down. He stepped into the green. "Always a park," he thought to himself. "I always find myself in these little man-made, mini re-creations of nature." He strolled along, soaking in his surroundings: children on swings, picnic tables filled with people, a young couple holding hands. The air was light and crisp. It smelled faintly of lilacs and strongly of hamburgers. The sun was beginning to drop west and it painted long elegant shadows of maples and children and tall plastic slides on the grass. Somewhere to Elmer's left, the long, mournful wail of a trumpet cut across the still air. He turned. The sound emanated from just beyond a small, green hill at the end of the park. Elmer made his way towards the instrument's cry, grinning as he stepped lightly through the grass. The trumpet's song continued, twisting and turning through the park, dashing behind boulders and climbing tree trunks, chasing children as they played tag. The music rose and fell in excited waves. Elmer looked up as the sound hovered between the canopy leaves and ducked as it plummeted towards his feet. He rounded the crest of the hill and squinted towards the barrage of sound that danced around him, nipping at his ankles and tickling his heart. His smile froze—wide and ridiculous, jaw hanging sloppily open—across his face. He spotted the musician.

The musician stood facing southeast, his profile turned towards Elmer, his back against the setting sun. He stood with his shoulders pressed back and his brass instrument level, the rich tones issuing smoothly and energetically from its bell. Dreadlocks fell across his skinny, dark arms.

Zach? Zach the street bum? No, it can't be…

Elmer cautiously approached the thin-framed man who was busy making magic with his trumpet. The musician's face reflected an odd mix of calm and concentration. He looked as if the music he spun was made with the threads of his soul. As Elmer approached, he realized that the man was not alone. Spread lazily on the cropped green grass were seven or eight long-haired, extremely dirty people. Their bare feet moved slightly to the music as they sprawled across the lawn and sometimes on top of each other, using one another as living pillows. Elmer scrunched his nose in disgust. They were a blemish on the smooth surface of City A.

Elmer stopped and peered towards the trumpeter. It wasn't Zach. He could see that now. The two men shared many of the same features and carried themselves in the same, straight-backed way, but the trumpeter was slightly broader and had a flatter nose, a squarer jaw, shorter hair—shoulder length instead of trailing down his back. But Elmer could see they loved their music in the same way. He could see their music was intrinsically entwined with their souls.

Elmer sighed. He had been hypnotized by the silvery tones of the trumpet, but the trance was now broken. He glanced from one grungy vagabond to the next. They were lounging around like they owned the place, idly listening to the tones that blanketed them like the moth-eaten blankets on which they lay. Their presence miffed Elmer. He had hoped to get away from this sort of people. He had hoped to leave them in the dust, along with the skyscrapers and pollution, along with Irene and the potato fields. Somehow, he had managed to ditch the skyscrapers and Irene, but not the scruffy low-lives which he despised to his very core.

The music stopped and the tall musician kneeled to put his trumpet in its case. He tucked it away like a sleeping child. The seven or eight on the grass did not applaud, but they each wore a look of quiet satisfaction and peace. The musician bent down to join them, but paused mid-stoop. He spied the watching old man to his left and turned towards him, the corners of his mouth raising just a little. He beckoned towards Elmer with a wave of his hand. His hand and his soft, welcoming face spoke wordlessly, inviting the stranger to join his bedraggled group.

Elmer blinked nervously. Grasping the handle of his cane, he silently turned and fled. The old man did not look back. He walked back over the hill, down the length of the park, and out the gates. He hobbled briskly, leaning heavily on his cane with each step. He was astounded by the tenacity of the trumpeter. He was astounded by his quiet invitation to join the scruffy, mangy group. Who did they think he was? A common bum like them?

Elmer walked, lopsided, along the neat sidewalks of City A. He passed plain, cream-colored buildings and well-manicured lawns. He wondered how such flea-bitten riff-raff could manage to crop up in a town like City A. They didn't fit. They didn't match the normalcy. They stood out like dandelions in a rose garden. Elmer shook his head in wonder as he walked through the city. The sidewalks were empty now. It was dark and the night sky was illuminated by evenly interspersed street lights that cast dark beige shadows on light beige buildings. All the good people of City A were inside, eating dinner and watching television. Elmer also wanted to be inside, eating dinner and watching television. He turned at the intersection of Second and Spruce and found his hotel at the end of the street.

When he settled into his room, he ordered room service and flicked on the black box that stared at him across the room. His thoughts were not on the weather channel. They focused on Zach and Levi and the trumpeter in the park. He didn't care that there was a thirty-five percent chance of rain tomorrow. He hardly saw the weather man as he grinned sloppily and told a joke. All he could see were faces. He saw the face of the trumpeter, eyes beaming warmly, inviting him to be part of the camaraderie. He saw Levi's face, friendly and smiling—smiling despite his two missing teeth. He saw the moon-shaped face of the lovely woman in purple robes as she advised him to starting digging, to recover the pieces of himself that he had buried long ago. He saw Irene. He saw Papa. He saw the mysterious, bare-footed woman in long green robes and the hawk-headed man who sat next to her. Suddenly, Elmer's body began to shake and vibrate. Rainbow colors flashed before his eyes and he saw the seven sages, perched on their mountaintop thrones, as if they were in the same room as the elderly man. He stood before them, small, insignificant, ashamed at his progress. The deep voice of the man in blue boomed towards him, "Stop running, Elmer. Stop. Turn and face your fears with a shovel in hand."

Elmer's eyes met the large, grey ones of the speaker. He blinked. The eyes disappeared and were replaced by a queen-sized bed, bad hotel art, and the weatherman's too-high voice talking excitedly about thunderstorms on Sunday. Elmer's heart raced; beads of sweat gathered on his forehead and trickled down his neck. He breathed in and out, in and out, steadying his pulse.

I've lost it. I am clearly out of my head.

He flicked off the television and closed his eyes. The rich, bass voice of the man in blue echoed through his head. "Stop running, Elmer. Stop. Stop! Stop!" Elmer grabbed a pillow and pressed it against his ears. He lay, face down, willing himself to go to sleep. The voice continued. "Stop Elmer! Stop! STOP!"

"Leave me alone!" Elmer shouted. The voice persisted, but this time more quietly, like a buzz in the back of Elmer's brain. "Stop—stop—stop—stop—stop…" Elmer fell asleep to the rhythm of this command. His dreams were disjointed and tangled. He saw bodiless faces and colors and cracks of lightning and clods of dirt and music notes jumping off the tops of oak trees. Image after absurd image passed through his head. When he woke up the next morning, every image faded into the mists of his subconscious. Every image, except one: the image of a hand beckoning towards an old man in a park and the old man reaching out and grasping it.

Chapter 12

Rain fell on City A. It drizzled lightly, pitter-pattering delicately on lawns and the tops of leaves, skipping off rooftops and sliding down the backs of passersby. Elmer watched it wearily from his window. Even after his second cup of coffee, he was still feeling groggy from his rollercoaster dreams. His head spun; his stomach gurgled with nausea. He was hungover from a wild night of sleep.

The tired old man stared at the streets below. Now that it was daytime, the incidents from the night before seemed distant and farfetched. The whirl of colors, the seven seated gurus, the deep, friendly voice—it was all fluff and pixie dust. It was the creation of a sleepy old man who had had a very long day. And yet...

Stop—stop—stop

The voice still called out to Elmer. Elmer squashed it down. It promptly rose up again.

Stop—stop—stop. Elmer shoved his fingers into his ears.

Good riddance. Stop? Stop running away, you say? I'm not running. I'm just...lost.

Elmer thought of the trumpeter in the park. *I didn't run from him. Not really. I just didn't accept his invitation. How is a scruffy musician supposed to help me dig myself out anyway?*

The rain continued to dampen the earth and concrete of City A. Elmer watched it and the people below, bustling around in orthopedic shoes and raincoats. He loved orthopedic shoes. At two in the afternoon, the rain let up and Elmer decided to venture outside. He velcroed his sneakers, slung his black duffle bag over his shoulder, and marched out the door, his cane click-clacking at his side. He shuffled down wet sidewalks, avoiding worms that had risen up from the dirt in order to save themselves from drowning. Someone once told him that robins are expert worm-catchers because they trick them into believing it is raining. They pinpoint the location of a worm and start pecking the ground at random intervals, imitating falling droplets. The worm crawls out of the soil and—SNAP—into the robin's jaws. "Poor worms," Elmer thought, realizing he never felt sorry for them before. *All they want in life is to be safe. All they try to do is survive.*

Elmer looked up. He noticed he was approaching the park he discovered yesterday and he immediately forgot about the worms. The lone note of a trumpet floated off in the distance. Elmer couldn't help himself; he walked towards the music once again. This time, the song was soft and mellow. It didn't dash and skip through the park. Instead, it wrapped its long, red-velvet arms around its listener and caressed his skin with its gentle tongue. Elmer shivered. The music continued, low in tone, subtle in movement. The old man followed the sound; he couldn't help himself. The sultry song whispered delicious promises in his ear and he believed every one. Eventually, it lured him to the crest of the same hill and once again Elmer spotted the musician. He was alone this time, standing straight as an arrow in the middle of a giant puddle of mud. But he didn't seem to notice. He simply played, painting melodies with his air and his brass.

Eventually, elegantly, the song stopped. The man lowered the bell of his trumpet in one smooth motion, as if it were bowing to the earth. He felt Elmer's eyes upon him and turned his neck in the old man's direction.

"Hey!" shouted the musician in a rich mahogany voice. "You, there! Come over here, don't be shy!"

Elmer jumped. "No, quite all right!" He shouted back. "Must be off!" He turned and scuttled away, his feet squish-squashing on the wet grass. The musician stared after him, smiling serenely.

When Elmer was a good distance away, he paused, spotted a coffee shop across the street, and marched up to the entrance. A tiny bell tinkled as he heaved open the heavy glass door. Friendly warm air rushed towards him and he breathed a sigh of relief as he sat down stiffly in one of the booths.

"Stop-stop-stop," the voice of the man in blue beat in his head.

"I'm not stopping for riffraff!" Elmer replied stubbornly. He frowned at his menu and ordered a cup of chamomile tea and an oatmeal cookie. Elmer looked at his feet. His shoes and woolen socks were soaked and his toes felt like small blocks of ice. The elderly man shivered as he crossed his arms, rubbing each one briskly as he tried to chase away the cold. He thought about the trumpeter in the park and questions began bubbling in his brain. *Why did I follow his music? What made me powerless to the wail of that damn trumpet? Why did that raggedy man have to call me over like that? Why didn't he just leave me alone? For Christ's sake, why can't people just leave me alone?!* Elmer glared ferociously at his oatmeal cookie, picked it up, and took a large angry bite.

He chomped and chewed and then attacked his tea. The warm liquid burned slightly as it slid down Elmer's throat, but he kept gulping. The old man felt restless and he wanted to get back to the hotel and slip into some warm socks. He set the tea cup aside, grabbed his black duffle bag and cane, and paced up to the counter to pay.

"Four-fifty," said the young woman behind the counter in a voice as dull and bored as the cloudy day. Elmer handed her a five and waited for change. He snatched up the fifty cents she tossed casually on the counter and shoved it into his duffle bag. He glowered at the girl behind the counter. *No tip for lousy service.*

Elmer turned to leave just as the heavens opened up and started pouring buckets of rain onto the earth. *Perfect. Just perfect.* The old man had neglected to wear a raincoat and was not about to walk several blocks in the rain. He turned around and settled his bony frame into the same booth. "Just my luck," he muttered as he stared daggers at the charcoal-colored sky. The rain ignored his glare and proceeded to do what rain does best: fall.

Elmer grabbed a newspaper and read about the goings-on of City A. Garage sales, the grand opening of a new bakery, the fifteenth annual chestnut festival—nothing captured the old man's attention for more than six or seven minutes. Elmer tossed the paper aside. It was now 5:30 p.m. and hoards of people were storming inside to grab a cup of coffee before heading home for the evening. Elmer watched as they poured into the tiny shop. They were about as entertaining as the newspaper. Serious-looking businessmen in glasses and red neckties chatted about the weather and the stock market; a pair of women in gym shoes laughed about something one of their husbands had said; a young couple in matching khaki pants stood silently looking at the menu, loosely holding hands as if they didn't want to catch some rare, deadly disease the other had. Elmer watched and waited as the people came and went, came and went from the coffee shop. He propped his elbows on the table and set his head in his hands, wearily observing the mundane tide of caffeine-deprived City A residents.

The rain stopped. Without overture or warning, it stopped. Elmer lifted his head. He had drifted to sleep listening to the soft patta-patta-pat on the shingled rooftop. The old man stretched his arms, yawned, and slowly, painfully arose from his wooden seat. *Finally. Finally I can go put on some dry socks.* He grabbed his cane and reached for his black duffle bag. His hand hit air.

Startled, Elmer looked at the empty booth. It stared vacantly back. The bag was gone. *Gone.* His world had vanished.

Chapter 13

Elmer clutched his stomach and ran out of the coffee shop. His insides squirmed, a lump of vomit climbed up his throat. He choked it down and ran wildly into the street, waving his arms up and down, shouting nonsense. He snapped his neck to the left and to the right, frantically searching for the thief. Car horns blared and angry drivers shouted. Elmer limped back to the sidewalk, a bowling ball weighing down his stomach.

He was too shocked to cry. He was too shocked to move. The old man stood, quivering on the sidewalk, his eyes fixed on nothing in particular. People in yellow raincoats jostled around him as he stood, statue-still. He was a stone in the river and the indifferent water rushed around him without pause.

My bag. My bag. My bag. My bag.

Elmer stared straight ahead.

No. No. No. No.

His mind buzzed. It was as heavy as his stomach.

I'm lost. I'm lost in the wilderness. I'm lost. I'm lost in the wilderness. No bread and water. No bread. No water. No shelter from the storm. Human. I'm human. I'm trapped on earth with nothing. No bread. No water. I'm lost. I'm lost.

The stiff yellow raincoats poured around him.

Help. Help. Help! Help? Help. I beg you. I'm just an old man. Why. Why? Why didn't you just leave me alone? Why didn't you leave an old man alone? I have nothing. I have nothing. I am lost. Without a friend or companion, I am lost. Ouch! My stomach is eating itself. The knots are twisting like snakes. Snakes slithering in a great pit. They are eating their way to freedom. Ouch! I hurt. I'm in pain. The pain is red. Dark red, like my guts. Dark red, like smashed worms on the sidewalks. Dark red, like the blood that runs through my heart.

Just an old lunatic on the sidewalk. Best to avoid him. Don't touch him with your yellow raincoat; he might stain it red.

My heart is frozen, frozen like my toes.

Step around him. There you go. Don't get too close. He might bite.

Ouch. It's so heavy—my heart too.

What old lunatic? Where? I don't see him.

A speeding car sped by Elmer and splashed him with mud. The old man's body convulsed violently and his brain snapped to attention. Murky, brown water dripped down his sweater and khaki trousers, pooling in the cuffs of his pants.

The police. I must go to the police.

Elmer uprooted himself from the sidewalk and stepped slowly to the east. A petite, nervous-looking woman gave him directions to the police station and he ambled on, eyes looking vaguely ahead to where the sun was disappearing behind the horizon. A plain, square building held the police station. Elmer wandered inside.

"May I help you?" the secretary forced her voice to sound polite. She looked disapprovingly at the elderly man's muddy clothing and vacant eyes.

"Yes," Elmer's voice was hollow and distant. He wasn't sure where it was coming from or how it was forming words. The voice continued, "My bag. It was stolen. Stolen. Just now."

"I see. Well you'll have to fill out a police report," she shoved a piece of paper and a clipboard into his thin, shaking hands. "Have a seat."

Elmer silently took the clipboard and sat down in one of the stiff, red chairs. The secretary watched him over the top of her glasses. Name—Date of Birth—Social Security Number—Phone Number—Address.

Oh god.

Elmer looked up. The secretary pretended to examine the sign behind him. "Erm, ma'am," he said quietly, his actual voice returning to his lungs. "Can't I just tell you what happened? Do you really need all of this other information?"

"Sorry," she said in a voice that sounded anything but sorry. "You have to fill out the entire form. It's protocol." Her smile was reminiscent of fake coffee sweetener.

"I see," said Elmer in a small, defeated voice. "Right now I don't have a permanent address."

"Ok then, where are you living?"

The question punched Elmer in the gut. He winced. He couldn't remember ever feeling so small. So embarrassed by merely existing. He reluctantly summoned up an answer. "At—at the hotel on Second Street. But—but not anymore I'm afraid. Now I'm not really sure where I'm going to live…"

The secretary looked as if she had just stepped in something unpleasant with her favorite pair of heels. "Ok, sir. Regardless, we need the entire form completed. We need to know who you are."

Who—you—are.

The words pierced the old man like three poisonous darts. "I don't know," he said in a voice, barely audible. "I don't know who I am."

"Sir?"

Elmer stood up quickly, the clipboard sliding off of his lap and clattering to the ground. "I—I have to go," he blurted and flew out the door, leaving the secretary blinking in his wake. She stared incredulously for a moment and then arose, walked around her desk, and picked up the discarded clipboard. She looked at the crumpled form attached to it. Elm— was scrawled across the top.

"Elm? What a bizarre old man. It's loonies like him that ruin the reputation of a respectable city like ours. If I see him in here again, I'll call the police." She tittered to herself. "They won't have to go very far."

Chapter 14

A week had crawled by since the robbery and life in City A was just about the same. Business went on as usual. Play went on as usual. Beige buildings continued being beige. Maybe some people noticed a sickly-looking old man roaming the streets, poking his head into dumpsters. Maybe they noticed him shivering as he slept on park benches and under the Main Street bridge and in the entry way of the Johnson-Heimler Elementary School. Maybe they noticed these things, but they probably didn't. Life marched on as usual.

But not for a frail, frightened old man from far away. His life did not march. Instead, it broke free from the marching line, seized the old man, and flung him out the window of a thirty-story building, laughing maniacally as he fell. His life had betrayed him.

At least, that's what Elmer thought as he prowled behind restaurants each night, waiting for them to close. That's what he thought as he dug through heaps of rubbish, seeking the edible bits that had been casually tossed aside. He thought—he felt—that life had betrayed him. It had eaten his food, shared his bed, worn his clothes, and then plucked out his eyes, slept with his wife, and left him in the desert to fend for himself. Elmer fended. He had no choice, but to fend. However, with only a week of homelessness under his belt, he was ready to quit. He was thin, cold, and his body ached with such intensity that he sometimes fell over from the violent waves of pain that coursed through him.

Mornings were the worst. Elmer felt pinned to the ground in the morning. His body reminded him every day that he was too old to be sleeping on park benches or cold cement or under low-hanging bushes. His hip bones jutted out from his body and the thin layer of skin that hung around them provided little padding for the old man. He would wake up with his joints on fire and his muscles bound up in tight balls. But the thing that hurt the most was Elmer's crushed dignity. The weight of his situation sat heavily on his shoulders, pressing him to the ground like the beefy hands of a schoolyard bully. The pressure was nearly unbearable. It nearly killed him every morning.

Elmer was a proud man. He built up his life, brick by painstaking brick, over the course of several decades. He had a decent job and a decent house and a couple of average, but well-maintained, cars. He sent two kids to college. He was never without food or clothing or a well-stocked bank account. He wondered how anyone could go hungry or be without an average, but well-maintained, car. He spent his brick-laying decades building up his life and building up his pride. And in a moment, it was gone. There were no fireworks or parades to send it off. There was only a wrecking ball. A crash. A pile of rubble. And an old man trapped inside the building as the beams clattered down.

So what if the building had been weak in the first place? Who cares if the skeleton was made of plastic Lego blocks and the exterior was sheets of aluminum foil? It still looked good, didn't it? It still kept the rain out. It was something to point to and say, "Look, would you. That's mine. That's my building. I have something pretty. I have something that stands. It's mine. And it fits in well with all the buildings around it, doesn't it? Not too showy, but not shabby either. It fits in well. Doesn't it? Doesn't it? Please say it does. You approve, don't you?"

At that moment, Elmer didn't care that his life had been built on fake dreams and rehearsed actions. It was all he knew. He was not prepared to start from scratch. He was not prepared to sweep away the rubble and start constructing a golden castle. He had simply wanted to remodel. He wanted to swap the plastic beams for steel. The structure was fine. Just fine.

Every morning, Elmer would eventually get up, but his body would stay buried under the rubble. It would lay, eyes blinking in the darkness, surrounded by bits of plastic and aluminum foil. It was too horrified to move.

Elmer walked through City A in a daze. He picked through Styrofoam to-go boxes and soggy paper bags with eyes glazed-over and limbs mechanical. He would eat out of habit and then find a place to sit. His will to explore was gone. Sitting was about all he could handle. Every now and then, Elmer would snap out of his zombified state and burst into tears. He would blubber like an idiot, screaming to the sky, shouting the names of Papa and Daisy and Irene and his two children. He would ask for forgiveness. He would criticize himself and admit they were right. They were all right. Papa was right—he had a good-for-nothing son that should have been content with fake walls and plastic beams. Elmer would sob and scream and then stop. His mouth would snap shut and the numbness would set in once again. He would sit and stare. Stare and sit. Life in City A flowed steadily around him like a river skipping over a rock.

Once a young woman with nylon stockings and a pair of patent leather pumps walked by Elmer, chatting noisily with a small group of older ladies to her left. She used proper grammar and stood ram-rod straight as she strolled and gabbed. The older women were enthralled and seemed to relish the fact that their younger companion had the limelight. When the group was level with the old man seated on a park bench, the young lady paused, dug purposefully in her handbag for a few long seconds, and emerged with a crisp dollar bill. The older ladies waited with bated breath as the woman delicately placed the bill on the mud-stained lap of the old man. She smiled a too-big grin, turned to the group, and walked away, continuing the thread of the conversation as if it had never stopped. The older women beamed and trotted alongside her.

Elmer was horrified. He stared at the dollar bill, perched mockingly in his lap, for several minutes. He hadn't asked for the money. He wasn't a beggar. No, not that. Surely the proud young woman had not mistaken him for a common tramp. Elmer examined his hands. The fingernails were black, the knuckles caked with mud. His pants were no longer khaki-colored, but yellowish-brown with grass stains marring the once-pristine knees. His pants and shirt were not laundered, starched, and pressed. His wispy white hair was not trimmed and neatly combed. Mud was caked on his left cheek—the one he normally slept on.

Of course the young woman with the stiff back and clear voice thought he was a charity case. Of course. What else would she think? Would she believe he had a family and a home and a steady job his entire life? Would she bother to ask? No. No, of course not. She was too busy looking at his grass stains and mud-smeared face and his dejected, vacant eyes. She was too busy earning social points.

The dollar bill stared at Elmer indifferently. It didn't care about the feelings of an old man. It didn't care about his wounded pride and crushed ego. It ignored his agony as he looked at his dirty hands, his black fingernails. The dollar bill simply stared. Elmer stuffed it into his pocket angrily.

Charity case. Bum. Tramp. That's all I am now. That's all I am. Bum. Tramp. Vagabond. Without a home. Without a purpose. I think I had a purpose once…

A week had gone by. Elmer was certain he could not last another.

* * *

It rained. Hard. It wasn't the same grey drizzle that had fallen on City A on the day Elmer's world was stolen. This rain was thick and jagged. It penetrated the earth like falling daggers and blackened the sky with its enormity. A few yellow rain coats scampered down the sidewalk, but most citizens of City A were tucked safely inside. It was not a day for walking down sidewalks.

It was also not a day for hiding in schoolyards. But that is precisely what one non-citizen of City A was doing. He was hiding in a plastic tube at the top of a plastic, twisted slide. His neck and back were hunched, his knees bent. Plastic tubes at the top of plastic slides are not very big. They are not meant for old men—old men who are hiding from the thick, jagged rain.

Elmer had no choice. The playground of the Johnson-Heimler Elementary School was the nearest refuge he could find when the rain set in. At first, he dashed under the entryway of the little brick schoolhouse, but security didn't stand for that very long. No perverted old men allowed near *this* establishment. Desperate and soaked, Elmer scrambled to the playground, plunging his cane into the mud and slllucking it out again with every step. He spotted the tube at the top of the slide. With great effort and plenty of pain, he climbed the small ladder that led to the top of the playground. He squeezed himself into the tube and rested his muddy cane on his lap. He willed himself to die.

Rock bottom. I've hit rock bottom.

He reached into his pocket and squeezed the dollar bill the young lady had given him yesterday. He looked around at his bright orange, plastic surroundings. He felt each vertebra in his back jutting against his skin.

And I thought yesterday was bad. I thought yesterday was rock bottom…

Elmer tried to lay on his side, his elbows bent, his legs dangling inside the plastic slide. He put his hands in front of his face to block the rain. The rain ignored his feeble efforts and came in anyway. It soaked his face and trickled down his neck and back. It mixed with his snot and dribbled down his chin. The rain made it difficult to be a zombie. The rain forced Elmer to think. Elmer cursed the rain.

Cursed and thought. Cursed and thought and willed himself to die. Things would be much easier. Then, he wouldn't have to think about his past. He wouldn't have to think about There and all the colors of the rainbow and plastic drums and missing teeth. He wouldn't have to think about the young girl on the train, curled up in the exact fetal position as himself, drool running down her face instead of icy rain. He cursed his thoughts and the rain and his aimless wandering.

Isn't that all I've done? Isn't that what I've done my entire life? I've never really known where I was going. It didn't matter as long as I put one foot in front of the other. It didn't matter as long as I looked like I knew where I was going.

Elmer closed his eyes tightly. The rain beat against his lids. *Seventy-eight. Seventy-eight and lost. So lost.*

The rain pounded against his wrinkled brow, forcing the old man deeper into his memories. He saw himself. He saw bare feet and grimy overalls clinging to a skinny, scrappy frame. He saw an impish smile and a fishing basket. He saw his hand, smooth and brown, pick up a flat stone by the river and skip it along the dancing water. He saw an oak tree, huge and crooked, its roots stretching towards the flowing water like the tentacles of a gigantic brown octopus. Old Elmer smiled sadly at little Elmer. Little Elmer smiled at the water and stretched out underneath the oak tree. He reached into his fishing basket and dug out a writhing, skinny worm. He hooked the worm, seized his fishing line, and cast it into the water with easy confidence.

Little Elmer was a fisherman. He was happy. He was in love with a young girl named Daisy and she was in love with him. He knew these things for sure. They were fact. He didn't bother with thinking about them too much, he just knew.

Elmer looked at the young boy. He couldn't look away. He loved him.

Where did I go wrong? When did I become unsure?

The little boy cast his line again. His confidence amazed Elmer. The boy had not yet been beaten to death with harsh words and disparaging remarks. He had not yet decided it was better to please others than to exercise free will. He had not yet started construction on his plastic world. There was no middle-management job or two kids or wife from a good and proper family.

The boy just fished. And smiled.

* * *

Four hours later, the rain stopped and Elmer emerged from his plastic cocoon. He stretched his limbs, one at a time, feeling the soreness in his muscles, feeling the mass of knots that ran along his spine. His head refused to look right until he massaged the bound-up muscles in his neck. It was late afternoon and the old man had nowhere to go. Nowhere to go but down the ladder. So he went down and felt his too-thin body shaking violently. He could not control it. His shoulders and knees and head moved by their own volition, making a rough epileptic dance across the playground.

Elmer leaned on his cane and willed his feet to shuffle across the road. If he was spotted by school security again, *they* would surely take him in. They. The impersonal mass of people who were suspicious and wary of the raggedy old man. They who continued living, unaffected by the homeless old man and his violent shaking. Some of them saw him, walking drunkenly down the street as he followed his vibrating limbs. They ignored him. They were better off ignoring him.

Eventually, Elmer found himself in a park. It was the park he liked to avoid. The park where the trumpeter played and the barefooted people gathered. It was the only place he knew he would be recognized and he certainly did not want to be recognized. But Elmer's shaking body led him there and he was powerless to stop it.

He was powerless to stop his knees as they buckled, powerless to stop his shaking shoulders as they thrust forward and hit the ground. He couldn't control his neck enough to raise his head above the sticky mud. So he lay on the ground. He let the mud leak in through his open mouth and his closed eyes. He lay there shaking, convulsing, trying to banish his thoughts. Trying to banish his pride.

His pride remained. It stuck by his side like a loyal dog.

Minutes ticked by slowly, painfully, like the movements of a sad, old man. Elmer lay helpless and shivering, thinking of death. And the distant memory of a little boy with a fishing basket. His thoughts mushed together and swam through his head—a swirl of colors and shapes. He felt helpless and small amongst the loud mish-mash of colors. They snuck up behind him and skirted around his legs, brushing against him smoothly like a horsehair brush. He tried to concentrate his thoughts, to tie all the wild hues together into one entity, but the colors continued swimming. In the midst of the colors and distorted shapes, two forms leaped into his mind—a green one and a red one. They were two women, one dancing, the other staring straight ahead and occasionally flicking her long, grey braid.

Elmer cried out to them. He hadn't seen them in years, he was sure of it. He had forgotten about them. Their memory had been buried between the folds of robbery and humiliation. Now, he forgot that he had forgotten. He reached out to them like a small child reaching towards its mother.

They smiled. Their smiles were kind and warm. Elmer smiled weakly back.

Without a word, the two stooped down, one on either side of the elderly man, and lifted him to his feet. His body was still; his mind was calm. He felt their hands, smooth and gentle, propping him up, filling his body with warmth and light. He smiled. They clasped his withered hands in theirs and they started walking. Elmer's strides were short and precise. They were not shaky.

Through the park, under the large shade trees, and over the saturated grass of a green hill they walked, hand-in-hand. Elmer forgot to shake. He forgot about his snot and wet socks and knotted back. He basked in the light of the two women—one green, wild, and sentimental, the other red, rhythmic, and passionate. He followed them as if in a trance. He had not felt so good in weeks.

They rounded the crest of the hill and Elmer heard music. It was the music of a trumpet. He jerked to attention, his eyes searching for the musician. He saw the profile of the man, this time alone, standing serenely at the base of the hill. His music was lovely and clear. Elmer stared at the man he had tried to avoid—the only man who had acknowledged his presence in City A. The only one. The old man bowed his head, his face humble. He stood, in between green and red, listening to the music that never failed to entrance him. Minutes passed and mud slid down Elmer's back and pooled at his belt. He didn't notice. All he noticed was the brassy lullaby that buzzed sweetly from the trumpeter's bell. No thoughts passed through the old man's head, only sensations.

The music stopped. The musician turned. He recognized the old man on the hill and once again beckoned to him with an open hand. The gesture was simple and sincere, like a single quarter note on a page.

Elmer looked at his shoes, mud-stained and soaked. He looked at his dirt-streaked pants. He looked up. This time, he was not too proud to follow the hand.

So he followed. One foot led the other as he slowly descended the wet, glistening hill. His shoes sunk slightly with each step and his feet felt heavy and bloated. Elmer grasped his cane. He realized with a start that his right hand no longer held onto the woman in red. The smooth wood of his cane had replaced the smooth skin of her hand and a panicky feeling welled up inside the fragile old man. He glanced to his left—no long braid, no green robe. Just long grass and green fields. His feet stopped moving. He felt empty and alone. His eyes darted to the bottom of the hill where the musician stood and waited patiently. Elmer wanted to cry out to him, to shout for help. Instead, his feet forgot how to walk and his hands forgot how to use a cane. The old man started to fall. For one clear, excruciating moment, right before he hit the ground with a dull thud, Elmer became painfully aware of his body. He felt every swollen joint, every knotted muscle. He became aware of his hollow stomach and parched throat. His soggy skin was covered in goosebumps from the rain and the cold. His breath came in short raspy gulps. He felt every pore and fingernail and internal organ as they worked tirelessly together to give him life.

And then he felt nothing. He didn't notice the ground as his cheek smashed against it. He didn't hear the trumpeter's cry as he tossed aside his beloved instrument and sprinted up the hill. All he saw was black. It was as black as a single quarter note on a page.

Chapter 15

Doors opened and closed. Footsteps trod on hardwood floors and through black dirt. Hands held each other and kitchen knives and overdue bills. Clothes cycled between bodies and the floor and the clothes line and back to bodies again. People woke up. People went to sleep. Some people worked in between. Most did not. All lived.

They lived together under one roof, in constant ebb and flow, in crescendo and decrescendo. They wove in and out of each other's lives, filling in the blank spaces that needed to be filled and stepping aside at the right moments to let others leave their mark on the page. They worked. They fit. They moved in harmony, but not like a machine. They moved like a dancer. Or a song.

An old man had been tossed into their midst. They had swallowed him up, like a stone under streaming lava, and continued to flow around him. Perhaps he would join them in their movement, but all in good time. These things could not be forced.

Elmer could feel life around him. As he dozed, he was dimly aware of the human energy that filled the small, clapboard house. He could sense it walking down the halls and tip-toeing up to his bed as he slept. Occasionally he woke up, acknowledged that he was awake, and drifted back to sleep. He slept for three days.

On the third day, he felt heavy rays of light playing on his face. He squeezed his eyelids tightly together, yawned, and stretched his thin arms. Slowly, he released his lids and his eyes became clouded with vision. It was the vision of a man who had spent the last three days seeing nothing but black, nothing but the inside of his own eyelids. He could see, but it was fuzzy around the edges and every shape seemed smooth and monochromatic. Elmer rubbed his eyes and felt around for his glasses. He found them on the nightstand and slid them behind his ears and over the bridge of his nose. Slowly, his eyes focused and his brain began to make sense of its surroundings.

He was in a room—a small bedroom—that was elaborately decorated, but comfortable. Fabric hung from the ceiling and formed glossy curtains around the twin bed, casting green and blue shadows on its sheets. The only furniture, besides the small bed and nightstand, was a square table with an antique lamp and a large bookcase, teeming with books of all sizes and shapes. The shelves of the bookcase sagged and the structure seemed ready to collapse from the weight of all the knowledge it held.

Elmer's gaze wandered from the bookcase to the walls. Artwork littered the space, cramming into every nook and cranny, elbowing for room and attention. There were paintings and charcoal drawings and mosaics and weavings and oil pastel drawings. They showed people and places and abstract shapes. They didn't follow certain subject matter or style, but Elmer knew they were from the same artist. They were like pages from a journal, ripped out and pasted on the wall. Elmer was a little embarrassed to look at them. He lowered his gaze and looked at the bed instead, examining the homemade quilt that covered his skeletal body. It was multi-colored and bright and held together with tight, careful stitches. He looked at his clothes. Someone had swapped his grimy, mud-caked pants and shirt for a worn, but clean, t-shirt and loosely-fitted linen pants.

The old man lifted the t-shirt and looked at his sunken belly. It stared back at him, pale, speckled, and hollow. He suddenly became sharply and painfully aware of his physical state. His muscles were sore and bruised and his brain pounded against his skull. His right shoulder felt like it was out of its socket. Elmer raised his left arm and rubbed his hand against his cheek. The skin was scratched and tender to the touch.

And then Elmer remembered falling. Twice. He remembered huddling in a plastic tube at the top of a slide. He remembered his hypothermic cold and the slippery mud that filled his shoes and tugged at his cane. He pictured himself lying pathetically in the dirt, willing himself to die. Why hadn't he died? Something had stopped him. Something had told him *NO* and walked him over to safety—to the beckoning hands of the trumpeter. Death had not been an option.

Where was the trumpeter now? For the first time, Elmer thought of the wiry black man in the park. This must be his home. Elmer glanced shyly at the hodge-podge of artwork on the walls. He felt voyeuristic and uncomfortable.

The plain wooden door in the corner creaked open with a low squeal. Elmer jumped.

"Well, well. You're awake. Roger will be pleased." A young woman stepped through the door. Her hair was blonde and stringy; it fell loosely over her shoulders, past her breasts. She wore a broad grin and a long, flowing skirt packed with reds and oranges and mauve paisley swirls. She turned and shouted over her shoulder, "Hey Ezzie, Onyx! He's awake!"

Elmer sat in bed, tight-lipped, blinking at the young lady. He heard a set of footsteps thub-thubbing up the stairs. The long-haired girl stepped aside and a short, heavy-set girl with shiny, jet-black hair cut in an asymmetrical bob walked into the room. Elmer eyed her suspiciously, glancing from her lip ring to her studded belt to the swallows and ships that encompassed her entire right arm. "*She has more ink than that bookcase,*" thought Elmer wryly.

To the old man's horror, the dark-haired girl walked up to the bed, stooped down, and wrapped her arms around his bent shoulders in a gentle hug. Elmer did not hug back. The girl released him and stepped back, smiling as broadly as the girl with the long skirt. "I was so worried about you, Old Turtle! Thank the goddess you're awake!"

Elmer stared at her as if she had just sprouted wings and started flapping around and around the room in manic circles. The girl continued grinning.

"I'm Onyx," she said, her face uncomfortably close to Elmer's. "And that," she pointed over her shoulder, "is Cecelia." The girl in the doorway waved and stepped forward a little.

"Jesus! Don't overwhelm him Ons." She looked at Elmer's wide eyes. A smile passed over her pale face, warm and understanding. She addressed the frail old man; her voice was soft and private, like she was telling him a secret. "You probably don't know what to think of all this, do you? For starters, we—Onyx and I, that is—have been calling you Old Turtle since you got here. No one else in the house has really picked it up—"

"—Especially not Ezzie," Onyx cut in. "She doesn't believe in spirit names or any of that. She says it's a load of hamster shit—her words, not mine—and that anyone who believes in that nonsense should be run over with a truck. Ezzie is a bit of an anomaly in this house—you'll see. Anyway, there are eight of us right now, nine if we count you, but people are in and out all the time. It's always sad to see people go, but new ones are always taking their places and at least things don't get stale. Besides, that's the natural way of things, isn't it? Ebb and flow, give and take, cycles of life and all that. You plant the corn, you nurture it, you watch it grow, and then you mow it down. You drink the water, you piss it out, it evaporates into the clouds, and then it returns with the rain. Cycles. That's what our whole world is about. Hell, that's what the whole universe is about. Just look at the moon. Just think about the earth revolving around the sun. Same number of days, same cosmic path. But I digress…"

Elmer stared, slack-jawed. He was at a loss for words, so he said nothing.

Cecelia gave him a small smile. She leaned forward. "Ons, I think we'd better let the poor man rest. He'll come down when he's ready. Come on."

"But he's been snoozing for three days straight," the dark-haired girl whined in protest, "he *can't* be tired."

"Three days?" The old man said in a low voice. The two girls looked in the direction of the voice.

"So, Old Turtle does talk after all," said Onyx, with a half-grin.

Elmer nodded silently.

"You're not tired, are you O.T? Tell Cecelia here that you're not tired and let's take you downstairs to meet the rest of the crew."

Elmer spoke in the same quiet voice, "No, I'm not tired." He glanced down at his sunken stomach. "Hungry perhaps, but not tired." Elmer looked up at the two young girls. He wondered why he said that. His honesty surprised him.

"Where on earth are our manners!" said Cecelia, shaking her head for emphasis. "Of course you're hungry—I'd be starving too! Onyx, let's go downstairs and make some tabouli salad or something. Come on."

"I—I mean—it's really ok. I'm not that hungry. Don't go through any trouble on my account. Please."

"Oh hush up!" said Onyx, laughing. "We're not going to let any old people starve today. No one ever goes hungry in this house, let alone some skinny-ass old man that we took in off the street—"

"Onyx!" Cecelia cut in. "You have no fucking tact, girl. You're making him feel like a stray dog."

"No, no. It's alright," muttered the old man. "It's true, I guess. I am an old stray dog."

Cecelia smiled sadly at the old man. Onyx started to say something, but bit back her words. Elmer squinted at the girls; their features were blurred through the uncomfortable air. He turned bright red. He was embarrassed by his candidness.

Cecelia broke the silence first. Her voice was soft and empathic—a mix between pity and awe. "You have quite a story, don't you?"

Elmer looked at her blue-grey eyes; they reminded him of a storm. He thought about what she had said. A story? Him? His life stretched before him like an endless wheat field, tan and stiff, swaying rigidly with the gentle breeze. A story? No. Not really. She was mistaken. There was nothing worth telling. There was only monochromatic rigidity. There were only the dull days of a dull man.

Cecelia spoke again. "Let's worry about stories later. How about this—I'll get you a towel. There's a shower down the hall and to the left. Take your time; rinse off all that mud. By the time you're finished we'll have something ready for you to eat." She gestured to Onyx, "Come on, let's leave him alone."

Elmer had no time to protest. Cecelia and Onyx marched out the door. The old man took a deep breath. In the not-so-distant past, he would have rejected the girls' invitation with a flat, "No thank you." They didn't fit with his world of pressed khaki slacks and clean, normal haircuts. They didn't speak or act in ways to which he was accustomed. They were foreign to him. But he was a visitor in their land, not vice-versa. He had washed up on their shores like a baby in a basket, helpless and innocent. Who was he to refuse a free meal? Pride—what was that?

A knock at the door interrupted Elmer's thoughts. Cecelia poked her head in. "Here you are." She tossed a faded green towel onto the table. "See you downstairs in a bit."

"Thank you," Elmer said as the door closed with a gentle click. He frowned at the green towel—it wasn't a frown of disapproval. It was a thoughtful frown. It remained static on Elmer's face as his world views crumbled a little—only a little.

She's so…nice. Why is she so nice? Why is a vile hippie helping an old man like me? What does she want? There is a motive for everything. If she thinks I'm going to join her free-love, Communist cult, she has another thing coming…

Elmer sneered at the towel. It was a half-hearted sneer. It convinced nobody, including the old man who wore the flimsy expression.

She must have a motive. And her friend too. It's tucked away behind her tattoos.

Elmer looked at his hands. Mud still clung to the tiny hairs on his knuckles; it was kneaded into the swirls of his fingerprints; it choked the white from underneath his fingernails. Elmer found it hard to care about ulterior motives when his skin ached so violently for a hot shower.

The old man crawled out of bed and straightened his spine as far as it would allow. His muscles remembered how to behave like muscles and they guided him out of the room and down the hallway. As Elmer stood in the warm stream of water, he felt his tension and suspicions melt away and swirl down the drain with the mud from his body. He opened his mouth and gulped down some of the liquid; it tasted exotic and sweet, like dark, rich coffee. Elmer savored the warmth and the smooth caress of the droplets on his skin. He stood facing the nozzle, letting the water hit him squarely on his narrow chest and trickle down his thin, pale legs. A few days ago, he had cursed the water as it fell from the sky, dribbling down his back and dampening his shoes and his spirits. Now, water was falling on him in a different form—one he thoroughly enjoyed. One he could control completely.

The old man spent half an hour basking in the clean heat of the shower. He scrubbed and soaked until his legs grew tired and his skin was even more wrinkled than usual. Then he stepped out of the tub, wrapped the worn green towel around his waist, and softly stepped back to the same room, leaving a trail of droplets and watery footprints behind him. His heart beat slowly and steadily. His breath came in full, even intervals. He wondered why he felt so calm in the strange house.

When he stepped back through the doorway of the artist's room, Elmer spotted his old clothes, washed and neatly folded, perched attentively on the bed. They seemed much too beige for the vibrant room. Nevertheless, Elmer was happy to see them and he picked up his pants and shirt tenderly, as if they were old friends he hadn't seen in a very long time. He dressed quickly, his mind on his hollow, gurgling stomach. Tantalizing odors from the kitchen had jumped off the frying pan, raced up the stairs, and were now tickling the hungry old man's nose, teasing him relentlessly. He followed the aromas (were they sweet or spicy? He couldn't decide) and ended up downstairs. When he quietly walked into the kitchen, a collective cheer broke loose. A million voices began talking at him, asking him a million questions and articulating a million different thoughts. Elmer was briefly swept up in the whirlwind of fan worship and let himself enjoy his brief celebrity.

"He's here!"

" Hooray, he's up!"

" Are you clean, O.T? Get all the mud off?"

"Good to see you old boy. Never thought you'd wake up."

"Come here! Have a seat. Let me dish you up some eggplant stir fry and tabouli. It's delicious. I made it myself."

"Come on, little one. Don't be shy. Pull up a chair."

Slightly dazed, Elmer walked to the kitchen table without saying a word. He looked at the sea of faces, grinning unabashedly, and quickly averted his eyes. The attention made him uncomfortable. Cecelia tapped him on the shoulder and slid a steaming plate of food under his elbow. Elmer murmured a thank you, nodded in the general direction of the crowd of people, and attacked his food. He didn't mean to attack it, but he couldn't hold back. The smells were teasing him again and he was in no position to resist. As he ate, the group smiled contentedly and chatted amongst themselves. A few of them also grabbed dishes of stir fry and ate quietly alongside their guest. They seemed to silently agree to let the old man enjoy his food in peace. Elmer was grateful. He was enjoying a near-holy moment with his food and did not want to be interrupted. He was not exactly sure what he was eating, but it tasted better than anything he could remember. It tasted like manna from heaven.

After he wolfed down the last bite of vegetables and licked his fork clean, Elmer looked up once again at the collection of people. They looked back. He suddenly felt like he was on stage and had just forgotten his lines.

"I—" Elmer began. He wasn't sure where his sentence wanted to go. "So—I—it was delicious. I mean—thank you."

"You're welcome," a few of them replied. There was a strong feeling in the room that something was about to happen. But no one spoke. The something could not be forced.

Elmer examined the group. There were five women and three men. Two black, five white, one Asian. His eyes rested on the musician from the park. He nodded. The musician nodded back. Nothing was said. The silence was slab-of-butter thick and Elmer grew more and more uncomfortable. When he couldn't bear it any longer, he sliced through the heavy silence with a quick, awkward cut.

"So…you all live here?" The question was stilted and forced. It would have made a less-gentle group ignore the speaker and carry on as if they hadn't heard him. Fortunately, this group was more than gentle and forgave the speaker's awkwardness.

"Yes," came the answer from the mouth of the musician, "Yes we do. It's the eight of us now, but that number is always changing. We tend to pick up stray dogs from time to time." The musician glanced over at Onyx and gave her a small wink and a crooked smile.

"Oh, cut it out, Roger. You know I didn't mean to insult him."

"I know, I know," came the reply. "I'm giving you a hard time. You were just being Onyx." He turned to the old man. Words rolled smoothly and gently over the musicians tongue. He didn't seem to know the difference between talking and singing. "Our group is always changing," he explained, "but while we're together, we're family. We're a collective of brothers and sisters: learning, growing, living together. We support each other in any way we can. Some of us work. Some of us garden or sew or cook the meals. All of us share our knowledge and experience. Everyone has something to offer. Everyone."

"Jesus Roger," a coarse voice cut in, juxtaposing roughly with his smooth one. "You make this place sound so fucking ideal, like all we do is sit around and sing kumbaya and talk about our feelings. Come on, now. You forget that the rest of the capitalist world doesn't like all this commune, lovey-dovey, 'let's share' bullshit. He's probably ready to fly the coop right now."

Roger ignored the speaker and turned back to the wide-eyed old man once again. "Allow me to introduce Ezzie. She's the resident pessimist of the bunch."

"Realist. Resident realist," Ezzie retorted. "And it's a damn good thing one of us doesn't skip around all day with her head in the clouds." She walked up to Elmer and extended a hand, "Esmeralda. Pleased to meet you."

Elmer grasped the hand and briefly shook it, gazing in wonder at the crass woman. She didn't seem to fit. For one, she was old—relatively speaking. Most of the group appeared to be in their twenties or thirties. They were bright-eyed, energetic, and full of life. Ezzie was none of these things. She was at least mid-fifties, tired-looking, and annoyed. She also seemed to be the only one that did not whole-heartedly embrace the spirit of the group. They were bound together by something higher—something more noble—than common human existence. Elmer could sense it. He wasn't sure what it was, but he was certain that Ezzie didn't completely buy into it. He didn't blame her. It was all a little strange and cult-like. Ezzie had hit the nail on the head—he had been ready to fly the coop. But where could he fly? His wings had been clipped. He could see no other option but to stay. For now, at least. At least for now.

"Ahem," said Esmeralda. It wasn't a cough, but a "hey you."

"Er—yes?" said Elmer, unsure what she wanted.

"And you are?"

"I—" Elmer hesitated. Was this a trick question? He remembered the secretary in the police station. Why was everyone so anxious to know who he is? He didn't know; how could they?

"Your name," Esmeralda prodded. "What is your name?"

"I—it's…Elmer." Elmer replied hesitantly. He felt as if he hadn't really answered the question. But the sea of nodding faces seemed to approve, so he left it at that.

"Elmer," Onyx said his name thoughtfully. She rolled the letters around in her mouth and spit them out again carefully. "Elm-er. That's definitely an old person name isn't it? Not nearly as good as Old Turtle, but I guess we can't help it if our parents had poor taste—"

"Onyx!" a new voice cut in. It was the strong, clear voice of a willowy black woman. She stood perfectly straight, despite the small child she balanced on the side of her hip. The child was quiet and discreet. Elmer had not noticed it until just that moment. The woman continued to chide Onyx, "Girl, a person's name is a very special thing. You shouldn't belittle it."

"I wasn't trying to, Maggie!" protested Onyx, blowing her jet-black bangs out of her face with more force than necessary. "I mean, you can't deny it's an old person name. Could be worse too. He could be a Harold or a Cornelius or a Milford or something. At least Elmer sounds kind of like a tree—an elm. Hey, that could even be his spirit name—Elm Tree—if he doesn't like Old Turtle, that is."

Ezzie rolled her eyes. "Isn't a 'spirit name' a label that's granted by a deity? That's the whole fucking point, isn't it? You can't just assign him a spirit name. Not that I believe any of that shit…"

"Ok, ok," Maggie stepped in between the two women in one fluid motion. Her child moved effortlessly with her as if it was another limb instead of a human being. "I'm sorry Elmer," she said, glancing over her right shoulder at Onyx and then over her left shoulder at Ezzie. "Sometimes we get a little excited about having a new body in the house. We completely forget our manners. And, by the way, your name is lovely and it suits you just fine. I remember when Onyx found out my name is short for Margaret. I was in for a solid week of heckling, but fortunately I'm from the South-side of The City. My feathers don't get ruffled too easily."

"Sorry Elm," Onyx muttered. "I didn't mean to offend."

Elmer shrugged. He wasn't offended. He didn't care one way or another about his name. He had never thought much about it. It was just another label that he carried through life. It held just as much significance as "man" or "thin" or "pale." It was just a way to distinguish himself from the billions of people on the planet. It was just a way to get a letter to his mailbox or money out of the bank.

"Well, *I* think your name is fabulous," said a young, petite Asian man to Elmer's left. "It's a strong name, you know."

"Is it? I didn't know."

"Oh yes. It sounds a lot like Elmo, the saint. St. Elmo is a protector, you know. He's also the patron saint of sailors. He protects them on their voyages across the sea—"

"Oh, Craig! You sound like a fucking encyclopedia!" said another young man, poking him in the ribs. He turned to Elmer. "Don't let him bother you with his ramblings. He does it all the time. Craig is totally interested in religion, especially Catholicism. That's what his whole family is, you know. I don't know why he spends so much time researching it and reading about it. I mean, they don't exactly approve of our lifestyle and he hasn't been to church in years." The young man shook his head. "But I don't want to bore you with all that. My name's Kyle, by the way, and this is obviously Craig. We've been together for a little more than a year now."

Kyle gave Craig a squeeze around the shoulders. Elmer stared at them, unblinking. It slowly occurred to him what "together" meant. He cringed. The rest of the party didn't seem to notice.

Roger stepped forward. "Well, I think you've met almost everyone now. Let's see…" He began counting on his fingers, "Onyx, Cecelia, Ezzie, Craig, Kyle, Maggie, me…oh yes. Hilo. There she is. Sweetheart, why didn't you say anything?"

A small-framed girl stepped forward. She shrugged. Onyx spoke for her.

"She didn't say anything, Roger, because she *never* says anything. If I get two words out of her in a day, I feel like I've accomplished something."

Hilo glared at Onyx, but remained silent.

"Hilo is her spirit name, you know," continued Onyx. "It means thread in Spanish. It's spelled H-I-L-O. The 'H' is silent. Eeeee-low!" She looked over at the girl whose mousy hair hung limply in her face, like a thin wall of protection. "Hilo, why dontcha tell Elmer why you're called Hilo."

Hilo glanced shyly at the old man, not meeting his eyes. "It's—" she began in a low voice. "It's because I like to sew." She spoke quickly and softly. Elmer couldn't hear a damn thing she said.

"IT'S BECAUSE SHE LIKES TO SEW," Onyx repeated in an overly loud voice.

"Oh, I see," said Elmer. He looked at the girl, an expression of curiosity etched blatantly across his face. She was so nervous, so fragile. She couldn't have been older than fourteen or fifteen. What on earth was she doing here?

Onyx noticed his expression of curiosity. She leaned over and whispered in the old man's ear, "You think *you* feel like a stray dog? You wouldn't believe how battered this little ragamuffin was when we first took her in. I mean..."

"Onyx!" chided Roger, "For the love of god!"

"Sorry, sorry," said Onyx. "But really, he's going to find out all this stuff anyway. I mean, if he stays, that is. Are you Elm? Are you going to stay a while?"

Elmer quickly looked down. He stared silently at the empty plate in front of him. There was nothing particularly interesting about it—just a cream colored plate, outlined with a bright blue circle—but it gave him an excuse to not look up. He knew if he looked up, his eyes would lock with eight other sets of eyes, staring intently and expectedly at him as if he was supposed to make a speech or perform a magic trick. He could feel the brown and blue and green orbs peering out of the faces, willing the man in front of them to talk. Willing him to move or gesture or show some sign of life. But the old man remained as dull as a sleeping lion in the zoo. He stared at the plate, his eyes chasing the blue circle around and around and around and around. He felt as if his eyes would eventually wear the blue paint clean off the dish.

Ezzie spoke and Elmer jumped a bit. She had snapped him out of his hypnosis and he was now watching her with the same weary expression he had used on the plate. Ezzie's voice was tinged with sarcasm and a touch of bitterness, "Well, I'm going to go read. Looks like the party's over." She stood up, yawned, and stretched. She held her arms above her head a bit too long; she yawned a bit too loudly. Her actions were infantile and exaggerated. "And Maggie," she gave the tall woman next to her a significant look, "don't talk about *our* bad manners. I've seen worse." She cocked her head towards Elmer and raised her eyebrows in a none-too-subtle gesture. She held the look until Elmer's cheeks blazed red and his eyes once again turned downward towards the plate. Then, with a sharp one hundred-eighty degree turn, she marched out of the room.

Silence. It rushed to fill the gap left by Ezzie, like newly poured cement, oozing into the space it was meant to fill. And everyone watched as it solidified and became harder to ignore or remove. Soon it would be a concrete block and they would have to break it with a sledge hammer—a sledge hammer and a pair of strong arms. Fortunately, the child cried and the silence melted away. The group let out a collective exhale. The little one wailed harder, blubbering nonsense words and pounding its little fist—perhaps because of the sudden elevation of carbon dioxide. Maggie shushed it and bounced it up and down on the side of her body. The rest of the group started shuffling about and hurriedly jump-started conversations with their neighbors. Only Roger approached the mute newcomer.

"Hey, Elmer," he said in a gentle voice, laden with understanding. "*A little too much understanding,*" Elmer thought. Roger stood in front of him, silently, until something inside the old man prompted him to speak. It kicked at his throat and he wheezed as the words jumped out of his mouth.

"I—I don't mean to seem ungrateful. I'm not ungrateful, really. I—it's just, I have a lot on my mind and—" Elmer choked back his words. It was better not to talk. It was better not to offend. For some reason, this place made him much too honest. There was no need to divulge what he really thought of the people in this house. There was no need to preach fire and brimstone and condemn single mothers and body piercings and homosexuals and crude language. There was no need to judge and throw thick clods of black dirt on the throats of his rescuers. There was no need, but he did it anyway, silently, as he thought of the vulgar people in this house—this strange, strange house in which he was a prisoner. In his head, Elmer could see dark figures; his body swayed with their motion; his ears rang with their chant. He shook his head to clear the image.

Roger was still watching him. His eyes held a knowing look as if they could see past the elderly man's skull and straight into his thoughts. Elmer turned red for the second time in ten minutes. How much had the man before him, the man with those too-empathetic eyes, guessed about his thoughts? How much had he read from the silence? Maybe Elmer had failed to bite back his words after all. Maybe they had tumbled, uncontrolled, out of his mouth and into Roger's ears. Had they? Elmer thought about it. He was pretty sure they had not.

"Tired?" Roger asked, ignoring Elmer's flushed cheeks and nervous eyes.

"A bit," Elmer replied, grateful for words. "I shouldn't be after sleeping for three solid days, but I am."

"I understand," said Roger simply. Elmer knew that he did. "You can go back upstairs to my room if you want. No one will bother you up there. I'll make sure of it."

Elmer smiled gratefully, "Ok." He got up slowly, letting each limb unfurl. He glanced at Roger. If his dark brown eyes had fingers and a wrist, they would be reaching out to Elmer, summoning him just like the thin hand had done in the park. Elmer followed.

They walked up the creaking stairs. Slowly. Methodically. Roger walked ahead of Elmer, but he did not lead. He let the old man determine their pace and he followed each footstep attentively. Elmer didn't notice. He was too distracted by the pain in his hips, the feeling of bruises spread all over his body. He was distracted by his disjointed thoughts that floated vaguely through his head and tried to cohere, tried to form something tangible, but could not. He concentrated. He furrowed his brow. But the fragments of thought didn't stick. All he could sense was a dim feeling of unease. All he could feel were his feet. They moved one—step—at—a—time.

Somehow the old man ended up in bed, his shoes off and his stiff clothing exchanged for a baggy t-shirt and shorts. His socks, however, stayed on and they hung loosely around his skinny legs. Roger was still there. Elmer knew it had been Roger who had helped him into bed when all he could do was move his feet. It had been Roger who had carefully rolled back the sheets and the patchwork quilt while the old man's thoughts fluttered and bounced off each other like frenzied moths. And then Roger was speaking.

And then Elmer tried to listen. He tried. But the best he could achieve was a vague impression of listening. It seemed like he was standing inside the caverns of his mind, watching the shapes of words bounce off the rocky walls.

The words stopped. The echo continued. Roger looked at the hollow eyes of the man in front of him. He put his hand on one of the thin shoulders. He closed his eyes and breathed in. He breathed out, slowly and forcefully, as if he was pushing his breath into the ground. Maybe it was the sudden human touch—a warm hand on a cold shoulder—or maybe it was the exaggerated breath that snapped Elmer out of his stupor. Whatever the case, the old man regained his consciousness and his thoughts scrambled to form a single picture in his head. He blinked, slowly, and focused on the two dark eyes that were fixed inches away from his, separated only by a sliver of air and a single dreadlock that hung playfully across his face. Elmer glanced to his left. Roger's wiry arm still clutched his shoulder. The old man jerked away quickly, his entire body jumping back several inches. A small, sad smile passed over Roger's face as he stood up and took a step backwards.

"Well, you seem like yourself again. I was a little worried; you took those stairs pretty slowly. You must have really hurt yourself the other day. It seems like your brain shut down entirely to avoid thinking about the pain. What happened to you?"

Elmer remained mute for a few long seconds. He was slightly embarrassed about jerking away from the young black man—it had been an automatic reaction, an impulse. Now, he wasn't at all sure how to talk to him. He looked at the dark, expectant eyes. "I—" he began, "I fell in the mud a couple of times. Pretty hard, I guess. I'm not exactly sure—it was hard to tell. I was soaked and miserable before I fell and then I was soaked and miserable and…horizontal."

Roger laughed. Elmer looked at him, amazed. He couldn't believe that he had just made light of his past situation. It had seemed like anything but light at the time. The old man chuckled softly. He could feel the tension melting and he was relieved.

"I'm surprised I didn't break a hip," he continued. "That's always happening to old people, isn't it? You'd think that's the only bone in our body. The rest must be made of Jell-o and cream of wheat."

Roger laughed again, shaking his head. "What do you know," he said, "old man Elmer has a sense of humor after all."

Elmer grinned back. He wasn't sure where his sentences were coming from or who was saying them. Something about the whole essence of the house made it hard to tell lies or censor oneself. Words seemed to spring right from the very pit of his stomach. It was incredible. His past life had been a cemetery of falsehoods and buried truths. Lies had come so easily and so often that he hardly paid attention to them, hardly acknowledged their presence as they slid past his teeth and into the air. Now, it seemed that years of suppressed truths were springing to his mouth and he was powerless to stop them. *Why was that?* He looked at Roger. It wasn't that he particularly trusted any of the people here—in fact, he really didn't trust them. He thought they were strange and much too wild. No, it was more of a feeling. It was a feeling of comfort that the entire house evoked. He wasn't sure where it came from, but he got the sense that it was comprised of many small parts, like words on a page or notes in a song. The small parts worked seamlessly together and wove a web of comfort that blanketed the entire house in its silk. Elmer sighed.

"I slept at the top of a plastic slide, you know," he said, looking in the general direction of Roger's face. He said it matter-of-factly, as if he was saying, "I drive a blue Ford" or "I ate a ham sandwich for lunch." He wasn't sure why he said it. He wasn't sure why it was the right thing to say. It was simply another bit of honesty that he couldn't keep from spewing out of his mouth and onto the nearest pair of ears.

Roger said nothing. Elmer looked away. How many times had his cheeks flushed red that day? How many times had he been caught in a humiliating act of truth?

Elmer let the sentence hang for a few seconds, then added quickly, "It was only for a little while, a couple of hours at most. I had to escape the rain. It was coming down hard and fast, so hard it burns your skin. You know the type? Nasty rain. Not at all like the kind you can walk in—with an umbrella and some rubber boots—and just enjoy. Not at all like the soft, pitter-patter rain that sounds so wonderful on roof shingles. No, not like that at all. This rain was nasty. Nasty, nasty rain that stings the skin and blinds the eyes. I had to go somewhere. I had to!"

Elmer gasped for air. His chest rose and fell quickly, his lungs wheezing. "Shhh," said Roger softly. His hand was once again on the old man's shoulder. This time, he did not pull away. "Shhh," he repeated. Elmer was shaking, his head bouncing around like a bobble-head doll. Roger did not let go of the brittle shoulder.

"Elmer," he said quietly. "You've come to the right place."

The old man breathed in deeply. His shaking subsided; his body calmed down. Eventually, the old man lifted his pale eyes to meet the dark ones in front of him.

Roger continued, "Elmer, you've suffered. You've cried out. Your call was answered—you were brought here. I can help you. *We* can help you."

Elmer's look was steady. "We?" he heard himself ask. His voice was barely audible. It sounded as if it was coming from deep inside him. "But…who are you? How could you possibly help?"

"We," said Roger, his voice sparkling like the notes that danced from his trumpet, "are healers. We are the Modern Shamans."

Part I: The Modern Shamans

Chapter 16

Irene Heartland paused and took a deep breath. A few stray hairs hung in her face and she serenely wiped them away, smearing them against her sticky forehead and coating them with the stray flour that clung to her hands. She was baking pie. Apple pie. She had never really cared for apple pie. But he had. It was his favorite.

She picked up a large chunk of dough for the pie crust and began kneading it between her fingers. She separated the dough into two equal parts, balled it up in her fists, and then squeezed her hands tightly, watching as the sticky concoction of flour, butter, and sugar oozed between the knuckles of her left hand and the knuckles of her right hand. She loved the slimy texture; it reminded her of clay. And she was its sculptor. Her hands molded it, guided it, told it precisely what to do. In the end, she would have a pie. But she didn't care much about that. She only cared about the soft popping of hot water as it boiled the apples; she only cared about the rhythm of her arm as it stir-stir-stirred the cinnamon and cloves and mushy apples; she only cared about the way the warm filling spread out over the homemade crust as she poured it, sliding gently to the edges of the circular pan and slowly leveling itself. Irene opened the oven door and felt the heavy rush of heat on her face. She carefully slid the pie into the oven and noticed the tinny ring of metal as the pan made contact with the oven rack. She closed the oven door, set the timer, and slumped down in a kitchen chair, staring absently at the wall for forty-five minutes while the pie cooked.

The timer rang. Irene answered its call. She paced around while the pie cooled. Then, she snatched up a knife and plunged it into the warm crust, cutting it down the middle with one long, precise stroke. She carefully carved the pie into six equal pieces. She took a step back and looked at her creation. Her work was done. She slid the pie into the trash can.

* * *

Esmeralda Huntington stood up and stretched her back. She had been hunched over the rich, black soil all morning and her spine felt frozen in a stiff, convex arch. She threw her head back, raised her arms, and felt a few stray vertebrae click back into place. She lowered her arms and returned to the soil, resuming her hunch. Sweat trickled down the back of her neck and along the ridge of her curved spine. Her t-shirt clung to it, but she hardly noticed. She continued digging. She continued pulling out weeds and tossing them into a green heap at the edge of her flower bed. It was late spring and several colors had already sprung from the earth. The purples and pinks of lupine and carnations had just replaced the yellows and oranges of daffodils. The last of the tulips were blooming and soon Esmeralda would trim them down to make room for the snapdragons that were just starting to rear their burgundy and pink heads.

She wondered for the thousandth time what kind of flowers Susan liked. Did she even like flowers? Of course she did—every normal little girl does.

Esmeralda wiped her sweaty forehead with the back of her hand, leaving a wide streak of dirt that paralleled her hairline. She liked some of the flowers; others she did not. She hated the carnations. They reminded her of Mother's Day and church. And they bloomed forever, their frilly heads poking around until late August or early September. She glared at a group of white and crimson carnations. The flowers waved serenely back. Esmeralda sighed. What if carnations were Susan's favorite flower? It was possible. Maybe she loved the snowy whites and the fluffy pinks and the top-heavy heads perched on thin, green stems. Maybe. Esmeralda fought the urge to pluck the carnations out of the soil and toss them onto the weed pile. She knew she wouldn't. She knew she would continue to plant carnations year after year.

Hot, noon sun beat down on Esmeralda's grey-streaked hair. She rarely wore a hat in the garden. She liked to feel the closeness of the sun; she liked to feel it hugging her skin and bleaching her hair. She didn't wear a hat for the same reason she didn't wear gloves. Gardening was intimate for her and she needed to touch it, to hold it close to her body, like the skin of a lover. She dug her hands into the soil and let the dirt pack under her fingernails.

A breeze swept over her bare skin and played with the delicate petals of the flowers. Esmeralda looked at them, an amused half-smile crept onto her face. She pulled a carnation towards her and cradled its showy head. What use did she have for flowers? Vegetables were much more practical.

Chapter 17

Elmer sat by the window, watching. A pane of glass sliced between him and the hot, sticky day. He observed the life outside like a spectator at the zoo. Nothing particularly exciting was happening, but somehow it felt distant and exotic.

Onyx was lying on her stomach in the tall grass. Her elbows were propped up and she was reading a book, her legs slowly kicking the air above her. Elmer watched her face as she skimmed through pages; it showed an odd mix of concentration and tranquility. To her right, and a little further away from the window, Ezzie was rooting around in her flower patch. Sun beat down on her naked skin. Elmer had never seen sunscreen touch those brown arms or tanned face. He wondered if she would get skin cancer someday. He wondered if she cared.

A robin flew past the window and landed lazily in a maple tree. Elmer's eyes followed it, but didn't linger long. The bird was dull. It just stood there. Stood and stared. Elmer looked away. His eyes darted around the lawn, looking for something to amuse them. He was restless once again. Today was worse than yesterday, which was worse than the day before. His restlessness had been growing exponentially during the week he had spent with the Modern Shamans and he felt like he was nearing a tipping point. He had a decision to make: either get out or get in.

No one told him he had to make this decision. It was something he sensed. He sensed it in their looks and in their questions. He sensed it through his restlessness and mounting unease. He felt himself growing comfortable with the people here. He started to notice their routines and their moods. He started to take note of their personalities. He felt himself growing comfortable with the hallways and bedrooms and bathrooms of the old wooden house. He slept easily in his bed at night, his body drifting off to sleep seconds after his head hit the pillow. The room that surrounded him was familiar and safe and almost seemed like his own. He slept soundly each night, but awoke each morning with a little more dread brewing in his stomach. He was growing comfortable and it scared him. It scared him because he wasn't sure he wanted to grow comfortable with...this.

This. What exactly was this? It was hard to put his finger on, but he was slowly starting to figure it out. He asked few questions, but the people here offered up bits and pieces of information on their own. They spoke lovingly about the house and all its inhabitants and Elmer often found himself listening for several minutes, even hours, as they rambled on and on. They talked about their philosophies and beliefs. They talked about their personal histories and how they ended up in the house of the Modern Shamans. They talked endlessly about recycling and veganism and cultural diversity. At first Elmer was overwhelmed. It seemed as if someone had tossed him several hundred puzzle pieces and asked, "What is it?" However, through the flurry of minute details, Elmer was starting to see the big picture.

A week ago, Roger had tried to explain the big picture. He sat by Elmer's bed and talked about shamans and healing and ancient remedies. He talked about the earth. He talked about the need to shed our laissez-faire greed and embrace collectivism. There was urgency in his voice as he spoke. It sounded like a call to action. Elmer heard the urgency, but not the words. He was tired and overwhelmed and didn't want to be bothered with Communist jibber-jabber right now. He had never really cared about politics or human rights or the environment. He knew nothing about alternative medicine and healing. The words that issued from Roger's mouth were foreign to him. He had trouble making sense of them.

Eventually, Elmer fell asleep. Roger's words stopped mid-sentence. He shook his head and placed his hand on the old man's shoulder for the third time that evening. "Be well, my friend," he said. "Be well." He quietly left as Elmer began to snore. The next day, the old man woke up refreshed. He stretched and tried to remember the night before. Dinner. Climbing the stairs with Roger. Stories of mud and plastic slides. Shaking. Hand. Shoulder. Hand on shoulder. Dark brown eyes. Quiet, understanding words. We are healers. We are the Modern Shamans. We are healers. We are the Modern Shamans. We are healers...

The words repeated over and over in Elmer's head that morning. He didn't know what to make of them. He forgot what they meant...or he never knew. He searched his brain for some explanation of the words, but the explanation was not there. All that remained was a vague feeling of urgency. And a call to action.

We are healers. We are the Modern Shamans. The words repeated and rolled around in Elmer's head day after day. They cropped up when he least expected it and startled him, like a prankster leaping out from behind a bush.

Sha-man. Heal-er. Man. Sha. Mod-ern. Mod-heal-man. Sha-er-dern. We. We are. Heal-man-mod. Elmer dissected the words and strung them together. He felt that they carried some profound significance wrapped tightly inside them. All he had to do was break them open and their meaning would spill out. Like cracking open a walnut.

"I came here almost three years ago," said Maggie one day. She was folding laundry in the living room and Elmer was sitting in a chair nearby. "It was the best decision I ever made. I was feeling lost and alone. I was six months pregnant. It was almost like the house found me, you know? It was almost like it called my name. Maybe that's ridiculous, but the first time I came here I felt like I was home. I hadn't really had a home in years, not since The City." Maggie's eyes glazed over a little. She spoke as if Elmer was not in the room. She spoke as if she was walking through her memories and her words were merely describing where her feet were taking her.

"But then I joined the army and it was one city after another. I went where they needed me. I went because there was nothing for me back in The City. I knew I would slip back into my old life and that was exactly why I ran away in the first place. The army was as good an option as any, I guess." Maggie flopped down on the dark green couch. The towel she was folding slipped out of her hands and onto the floor. She didn't seem to notice.

"I'm not exactly proud of my decision to join the army. I don't like what it stands for and I'm certainly not in favor of senseless wars. But I see its function. It stimulates the economy. It gives us a sense of security and unity, I suppose. It takes people like me out of the ghetto and away from all the shit we have to deal with. It's really just a great distraction—kind of like a drug. Or a tropical island. It was my way of checking out of reality for a while."

Maggie's thin hand tugged absentmindedly on a loose thread on the couch. Elmer watched her slender fingers and tried to picture her in uniform. He tried to picture her holding a gun. He could not.

"Five years. That's how long I served our country. It was like a five-year trip. A five-year distraction. It was Zach who snapped me back to reality. He's the one who reminded me that life exists outside the barracks."

Maggie's son was playing quietly in the corner with a toy truck. He rolled it under a chair and over the wide green flowers that were woven into the rug. He didn't make a sound, but his face held a small smile.

Elmer looked at the tiny child. "Zach," he said quietly. "That's a good name."

Maggie looked up from the dark green thread and into the light green eyes of the old man. She seemed to just remember that he was still in the room. Maggie nodded, her eyes still distant. "Yes," she said to herself, "it is a good name." She looked at her son. "I quit the army for him. I quit so that he could have a normal childhood and go to school and have a yard with a dog and a vegetable garden. At least, that's what I told everyone. That's what I told myself. But really, I think I did it for me. I think I did it because I wasn't content. I felt like a part of my soul was missing—like it had floated off somewhere. I needed to tether myself down for a bit and retrieve that missing piece. And that's exactly what this house has done for me. For the first time in my life I feel grounded. I feel…happy."

Maggie paused and picked up the towel she had dropped on the floor. She silently folded it and placed it on the coffee table. "I've figured out a lot of things in this house. About me, mostly. I've learned how to live well and be healthy. Healthy in every sense of the word. Mind, body, soul. I feel centered here. I don't know, maybe that sounds a little selfish. Maybe it sounds like all I care about is myself and my own well-being. But how can you heal others if you can't heal yourself?"

Maggie raised her head and looked out the window. "Do you see that maple tree over there?"

Elmer nodded.

"We're all like that tree. We have to gather nutrients from the soil. We have to absorb sunlight and water. We have to grow—we have to grow strong and tall and healthy and then, *then*, we can provide shade or lumber or a place for birds to nest. *Then* we can serve others. If we don't take care of ourselves, if we don't take time to soak in the sunlight, then our branches will be brittle and our leaves will shrivel up. We'll be no good for anyone, including ourselves. We'll only take up space. Trees don't have to think about this—they just live. There should be more 'just living' in the world."

Maggie paused and continued to look at the maple tree. The maple tree stood, waving its three-pronged leaves. Elmer looked from one to the other. Their limbs were long and graceful. After several silent minutes, Maggie turned her head away from the tree and towards the old man once again. Zach buzzed his lips and continued to wheel the truck around the chair.

"I'm twenty-eight now," said Maggie. "But I feel much older than that. Not in a bad way, either. I feel like I've gained one-hundred years of wisdom in the last three. When I was twenty-five I still felt like a child. I was a baby having a baby. That scared me. This house helped me mature, to grow. I keep using that word—grow—but I think that's the best way to describe what's happened to me here. I've grown. I've grown into my own skin."

Later that day, Elmer stood naked in front of the mirror. He held up his arms; the skin flopped loosely underneath them. He ran his hands over his sides, grabbing a handful of flesh that clung to his torso. He stretched out one leg. Then the other.

After seventy-eight years, his skin still did not fit.

* * *

Onyx read. Ezzie gardened. Elmer watched. He glanced at the maple tree for a moment, remembering his conversation with Maggie a few days before. He didn't want to like her. He wanted to think she was over the top, a complete lunatic. But, somehow she made sense. Somehow, he felt more comfortable with himself when she was around.

The same was true for the rest of them. They had all talked to him that week, easily and candidly, with the exception of Ezzie. She generally ignored Elmer. She only talked to him when he was in the way, if you could even call her snappish remarks talking. Elmer began to avoid her and their distant relationship—or lack of—seemed to work well for both of them.

Elmer kept his eyes on the maple tree. *One week. One week has passed and I have a decision to make. Get in or get out. Stay or go. You've never had to make that decision, maple tree, have you? You're a tree. You stay put. You find soil that works for you and you stick by it for the rest of your life—through thick and thin, for better or worse. It must be nice being a tree and having roots that anchor you firmly to the earth.*

Elmer thought of Maggie again. He thought of her calm wisdom, delivered casually like an old woman teaching her grandchildren how to sew a quilt. In his past life, Elmer had had few interactions with young, black women. They made him nervous, so he avoided them. It was easy to do. He grew up in a rural, white town and the only dark skin he saw was on the necks and forearms of farmers at the end of growing season. Maggie surprised him—she was surprisingly comfortable. She spoke with maturity, dignity, and proper grammar (which Elmer especially appreciated). She didn't speak quickly or loudly, but her very presence commanded attention.

She kept her shoulders back and her head straight when she stood; she never slouched. She was a proud six feet. Elmer got the sense that she was part human, part willow tree. Her long, elegant limbs carried her smoothly through the house; her feet barely whispered as they carried her down the hardwood hallways. Elmer thought of her movement. He thought of how trees sway in the wind, but keep their roots planted firmly in the earth. That was Maggie.

He wondered what she had been like before she came to the house. He wondered how she became so grounded. Elmer envied her—the calm, the self-assuredness, the way she "just lived." Did she learn that from the people here? Or maybe from the house itself? Maggie's words passed through his head. "It was almost like the house found me, you know? It was almost like it called my name."

It does seem like that, doesn't it? This house seems just as alive as its inhabitants. It swallows you up and makes you comfortable in its innards. It makes you want to stop and stay a while. Maybe I'll stay a while. Maybe I will…

Elmer looked away from the window and into the living room of the house. Paper lanterns hung in each corner, softening the angles of the square room. The dark green couch was situated to his left, empty and inviting. A couple of mismatched chairs sat facing a small, beat-up piano made of some kind of rich, dark wood. The pedal was sticky and a couple of the keys were loose and made loud clicking noises whenever they were played. Despite its flaws, the piano was well-loved and often played, mostly by Cecelia and Craig. They sat in front of the eighty-eight keys and lost themselves in the sounds of sharps and flats, sometimes for hours. Neither of them used sheet music.

Elmer loved the music. He would sneak into the living room whenever he heard the tinkling of keys and settle into one of the easy chairs, rest his head against the chair back, close his eyes, and listen. He became familiar with their different styles and techniques. Craig liked jazz and blues. His music was filled with sharps and irregular beats; it kept you guessing. He played quickly and smoothly, his fingers barely touching the keys. Cecelia's style was more traditional. When she wasn't improvising, she was playing the classics. She especially loved Clementi.

One time, Elmer was in the kitchen when he heard the piano come to life. He didn't recognize the style. It was a short, clipped staccato, almost like a horse race or a quick Russian dance. Elmer hobbled into the living room and stopped abruptly when he saw the pianist. It was Hilo. She was playing effortlessly, her eyes closed, her fingers flying across the black and white. Elmer quietly snuck over to his favorite chair, a burgundy-colored easy chair with a footrest that popped out reluctantly at the tug of a wooden handle. He sat down, settled his hip bones deep in the cushion of the chair, and commanded the footrest to open. It did, with a loud squeal and a pop. Hilo wheeled around, spotted the old man looking guiltily across the room, and ran outside.

Elmer thought about the young girl and a sharp pang seized-up his heart. He grabbed his chest. *What was her story? How did she end up here?* He asked himself the same questions whenever he thought about the timid little girl. He wondered if she had a family and if they knew where she was. He wondered how she learned to play the piano with her eyes closed.

Elmer's gaze returned outside. Restless. Restless. Restless. His leg twitched. He watched Ezzie scritch-scratching in the dirt. He watched Onyx flip a page. He watched Craig and Kyle step outside and walk across the lawn. They were holding hands and talking animatedly. Elmer did not approve. He directed his gaze elsewhere. To his left, the maple tree waved serenely in the light summer breeze. The robin, who had been sitting benignly on a branch, suddenly decided to move. She spread her charcoal wings and flew to another tree. Elmer wondered why that tree was any better than the other one. He watched the sunlight as it trickled past the tree branches and spilled onto the lawn and the back of Ezzie's head and his own cheek. It felt like an invitation to join the world outside. Elmer accepted. His leg immediately stopped twitching.

It was the first time he stepped past the doorframe of the wooden house since he arrived. A full week had passed. He had watched seven sunrises; he watched the moon change from a quarter to a half; he consumed eight cups of tea. Elmer walked carefully down the steps, gripping the railing in his right hand and his cane in his left. Onyx looked up from her book and waved. Elmer nodded. Ezzie looked up from her gardening and did not wave. Elmer looked away. His feet landed on flat, smooth pavement and he started walking stiffly, but steadily, his right foot and his cane hitting the ground at the same moment as if they were waltzing. He held his head high and breathed in slowly. The air tasted delicious and fresh. This was exactly what he needed—some fresh air to unclog his mind and some exercise to loosen his limbs. For a while, he thought of nothing but different shades of green and different shapes of houses. He was walking in a neighborhood, down a tree-lined street, and he took great pleasure in carefully soaking up his surroundings, basking in their images and their smells and tastes.

Elmer walked like this for a while. He tried to remain relaxed and calm; he tried to focus on the custard-colored houses and the shady lawns, but they couldn't distract him for long. Underneath the thin film of images, his thoughts were brewing and bubbling like a witch's cauldron. Or like the storm that had pounded his brain for so many years. It wasn't the same storm—not at all—it was more like a little brother. It was the next hurricane in the alphabetical lineup. Elmer wanted to ignore it, but he couldn't. He prepared to face the storm.

I need to decide. The time is now.

He pictured them, one after another, living in the old wooden house. He saw Maggie reclined on the dark green couch. He saw Onyx' round face leaning over Cecelia's shoulder as she cooked dinner. He saw Hilo playing the piano, her eyes closed, a small smile filling the space between dimples. Elmer shook his head roughly, like a clogged salt shaker.

Why do they haunt me? Why am I tempted to stay with this band of hooligans? Surely the people back home would be horrified. I can just picture Irene's face…

He shook his head again.

But I'm not back home. I'm far from it. I wanted a fresh start, didn't I? Well, this will work, I guess. He paused. The image of Craig and Kyle holding hands floated into his head. He thought of Onyx' piercings and tattoos. He thought of all of them together and the odd group they formed—a group that had a name. *The Modern Shamans. What the devil? I still haven't figured it out exactly. I'm not sure I like it. No, I'm not sure I like it at all.*

Elmer turned into a park and continued to walk. He realized he had been muttering to himself and he turned around nervously to make sure no one was watching. No one was. It was one o'clock in the afternoon and the park was mostly empty. A few children played on the swings in the distance; their mothers sat at a nearby picnic table, chatting. Elmer's presence did not upset the park's normalcy.

They're fine individually. Really, they are. Even Onyx is starting to grow on me, annoying little chatterbox that she may be. It's the group that I'm afraid of. Together, they comprise something very strange. Healers? That's what they call themselves, isn't it? Shamans. What do they think this is? The year 12 B.C? I don't like any of it; it makes me nervous.

Elmer glanced at the children swinging. He thought of Maggie and Zach. He thought of the little boy quietly buzzing his lips as he played with his toy truck. He thought of Maggie's tranquil presence. *This house has helped me mature, to grow…I've grown into my own skin.*

I want that. I want my skin to fit. I want to be comfortable with life and with myself. My. Self. Myself—I want to know what that is. Maggie used to be lost. The house found her, it rescued her. She told me that. She said it found her. Maybe it found me too. Maybe I should give it a chance. Maybe I should stop running for a while.

Suddenly, Elmer thought of the man in blue robes. He came into his head, unbeckoned, the blue-clad figure sitting amongst six other colors. Elmer saw his large brown eyes, his bearded face. He heard his clear, deep voice. He saw him lean forward and repeat the advice he had given him long ago: "Stop running." *At least it seems like long ago…* "Stop running, Elmer." *So much has happened since then.* "Stop. Turn and face your fears with a shovel in hand." *Dig myself out; find myself. Stop. Stop running. Stop.*

Elmer thought of the man's kind eyes. He had seldom thought of the seven robed guides since he had moved into the house of the Modern Shamans. The seven from his dream had been replaced by the eight from reality. He had enough faces and personalities to think about without seven more clogging his head. Elmer felt vaguely sorry that he had neglected them. He thought of the day—it seemed like a long time ago—he rode the bus to City A. He thought of his confusion, of the thoughts tumbling through his head, and of his decision to believe—to believe in the messages of the seven, to believe in their guidance. He believed because *why not? What is there to lose from belief? They gave me a glimmer of hope. Dream or not, they made me remember joy. So, why shouldn't I trust them now? Didn't the one in yellow tell me to trust my intuition? I think I will. I will trust.*

Elmer heard the words of the man in blue repeat. "Stop running. Turn and face your fears with a shovel in hand." *Yes. Yes, I will. I need to stop being afraid. I need to stop running.*

The old man paused in the middle of the park. The bright green grass sprang up around his shoes. He stood as tall as his stooped back would allow, looking straight ahead. Slowly, he clenched his fists. *Ok. You win.* He wasn't exactly sure who he was talking to, but he got the sense that *someone* had just triumphed. *I'm going to listen this time. I'll stop running. I'll stay. This may be a mistake, but I have to take that chance. I'll regret it if I don't. Ok.* He tilted his chin upward. *Can you hear me? Can you!? I will stay. I'm staying! I am. I'm staying…*

He slowly dropped his chin and unclenched his fists. With one long sigh, he let the air out of his lungs. He realized he had been holding his breath.

Chapter 18

Elmer glanced to his right. The children on the swings squealed as they pumped their thin legs and sailed higher. The old man watched their motion as they sliced through the summer air, back and forth, back and forth. Their mothers ignored them. They had chatting to do.

Elmer looked at his hands. His hands had just unclenched and blood was gratefully refilling his fingertips. Elmer knew he had a body. He knew he had two feet planted firmly on the ground—two feet attached to legs, attached to torso, attached to neck and skull. He knew these things very well, but at that moment he forgot them. At that moment, he felt like he was made of wind and dandelion fluff. He could fly; he was certain of it. All he had to do was pump his arms back and forth, back and forth.

He closed his eyes. He stretched his arms towards the sun. The warm rays kissed his face. A light breeze brushed past him and lifted him gently into the air. And then he heard the low whoosh of wings and he was once again on the back of a giant black bird, soaring through thin mountain air. They flew together, Elmer's pale arms moving in cadence with the bird's giant wings. BOOM-batta-BOOM-batta-BOOM-BOOM-BOOM. The wings sounded like drums. Elmer swayed to their rhythm and pictured the woman in red. Her hips shook, her body complimented the rhythm and added to it at the same time. He pictured Levi and his grungy stocking cap and gummy grin. He pictured Zach. Zach, who shared his name with Maggie's son. Zach, with his long dreadlocks and straight back, who reminded him so much of Roger. Especially when they played music. Especially when channeled bits of their souls through the percussion and brass. They were naked in these moments—naked and pure. Elmer could hardly think of it without turning red.

But he did think of it. He thought of it as he soared through the air and watched black feathers ruffle under his legs. He thought of the musicians and their looks of unabashed joy. He thought of the way they simultaneously lost *and* found themselves through their music. *Lost and found.* His mind lingered a moment. *Lost and found. Lost and found. Although they surrender themselves to their music, they are never really lost, are they? No—they lose themselves completely in order to be found.*

Elmer held onto that thought for a few moments—it was clear and refreshing, like cold water—but then it slipped out of his head and blew away in the wind. He looked down and thought about the absurdity of riding on a giant bird. *Completely ridiculous…*

The bird disappeared. The mountains and cool air disappeared. Elmer was aware of the soft sensation of grass under his feet. He opened his eyes. The children were still in the park. They were swinging back and forth, back and forth.

* * *

Elmer walked home quickly. *Home.* It was starting to feel close to that. He was desperate to see their faces, hear their familiar voices. He wanted to tell them his decision slowly and deliberately, building up their anticipation, until he delicately unleashed the climax. They would applaud and cheer, he was sure of it—just like they did on the first evening he met them. Yes, he was looking forward to telling them, but mostly he was looking forward to being amongst them again. His vision in the park had scared him and he needed their affirmation, their assurance that he was not just a crazy old man.

The house of the Modern Shamans was an odd kind of refuge. It lent protection and comfort against the storm that raged outside its wooden walls. It soothed his mind and kept his thoughts away from his troubles. Amidst the band of free-spirits, outcasts, damaged souls, and one ornery-ass lady, Elmer felt at peace. He didn't know why. It puzzled him. But he decided to accept it.

As Elmer's feet turned into the driveway of the house of the Modern Shamans, he inhaled deeply. The crisp scent of fresh flowers and newly turned dirt filled his lungs. He exhaled and paused for a moment. *Here I am sane. I am safe. I could fly on the back of a giant black bird if I wanted to and no one would bat an eye. In fact, they might join me.*

He smiled. It was satisfying to smile. He found himself doing it more often than ever before, as if he was making up for lost time that had slipped away in the grey, dull past. He walked up the steps of the creaky, wooden house. Elmer wondered how old it was. He wondered how many people had called it home. The stairs moaned under Elmer's feet as he slowly conquered each step.

"Hello, Elmer."

Elmer jumped, awakened from his thoughts by the sound of Roger's voice. He looked to his right. Roger was standing on the porch, a paintbrush in hand, an easel and canvass propped in front of him.

"Oh, 'llo," said Elmer, "I didn't see you there." He climbed the last step and turned to face Roger. "What are you making?"

"What, this?" said Roger, casually swinging his paintbrush towards the easel. "This is just something I do to release tension. I never know what I'm going to paint; I just let the brush do the talking."

"Oh. I see," murmured Elmer. He really didn't see, but he humored Roger anyway. After everything he had done for him, it was the least he could do. "So…" began Elmer. The notion of making a grandiose speech faded from his mind. Now it seemed utterly ridiculous and he decided to get straight to the point. "I guess—if you'll have me that is—I'd like to stay a while." He quickly looked away from the porch and stared vaguely in the direction of a grove of oak trees across the road.

Roger set down his paintbrush. "Well, that's great news! Just excellent. Wait until I tell the others; they'll be thrilled!" He threw his arms around the old man while Elmer stood rigidly, not quite sure what to do with his hands. Roger dropped his arms and walked over to a plain, pine bench on the other side of the porch. "Here," he said, "have a seat. I feel like we should talk for a bit."

"But what about your painting?"

"Ah, no matter. That can wait. Sit down for a while, you look a little flushed."

Elmer hated to admit it, but Roger was once again correct. He was still feeling a little tired from his long walk and a bit overwhelmed by his vision of riding on the giant black bird. Silently, Elmer hobbled to the bench and sat down, leaning on his cane like an extra limb. He adjusted his seat, laid his cane across his lap, and looked at Roger expectantly, waiting for him to speak first. Roger smiled and sat down in a folding chair. He stretched his legs and folded his arms across his lap. He closed his eyes and didn't say a thing for several long seconds. He just breathed in and out. Steadily. Elmer watched him and squirmed in his seat—the silence made him uncomfortable. Just when he was about to say something, Roger's eyes blinked open.

"You know," Roger began without preamble, "I bought this house seven years ago when I was twenty-six. Best decision I ever made."

It took Elmer a second to soak in the words. "Really?" he said.

"Yes indeed. Paid in full on the day I bought her. She's been home ever since."

"You bought it yourself? I mean, it wasn't in the family or anything? I mean—" Elmer's cheeks glowed red, "I didn't mean to sound surprised, it's just that—"

"It's just that, you've never seen me working? You wonder how a dirty hippie can afford to buy a house?"

"I—uh—no, not that. I mean, not quite—"

Roger laughed, "No worries. I'd be perplexed too." He straightened up in his chair, placed his feet on the floor, and leaned forward. "I don't really like to admit this," he said in a low voice, "but I used to be a rising star in the corporate world. I made top dollar marketing different products to average-Joe citizens and damn…I was good at it."

Elmer blinked at him incredulously.

"I know, I know. It's hard to believe, isn't it? But it's true. I sold my soul at an early age—right out of college, in fact—and I didn't look back for almost five years," Roger's gaze wandered across the road to the same grove of oak trees that seemed to catch Elmer's attention a few minutes before. "I wanted to be an artist," he said, almost to himself. Elmer leaned forward, straining to hear. "A professional painter. But everyone—my parents, my teachers—said the same thing: 'it's not practical. It won't earn you any money. Go into graphic design instead…' So I did. I listened. I was a fucking star at the design table. I graduated with honors, was top of my class, and the minute after I tossed my cap into the air, I was snapped up by a well-known design company. I thought I was going to design business cards and company letterheads and things like that, but they ended shuffling me into their advertising branch. Before I knew it, I was designing backgrounds for cereal commercials and logos for massive hotel chains. The work never stopped flowing. I was the popular new kid on the block because frankly, my shit sold. Companies knew they could count on me to come up with something brilliant. I always did. The public always bought it."

Roger sighed and leaned back again. He turned his head towards Elmer. His expression was serious and grim; Elmer had never seen him look so troubled. "Look," Roger continued, "I'm not telling you these things to toot my own horn. Not at all. It still amazes me that I was able to look past the scummy corporate wrongdoings, go about my work, and then hold out my hand for a paycheck. It makes me absolutely ill."

"But—" Elmer spoke up for the first time, "I don't see what's so terrible about earning money. You have to do it one way or another. Why not help corporations advertise?"

Roger nodded. "Ok, valid question. I guess there are two main reasons I feel so terrible about what I did. First of all, I think differently than most people; my brain just processes things on a different level, an emotional level. And secondly, I worked for a few corporations that are especially evil." He looked over at Elmer, "I can see you're confused, so let me explain. Ever since I can remember, I have been highly in tuned with people's emotions. I can easily sense when someone is angry, sad, uncomfortable, jealous, whatever. Maybe it's a skill I developed because I had a big family—I was the youngest of seven—or maybe it was just something I was born with. Who knows. All I know is that I can read people like a book. It used to drive my mother crazy. I could always tell when she was worried about paying the bills, no matter how hard she tried to hide it from us. Anyway, the important part of all this is that I can also tell how people react to their surroundings, including how they react to art. I knew I had painted something brilliant when it evoked some kind of strong emotion. I've made people cry and laugh and clench their fists in rage. It was all just for fun until I got into advertising…"

Roger trailed off and paused. He seemed to be gathering his thoughts, arranging them logically before they spilled out his mouth. Elmer thought about how he used to do that back in Here. Every sentence meticulously planned.

Roger began again, "You know how superheroes can choose to use their powers for good or evil?" Elmer nodded. "It was kind of like that. I mean—I was no superhero, not even close, but I had this power, if you want to call it that. And I used it to sell people shit they didn't need. You see, advertising is all about subliminal messaging. Different colors, shapes, phrases cause different reactions from people. Most of it is hardly noticeable. For instance, think about an arrow. It's bold and green. Think about it pointing upward and to the right. What does that mean to you? Progress, right? Now, think about that arrow pointing straight down. It's thin and red. That means something is going downhill fast; there's no stopping it. And there's no stopping your brain from reading it this way. I learned how to articulate these things in school, but I've been aware of the concepts since I was a child. So, long story short, I used my powers for evil."

"And the evil companies you worked for?" asked Elmer. "Who were they? Why were they so bad?"

Roger sighed. "Right. Them." He smiled sadly, took a deep breath, and continued. "Eventually, I was snatched up by the pharmaceutical industry. They heard that I'd had some success working for the hospitality industry—restaurants, hotels, etc.—and they wanted to give me a shot. At this point, I had moved beyond the graphic design side of things. Instead of just designing backgrounds and logos for advertisers, I was involved in producing entire commercials. They would have me design sets and position the actors in a scene. I was even given a script a time or two so I could edit the content. Anyway, the pharma people get wind of my work and offer me a lot, I mean *a lot* of money to work for them full-time. So I did. And it was great for a while. I made tons of money and kept busy. I was even able to send a couple of my older siblings to college who never got the chance. But then everything changed…"

Roger trailed off again. Elmer was at the edge of his seat, his eyes glued on Roger. "What changed? What?"

Roger looked at him and said in a quiet voice, "The drugs I was selling began killing people."

Elmer's eyes grew wide. "What? No!" he said, bringing his hand to his forehead and shaking his head. His cane slid off his lap and clattered loudly on the porch.

"I'm afraid so," said Roger in the same low tone. "I didn't want to believe it, but the evidence was undeniable. First, I heard some of the pharma guys talking about recent problems they had in the lab with one of their products. Nothing major, just a few lab rats ending up with cancer after prolonged treatment. Probably just a fluke. Then, my sister sent me an article about some elderly people winding up dead after using this particular product. I decided to take matters into my own hands and did a little research myself. As it turns out, this was not the first time my friends in the pharmaceutical industry had been accused of marketing deadly medicine. This particular branch had a long history of lawsuits and were known for marketing products prematurely, products that had received mixed results from the lab or sometimes even negative results. It made me sick, but for some reason I said nothing. I continued to show up for work like everything was normal, a smile on my face and a sketchpad in my hand. I knew better. I still haven't forgiven myself for it."

Roger's voice stuck in his throat for a second. His eyes glistened and he blinked away the moisture. A couple of fat tears rolled down his dark cheeks. Elmer looked away. He wanted to pat him on the back. He wanted to tell him, "Everything is fine now. You aren't a monster. You are a good person. Truly. Truly…" But he couldn't. He looked at Roger's wet cheeks and stooped shoulders and said the first thing that came to mind. "Then what happened?"

Roger looked up. He cleared his throat, stared straight ahead, and picked up the thread of his story as though he had never lost it. "Then," he said, "I met Luke. Good old Luke." He looked away for a second, lost in his web of memories, and then began again. "Luke was in his mid-sixties. He had just retired from his work as a commercial fisherman. It was work he loved—he had been in the business over forty years—but his back was bad and things simply weren't the same as they used to be. The fish he thought were so majestic and beautiful became smaller and harder to find. He got out of the industry while there were still a few fish left to catch. But I didn't know any of this when I first met Luke. Or the first few times I met Luke. I only knew him as the 'dirty protester.'"

Roger smiled a little and went on, "He would sit outside our building, day in, day out, with a ratty cardboard sign that read APOLOGIZE TO ME BECAUSE YOU CAN'T APOLOGIZE TO HER. The sign had a photograph of a woman's smiling face glued to its corner. We avoided talking about 'the dirty protester' at the office. It tended to ruin our spirits."

"I walked past that sign at least a dozen times on my way up the steps to work. I usually turned my head as I walked by and ran inside as quickly as I could. One day, I simply couldn't. I remember the weather was colder than usual. The man was bundled in a khaki-colored jacket with a stocking hat pulled low over his head. He paced back and forth with the sign, shaking his legs occasionally to try to stay warm. I watched him for a while and decided I couldn't resist any longer. I walked up to the man, held out my hand, and said, 'I'm sorry.'"

"Luke started to cry. I started to cry. Before I knew it, I was patting him on the back and then I was sitting with him on the sidewalk as he told me the story of his sister and how our medicine had poisoned her body. I didn't doubt him for a second. He was an intelligent, humble man and I knew he wasn't lying."

"I didn't go to work that day. Instead, I sat and talked and listened and remembered what it was like to care about people more than money. I hadn't done that in a long time. When my co-workers streamed out of the building after work, they hardly looked at me. They knew I had crossed over to the 'dark side,' to the civilian side. My boss gave me a nod as he walked to his car and that was that. A chapter in my life had concluded and a new one was about to begin. I could sense it. I said goodbye to Luke and sped off in my car. I've never seen Luke since, but I think about him every day and hope he has found some peace."

Chapter 19

"And then you bought the house of the Modern Shamans?" asked Elmer. He didn't want the story to end, not before he knew every detail, not before he discovered how Roger pieced himself together after the storm.

"Well, not right away," Roger replied. "At first, I felt fragmented and directionless. I had no idea what to do with myself. I had forgotten what it was like to have free time. My limbs felt heavy and my joints began to ache. One of my friends suggested I try Reiki, which is a kind of spiritual healing. The Reiki master works with your aura, identifies your problems—your blockages—and helps fix them. They channel energy through their hands and heal the damaged parts of your aura. They restore your body to its natural rhythm and flow."

Elmer blinked at Roger. His face was screwed up in a comical mixture of confusion and disgust. He cleared his throat, but remained silent, his eyes fixed on the man across from him.

Roger laughed. "I know, I know. I was skeptical too, at first. But I decided to go in with an open mind and an open heart and, what do you know, it worked. My joints stopped hurting; my head felt lighter. I felt like a completely new person—revitalized and ready to take on the world. Ready to live. A week later I went back to the Reiki studio for more work. Then I went back again. And again. I grew addicted to the high I felt after every session. I was light and free. My head felt clear. I loved the feeling so much that I decided I couldn't keep it to myself. I wanted the entire world to experience it."

"So, I decided to study the healing arts myself, starting with mastering Reiki. And, wouldn't you know, in the very first class I attended I met Cecelia and Onyx. The three of us became instant friends and we all learned worlds of knowledge from each other. They knew a lot more about healing than I did and they were very patient with me when I pestered them with an endless stream of questions. There is an entire world out there devoted to the healing arts that I knew absolutely *nothing* about. I felt like I had landed on the shores of a foreign country and was trying desperately to understand my surroundings. Cecelia and Onyx were my guides. Within a month, I considered them my best friends. That's when we began discussing buying a house—a house for healing. A house for anyone who needs comfort or support or guidance or a place to rest weary bones. When I stumbled upon our lovely house, I knew she was perfect."

He looked fondly at the wooden clapboard next to him, as if it was a favorite pet or a beloved grandparent. He turned back to Elmer. "There is no single way to heal. Different people have different methods—some meditate, some run marathons, some garden…" He looked across the lawn to where Ezzie's flowers swayed serenely in the afternoon sun. "There is no magic phrase or practice. There is only guidance and personal belief. Elmer, let me tell you something—I know for certain that if I walked into that Reiki studio seven years ago with a closed, narrow mind, nothing would have happened. I would have finished the session, driven home, and told my friends, 'See! It's just like I thought, a New Age scam to get gullible people to fork over money.' But I was open. I let myself believe in the high I experienced. I let my brain believe in my mended joints and my euphoria. I found comfort in my belief." He locked eyes with Elmer, "What do you believe?"

Elmer stammered for a moment. He tried to respond, but choked on his words and began to cough violently.

Roger looked at him, startled. "It was…more of a rhetorical question."

Elmer looked up. "I—yeah. Of course, of course. Rhetorical…"

Roger chuckled a little. "You get nervous talking about yourself, don't you? That's ok, not everyone likes to do it. And then there's Onyx," he smiled. Elmer felt himself relax once more. "Onyx has probably talked your ear off about her beliefs. Well, they're pretty much in line with my own. We both believe in ancient medicinal practices—traditional shamanism and healing with herbs and all that. And we also think the earth is full of energy or spirits, if you want to call them that. Cecelia believes in most of that stuff, but she also believes in a higher power that watches over us and protects us. I guess her Catholic upbringing never fully left her."

"I was raised Catholic too," said Elmer quietly, almost to himself.

"Were you?" said Roger. "You should tell us about it sometime. No pressure. We just love to hear people's stories, that's all."

Elmer nodded stiffly. He wasn't convinced that he had enough of a story to hold their attention for five minutes.

"The three of us—Onyx, Cecelia, and I—are really the only ones in the house that think and believe the way we do. Maggie buys into some of it, especially the healing with your hands, Reiki-type stuff. But everyone else has their own set of beliefs, their own way to practice healing. Kyle's an atheist, Craig is Unitarian, Ezzie's agnostic, Hilo…well, I'm not exactly sure what Hilo believes. She's never really told anyone. But there's no doubt in my mind that she's finding her own way of mending that tattered little soul of hers." He shook his head sadly.

"Look Elmer," he said softly. "I'm telling you all these things because I don't want you to be afraid of us. I want you to know that we will accept you for whoever you are, even if we don't necessarily agree with it. I mean, look at Ezzie. If that pessimistic naysayer can stick around, so can you." He grinned. "We love Ezzie, we really do. She may be negative, but she's usually willing to give new things, new experiences, half a chance, even if she doubts their validity. I actually performed an Incan healing ritual on her last week, complete with palm fronds and smoke that I blew across her body. She sat quietly in her chair and let me finish the whole process before she scoffed at me and told me it was all a load of shit and that I would be better off giving my patients a shot of whiskey and a fat joint to take away their pain." Roger laughed, "I didn't think it was too funny at the time, but looking back it was pretty hilarious. Ezzie definitely adds character to our house; I wouldn't trade her for any Reiki master in the world."

Again, Roger and Elmer locked eyes. "We are all different here—all unique—but we share a couple of important similarities. The most important one, in my opinion, is that we are all open-minded. We may not agree with everyone's lifestyles or beliefs, but we respect them. That is why our little community works. That is why we all get along, for the most part. It's sort of a live and let live kind of philosophy. If more people practiced this philosophy, the world would be a much better place. And would have *been* a much better place too. You don't have to look very closely at history to realize that the root of most of our troubles is intolerance. The eradication or 'taming' of different people, our great wars, the squashing of cultures all stems from intolerance. It is just about as strong today as it was two-thousand years ago. It bleeds into our political systems. It's taught in Sunday school and on TV and in the playground. We are instructed at a young age to fear and mistrust all things that stray from the status quo."

"But I have faith. I have faith that this nation, this world is slowly coming around. I have faith that someday the differences between people will be embraced rather than fought over. I look at our children—I look at Zach—and I see hope. I look at adults who are trying to overcome narrow-mindedness and a tradition of mistrust, and I see hope. I look at you, Elmer, and I see hope."

Elmer swallowed. He wished Roger would stop putting him on the spot.

Roger continued, "Tolerance, respect, open-mindedness—these are all things we value in this house and these are things we expect everyone to practice. The other thing we expect is growth. This is not a house for stagnation. This is not a house for the pleasantly content. This is a house for those who want to learn and teach and share their wisdom. This is a place for healing and fixing what is broken. And believe me, if you're not broken, someone else is."

The tone of Roger's voice was serious. Serious and urgent. His eyes had not left Elmer's for a long time and the old man was beginning to squirm under the fixed gaze. "Open-mindedness and growth," he said. "These are the key ingredients of a Modern Shaman. Elmer—do you think you can do that? Can you have an open mind? Can you constantly strive for growth?"

Roger leaned forward and waited for Elmer's reply. The silence was thick and heavy, like a large slice of rye bread. "This is not a rhetorical question, by the way," said Roger, winking.

Elmer laughed. "Yes," he replied, a grin spreading across his face. "Yes, I believe I can do those things."

Roger nodded and leaned back. "I know you can, Elmer. I know you can." He beamed at the old man and then let his gaze wander to his right until it fell once again on the outside wall of his beloved house. He reached over and gave the wooden slats a quick pat. "Welcome, Elmer," he said. "Welcome to the house of the Modern Shamans."

Chapter 20

Elmer sighed as he sunk into the creaky burgundy arm chair. He reached down and grasped the stiff, wooden handle on the side of the chair and gave it a rough tug. The footrest popped out with a squeeeak-click. The pianist did not run away. She continued to play smoothly, gracefully, her fingers effortlessly recalling the notes of Sonata in G minor by Clementi.

Elmer closed his eyes. His skin tingled from the staccato beats that flew away from Cecelia's fingers. He pictured himself dancing. Dancing, dancing, dancing. Dancing in a field. He could see the tall grass. He could see it swaying as he danced. And danced and danced. The afternoon sun beat down on his cheeks and ran its warm fingers through his hair. His forehead glistened with sweat. And so did hers. She smiled. He smiled back. Around and around they danced. Danced. Their hands were slippery with sweat, but they hardly noticed as they kept their eyes on each other and their fingers tightly entwined. Dancing, dancing, dancing. They flew around in circles until they grew weary and dizzy and fell over in a fit of laughter. Their hands remained entwined. Her hair was blonde. Blonde from the sun. Their skin was tan and rough. It always got tan and rough by the end of summer. She sighed, stretching her arms outward. He reluctantly let go of her fingers.

Elmer's eyes snapped open. In front of him was a sheet of ashy-blonde hair. Swaying, swaying in time with the music. It flowed over Cecelia's shoulders and hit the top of her back. A shiver passed through his body and his shoulders jerked from the force of it.

Where did she come from? She was so real. I forgot about the time we danced together in the field…

Elmer rarely thought of Daisy.

Where did she come from? Where? Do I really need to be haunted by more spirits?

* * *

Joy and camaraderie filled the kitchen of the house of the Modern Shamans. It was potent and contagious. Soon, everyone was drunk from the thick stew of glee and giddiness that hung in the air, swirling around and around, drenching people in its optimism.

"Elmer is staying! He's staying!"

Elmer was slightly embarrassed that the hubbub was for him. But mostly, he was happy. He stood quietly in the kitchen as the eight other members of the household flittered around him, grinning and laughing, holding glasses of wine and crackers topped with spinach artichoke dip. Elmer had insisted that there be no party. He pled. He told Onyx that he was tired and would really rather go to bed. "Nonsense!" was her reply. "This is your night!"

And so the house began planning the party. In an hour and a half it was ready. Elmer had never seen such efficient, pleasant teamwork. They quickly divvied out tasks and went about chopping, boiling, stewing, sweeping, washing, painting, stirring, and pouring until the table was laden with food and drinks, the kitchen was spotless, and a large banner hung across the back wall in the kitchen. Elmer looked up at the painted cloth banner for the millionth time, "WELCOME ELMER! YOU ARE FAMILY."

Family. I suppose they're becoming just as close as family.

Elmer shuffled over to the kitchen table and helped himself to some chips with dip, a few pickles, raspberry punch, homemade strawberry pie, and a couple of bite-sized sandwiches. He settled down in a nearby chair and admired the lilies and carnations that adorned the table. He brought one to his nose and breathed deeply. Elmer was, of course, pleased with the lovely food and the wonderful banner, but these—these were truly special. They were Ezzie's contribution and they were arranged on the table with painstaking, meticulous care. To Elmer, they were a peace offering. They signified a glimmer of potential, a spark of understanding. They also seemed, ever so slightly, to ask for forgiveness.

Or maybe they didn't. It was hard to tell. Perhaps they were just flowers.

Elmer picked up a pickle and chomped down on its tangy flesh. He realized he was enjoying himself. He had not really enjoyed himself at a party since…well, he had *never* actually enjoyed himself at a party. He chewed the pickle and grinned.

"Old-Turtle-Elm-Tree!!" Onyx made her way across the room and sat next to the man of the moment. "I can't bee-lieve you're staying! It's fantastic. I remember the first day you were here—awake, that is—and you were so pathetic and scared! Woo-eee, I would have never, *ever* guessed that you would stay. No way! I thought you didn't really like us."

Elmer coughed and choked a bit on his pickle. "I—no, it wasn't that—" he gasped as the pickle reluctantly slid down his throat. He reached for his glass of punch and gulped it down. "I like you all just fine," he said. "It's just that, this is all very new to me. It's just that…I'm a little lost." Elmer avoided Onyx's eyes and continued. He wasn't sure why he continued, but he did anyway. "I know I've been a bit elusive around here. I know I've kept to myself and avoided talking to people when I could. To be completely frank, you all made—make—me a little nervous. You're completely different from what I'm used to. I never really knew people like you. In fact, I tried to avoid them whenever I could. I only associated with people my age. No, that's much too broad—I only associated with *stuffy, boring, ordinary, 'I have a wife and two kids and a house with a picket fence'* people my age. They were all I knew and I learned how to live amongst them, to thrive amongst them. I was one of them, in a way. I was one of them on the surface. They aren't exactly a tough group to figure out. I had it down to a tee." He paused. "Why on earth am I telling you all this?"

Onyx laughed, "That's what tends to happen in this house. Word vomit. Or baring your soul. However you'd like to think about it. This place tends to crack even the hardest nuts. I mean, even Ezzie has opened up and cried like a baby when we were having one of our meetings." She dropped her voice, "Don't tell her I told you that. She's still embarrassed about it. But really, it's nothing to be ashamed of. We've all done it. If you haven't noticed, we are all a bunch of raggedy, damaged souls. Or, at least, we *were* a bunch of damaged souls. We all kind of lean on each other and help to fix what is broken. And yes, part of that inevitably involves spilling your guts. So, no worries. I like hearing about your past. I hope I'll hear more soon."

She smiled and gently squeezed Elmer's shoulder. "And Elm—don't worry about feeling lost. Only those who've been lost can truly appreciate the pleasure of being found."

* * *

Meeting number one. Elmer stared at the ancient chalkboard. It was gigantic and black. It looked like a relic from his youth.

Onyx dusted her hands and stepped away. She admired her neat handwriting. It sprawled across the board in wide, commanding letters:

<u>Tenets of the Modern Shamans</u>

Tenet 1: Constantly Strive for Knowledge

Tenet 2: Heal (Yourself and Others)

Tenet 3: Walk With the Earth, Not Against It

Tenet 4: Live in Harmony; Live as One

Elmer wondered where they had acquired such a chalkboard. He wondered if they used it for all their meetings.

Meetings. They happen often, I'm told. I hate meetings.

Onyx stepped forward and poked Elmer in the side. She stood ramrod straight and looked sternly at the eight sets of eyes that peered expectantly at her. Or, at least she liked to think that they were staring expectantly at her. She liked to think that her audience was waiting with bated breath to hear the lecture she had prepared. In reality, they were not. Their gazes and minds wandered. They had all—minus Elmer—heard this speech before and were simply offering their support to the newest member of the household. They sat quietly while Onyx focused her eyes on Elmer and began speaking in a voice as authoritative as her stance.

"Elm. Tell me what you see in the four tenets listed on the board."

"What I *see*? I'm not sure I know what you mean."

"Oh, for Pete's sake, Elmer! Just tell me what you make of them. How do you interpret their messages? What do these words mean to you?"

Elmer pressed his glasses against his face and squinted at the board. "Well," he began, his voice slow and unsure, "I suppose they are good general rules to live by. I certainly don't oppose striving for knowledge or living in harmony—"

"Ok, ok," Onyx cut him off impatiently. "But how do these words make you feel?"

"Good, I suppose," said Elmer lamely.

"For the love of the goddess, you're pathetic," said Onyx, exasperated. "We're going to have to work on your emotional education. You can express yourself about as well as a lumpy sofa."

"Come on Ons," said Kyle. He was sitting next to Elmer and he reached over and gave him a small thump on the back. "Don't be too hard on him. It's his first meeting—we don't want to chase him away yet."

"Yeah, seriously Ons," chimed in Maggie. "This isn't boot camp."

"Alright, alright," said Onyx, still exasperated. "I can see this is a tough crowd today. I'll just give you my own interpretation of the Tenets." She cleared her throat and picked up the pool cue she was using as a pointer. She slapped the stick across the board and pointed to the first line of words.

"Tenet one. Constantly strive for knowledge," her eyes slowly scanned the audience. "If you're not learning, you might as well be dead. There is an entire world of knowledge out there and no way in *hell* can you learn everything. But you can at least learn something and *that* is very important." She raised her voice slightly and started pacing in front of the chalkboard. "We live in an ignorant society. We live in a society that is content with the status quo because they don't know any better. They are lost sheep and they don't even know it! We—,"she pointed the pool cue at her audience and slowly swept it in a wide arc, "we are found sheep. We need to rise above the fray and *constantly strive for knowledge.* It only helps you to be a better person. And it helps you to help others become better people." She shouted at her audience, swinging the stick for emphasis. "Knowledge is power, people! Educate yourselves!" She jumped up on an empty chair near the chalkboard and continued speaking loudly and forcefully, enunciating each word as it sprang from her mouth. The stick moved up and down with ev-er-y-care-ful-syl-la-ble. "We've become a distracted society, shuffling from one social feeding trough to the next. Separate yourselves from the herd! Snap out of your hypnosis! Stick it to the man! Show him that you don't give in to distraction and tedium! You were born to have an active mind. For the love of god, USE IT! ...That is all."

She bowed. Kyle and Roger burst into applause. Craig shouted, "Right on, girlfriend! Tell it like it is!" The rest, even Ezzie, nodded their approval. Elmer just looked around awkwardly.

Onyx smiled at her audience. "Thank you, thank you. Seems like you're more awake now, at least." She paced over to Elmer's chair and stooped down so their eyes were on the same plane. "Where do you think we get our knowledge, Elm?" she asked.

Elmer paused and ventured a guess, "From books?"

Onyx straightened up. She held the pool cue so that it rested on her right shoulder, just above her sparrow tattoo and began pacing in front of the chalkboard once more. She looked very much like an armed soldier keeping watch. "Well, sure. There's some of that, of course. I give that answer a C+. Anyone else?"

Roger spoke up, "We gain most of our knowledge from each other. Everyone has a story. Everyone has something, or multiple somethings, at which they excel. Everyone has something to teach. And it is our duty to learn. Listen and learn. That's what our ancestors did. They didn't have computers or books or even the written word for quite a while. They told stories and they kept their history alive through their words. Our personal histories may not be written down, but they can be told and we can learn from them. Listen and learn…"

"Always the sentimentalist, Roger," said Ezzie from the back of the room.

Roger smiled and said nothing.

Onyx looked at him and nodded. "Good answer, Rog. Although, I probably learn more from Wikipedia than most of the clowns in this house. Kidding, Cecelia, kidding—don't look at me like that. Anyway," she turned back to Elmer, "did I get the point across? Is Tenet numero uno crystal clear?"

Elmer nodded.

"Good. On to number two."

Onyx climbed down from her chair and plopped down in the seat with a THUD. She scanned the room. "I'm a little worn out from my speech. Does someone else want to take the floor for a bit? Hilo?" Hilo stared at her with wide eyes. "Joking, Hilo. Obviously. Jesus, Cecelia, I think that look singed my skin a little."

"Oh, for Pete's sake," Cecelia stood up, green skirt swishing. "I'll take the floor for a while if it means you'll stop antagonizing people."

"Not antagonizing, just lightening the mood a bit. Things can get a bit stuffy around here, especially after a 'Roger speech.'" Onyx glanced over at Cecelia, "Honestly, why do you *still* take me so seriously…"

"I'm sorry, weren't you the one who was just wielding a stick and tromping around in front of us like Mussolini?"

"Touché. Alright, I'll stop. Anyway, the floor is yours, sistah."

Cecelia shook her head and sighed. She turned to face her audience and took a small step towards them. "First of all, your speeches aren't boring, Roger. They're inspiring. Don't stop sharing your wisdom." Onyx rolled her eyes. Cecelia continued, "Secondly…healing. That's our second Tenet. Heal yourself; heal others." She paused. "When I look around the room I see people who have had tough lives. I see people who have struggled, who've been lost and battered and trampled upon by others. I see people who have battled through life because they are different from the mainstream, because they flow the other way down the river."

Kyle reached over and squeezed Craig's hand. Craig squeezed back.

"But, more importantly, I also see people who are strong, who haven't given up, who cling to hope and bits of light when everything seems dark. I don't need to explain to any of you the importance of healing. It is essential. It is the only way to make it through this life." She cleared her throat and gathered her thoughts for a few seconds.

"I'm not trying to be dramatic. I'm just telling it like it is. I have seen dozens of people pass through this house in the last seven years. They've all had vastly different personalities and come from different backgrounds. But they all have one thing in common—they hurt enough to seek refuge. They all found this place. It called their names. Maybe you don't think a place holds memories," she glanced over at Ezzie, "but I do. I think they soak into the pores of the ceiling and take root in the walls. I think a home is an echo of the people who live in it. Believe what you will, but I think this home is especially powerful."

Her storm-colored eyes locked with Elmer's. He nodded. He knew what she meant.

She peeled her eyes away from the old man and continued, "It is a rare person who walks through the world with no pain pressing on their back. But it's not unheard of. I have seen some of these damaged souls become those rare people. I have seen amazing transformations. I have seen ratty caterpillars morph into butterflies. I see it all the time. I see it in this room."

She glanced around the room lovingly, like a mother watching her children sleep. They fought the urge to jump up and hug her.

"I believe in healing," she said quietly. "I believe it holds an important place in a world that is often chaotic and terrible. We live in a messy place—you all know that, but before any of us sets out to heal the world, we have to remember ourselves. Healing starts right here." She placed her hand above her heart. "It starts with you."

She rocked back and forth on her heels, her long, apple-green skirt whooshed softly with her movement. "I'm not saying 'don't help others.' Not at all. Just remember, it's easy to get wrapped up in others' lives and neglect your own. Never, *never* let that happen. You would be doing your own life a disservice."

Elmer's eyes became heavy with tears. He tried to blink them back. He was unsuccessful.

You would be doing your own life a disservice.

Elmer wasn't quite sure who he had been living for for all these years, but he knew it wasn't himself.

Cecelia pretended not to notice the old man's glistening eyes. She gently picked up the thread of her speech. "The beautiful thing about healing is that there are endless ways to do it. Onyx, Roger, and I practice shamanism and Reiki. We work with herbs and chakras and energy healing."

Onyx chimed in, "I like to call it 'old school healing meets New Age fabulous.'"

Ezzie rolled her eyes and made a "hmph" sound in the back of her throat.

Cecelia looked from Onyx to Ezzie. She continued as if there had been no interruption. "Of course, that's not the only way to practice healing. It's not a 'one-size-fits-all' thing. Different people find different methods that work for them. The only trick is finding that special method, that special outlet that helps *you.* I sincerely believe this house helps foster a closer relationship with yourself that allows you to understand how to Be. Just Be. Much easier said than done."

Elmer glanced over at Maggie. He thought of her absentmindedly tugging on a loose thread, her long limbs sprawled across the green couch. Looking like a tree. Her voice soft, but strong.

"It's so important to Be," said Cecelia. "It's so important to live in harmony with yourself."

If we don't take care of ourselves, if we don't take time to soak in the sunlight, then our branches will be brittle and our leaves will shrivel up. We'll be no good for anyone, including ourselves.

"Healing is contagious. Your light inevitably shines on others."

Trees don't have to think about this—they just live. There should be more "just living" in the world.

"Practice being comfortable in your own skin."

I've grown. I've grown into my own skin.

Cecelia paused. Elmer's thoughts calmed down. He glanced at Maggie. Her left leg rested on the floor and the other was bent in front of her, her foot situated on the seat and her right elbow propped on the bent leg. Her chin rested comfortably on the back of her hand. She watched Cecelia with dark, thoughtful eyes.

Elmer turned back to Cecelia. *These young people are wise for their years. But age is a funny thing…*

"Anyway," said Cecelia. "The long and short of what I'm saying is that healing is important. It's important to heal yourself first; others will naturally follow. And one more thing," her eyes swept over the room. "Don't forget to try new things. You might find a way of healing that works for you, but there may also be something out there that offers a fuller, richer experience that you might have trouble imagining if you never venture from your rut."

Cecelia looked at her audience once more, nodded, and quietly sat down in her seat. No one applauded; applause was not appropriate. Instead, the room was filled with a thoughtful silence and a heaviness as Cecelia's words saturated the air. Elmer looked at the wooden walls around him. He wondered if Cecelia's wisdom had soaked into its cellulose, locked inside the wood forever.

After a while, Onyx stood up. "I think it's about time we take a little break, yeah? How about everyone go outside for a little while and we'll meet back in half an hour. Sound good? Ready, go."

They arose lethargically and shuffled away from the room. Only Elmer remained. He didn't want them to see his tears.

Elmer watched the group of eight from the living room window. They looked like a painting—a painting of an idyllic summer scene that makes you long to step inside the canvas and dance amongst the subjects. Everyone was tranquil and happy…comfortable in their skins. Onyx was braiding Hilo's hair as the spindly girl sat cross-legged in the sun. She picked dandelions and carefully removed each tiny yellow pedal and placed them in a small pile in front of her. She waited patiently as Onyx braided and re-braided her thin hair, trying different methods and styles. Ezzie was nearby, poking around in her garden. Dirt already clung to her knees and the cuffs of her pants. It clung to her like it was part of her body. The rest were sprawled out in the short, bright grass. They looked like statues lounging in various positions, faces upturned, bodies still, skin warm and bright.

Elmer could feel a wall of water pushing against the backs of his eyes. He feebly tried to resist, to push against the flow. He knew it was useless. The plastic dam burst several weeks ago in There and all the brittle pieces had washed away with the force of seventy years. His shoulders and thin back shook as tears sprang from his eyes. He wiped his cheeks with the back of a sleeve and looked out the window. He cried harder.

Words and images pounced into his mind, grabbed hold of his thoughts for a moment, and then left again.

Irene. Papa. The train. Drums, drums, drums

Mud, lots of mud

Streets humming, city buzzing, people surrounding me like a stream

"Dig. Dig yourself out. Dig. Dig yourself out. Dig…"

Irene, Papa, Maggie, Arnie

Levi and Zach, Maggie and Zach

Onyx-Craig-Cecelia-Roger-Maggie-Hilo-Kyle-Ezzie

Ezzie.

His thoughts rose up like a giant wave. They gathered momentum. They were clear and bright.

Plastic slide. Rain, rain like tears, rain that beckoned the worms, rain that made me slip, rain that made me fall

into the mud.

"Dig. Dig yourself out. Skin. Feel comfortable in your skin. Heal."

Seven colors of the rainbow. Seven colors smiling at me, guiding my actions, helping me. Wisdom pouring through their mouths and into my ears and into this house. Wisdom and belief.

WELCOME ELMER. YOU ARE FAMILY.

Flowers.

"There should be more 'just living' in the world."

The seven sages sprang back into his head. This time, one at a time. He still believed in them, like he believed in the wooden house. Maybe they were connected. Maybe they were the same thing…

Violet, indigo, blue, green, yellow, orange, red.

Woman, man, man, woman, half-man, man, woman.

Soft, grey, powerful, wild and gnarled, proud, tranquil, dancing

Elmer sobbed. The wave had reached its pinnacle and began to crash down. The images and words came fast. Fast and frantic. They flooded his head.

Irene—Papa—Daisy—train—Maggie—slide—dig—Spud! Hey Spud!—heal—orange—red—yellow—There—City A—Onyx—rain, rain, rain—green—blue—Here—bird, giant black bird—streets—drums—pillars, tall carved pillars—parks—a trumpet—Cecelia, Kyle, Roger—Daisy, my Daisy—sleep—trees—indigo—violet—mountains—train conductor—cane—Craig—walls, wooden walls—Irene, Papa—glasses—the woman at the police station, judging—Hilo—drums—bird, cat, pit of writhing snakes—flowers—walls made of wood—Zach—Ezzie—Irene—dig. Heal. Dig. Dig. Dig…

The wave flattened out and spread its watery fingers along the shores of Elmer's brain. The old man lay still on the floor, blood quietly pooling behind his ear.

Chapter 21

"Tenet number three. Walk with the earth, not against it."

She looks like the green-robed woman, somehow.

"This one is very important to me."

They both look like they would be happy planted in the ground. They would thrive.

"The earth is where we live. It's our one and only home. We should be grateful for the soil under our feet and the trees over our heads. We should appreciate every creature that crawls on the ground or flies in the air—every creature that is worth gathering two-by-two and rescuing from the angry flood of humanity."

Maggie paused, bounced Zach a little higher up her hip, and looked at her audience. Her face was grave and slightly anxious. "We don't have to fight against the earth. We don't have to struggle to control her. We can walk with her instead, like we were meant to."

Elmer sat in the audience once again. A thick pad of gauze was taped behind his right ear. He placed his hand against it. The skin underneath the bandage still ached and throbbed with each heartbeat.

"The industrial revolution stroked our enormous human egos. We began to think we're superior to mother earth, that we can rape her and toss her aside. That was *never* how it was supposed to be. Craig," she locked eyes with the petite Asian man sitting attentively in front of her. "You know the Bible like the back of your hand. What does it have to say about all this?"

Craig nodded gravely. "Well Maggie, it really says whatever you want to hear." A few people snickered and Craig hushed them with a wave of his hand. "No really. If you're looking for a passage that says 'ravage and abuse the earth,' you'll find it. But I truly don't believe that is the bigger picture. Yes, the Bible tells us to populate the earth, but you have to remember when this thing was written—hundreds and hundreds of years ago. Back then, there were fewer people and they constantly struggled to survive. I mean, when people are dying left and right from diseases and warfare and childbirth, *of course* the goal is to populate the earth. And they wanted the earth to be populated with *believers*. In my opinion, the deed is done. Good job. Earth populated. That's Old Testament stuff. If you look to the New Testament, the message changes significantly. We are told to love and practice empathy. We are told to be good stewards of the earth. We are instructed to reject greed and to remember that it's 'harder for a camel to pass through the eye of a needle than for a rich man to enter the kingdom of heaven.' If that's not a case for living simply, than I don't know what is."

"Thank you, Craig," said Maggie. "Your expertise is always appreciated."

A sharp pain rocketed through Elmer's head and his hand shot up to cradle the spot behind his ear. Maggie's eyes followed the movement.

"Oh no. Elmer honey, are you ok? I knew we shouldn't have continued this meeting so soon…"

Elmer reddened. He didn't like being the frail one, the one with an old, brittle body and a fragile mind. He steeled himself against the pain. "No, no. I'm alright. Don't worry about me. I've had two days to recover. I'm perfectly fine."

The room stared at him. Lies didn't come easily in this house.

"Get on with it," Elmer insisted, his voice gruff and his face sullen. "I want to hear more about the earth. I never really gave it much thought until now."

Maggie shot him a worried glance, but she could tell it was no use arguing with him. He was as stubborn as an ox. "The earth," she continued, "provides us everything we need…as long as we're not too greedy. It's easy to be greedy. It's easy to always want more, more, more. It's easy to want bigger and better. We live in a society that encourages those thoughts, that encourages greed. We all have to learn how to resist, to hold back, to live frugally. We have to live consciously. It's easy to wander through life aimlessly, buying whatever they're selling. Don't. Do. It. Think before you act. Think about the repercussions. Think about the trees that were uprooted in order to make your mahogany cupboards. Your actions *do* make a difference, believe me. "

She looked at the child resting serenely at her side. "If not for yourselves, do it for him. Do it for the future."

Maggie walked—or floated, maybe—to a folding chair that faced the audience. She sat down. "Just so we're clear, I'm not telling you to sell all your possessions and live in a cave in the woods. That's not the point. The point is moderation. The point is showing respect. The earth has done so much for us, the least we can do is take care of her a bit. Small changes make a huge difference—remember that."

She sighed and looked at her son. His tiny chest moved up and down, up and down, keeping a steady rhythm while he slept.

Elmer thought of the earth and Papa's potato farm. He thought of dry, barren years when only a few scraggly potato plants managed to poke their heads through the soil and bare their pathetic, lumpy fruit. He thought of his father cursing the soil and throwing clods of dirt at the dusty earth below his feet. He thought of lush, plentiful years when rows of green carried hundreds of hidden treasures below the earth, guarding them like leafy soldiers. Papa praised the earth during those times. Its whims controlled his mood. Elmer had never thought of these things before. But he thought of them now as he watched the beautiful woman in front of him calmly explain the importance of the earth and mankind's connection with her. To Elmer, it sounded like poetry.

The old man glanced outside and watched the long shadows of the afternoon trees dance on the lawn. They moved smoothly with the tug of the wind. It was something very close to the tug of the wind that had yanked Elmer onto the train and away from Here—an external pull, neither friendly nor vicious.

Maggie was standing now; her speech was complete. It ended much like Cecelia's—with thoughtful silence rather than raucous applause. Maggie walked to the window and gazed at the trees that Elmer had been watching. He hardly noticed as she stepped into his line of sight. Her figure and movements blended with the life outside.

* * *

When they found him two days ago, his body was eerily still. Ezzie walked through the doorway first. She spotted him. She screamed. They had never heard Ezzie scream. They clambered to get inside, to see the horrible thing that made the usually emotionless woman cry out.

They saw him, one-by-one, lying eerily still.

Some gasped, some cursed under their breath, all piled frantically around him.

Through his haze, Elmer heard voices. They melded together in an amorphous lump, rising and falling like waves. Someone cradled his head in their palm, covering the gash with their fingers.

"Is he ok?" they asked. "Will he be alright?"

"Yes, yes," the one cradling his head replied. "He'll be alright."

"Iren-pa," Elmer muttered. "Drm-brd."

"Oh, Elmer, Elmer. Be ok. Be well."

"Dais-brd-svn," Elmer replied.

They put him to bed.

* * *

"Live in harmony; live as one," the speaker paused and glared at her audience. "That is the fourth tenet."

Elmer stared incredulously at the speaker in front of him. He wasn't sure if Ezzie volunteered to speak or if she was coerced into it, but there she was, looking very much like her usual catty self.

"I'm not one for long, flowery speeches, so I'll keep this brief," she said in a clipped, curt tone. "This one's pretty self explanatory anyway." Ezzie did not move as she stood, straight-backed in front of her audience. Her head was fixed forward; her eyes locked with no one's as they scanned the room. "We are all people living on the same earth. We are all equals. Sure, I don't agree with everyone's choices and everyone's opinions, but it doesn't mean they're not damn-well entitled to those choices and opinions. Things would be *much* better if we all fucking got along. That's that. Simple."

She finally locked eyes with one member of her audience. Elmer was horrified that it was him.

"That's how we live, Elmer. We choose to live in a community. Now *obviously*," she glanced at Onyx, "we're not all alike. I don't buy into a lot of the hocus pocus that goes on in this house, but it doesn't mean I'm going to try to stop it. It doesn't mean I'm going to shut my trap either. Opinions are meant to be shared, if you ask me. But anyway, even if I'm not thrilled about sacred gemstones and aligning my chakras, it doesn't mean I'm going to become violent and lash out and threaten to bomb the shit out of everyone who doesn't agree with me. No. Life is better when we live as a community, when we live as one."

She looked around the room. "That's the idea behind our little community here. We live as one organism, helping and supporting each other, leaning on each other when we need to. Everyone pitches in. We all have *some* positive attribute we can tap into for the good of the household. And so we do. It's a very natural thing, really. And it works well for all of us."

She turned back to Elmer. "Pretty fucking idyllic, isn't it?"

"Yes, yes it is. But I don't quite see how it works. I mean, isn't money ever a problem? What do you do about that?"

"Oh, that," Ezzie said, her voice edged with sarcasm. "That wasn't such a problem for me, but I can see how some people wouldn't like our little system here. You see, what we do is put all the money that we earn in a communal pot. Some of us have jobs—"

"I work at the co-op in town!" said Onyx enthusiastically. "They let me take home all the old veggies and fruit too. It's usually perfectly fine, just a little rusty around the edges—"

"Did anyone ask you?" Ezzie snapped.

Onyx replied, "No, I just—"

"Then keep your trap shut," snarled Ezzie. She turned to Elmer once again. "Now where was I? So, money. Yes. We throw all our money into a single fund and use it as we need it. Anyone can request to take money out of the fund for any reason. It can be as stupid as Cecelia's new yoga mat or replacement light bulbs. Like I said, it wasn't ever a problem for me—sharing from a communal pool of money, that is—but I can see how some people would loathe it. Most people, probably. But that's just because we've all been brought up to worship money and material goods. It really ties into tenet three—walking with the earth."

Elmer hesitated for a moment and then decided to speak. "It all sounds a bit…I don't know…Communist."

"Goddamn it, Elmer!" Ezzie shouted. "I know you're old, but at least try to open your eyes a bit."

Elmer blinked back at her. *Old? Isn't she just a decade or two behind me?*

"Communism," Ezzie continued. "You say the word with such disdain. Sure, it was a form of government that's been fairly unsuccessful in *practice*, but that doesn't mean the ideas behind it weren't any good. I mean, what's wrong with everyone being equal? What's wrong with fewer possessions and frivolity? Ok, ok—I know the government lets all its power go to its head, but that's the beauty of our household—no one is 'in charge.' And when no one is in charge, *and* everyone is equal, it's really quite liberating."

Ezzie paused and chewed on her lip as she searched for her next words. "To be perfectly candid with you, I'm not so sure some aspects of our household would work on a larger scale. There are just too many lazy assholes out there that would screw over all the hardworking, fair people.

With just eight of us—now nine, I guess—it's easy to give people a kick in the pants every once in a while if they're not pulling their weight. It's easy to hold everyone accountable. But Elmer—"

Her eyes were pleading. Elmer thought he saw tears forming in their corners, but he was sure it was only his imagination…

"Try to see the bigger picture. Try to see beyond the minute details like money. There are more important things in the world than dollar bills. Think back to my first point. Do you remember what I said?"

Elmer squeezed his eyebrows together in thought. The puffy skin under his bandage ached. "Yes, I remember," he said. "You said we are all equals and we should all try to f-ing get along."

A few people chuckled. Ezzie remained serious. "Now it's Elmer the comedian, is it? Anyway, that's right. We *are* all equals. And that's why this is a tenet for the world, not just this household. Sure, we choose to take this tenet to the extreme and literally *live* in harmony with each other, but as for the rest of the world, this tenet simply means to coexist. Coexist and remember to respect and value every human life. *Every—human—life.*"

Now Elmer was certain he wasn't imagining it—Ezzie's eyes glistened with tears as she continued speaking.

"To me, it's a sacred tenet. Don't judge. Don't shun or show disrespect. Don't spit at people and throw stones. At the *very* least, tolerate. Is that too much to ask? You don't have to agree with my lifestyle, but at the very least you can tolerate it, damn it!"

Nobody moved. They hardly dared to breathe.

Ezzie choked on her words, but still managed to spit them out. "We can be evil and downright cruel to other people. We can trample their hearts with words and crush their spirits with actions. Why? Why do we do these things? WHY?" She breathed in deeply, looking at the floor and began muttering under her breath. The room disappeared in front of her; all she could see were her own feet. "I can't understand it. I'm only trying to be true to myself for the *very* first time in my life and you have to add to my turmoil? Why? Why would you do that? You're still my daughter, aren't you? And I'm still your mother? What changed? What changed—what changed—*what* changed? Why can't you just let me be? Why did you have to lose your respect? Why did you trample and crush, trample and crush, trample and crush…"

Ezzie suddenly dissolved into tears. She crumpled in a heap on the floor and buried her head in her hands.

Maggie was the first to dash to the front of the room and wrap her arm around the woman's broad shoulders. The others jumped to their feet and closed in on Ezzie—or the whimpering shell of a woman that looked like Ezzie—and began to comfort her. Ezzie cried uncontrollably into her palms.

Even Elmer struggled to his feet and leaned on his cane as he watched the seven pat her on the back and stroke her hair, easing her with soft, kind words. Two days ago, he had been the one sobbing in the living room. He had been the one who was so overcome with emotion that he couldn't control his body or his thoughts. They both went wherever they wanted to go and his body, unfortunately, wanted to slide off his chair and smack his head against the leg of the piano.

Elmer reached behind his right ear and gently pressed his bandage. They had quickly and carefully healed his wound in the same way they were healing Ezzie's: with love and solidarity. Elmer didn't remember who stopped his blood from seeping on the floor. He didn't remember who bandaged the back of his head or who carried him upstairs and tucked him into bed. What he did remember were the looks on each of their faces as he struggled downstairs for the first time after his fall, almost a full day later. They each wore an expression of care and concern. Deep, true care and concern. The memory of their faces almost made Elmer melt into tears once again.

Now, as they stood or kneeled or sat by Ezzie, the same care and concern radiated from each member of the Modern Shamans. Elmer stood back. Ezzie was in good hands.

* * *

Later that day, Roger sat down next to Elmer. The old man was relaxing in his favorite burgundy chair and opened his eyes when he heard Roger approach.

"Mind if I join you?"

"Go right ahead."

"Elmer, I'm sure what you saw today confused you."

Elmer nodded.

"There are a few things you should know about Ezzie."

Chapter 22

It was the day of Summer Fest and everyone was in a good mood. Faces smiled; voices were light. They tittered and chuckled about nothing at all and grinned at the sunshine. Craig, Onyx, and Roger all wore matching green robes that looked like long, plain kimonos. They talked excitably with the others as they loaded their instruments into Roger's car.

"Today's the big day!" said Onyx. "I finally get to show off my mad drumming skills."

"Skills?" teased Ezzie. "Don't you have to be able to keep a rhythm in order to claim you have drumming skills?"

Onyx poked her in the ribs in reply.

Craig loaded an electric keyboard that Elmer had never seen before into the car. He turned and noticed the old man's inquisitive eyes. "Rummage sale," he said, pointing to the keyboard. "I got this baby for thirty-five bucks. Almost like new. The living room piano was just a *tad* too big to fit in the old car." He winked at Elmer and the old man smiled in return.

Onyx skipped over to Elmer and threw her arms around him in a rough hug. "Wish me luck Old Turtle, Elm Tree!" she exclaimed.

"Good luck," Elmer managed to say once he caught his breath. "To be honest, Onyx, I didn't know you played percussion until just today."

"Well, that's just because I'm too *shy* to practice at home."

They all laughed. Onyx stuck out her tongue. "Seriously!" she said. "I get all nervous and self-conscious when I'm playing, especially when I'm surrounded by all the honest-to-god, real musicians that live in this house. I mean, we have Louis Armstrong and George Gershwin here." She motioned to Roger and Craig, "and the female equivalent of Bach over there." She motioned to Cecelia. "And," she paused theatrically and looked at the mousy girl in the back of the group, "rumor has it lil' Hilo over there is quite the Wolfgang Amadeus Mozart herself."

Hilo reddened and looked down at her shoes. She suddenly became very interested in tracing circles in the dirt with her right foot.

Roger walked over to Onyx and put his arm around her shoulder. "About ready to go, little imp?"

Onyx laughed and hopped into the car. Craig clambered into the back.

The remaining six waved. Cecelia shouted, "See you in a bit! Good luck!"

"Thanks!" Roger replied as he started the car. "See you all soon!"

The car rolled down the driveway and out of sight. The group dispersed and went back inside one by one. Only Cecelia and Elmer remained standing on the driveway. Cecelia turned to the elderly man, her voice smiling as she spoke. "They're going to be wonderful, I just know it."

Elmer looked at the young woman. The sun shone on a few golden strands mixed into her ashy hair. "But what about you?" he asked.

"What do you mean?"

"Why aren't you performing?"

"Ah, that," said Cecelia. "I'm just not a performer. I love to play by myself, to feel the keys beneath my fingers, but I don't love to showcase it in front of the world. Besides, I'm not so sure the folks at Summer Fest would be too excited to hear Clementi."

"I think it's beautiful."

She looked into the old man's green eyes for a moment. "Thank you, Elmer."

* * *

Hilo watched Ezzie's car pull out of the driveway, turn left, and accelerate down the road. They were all—all five of them—going to Summer Fest to eat, socialize, and watch Roger, Onyx, and Craig perform on the makeshift stage. Every summer the central plaza of City A transformed into a mini festival filled with arts and crafts, food booths, and family-friendly entertainment. It was called Summer Fest. It was good, wholesome fun. There was something to do for everyone. But Hilo wouldn't know. She had never been there.

Ezzie's car had kicked up a cloud of dust above the short, gravel driveway and Hilo watched it settle. They tried to convince her to go. They pleaded and promised good times and endless fun. Hilo would have none of it. To her, the prospect of mingling with a gigantic, noisy crowd was terrifying and the terror trumped the promise of endless good fun. So they went. And Hilo stayed.

Hilo ran her hand along the window ledge, feeling the smooth wood beneath her palm. She plucked a hair tie from her wrist and threw her hair back in a thin ponytail. The house was silent and her footsteps sounded unnaturally loud as she walked across the hardware floors of the kitchen and into the living room. She tiptoed to the stereo in the corner and turned it on. Miles Davis sprang from the speakers and she caught hold of the rhythm and let it guide her while she danced.

She stepped elegantly through the house, her feet hitting the floor in perfect time with the irregular beat. One-a-two-a-three-and four and, one-two-and three, four. She held her arms off to the left as if she was dancing with an invisible partner.

One-a-two-a-three.

The saxophones and trumpets continued. Hilo lost herself in the music. She found herself at the piano.

She sat down, her back straight, her shoulders held back. When she was a young girl, her mother made her take lessons. That was part of being a lady. No man wanted to marry a woman who wasn't raised properly. At least, that was the expectation of all females in her family's social circles. Ladies were to speak French, quote classical literature, and play the piano. To Hilo, it was something freakish out of the pages of War and Peace. She would know; she had read it.

She didn't like to think about her past, but it had a way of sneaking into her head. At times it seemed dim and far away, but it always surrounded her, like a blanket of thin fog. She breathed in and out deeply, clearing the mist from her brain, and looked at the humble dark face of the piano. She placed her right thumb on middle C and carefully aligned the rest of her fingers on the keyboard. That was the way she'd always done it. She liked to slowly prepare her hands for making music; she liked to build a little anticipation for the main event. Even if the main event was only for herself.

When her hands were in place, Hilo shut her eyes. She began to play, quickly and a bit irregularly, complementing the jazz chords in the background. Her shoulders and head swayed as her fingers swept across the keys. She wondered if there were pianos in heaven.

Time flew by with the notes—a half hour, an hour, an hour and a half. Hilo did not notice. She played and played, making up for lost time when she didn't play at all. At times, she played furiously, desperately, vomiting her bundled up emotions onto the keyboard. These spasms of emotion were brought on by the voices—the voices that haunted her from the past.

Occasionally, they would crop up, taunting her, and she would beat them down with her nimble fingers.

"You had better take cooking lessons, young lady," her mother's snide voice lectured. "Do you think any of the eligible young men are going to marry you for your *looks*?"

Hilo slammed a C minor chord in reply.

"Young lady!" her father's baritone voice called this time. "There is a guest here to see you. Come downstairs and greet Mr. Ivanov, will you?"

Frantically, Hilo shook his voice out of her head and played faster, harder.

She became entranced by the music. She couldn't stop. Whenever she lost her focus the unwelcome voices returned. She let herself sink deeper and deeper into the music. She became part of the melody. Eventually, her heart rate slowed, her fingers became less violent. She could hardly tell where her arm stopped and the piano began. It was entwined with her body and filled her up like a cup of mint tea. And then—

CRASH!

The window shattered along with her concentration. A rock sailed past her ear and struck the piano's front, smashing its ancient face.

* * *

The sun shone on Summer Fest and warmed the faces of the good people of City A. Roger, Onyx, and Craig had just finished their performance and exited the stage quickly, whisked away by thunderous applause and a desire to be a part of the action. Kyle was the first one to meet them and he gave each of them a bone-crushing hug. "Oh-my-god, you were great! They loved you!"

"I know, right?" said Onyx, grinning. "We had them eating out of the palms of our hands. Looks like the uptight citizens of City A can appreciate good music after all."

"Damn straight!" said Roger. "Let's go celebrate with some fair food. I'm dying for a soft pretzel with cheese."

Two and a half hours and several pounds of fair food later, the group of eight piled back into their cars and drove home. They chatted amiably and laughed easily.

Car one slid into the driveway; car two followed its lead. The group disembarked and ambled up the stairs of the wooden house. Cecelia led the way. She reached for the door handle and paused, her hand resting on the knob and her brows furrowed.

"Something's not right," she said in a whisper. "I know it."

"Don't be ridiculous, Cecelia, open the door," said Ezzie.

She didn't need to be told twice. Cecelia ripped open the door and rushed inside shouting, "Hilo! Hilo, darling, where are you? Hilo! HILO! Come here!"

Her panic was contagious. The rest of the group scurried around the house, looking for the young girl. The search was short-lived. Craig spotted the battered piano first and rushed to see what happened to his beloved instrument. Then, he spotted a pair of bare feet poking out from the narrow space behind the piano.

"Hilo? What on earth? Are you ok? What happened?"

Craig held out his hand to the girl, but she ignored it. Her arms were wrapped around her knees and her body shook feverishly as she stared blankly ahead.

"Oh my god. What the hell happened?" Craig muttered. He turned and called out, "You guys! She's in here!"

Seven pairs of feet ran into the living room. One-by-one they spotted the piano. Cecelia clasped her hands over her mouth and gasped. Her eyes welled with tears.

Roger walked forward and picked up an object that was resting by one of the legs of the piano. It was a rock.

"Hey, there's a note attached!" said Kyle. "What does it say?"

Roger slowly untied the string that was holding the small piece of paper to the rock. He opened it and silently read the thin, sloping handwriting. He stared at the note for several long seconds, saying nothing. Elmer studied his face. He had never seen Roger wear such an expression; it was a confused mix of anger, disappointment, and fear. It was the fear that made Elmer shiver.

After several heavy seconds, Onyx snatched the note from Roger's stiff hand. She gasped, crumpled the note, and threw it on the floor. It landed face up and its edges began to slowly uncurl, like a monster lethargically stretching its limbs after a deep sleep. The rest of the group gathered around the small piece of paper. Ezzie smoothed its edges with her foot and the neat, cursive letters stared up at them.

Burn in hell, dirty Communist hippies.

You aren't welcome here.

Chapter 23

The mood was somber in the house of the Modern Shamans. Elmer felt as if he was living amongst eight ghosts. No one talked about the incident; they went about their days silently and methodically, avoiding eye contact. They only exchanged words when absolutely necessary and when they did, the words came out terse and short. Even Onyx was eerily silent.

In fact, the last words Elmer heard her utter occurred on the day of the incident. After everyone had read the piece of paper, Onyx snatched it from the floor and said, "Burn in hell, huh? Why don't *you* burn in hell!" She yanked a lighter from her pocket and held it to the edge of the paper. It blackened and smoked as the flame greedily fed on the hateful words. A tiny pile of ash was left on the floor.

"Oh great, Onyx," Ezzie moaned. "You've destroyed the evidence! Now we can't file a police report."

"Fuck them," Onyx said. She turned and ran up the stairs. That was three days ago and Elmer had hardly seen her, let alone heard her speak, since. Onyx mostly stayed in the room she shared with Cecelia, listening to vinyl records from her collection and staring at the ceiling.

Elmer followed the ghosts' leads and tiptoed around the house too. He hated it. It reminded him of church. Or the way he used to walk on eggshells around Papa when he was in a bad mood. Besides, he didn't really feel like the note was directed at him. Sure, he understood how it could strike a nerve with the others (I mean, they were all a little odd, weren't they?), but he did not understand their reaction to the note. *Why did it have such a profound effect on them? Why was it heavy enough to weigh down the entire collective?* He didn't know. But there was one thing he *did* know—he was getting damn sick of living in a place more solemn than a tomb.

But Elmer continued to tiptoe. He didn't know what else to do. He dreaded getting up each morning and filling another long day inside the silent house. He found himself with a lot of free time to think. He went on countless walks. He meditated quietly in his burgundy chair for hours on end. He paced shakily around the house, grasping his cane with his right hand and leaning on it heavily with each step. He thought about Here and There. He thought about the seven robed sages. He thought about the light, sunny mood of Summer Fest before it came crashing down…

After they watched the horrible note go up in flames, the group was silent and still. They shifted their weight awkwardly and looked at the floor. Finally, Craig snapped out of his trance and said, "Come on, Kyle. Let's get Hilo out of here."

The two men walked silently to the piano and dragged it away from the terrified young girl, still curled in an embryonic ball, rocking back and forth, seemingly unaware her shelter had been removed.

"Let's go, Hilo," said Kyle gently. "Come on, honey. Let's go upstairs."

He lifted her right arm and placed it around his neck. She didn't struggle. She didn't even move.

"Craig, get her left arm. Looks like we're going to have to help her up the stairs."

Craig silently obeyed. Soon Hilo was strung between the two men and they half-dragged, half-carried her up the creaky, wooden stairs. As Elmer watched them ascend, the sharp feeling of déjà vu kicked him in the gut. His jaw dropped open. Craig was wearing a red polo shirt and Kyle was wearing a green t-shirt. They held onto the girl so loosely she appeared to be floating between them. When they reached the top of the stairs, the three stepped into a thick beam of light and for just a moment, Elmer saw the wide, swaying hips of the woman in red and the fly-away, grey braid of the woman in green. His thoughts were suddenly hurled back to a day filled with mud and rain and the agonizing feeling of helplessness. He remembered how the women steadied him with their warm, sturdy arms and led him through the damp park to the trumpet player, who seemed to be waiting for him to arrive.

The three turned to the left, stepping out of the sunbeam and back into their original bodies. Elmer stared at the top of the stairs for several seconds. He opened his mouth to say something, glanced at his four remaining housemates who stared blankly at the ground, and clamped his lips shut. Now was not the time.

Five days later. Elmer was sick of living by himself. He was sick of spending long days in silence. He was sick of tiptoeing. He often found his thoughts turning to the past and Elmer was driven half-mad attempting to fill his head with things other than his faraway wife and his long-lost love.

Elmer got up from his burgundy chair. He walked slowly to the window and leaned against the ledge. Rain trickled down the glass and muddied the ground below. No walk in the park today. Elmer paced back and forth, back and forth. He thought of swings swaying in the park. He thought of the handsome black woman in red and the wild woman in green. They seldom left his thoughts these days and he was almost as sick of them as he was of Daisy, Irene, and Papa. He stopped pacing mid-stride. His thoughts raced excitedly as he looked out the window.

Maybe they're trying to tell me something. It's a crazy thought, but really…when was the last time my life was truly sane?

Elmer stared at his reflection in the glass. The rain filled the backdrop and it almost looked as if he was standing outside.

Is it really that simple?

Elmer locked eyes with his reflection.

Yes. Yes, I think it is.

Elmer turned around and walked purposefully out of the room. It was his turn to offer a friendly arm and guide his friends through the rain.

* * *

"I call this meeting to order!" said Elmer firmly, standing rigidly in front of his audience.

"Geez, Elm. Don't let all the power get to your head."

Elmer turned and smiled at Onyx. He had never been so happy to hear one of her wisecracks. "Today's meeting," he continued, "is long overdue. We've all been moping around the house, avoiding eye contact and avoiding talking about the incident that we know is on everyone's minds. It's the elephant in the room that no one wants to bring up. So, I decided to finally confront that elephant head on and see if we can't put it in a harness and train the bugger."

A few people chuckled. Elmer was thoroughly enjoying himself. He was usually not one for showmanship and certainly preferred to be in the crowd, rather than speaking to it, but today was an exception. Something had driven him to initiate this meeting and he felt like it was his duty to carry it out. It also didn't hurt that each of his housemates had welcomed the idea with open arms, thankful that *someone* had stepped forward to help the dismal, dreary group. When Elmer had presented his idea to Onyx, she leaped across the room and planted a big kiss on Elmer's cheek saying, "Oh, Elm Tree! I knew you were a wonderful person the moment you came into our lives. I just knew it! Thank you so much. You don't know what this means to me. You really don't."

The rest had responded in a similar vein, their voices filled with gratitude and relief when they thanked Elmer for coming forward to help. Buoyed by their encouragement, Elmer decided to conduct the meeting immediately. They quickly agreed.

"Now, I'm not usually one for meetings," said Elmer, grinning like a schoolboy at his audience, "but they are a whole heck of a lot better than burying our problems under a heap of silence."

"Here, here!" said Kyle. The others nodded.

"I do think we should talk about what happened," said Elmer, "but first I think we all need to get in a better frame of mind. When my son was in the Cub Scouts—" Elmer paused and cleared his throat. He knew it wasn't going to be easy to talk about his family and he had mentally prepared himself for this moment before the meeting. It was still difficult.

Elmer cleared his throat again and pressed on, trying not to think too much about the lines he rehearsed as they spilled out of his mouth. "When my son was in the Cub Scouts, I went to a few of their campfire meetings. Those boys knew how to laugh and have a good time better than most people I know. It always lifted my spirits just being around them."

"Awww," said Onyx. Elmer reddened.

"So, anyway," he continued, "the troop leaders had this game where everyone went around the circle and told about the best moment or day of their lives. At the time, I thought it was just a silly game, but now I realize the value of it. It's easy to dwell on the sour moments and the rotten days. It's not always easy to hold onto the good times in our lives and truly appreciate them. So that's what we're going to do right now. We've all been a brooding mass of negativity for the past week and it's time we change that. Who wants to go first?"

* * *

Two and a half hours and nine stories later, the heavy fog that surrounded the house of the Modern Shamans finally lifted. Hearts and voices were lighter and the group felt comfortable with each other once again. And comfortable with themselves. When the rock was hurled through the window, it shattered more than glass. It shattered the confidence and self-assuredness of everyone in the house. It made them uneasy; it made them question their beliefs and the foundations on which they stood. Elmer helped them pick up the pieces and reassemble what was broken.

In a past life not long ago, Elmer would never have imagined he would help a group of people like the Modern Shamans. But Elmer had been reborn. He wasn't quite sure when it had happened. In There? After his vivid dream? When he had crossed the threshold of this house? Or maybe it happened as soon as he stepped onto the train…

Regardless, Elmer could sense a change. When his eight companions began telling their stories, Elmer realized he felt an intimacy with these people he had not felt in years. Many years. He felt friendship.

Elmer smiled. He looked at the group seated before him. "Who wants to go first?"

Cecelia volunteered. She smiled gratefully at Elmer as she rose to speak. Her voice was even and matter-of-fact as she described her happiest day—the day she decided to seek her own fortune and abandon the home in which she grew up: a shabby foster home littered with dozens of children.

"But, but—" Elmer stuttered after Cecelia had finished speaking. He stared at her wide-eyed, his crinkled mouth hanging open. "But, I would have never guessed. You seem so, so—"

"Put together?" finished Cecelia. "Normal? Innocent? Content?"

"Yes, any of those adjectives will do," said Elmer sheepishly, a small grin on his face.

"It's fine," said Cecelia. "Most people react about the same way when they find out. At least you were a little more tactful than Onyx," she shot a wink at her friend. Onyx stuck out her tongue in reply. "I guess," she continued, "my mother had me when she was very young and didn't know what to do with me, so she dropped me off at the doorstep of Mrs. Terwilliger's Foster Care and Berry Patch. It was the kind of dumpy place where kids don't get adopted—they simply stick around until they can't take it anymore and then run away. Like me."

"Excuse me, Foster Care and *Berry Patch*?" said Kyle. "Umm…I don't remember you telling me about that part before."

Cecelia laughed. "Yeah, that was just another way for Mrs. Terwilliger to make a little profit off of us. While she raked in money from the government for every chick she kept under her fat wings, she made us work in her strawberry patch so she could earn a few dollars on the side. A smart business venture, really."

"Oh my god," said Kyle. "That is so disgusting."

"I guess so," said Cecelia, "but I got out early; I was only fourteen. I moved to the next town over and continued going to school and—"

"And met me!" Onyx cut in.

"Yes, I was getting to that part."

"Well, hurry up!" Onyx grinned, "It's clearly the best part."

"Right, right. So I move to the next town over with only a backpack and one pair of shoes and start working at this little café to start earning money—"

"Wanda's." Onyx interjected again.

"Oh, for the love of god, Onyx! That's not an important detail!"

"It is to Wanda."

Cecelia rolled her eyes and continued. "Onyx was a few years younger than me and she loved coming into *Wanda's*. She was pretty nosey—clearly not much has changed—and she began asking me about myself and soon discovered that I was homeless. I think this came as quite a shock to her because in all her twelve years, Beatrice McFadden had never known anything harder than her weekly tennis lessons."

"Come on Cecelia, what did I tell you about using that name?"

"Woah, woah, woah. Hold up, girl friend!" said Kyle. "Be-a-trice? That's your real name?"

"And you made fun of me for 'Margaret,'" said Maggie with a wink.

Beatrice "Onyx" McFadden rolled her eyes. "Yes," she mumbled. "That was my name. Can we move on please?"

"Tennis lessons, really?" said Ezzie. "I never knew, *Beatrice*."

Onyx jumped to her feet. "Would you cut it out!" she shouted. "I changed my name for a reason. And clearly the tennis lessons weren't my choice. And, as much as I dislike my parents and their fancy cars and their stuffy dinner parties and their tiny, obnoxious dogs, they *did* bring Cecelia in off the street. And for that, I will always be grateful." Onyx plopped down and crossed her arms.

Elmer stared. The ghosts of the house had suddenly sprung back to life. He faced the room and cleared his throat, searching for the right words to say. "Erm…Cecelia, did you want to finish your story?"

"Sure, sure. Ok, so anyway, little Onyx befriends me at Wanda's Café and ends up telling her parents about me. They must have been feeling generous—or maybe they were in need of a little cheap labor—because they agreed to give me room and board and…" she paused and smiled to herself, "and piano lessons in exchange for doing a few odd jobs around the estate. And that," she concluded, "was the best day of my life."

"Oh my god," Onyx moaned, burying her face in her hands. "No one is ever going to want to be friends with me again. I grew up on an *estate*."

Silence.

Then Craig snickered a little. Then Ezzie. The flood gates opened. Laughter bounced off the rafters and dancing crazily around the room until they were dizzy from its force and out of breath.

"Whew," panted Kyle, "I needed that. But shit, who's going to go next? It's a little hard to top running away from a foster home, isn't it?"

They laughed again.

* * *

Elmer sat with his *friends* and savored their words. The flavor of each sentence marinated in his brain; he could taste their experiences; he could feel their joys. They were master storytellers—at least, that's what Elmer thought as he listened to tales of discovery and triumph and the death of past hurts and the birth of new beginnings. He listened as Maggie talked about Zach and Roger talked about painting. He listened as layers peeled back and new skin was revealed. The new skin fit well. Even Hilo was comfortable as she told about the day *she* ran away from home.

With each tick of the clock and each spoken word, the Modern Shamans healed. Before the meeting, the rock and the scathing scrap of paper seemed enormous—giant demons that filled their house and sucked out the air. The paper shrank and continued to shrink after each story, each moment of joy they shared. Elmer looked around the room and smiled. They were happy. And he had been the catalyst. His stooped shoulders straightened just a little.

"Wait just a minute! Elmer—you need to go!"

Onyx jolted Elmer out of his daydreams. "Wha? I—I mean, I don't know. This was really just intended for you. I'm just the monitor."

Roger spoke up, "Onyx has a point, you know. You *are* part of this family too."

"Yeah, Elmer, come on!" said Ezzie. "Even Hilo went." She glanced over at the wisp of a girl sitting cross-legged on the floor. "You're a brave girl Hilo," she said in a low, private voice, "I underestimated you, my dear."

Hilo blushed. Onyx tugged on Elmer's sleeve, "C'mon Elm! We all want to hear your story. What was your best day? Tell us! We're dying to know…"

A sea of faces nodded.

Maggie stood up. "Ok, ok. Listen up everyone. Elmer will go if he wants to. No one is ever forced to do anything in this house." She turned and faced the old man. "Elmer, do what you'd like. It's up to you." She gave him a small nod and sat down. Elmer looked at the quiet child nestled against her hip. He closed his eyes for a moment.

"Ok," he said softly. "I'll go."

Chapter 24

Once long ago, there lived a scrappy little boy named Elmer William Heartland. He grew up on his father's potato farm in the far off land of Here. Elmer loved his life. In the summers, he never wore shoes and grew very tan and very dirty. He would run through the potato fields, playing tag or kick the can with his younger siblings. Or he would sneak away on his own to fish for brook trout in the chilly river. He loved to dip his feet in the water as he fished and feel the icy current rush around his toes and turn them numb.

But little Elmer's life was not always wonderful. His Papa was strict and rarely uttered a kind word. He sometimes beat little Elmer if he forgot to do his chores or if he caught him fishing in the chilly river. But mostly he hurt Elmer with his words. Poor little Elmer was never the son his father wanted him to be—he was never a potato farmer.

Elmer tried to escape whenever he could. He went on long walks that he called "expeditions" and would sometime trek across the countryside for miles and miles. He was always in tremendous trouble when he returned from his journeys, but the punishments never stopped him from going.

On one of his expeditions, Elmer wandered all the way to town. Elmer rarely went to town. In fact, in all his eight years he had only ever set foot inside Peckham's General Store to help his mother buy supplies. The Heartland children didn't go to school; they were taught at home by their mother in order to keep them close to the farm. The potato farm needed as many hands as it could get and that certainly included the children. So when Elmer spied the Here public schoolhouse, he was naturally curious.

He walked s-l-o-w-l-y and carefully towards one of the tall windows of the plain, grey building. The window loomed above his head; he pressed his ear to the wall and listened. A symphony of tiny voices vibrated through the wooden slats and tickled his ear. The voices were reciting lines—lines from a poem? Or a story? Little Elmer couldn't be sure. The words melded together and blurred inside the crude wooden walls. Maybe the window glass would offer more clarity…

Elmer stretched his tan, wiry arms up towards the window ledge and grabbed a hold of the rough wood. In one quick motion, he simultaneous jumped and pulled himself up so that his head peaked over the ledge. The young boy rested his feet against the top of one of the wooden slats and clung to the window sill. He peered inside. Soon, the teacher would spot him. Soon, he would fall from the ledge, startled, and scamper away. Soon he would be back at Papa's farm.

But for now—for a few sublime moments—he clung to the ledge and soaked in the idyllic classroom that spread before him. It was the most wonderful thing he had ever seen. Rows of desks faced a big, black chalkboard and a tall, handsome woman in a long, blue cotton dress. The desks were filled, *filled*, with children his age. They smiled as they recited the words that their teacher had scrawled across the big, black chalkboard.

Tyger! Tyger! burning bright

In the forests of the night…

Elmer closed his eyes. He loved the words. He loved how they sounded when a dozen voices embraced them in their mouths and spit them into the air to mingle with each other. It sounded much better than church.

The voices stopped. The poem was over. Elmer opened his eyes and ran them across the colorful walls of the classroom. A glint of honey-gold caught his eye and he found himself staring at the most beautiful hair he had ever seen. It tumbled down her back, long and wavy, like soft timothy grass on a sunny spring day. Elmer was mesmerized. He kept his eyes glued to the young girl as she leaned across the aisle, whispered something to the tiny girl sitting next to her, and giggled softly, her shoulders subtly shaking the mane of hair that fell around them.

"Daisy!" the teacher snapped.

Daisy froze. "Yes, Miss Anne?"

"How many times do I have to tell you—" Miss Anne paused. Elmer's eyes widened as they met hers. "What on earth?!" Miss Anne shouted. "Hey you! Young man!"

But Elmer had slipped off the ledge, sprang to his feet, and began sprinting away before Miss Anne could make it to the window.

That night, little Elmer dreamed of timothy grass and golden hair.

Once Elmer had tasted a tiny morsel of the outside world, he wanted more. He found it harder and harder to put up with the monotony of Papa's farm and would often daydream about the humble school house, the rows of desks, the girl with the lovely hair…

"*Daisy*," he said to himself as he pulled weeds in the field. "Daisy, Daisy, Daisy." He had to see her again.

And so he did. Once a week—or more if he could manage it—Elmer snuck back to town. He would sit underneath the window of the schoolhouse and listen to the cadence of the voices inside. He liked to imagine the children, their backs straight, their mouths smiling. He liked to picture Daisy alongside them, an angel amongst chubby cherubs.

Occasionally, he would get the courage to hoist himself up on the window ledge. Every time, Miss Anne would eventually spot him. At first, she shouted and made a fuss whenever she saw the small, brown face in her window and Elmer would clamber down and run home. But eventually, Miss Anne simply ignored the child in her window and continued teaching as if there was not an additional pair of eyes watching her.

One day, Elmer began climbing to the wooden ledge as usual, when a hand shot out of the open window and grasped him around the wrist. Elmer cried out and almost lost his balance, but continued to cling to the narrow ledge as he stared into the dark eyes of Miss Anne. A moment of anxious silence passed between them. Miss Anne broke it first.

"Young man," she began in a stern voice, "you simply cannot continue to listen outside of our classroom like this. You are a distraction to the children and myself and I will not tolerate it any longer. Do I make myself clear?"

Elmer nodded. His left arm was shaking as it clung to the ledge.

"There is only one thing to be done," said Miss Anne, pursing her mouth in determination. "I need to talk to your parents."

Not a word was spoken as little Elmer led the schoolteacher across hay fields and through a patch of woods on the way to Papa's farm. His heart was pounding with dread and his mind raced crazily within his skull, blurring all coherent thought. Miss Anne paced alongside him, still clutching his wrist. She dismissed class early that day in order to make this *special visit* and the children scampered away gleefully—all except the one child outside.

Elmer considered dashing away, but before he could make a run for it, Miss Anne seized his wrist once again and said tersely, "Ok then, lead the way."

So Elmer led the way. And they finally arrived to the edge of the potato fields. And then to the barn. And then to the doorway of the shabby farm house. Miss Anne rapped on the door sharply.

Elmer's mother answered, looking startled. She glanced from Elmer to Miss Anne and back to Elmer. "Papa!" she called. "Come here please!"

Elmer didn't think it was possible to feel more dread than he already did. But as the CLUMP-CLUMP of Papa's boots sounded in the hallway, his heart nearly froze in terror.

Miss Anne extended her hand and introduced herself. Papa did the same.

Then the miracle happened.

"Are you this young man's father?" asked Miss Anne sternly.

"Yes," said Papa.

"And why, sir, is he not enrolled at the public school? A boy his age should be getting an education, not hiding out on a potato farm. You ought to be ashamed of yourself."

Elmer stared.

Papa stared.

Miss Anne continued. "Did you know it is compulsory for children to attend school in this state from ages eight to fourteen years old? He has to be at least that old. You don't want to be in trouble with the law, do you?"

Papa suddenly found his voice. "Now listen here, ma'am! I don't need some uppity school teacher waltzing onto *my* property and telling me how to raise my children! You've got no right! No right at all. I'm calling the police!"

"I believe, *sir*, that it is *I* who will be calling the police," Miss Anne retorted.

"On what grounds?" snarled Papa. His voice was gruff and menacing, but Elmer noticed his bright green eyes shifting nervously. "He gets a fine education here at home. A *damn* fine education."

"And are you registered with the state?"

Papa glared back in reply.

"I asked you a question, sir," Miss Anne persisted. "Are you registered with the state to teach this young man?"

"No," Papa muttered, looking away from the straight-backed school teacher. "No we're not."

"I see. Come by the Here Public Schoolhouse this Saturday and we'll get your son enrolled. I've had enough of his sneaking around my classroom window."

With that, Miss Anne turned on her heel and marched away. And Elmer felt the lash of Papa's tongue and the sting of his belt.

But he didn't mind. A window had opened.

Chapter 25

Two months. Two months had passed since Elmer first set foot in the house of the Modern Shamans. He couldn't believe it. A million things had happened in those months. A million emotions; a million new thoughts. Elmer felt more cognitive and awake than at any other time in his life. He felt sharper. More alive. Free.

Today, Elmer was sitting on a chair under one of the Red Maple trees. He looked up at the pointed leaves as they scuttled around in the breeze. *In a few months, they will turn bright red and fall and dry out on the soil. They will crunch when I walk on them. They will dissolve into the soil and become part of it. But for now, they are green.*

He closed his eyes and listened to the chatter of the leaves as they rubbed against each other and against the branches of the Red Maple. He never used to pay attention to things like this. But here he could; here he was encouraged to pay attention. He inhaled deeply and swore he could hear the earth inhaling with him. *Tenet Three: Walk With the Earth, Not Against It.*

Elmer listened. Piano music was issuing from the house. Clementi.

After the rock had smashed in the face of the piano, Roger immediately found a slab of wood and went about crafting a new front for the beloved piano. He carved its face with an intricate pattern of vines and leaves. His love was entwined in each twist. When he finished, Craig and Cecelia hugged Roger and immediately clambered to the piano to give it a try and listen to the resonance of the new wood. Hilo stood by watching, her eyes were wet, her mouth curled slightly upward in a grateful smile. *Tenet 4: Live in Harmony; Live as One.*

That is the way of things here. They all live for each other. I think I love them…or at least the idea of them…

It was a sunny day. Hilo sat on the porch, her brow knitted in concentration, her shoulders stooped over a colorful quilt she was sewing by hand. Ezzie was rooting around in her garden—the garden she planted for Susan, the garden full of flowers. Elmer looked at Ezzie for a long time. He watched her movements as she plucked weeds from the soil and flung them into haphazard piles. Sometimes her movements were soft and fluid, other times they were violent and rough. Elmer wondered what she was thinking about during the violent, rough patches. Her daughter, maybe.

When the Modern Shamans told their tales about the best days of their lives, Ezzie spoke about her daughter. She reminisced about the day she was born—a tiny human being eager to come into the world—so eager, in fact, that she refused to stay put for the full nine months and insisted on emerging almost a full month early. Ezzie talked about the magic she felt when she beheld the miniscule new life she had created; she spoke of her joy when she looked into her daughter's tiny, squinting eyes and touched her delicate fingers. Ezzie spoke until tears began to form in the corners of her eyes. She didn't speak long.

Despite everything, Ezzie stilled loved her daughter. She thought about her every day.

Ezzie straightened her back, uncurling from the hunched position she maintained when she ripped out weeds. She admired her work. The late spring flowers were mature and starting to wilt, but the Mountain Laurels and Irises of early summer were bursting with life and painting the flower patch purple and white and cotton candy pink.

Ezzie thought about her daughter every day, but the garden wasn't planted for her. It was planted for Susan.

* * *

Tenet One: Constantly Strive for Knowledge.

"Tell me again why the Summer Solstice is so important. Onyx tried to explain it to me, but she got carried away blabbering about ancient Andean civilizations or some such nonsense."

Maggie laughed. "That doesn't surprise me in the least. Onyx spent a semester abroad in Ecuador and loves talking about the time she went to Otavalo to celebrate the Solstice with the indigenous people that live there. She was writing a paper about the village and one of the shamans she interviewed invited her to the festivities. Apparently they all went to a sacred waterfall at midnight, hit themselves with stinging nettles, and jumped into the water naked."

Elmer stared at Maggie, wide-eyed.

She looked at the expression on the old man's face and burst out laughing, clutching her sides and shaking her head. "No worries, Elmer! We won't be doing that here!"

Elmer sighed and shook his head. "To tell you the truth, I *never* know what to expect from you young people."

"Fair enough," said Maggie, grinning. "So you want to know more about the Solstice?"

"Constantly strive for knowledge," replied Elmer with a wink.

"Right you are. Just a warning, though—I may not be the best person to ask about this. Roger is more of an expert on Solstice traditions and Craig could tell you all about the religious iconography associated with Solstice celebrations—"

"I'd rather hear about it from you," said Elmer.

Maggie nodded, smiling quietly at the man in front of her. "Ok then, Elmer. I'll take a stab at it," she paused for a moment to collect her thoughts. "The Solstice is a time of change," she began in her soft, firm voice. "It is a time of celebration. It is a time to be grateful. Grateful—"she paused and looked out the window, "—for the sun."

Elmer chuckled. Maggie continued as if she hadn't heard him, "There is something to be said for worshipping the sun. It is the root of all life. Without it, we wouldn't exist; *nothing* on earth would exist. So, it makes sense that so many cultures worshipped it and celebrated the Solstice—the Incans, the ancient Egyptians, the Natchez Indians. Even the Christians honor the Solstice in a way."

Elmer looked at her skeptically. Maggie smiled at the old man's expression. "Craig told me," she said, "so I believe it. Apparently, St. John's Day is held right after the Solstice to honor John the Baptist. It's fitting, really, because St. John's role in Christianity is to give people new life—a rebirth—and the sun is the facilitator of all new life. And they both rely, or relied, on water to create a fresh start. St. John used the River Jordan for his baptisms, whereas the sun partners with the rain to make life spring out of the ground. Anyway, where was I…"

Maggie let her hand rest quietly on Zach's tight curls. He had been softly tugging at the bottom of her t-shirt, but stopped abruptly when he felt his mother's touch. He looked up at the mahogany-brown hand and long fingers entwined in his hair. He reached up.

Maggie squeezed the tiny hand with her thumb and forefinger and turned her attention back to Elmer. "So the sun...," she said, looking into the old man's eyes. He felt comfortable as he returned her gaze. "The sun possesses a lot of power even if you don't think about it symbolically. During the summer months, the days are longer, the air is warmer. Things grow. Life is abundant. People praise the sun during this time even if they are unaware of the mysticism surrounding sun-worship."

"Like farmers," Elmer interjected. "Farmers are grateful for the warm summer months."

Maggie nodded, "Precisely. The celebration of the Solstice can be as practical or as religious an experience as you want it to be. I think you'll find that right here in our little community, we run the gamut of how people interpret the Solstice. But that, to me, is the beauty of it. It's ok to see things differently. We might be given the same ingredients, but we each use them to prepare different meals."

"I like that metaphor," said Elmer softly.

"Thank you," said Maggie, smiling, "Just thought of it now. Anyway, you see my point. The Solstice has deep religious connotations, but it is also rooted in practicalities. It's basically a time for all of us to come together and be grateful for what we have. I'm not quite sure if that's the explanation you wanted, but that's my take on the Solstice in a nutshell."

"Sounds like an ancient version of Thanksgiving," commented Elmer with a grin.

"If Onyx was here she would tell you it's more of a time when the earth is full of cosmic energy that we can tap into in order to gain clairvoyance and healing powers." She reached a willowy arm towards Elmer and clasped his hand. "But I like your take on it."

Elmer smiled.

* * *

Hilo watched Onyx in the kitchen. She was stirring a large batch of chicha that she had made from fermented corn. The spoon swirled around; the liquid sloshed against the side of the bowl. Onyx paused to taste her concoction. She muttered something to herself and added a little sugar from the cupboard.

Hilo remembered holidays at her parents' house—especially Christmas. The maids would make cabbage rolls and pelmeni dumplings and roast pheasant smothered in mushroom sauce. They would spend hours perfecting the plum and almond tarts and the cottage cheese pancakes. Hilo loved sneaking down into the kitchen and helping the maids prepare her family's traditional cuisine. She loved the aroma of the kitchen. She loved feeling fresh dough in her hands.

Her parents were never completely satisfied with the holiday meal. There was always a tart that was undercooked or a dumpling that was too dry. Hilo tuned out their complaints. She chewed slowly, letting the flavors of each bite dissolve on her tongue.

Hilo watched as Onyx poured the chicha into three glass pitchers and placed them tenderly in the refrigerator. They both came from money and affluence. They both took lessons their parents forced upon them. They never talked about their backgrounds.

Hilo studied her shoes. The soles were cracking and the once-white laces were a dull grey. She would take her ratty sneakers over her old life any day.

Onyx breezed by her with a quick "Hey Hil" and rushed outside. Hilo watched her short, dark hair move through the doorframe and across the porch. Yes, they both came from money and affluence. Yes, they had both taken unwanted lessons. But at least Onyx' parents still cared. They still sent her birthday cards and an occasional check.

Hilo walked to the window and watched Onyx' dark hair bounce excitedly as she conversed with Roger. She knew she would never see her parents again. And she didn't mind.

* * *

Onyx watched the timid girl out of the corner of her eye as she stirred her bowl of homemade chicha. She was standing awkwardly in the living room, gazing alternatively at the floor and Onyx' hand as she stirred the effervescent liquid. Onyx paused and tasted the liquid, sneaking a glance at the gangly girl out of the corner of her eye.

"That skinny thing is always so nervous," Onyx thought. "A good lay would do her wonders."

* * *

It was the day before the Solstice and the Modern Shamans were happy. Many of them did not know why they were happy, but they sensed that this was the prevalent emotion of the day and didn't mind embracing it. They bustled around, grinning, preparing for the evening. Onyx was the undisputed leader of the goings-on.

"Craig, go get my drums, will you? And Roger, make sure your trumpet is there tonight too. I want to make a racket; I want to welcome the new season in style."

"I'm not sure the neighbors will be too happy about that," commented Roger.

A dark look passed across Onyx' face for a moment. "Fuck the neighbors," she said, turning to Cecelia. "Celia, will you check and make sure the chicken is ready to put in the oven. Oh don't make that face—there's a veggie dish for you and Roger and Craig. Why do vegetarians have to be so damn difficult? Kidding Cecelia—you know that—but seriously, check the chicken."

Onyx pranced over to Elmer and planted a large, wet kiss on his cheek. "Muah! How're you holdin' up Old Turtle? Don't get too excited—I wouldn't want the ol' ticker to go into overdrive."

Elmer smiled. He had been sitting on the porch watching the preparations unfold and soaking in the excitement. "I'm doing just fine," he said.

And he was.

"Good, good," said Onyx and scampered off, dark hair bouncing. "Has anyone seen the table cloth?" she shouted at no one in particular. "I just ironed it and I swear I put it right here. Come on people! A table cloth doesn't just sprout legs and skitter away…"

Elmer stretched one leg and then the other. He smiled at his limbs. His bones didn't creak quite as much as they used to. Elmer leaned forward and rose from the cushioned chair. He grabbed his cane out of habit and strolled across the lawn. The air was hot and muggy, but his spirit was light and it lifted him across the grass and towards Ezzie's flower patch. He paused to enjoy the lavender and crimson blossoms. He wondered what their names were. Once upon a time, his mother grew flowers. Papa hated it. "What's the goddamn point?" he would say and shake his head in exasperation. Elmer's mother simply smiled and continued to garden. It was one of the rare occasions when she dared to defy him. *I wish I would have asked her about the flowers. I wish I would have asked her their names.*

Elmer reached out a thin hand and cradled a showy pink flower with splashes of scarlet in the center and around its edges. "I've always loathed carnations," a rough voice opined behind him.

Elmer turned around slowly. "Then why do you grow them?" he asked, before he could stop himself. He turned his eyes sheepishly towards the flower he still held in his hand, his cheeks flushed to match its piping.

Ezzie sighed and walked closer to Elmer. "Good question," she said softly as she stretched her fingers towards the carnation and caressed its silky petals.

Elmer turned and looked at her in surprise. She seemed small just then, breakable.

"I didn't mean to pry—" began Elmer.

"No need for apologies," said Ezzie gently. "It really was a valid question. And I—" she paused for a moment, "—have a valid answer."

Elmer's eyes did not leave the woman at his side. He looked at the tan skin on her arms, sagging a little. He noticed the creases in the corners of her eyes and the smattering of light freckles on her nose. He felt like he had never seen her before.

"I plant the carnations," began Ezzie, "because they are not really for me at all. They are for my granddaughter, Susan."

Elmer frowned thoughtfully and continued to study her face.

"I haven't seen her since she was an infant and I don't know what flowers she might like. So—" she waved her hand in a wide arc, "I plant them all. I do it to honor her. And—," her voice caught slightly in her throat, "I do it just in case she visits me someday."

"Ezzie," said Elmer gently. He reached out and grasped her hand. She did not resist. "Roger told me about the trouble you've had with your daughter—that she doesn't let you see her or your granddaughter because she doesn't approve of your…lifestyle." He squeezed Ezzie's hand a little tighter. "I'm so sorry."

"Me too," said Ezzie. "Me too." She looked vaguely in the distance. "Sandra never could stand that her own mother turned out to be gay. She refused to come to terms with it, but at least I got to see her every once in a while, despite our differences. But when the baby came, forget it. She didn't want me spreading my sin all over the child. As if I was a leper. As if what I have is contagious. Wouldn't want little Susan to catch the 'gay bug,' now would I?"

A chuckle escaped Elmer's throat. Ezzie turned to him and smiled a little sadly. "It is ridiculous, isn't it?"

"Yes," said Elmer, "it is. But I have a confession to make." Ezzie looked at his creased face. Someday she might wear that many wrinkles. She hoped she would wear them proudly.

"What is it?"

"Not too long ago, I might have believed that someone could *actually* catch the 'gay bug.'"

His eyes twinkled. They laughed.

Ezzie gave his hand a final squeeze and let go. "Come on," she said, "let's help the others prepare for this pagan holiday thing we're celebrating. We wouldn't want Onyx' panties to get in a bunch because the ceremonial drums aren't in place."

She winked at Elmer and they started walking across the lawn. Together.

* * *

Greens and yellows and dark browns and reds adorned the long picnic table of the Modern Shamans. Elmer admired the colorful spread that lay before him, tantalizing his olfactory system with an array of tangy odors. Ears of roasted corn, cucumber salad, homemade tortilla chips and salsa, lemon-pepper chicken marinated in citrus juices, fresh-baked garlic bread, garden vegetables and hummus, stuffed green peppers, basmati rice, blackberry pie, fried plantains, and a variety of culinary concoctions that Elmer had never laid eyes on were spread decorously along the checkered table cloth. He breathed in deeply. His lungs were filled with heavy, flavorful air.

"Excuse me," said Onyx, setting down a few pitchers of cloudy liquid by Elmer's left elbow.

"Onyx," Elmer said softly, "it's beautiful."

The girl turned to the old man and placed a pale, smooth hand on his shoulder. "Thank you, Elmer. Really. Thank you. I hope you enjoy it. Want a glass of chicha?" She gestured towards the cloudy liquid.

"Um…I dunno. Do I?" said Elmer, looking doubtful. "What is it?"

"It's a traditional Andean drink—the Incans used to drink it, in fact. It's slightly alcoholic. Made out of fermented corn. This is the finest batch I've ever made," she said proudly.

Elmer still looked doubtful. "Ok. I guess it doesn't hurt to try something new."

"Atta boy, Elm!" said Onyx, pouring him a large glass of chicha. "Drink up. Salud!"

The feast began; the Modern Shamans dug in. Elmer grinned and laughed and fed off everyone's good mood along with citrus chicken and roasted corn. The fact that the chicha wasn't half bad emboldened Elmer to reach for the most exotic food on the table and try things like octopus ceviche and mushroom albondigas stew. Or perhaps the glass of chicha made him just tipsy enough to lose a few inhibitions and gain a bit of courage.

When everyone finished eating and conversation mellowed to a dull roar, Onyx leapt to her feet and clinked her glass. "Everyone! Hey everyone! Attention please. I have a few things I'd like to say." Eight sets of eyes turned towards her. Onyx brushed her dark bangs out of her face and began, "First of all, thank you to everyone for making this fabulous meal possible. Couldn't have done it without you. And I hope you're all feeling as stuffed and satisfied as I am." They nodded in agreement. Elmer gave his full belly a loving pat.

"As many of you know," Onyx continued, "the Solstice is a time of heightened awareness and clairvoyance. The energy that flows around us is especially active and is able to manifest itself in different ways, which is how I was granted my spirit name several years ago. I was able to channel some of the heightened Solstice energy in a vivid dream, a dream filled with spirit guides who called me Onyx."

"Dream or peyote trip?" Ezzie called from across the table.

Onyx stuck out her tongue and casually flipped her middle finger towards her friend. Ezzie winked in reply.

"Anyway," said Onyx, "I want to emphasize the importance of the Solstice. It is a time of transformation and growth. I hope you're all feeling positive energy right now the way I am. Thanks! That is all."

She sat down to light applause. Elmer looked at her for a moment, furrowed his bushy white eyebrows, and blurted, "So you're saying spirits can channel themselves through our dreams?"

The table fell silent. They looked at Elmer curiously.

"Yes Elm, that's what I'm saying," said Onyx. "Do you have something you'd like to share with the class?"

"I don't know," Elmer hesitated. "It's probably nothing, but three months ago I had a pretty vivid dream myself. There might have been spirits in it. Who knows." He looked self-consciously at his plate, wishing he hadn't said anything.

"You know," said Cecelia from across the table, raising an eyebrow at the old man, "three months ago was the Spring Equinox—another high-energy time of year."

"Sure it is!" piped up Onyx. "Come on Ol' Turtle! Tell us about your dream."

Elmer bit his lip, glanced nervously at the expectant eyes around him, and took a deep breath. "Oh, alright. Here goes…"

And suddenly Elmer was flying—flying on the back of a gigantic black bird. Mountains loomed. The cold air nipped at his face. His thoughts whirled around his head like wind passing through smooth, black feathers. And then a wall of mountains. And a quick decent. And a surprisingly fluid landing. Mountain, cavernous room, gigantic pillars. Walking from pillar to pillar, looking at their shapes. Lamb, skull, turtle, horse. Running—or something close to it. Limp-running away from the shadow of the giant cat. Then out of the frying pan and into the fire—a writhing, squirming, live fire. Snakes. Loathsome, slippery snakes. Snakes that squirmed, but did not bite. Snakes he surrendered to and, in one synchronized effort, seized up and moved no more. He had asked for help and help was given. The feline asleep by the pit. And colors—colors that danced—and a feeling that washed over him. An old feeling, one that had been buried under layers of carefully laid plastic bricks. Happiness. And the giant thrones. Thrones that had voices; thrones that had eyes. One-two-three-four-five-six-seven. The third one was the orator—the man in blue, with the commanding beard—he spoke first. And then a few more spoke. And a few had remained mute—mute, but not silent. Speaking with eyes and hands and hips. Moving to the beat of drums. The moon-faced woman in purple. Joy—she spoke of Joy. *It's not the only thing you've buried, Elmer. You've been burying bits of yourself for years.* Dig. *Dig yourself out.* Each a different color, the colors of the rainbow. Violet to red. Full of advice and wisdom. Telling him to seek himself, telling him to keep trying. Saying he is reborn. And then sleep. Sleep with the giant cat. And slipping out of their world and into ours.

"…and then I woke up in a very ordinary park in There."

Chapter 26

They stared. Elmer stared back.

"Elmer," whispered Maggie, clutching Zach to her chest as it heaved up and down, as if she just ran several miles. "Elmer," she said again, barely audible. "That—that's incredible."

Onyx let out a low whistle. "Whew. Good goddess, Old Turtle, how long were you asleep?"

"About a day, I was told."

"No kidding," she replied. "And I bet you woke up exhausted after such an intense spirit journey."

"Huh?" said Elmer. "A what?" His head was pounding and his limbs felt heavy after reliving the vivid dream.

"My goodness, I know!" exclaimed Cecelia. "Elmer, I didn't realize you are so....prophetic. I mean, you were visited by some very powerful figures in your dream. I'm not even sure it was a dream. It was more like a vision. Elmer, there's no doubt in my mind—you are a seer."

"What? I—what?" Elmer found himself at a loss for words and simply stared at Cecelia, his mouth flapping open like a land-bound fish suddenly realizing his gills are dry.

"A sage, a shaman, a guru," continued Cecelia. "—you know, someone who has visions, who can tap into cosmic energy, who can communicate with spirit guides and derive messages from them. A *seer*. Someone who *sees*. You have a gift, my friend."

Elmer continued to stare. He was confused and tired and uncomfortable. He looked around him. The Modern Shamans stared back with a strange mixture of expressions. He sensed trepidation and awe and interest emanating from their faces and something else that startled him—reverence. Hero-worship, almost. It scared him.

"I—," stammered Elmer, "I should go. I should lie down."

"What!" said Onyx. "No way! Not until we hash this dream out. I have some thoughts I want you to hear. Come on O.T! Don't puss out on us now!"

Elmer hesitated.

"Elmer," said a low voice. Elmer turned and looked at Ezzie. He sighed. She didn't wear the same expression of admiration that everyone else had plastered across their faces. "You might want to hear what they have to say. It sounds like you've been thinking about this dream for a long time and this might help put it to rest." She gave Onyx a sidelong glance. "I mean, take it with a grain of salt, but they might have some worthwhile input."

Elmer gave a small, grateful smile. "I suppose I *have* been grappling with this dream for some time now. It's a relief to get it out in the open." He turned to his left, "Ok, Onyx. What do you make of that hodge-podge, willy-nilly dream? And for Pete's sake, stop calling me a prophet or a seer or what-have-you. I'm not. And that's that." Elmer crossed his arms and looked sternly at the crowd. He sensed protest in some of their eyes, but no one dared challenge him. His words had a tone of finality that only the foolish or the painfully obtuse would defy.

"Alrighty then!" said Onyx, quickly regaining her usual enthusiasm. "I think—no, correction—I *know* that you have three ancient Andean symbols in your dream—"

"You can't *know* that," interrupted Ezzie. "Did you listen to that dream? It's a complete cluster fuck. These are all just guesses, shots in the dark."

"No, wait!" said Craig from across the table, his eyes bulging, his voice quivering. "Hear her out, Ez. She's right! Good god, it makes so much sense! Why didn't I see it before?"

"Anyway," continued Onyx, cheerfully unperturbed. "In traditional Andean culture, there are three levels of being—heaven, earth, and the underworld or hell. Each level—or 'plane,' you could call them—is depicted by three different animals. A condor. A puma. And a snake."

Onyx paused and waited for her words to sink in. A few people gasped. Kyle exclaimed, "Oh, wo-ah! No freaking way!" Onyx smiled smugly and continued after her words achieved their full effect. She turned to Elmer, "Your giant black bird—that was *clearly* a condor. The big cat was a puma. And the pit of snakes were, obviously, snakes. In one dream, you flew with the condor of heaven, ran with the puma of earth, and struggled against snakes in the pit of hell! But," she said, giving Elmer a mischievous smile and a wink, "I won't say you're a prophet. I promise."

Elmer's jaw hung open once again. His features were frozen and his throat closed up. He couldn't move; he couldn't think; he couldn't speak. Roger spoke for him.

"That's truly amazing, Ons. The symbols are pretty damn clear if you know what to look for."

"Well, to be fair," said Onyx, "I was tipped off by the cat's name. Tierra means 'earth' or 'ground' in Spanish."

"Amazing," whispered Kyle.

"The pillars were also a clue," continued Onyx. "Elmer described them as full of carvings of things like a horse and a skull and a plow—all things 'of the earth.' So, the pieces just kind of fit. I have to say, I'm a little jealous, Elmer. I'd like to ride on a giant bird from heaven. Shit, I'd even take a pit full of hell-snakes!"

They all laughed. Elmer continued to stare.

"I gathered something different from the dream," a voice spoke up excitedly. The group turned towards the excited blue-grey eyes of Cecelia and cocked their heads inquisitively. "Not that I disagree with your interpretation, Onyx," Cecelia continued, "but I think there might be another layer of meaning tucked into Elmer's vision."

"Or several layers," spoke up Craig. "The potential religious iconography alone is staggering. I mean, if you look at—hey!"

Kyle poked Craig in the ribs. "Now, now smarty pants. It's Cecelia's turn to speak."

"Ok, ok. You're right. You know how I get riled up about these kinds of things."

"Oh I know. I have to deal with your inane rants." Kyle gave him a wink and turned to Cecelia. "Proceed, darling."

"Right," said Cecelia, tugging thoughtfully on her braided hair. "When I heard Elmer's tale I couldn't stop thinking about the seven spirit guides. I mean, it can't be a coincidence—one of every color of the rainbow. Elmer," she turned to the old man. He looked reluctantly back. "I think your seven spirit guides represent the seven chakras."

"The what?" asked Elmer brusquely. He was annoyed by all the attention and admiration they were tossing at him.

"Chakras," Cecelia answered. "Spheres of energy that appear in a column in every human body. There are seven spheres and each one represents a different aspect of your being. The goal is to keep your chakras in balance, so that one sphere is no stronger than any other sphere. Ideally, they should all work in cadence to guide you through life."

"Spheres in the body?" said Elmer skeptically.

"Yes," Cecelia replied. "*And*—here's the kicker—each sphere is a different color of the rainbow, red through violet."

"That makes complete sense!" Roger jumped in, his dark eyes shining. "Each robed figure represents a chakra—violet, indigo, blue, green, yellow, orange, red—each with their own unique personality and characteristics. For instance, your throat chakra is associated with the color blue. It governs honesty and expression; it reacts well to truth and reacts poorly to lies and deceit. It also represents growth and maturation. Your sage in blue was the key orator of the bunch, the most vocal. I think that's very fitting, don't you?"

"I suppose," Elmer replied. He avoided their eager, fawning eyes. "I should really go inside and rest for a bit," he said, leaping to his feet. "All that food is making me sleepy. Delicious meal, very tasty…" He took off before they had time to protest. He marched resolutely towards the house, ignoring the feeling of eyes on his back. "What's wrong with them?" he muttered to himself. "I'm just a painfully dull old man. I'm just Elmer."

* * *

Fire punctured the darkness; drums punctured the silence. Nine figures sat near the orange flames, some swayed, some sang, some pounded drunkenly on their instruments. The low wail of a trumpet mingled with the percussion. Voices were flung into the air and swept up by the thin, dark smoke. Elmer sat with them, by himself. His elbows brushed theirs, his chair was a link in their circle, but his mind was feverishly churning, chugging, somewhere else. Somewhere in the mountains.

Elmer watched as Onyx poured several tall shots of dark liquid and passed them around. Kyle reclined on the grass, his head nestled against Craig's arm. He smiled as Onyx passed him a shot and clinked glasses with Craig before he swallowed it in one gulp. Red and orange shadows passed over his face as the flames danced and shimmied over birch logs. Elmer thought of hips swaying—large, smooth hips, covered in red. Hips attached to a body that commanded them like a snake charmer. Sway here, float there, move, move, feel, move.

The Modern Shamans seemed to think he saw something spectacular in his trip to the mountains. They seemed to imagine he was some kind of prophet or guru. Elmer watched the fire dance and rubbed a sore spot along his spine. He didn't feel gifted. He didn't feel like anything but an ordinary, seventy-eight year old man.

He thought about Onyx and Cecelia's interpretations of his vision—Andean symbols and energy spheres. Foreign concepts to a sheltered old man. But the ideas were intriguing and he thought about them as he looked at the fire. Seven rainbows colors and a condor and writhing snakes mixed together in his thoughts and he found himself wondering if the Modern Shamans were onto something. Maybe he had experienced a powerful spirit journey. But then again, maybe it was all just a dream.

No, it was more than that. It is more than that.

Elmer glanced out of the corner of his eye and noticed Roger and Maggie whispering and staring at him. Even if he *had* experienced something profound, there was no need to treat him like a celebrity. It made him uncomfortable and self-conscious. He kept his eyes trained stubbornly on the fire.

A hand reached out and touched the old man's shoulder. Elmer lurched forward, out of the mountains and into a stiff, wooden chair by the fire.

"Hello, Hilo."

"Hi, Elm. Sorry to startle you."

"That's quite all right. I—I was in my own world."

Hilo nodded. She sat down in the grass next to the old man's chair. "I hope it's ok if I join you," she said softly.

"Of course."

They stared at the fire, watching the drum-playing, shoulder-swinging figures that sat in front of them. Hilo hugged her knees almost to her chin and tapped her foot a little. She glanced at Elmer and back to the fire. She chewed on her lip as she lost herself in the crackling embers and tiny showers of neon sparks.

"Elmer," her voice was distant, as if it had traveled halfway across the globe before settling in Elmer's ear.

He turned towards the speaker.

The distant voice reached his ears again, "Do you ever miss home?"

And Elmer was swept back to a place where pale curtains hung by plain, maple cupboards filled with complete sets of dishes. A place where his children lived in dusty frames perched along the ivory-colored wall or displayed on end tables. He was transported before his wife's grinning lips and wide, bubbly thighs. She chatted into the air; the air did not answer but occasionally nodded and smiled. Elmer looked deeper into the place—across fields and uncluttered roads, past the tiny hospital and peeling paint of the Lions Club building, past clapboard churches, alongside a river that cut deeply across rows and rows of potatoes. He looked longer, harder, past a small patch of forest and into the open window of an ancient school house.

"Yes," he answered. "Sometimes I miss home."

"Will you ever go back?"

Elmer swallowed and stared into the fire. He shrugged.

"Yeah," responded Hilo, "that's about how I feel too." Her gaze paralleled his and looked absently into the space across from the fire. "Home was never anything to…well, write home about. In fact, it was usually awful. But sometimes—and I never can explain this—I get a vague pain right here," she tapped the left-hand side of her chest, "that makes me want to drop everything and run back."

Elmer nodded and continued to stare.

"It's almost like a nagging rainstorm that never truly goes away. Try as it might, the sun cannot shake the murky grey clouds and gusts of wind that drum against my heart when I least expect it."

Elmer looked away from the fire and towards the petite girl who usually strung no more than three or four words together at a time. "I understand," he whispered.

Hilo reached up from her spot on the ground and clasped Elmer's hand. "I knew you would." She dropped her voice. Her words were meant for his ears only. "I knew ever since I met you, but I've been too afraid to talk to you until now—that is, until you told us all about your dream and everything."

Elmer looked down at his hand. Her palms were cool and slightly clammy against his rough, dry skin. "I don't mean to disappoint you, Hilo," he said quietly, "but I'm none of the things you all say I am. I'm just a bitter, old man who's lost his way."

She shook her head, "You're wrong, Elmer. You are much, much more than that. I hope you can see it someday like all of us can."

He glanced down at the small frame of the girl nestled in the grass by his side. He thought of her fingers flying across the keyboard, dancing like sunbeams across the water. "And I wish the same for you," he said. "I hope you can recognize all the beauty you are, all the beauty others see."

Hilo said nothing, but hugged her knees tighter with her right arm and squeezed Elmer's fingers with her free hand. They didn't speak for several minutes, but the air around them vibrated with sound. Sound. And color and emotion. It passed between them, as iridescent as oil.

Hilo broke the silence and the colors splattered against the grass. "I never had a father, you know. Not really. Or a mother. They were just two people who had fun mixing their DNA and then, when the experiment was over, abandoned it and moved on with their lives."

The fire glistened off of Hilo's eyes. "They wanted to get me out of the house as soon as possible—such a nuisance I was. I completely interrupted their aristocratic social lives and they couldn't wait to auction me off to the lowest bidder."

Hilo's shoulders shook, but her voice remained steady. "I haven't told anyone the details about all this," she said, leaning towards the old man. "They know I ran away," she said, glancing across the fire at the other Modern Shamans, "they know I was mistreated, but they don't know the details. Elmer, I know I can trust you. I know you'll know exactly what to say. As always."

"Hilo—"

"—No, don't protest. I have faith in you, even if you don't. And I have to tell someone; this secret is slowly eating me from the inside." She looked at her fingers curled around the old man's hand. "My parents came from the Old Country. They held outdated ideals and ideas; they reveled in upholding traditions, no matter how arbitrary or ridiculous. I was part of their ancient worldviews and that is why they arranged for me to marry a man three times my age."

Elmer's eyes lurched out of distance and fell upon the thin girl at his side. A strange mingling of emotions passed through him as he looked at her bowed head, her slouched shoulders. Shock and outrage and profound sadness. *How could they? It wasn't fair! She should choose her own path, be with whomever she desires...*

The words were oddly familiar in Elmer's head. They drummed up the ghostly image of a small girl with piercing brown eyes and a tiny boy who loved her blonde hair very, very much.

"I was fourteen at the time," Hilo continued. "Pre-pubescent and untarnished. The perfect vessel to satisfy his ugly desires." She closed her eyes and shook her head with a quick shiver. "So I ran away. I never really had a family. I didn't care about my dolls and dresses and china tea set and nanny. They were all part of the elaborate fairy-world my parents created to impress their peers. They were all part of the façade. That was four years ago and I rarely look back. Rarely. I like my life now, but like I said, sometimes my heart goes rogue. Sometimes it pines for the mother and father I liked to imagine I had. It tries to trick me into believing that I was loved and content and cared for. But those moments are short-lived and I have no trouble talking my heart down from the ledge when it's ready to do something crazy." Her voice trailed off, "No trouble at all…"

Hilo picked at the grass by her side, tossing it absent-mindedly into a small pile. "Five long years ago," she said distantly. "Four good years."

"You're eighteen?"

"You sound surprised, Elm," she winked. "How old did you think I was? Thirteen?"

Elmer was thankful she couldn't see the flush of his cheeks. "No—I—I don't know. I had no idea, I guess."

"Meh, it's ok. Onyx demanded to see a driver's license when I told her how old I am. I don't have one, so she just had to take my word for it." She paused and looked thoughtfully at the growing pile of hand-hewn grass by her side. "Come to think of it, she still might not believe me."

Elmer laughed. "That's Onyx for you." He looked at the thin shoulders of the girl—woman—by his side. He squeezed her hand and gazed back at the fire. "Hilo," he began. Her hand paused mid-tear over the grass. She turned to him, her large brown eyes resting on his profile.

"Everyone has a past. You don't have to be ashamed of what you've been through. Anyone can see you are a strong, capable woman if they look hard enough. And Hilo—" he paused, meeting her brown doe-eyes with his green ones, "you are *not* your parents."

Hilo held his gaze for several seconds and then closed her eyes and turned away, attempting—and failing miserably—to hide the thin rivulets that streamed out of the corners of her eyes and down her china-doll cheeks. She wiped the tears carefully with her sleeve.

"I knew you'd know just what to say."

Chapter 27

The seven robed figures were present all the time now. It wasn't an uncomfortable presence. It was more like the presence of an old clerk at the tiny grocery store down the street—familiar and friendly and expected. Elmer called upon the seven when he was feeling lonely or upset. He thought of them when his housemates came to him for advice. They coaxed him to sleep at night at the end of long, trying days.

Elmer's role in the House of the Modern Shamans had changed. He no longer sat on the sidelines, observing. He shifted to the center, right in the thick of things with the world swirling quickly and precariously around him. At first he was wary of his new position in the house. He tried to avoid people and questions by scuttling the other way whenever someone approached him, but eventually he settled into his role and started to actually enjoy his new presence in their small community.

"Elmer the Elder," Cecelia called him. Elmer smiled. He wasn't sure if he deserved the title, but he thought it had quite a nice ring to it.

The milk and honey sun beat down on Elmer's upturned face. Elmer loved summer. It reminded him of fishing and fresh, green fields and falling in love. He savored the sun as it soaked into his weathered skin. He smiled. At the moment, it was only the two of them—Elmer and the sun—enjoying a quiet afternoon on the lawn. The sunshine traveled ninety-three million miles to join him that day; now *that* was a loyal friend.

Elmer's thoughts and solitude were interrupted by someone clearing their throat.

"A-hem. Hey there, Elmer. I don't mean to interrupt," said Roger.

"Oh, it's no trouble," Elmer responded. He meant it.

"I wanted to talk to you and let you know how much I appreciate what you've done for our household. I've noticed a change in almost everyone. They're all much lighter—more confident—than they used to be. Especially Hilo. I mean, Jesus, what on earth did you say to her? She's so chatty these days that Ezzie had to tell her the other day to 'hush up because she couldn't hear herself think.'"

Elmer smiled. "Well, I have a confession to make, Roger. I don't think I've really done anything. I've mostly just listened. They've come to me with their troubles and I've nodded and patted them on the back and sent them on their way. I don't pretend to know any answers, but for some reason they all think I do."

"And that," said Roger with a crooked smile, "says quite a bit, doesn't it?"

Elmer looked at him thoughtfully for a few seconds. "I suppose so…"

"People generally believe what they want to believe. It just so happens, they want to believe in you."

Elmer gazed towards the plain, wooden house with its creaking floorboards and grumbling joints. He thought about the people it held in its gut—the people who warmed it with laughter and stories and baking bread. They were his people now; he would do just about anything for them. The least he could do was give them a sliver of hope.

"They see you as a gift, Elmer—someone who was sent to them. You know, I wasn't quite sure how you would handle all of them after the Solstice. I mean, they were all—myself included—a little star-struck after you told them about the dream you channeled. You became something of a celebrity. It's not every day, you know, that a prophet is dropped into our midst. Oh, don't give me that look Elmer—you know that's what everyone thinks. And if you *really* wanted to discourage that point-of-view, you would stop counseling when they come to you for advice."

Elmer could feel the redness in his cheeks. He kept his eyes trained on the house, avoiding Roger's gaze.

"I'm sorry Elm. I didn't mean to imply that you are basking in your new-found limelight. All I'm saying is that part of you must believe that you really do have a gift, that you really are some sort of prophet."

Elmer chewed on his lip and continued to study the side of the house.

"It's not a bad thing, you know. Just something to gnaw on and come to terms with eventually." Roger studied the old man's face. He noticed the set jaw, the vein ticking alongside his temple. He set a smooth, brown hand on his shoulder.

"Life throws us all kinds of twists and turns, doesn't it? But that's not why I came to see you this afternoon. I had no intention of discussing all this. What I really wanted to do was give you a present."

Elmer turned to the trumpet player—his rescuer and first friend in the house—and studied his chestnut-colored hand. "What is it?"

He stooped down and picked up a flat, square object that had been resting against the back of Elmer's chair. He set it gently in the old man's lap and took a few steps back, continuing to watch the lines and features of his face as if he were reading a complicated text book.

Elmer studied the object in his lap for a moment and began to unwrap the plain, brown paper that concealed its identity. He carefully sought the edges of thc wrapping and peeled back the tape that bound it together. When he was finished he folded the paper neatly and set it by his side. He slowly flipped the canvas over.

Splashed across its surface was an abstract picture of a small wooden house surrounded by gigantic trees and a dazzling night sky. The house almost seemed to look up at the stars as they shined down on its glimmering windows. Elmer studied the sky. Dancing across the tree line were seven bright points of light—one of each color of the rainbow. He let his gnarled fingers caress the surface of the canvas, tracing its thick lines of texture with the grooves of his skin.

"It's something to remember us by," said Roger softly. "I hope you like it."

Elmer didn't say anything for several seconds. His eyes ran across the painting with his fingertips. He turned the canvas and examined it in the generous sunlight. Eventually, he turned towards Roger and nodded. "Yes," he whispered, as if afraid he would wake the people sleeping in the starry house. "I like it."

They lingered in silence several seconds longer. Elmer turned towards Roger once again, "but why do I need a memento to remember you all? Is someone leaving? Are *you* leaving?"

"No, not at the moment," he replied. "But you can never tell. Truly beautiful times are often ephemeral and I wanted to make sure I captured a piece of the beauty for you."

Elmer nodded and faintly heard the soft murmuring of a creek bubbling up from the banks of his memory. "Yes," he said, "it's fleeting isn't it?" He lifted his chin towards the warmth of the sun. "Fleeting…"

Chapter 28

It was Ezzie's birthday and she was annoyed.

"Goddamn it! I told you all I hate turning a year older. Can't we just ignore it like normal fifty-five year olds? Jesus. I was hoping it would just slip on by, but Mr. Korean super-historian here has a mind like a steel trap. Thanks a lot, Craig!"

Craig just smiled and continued frosting a row of cupcakes spread across the counter.

"Oh get that smug look off your face," growled Ezzie and stormed outside.

"Woah," said Kyle, sidling up to Craig's right shoulder. "I never knew anyone who hated their own birthday so much."

"I think it's hard for her to turn a year older without her family around to celebrate. Her good-for-nothing daughter never calls or writes or acknowledges her existence in *any* way and I think special occasions give Ezzie an extra stab in the side. Just another reminder that she is mostly forgotten."

"Yeah," said Kyle quietly, staring blankly at the white tops of the cupcakes. "It's sometimes really hard to stomach your family's opinion of you. And even harder to ignore…"

Craig looked up from his bowl of frosting and into Kyle's lost stare. He reached his arm around his waist and pulled him close.

* * *

Ezzie walked through her flower garden, looking and smelling mostly, but occasionally touching. She reached towards the head of a quietly swaying Black-eyed Susan and rubbed her fingers against its canary-colored petals, admiring the velvet sliding under her skin. She plucked the yellow appendages away from the dark center, one by one, and hurled them into the air, watching them flutter away in the breeze. They landed softly in the grass and were lost amongst the carpet of green.

She smiled sadly at the ground and continued to pace around the small plot of blossoms, stopping every now and then to stare intensely into the striped face of a lily or the bottlebrush shape of a lupine. When she reached the carnations, a tiny fire welled up inside her as she stared at their decorative faces. "Pah!" she grunted as she lashed out her arm and swiftly decapitated a crimson head. It landed noiselessly on the ground and stared up at her benignly, like a small puddle of blood.

Ezzie glared back, her fists clenched and shaking. She stood that way for several seconds and then slowly released her fingers, dropping her hands to her sides. Her shoulders drooped and she closed her eyes. She felt deflated. Slowly, she opened her eyes and took a few steps towards the disembodied flower. She reached down and delicately scooped it off of the ground. Carefully, she bent her knees and settled her hip bones on the ground, crossing her legs in front of her. She cradled the flower head in the palm of her hand and rocked it back and forth, back and forth, whispering to it softly, "I'm sorry. I'm so sorry." She paused, looked at the flower, and pressed it to her chest.

The flower petals made a bright red smudge on Ezzie's t-shirt as she burst into tears.

* * *

"WELCOME ELMER! YOU ARE FAMILY" had been painted over with white acrylic paint and in its place the words "HAPPY BIRTHDAY EZZIE!" gleamed from the wide cloth banner. It was orange and pink with yellow accents and perfectly matched the plate of cupcakes Craig had decorated earlier.

"Dig in, Ezzie!" said Craig, offering her the plate. "You're only fifty-five once."

"Don't remind me," Ezzie replied with a wink. She was feeling better. Lighter. She had cried away several years of frustration in the garden and watered the soil with bitterness and anguish. She wondered what kind of thorny, devil-plant might spring from that soil.

Ezzie grabbed a vanilla cupcake decorated with delicate pink daisies. "Really, Craig. These cupcakes are so gay, the only thing they're missing are sequins and boas."

They laughed. Elmer laughed too. Three months ago he would have been horrified by the comment, but now he felt comfortable and safe. He felt free to laugh with them.

"Fairy cupcakes for our fairy princess," said Onyx, grinning. "Have another, Ezzie. It's your birthday, after all and Hilo's already had two. You've got to be able to out eat her!"

Hilo poked Onyx in the ribs. "Hey! I'm just building up some fat for winter. It'll come before you know it."

Onyx laughed, "How about building up some fat for summer first? There have been days when I swear you'll blow away in the breeze."

Elmer smiled at the two young women seated across the table from him. Hilo looked happier, healthier than ever before. She was like a silky garter snake that had shed its dry, old skin and left it to rot in the dust. Elmer liked to think that he helped facilitate the change—and maybe he did play a small role—but he knew that it was mostly Hilo's doing. She was the one who decided to wriggle free of the past.

"Elmer, you've been awfully quiet tonight," said Onyx, meeting his distant gaze.

"Oh, yeah, I guess," said Elmer, shaking himself from his thoughts.

"Yeah," Cecelia chimed in, "what is Elmer the Elder thinking about tonight?"

Elmer blushed and grinned at the same time. "Nothing too profound, I'm afraid. Just thinking about you young people and how lucky I am to have met you all."

"Aww, Elmer," said Cecelia, "that's so sweet."

"You young people?" said Onyx. "Good grief, Elm, are you going out of your way to sound like an old timer or are you really just that much of a fogy?" She grinned at him from across the table. He grinned back.

* * *

That night, Elmer tiptoed outside and strode across the lawn. He found a bald spot in the tree cover and looked up at the stars winking down at him. Wind rustled the trees and sent them swaying like hips. Elmer watched their movement. It was smooth and supple, like his knees these days. He rocked his body with the wind. Left, right, left. He closed his eyes. The same wind that rustled the branches kissed his face.

The wind made him restless. It made him want to soar on the back of a gigantic black bird. It made him want to dance to the BOOM-batta-BOOM of drums. It made him want to run through golden fields of wheat, trailing a head of hair that matched the flaxen stalks.

Elmer moved one foot in front of the other, swaying to the rhythm of the wind. He thought of Ezzie and vanilla frosting and Onyx grinning from across the table. He thought of Maggie's willowy limbs. And Hilo's shy smile.

Sway, sway, sway.

He threw his hands into the air, embracing the world around him. His cane clattered to the ground.

Eventually, Elmer lowered his arms and looked at the stiff piece of wood lying on the ground. He bent over, picked up the cane, and walked back to the house with it tucked under his arm.

Before he fell asleep that night, Elmer studied the painting he had propped on his bedside table. Swirling stars. Dark, rigid tree trunks. Cozy wooden house. We wondered how the house could sleep amidst the brilliant chaos of the world outside.

Elmer closed his eyes and slipped into a kaleidoscope world created in his mind. In his dreams, he was dancing. He danced amongst the stars, hopping from one point of light to the next, twirling and bowing, feeling as light as a flake of snow or a glossy black feather. All around him people smiled. They smiled and swayed, their brightly-colored robes swishing from side to side.

Elmer smiled and swayed back. Smiled and swayed.

* * *

A single scream pierced Elmer's dream world. It was shrill and desperate. It sliced happiness like a razor slitting a canyon down a trail of soft flesh.

Elmer's eyes snapped open. The scream echoed in the caverns of his brain.

Another scream. This one more like a shout. And voices. A cacophony of voices piling on top of each other, frantically climbing to the top of the heap.

Elmer shivered. He was wide-eyed and alert. He clung to the hem of his homemade quilt.

Footsteps. More shouting. A thud at the top of the stairs and a shoulder crashing through his door.

Now Elmer screamed. Smoke billowed in behind the figure that rushed to his bed. He recognized the long dreadlocks, the wide, brown eyes.

"Roger!" he tried to shout. "Roger!" The words caught in his throat and he choked on the dust and smoke that now encompassed him in the little room. Elmer coughed and sputtered. All thoughts of dancing had been chased away by the heavy black smoke that filled his lungs and fogged his brain.

"Come on, Elmer! We have to go. Let's move!"

Elmer nodded, losing himself in the haze. He reached up to Roger, like a tiny child desperate to be held. His arms looked brittle and pale. Roger bent down and scooped up the old man in one quick motion. Elmer locked his hands around his neck, shaking violently. They started towards the door and Elmer's voice leaped back into his throat.

"Stop! Stop! The painting! Roger, please! Please stop!"

"No, Elmer. It's just a painting! We need to get the hell out of here!"

"No, Roger! Please! Please stop!"

Elmer's eyes were wild. He began to flail spastically.

"NO!" he screamed. "Stop! Stop! STOP!"

They passed Hilo on the stairs. She looked like a pale Grecian statue, frozen and white.

"Hilo, let's go!" Roger shouted. "Let's fucking go!"

"What's wrong with Elmer!" she wailed. "Why is he screaming?"

"The painting!" Elmer whimpered, his eyes red from smoke; he strained to see her wispy form. "I need my painting. My—" his voice trailed off. He started to sob. He hiccupped violently with every breath he took and his body shook with the force.

"I'm going to get it," said Hilo quietly and she dashed up the starts, ducking around Roger's arm as he tried to grab her.

"HILO! Are you out of your fucking mind!? It's just a painting! Let's go!"

"You go!" She called from the top of the stairs. "Get Elmer to safety."

Roger hesitated a moment. Hot smoke jammed itself down his throat. The flames gorged themselves on the beams of the house, feasting on the dry timber. The house was under siege and the fire was winning. "Jesus," he murmured, clinging tightly to Elmer and sprinting past vibrant orange and blue flames. "She's crazy. I swear to god, Elmer, if anything happens to her I don't know what I'll do."

Elmer was bawling like an infant, kicking his feet in protest as Roger ran forward. "Hilo!" he cried softly. "Hilo, no! I didn't want you to go back. Stupid! Stupid! I'm sorry. Come back. Come back. Come back. Come back!"

Roger stumbled ahead, the smoke making him blind and mute. It suffocated his senses; his thoughts moved in a thick haze. He was moving, but didn't know what propelled him. His mind was too heavy to command limbs. They must have acted on their own volition as they carried and cradled and hurled themselves towards the door.

The door.

There it is. Just a few more steps. Through the fiery frame and born again like the phoenix.

Roger's shoulder rammed the door and they burst through the frame and into the oxygen of the dark, outside world. He stumbled across the yard to the group of six and fell into the waiting arms of their embraces.

"Roger—Elm—is that you—I can't see a thing—you're safe—thank the goddess you made it—we were so worried—look at you, you're shaking—oh, Elm, oh Rog—come here, I have a blanket—oh shit, oh shit—I can't believe this—but you're safe, so everything's fine—let's get you some water—where's Hilo?"

Hilo's absence struck the group like a kick in the groin.

"It's all my fault!" wailed Roger. "I should have never let her go back in there, crazy girl! Now she's trapped. Trapped! I—I—I have to go get her!" He stumbled fordward, tripped, and collapsed on the ground. His legs turned to jelly; he couldn't move. "HILO!" he screamed. "HILO!" He spasmed and writhed on the ground as six sets of hands pinned him down and hugged him, while six voices told him everything would be ok. Be ok. Be ok…

"NO!" Elmer shouted from his spot on the grass. He had been set down by Roger in the midst of their embraces and now he lay in a fetal position on the lawn, his hands clutching his head, nails digging into its crown. He rocked back and forth. "NO!" he said again. "It's my fault! Mine! Stupid, stupid! Why did I want that painting!? Why did she listen to me!? Raving, stupid old man! AH! Hilo! No. NO!"

And now hands were on Elmer, pinning, hugging. They cradled his head, removed his claws.

"Hilo!" he whimpered. "Hilo. My girl. My lovely, lovely girl. Hilo…"

From Maggie's arms, Zach's desperate sobs matched Elmer's.

Onyx growled, "It's all their fault! *They* are the ones who did this! I know it! The same ones who threw a rock through our window. The same ones who blindly hate anything that's different from them. That's what they do! They hate! They are fucking *good* at hating. Well, I hate them! I hate them; I hate them; I HATE THEM! Look what they did! Just look at what they fucking DID!"

An arm wrapped around Onyx' shoulder and held her tightly. "Shhh," said Ezzie, rocking her back and forth, back and forth. "Shh, child. Everything will be alright. You'll see. Everything will be alright."

Onyx turned to face Ezzie. She threw her arms around her neck, buried her face in her shoulder and began to cry.

Elmer couldn't watch. "All my fault," he whispered. "All my fault."

A hand landed softly on his shoulder. He opened his eyes just enough to see the smooth outline of Maggie. Elmer cried harder.

"Maggie! It's all my fault; it's all my fault."

"No," she whispered. "No it isn't. It's not your fault. Things happen. Life happens. You can't always explain these things, but don't blame yourself. Please Elmer, don't blame yourself."

Elmer sat up and allowed himself to be held in the crook of Maggie's right arm while she cradled Zach in her left. She patted him on the back and whispered something Elmer couldn't quite make out. It sounded like a soft breeze making its way through tree branches. Elmer rested his heavy head on her shoulder and closed his eyes.

And then he heard the crying.

It wasn't like anything he had heard before. It was an other-worldly sobbing that seemed to spring from the soil beneath him. The sound touched his ears and sent shivers through his body, raising goosebumps on his thin arms and legs and causing his breath to freeze in his throat. His eyes opened; he looked around.

The others noticed it too. A hush fell over the Modern Shamans as they tried to identify the source of the sound. Roger sat up. Onyx turned away from Ezzie's embrace. All eyes fixed across the lawn.

"No, it can't be" whispered Cecelia softly. "It's crying…"

The low, whiney sobs creaked across the lawn. The Modern Shamans gazed, transfixed. Elmer shook his head vaguely, wondering if they were all losing their minds in one cooperative lunacy.

Across the lawn, the house wailed in agony as the flames chewed it to the ground. The timbers shook like quaking shoulders and bits of floorboards and window frames fell to the ground like fiery tears. Through it all, the air was permeated with a low, anguished groan that sounded like a mix of creaking floor boards and the wails of a newly widowed woman. They watched in silence as the house moaned and shook, slowly expiring under the hot fingers that pressed it to the ground.

Hilo's in there. Maybe the house is crying for her. Maybe it's crying for all of us…

A siren screamed in the distance. The sound grew closer and the Modern Shamans watched as fire trucks streamed up the driveway and sidled alongside the house. The firemen sprang from their truck and yanked the heavy hose across the lawn. The water turned on. The spray hit the blackened boards of the house.

What's the use? It's already dead.

She's already dead.

The boards hissed; the wailing diminished; the Modern Shamans watched. They piled next to each other on the lawn. They held each other closely as they watched—as they watched their house die. The ruby edge of the sun peered over the trees and mused at the house below. The morning was misty and delicate and probably very pretty.

Elmer rested his head against Maggie's lap. Through the fog, the slight figure of a young woman approached his side. Elmer smiled and reached out his hands towards her. She tiptoed quietly to his side, kissed him lightly on the cheek, and tucked a small painting under his arm.

He watched as she slowly walked away.

END OF PART I

-LIMBO-

Winter was on Irene's mind as she reclined under the beige umbrella. Iced tea in her hand, she felt like the ice cubes that floated and drifted, bob-bob-bobbing along aimlessly. She took a sip. An ice cube slipped past her lips and onto the patio stones below. She watched it as it sat helplessly in the sun, icy guts spreading thinly along the stone as it melted a—little—more—and—more—each—minute. And then it was gone.

"Fleeting," she thought. She also thought about winter.

* * *

The McFaddens' home was perched on the edge of a cliff. It was a caricature of a real mansion. A Faberge egg ridiculously nestled in a plain, straw nest. Obnoxious, loud, and frivolous. Its massive pillars were elaborately carved and trimmed with golden, frilly leaves. Its brass door knobs had tiny ropes of ivy carved around the handles with miniscule emeralds tucked into a few of the leaves. There was a room for every occasion and few occasions to use the rooms. The McFaddens were elated when their daughter gave them a chance to put a few of the dusty rooms to use.

There was a great fuss and a shifting around of tables and lamps and beds. The servants fluffed pillows and turned down sheets. Each room had a pitcher of cucumber-mint water, a packet of crisps, and a set of matching crimson robe and slippers—both overly fluffy and sickeningly soft. Onyx looked at the crimson offerings with disgust and hurled them across the room and into the closet.

"Fucking embarrassing…" she mumbled.

* * *

The sun shifted and the umbrella's shadow no longer spread across Irene's wide, spotty legs. She wriggled uncomfortably and wished she had someone to adjust the beige cover just a little bit more.

"Elmer!" she called. "Adjust this umbrella, why don't you!"

She cocked an ear and listened. No answer.

Irene never really expected an answer, but it didn't stop her from trying to summon Elmer's body back from the dead. She washed and rewashed his clothes. She ironed his shirts and laid them out on his bed. Sometimes she cooked him dinner and dished him up a large helping of tuna noodle casserole or chicken dumpling soup and tried to make small talk with his chair. The chair never answered. It behaved rather like Elmer.

* * *

Elmer padded quietly down the hall and past Onyx's room. He was returning from the bath house and had his robe tightly wound around his thin waist. The hot bath had left his skin feeling raw and vulnerable. He pulled the robe closer around his shoulders.

"What are you wearing that thing for?" Onyx shouted as he passed her open door. "It's hideous! This whole place is so goddamn hideous!"

Elmer didn't answer. His skin shuddered under the velvet touch of the robe. He hurried to his room. A glass of cucumber-mint water might help.

* * *

"Another meeting to call to order. Gosh, it just ain't the same without old Spud here. He was the only one who was always on time, he was."

"Geezus Arnie, just go up there, bang the gavel, and get on with it. Spud's been gone for months now and we have a full agenda today. The raffle's next week, you know."

"Yah, yah, I know. Alright, Bill. I'll get on with it."

* * *

The cucumber-mint water was cold as it passed through Elmer's toasty organs. It made him think of a river cutting through warm fields of crops.

That's better. Much better.

Most of them had left by now. It was only Onyx and himself that remained. And soon that would change.

Soon. That will change soon. Very soon…

* * *

Irene adjusted her legs. "Darn sun," she muttered. "Why can't winter hurry up and get here? Why does it have to make me wait? All I want is to nestle under a pile of blankets and sleep, sleep, sleep. Because that is what winter is for—hibernation—and the neighbors won't bother about my whereabouts because they'll be too busy hibernating as well."

She glared at the sun. "Then maybe I'll get some peace and quiet to drift and float and bob aimlessly and do whatever I please."

The sun glared back. It glared at her wide, spotty legs.

* * *

After the tragedy, they had all piled into the McFaddens' home like so many refugees. They were miserable and singed, downtrodden and sooty. The McFaddens took them in, embraced their daughter, and went about cleaning things up. Or rather, they ordered a platoon of workers to begin cleaning things up. Starting with the old man.

"Good god," Esther whispered. "He must be close to eighty years old. Just look at his poor, little dirty arms!"

"Hush Mom!" Onyx whispered back sharply. "That's Elmer you're talking about."

The eight scruffy Modern Shamans were ushered into the house and led to a stuffy parlor at the end of a long corridor. They weren't themselves. They felt suspended in an odd kind of purgatory. They waited in the stuffy parlor while their rooms were prepared and Esther McFadden apologized dozens of times for the delay. Ernest McFadden said nothing, but cringed every time their ashy arms brushed against the furniture's leather ones. After the guests were led to their separate rooms, he spent several minutes studying the creases in the tan leather chairs and bellowing orders to maids with tiny polishing cloths. They buffed and polished the chairs until his wife retrieved him and dragged him to the banquet hall.

"Poor dears," she said. "They must be starving."

"Hmph," he replied and allowed himself to be escorted by his petite wife. Before they turned into the banquet hall he paused and beckoned to a nearby servant. "Count the silverware, will you. I won't have these vagrants running off with my soup spoons."

Esther rolled her eyes, but said nothing. They pushed open the heavy oak doors of the banquet hall and stepped inside.

* * *

In There, the restaurant owner was closing down for the night. She shut off the burners; she wiped down the counters. She placed her hands on her hips and arched her back, feeling the vertebrae pop-pop down her spine. As usual, she gathered up the extra food scraps that had accumulated in the kitchen throughout the day. She tossed them in a cardboard box and opened the back door. Seven or eight pairs of eyes stared at her expectantly from the ally. She glanced at them for a moment and they skittishly looked away. The restaurant owner stepped outside and gingerly placed her offering on the cold cement. She backed inside and quickly locked the door behind her. With a howl, the pack of homeless people pounced on the box, frantically clawing for choice bits of meat, and scampered away as soon as they had filled their pockets and hands with the leftover bits of food. The restaurant owner watched silently from a window.

* * *

"Elmer," said Esther McFadden in a sugary voice, "why don't you tell us a little about yourself."

Elmer looked up from his honey-walnut glazed ham and baby asparagus. The guests at the massive banquet table were silent, aside from the occasional click of a fork or a spoon against china dishes. They looked at him expectantly.

"Not much to tell," he muttered and looked at the ham. It glistened gelatinously back.

"Surely there must be something," insisted Mrs. McFadden. "What about your family. Where are they?"

Elmer remained tight-lipped and began to absently push the ham around his plate in small circles.

"Jesus, Mother," snarled Onyx. "We've all had a very long day. Maybe we want a little peace and quiet, yes? Can you let him eat his fucking ham?"

"Young lady," her father vaguely warned.

"I knew this was a bad idea!" said Onyx and stormed out of the room, letting the heavy doors swing violently after her. The room filled with silence. The Modern Shamans ate the rest of their meal quickly and quietly. They excused themselves and rushed off to their respective rooms. They undressed, climbed into bed, and fell into restless sleeps.

Ernest McFadden supervised as the servants counted the silver.

* * *

Irene wrestled with the umbrella stand. She tugged and prodded it until its shadow once again fell across her lounge chair. The ice in her drink had melted and now it was simply a watered down version of what it used to be. Irene didn't catch the metaphor. She didn't think about things aging and becoming dull and tasteless. She didn't think about the way people can lose their zest for life. Instead, she gulped down the last of the iced tea, arranged her wide hips on the lounge chair, and admired the long shadow that fell across her legs.

* * *

First Kyle and Craig left. They found a quiet apartment complex on the edge of City A and decided to move in. The carpet smelled like cat pee and the drapes were velvet burgundy, but that could be fixed. They were anxious to leave the dead expanse of the mansion and settle into somewhere real, somewhere with life in its walls. They left with little ceremony, only a few hugs and kind words. The Modern Shamans waved as the McFaddens' Mercedes Benz slowly rolled down the driveway. Kyle and Craig waved back. Few words were exchanged. Few needed to be.

And then there were six.

* * *

Irene fell asleep. The sun continued to shift. It sidled around the umbrella and found her helpless legs. It proceeded to roast the pale, spotty skin.

* * *

Next was Ezzie. A dark blue minivan crept through the McFaddens' iron gate one day and stopped in front of the ornate main doors. The occupant checked the address scrawled across a scrap of paper, gave the mansion a quizzical look, shrugged, and stepped out of the van. She walked up to the doors. They were opened by her mother.

Ezzie looked at her daughter. Sandra looked back. Ezzie hesitantly stepped through the doors. Sandra wrapped her arms around her quickly, squeezed, and stepped away silently. Ezzie did not squeeze back, but the hint of a smile crossed her face.

They silently climbed into the dark blue minivan and took off. The Modern Shamans watched from inside. That was how Ezzie had wanted it.

* * *

The vagrants of There were settling down for the night. Some were lucky; some had eaten dinner. They piled together for warmth. Summer was playing tricks on them. It made them pant and sweat at times and then would abandon them and shower them with cool air and stiff breezes. Tonight was a night for stiff breezes. The bums gathered together and hid their faces. Prickly rain beat against the sidewalk and against their exposed feet. They shivered.

A boy with a large backpack marched past the bums. He had spent several months in There with the love of his life. Or, at least, she was supposed to be the love of his life. It didn't work out. He was going back. He marched past the bums and towards the train station. "Back on the train," he thought. "Back on the train."

* * *

After the fire, Ezzie called her daughter and left a message on her answering machine. Her daughter never answered. It was not a surprise she didn't answer this time. Ezzie let the machine beep and paused for a moment to collect her thoughts. Her message sounded hollow and distant.

"Sandra. Mom. There's been a fire. I have no place to go. I'll be staying with the McFaddens on Chester Hill for a while. You can reach me there." She paused. "This is not a desperate ploy to see Susan. I really am in trouble. If you can find a little mercy in your heart, please help."

She hung up the phone and turned to Elmer. "She'll never come find me. No goddamn way."

Elmer reached a shaky arm around her waist and patted her side. She buried her head on his bony shoulder and cried. The tears soaked through his shirt and dampened his skin.

And then he was crying too. Crying for Hilo, crying for the house. He cried for the time he was homeless and sought shelter in a plastic tube. He cried for Here and Irene and There and the damaged piano and the homeless drummer he met in the park. He cried for the painting that was lost in the fire.

They clung to each other and sobbed until their knees were weak and their throats were sore and their heads felt light and dizzy. And then the storm was over and only little hiccups escaped their mouths, only occasional teardrops slid down their cheeks. They found a park bench and sat down, their arms entwined, until the McFaddens' chauffeurs picked them up and drove them all to Chester Hill.

* * *

Maggie was next to leave. With little Zach in her arms, she smiled as she hugged each of the remaining Modern Shamans. Roger—Cecelia—Onyx—Elmer. Her arms lingered around the old man.

"Elmer, you've done me proud, you really have."

Elmer blushed and avoided her eyes,

"Now, I'm serious, Elm. I have seen such growth and change from you, it's incredible. You've been a real inspiration to me. You've made me realize that it's never too late to change my ways. Thanks to you, I now have the courage to go back to The City and face my past." She cradled the child on her side and with her spare arm stroked Elmer's cheek. Her skin felt like a feathery spring leaf.

Elmer finally met her eyes.

"Elm," she lowered her voice. "Please don't be too hard on yourself. Life is a wild thing. You can't tame it and sometimes it spirals out of control. It's up to us to grab a hold as best we can and ride out the madness." She stroked his cheek again, her smooth fingers tracing the creases of his face. "You can do it, Elm. Ride out the storm. It will pass, I promise."

Elmer swallowed and nodded. She nodded back.

And then there were four.

* * *

The Modern Shamans watched as the house wailed and moaned and eventually hissssed quietly as it became a pile of smoldering ash. They let out a collective sigh as the house desperately gasped one last time and expired. They felt strangely relieved and their lungs filled and they began to breath normally again. The neighborhood was waking up and oddly normal sounds issued from their surroundings. Birds chirped noisily in the trees. Doors clicked shut. Car engines started. Elmer wondered how the world could sound so typical.

The only out-of-place sound that morning was the steady gush of water as the firemen drowned the blackened planks of the house. They watched. Eventually the firemen finished their job and walked over to the little group. "Where to?" they asked. "Town," the group replied. "Ok."

The firemen hauled them to town. They clambered into a gas station and begged to use the phone. The clerk agreed. The McFaddens were called. Sandra was called. The clerk said, "Ok, ok, that's enough. Please wait outside." They did.

*   *   *

"Damn!" said Irene as she awoke in the full, blistery sun. She rarely swore. "Damn!" she said again and shook her fist at the sun.

*   *   *

Elmer set his glass of fancy water on the bedside table. The McFaddens had been good to them. They had tended them like a herd of lost sheep, lending them shelter and safety. But Elmer understood why Onyx had left.

And now we are two. And her anxiety grows every day. It's palpable.

Elmer understood very well why she had left. He looked at his surroundings, he touched the edge of a marble sink and looked at himself in the gold-gilded mirror. He understood very well.

He thought of Here and falsely upbeat conversations and perfectly calculated nods of interest and agreement. He understood.

*   *   *

In City A, it was time for the young boy's haircut, so his mother took him into the family barber. "Just a little off the top," she smiled through lipsticked mouth and chemically whitened teeth. The little boy pouted, but said nothing as the barber retrieved his clippers from a neatly organized drawer. They made small talk—the mother and the barber—as the little boy watched bits of his hair fall to the floor. They didn't realize they were making small talk. To them, it was just talk. There was no size to it.

The barber trimmed around the boy's ears and commented on how much he had grown. The boy remained silent. His mother responded for him. They bantered on about the weather and the school system and the recent success of the high school football team and a new recipe she had discovered for chicken chili. They nodded and smiled and the boy's hair went from shaggy to neatly trimmed. He hated it.

"All done. How do you like it?" the barber asked.

The boy nodded in approval.

City A was training him well.

*   *   *

When the McFaddens' drivers pulled up to the Faberge egg mansion, they braced themselves for the shower of empty compliments and praises that were usually aimed towards the house. The Modern Shamans said nothing. The drivers breathed a collective sigh of relief. They were sick of the house and the empty compliments. The guests never meant a word of what they said. They praised and complimented because they couldn't think of anything else to do with their lips.

The Modern Shamans looked at the mansion and thought about the home they had lost in the fire. It was honest and humble and alive. The mansion was sarcastic and frilly and dead. They did not believe their situation had improved much. But in the end, they were walls, were they not? They contained beds and refrigerators and hot showers. That was enough for now.

They all left within two weeks.

* * *

Irene's afternoon nap was over. She waddled back inside, absently carrying the iced tea glass to the sink. She tossed it on the counter. She would clean it later. The clock read 4:43 p.m., which really meant it was 4:40 p.m. Elmer had always liked his clocks set three minutes into the future. He felt like it gave him a leg up on the day and a distinct advantage over those who were strictly stuck in the present. Irene didn't understand why he set all the clocks three minutes into the future, but she humored him. He didn't ask for much.

4:40 p.m. Her book club started in twenty minutes. She hadn't touched Wuthering Heights. Irene stared at the empty iced tea glass on the counter and then at her sun-reddened legs. No book club this week.

* * *

Elmer stayed in his room for most of the day. Occasionally, the seven sages visited him—mostly, the women. They would stroke his hair and cradle his head and he would stare as they held him in their velvet arms and rocked him back and forth. Back and forth. They spoke few words, but their presence was strong and vocal. Elmer tried to listen. He tried to understand. Mostly, it helped to just stare.

* * *

Two more left the mansion and only Onyx and Elmer remained. Cecelia and Roger decided to rebuild. Earlier that week, Roger watched Ezzie climb into the dark blue minivan and roll away from Chester Hill with her daughter. He didn't know if Ezzie stayed with Sandra or if she simply took her from Point A and dumped her at Point B. He didn't know if they talked or argued or laughed. He didn't know if Ezzie finally had a chance to see her granddaughter. None of the unknowns mattered much. He felt a tiny ray of hope. For the first time since the fire, he felt a glimmer of inspiration. He would rebuild.

He talked to Cecelia and Onyx and Elmer and Maggie. Cecelia agreed to help. The others breathed a sigh of relief. They liked the idea well enough, but it made them nervous. They weren't ready to go back. They weren't ready to face the charred timbers and blackened foundation of the house. They weren't prepared to cope with the gallons of memories that would flood their brains when they stepped into the empty lot.

Maggie held Zach a little tighter and thanked Cecelia for volunteering. "No problem," said Cecelia. "You're the best," said Maggie. Maggie turned to Elmer to say goodbye. Then she left.

Three days later, Roger and Cecelia left too.

"I have enough money socked away," he insisted. Esther McFadden nodded and continued to write him a large check. "Just the same dear, it doesn't hurt to have a little extra. I know how much that house meant to our Beatrice."

Onyx grimaced and bit her tongue. Now was not the time to quarrel about her name.

Roger stopped protesting and took the check. "Thank you," he said. "Thanks for everything." Esther McFadden grinned saccharinely. "No trouble, dearie. No trouble at all."

Hugs. Kisses. Words of encouragement.

And then there were two.

* * *

Elmer paced nervously around his room. His slippers pad-padded on the floor. Seven sets of eyes watched him. They were all present today.

Soon. I will leave soon. I must.

His shaky hand poured minty water into a glass. Most of it spilled out the side.

The time is right. The time is now.

Elmer pictured the glaring eyes of a taxi, the young, bored ticket seller, the thick steel sides of the train as it ground to a whining, whirring halt in front of the station. He pictured himself on the bus ride from There to City

A, deep in thought, watching the giant black bird dive and swoop and brush the tops of wheat grass with its wings.

The time is right. The time is now.

Elmer felt the eyes. Felt them nodding, encouraging. Felt colors rushing out of the irises and swirling serenely in his brain.

Yes, the time is clearly now.

The colors swirled, but they didn't rage. They didn't feel like a storm. They were more like water in a lap pool, slosh-slosh-sloshing against the sides of his brain, subtly beating him into submission.

I need to talk to Onyx.

* * *

Irene picked up her copy of Wuthering Heights and set it down again. The phone rang for the third time. She ignored it for the third time.

She had meant to read the book, she really had. She had meant to go to her book club. Instead she decided to say "Fuck it" and stay home. Or, at least she would have said "Fuck it" if she was the swearing type. In reality, she didn't say anything. She just stayed home.

* * *

Onyx crossed her arms and looked away as her mother handed Elmer a thick roll of hundred-dollar bills. He had refused point-blank to take a check. A cashed check meant losing his anonymity. It meant losing his freedom.

"You really didn't have to," he protested half-heartedly. "I would have figured something out."

"Don't be silly, Elmer!" Esther gushed. "I wouldn't be able to sleep at night knowing you were out there with not a penny to your name."

Elmer nodded and gingerly took the money from her extended hand, as if it was a dove that might startle and take flight at any second.

"Well, thanks," he said. "Thanks for everything."

"My pleasure." Her words were sticky and slow. Elmer thought of caramel rolls. "Now, I'll let you two say your goodbyes. You take care of yourself, Mr. Heartland." She hugged him stiffly and Elmer hugged her stiffly in return. She turned on her heels and marched inside.

Elmer watched her purple cardigan disappear through the door frame and then turned to Onyx. She avoided his eyes. "Onyx," he began. "Onyx, look at me."

Reluctantly, she turned her head.

"Onyx, I'm sorry, but you know I have to go. Everyone else left. Now it's my turn. My time. I don't have a choice."

"Bullshit," said Onyx. Elmer noticed how tired her eyes looked. "You don't have to leave. You can stay here with me. Where are you going to go anyway?"

"No Onyx," said Elmer quietly. "I have to leave. Please believe me. I *have* to leave. I'm not sure where I'm going—wherever the next train is headed, I suppose."

Onyx scoffed, but didn't argue. She noticed the quiet fire in his eyes, the flash of steel that meant his mind was made up. He was determined to leave. And that was that.

"Oh, Elm!" she exclaimed and threw her arms around him. "I know you have to go. I know it! I'm just being selfish. I wish you could stay with me always and teach me things. I have so much to learn and I *know* you have endless wisdom inside that wrinkled, old head of yours. What am I going to do, Elm!? What, oh what, am I going to do?"

Elmer chuckled. "Wrinkled, old head, huh?"

Onyx wiped away a few tears. "No offense," she laughed.

"None taken," he replied. "Look, Onyx, you'll do just fine. Wait and see. Things will work themselves out for the best. And don't be afraid to follow your heart. It took me over seventy years to figure out that one, but I'm so happy I did." He placed his hands on her shoulders and gave her a significant look. "So happy I did…" She nodded.

"I'm happy you did too," she said. "We are *all* happy you did." She stroked his cheek and hugged him again. He hugged back. "Good luck, Elm," she whispered. "Wherever the road leads you, good luck."

* * *

Elmer sighed, deeply and fully, as the train lurched forward. He kept his eyes on the afternoon sun of City A as the train slowly gained speed and barreled down the tracks. It rounded a bend and the sun slipped out of sight. Elmer sighed again. He was tired, but content and he could feel the wad of hundreds pressing mildly against his pocket.

The trained bellowed down the tracks. The square, beige buildings of City A thinned and disappeared. Elmer picked out trees on the horizon and watched as they grew closer and closer and then paralleled the train and then fell behind it, embracing the thin sheet of dust that stained their branches. He tried to identify the trees as they streamed past. *Maple, aspen, box elder…* But many were different than the trees from Here and he soon gave up his game.

Elmer's attention wandered from the passing landscape to the handful of sleepy passengers to the geometric pattern on the seat in front of him to the ticket stub in his hand. Elmer's glance lingered on the date printed across the top of the ticket stub. He smiled. Carefully, tenderly, he folded the ticket stub and put it in his back pocket. Today was his birthday.

Part II: Dueling Soup Kitchens

Chapter 29

The first thing Elmer noticed about City B was the abundance of friendly, helpful people. The second thing he noticed was that they made him feel uneasy.

As soon as he stretched his back, rubbed the sleep from his eyes, and disembarked from the train, he was bombarded by a gaggle of City Beeans who insisted on being helpful.

"Hey there feller! Let me take that bag for you. Looks mighty heavy." "Hello there! Do you need some help crossing the street? Traffic can be awful this time o' day. 'specially with a cane there." "Hi mister! You hungry? Mah wife's makin' beef stew tonight. It'd be no trouble at all—we love havin' guests!" "Ah, he don't want beef stew, Jerry! How 'bout some lasagna to fill the gullet?"

Elmer stood, blinking, at the half dozen people who crowded around him on the platform. They tugged at his bag and at his arm. "Here, lemme take that!" "Here, lemme help you cross the street!"

"No thanks," Elmer murmured and dashed (or, rather, hobbled quickly) across the road and into the nearest store. He didn't dare look behind him until he had zig-zagged down several aisles and hidden himself behind a shelf filled with thick books. He caught his breath and peeped around the corner. Not a soul in sight. Elmer sighed. He shifted the weight of his duffle bag on his shoulder. The McFaddens had been kind enough to buy him a new bag—remarkably like his old one—and fill it with a few articles of clothing and some toiletries. Elmer appreciated the clothes, even though he had never much cared for polo shirts and argyle socks. He was certainly not in a position to be picky.

"Hey mister!"

Elmer jumped. "Umm, yes?" he replied, annoyed at being discovered. He glared at the fleshy man standing in front of him, blocking his path out of the aisle.

"Can I help you find something?"

"No, no," said Elmer hastily. "I just got off the train and I came in here for a moment and now I'm leaving. Yes. Must be off. Bye now…"

"Now wait a cotton-pickin' minute! Just got off the train? Does that mean you're new in town, mah boy?"

Elmer cringed at his enthusiasm. And at being called "mah boy." "Uh, yes. Yes I am."

"Well, praise be! Welcome! Welcome to City B. And welcome to the Bible Lot! I'm Freddie Keys, owner of this here fine establishment." He held out a fat, clammy palm to Elmer. "And you are…"

Elmer picked up the offered hand briefly and let it quickly fall. Keys didn't seem to notice the look of disgust that passed over the old man's face. "Elmer," Elmer muttered, wiping the moisture off his right palm on the leg of his pants. It left a few oily speckles on the khaki material.

"Elmer. Elmer what?"

"Just Elmer should do," Elmer replied waspishly.

"Alright 'Just Elmer,'" chuckled Keys wetly. "Where are ya stayin' in City B?"

Elmer tried to quickly fabricate a story, but the truth jumped from his lips. "I'm not sure at the moment," he said and immediately thought, "Oh shit…"

"Don't know where you're gonna stay!? Well, that's preposterous. E'ryone's got a place tah stay in City B! 'n fact, my wife was just talkin' 'bout how she'd really like to rent out the spare bedroom. I mean, now that Samuel's moved out and all, we gots the space. And tah me, it's sinful if ya got all that extry space and ya ain't sharin' with folks that need it. Am I right?" He didn't wait for a reply. "Course I'm right. And you're gonna come home wit' me. No ifs, ands, or buts about it!"

Elmer tried to protest. He tried to say it was no trouble, that he'd find a place on his own. But Keys wouldn't hear any of it. He went bustling around the store, cleaning things up and closing things down, as he talked loudly and boisterously to himself. "Just wait 'til you taste my Nel's cooking. If she doesn't make the best beef stroganoff in the county, I'll eat my hat! Course Samuel's room hasn't been touched since he left, but that wasn't more than a year ago and he always was a neat kid. Married the Anderson girl last March—my, what a beauty she was! All white lace and orchids. Now that was a weddin', *that* was a weddin'. Never saw so many damn orchids in mah life! Lord knows they spent a pretty penny on that weddin', but Sam never asked for a dime, not a dime, mind you! Always was a proud kid. Some might say the weddin' was a bit extravagant, but I say hey, they're sealing their bond through God, the Father and you don't want to skimp on that, now do ya? Don't want tah penny-pinch when you're marrying God, now do ya?"

Elmer nodded silently and watched the large mass of jabbering, jiggling human flesh move deftly through the narrow aisles of the store. *How on earth did he manage to avoid knocking things over with that large, swaying gut of his? Amazing.*

After a few more minutes of bustling and arranging things, Keys closed the register, locked it, and turned to Elmer. "A'right 'Just Elmer,' let's get a move on. Nel likes to serve dinner at half past six and—," he glanced at the enormous watch cinched around his wrist, "it's a quarter past now."

Elmer followed Keys out the door and around the corner to a dirt parking lot. They found Keys' vehicle—a small, burgundy pickup truck with a few spots of peeling paint—hopped inside, and took off down the road. Keys chatted amiably and loudly for ten minutes. Elmer stared straight ahead in silence for ten minutes. When they arrived, the trip seemed to take a matter of seconds for Keys, several years for Elmer.

"Home, sweet home!" Keys bellowed as he oozed out of the driver's seat.

Elmer stared stiffly at the weathered boards of a split-level house that protruded awkwardly from the surrounding land like a pimple. Perhaps at one time, trees had sprouted and flourished in this land, but there was no sign of them now and yellow-grey fields stretched flat and endlessly behind the house. They reached the horizon and bled together with the dull sky and Elmer grew bored with the lifeless scenery in a matter of seconds.

Keys didn't notice his guest's critical eyes and stepped cheerfully to the passenger door and yanked it open. "Whatcha dilly-dallying fer, Elm? Get outta the car and let's get you some dinner."

The food wasn't too bad—minus a little extra gristle on the pork chops—but the dinner was painful. Elmer wanted desperately to avoid conversation; Keys wanted desperately to start it. Nel and the three youngest children sat in relative silence as Keys prattled on and on about his family tree, his Christian gift shop, the sorry state of the City B school board, and the horrible things that appear on TV these days. He asked Elmer about his background, his religious preference, his education, his heritage, his height, and a host of other questions that Elmer felt were both intrusive and entirely unnecessary. He was surprised Keys didn't ask him for his blood type. Or whether he preferred to dress to the left or to the right.

Elmer answered the barrage of questions tersely with as few words as possible and Nel and the children spent a lot of time staring at their plates in order to avoid the painful conversation. They got the sense that if they looked up, they would be blinded by the glaring embarrassment that sprang from Elmer and Keys' interactions. Occasionally Nel would mutter, "Would you like some more peas, Elmer?" or "A little barbeque sauce, Elmer?" Elmer would politely decline and she would sit in silence again, focusing hard on cutting a bit of pork chop into the perfect sized bite.

After dessert (an apple crisp) had been served and devoured, Nel jumped up from the table, cleared the dishes, and beckoned to Elmer to follow her to his room. Elmer gratefully obeyed.

"But Nel, I was just askin' him 'bout which football team he rooted for in last year's finals! C'mon! We was right in the middle of conversation."

Elmer turned. "I'm not much of a football fan," he said quickly and followed Nel down the long hallway on his left.

Keys watched him go and turned to his youngest child, shaking his head. "Not much of a football fan? What kind of male citizen is he?"

The child shrugged and licked a bit of apple crisp off his fork.

Elmer shuffled behind Nel as they passed several doors cluttered with stickers and posters that displayed well-groomed pop stars and cute animals and Jesus fish. Elmer paused at one door that had five painted wooden letters tacked neatly to the outside. I-R-E-N-E. Nel noticed the absence of footsteps behind her and also paused. She followed Elmer's eyes.

"Irene is our eldest. She moved out of the house several years ago. She was always the artistic one—painted those letters herself."

Elmer nodded and pried his eyes away from the door. Rumblings of the past mixed with the porkchop in his belly. He met Nel's eyes for a moment. "Nice," he said. "Very nice work."

Nel nodded, a quizzical look passing over her face. "Yes, very nice indeed."

They continued walking. At the end of the hall, on the right hand side, they reached a door covered mostly in race cars and a few burly football players making impossible catches in mid-air. Next to one of the football players, a large sticker clung to the door. It displayed a spoon angled diagonally, hugged by the curlicue letters "E" and "B." Its corners were peeling away from the wood and its crimson background looked dusty and faded. The peeling corners annoyed Elmer and he fought the urge to smooth them with his finger.

"This here was Sam's room," said Nel. "Moved out after he married the Anderson girl. Make yourself at home. Holler if you need anything."

Elmer studied Nel for the first time. She was a short, squattish woman with greyish-brown hair tied back in a loose bun. Her face was lined and tired, but her eyes were bright blue and she looked like she had been quite the beauty at one point in her life. Probably a very brief point—a point between puberty and her first child. Elmer wondered if she looked back fondly at that time.

"Thank you very much, Nel," he said. "I appreciate your hospitality."

He said "your" with subtle emphasis, implying that he didn't necessarily appreciate the hospitality as a whole, but her part had been played rather well. She nodded, a glimmer of understanding in her eyes.

"Sleep well," she said and shut the door behind her.

He didn't. All night, Elmer tossed and turned, sleeping for fifteen minutes or half an hour and waking up feverish from his nightmares. They featured a girl—a young girl—and she wanted something. She wanted something from him and she was very persistent about it. She chased him, screaming and flailing her arms, sometimes striking the back of his head, sometimes swinging a small knife at his spine. Elmer tried to run away, but his footsteps were heavy and his balance was that of a drunken housewife in five-inch heels.

"I'm sorry!" he would shout. "I'm sorry!"

She never said anything, just continued screaming unintelligibly and flailing her arms. Elmer tried to look at her, to examine her face, but she was like a specter—as hazy as fog. The one thing he could discern were her eyes. They stared hollowly out of her misty face, like large, dull coins. There were no eye whites, no irises. Just pupil. Elmer felt as if they could suck the marrow from his bones or the soul from his body. He screamed. The vision would disappear and he would wake up in Samuel Keys' old bed, sweaty and shaking for several minutes. Then he would settle down again, close his eyes, and the same girl would haunt his dreams all over again. Eventually, he was too afraid to fall back asleep and he clung desperately to his pillow, eyes wide and body curled tightly, until he spotted the dull sun rising above the tan prairie grass.

Elmer ate breakfast in silence, poking his eggs around his plate and avoiding Keys' questions with a tight lip. Eventually Keys gave up and said with a shrug, "Well, someone woke up on the wrong side of the bed today. Are you ready to go to town, 'Just Elmer?' I've got to open the store in a few minutes here."

As a reply, Elmer finished the last of his orange juice and stood up. They walked together in silence towards the burgundy truck. Elmer carried the duffle bag that held all his belongings. He was getting the hell out of dodge. He didn't care where; anywhere was better than this place where the chatter was nonstop and a hollow-eyed girl haunted his dreams.

Then again, she might haunt my dreams anywhere. She might follow me to the ends of the earth.

Elmer shivered. *Those eyes.* Keys started the truck and roared down the road. "Bit late today, Elmer, mah boy! Gotta make time."

They rumbled up to the parking lot behind the Bible Lot at precisely 9:55 a.m. "Made it, praise the Lord!" bellowed Keys. He ambled to the front door and pulled a large key loop out of his pocket. The keys scraped and clinked together as his sausage fingers searched for the right one. He found it and thrust it into the lock. "Coming inside, Elmer? You can help me run the store today if you'd like."

Elmer could think of very few things he would like to do less. "No thanks," he said, attempting to sound polite, but aware his voice blatantly betrayed his disinterest. "Erm, tempting offer, but I've got a few things to get done. Must be off."

Elmer didn't wait for a reply, but spun on his heel, struck his cane against the sidewalk, and strode off down the street. Keys called after him, "Suit yerself! Tomorrow maybe!" Elmer didn't reply. He walked quickly and determinedly north, putting as much distance between himself and the Bible Lot as he could before he lost momentum and had to rest. Elmer found a narrow bench by the sidewalk and settled down on its wooden planks. He sighed. At some point he would have to double back and return to the train station, but for now he needed some quiet time to think.

Where to next? Where can an old man like me find a place to rest his bones? Is there a place? Or am I meant to wander this lonely road for the rest of my life? I wonder, is there a destination? Is there a resting place?

Elmer closed his weary eyes against the midmorning sun. Immediately, the girl from his dreams jumped back into his head, but she was not nearly as terrifying as she was night before. Instead, she seemed tired and listless, her hollow eyes as distant as cars from an airplane seat. Elmer pictured her thin frame, her wild hair. He almost felt sorry for her, but she still gave him the shivers.

"Hilo?" he whispered. "Is that you?" The image in his head stared blankly ahead. "Daisy?" he ventured. "Irene?"

The phantom girl didn't exactly look like any of the women he mentioned, but at the same time, she seemed to embody them all.

All the women I've wronged. God, I'm a fool. A prize idiot.

Elmer's shut his eyelids tighter. He pictured the ghostly girl walking towards him and leaning close to his face. Her eyes, her nose, were inches from his. She coughed roughly.

Elmer jumped; his eyes sprang open. A pair of light brown eyes stared back, inches from his nose. "Holy-Jesus-living-shit! Wha-what? Who? What on earth? You scared the living daylights out of me." Elmer steadied himself with his cane and stared into the chestnut eyes that hovered near his face and belonged to a body he had seen before. For a moment, he thought it was Roger, but the face was too thin, the nose too pointed, the skin several shades lighter, and the wiry body stood several inches taller than Roger's. It dawned on him.

"What on earth! Zacchaeus? Is that really you?"

"Didn't I tell you to call me Zach?" the man said with a wink, flecks of gold shining from his brown eyes. "Good to see you again, Elmer."

"But, but I don't understand. What are you doing here? Why did you leave There?"

"Living the dream in There, was I?"

"Well, no," said Elmer, his cheeks flushing red. Begging in a city park did not exactly qualify as "living the dream," but Elmer had assumed that that was all there was for Zach. That was what he would do for the rest of his life, right? How does a street bum just pack up and move on to a new city when he got the urge? That just didn't happen.

"But, Zach," Elmer pressed on, "how *did* you manage to get out of There? I mean, no offense, but a train ticket isn't exactly cheap."

"Who says I took the train? I have a thumb, don't I?" he said, balling up his right fist and sticking out his thumb.

"Ahh, hitchhiking. I didn't think people did that anymore."

"Well, not many. And I had a hell of a time getting someone to pick up my raggedy ass and drive me to City B. But I eventually made it and here I am—been here for a month now."

"That's great Zach," said Elmer, "but why on earth would you choose to come to City B in the first place? This place is a nightmare. It's awful. In fact, I was planning to take the next train out of here."

Zach nodded. "Yeah, I can see why it would make you uneasy. It can be a little strange here, but the town folks really do mean well, once you get past their overbearing helpfulness."

"Yeah, that," said Elmer. "Don't you find it strange? As soon as I stepped off the train, I was bombarded by a herd of do-gooders. It seems to me that they are all competing to be the most helpful, the most selfless."

"That's exactly what they're doing," said Zach. "And that's exactly why I came here. I came because of the dueling soup kitchens."

Chapter 30

"The what?"

"The dueling soup kitchens."

"I see," said Elmer. "And what exactly do these dueling soup kitchens do? And why are they fighting? Is there a food shortage here or something? Are the owners in some sort of feud? Like the Hatfields and the McCoys?"

"Not quite," Zach replied. "But the owners do loath each other with a deep passion that dates back as far as anyone can remember. But it has nothing to do with family."

"Ok…" said Elmer. "So what is the duel about?"

"It's a duel about who is the most generous."

"The most generous? What? I've never heard of such a silly thing in my entire life."

"Yes you have," said Zach, his face as serious as stone. "You've been to church, haven't you?"

"Well, yes, of course I've been to church, but what does that have to do with anything?"

"I think we should take a little field trip."

* * *

The first thing Elmer noticed about Ezekiel Banks' Soup Kitchen was the sheer size of it. It sprang from the sidewalk like a medieval castle, all cinder blocks and windows, and rose some seven stories into the sky. Elmer clutched his duffel bag to his chest and stared at the top of the massive building. It towered over him, huge and proud, like a haughty grey elephant.

The second thing Elmer noticed about Ezekiel Banks' Soup Kitchen was the emblem hanging neatly on an engraved wooden sign above the door. A wide soup spoon split the sign in half diagonally. An ornate E filled the top left corner and a matching B claimed the bottom right. The background was crimson and resembled a family crest.

"I—I've seen that before," said Elmer. "On the door of the Keys' kid's room. There was a sticker that looked just like that." He pointed at the sign. Zach nodded.

"That would be part of the Ezekiel Banks merchandise line. The stickers are pretty popular with the kids. Only a buck a piece."

"Merchandise line?" said Elmer in a disapproving voice. "A soup kitchen has a merchandise line? What is this world coming to?"

Zach grinned. "Oh, you haven't seen the half of it." He pressed his hand against one of the heavy wooden doors and gave it a shove. "Welcome to bums' paradise."

They stepped inside and were greeted with the warm smell of freshly baked rolls and corned beef hash. Tables were scattered around the one, large room and teemed with board games and steaming beverages and a whole host of rag-tag, filthy people. Scarlet and gold tapestries hung elegantly on the walls and matched the hand-woven rugs that ran between tables. On the right hand side, an instrumental quintet played violins, cello, saxophone, and piano quietly and subtly like elevator music. Two of the grimy guests danced slowly to the music, holding each other in their arms and looking fondly into each others' eyes as they swayed.

Elmer blinked in amazement. "Don't tell me *this* is the soup kitchen? It's like a five-star hotel in here."

"Can I take your shoes sir?" squeaked a tiny man on Elmer's left. The top of his head barely reached Elmer's shoulders and his delicate spine was poised straight as an arrow. He wore a black suit with a gold tie and matching gold apron. Elmer noticed his polished black shoes were strung with black laces with gold bobbles on the ends. He stared, speechless, at the prim little man.

"Yes," said Zach, "please take his shoes."

"Alright, sir. And you? Can I take yours as well?"

"Sure thing."

"Alright then. I'll be back in a jiffy. Please," he gestured at a couple of overstuffed chairs, "make yourselves at home. And don't forget to sign the guest book." The man scuttled off and left Elmer staring at his narrow back and Zach laughing at Elmer's expression.

"You're not in Kansas anymore, are you Dorothy?" Zach chuckled. "Welcome to Ezekiel Banks' Soup Kitchen."

"This is incredible," said Elmer, still staring at the spot down the hallway where the man in the black suit disappeared. "Is all this really free for the taking? What's the catch?"

"Yes, it's all free. No catch. Not really, anyway. The only downfall is you are expected to be loyal to one soup kitchen over the other and spread the word about the clear superiority of your chosen kitchen. But that's not really for me. I switch back and forth all the time, depending on my mood and what's on the menu that day. Some of us do it that way, but it's not exactly smiled upon by the Loyals."

"I see," said Elmer distantly. He didn't really see. He didn't really understand what was happening in this fairytale world he stumbled into and he wasn't at all sure he liked it. For some reason, he felt something sinister lurking beneath the glittery scarlet and gold tapestries and polished marble floors. Something as contrived and phony as his previous life in Here.

"Size eight and a half," said the miniature man, returning to Elmer's side. He placed a pair of fuzzy red slippers at his feet. "And size twelve," he said, handing Zach his pair of slippers—also fuzzy, also red. "Anything else I can do for you gentlemen?" he asked in a too-high, simpering voice.

"No, thanks," Zach replied. "We're just going to have a look around for a bit."

"Guided tour?" asked the man.

"No, I think we'll be fine on our own."

"Very well, sir. Enjoy your stay and do join us for a bit of lunch when you're done."

"Thank you very much," said Zach.

The little man bowed slightly and rushed to the refill the water pitchers at the occupied tables. Elmer shook his head.

"Strange, strange. Ok, let's get this tour over with. I'm feeling a little stifled and I think I'll need some air soon."

Zach nodded and stepped forward. Elmer padded softly behind in his cushy purple slippers. They reached an old-fashioned caged elevator on the other side of the room and Zach instructed it with the push of a button to take them to the second floor. They passed the eight-second ride in silence and disembarked into a cool, lemon-scented room. Floor mats hugged the wall and a giant mirror wrapped around two sides of the gigantic square space. In the center, treadmills and stationary bicycles and an array of weight machines were packed together to form a small fitness city. A few people leisurely pedaled as they read magazines or watched one of several TVs. On the other side of the room, two full-length basketball courts and a rock-climbing wall filled the enormous space.

"This," said Zach, gesturing an open palm at the room, "is the E.B. gym and fitness center. Open twenty-four hours per day, seven days a week. Group fitness and dance classes take place over there," he motioned to an open area by the mats, "and competitive basketball league is Monday, Wednesday, Friday."

"What," said Elmer sarcastically, "no swimming pool?"

"That'll be on the next floor," said Zach with a wink.

Elmer rolled his eyes and followed him back to the elevator. "Of course it is," he muttered.

The next floor was a large wellness center and spa, complete with massage tables, several jacuzzi tubs, a yoga room, and of course a swimming pool. "There's also a rehab center on this floor," Zach informed Elmer. "I'll be the first to admit that my homeless brethren are not all angels and saints. But you'd be surprised how quickly people shape up once they're treated like royalty."

"Hmph," said Elmer, furrowing his brow.

The fourth floor was a library with an expansive collection of books and periodicals, as well as a newly remodeled computer lab and a large auditorium. The fifth floor held sleeping quarters, complete with individual and family rooms and a huge lounge area with several nooks for couches and flat screen TVs. The main area housed a large movie projector surrounded by a wraparound couch. A small bedraggled child had connected a video game console to the projector and was racing a shiny convertible through the city. He made "vroooom-vroooooooom-screeech!" sounds as he raced, ignoring the two men as they passed by.

Elmer took in the rooms passively, nodding politely as Zach explained their features, but asking no questions and offering no comments. On floor six, however, Elmer jolted back to life.

"What on earth!" he exclaimed as they stepped through the caged doors of the elevator. "What is *he* doing here?"

An enormous painting of a man hung before them, arms outstretched, light blue robe billowing, a serene look hung on his face, like laundry swaying on a clothesline. It was Jesus. Elmer studied the portrait. It didn't seem to fit. It didn't seem comfortable. It was like hosting a wedding at the circus—tacky and void of meaning. The painting stared vapidly at the ceiling. It was large enough to dwarf the surrounding room and that was saying something, considering the room could easily hold three-hundred people without anyone rubbing elbows. It commanded attention, but could not hold it for long. Elmer wondered if the painter got bored halfway through his commission.

"Who? Him?" asked Zach, pointing to the painting. "What, don't you think he belongs here? This is a chapel, isn't it?"

"I can see this room is *trying* to be a chapel and failing miserably," growled Elmer irritably. "But it's not right. It's just not right. He doesn't belong here. Not in this phony place." Elmer scowled at the room and its decadent stained glass windows, gleaming golden altar, and ornately carved pillars.

"Well," said Zach, suddenly losing the natural playfulness in his voice, "I happen to agree with you. I've been trying to be a neutral tour guide and let you see things for yourself, but I might as well tell you I'm pretty disappointed in the kitchens. I don't much care for the way they operate and I find it hard to believe a place like this," he made a wide gesture with his arm and glanced up at the giant painting, "truly embraces *his* teachings and that *he* would truly embrace this place."

"Damn right, he wouldn't!" declared Elmer. "Just look at it! Decadent and frilly. Competing with another poor, little soup kitchen. It's despicable."

"Ha. You won't be calling Abe's Soup Kitchen 'poor and little' once you see it. But anyway, I'm surprised you're so worked up about the chapel. You don't strike me as the religious type, Elmer. No offense."

Elmer's cheeks burned, partly from rage, partly from embarrassment. "I, well, I'm not. Not particularly. I grew up Catholic, but haven't felt especially loyal to the Catholic church in years. But," said Elmer firmly, "that doesn't mean I think it should be treated with blatant disrespect. I mean, it still means something to lots of folks, doesn't it? Who am I to trample on their values, their beliefs? I can respectfully disagree, can't I? I don't have to ravage their whole way of thinking, do I?"

Zach studied the old man's face—lips pursed tightly, chin jutted out. Beads of sweat formed across his brow and he wiped at them angrily with his sleeve. "Elmer," said Zach quietly, "that's very understanding of you. I didn't get a chance to know you very well in There, but from what I can tell you seem…different somehow. Changed. I'm not sure where life took you between then and now, but it must have led you to some miraculous places. It must have taught you some valuable lessons."

Elmer paused. His mouth loosened; he lowered his head. His pulse slowed to a steady THUB-THUB-THUB and he listened to his heartbeat for several seconds. "Yes," he said and thought of Hilo and Ezzie and Maggie and little Zach and Roger and Onyx and Kyle and Craig and Cecelia. He thought of his distaste for their alternative lifestyles and the way he gradually softened and eventually warmed up to them. He thought of mutual respect and learning and something close to love. "Yes," he repeated. "I've learned a lot since There. And I suppose that means I've changed."

"Change can be good," said Zach, patting Elmer gently on the shoulder. Elmer was once again reminded of Roger. "Come on. Let's get out of here. Not much to see, just a bunch of pews and statues and stuff. Let's go back downstairs and get us some lunch."

"What about the seventh floor? We haven't toured there yet."

"The seventh floor is strictly off-limits. That's where Mr. Banks lives and he rarely lets in visitors. Come on, let's go."

* * *

It was two o'clock in the afternoon by the time they left Ezekiel Banks' Soup Kitchen. They patted their rounded bellies and stretched like cats after an afternoon nap in the sunlight. Elmer hadn't wanted to eat the corned beef hash, hadn't wanted to be a part of the workings of the kitchen, but in the end he could not resist the large steaming plate that was placed before him. He ate hastily, shoveling the delicious, tender meat into his mouth and paused only to glare at Zach and say, "This doesn't mean I support any of this. I was just hungry, ok?"

Zach grinned. "Ok, Elm, whatever you say."

Elm. Onyx used to call me that. Then they all did. Elm…

"…does that sound like a plan? Elmer?"

"Huh? Yeah. Sure, a plan. Whatever you want."

"Great. The fifth floor is the perfect place for an after-lunch nap. And it shouldn't be too crowded right now because there's an event in the library auditorium. Some author is visiting from overseas. I think she writes Christian romance novels."

Elmer wrinkled his nose. "Yeah, a nap sounds fine. Let's go."

Elmer and Zach were finally coming out of their post-nap haze when they arrived at the doorstep of the Ibrahim Anbar Soup Kitchen. They paused at the entrance of the building and looked up. It was only three blocks away from Ezekiel Banks' Kitchen and when Elmer turned around he could see the seven-story structure glaring at them from down the street. He turned back to the building in front of them. "*Abe's Kitchen*" was painted in colorful letters across a sign that perched above the door. Underneath the sign, hung another smaller sign with a deep purple crest and the letters *I* and *A* suspended over a silver bowl.

"Let me guess," said Elmer, "That stands for Ibrahim Anbar. And I bet they also have merchandise for sale with that crest on it."

"Correct on both accounts," said Zach.

"Ok. But why is it called Abe's Kitchen and not Ibrahim's Kitchen?"

Zach shrugged. "I don't know for sure, but supposedly everyone calls Mr. Anbar 'Abe' for short. I've never actually seen him. He doesn't come down from his tower very often." Zach pointed to their right. Elmer took a step back. How had he not noticed it before?

At the far end of the long, one-story building jutted a silver-plated turret. It looked awkward and self-conscious, like an unwanted erection. Elmer chuckled to himself. "What in the world? Does he think he's a king or something?"

"Maybe," said Zach. Elmer could not detect any sarcasm in his voice and it made him slightly disconcerted.

"Hmm, ok. Well, let's get inside then."

They pushed open the double doors and strode inside. Smooth jazz and warm air tickled their ears, purple bombarded their eyes. Rugs, wall hangings, placemats, chair covers—all a deep, rich purple. Elmer sniffed at the decadent color.

"Your sweater, sir?" said a neatly-dressed black woman in a dark, plum-colored velvet coat with silver trim. The bun she kept in her hair was as rigid as her backbone.

"No thanks," said Elmer. "I might need it later."

"But sir," she protested, purple arm waving agitatedly, "I assure you our robes are made of the finest quality cashmere and will surely keep you warm during your stay."

Elmer stared. Zach grinned. "Umm, sure. Ok. Robe it is." He surrendered his sweater, Zach gave up his grimy denim coat, and the attendant marched away down the hall. "Don't forget to sign your name in the guest book!" she called over her shoulder.

"This seems awfully familiar," said Elmer.

"Just you wait."

The woman returned promptly with two matching silver cashmere robes with lavender embroidery on the sleeves and front pockets. "Anything else I can help you with today?" she asked.

"No, no. We're just having a look around."

"Guided tour?"

"No thanks. I know my way around."

"Very well, sir. Enjoy your stay."

"Thank you."

She glided away and began clearing dishes from the long banquet tables that filled the room.

"To the left is the kitchen," said Zach. "To the right is everything else." He guided Elmer by the elbow to the right, past long tables with hand-sewn placemats, past large landscape paintings with ornate silver frames, past the members of the jazz band that were just putting their instruments away for the afternoon. They walked through an open archway and into the next room.

"Step up!" said Zach and walked onto a sort of conveyor belt on the floor. Elmer obeyed. He hopped onto the moving belt, placed one hand on the parallel railing, and let the walkway move him down the long, narrow corridor. They were flanked by an identical belt moving in the opposite direction on the left and a colorfully painted wall on the right. The wall was decorated with geometric shapes that climbed up to the ceiling and littered the space above their heads with color. It was also crammed with doors, evenly spaced and uniform in size.

"What will they think of next?" said Elmer, looking down and patting the moving railing.

Zach looked at Elmer quizzically. "Haven't you seen these walkways in an airport before?" he asked.

Elmer reddened. "Well, no," he answered. "I suppose I haven't. I—I've never traveled by plane before. Have you?" he asked indignantly.

"Well, sure," Zach replied. "I've flown lots of times. I wasn't always dirt poor, you know. I *was* in med school once."

Elmer nodded briskly, shaking off his embarrassment with the movement. "That's right. I think your friend in the park mentioned that. What happened to med school?"

Zach was silent for several seconds. Elmer reddened, stammered, "I—I mean, you don't have to tell me. Rude of me to ask. I—"

"No, no. It's fine," Zach replied. "You asked a direct question. You deserve a direct answer." Zach stared at the wall for a second, watching the mosaic patterns slide past them in. "I quit med school. It was tough to concentrate after my parents died in a car crash. They were actually coming to visit me, you know. Thought they would stop by the university and see how I was doing…"

"Zach," said Elmer quietly, looking away, "I'm so sorry."

Zach shrugged. "Yeah, it was terrible, but I definitely could have handled it better. I drank too much and spent all my money on trying to start a rock band—an endeavor that proved to be less than successful, as you can see. So here I am. Just another person who made bad choices in life."

Elmer chewed on his lip and let his eyes wander back to the thin-framed man. He didn't know what to say, so he awkwardly patted Zach's back and changed the subject. "Say, whatever happened to your friend in the park? Why didn't he come with you to 'bums' paradise?'"

"Levi?" said Zach, pulling his eyes away from Elmer's. "I'm sure he would have loved to join me, but he passed away. Shortly before I took off."

"Oh no," Elmer moaned. "I'm on a roll for bringing up touchy subjects today. What happened to poor Levi? What did he have?"

"Pneumonia, I think. Although it's hard to diagnose someone without the proper equipment. Anyway, it happened quickly. Not much suffering. And then they took him away. Just another dead homeless man in the park."

Elmer gaped at Zach. "But," he said, struggling to find the right words, "he was *not* just another dead homeless man. He had a name! He was Levi!"

Elmer's lips quivered. He leaned heavily on the railing. He felt his emotions bubbling inside him, ready to explode with any slight tap of the trigger. Zach patted him on the back, "You're a good man, Elmer. You know that? Levi would have been pleased that I found you here in City B."

Elmer nodded and swallowed. The acidity of his emotions burned his stomach. "So, the tour, then?"

"Right," said Zach, removing his hand from Elmer's back. "Those doors we're passing on our right, they're the dormitories. Individual and family rooms. All with private bathrooms." They reached the end of the corridor and entered a wide room that looked remarkably like the fitness center at Ezekiel Banks' facility. They stepped off the moving walkway.

"This is the fitness center," said Zach. "Weights, basketball courts, climbing wall—"

"—dance classes, bicycle machines, treadmills," Elmer finished.

Zach grinned. Precisely. "Want to hop back on the walkway? I can see this is going to be a quick tour."

It was. The Ibrahim Anbar Soup Kitchen had almost the same amenities as Ezekiel Banks' Kitchen. There were a few modifications, a few alternative features, different decorations, but when viewed with a not-so-critical eye, it was basically the same.

"Abe's Kitchen has a barber shop in the wellness center, which is kind of nice," said Zach. "But I hear that Ezekiel is planning to install one soon, so that won't be a novelty much longer." Elmer rolled his eyes and they moved on.

The final room loomed ahead and Elmer braced himself for its inevitable content. They passed through the archway. Elmer gasped. As he suspected, the room contained some sort of worship place, but it was much different than the space that occupied the sixth floor of the E.B. building. This room had the same geometric patterns he had seen in the corridor, except they wound their way up pillars and archways, cluttering the space with different hues and shapes.

"Wow," Elmer whispered, his vision overpowered by patterns of stars and triangles and hexagons.

They continued to walk into the space of worship, side-by-side, soaking in the kaleidoscope walls around them. Each step sounded loud and clangy in the immense space and Elmer found himself wishing he had kept his slippers from Ezekiel's. They walked through the archways, rounded a bend, and found themselves looking into a gigantic room.

"Oh dear god," said Elmer with disgust. His reverence for the place washed away like spit in a river. "A little overkill, wouldn't you say?"

"Depends on where your priorities lie," responded Zach. "If you think it's of the utmost importance to plate your place of worship with twenty-four karat gold, then this room certainly meets the expectations."

"Meets the expectations? It's like pissing on a pile of money! Useless, disgusting, wasteful!"

"Ok, ok. Keep your voice down, Elm. Look, I happen to agree with you, but there's no need to shout about it."

Elmer's mouth frothed a little at the corners. He frowned at the offending room. It glittered back. Everywhere he looked, he was blinded by the abundance of gold. Golden archways, solid gold pillars, golden ceiling that sprouted a crystal and gold chandelier. He felt like he walked into the vault of a rich, tyrannical banker. Or the grimy mouth of a gold-toothed farmer. The gold swirled around him, overpowered him, attempted to be whimsical and cute with its geometric shapes swimming across pillars and walls and ceiling. Elmer found nothing cute about it.

"Twenty-four karat?" he muttered. "What a waste. It's so decadent, so tacky and tasteless. So in-your-face and taunting. I thought I might like this place, but it's just as bad—maybe worse—than the last." Elmer turned to Zach. "How," he asked in a strangely calm voice, "can anyone worship here? How can anyone muster actual respect for this sickeningly overdone, candy-sweet, artificial place? How?"

"Not everyone sees it like you, Elmer," Zach replied quietly. "Some people think the gold and glitz is a sign of great respect. They think Abe's mosque is beautiful, just like Ezekiel's chapel. They don't see it as overdone and materialistic. They see it as a genuine tribute to a higher power or," Zach paused for a moment and raised his eyebrows, "they at least see it as proof that Abe cares just a little bit more about faith than Ezekiel. Although," he added, "I hear that E.B. is going to gold-plate his pillars next year, so we'll see who has the better worship place after that."

Elmer opened his mouth. He wanted to scream. To flail his arms and preach about the wrongness of gaudiness and materialism. He wanted to tell anyone who would listen that this strange competition between soup kitchens was wrong. Wrong to its very core. But he ended up just opening his mouth and letting out a prolonged, exaggerated sigh.

"I know it, Elm. Twisted, isn't it? You haven't seen the half of it."

Zach turned and walked back towards the moving walkway. Elmer stared at his back for a moment. He wondered what other surprises the soup kitchens had in store for him. He wondered how much worse it could possibly get. Then he stopped wondering, looked anxiously around the hollow chamber, and shuddered. He hobbled quickly out of the room, sweaty palms slipping across the crown of his cane as he desperately clutched it. He was struck with the sudden and intense feeling that someone was watching him.

Chapter 31

Grace awoke in a queen-sized bed on the fifth floor. She rolled over and patted her sleeping son's head and tucked his shaggy hair behind his ear. He moaned softly, tugged at the covers, and slipped back into his dreams. Grace tip-toed into the changing room and put on running clothes and a pair of sneakers. Like usual, she would hit the gym for an hour before breakfast. Maybe she would take a dip in the pool. "Yes," she thought, "a dip in the pool sounds nice."

She stepped off the elevator on the second floor and strode to the treadmills. Several people already populated the machines, but she managed to find a free one at the far end of the row. She recognized the man on the next treadmill over. "Mornin', Grace." "Morning, Earl. Nice to see you."

The belt started. As usual, she started out at a brisk walk, stretch-stretch-stretching her morning muscles until she felt ready to break into a run. She had never been in such great shape in her life. After a few minutes, she increased the speed. Her legs flew; her arms pumped up and down in a marching band-like rhythm. Right arm-left arm-right arm-left arm. Legs flying, heart pumping. Beads of sweat dripping down her forehead and off her chin.

In these moments, she felt free. She felt light and careless. She felt like she was on top of the world; like she was in control. But then her legs grew tired, her lungs cried for air, and she had to stop. The belt ground to a halt. The heaviness returned. She should be grateful for this place. She should be grateful for the regular meals and fitness center and place to sleep. But she wasn't. As much as she tried, gratitude did not come naturally to her. No. Gratitude was lost in a sea of other emotions, buried under unease and distaste and caution.

Just last week she was approached by some of the Loyals from Banks' Kitchen. "Join us," they said. "Commit to Ezekiel Banks. Do you see everything he has done for us? Do you notice his bountiful generosity? His unending good works? Don't you feel cared for and secure and happy? Don't you feel *loved*?" She ran away from them. She scooped up her son in her arms and jogged down the sidewalk to Abe's. They took her in, lent her a robe, fed her the lunch de jour—curried rice with lamb, and told her with a smile that she was always welcome at Abe's. She breathed a sigh of relief.

But it was a tentative sigh. Within five days she couldn't have sighed if she wanted to. Her breaths came in short, restrictive gasps. Her lungs felt like they had a leather belt around them that squeezed and squeezed until she burst out the door of Abe's and ran, once again, into the street. She hadn't stayed anonymous at Abe's for long. She was watched with the hawkish eyes of the Loyals as soon as she stepped through the doors, as soon as she took her first bite of curried rice. First she felt the eyes. Then, she heard the voices. The voices that praised and complimented her, the voices that tried to set her at ease, tried to make her feel comfortable and at home. She listened to the voices suspiciously and nodded and smiled at the faces to whom they belonged. The faces nodded and smiled in return. The hints mounted; the voices became more persistent. Then one day, one of the voices said, "Join us" and that's when she fled, heart pounding, arms clutching her son, back into the street.

"Son," she said. "It's back to Banks' Kitchen.

They had been at Ezekiel Banks' Kitchen a week now and the Loyals were keeping their distance. She was a tiny antelope at a watering hole, cautious and alert, and they knew they had to approach her carefully. Had to make her feel comfortable, safe. Had to let her take large, greedy gulps of the sweet water before they pounced. Before they sprang. Before they sunk their claws deep into her tender hide and brought her to her delicate knees.

That time would come, but that time wasn't now. Not quite. They would have to be patient, lest they destroy another opportunity to usher another one into their pack. Patience. Calculated patience. Just as Ezekiel would want it.

Grace felt their eyes upon her as she stepped off the treadmill and wiped her neck with a little, white towel. She felt their eyes as she unlaced her sneakers and stepped, barefoot back into the elevator. Their eyes watched her fingers linger over the "Three" button and finally opt for the "Five." No swimming today. She thought she would probably throw up in the pool if she tried. No, five it is. Time to get back to her son. Time to get back to something certain, something she could believe in and trust.

She knotted the laces of her sneakers, threw them over her shoulder, and waited for the gold caged doors to clank shut. The elevator creaked upward. She wondered how it could rise with all the weight she felt pressing on her shoulders.

Chapter 32

Elmer stretched. A couple vertebrae snapped into place with a loud POP and he rubbed a tender spot in his lower back. Maybe he would go to the masseuse later. He had been here three days and was meaning to stop by at some point. Yes, today was the day. Again, Elmer stretched lazily and yawned like a cat. Time to get up, he supposed, but he wasn't quite sure. There weren't many clocks inside Abe's Kitchen. Elmer lifted one knee, then the other. He slid his feet into sheepskin slippers and wrapped a robe around his narrow shoulders, tying it securely around his waist. The excess length of belt almost reached the floor. *I should eat something, I suppose.* He examined his skinny arms, his scrawny legs. *I should definitely eat something.*

He had to constantly remind himself to eat these days. He had no appetite. Mostly, he thought of Hilo and her small features and the sophisticated way she played the piano. Always her own style. Always making it up as she went along. He thought of her long, dull hair, her shy smile. He thought of the way she came to him for advice, thought of the time she told him her story. An unbelievable story of arranged marriage and negligent parents and running away. *She was always so brave, my Hilo. Underneath that fragile shell, she was as hard as a diamond. And as spectacular.*

Elmer cried a lot lately. He cried to make up for all the moments he did not cry after her death. At the McFaddens, he was too shell-shocked, too traumatized to consider crying. He walked the halls of the Faberge mansion, barely alive. A ghost inhabiting Elmer's skin for a while. Now, the ghost was gone. He felt his heart beating and his skin sweating. He felt the familiar aches in his hips and in his knees. He felt the heaviness of emotion. And so he cried. He cried because he felt human; he cried because he hurt.

He paced the halls of Abe's Kitchen for three days. He went to the library. He went to the spa. At some point during the day, Zach would find him, prod him to go eat, and they would spend the rest of the day together. And so it went. But it wasn't quite as simple as that.

Elmer began to notice prolonged stares and sideways glances. He began to hear murmurs when he stepped into a room. Sometimes he thought he recognized familiar faces, bunched together and staring at him, but it was impossible to tell. Everyone looked about the same to him—an indistinguishable blob of humanity, sucking on the fat of its host.

Last night he hardly slept. The stares and glances filled his head, commandeered his thoughts. When he did fall into a restless sleep, their eyes mingled with hers—the ghost girl who was first his wife, no wait, Hilo, no, obviously Daisy, well, maybe Irene. He tossed and flailed like a madman, beating away the hollow, woman eyes and the staring, human blob eyes. He didn't calm down until a new group of eyes filled his head, a group of seven pairs. Elmer gave a little yip of joy when he saw the eyes of the seven sages and whispered softly, "Oh thank you, thank you. You've saved me. Again. Oh thank you." The sages nodded, their eyes warm and comforting, and Elmer slipped into a heavy, dark, dreamless sleep. It filled his head like a bowling ball.

In the morning he stretched and decided to go to the masseuse. He also decided to get the hell out of there.

At one o'clock in the afternoon, after a shower, a shave, and an hour-long massage with Mindy, the bubbly masseuse, Elmer stepped out the door of Abe's Kitchen with his black duffel bag. "Don't forget to sign out every time you leave," reminded a spindly young worker with curly blonde locks. "That's the one rule we have around here. Gotta keep the guest book up to date." He grinned widely at Elmer and tapped with his index finger a massive, leather-bound book on a pedestal beside him. Elmer sneered back and signed the book:

Elmer H.

"Hey mister, dontcha have a last name?" yelled the young attendant. But Elmer was out the door and the words fell on his sweater-clad back.

Elmer breathed in deeply and the outside air rushed to fill his lungs. *Delicious.* He smacked his lips, pushed back his shoulders, and strode down the sidewalk, humming as he walked. He wasn't sure where he was going, but at that moment, it didn't matter. The only things that mattered were the blue sky, the shoes on his feet, and his beating heart. Elmer smiled at the neat houses and tiny flower gardens with their late summer blooms. He thought of Ezzie. Nothing could ruin his mood. Nothing—

"Well, howdy there 'Just Elmer!'" Elmer's mood deflated like a helium balloon shot with an arrow. "Where in tarnation you been hidin' yerself? The missus and me bin speculating for days now 'bout where you run off to. Almos' thought you skipped town."

Elmer wished he had. He nodded tersely at Freddie Keys and said, "Good afternoon. Good to see you. Must be going." He turned ninety degrees to his right and attempted to scurry away, but Keys' fleshy fingers grabbed his shoulder.

"Now, not so fast there, 'Just Elmer!' Us citizens of City B care 'bout each other and I consider it my God-given duty to make sure I know yer ok. Now, I see you've come from the North side o' town. Where 'bouts you been staying?"

"Abe's Kitchen," Elmer muttered and attempted to shake the pudgy hand from his shoulder. The hand clamped tighter.

"*Abe's* Kitchen? Did I hear you correc'ly mah boy? Crim'ny bless, you do *not* want to get mixed up with that ilk. Their kind's no good. Jus' a bunch of low-down, scummy, false prophets. That's what they are. You listen to me 'Just Elmer.' Stay as far from them as you possibly can or you'll regret it."

Elmer turned and looked at Keys for a moment. Took in his serious mouth, his knit brows. It was the first time he had seen the flabby man without a silly grin pasted across his face. "I agree," he thought. "For the first time yet, I agree with this man. Abe's Kitchen is trouble. It *is* a shady, no-good place. Does Keys really sense that the way I do?"

Then Elmer remembered the sticker on his son's door. E.B. And it dawned on him. He looked at Keys' beady, unblinking eyes and said, "You're telling me to avoid Abe's Kitchen because you support Ezekiel Banks, is that right?"

"Well, of course," Keys declared, the sloppy grin once again pasted across his face. "What kind of delusional idiot doesn't support the noble Ezekiel Banks and his efforts to feed and shelter the homeless? Gosh, you've gotta lot to learn, Elmer. Only infidels and lunatics support Ibrahim Anbar—the filthy non-believer." He wrinkled his nose as if he had just stepped in a large, steaming pile of dung. "Elmer good thing I caught you 'fore it's too late. Now you listen to me. The only way—," he pointed his finger at the middle of Elmer's face; it came centimeters away from hitting his nose. "The *only* way to receive the Reward is to follow Ezekiel Banks. Anyone who's worth their salt knows that. Following Ibrahim Anbar's lil' cult is a pure waste o' time. A pure, r'diculous waste o' time! Now come with me 'Just Elmer.' We're going to check you into ol' Ezekiel Banks' Kitchen 'fore you can say chicken dumplin' soup! Now come along!"

Elmer didn't have time to think or resist or ask "What the hell is 'the Reward' and why should I give two shits about it?" Keys swooped in on him like a ravenous red-tailed hawk and half-dragged, half-pulled him to his burgundy truck and shoved him inside. Elmer slumped, defeated, into the passenger seat. He remained tight-lipped for the seven minute drive to Ezekiel Banks' Kitchen while Keys prattled on and on about scummy infidels and their schemes to corrupt good, wholesome, God-fearing folk. To Keys, the world was black and white. There were two sides and no room for middle ground. Perhaps that was why Elmer made Keys nervous. The old man didn't fall neatly into one camp or the other and that troubled him. Something had to be done.

"Here we are!" shouted Keys enthusiastically as they pulled next to the hulking grey building. "E.B.'s Kitchen!" Keys' enthusiasm sounded hollow and fake. Elmer had heard this exact tone of enthusiasm during some of his Lions Club meetings. It was a tone that said, "I'm trying really hard to convince you that this next endeavor is exciting and worthwhile…even though I'm none too sure of it myself." Elmer smirked at Keys and allowed himself to be led by the elbow into the reception hall. He clutched his duffel bag tightly and began planning his escape from Banks' Kitchen. Inside, Keys released his elbow.

"A'right now, Elmer. As soon as you sign the guest book, I'll be on mah way. I know yer in safe hands here. Good ol' Ezekiel and his crew will take good care of you."

Elmer turned away from the fleshy man and signed the large book in front of him. Elmer H.

Keys peered over his shoulder.

"H, huh? What does that stand for? Harrison? Hamilton? Huckleberry?"

"If I wanted the world to know my last name, I would tell it," said Elmer tersely. His voice was low and menacing, like the growl from the throat of a mountain lion. Keys heeded its warning and changed the subject.

"Right, right. Well, the lunch hour is 'bout done. I'd better run back to the store an' open her up again. Right. Be seein' you, Elmer." He clapped him on the back with his wide palm and shuffled out the door. Elmer stared behind him. He counted to forty—an amount of time he thought was sufficient to let Keys amble to his burgundy truck, start the engine, and take off—and then headed towards the door. A leg blocked his path.

Elmer looked into the face of the person the leg belonged to. It was the little man that had taken his shoes on his first visit to Banks' Kitchen. Now, he stood in front of Elmer, one thin eyebrow raised, smile plastered across his smooth, baby face, right leg outstretched and blocking his way with a pointy, elf-like shoe. The man nodded familiarly at Elmer.

"Well 'llo again sir!" he tittered.

Elmer crinkled his nose at the thin voice. "Well?" he demanded.

"Won't you staying for a bit? You *did* sign the guest book."

"The *guest book*? The bloody, blooming guest book?!" Elmer was furious. "Did I sign away my life then? Well? Did I?"

The miniature man hesitated. "Well, no sir. No, you didn't. It's just that it's highly irregular to sign in and then step out the door less than a minute later. Highly irregular. Everyone stays a while, you see. Everyone wants to stay a while. This is Ezekiel Banks' Soup Kitchen, you see. It's a happy place." His voice sounded puzzled. "Why wouldn't you want to stay? Everyone wants to stay."

Elmer sneered at the man, but his voice softened a little. He felt a minutia of pity for the tiny, loyal soul. "Not everyone," he said. "Not everyone wants to stay."

"Ok, sir. I hope you come back soon. There's always a place for you at E.B.'s Kitchen." He reluctantly moved his spindly leg aside.

"Thank you," Elmer murmured as he made a move to leave.

"Oh wait!" the man yipped. Elmer turned.

"Yes?"

"You forgot to sign out, sir. The guest book. Here." He motioned to the leather-bound book and shoved a feather-plumed pen into Elmer's right hand.

"Oh, for Pete's sake," Elmer muttered as he signed the book.

For the second time that day, Elmer stepped into the sunshine. He squinted at the luminous orb that beat down on him high overhead. Elmer knew immediately that it was shortly after one o'clock. Gauging the time from the sun was a skill he had acquired while growing up on the potato farm. Papa never owned a wristwatch. He believed them to be frivolous, unnecessary items when "all a fellow needs is the sun and a good sense of direction."

Elmer glanced at the sun again, adjusted his glasses, and made his way to the far sidewalk. He walked towards the train station. Twenty minutes and several hundred footsteps later, he arrived at the familiar platform and wearily sank down into one of the cushy lobby-room chairs. He pulled a clean, white handkerchief from his pocket and mopped his damp brow. He had walked quickly and militantly to the station, not pausing to take a break lest someone should again stop him, scoop him up, and haul him away to one of the soup kitchens. Now he sighed and rested his hands on his bony knees. The muscles twitched, agitated by the hasty journey. Elmer patted them lovingly and silently thanked them for holding up.

He sat back and looked up at the day's train schedule, scrawled by hand across a wide chalk board. There were three more trains that day: one to The City, one to There, and one to City A.

City A. Roger and Cecelia are in City A. I could help them rebuild. I could help them rebuild their charred dreams.

Elmer stared at the schedule for a long time. *City A.* He wondered if he could really go back. He wondered if he was strong enough to face the place where Hilo had died, where her little body had turned into black, smeary ash, where her spirit undoubtedly lingered. Elmer pictured her, small and afraid, clutching his painting tightly to her chest, as burning timbers fell around her and dense smoke curled its way into her lungs. He shuddered.

City A. He couldn't do it. He couldn't go back. Not yet. The memories and ashes were too fresh.

Elmer heard the rumble of a train in the distance. It was the train bound for The City. Its beating diesel heart grew closer with each second, pounding violently and filling the ground with heavy vibrations. Elmer squeezed his knees again. He could feel the pulse of the train traveling through his skin. He heard the squealing of breaks and the grating of steel. He watched as the head of the great machine came into view and wheezed to a stop in front of the station, creaking and groaning dramatically. The doors opened. A few people got off. A few people got on. Doors shut. Engine primed. Wheels turn slowly, then gather speed, heart beating faster, rounded nose pressing down the track. Gone.

Elmer watched the train depart, tasted the dust it left in its wake. No City for him today. No There either. Certainly no City A. He felt vaguely defeated and a little annoyed. *Now what?*

He decided to take a walk and delay the decision. He stepped away from the train station and studied the angle of the sun. Three o'clock.

* * *

"Grace, my darling, sit down!" the woman in red motioned with a flabby arm. "I thought you'd left us for good. You were gone for what, five days? Abe's Kitchen wasn't all it was cracked up to be then? No, of course it wasn't. Sit down, sit down! Don't be shy. The manicotti's not half bad today, is it? Last time they served it the noodles were a bit dry, I thought. But I wrote a little note for the comment box and it seems they fixed it, didn't they? How sweet of them, really. That's why E.B.'s Kitchen is the best. And not just the best because they listen to their people and provide us with the best little meals. Oh no. It goes way beyond that, indeed it does. Way beyond that."

Grace nodded stiffly and scurried to a different table.

* * *

It was getting dark and Elmer was tired. He had spent the afternoon alone with his thoughts and they were starting to weigh on him like a two-ton wrecking ball. He was in a bind and he knew it. Trapped. He didn't want to stay in City B, but didn't know where to go. Where could he go? He longed for human affection, a group like the Modern Shamans, to distract him from his morbid notions and his aching heart, but that group had disbanded and now the only bunches of people in his life were the lurking, amorphous groups that haunted the spas and fitness centers of the soup kitchens. He paused and drew in a breath. The air rattled in his lungs. He felt empty and unsure. He wondered how many people sometimes paused and asked themselves, "What does it all mean?"

He passed a tiny grocery store on the corner, remembered he was thirsty, and walked inside. While he was standing at the counter, paying for his bottle of iced tea, he heard it. Drums.

BOOM-batta-BOOM-batta-BOOM-BOOM-BOOM

He collected his change and hustled outside. He stopped short at the doorway, cocked his head for a moment, and then followed the sound of drums to his right. North.

batta-BOOM-batta-BOOM-batta-batta-batta-BOOM

Elmer's footsteps matched the rhythm, an excited staccato. He drew closer and closer to the sound. His left arm swung the bottle of iced tea; his right arm, the cane. BOOM-batta-BOOM-batta-BOOM-BOOM-BOOM. On his right, the sidewalk opened up. A small, brick-paved open space, lined with a few trees and wooden benches, held the sound. He squinted his eyes. He smiled.

Pounding away on several overturned five-gallon buckets, Zach's head and shoulders moved to the beat. A small crowd started to gather around the musician, hypnotized by his steady hands, his swaying dreadlocks. Zach paid them little attention. He was lost in the percussive sounds he wove. Or maybe the sounds wove him.

Elmer joined the crowd, transfixed. He remembered the Solstice party with the Modern Shamans. He remembered their wide smiles and benevolent eyes. He missed them, but right now he was not sad. He rejoiced. He rejoiced in their memory and in their presence. He swayed to the rhythm of the drums, imaging they were there with him, their arms entwined with his. A silly grin spread across his face. He felt drunk with bliss. He wondered if the rest of the crowd was as caught up in the music as he was. He glanced to his left.

They were dancing. They were all dancing. Jumping up and down, spinning, rocking on their legs. Elmer's eyes widened. Among the crowd, dancing and jumping in between the bodies, were seven robed figures, each a different color. The bearded man in blue turned his head and winked at Elmer. Elmer stared back. He felt a hand grasp his. The moon-faced woman in gleaming purple robes smiled as she swept him towards her and began dancing a kind of quick waltz. Elmer followed along, less startled now and grateful for company, even if the company happened to be seven spirit guides that he was quite certain had sprung from his own head. When the drumsticks stopped pounding, he nodded graciously at the moon-faced woman and stepped away. He was out of breath and feeling more than a little confused. He slid onto one of the wooden benches at the edge of the open space and gulped down some iced tea. He closed his eyes and instantly fell asleep.

In his dream, Elmer was a young warrior clad in animal pelts that had just returned from a hunt. He held up a glistening spear as he danced around a fire. Danced and danced. Danced to the beat of drums. Bare feet hit the ground and kicked up a dusty film that muted the fire. The fire shone, bright and warm, on his victorious face. He knitted his brows. He was suddenly aware that he was not alone. Rings of people surrounded him. They danced too. Danced and danced. Around him. Circling. Revolving around him in tight rings. He felt like everyone in creation was holding him in their arms. Safe in their arms. It was a good feeling, a feeling of maternal security.

A hand patted his shoulder, jostling him from his dream. "Elmer. Elmer, wake up! Elmer, what the hell are you doing? You ok? Come on, speak to me."

"Hrm?" said Elmer.

"Hey old man," the voice continued. "It's me, Zach."

Elmer rubbed his bleary eyes and tried to focus on the light brown face in front of him. It was dark now and a few street lamps shone, lighting up the bricks below. Elmer's brain clicked into gear.

"Hmm. Oh, Zach. Hi, hi. How're you doing? Just enjoying your music. Must've fallen asleep. Was dancing, you know. Plumb wore me out."

Zach smiled. "Glad you liked it, Elm, but it's getting late. Let's get you back to the kitchen. Eaten anything today?"

Elmer tried to remember. "Some eggs for breakfast, I think."

"You think? Oh no, Elm. Not good enough. Not on my watch. Come on, let's get some food in you and get you to bed. I decided to move on to E.B.'s tonight; I hope that's ok."

"NO!" Elmer yelled, all the sleep-induced fog dissipating from his brain. "I was there today and I'm not going back. That place gives me the chills."

Zach gave him a puzzled look. "Ok, Elm. Did you have a bad experience there or something? We can always go to Abe's—"

"No. I'm not going there either. I'd rather sleep on that old park bench than have anything to do with either of those places. I mean it!"

"Ok, ok. It's just that—I—I mean—there's this woman, name of Grace, who is sort of a friend. She's staying at Banks' Kitchen and I was kind of hoping to meet up with her there."

"Well you go right ahead," said Elmer, crossing his arms stubbornly across his chest. "Don't let me stop you."

"Come on, Elmer," Zach persisted. "I think she's in trouble. Things have been really hard for her and her son. Moving back and forth between soup kitchens, trying to avoid the Loyals. It's been pretty tough for her and little Levi."

Elmer's frown softened. "Levi, you say? That's the boy's name?" He thought of the spare-toothed grin of the bum in There. He thought of Maggie and Zach. He pictured her balancing the little boy on her hip as she bustled around the house. He sighed—a big, full-bodied sigh—and turned to Zach. "You win," he muttered, shaking his head. "We'll go to Banks' Kitchen. But I'm warning you," Elmer waved a gnarled finger at his friend's narrow chest, "if I detect any funny business from that place, I'm high-tailing it and *that* is that!"

The corners of Zach's mouth twitched upward. "Excellent," he said. "Let's go. I think you'll really like Grace. Sweet girl." He strode ahead, mumbling a song as he went.

Elmer rolled his eyes and followed. The large grey building lurked down the street and his heart pounded warily in his chest. He imagined he was Daniel. Every step led him closer to the lion's den.

Chapter 33

"Dear God 'n heaven, please bless this here food on our table and bless the hands that made it. Thank you for our health and happiness, Lord. Please let this food nourish and strengthen our bodies so we'll be able to perform your work and the work of Mr. Ezekiel Banks, yer wise and noble servant. Please keep Mr. Banks happy and in good health as he endeavors to do yer bidding. And please let all the nonbelievers open their eyes and see the one, true way. In yer name, we pray. Amen."

"Amen."

"Nel, pass the corn, will ya? Jake, you want some? Come on, you gotta eat yer veggies. How else do ya expect to be a big, tough football player like your brother Samuel was? That's right. Take another scoop."

"Dad, can I go over to Jimmy's tomorrow night? Please?"

"Jimmy—Jimmy Mullin? Son of Cynthia and Marve Mullin? They're the tall family that sits in the back of the E.B. Chapel, aren't they? Well, I don't much approve of people who sit in the back, but at least they go to the right chapel, eh? Yeah, I suppose that'd be alright. What'd ya think Nel?"

A nod.

"Fine, fine. To Jimmy's it is. That'll be fun. Yes, that'll be good fun."

* * *

Miniature shepherd's pies dotted the kitchen counter of Ezekiel Banks' Kitchen. They were divided into three clusters, each cluster with their own sign. CHICKEN. BEEF. VEGETABLE. The pies were fresh and a pleasant odor wafted from their crusts. A petite woman in a brilliant crimson blouse stepped primly to the counter and inhaled deeply.

"Ahh, perfect," she thought. "I've been told he loves shepherd's pies."

She chose two chicken pies and placed them delicately on a gleaming gold tray. She continued to walk the counter line and picked up a dinner roll, steamed broccoli, and two deviled eggs and placed them lovingly on a plate next to the shepherd pies. At the end of the counter, she found rows of German chocolate cake and selected the piece she deemed the most lovely. She set the tray on the counter for a moment and arranged the food and scarlet napkin in a way that was both aesthetically pleasing and logical. She stepped back and looked at it.

"Perfect."

She placed a matching gold cover over the tray and walked rapidly to the golden caged elevator, her quick steps even and careful. She stepped inside, scanned her security card, and punched the number seven button with authority. The elevator doors creaked shut.

On the seventh floor, she stepped quietly from the elevator, the tray of food balanced elegantly on her right hand. She looked at the large, gold-trimmed oak doors in front of her. They stood about fifteen feet high and were covered in delicate, vine-like engravings. A chill ran through her body; her forehead began to bead sweat, but she ignored it. Softly, she inched towards the door and pulled the supple, gold tasseled cable that paralleled the door and disappeared into the ceiling. A faint gong sounded somewhere in the caverns of the room beyond.

Almost instantly, a small door situated at shoulder height sprang open; a metal platform slid out the door and stuck out like a tiny gangplank. The petite woman crept up to the platform and placed the golden tray gingerly on top of it. She stepped back and watched the platform sink into the room with the tray as its prisoner. The small door clanged shut.

She scurried back to the elevator and punched number one. The elevator rattled to life and started slowly descending back to the ground floor. She kept her eyes on the massive oak doors as they sank upward, away from her vision. "Towards heaven," she thought.

* * *

The group sat down and began silently eating their shepherd's pies. The silence was tense. The group was aware of rows of eyes trained on their backs and faces. For a while, they chewed on the food in front of them, avoiding eye contact, listening to the masticating of chicken, the rolling around of vegetables and crust in their mouths. Finally, gratefully, Grace broke the silence.

"So Elmer, tell me a little about yourself. Zach says he met you in There. Is that where you're from?"

Usually, Elmer loathed questions about himself or his background. He was afraid that the secrets of his past might slip into the open and muddy things up. He was afraid he might have a panic attack if he started talking about his former life. At the moment, however, he was grateful for any chance to stir up the stagnating silence.

"No, ma'am, I'm not from There. I'm from the town of Here."

"Here. Hmm, *Here*. I don't believe I've heard of it."

"I'm not surprised. Small place. Agricultural. My Papa used to farm potatoes there."

"Ok. Very nice. And do you still own the family farm?"

Elmer chuckled a little. "Hell, no. I sold that thing the first chance I got. Do you have any idea how horrible potato farming is?"

Grace cracked a smile. "I haven't the faintest idea."

"Well," Elmer replied, "it's pretty damn horrible, just take it from me. If there wasn't a drought, there were plagues of greedy potato beetles. And if you didn't lose the entire crop, there was the long, tedious harvesting. We did most of the work by hand then, you know."

"Fascinating," said Grace. She meant it. "I've never much thought about where they come from," she said, digging a chunk of potato out of her shepherd's pie and scrutinizing it as if it had just dropped to earth from outer space. She looked back at Elmer. "What are potato beetles?"

"They're these ugly black and yellow things with a semi-hard shell, like a ladybug. They lay bright orange eggs under the leaves of the potato plants. The eggs hatch and before you know it, there are hundreds—or even thousands—of these pests, chewing down the leaves of your potatoes, leaving the plants weak and defenseless, and essentially ruining the crop. They're bad, those potato bugs. And nearly impossible to get rid of unless you walk down each row of potatoes, turning over their leaves one by one, and crushing the egg sacks you find below. At least, that was the old fashioned way to do it. Now, I suppose they just use pesticides and get rid of the whole blight at once."

"I know of some other pests that are nearly impossible to eliminate," said Grace darkly, looking over Elmer's shoulder at one of the whispering clusters of humanity. Their eyes darted away quickly. Grace emitted a sound somewhere between a growl and a sigh. She shifted the weight of the little boy sitting on her lap and hugged him closely to her chest.

"Now, Grace," said Zach, reaching over and patting her hand. "Don't let them get to you. The moment you let them take over your reasoning is the moment they've won."

"Hmph," said Grace. "Let them try."

"Oh, believe me," Zach replied. "They will. And they are."

The group was silent again for a few long seconds. Zach squeezed Grace's hand tightly and looked into her eyes encouragingly. His gold-flecked eyes lingered on hers. He often found it hard to drop her gaze. Those eyes. They were round and luminous and so startling green that they often made people stop whatever they were doing and stare. They were haunting, those eyes. Haunting and lovely. Zach wondered if they would have seemed more ordinary if they were set against a backdrop of pale, Caucasian skin. But as it was, the emerald eyes were juxtaposed against a dark olive background, a background that entertained a mix of cultures, a stew of diversity. It was impossible to tell where her skin had come from; it looked as if the different ethnicities of the world were set at her feet in giant paint cans and she had been dipped in only the loveliest colors. Zach shook the image out of his head and continued where he left off.

"But we shouldn't worry about them. In fact, we shouldn't heed their stares at all. That's just what they want. Come on, who's up for some dessert?"

A mass of eyes watched as they sought the German chocolate cake.

* * *

Levi was bored. They were always talking, the grownups. For the last three days all they seemed to do was talk and talk and talk from sunup to sundown. Today, he had waited patiently while the group of three finished their sandwiches, but now he wanted to play. He tugged impatiently on his mother's sleeve. She calmly removed his tiny fist and continued chatting. Levi stuck out his lip. His favorite toy truck was waiting for him in the playroom—the blue one with big, bumpy tires and a button on top that made the car go Vrrrr-vrrrrr-vrrrrrOOOMMmmmmm. That one. But no one seemed to care. He tugged on his mother's sleeve again and this time made a tiny whimpering noise.

"Levi, come on. Mommy's trying to have a conversation."

Levi crossed his arms and looked away. He scanned the room, seeking something, *anything* that would entertain him. His roving eyes came to a sudden halt. A cluster of eyeballs stared at him from across the room. Levi's lip trembled. A tiny squeak escaped his lips and he buried his shaggy head underneath his mother's arm.

"Levi, will you quit squirming! What's gotten into you today?" Grace shifted her son on her lap; he hugged her closely. She looked down inquisitively at the dark, curly locks that hid her son's round face. They bobbed up and down slightly, in cadence with his shivers. She shrugged.

"Like I was saying," she said, turning her attention back to Elmer and Zach, "I know we're not the only ones here who think the Loyals have gotten out of hand. Just yesterday, I was talking to Lucinda and she reckons she'll be moving back to Abe's any day now—not that Abe's is much better. But that's the thing. It's like, once you're in one place you start to feel nostalgic for the other and think to yourself, 'Oh, Abe's wasn't that bad' or 'Ezekiel's place was nice and homey, wasn't it?' And then you trick yourself into going back once again. It's an endless cycle."

"Well, I for one am sick of it," growled Zach. "I came to this city because I wanted to better my life, to feel safe and cared for. Hmph. I certainly can't say that 'safe' is one of the adjectives that comes to mind when I think of the kitchens. More like 'unnerving' or 'eerie.' It shouldn't be that way. Think about it. These are *soup kitchens.* They are supposed to provide a little food, a little comfort to those who need it most. Simple. So, how did such a beautiful, straightforward concept get twisted around into these, these…cults? How did the concept of 'love one another' become expounded into a profitability ploy. And the worst part is, we just sit back and accept it. We let ourselves be lied to and led around like sheep. It really shatters my faith, you know."

Elmer didn't say anything. His mind was on a place, far from City B, where he had lost his faith in other things, things that seemed simple at one time. He saw himself as a young boy getting ready for church. He saw his mother's gloved hand leading him down the aisle while his father sought an empty pew. His eyes roved around the immense building and settled on the stained glass windows in the front. They always settled on those windows. He swore they were magic. The way the sun shone through them and cast multi-colored shadows on the floor. The way those shadows danced. Danced. Blues and oranges and greens all rippling across the altar and down the tiled floor. Those colors danced. Little Elmer was mesmerized. He loved the windows. He loved going to church just to see them.

"What do you think Elmer? Elmer?"

Elmer shook himself from his daydreams. "Huh? Oh, sorry. Must've gotten lost in my thoughts."

"That's alright," Zach replied. "I was just asking if you and Grace think it's a good idea to put our plan into action—you know, the one we've been discussing. What do you think?"

"I suppose now's as good a time as any," said Elmer.

Grace nodded, eyes flashing. "I agree. We know we're not alone and we know there are plenty of people who are just as fed up with those zealots as we are." She shot one of the groups in the dining room an angry look. Their eyes scattered like cockroaches from light. "I say we go for it."

Zach nodded. "Ok, but we're going to have to be subtle. No need to get the Loyals all stirred up. Who knows, they might try to get the Bookkeeper involved if they get too riled."

"Who now?" Elmer asked. "The Bookkeeper? Who's that?"

Both Grace and Zach shot Elmer surprised looks. "You know," said Grace, "The Bookkeeper. Old guy, really important. No?"

Elmer shook his head, a blank look on his face.

"Hmm," said Zach. "Sometimes I forget how new you are here. No matter." He shrugged. "Grace, want to explain? You've been here the longest."

"Don't remind me," she groaned. She turned to Elmer and cleared her throat. Their green eyes met and she started talking. "Each soup kitchen has a Bookkeeper. He is the right-hand man to the boss—either Ezekiel or Abe. You've probably noticed that old E.B. and Abe never mingle with the lowly kitchen guests. They just don't. That's the way it is. But they send messages through their Bookkeepers. Sometimes you'll see them—scrounging around in the kitchen, inspecting the fitness center, observing the goings-on in the library—but they don't really go out of their way to talk to us. We're all beneath them, you see. Lousy bums."

"That's not exactly fair, Grace," Zach cut in. "I don't think it even crosses their minds that we fall into some kind of pecking order with them on top. I think they hardly look at us as *people*. In reality, the only thing that concerns the Bookkeepers is the numbers. That and keeping their bosses happy. Although, the two are not mutually exclusive."

"You're right," Grace continued. "That is a better way of putting it. They don't look at us and see people. They look at us and see numbers, quantities, things to be measured. All the Bookkeepers care about is whether or not their boss' soup kitchen is the best or, at least, better than their rival's.

They look at us and think, 'Hmm. I wonder why no one has used the jacuzzi lately. Is it too hot? Are the jets too weak? Could this possibly drive them to go to the other kitchen?' They keep track of everything. They measure the popularity of each meal. They keep track of the books we check out in the library. They tally the number of active participants in the basketball league. All of it. They measure all of it."

Elmer looked at her, stunned. "That is incredible," he said. "And eerie. And just—just—awful. How—" he looked at Grace anxiously, "how did you find out so much about this Bookkeeper fellow and what he does?"

"Observing, mostly. Observing and listening. If you've been here a while like I have, you start to pick up on things—little phrases people say, a certain hush in the dining hall when the Bookkeeper is around. Plus, they're always alluding to the numbers in their lectures. At least twice a week there are lectures in Abe's mosque and Ezekiel's chapel. I used to be a regular. I thought it'd be good for Levi to get some exposure to religion and faith and all that and—" she paused and squeezed her son a little closer, "I hoped I would regain my own. But I didn't. And I won't. Not here, at least..." she let the sentence dangle in the air. Her thoughts hung for a moment. Then she shook her head and looked back at Elmer. "Have you been to any of the lectures?"

He shook his head.

"Go sometime. You'll see what I mean. Not a lecture goes by where they don't talk about the numbers. Go. You'll see. You'll see they keep track of everything. Keep track of us. Like bears with tags clipped in their ears. Like things meant to be studied."

Elmer stared at the lovely woman in front of him. His eyes were fixed somewhere around her mouth, as if he was trying to comprehend the words that had just left it. He shuddered and blinked, breaking the trance. He looked at Grace and then Zach and then back to Grace. When he spoke, the words came out in a whisper. "It makes the hairs stand up on the back of my neck," he said. "I knew from the start these places were bad news. I knew it. Always got a creepy feeling walking around here, like every move I made was being tracked, like I was being hunted by some animal. Now I know it's true." He looked around nervously, his eyes bouncing from one end of the room to the next. "Good god," he said tersely, "what the hell are we doing here? Why don't we get out? Now. Please. Let's get out of here!"

The old man stood up, teetered on his feet for a minute, and started towards the door.

"Elmer!" Zach called. "Elmer!" He leaped to his feet and dashed in front of the shaking, anxious man. He grabbed his arm. Elmer stopped. "Come on Elm, be reasonable. You've been in one soup kitchen or the other for a couple of weeks now and no harm has come to you. Seriously. Look around. You're well-cared for here, despite the Big Brother factor. Besides, that's exactly why we have to stay—to help the others."

Elmer turned around. Several people watched him from across the dining room, but he ignored their stares. Instead, he looked back at Grace. She was still holding Levi tightly to her chest and bumping him up and down as she looked at Elmer, her eyes round and pleading.

Elmer grunted, "Oh all right. All right, I'll stay. I don't like it much, but I'll stay."

"Oh good. That's great," said Zach, exhaling and letting the tension in his shoulders melt away. "That's really great." He gave Elmer a brief hug. Elmer's stubbornness would not allow him to hug back. Together, they walked back to the table.

"Ok," said Elmer as he sat down beside Grace. She put an arm around his bony shoulder. He was still shaking slightly, but his eyes no longer looked anxious. Instead, there was a glint of determination and defiance in them. A glint that had rarely appeared in the old man's life. He straightened his shoulders and gripped the table to stop his body from shaking. He turned towards the others.

"When do we begin?"

Grace gave his shoulder a squeeze and winked across the table at Zach. "No time like the present."

Chapter 34

"...and the third key to building a good, moral character is unwavering loyalty. That's right, loyalty. Loyalty is a word we use hastily and without much thought. We might be loyal to the local basketball team. We might be loyal to a certain brand of chocolate. Today, I say to you, let us reconsider this sloppy usage of the word. Let us restore its true and proper meaning. Let us give it the gravity and importance it deserves. Think about the important components of your life. Think about the things that matter. Your friends? Your family? The roof over your head? The food in your belly? Think about these things and ask yourself, 'Am I loyal to them? Do I give them my steadfast and constant attention?' Chances are, you take for granted most of these important components. Chances are, your loyalty has wavered at some time or another and you have forgotten to be true to these components. You have forgotten to be true to that which matters most."

The speaker paused and glared at the crowd. His beady brown eyes scanned the audience as he kept up the uncomfortably long paused. The corners of his wrinkled mouth upturned slightly in a satisfied smirk. He loved watching them squirm. He loved watching their guilty, anxious expressions. He had them in the palm of his sweaty, little hand. He took a long drink of water and continued.

"It has been written, my friends, that loyalty can be demanding. It can take sacrifice. You have to be willing to steel your hearts, willing to take on heavy loads, willing to resist opposition. And there will be opposition, of that I'm sure. There will be those who will attempt to rip you away from the things that matter, the important components. There will be those who will tell you, 'This really can't matter *that* much' or 'Why are you loyal to *that*? My way is much better. Come, follow me.' These, my friends, are the questioners. The unbelievers. These are the people who have nothing better to do than to plague the lives of others with their doubts. They will try to seduce you. They will try to lure you in with their wily, scheming ways. Pay attention, I say! Listen not to their riddles and lullabies. They will only do you harm. Follow what you know is true, my friends. Follow that straight and narrow path, that path laid down for us all by our benevolent benefactor, Mr. Ezekiel M. Banks."

Nods from the audience. A few encouraging shouts. The speaker's smirk amplified. He pulled his narrow, hunched frame a little closer to the podium, his thin arms firmly grasping the wooden sides. Bits of froth clung to the corners of his mouth and periodically launched themselves across the room during his speech. The first couple rows of people became accustomed to looking away and ducking slightly whenever he got riled up and began placing particularly strong emphases on his words. They could tell they were in for a dousing and subtly braced themselves.

"That's right! Mr. Banks. How many of you thought of him when you imagined the important components in your life? How many of you felt loyalty and devotion to the man who has given so much and asked for so little? He has provided you with food *and* shelter *and* security. He has given you this glorious chapel, provided you with clean beds, wholesome entertainment, and most importantly, a sense of community."

The audience nodded collectively. "Yes!" they chanted. "Yes he has!"

"So much! He has done so much for you all! And how many, I ask, *how many* of you forget all this? How many of you have stood up for Mr. Banks this past week and loyally defended his kitchen? I want to see hands! Come on! Raise your hands if you've practiced unwavering loyalty to Mr. Banks this week."

The speaker scanned the audience briefly. "Des*pic*able!" he spat.

The front row ducked slightly.

"Friends and allies, if you want to know loyalty, look no further than our esteemed benefactor. Mr. Banks is a man of implacable loyalty. He is a family man, a devoted friend, a hard worker. He has dedicated his life to the well-being of this establishment and has not faltered in his mission to make E.B.'s Kitchen the best, *the* best, soup kitchen in town. Or the world, for that matter."

"That's right!" they shouted, their eyes glued to the speaker. "The best. Best in the world!"

"That's how lofty his ambitions are. That's how dedicated he is to *you*. That's how great he is, how *loyal*. Listen, friends. Has he ever let you go hungry? Has he ever turned his back on you when you've needed a place to stay? Has he ever ignored a request or complaint?"

The speaker pounded the podium with each question; his thin body jolted from the force of his fist and made the long strands of his beard quaver. The crowd quaked and shook their heads.

"And all he asks, all he'll ever ask, is that you offer him some of the same loyalty that he has shown you. Friends and allies, it has been written that loyalty is not truly shown by your *words*, but by your *actions*. Actions. Doing. Show Mr. Banks that you are loyal. Don't just talk about it. Talk is cheap! Talk never prevails! *Actions* prevail. Doing. Do something! Act!"

A froth missile struck a woman in the second row and she hastily wiped her cheek.

"I challenge you all," the speaker's tiny, beetle-colored eyes swept across the room once again. His voice dropped; his posture relaxed. The audience leaned forward to hear his words, "to practice loyalty this week. Practice it in conjunction with the other two principles I talked about today—gratitude and compassion—in order to build good, moral character. Gratitude. Compassion. Loyalty. This trio, my friends, will never let you down. If you practice these traits religiously, if you keep them at the forefront of your consciousness, then you will surely earn the Reward when the time comes."

Cheers from the audience. An eruption of whoops and shouts. A few people stood up and applauded. The speaker bowed his head in mock humility.

"No, friends. No need to applaud me, your humble orator. I am but the bearer of truth. I am but a vessel that pours out the good news. No, friends. No need to applause."

They applauded harder. More people leapt to their feet.

After several minutes of basking in the noise of palms slapping against each other, the speaker held up his hands. A hush fell over the crowd.

"Thank you, friends. You make my heart quite full. Now—" he paused for dramatic effect and leaned forward, as if spilling a grave secret along with his saliva, "I have a message for you all, a message from our benefactor, Mr. Ezekiel M. Banks."

More cheers. The speaker quickly quelled them with a wave of his hand.

"Mr. Banks knew we'd be speaking about gratitude, compassion, and loyalty today, so he wanted to show you how much he cares about these traits. Because that's just the kind of leader he is. One of us. Someone who cares about the same good, moral principles we care about and leads us by example. He is grateful for your company; he is compassionate about your well-being; he is loyal to his followers. So, Mr. Banks is starting a brand—new—Points Program!"

The crowd roared with applause and wolf whistles. Several children jumped up and down. A few people clapped each other on the back, wide grins spread across their faces. The speaker silently watched them. His smirk was no longer subtle. A smug look of satisfaction filled the lines of his face. Once again, he waved his hands; once again, the audience quieted.

"The program," he continued, "will be called 'Pages for Points.' We have noticed," he stared at them accusingly, "that attendance has dropped in our fine library. This is greatly troubling to Mr. Banks and me. It makes us wonder if you are getting your books and videos from someplace else—some *other* source that might provide you with a better selection. It makes us wonder, indeed."

A few guilty faces turned away. The speaker glared.

"We have considered this trend, Mr. Banks and I, and we have decided that a new Points Program is just what this facility needs to encourage readership and *loyalty*. It will work very similarly to the Points Program we ran last month for the fitness center. For every book you read, you get a point, which will be recorded by our staff librarians. You can collect as many points as you wish and redeem them for E.B. merchandise in the gift shop. I know some of you were eying the new E.B. tote bags and baseball caps. Now is your chance! Read away! Read and earn prizes that you can use proudly."

The speaker paused, gulped down some water, wiped his mouth with a sleeve, and continued.

"Now some of you may be asking yourselves, 'Why? Why on earth would Mr. Banks do all this for me? What's in it for him?' Well, doubters, listen closely. Mr. Banks does this for you because he firmly adheres to the three principles we discussed today. He does this for you because *he cares*. He cares. Remember that and remember where your loyalty stands. Thank you!"

The speaker stepped away from the podium amidst ear-shattering applause. His thin mouth smiled as he waved two bony arms above his head and backed away from his audience. They continued applauding. They wanted an encore. He shook his head playfully, clicked his heels together, and made a slight bow. In one fluid motion, he exited the pulpit and disappeared behind a red velvet curtain.

Elmer steadied himself against his cane and reached for Grace's hand. He tugged it like an anxious child. She looked at him and nodded. Quietly, the group of three exited the chapel and clambered into the golden caged elevator. Elmer leaned heavily against the side, clutching his stomach. He was sick.

* * *

"Right this way," Grace said as the group turned to the left and walked down a corridor lined with blood-red tapestries and gold-framed paintings. They made their way past the sleeping quarters on level five. "Here we are," Grace said. Zach and Elmer nodded silently, their thoughts trapped inside the chapel on level six.

"Hey little man," said Grace warmly, crouching down and stretching out her arms. Levi scampered towards her and threw his arms around her neck.

"Hi Mommy."

Grace picked up her son and hugged him tightly. She signed him out of daycare and they stepped back into the hallway. Elmer watched the pair—Levi playing with strands of her dark hair, Grace smiling softly—and thought of Maggie and Zach.

Grace bounced Levi against her body and stroked his mop of hair. "My, you're getting heavy little man. What did they feed you in daycare? Bricks?"

"Graham crackers," said Levi seriously, his moon face looking towards his mother.

Grace smiled. For a moment she lost herself in her son's shaggy curls, in his bright green irises that matched hers. She stroked his hair. Zach and Elmer watched her distantly, their eyes unfocused and oddly empty. Grace remembered their presence and tore her eyes away from her son. "You two look like you've seen a ghost. Come on. Let's get out of here for a little while. Let's get some air."

She walked past the two men and squeezed Elmer's shoulder. He smiled weakly and followed her, leaning heavily on his cane. Zach trailed behind, walking as if in a trance. Grace punched the elevator button for the main floor and they descended to the dining hall.

"Don't forget to sign out in the guest book!" chirped the same curly haired youth Elmer had seen a few days before.

Elmer glared at him and picked up the pen.

The trio stepped into the sunlight and breathed a collective sigh of relief. The air was crisp and a little chilly that day, but the sunshine was bright and it warmed their shoulders and the tops of their heads as they strode down the sidewalk in silence. Every now and then, Grace would murmur something in Levi's ear or kiss him on the forehead, but other than her quiet interruptions, the group maintained a thoughtful silence. After a mile or so, a park appeared on the right. Without speaking, the trio turned and walked through the downy grass until they found a shabby picnic table bathing itself in the sunlight. They sat down. Levi immediately spotted a sandbox and scuttled off to play in it. Grace's eyes lingered over her son affectionately.

They sat in silence for several seconds, feeling the sun's warmth radiate through their skin. Elmer thought of Ezzie and how she never used sunscreen. He wondered if she would start using it now that she had contact with her daughter again. He hoped so.

Zach began to speak and the other two snapped to attention. "So, Elmer," he tried to sound casual, but his voice seemed slightly pinched, "you've finally seen the Bookkeeper."

"Yes, I suppose I have," Elmer replied. "He's just as horrible as I thought he'd be. No. Worse, actually."

"Isn't he awful?" said Zach. "That's only the third lecture I've ever attended, but I swear they're getting worse. I don't remember the other two being so hateful, so blatantly...self-indulgent. It was shameless."

"No, they've always been like that," said Grace quietly. "Some are worse than others but, believe me, they are always bad."

"I can't believe this Points Program nonsense," Elmer growled. "It makes me ill, utterly and completely ill. The Bookkeeper promotes gratitude, compassion, and loyalty in one breath and promotes materialism, pettiness, and bribery in another. It's so backwards. So wrong..."

"I know it, Elm. I know it." Zach shook his head sadly. "And the thing is, it all looks innocent on the surface. I mean, what was the topic of today's lecture? Building a good, moral character through gratitude, compassion, and loyalty. Well, that sounds safe enough, doesn't it? On the surface, sure, but when you listen to the Bookkeeper's examples of each of these attributes, when you listen to the tone of the speech, to the subtle changes in his voice, that's when you realize the lecture is not so innocent after all. That's when you realize it has dangerous undercurrents. That it has an *agenda.* These are scary institutions we're dealing with here. I'm only just beginning to realize how tremendous their power and how wide their reach really is. It's terrifying."

"I know it is," said Grace softly. "At first, I was quite taken with the lectures. I stamped my feet and clapped my hands with everyone else. I agreed with the lectures' principles. I supported the Bookkeeper and thought of him as noble and wise. But one day, I decided to sit in the front row. I remember being swept up in the fervor of the crowd. I remember applauding vigorously and standing up in solidarity with the rest of the crowd. Then I looked up. I will never forget the look on the Bookkeeper's face—a self-satisfied grin and devious, greedy eyes. It frightened me and it planted a seed of doubt in my head I couldn't ignore. I went to a few more lectures after that, hoping to regain the initial enthusiasm I felt when I first attended the lectures. I didn't. The doubt only grew stronger until I could only hear false words and empty promises. I could only hear greed and power-lust in the Bookkeeper's voice. I wondered how I was so completely hoodwinked in the first place."

Grace shook her head and buried her face in her hands. "I don't know how I was so stupid. I don't know how I let them fool me like that. It's so embarrassing. So awful." Her shoulders shook as teardrops escaped through cracks in her fingers.

"Grace, my Grace, it's ok," said Zach. He scooted next to her and wrapped a long arm around her shoulders. "You'll be alright. You're clearly not the only one. There are plenty of people who have been hoodwinked by E.B. and by Abe as well."

She cried harder. "I know!" she sobbed. "It's horrible! That's why we have to do something. We have to rescue those poor people."

"We will, we will," said Zach, rocking her back and forth in his arms. "We'll do our best, Gracie. We'll do our best."

Grace rubbed her eyes and looked up at them. "I wanted to leave, you know. After I discovered that Abe's is just as bad as Ezekiel's, I tried to get the hell out of town. But I couldn't. I simply couldn't bring myself to leave all those people and besides, where would I go? That's just it. They trap you, those soup kitchens. They lure you with their endless food and entertainment and warm beds and then, BAM! You're trapped! Because you get used to a cushy life. You forget how to live on the street with only one meal a day and a cardboard box over your head. You're like a wild animal in the zoo who's forgotten how to hunt. You can't just leave the zoo. You'll perish. What do I have outside the soup kitchens? Nothing! I haven't a penny to my name. I have no home, no food, no bed. How can I raise a child in an environment like that? So I stay. I choose the lesser of two evils and stay."

Grace was panting and Zach softly rubbed her back. "It's ok, Grace. You're ok. I know it doesn't seem like you have a choice right now, but you do. You can get out of there if you really try. You can get a job in town, save some money, leave when you can. We'll take care of Levi while you work, won't we, Elm?"

Elmer nodded.

"See. See, Grace. You have allies. You have friends."

Grace's lips curled in an ironic, little smile. "Funny," she said, "all I associate with the words 'allies' and 'friends' now is that damned Bookkeeper. I wish he wouldn't plague my thoughts. I wish I could just blindly enjoy the soup kitchens like so many do. They eat; they play; they sleep. They listen to the lectures and *love* them. They're happy."

"Happy?" queried Zach, "Do you really think they're happy? They might seem blind to you, but there is a difference between being blinding and choosing to be blind. How many of the residents would you guess *truly* believe in the bullshit they're spooned? My guess is not many. They're purposefully turning away from the kitchens' flaws. They are ignoring the shady goings-on that happen there. No, I highly doubt they're happy. I think they are exactly like you. They feel hopeless and lost and are grateful for a bed and a warm meal. They don't know what else to do with themselves, so they might as well devote themselves entirely to their host. I would call it parasitic, but the host is inviting the fleas and ticks of society to suck on its body. What would that be called?"

"Perverse," said Elmer brusquely. He had been listening to Zach and Grace's conversation with increasing anxiety and hopelessness. He wanted to throw up. He wanted to hurl his cane across the park and start running. To where, he had no idea. Anywhere at this point. This place was nauseating. This place felt hopeless and dark and cultish and wrong and—"Perverse," Elmer repeated. "I'm sorry," he said, shaking his head, "but I haven't the faintest idea about what to do. It seems beyond our control. It's monstrous. Besides," he looked away and fought the tears stinging the backs of his eyes, "I'm the wrong person to go about fixing things. When things get tough for me, I just run away."

Grace and Zach exchanged a look and got up. They walked around the table and sat next to Elmer, one on each side, and put their arms around him. They held him closely, saying nothing, but speaking volumes at the same time. Elmer closed his eyes. He felt the touch of Cecelia and Roger and Maggie and the rest of them as they comforted him after Hilo's death. He felt the touch of the wild, green-lady and the swaying, rhythmic red-lady as they guided him towards the trumpet music. He felt the touch of his wife. He felt the touch of his mother's hand as she guided him down the aisle in church. He felt the warmth of light from the stained glass windows as it danced amongst the pews and kissed his face. He felt Daisy's soft hand as they danced and swirled in a golden field of grass such a long, long time ago…

"Thank you," he said and looked up. "Thank you for being here. I will try to be there for you."

They gave small smiles and patted his back.

"But I'm warning you," Elmer continued, "I haven't the faintest idea about what to do to help these people. We have the vague workings of a plan, but I'm afraid I don't know how to implement it. I don't think I'll be much help to you two."

"You will, Elm," said Zach sincerely. "Don't worry about that. Besides, won't it feel good to stay in one place for a while? To not run away."

"Yes," said Elmer. "That will feel good."

Grace looked at the elderly man by her side. She took in his thinning white hair, the creases around his eyes, his wide knuckles and gnarled fingers. "Elmer," she said, placing her hand on top of his. "Why don't you tell us a story about yourself? It's been a long, bitter day for everyone and I would love to talk about something else besides hate and deceit."

He hesitated.

"Please?"

He looked at her round, luminous eyes. "Oh, all right."

Chapter 35

Once there was a young boy named Elmer who finally got the chance to go to school. He walked the earth eight long years without setting foot in a schoolhouse, without reading a text book, without reciting lines, but one Monday in March all that changed. Elmer William Heartland set foot inside the Here Public Schoolhouse.

He wore his smartest outfit—a pair of grey knickers and a matching vest, polished his shoes, and hovered over his mother's shoulders as she packed his lunch in a tin pail. At seven-thirty a.m., the team of Quarter Horses left Papa's potato farm, pulling the wooden cart behind them. Father and son sat in silence. Elmer looked out the side of the cart, peering across the foggy morning grass, avoiding any interaction with Papa. Papa sat rigidly, his back straight, his arms mechanically holding the reins and occasionally flicking the whip. They rode for twenty-three minutes in silence until the Here Public Schoolhouse arose in the distance. Elmer gave a little joyful squeak. Papa grunted disapprovingly.

"Boy, I don't know where you get yer high-faluting notions. Never were grateful for a damned thing. Not a damned thing."

Silence from Elmer.

"All I know is, you ain't never were *my* son. I don't know where you came from, but you ain't never were mine."

Elmer focused on the schoolhouse. He focused on the children inside and the blackboard and Miss Anne.

"All right. Now git on with you. Git! And don't think this schooling will get you outta chores tonight, because it won't. Now, on with you!"

Elmer scooted out of the wooden cart, clutching his lunch pail tightly. He patted the closest horse on the shoulder and strode towards the schoolhouse. "I'll be back at three, sharp!" he heard Papa bellow behind him. The whip cracked, the cart creaked into motion. Elmer didn't turn around. He kept his back resolutely facing Papa, his eyes towards the future.

The first thing little Elmer noticed when he climbed the stairs of the schoolhouse and stepped through the doorway was a flurry of children, a cacophony of undeveloped voices. The second thing he noticed was her. She was sitting on the far side of the room, leaning over and whispering to a dark-haired girl next to her. The girl giggled. She giggled. A row of perfect teeth gleamed from between rosy lips and her entire face seemed illuminated by her smile.

"Daisy," Elmer whispered.

"Hey," called a ruddy boy on Elmer's left, "you lost or somethin'?"

"Yeah," chimed in a second, taller boy, "who's you? Did they find you rollin' around in a field or somethin'? Was you out with the pigs?"

"Hey farm boy," a third boy with thick-rimmed glasses piped up, stepping in front of Elmer menacingly, "nice outfit."

Elmer blushed and looked at his shoes. For the first time, he noticed the red dirt caked to the bottom of them. He noticed the grass stains on the knees of his knickers and the tear on the right hand side of his vest where he had snagged it on some barbed wire. He suddenly felt small and raggedy and much less victorious than when he left the wagon five minutes earlier. He continued to stare at his muddied shoes. Hadn't he carefully polished them yesterday? *Why, oh why, did Papa make me muck out the barn this morning? He knew this was my big day…*

The boys started to gather around him, intent on teasing him some more, when Miss Anne marched through the door and breezed past. They quickly scurried to their desks, leaving Elmer standing awkwardly by the doorway. Miss Anne turned and faced the class. "Elmer!" she shouted. Elmer jumped a little. "Get up here. We need to introduce you to everyone."

Elmer's face burned deep crimson. He shuffled slowly to the front of the room. Twenty-some faces turned towards him as he went, watching him closely with twenty-some sets of eyes. The front of the classroom loomed before him and Elmer thought about how he would rather be anywhere else in the world but there. But he inevitably reached the front of the room and he forced himself to turn and face all those blinking eyes, those judging faces. He tugged awkwardly on his tweed vest, attempting to hide the tear.

"Everyone," said Miss Anne in a voice that commanded obedience, "I want you to welcome our new student, Elmer Heartland. Elmer will be joining you from now on in your lessons and I expect everyone to be helpful and courteous to him. He may need some assistance at first to get settled in and I am *certain* all of you will represent Here Public Schoolhouse very well and lend him the help he needs." She cast a stern eye across her students. "Ok then," she continued, "I want everyone to greet Elmer now. Say 'Welcome, Elmer.'"

"Welcome Elmer," twenty-some voices chimed.

"Great. Now take a seat, Elmer. There's a free one in the back there. Right there on the far side of the room."

Elmer walked quickly to the open seat, keeping his eyes set carefully ahead so as to avoid his fellow classmates' stares. He hastily sat down and folded his hands on his lap. He watched Miss Anne as she paraded in front of the classroom, pointing at things she had written on the blackboard and periodically calling on students to answer questions. Elmer watched her, but didn't hear a word she said. He was too busy feeling embarrassed and self-conscious. He felt desperate to fit in and desperate to get out. He was so distracted by the myriad of thoughts coursing through his brain that it took him several minutes before he realized he had been seated right behind Daisy. He started slightly when his eyes focused on the curtain of golden hair in front of him. Little Elmer blushed for no good reason and tried to pry his eyes away from the back of her head and towards the blackboard. He resisted reaching out and touching the hair in front of him and he found his fingers inching towards the golden strands…

"Elmer!"

Elmer jumped so hard, his knees hit the bottom of his desk and his book crashed to the floor. Every adolescent face turned towards him, grinning and snickering at the commotion. He swallowed. "Yes, ma'am?" he asked sheepishly.

"Elmer, aren't you paying attention, boy? I asked you to read the next two lines on the board. I'll have you know that in *my* classroom, children pay attention. I don't know where your head was, but you'd better keep it out of the clouds and in the classroom. Now, read those two lines. And as for the rest of you," she peered humorlessly over her spectacles, "face forward. This isn't the circus."

At three o'clock sharp, Elmer bolted out of the classroom door and leapt into Papa's wooden wagon. His eyes stared stonily ahead as Papa clucked to the team of horses and sent the cart moving towards home. After a few minutes, Papa turned to his expressionless son and said, "So, how was it?" The question sounded forced and awkward. Elmer shrugged.

"It was all right."

Elmer spent the next couple of months avoiding most of the children in the Here Public Schoolhouse. He arrived right before lessons, steered clear of any unnecessary interactions with his peers, and left as soon as they were dismissed. Recess was the worst hour of the day. No matter how hard he tried to stay within Miss Anne's range of vision, somehow the gang of three would find a way to corner him and tease him relentlessly. It became their favorite pastime to pick out new insults to hurl at the young boy and see if they could make him lose his cool. He rarely did. If he had learned anything from growing up with Papa, it was that getting overly upset rarely paid off. So, Elmer listened to their insults, quietly acknowledged them, and waited for them to grow bored with their game and scamper off. Elmer would breathe a sigh of relief and spend the rest of the hour playing by himself. The rest of the children were terrified of getting on the bullies' bad sides and avoided Little Elmer like the plague. Elmer understood.

Since he had no friends or distractions (minus Daisy), Elmer poured his heart and soul into his lessons. When he arrived at the Here Public Schoolhouse, he lagged behind the other children in the daily lessons. He was a slow reader, knew nothing about mathematics, and couldn't spell "blackboard" or "pencil" to save his life. However, he was a quick learner and dedicated several hours each night to studying. He would light a candle by his bedside table and absorb himself in limericks and equations and the Periodic Table of Elements until his eyes became bleary and his head heavy with sleep. He usually drifted off with an open book sprawled across his lap.

Soon, Elmer was at the top of the class. Miss Anne smiled whenever his hand shot up and made sure to only call on him for the most difficult questions. He smiled back at Miss Anne. He was determined to let her know that she hadn't made a mistake in bringing him in.

Elmer's insatiable appetite for learning sustained him through the school days. It almost made the bullying and ridiculing worth it. Almost. Although Elmer was unsure if he would be able to tolerate the bullying half as well if Daisy wasn't around. She gave him a reason to keep his head up and his eyes dry when the gang of three went about their daily harassment. She was the impetus for maintaining his dignity. He wondered if she ever gave him a second thought.

In May, he didn't have to wonder anymore.

It was a sunny day and the children of Here School were spread out across the wide field in front of the schoolhouse. Many of the girls sat in a circle, playing some sort of game involving hand-clapping and excessive amounts of giggling. Most of the boys ran around and pretended to shoot each other with their thumbs and pointer fingers. "Bang!" went the finger guns. "Missed me!" shouted the boys. Elmer watched in amusement. He felt a tap on his shoulder.

"Hey smarty-pants." It was the ruddy boy. The sun gleamed off his reddish brown hair and veiny arms. "Where's your precious Miss Anne today? Not around to protect you, I see."

"Yeah, teacher's pet," mocked the boy with dark-rimmed glasses. "Where's your girlfriend, Miss Anne? Sitting in the classroom, dreaming of you?"

They sniggered. Elmer remained silent.

"What's wrong, little potato farmer? Little Spud?" continued the first boy. "Cat gotchur tongue?"

Elmer looked away and waited for the game to end. Today it didn't.

"Answer me, Spud!" said the boy.

"Yeah, answer him." The tall, gangly boy spoke up for the first time.

"Now, farm boy," the ruddy boy whispered, his dirt-brown eyes shining. "You're making me very, very angry. I've put up with your shit for long enough. You answer me when you're spoken to!"

He swung a calloused fist. It connected with Elmer's jaw.

"Ah!" cried Elmer, bringing his hand to his face. His jaw stung where the fist made contact.

"Not so tough now are you, Spud? Not tough at all!"

Another swing, this time straight to his nose. Blood spurted out both nostrils. "Aha!" the boy shouted. "Not so invincible out here, are you?" He attacked again, his straight arms shoving Elmer squarely in the chest and knocking him over. The other two hung back, shouting words of encouragement, but hesitating to jump into the fray. Elmer clutched his chest and curled up on his side, wheezing a little. Blood pooled under his cheek and turned the dusty ground into thick, red mud. The boy stood over him, blocking the sun. His shadow fell across Elmer's face. He pulled one fist back as if he were about to release a rock from a sling shot. Elmer cowered beneath him and buried his head under his arms. He braced himself for the impact. It never came.

"Stop!" a voice shouted. The shadow over Elmer's body stilled. "Stop! Stop that! Get off of him!" The voice grew louder. "What do you think you're doing, you big bully!? You might kill him! Get off!"

"Daisy, what the hell! This doesn't concern you. Get outta here!"

"No! I won't. You get away from him or I'll go get Miss Anne. I mean it." She crouched over Elmer's body, shielding him from the hovering fist.

"Jesus, Daisy. Oh alright. I'll leave you with your little boyfriend here. But this ain't over. Hear that, Elmer? This ain't over!" The boy stormed off, his posse trailing behind him.

It took Elmer several seconds to realize what had just happened. He sat up hastily and turned his head away from Daisy, hoping she didn't catch a glimpse of his tear-streaked face. His head was a whirl of emotions and he didn't know whether to feel sorry for himself or outraged or happy as a lark. In the end, he just sat their dumbly as Daisy fussed about his bloody nose.

"I can take care of it myself. Please. Don't bother." He protested.

She would hear none of it. "Oh, it's no trouble. I have my handkerchief right here and I will not have you walking around school with blood running all over your face."

"No really, I can do it." Elmer added embarrassment to the cluster of emotions crowding his head. "Just hand me the handkerchief."

"No, no. I insist. You can't see where the blood is." She wet the handkerchief with her mouth and wiped the area above his upper lip. She leaned back slightly and examined her patient. "There," she said. "All done. Now that wasn't so painful, was it?"

Elmer didn't say anything.

"You know," Daisy continued, unphased, "Most of the boys in the schoolroom are farm kids, including your nemesis there." She cocked her head towards an oak tree in the middle of the schoolyard where the ruddy boy was huddled with his two cronies. "But they would all love to be bankers' kids or kids of the candy shop owner or anything but what they are. So they pretend that they're not. They pretend that they're better than what they are. It's nothing personal, Elmer. They always gang up on the new kid. I've seen it time and again. Shame, really, how they run this school and Miss Anne doesn't even know it. Or maybe she does, but she's just as scared of them as we are. I'm not sure. All I know is that the situation has gotten plain out of hand and someone ought to do something."

"No, that's ok. Really" said Elmer quickly. "I mean, yes, something should be done, but I don't want you to get hurt. Or me," he added as an afterthought, "I don't want to get hurt anymore either. I just don't think we should meddle."

Daisy paused and looked at him for a long time. She heard the concern for her in his voice, felt the caring in his eyes. She smiled. "Ok, Elmer," she said. "I won't say anything for now, but if this nonsense continues, you bet your boots Miss Anne will get an earful. Now, come on," she said, extending a hand, "we're going to be late for class."

Elmer gently clasped her hand with his and she pulled him to his feet. His insides felt warm and fluttery. He tried to remember how to walk in a straight line.

"Anyway," continued Daisy. A cocky look spread across her face and she gave an impish half-grin. "I think those boys are more scared of me than Miss Anne anyway. I *am* a banker's kid and my daddy's done his fair share of favors for their parents. They won't mess with me if they know what's good for them."

She marched towards the schoolhouse, her head held high and her flaxen hair swinging rhythmically behind her. Elmer looked fondly after her for a moment, then shook his head and scurried to catch up. The bloody handkerchief stared at their disappearing backs from its place on the ground where they had left it.

Chapter 36

"Hey, Lucinda. It's me, Zach. Grace introduced us the other day in the library. Remember? Good, good. Say, I wanted to talk to you about something."

"Mary? Mary Parker? I thought that was you. The cheesecake looks good today, doesn't it? Not bad for a bunch of bums like us, huh? I have to keep a close eye on little Levi here so he doesn't sneak an extra piece while I'm not looking. Little rascal. So, are you sitting with anyone at lunch? Mind if I join you?"

"Hi there, sir. Allow me to introduce myself. My name's Elmer. I'm pretty new here, but Zach and Grace have taken me under their wings and shown me around a bit. You know them, right? I thought so. And your name's Nathan if I'm not correct? That's what I thought. Grace recommended I talk to you. She said you were pretty easy to get along with. Are you on your way to the library? Me too. Maybe you can help me pick out a book. It's been a while since I've read for pleasure and I can't say I know a darned thing about any of these new authors. Well, great. I'd appreciate that."

"You see Lucinda, it's getting out of hand. They're turning us against one another. They're luring in a bunch of people who are down on their luck and then using us for their own slimy purposes. I know you see it. I know you feel the same way that I do—that the Loyals are getting out of hand. Grace mentioned you felt that way. No, please don't walk away! Don't go, Lucinda. I'm not a spy. You can trust me, I promise."

"This cheesecake is absolutely divine. I haven't eaten so well in years, how 'bout you? I know it, I know it. Too bad it comes with such a price. Oh, I think you know exactly what I'm talking about. Yes you do, just look around you. *The Loyals*. They have made this place insufferable. But I know it's not their fault. Not really. They're just acting out orders sent from the top. They go to too many lectures and listen to that abominable Bookkeeper. I've noticed you've stopped attending the lectures, is that right? Now, now, no need to get defensive. Who am I to judge, honestly. I'm with you. They are a complete and utter waste of time."

"What do you think about this new Pages for Points program? Do you think it'll increase readership? Yeah, I don't doubt that it will. Sad what some people will do for a few cheap trinkets. Now, I know we are people of few possessions, but that doesn't mean we don't have a bit of pride left, am I right? I'm glad you agree. In fact, I think it's downright despicable the way they buy our loyalty like that. We aren't just numbers for Pete's sake! They shouldn't try to hold us captive in order to gloat to the other soup kitchen that they have more residents. It's nonsense. It's nonsense and I don't buy into any of it. I'm not sure about you, Nathan, but it doesn't matter to me whether I'm eating a cheeseburger at Abe's or at Ezekiel's. Six of one, half dozen of the other. What do you mean, keep my voice down? It's a free country, isn't it? Oh, all right. I just get riled up about it, you know. Well, I noticed that you just switched back from Abe's to Ezekiel's, is that right? No, I don't care. Just curious."

"See, this is exactly what I mean. You think I'm spying for them. They are sowing distrust and making us tread lightly. That is no way to live. Perhaps the kitchens started off with good intentions, but they have turned into absolute beasts. That's why we're aiming to do something about it."

"In fact, I went to a lecture just the other day and I damn near walked out. It was the first one I'd been to in a long, long time—disillusioned with them, you know—but I went for the sake of a friend. He'd never been to one before. Woo-wee! You should have seen his face afterward. I don't know if I've seen that shade of green on anything but moldy fruit. What's that? What was it about? Oh, the usual. Building a good, moral character through gratitude, compassion, loyalty. Emphasis on the loyalty. They started up a new points program for the library, have you heard? Yes, of course you have. There are signs everywhere promoting it. Sick, isn't it? And the thing is, it works. Well, I know—not on you and I, of course—but it really does work. You should have heard the whooping and hollering when the Bookkeeper rolled it out. You'd have thought that Jesus Christ himself was dropping by next week for tea. Yeah, I know it's disgusting. I'm glad you agree."

"I think you have the right to switch if you want. Heck, I've done it. And I'll do it again. Keeps them on their toes. In fact, that leads me to a little proposition that Zach, Grace, and I have been working on. You see, we think things have gotten pretty ugly lately in the kitchens and we want to send a message to the people on top. Let them know we're not done fighting, that we aren't going to sit back as they tamper with our lives. Of course it's not impossible. Hear me out."

"We have to do something about it or we'll continue tearing each other apart. We'll continue distrusting each other and breaking off into sects. That's no way to live, especially since we didn't orchestrate all this in the first place. It all comes from the top; I know you can see that. Yes, I thought you could. I know you're as fearful of the Loyals as I am. I've seen you dodging their stares. That's exactly why we have to do something. Yes, of course it has to be right now! This can't wait."

"And that's exactly why ordinary people—people like you and I, Mary—have to do something. We have to resist the machine or it will swallow us up. Lord knows, they're trying. I know. I see the look in your eyes. You're scared. You think they're too big and too powerful to resist. You're wondering what a rag-tag group of bums can do about two big, monstrous dueling soup kitchens. Well, I'll tell you Mary, we have a plan. And it's a damn good one, if I do say so myself."

"Yeah, I know it's a clever plan. I wish I could take credit for devising it, but that was all Zach and Grace's doing. Smart cookies, those two. Did you know Zach was in med school at one time?"

"So, Lucinda, that's the plan in a nutshell. Take it or leave it. Just remember Sunday is the day. Good. Well, that's great. I knew we could count on you. It's not much, but it's a start and it will certainly leave them scratching their heads. Great. I'll see you at the shuffleboard tournament later? Perfect. Ha, I don't think so. Our team is undefeated so far. Ok, see you there. Thanks for talking with me. You're a real peach, you know that?"

"Can we count you in? Great. Oh, that's wonderful, Mary. You always seemed like a real fighter to me. Now, don't be so modest, it's true. Well, let me just say that I appreciate it and little Levi appreciates it as well, he just doesn't know it yet. He *is* getting big, isn't he? Growing like a weed. Maybe I should sign up for the Pages for Points program so I can get him a new t-shirt with the E.B. crest on it. Kidding Mary, just kidding."

"So Sunday? Can we count on you? That's great. That's really great. Zach and Grace were right about you. They said you were just as sick of the bullshit as we are. Hey now, what's so funny? What do you mean, you didn't take me as the 'swearing type?' Just because I'm old, doesn't mean I've lost my piss and vinegar, young man. Ok, ok. I know you didn't mean anything by it. Truth be told, I've got a lot to learn about you young people. I've never had so many younger acquaintances in all my life. But that's neither here nor there. So, you're in for Sunday? Ok, just making sure. That's great."

* * *

The wheels were in motion. All week, Zach, Grace, and Elmer set the stage for their plan. First step: allies. They spent the better part of a day comprising a list of people they called the "Hopefuls." These were people in both Abe's and Ezekiel's kitchens who seemed fed up with the Loyals and actively avoided them. They selected their potential allies carefully, choosing only those who were clearly independent from the Loyals and who could practice discretion. Loudmouths and gossips were quickly eliminated, as well as those who seemed too timid to act. The list of Hopefuls was not long.

After they had their list, the trio began working on the second step: recruitment. They talked about the best way to approach people, what to say, and how to say it. They created a loose script and practiced it with each other. Elmer was the most nervous about recruitment and constantly ran through the script outline in his head.

...Introduction, small talk, transition to problems with the kitchens, discuss kitchens' problems, gauge level of agreement, gauge willingness to act, reveal plan if appropriate,

words of encouragement, reiterate plan details, thank you. Again. Introduction, small talk, transition…

Grace and Zach assured Elmer he would do just fine. He could recruit Nathan first. Nathan was easygoing, very friendly. A real jokester too, that Nathan.

They recruited well. Every Hopeful they approached agreed—with varying degrees of excitement—to participate in their plan. The trio's call for action was a welcomed breath of fresh air in a polluted world.

The stage was set. The actors were in place. All they had to do was lift the curtain.

Third step: action.

* * *

Sunday. Today was the day. The lectures started at 9:30 a.m. at Abe's and 10:00 a.m. at Ezekiel's. They waited for the Loyals to file past and crowd into the golden caged elevator. "Come with us," some of them encouraged. "The lecture is supposed to be especially riveting today." The Hopefuls respectfully declined.

When the last Loyal punched the number six button and clattered upward towards the chapel, the Hopefuls sprang into action.

"I'd like to check out, please. The name's Mary, Mary Parker."

"Ok. Sign the guest book then."

"Great, thank you very much."

"Hi there. Signing out. Where's the guest book?"

"Right here, sir. Ok then, have a nice day."

"Thank you."

"Hi there young fellow."

"Hi Elmer H. Going out? You too? All right then, here's the guest book. Great."

"I'd like to check out of Ezekiel's please."

"Woah, what's going on here? Is the circus in town? All right ma'am. Here's the guest book."

They checked out in three-minute intervals, a steady stream of them. Conversation was light and cordial. They smiled at the greeter's questions. They felt a little sorry for his wide-eyed innocence.

Outside, the Hopefuls gathered in a group. They were twelve. They chatted eagerly amongst themselves, excited stage one of the plan was complete. Only Zach, Grace, and Elmer kept to themselves, oddly quiet, peering expectantly up the street.

"They should be here by now," Elmer muttered.

"Patience, Elmer. They'll come."

"And if they don't? The whole thing will be ruined. The entire plan will lose its potency. At least we could supervise the folks here at E.B.'s. We haven't a clue about what's happening at Abe's. Maybe the Loyals got wind of our plan. Maybe the Hopefuls decided to chicken out at the last minute. Maybe—"

"Elmer, will you stop it! Let's just wait and see. It isn't too late yet. Have a little faith."

"Hmph," said Elmer. He crossed his arms defiantly, but didn't utter another word. The trio resumed their vigilance.

"There!" Zach broke the silence. "I see them!"

Grace shifted Levi to her left arm and held her free hand flat over her eyes to block the sun. "Oh yeah! I see them too. Elmer, I see them! They followed through after all." There was a smile in her voice and she started hopping from one foot to the other in an excited, little dance. Levi giggled.

"Well, all be," said Elmer quietly. "It's happening."

Walking towards them, chatting happily as they went, was a group of twelve—the twelve Hopefuls they recruited from Abe's. As the group approached, the residents from Ezekiel Banks' kitchen fell silent. They watched excitedly as their counterparts neared. The groups met in a great collision of enthusiasm and happiness and hope. They shook hands with each other, smiling faces beaming. They talked eagerly for a while until Nathan let fly a sharp whistle. The groups snapped to attention.

"Hey everybody! I think we owe a big thanks to our organizers here. You know we would all be sitting on our bums, twittling our thumbs and doing nothing today if it wasn't for them. Doesn't it feel good to be doing *something*? Down with the Loyals! Let's give it up for Elmer, Grace, and Zach!"

Cheers erupted. The heroes looked at each other nervously. Zach held up a hand to quiet them down.

"Ok, ok. Thank you all. We really appreciate your enthusiasm and your dedication to the plan. Things are happening and it's about time, I say."

More applause.

"But let's get one thing straight," Zach continued. "This is *not* about us versus the Loyals. We don't see them as adversaries. We see them as part of us…just a misguided part, that's all. If you're out here today because you want to wage a war against the Loyals, you might as well bow out now because you're going to be sorely disappointed." He paused and looked at the crowd, waiting to see if anyone would oppose him. No one did. He continued, "This is about the bigger picture. This is about bringing change to the top. They're the ones who hold the real power, not the Loyals. The Loyals are just pawns on their chess board. They are just the unfortunate ones who got caught up in the fervor of the kitchens and couldn't get out. They're stuck, can't you see? They're in so deep now it's hard for them to take a step back and look at their situation the way we see it. Anyway—," he paused again and looked at the twenty-three faces staring back at him, "if you're still with me, stay put. If not, please go back. We need to be singular of purpose here. We're too small to be divided. So," he straightened his narrow shoulders. Elmer had never seen him look so tall or commanding. "Who's with me?"

Cheers and whoops. Clapping of hands.

"Good, good," said Zach. "Now, I want you all to know you're part of a *team*. We are all equals here. If you think part of the plan can be improved or you'd like to see some sort of change, by all means let one of us know." He gestured to Grace and Elmer. "We want to work with you, not above you."

Heads nodded.

"Ok, now," he went on. "Let's get rolling. Time's a wasting."

The groups resumed their eager chit-chat. Zach looked at them proudly. They had all lived on the street. They all knew immeasurable amounts of pain and suffering. They had all been hungry and thirsty and penniless at some point in their lives. They had been kicked around and sneered at and ignored. They knew what it was like to be at rock bottom, to feel lower than the dirt they tread on. They were humble people. There had rarely been room for pride in their lives. Yet here they were. Standing up for themselves. Aware they could make something better. Being proactive, making change. And they were acting in cadence. A team. Zach fought back tears. His heart swelled with joy.

He stole a look at Grace. She wore a similar expression. Her eyes and smile beamed. She held Levi tightly.

Elmer took in the scene: Bright sunshine overhead, a gaggle of homeless folk gabbing and gesturing animatedly with their arms, and Zach and Grace looking over them as if they were all their children. So much had changed in a matter of months. He would never have imagined himself associating with such a group of people. But that was before. Now, anything was possible. Elmer smiled at the thought.

Anything is possible.

Zach walked over to a member of Abe's group and pulled her aside. She was lanky and dark and wore several large, faux gold necklaces. Elmer looked at her willowy limbs and thought of Maggie. He wondered how she and little Zach were doing. He wondered if she had made peace with The City.

Zach and the woman exchanged a few hurried words. She gave a little nod and immediately began darting around, gathering her group together. Zach did the same. Soon, they were once again separated into two collections of Hopefuls. The groups smiled and waved, some blew kisses. And then they were off. The E.B. group marched towards Abe's Kitchen; Abe's group towards E.B.'s Kitchen.

Elmer walked in the back of his group, listening to the hum of chatter and the steady click-click-click of his cane. Soon, Abe's lengthy kitchen stretched before them. The chatter halted. They quietly approached the heavy wooden doors.

"Ok," said Grace in a hushed voice. "You know what to do. One person every three minutes. We're running on a tight schedule now. Today's lecture will be over shortly. Ready? Lucinda, why don't you go first this time. Ok. Go."

They entered the building one at a time, smiling at the greeter in her purple velvet coat. She made no comment as they entered, but eyed them suspiciously. The Hopefuls settled in, carefully grouping themselves in twos or threes so as to avoid extra attention. Grace hopped on the moving sidewalk and took Levi to the library. Zach started up a card game with one of the other Hopefuls. Elmer took a nap. He was exhausted.

* * *

"That's it?" Lucinda had said. "That's all there is to your grand plan? You're simply going to gather two teams of people—one at Abe's, one here—and have us switch kitchens every week? Sounds a little simplistic to me."

"Yes, but that's the beauty of it," Zach countered. "It's subtle. It will take them a while to catch on. They're used to looking at us as numbers. Since we'll be switching the same number of residents from each kitchen, the only way they'll notice the change is if they finally look at us as people."

"Ok, but I still—"

"And that will freak them out. They'll have to go back to their guest book, figure out when the switches started happening. Then they'll check their surveillance cameras. They'll realize we're leaving or arriving every three minutes. They'll see we're organized. Stealthy. Quietly rebellious. Believe me Lucinda, it will cause panic. I can't wait to see if unfold."

Lucinda looked at him. Quiet understanding shone in her eyes. She nodded slightly.

"So, Lucinda, that's the plan in a nutshell. Take it or leave it. Just remember Sunday is the day."

"Sunday," she repeated. "Ok." Her eyes glinted like steel and she held her neck and shoulders a little straighter. "I'll do it."

"Good. Well, that's great. I knew we could count on you. It's not much, but it's a start and it will certainly leave them scratching their heads."

"That it will. Yes, you can certainly count me in."

"Great. I'll see you at the shuffleboard tournament later?"

"You know it."

"Perfect."

"Your team's going down this time," she teased. "We're going to send you away whimpering with your tails between your legs."

"Ha, I don't think so. Our team is undefeated so far."

"We'll see, we'll see."

"Ok, see you there. Thanks for talking with me."

She smiled and patted him on the shoulder. "Any time, Zach. Any time."

He grinned. "You're a real peach, you know that?"

* * *

Abe's Bookkeeper sat in the tower, licking his lips and wiping his greasy fingers with an elegant silver napkin. The napkin stained dark grey where his fingers had touched it and he tossed it away after a few wipes into a bin on the floor. Dinner had been satisfactory tonight. Quite satisfactory. One of the attendants had delivered a steaming plate of baked parmesan chicken, boiled potatoes, steamed asparagus, and hot apple cider to the door. They set the tray down on a ledge, turned a dial, and watched as the tray was taken away by conveyor belt into the forbidden room beyond. As soon as the room had swallowed the tray of food, the attendant scurried away nervously, tripping a bit as he rushed through the door that led to the golden mosque. The Bookkeeper watched amusedly on a surveillance screen.

"Oh, how they quiver," he said to himself. "Oh how they quake with fear when they approach Abe's tower." He smiled smugly and allowed himself a glance in the wide gilded mirror on his right. A toffee-colored face stared back, lined from many years of frowning. His eyes were wide-set and dark. They glared back at him in the mirror.

"Yes. Yes," he thought. "That is a face to be feared. That is the mouth that delivered today's lecture. Those are the eyes that looked upon a sea of devote faces. There must have been at least seventy or eighty Loyals at the lecture today. At least. That's good. That's very good. Attendance has been strong. I intend to keep it that way."

He gave himself one last look in the mirror, wiped away a few crumbs clinging to the white strands of his beard, and turned back to his plate. He stabbed a piece of asparagus and shoved it into his gaping mouth. He didn't bother to close his mouth when he chewed. He was the Bookkeeper.

"Attendance has been strong," he mused, "but Ezekiel's Bookkeeper has been scheming. He started a new program. Brilliant, those programs. We must do something similar, and quickly. We are losing our edge. Yes, our spa is better equipped. Yes, our place of worship is more spectacular. But we aren't appealing to the human nature of consumption. Everyone loves free merchandise. Everyone is still a kid at heart, a kid who longs to be surrounded by candy and toys." He frowned at his fork. "But we can't just copy Ezekiel. We'll be seen as unoriginal. Boring. Yesterday's news. No, it must be fresh. We must appeal to that base instinct, the instinct to consume. Kid in a candy shop," he thought. "Kid in a candy shop..."

His eyes lit up. He banged his fist on the table. "That's it!" he said out loud. "Oh, it's brilliant." He picked up his mug of apple cider and began to slurp it down, mulling his plan over, working out the details. He slapped the mug down on the table, slopping some of the liquid over the edge. Droplets of cider nestled in his thick beard like morning dew in a spider web. He wiped them away with his sleeve. Again, he turned and looked at himself in the mirror. "Bookkeeper," he said waggishly, "you've outdone yourself again." He admired his reflection, smoothed a furry white eyebrow. "No time to waste," he said, leaping to his feet. He strode across the room to an ancient looking telephone. As he reached for the dial pad, he admired the ring that stuck out gaudily from his right index finger. It was twenty-four karat gold and encrusted with several small, exquisitely-cut rubies. It looked expensive. It looked powerful. The Bookkeeper pulled his hand away from the phone for a moment, gave the ring a loving stroke and a smile, and reached to the phone again.

He dialed. A female voice answered. "Yes, Ophelia? Hello. It's the Bookkeeper. Yes, all is well. I'd like you to arrange a Council meeting for me. The usual crowd. Tell them it's regarding an upgrade I'd like to make to the facility. Yes, tomorrow evening would be splendid. Right. Please let everyone know immediately. Tell them it's urgent. Excellent. Thank you, Ophelia. Let me know when everyone has been contacted. Ok, great. Goodbye."

He hung up the phone, let his hand linger under the light so his jewelry glittered obscenely, then shuffled back to his dining table. He arranged his hip bones on the wooden chair and attacked his asparagus once again. He muttered to himself, "Yes, attendance has been strong. Attendance has been strong. I must keep it that way. I must."

* * *

Another Sunday. Another switch. The groups smiled as they parted ways again. Abe's to Ezekiel's, Ezekiel's to Abe's. The Loyals hadn't suspected a thing. But that was to be expected at first. They were anxious to see what would happen the second week.

The greeters gave them exasperated looks as they signed in. "Back again?" asked the curly-haired youth at Ezekiel's. "Just couldn't stay away, could you? Well I don't blame you. I wouldn't want to be stuck with the heathens over at Abe's. Just beastly, them." The Hopefuls nodded and signed the guest book. They prepared to settle in for another week.

Another week. It passed by slowly. The Hopefuls counted the days, the hours, until Sunday. They tried to distract themselves, to numb their minds with television and food and board games, but despite their efforts, they often caught themselves looking at the clock. Time ticked on and little action was had. Occasionally a Loyal would approach one of the Hopefuls. Their palms would start to sweat, their pulse would quicken. They envisioned a barrage of questions and accusations. But the barrage never happened. Instead, the Loyal would make an off-handed comment about how it was nice to see them back at the *proper* kitchen and then be on their way. They hadn't caught on. They had no idea. It was driving the Hopefuls nuts.

Another week. More comments from the Loyals. More strange looks from the greeters. They were still none the wiser. The Hopefuls spent obscene amounts of time at the gym and in the library. They watched hours of television and breezed through dozens of board games. They were the most active people in the kitchens. They were aggravated and irritable. They could hardly take it. *Something* had to happen. Nothing did. Just the slow, cyclical passage of time. Another day, another night. Another breakfast, another lunch. Eat, play basketball. Calories gained, calories lost. If they paused, they would hear their hearts beating, hear their loud breaths as the air rattled around in their lungs. Their bodies were tense, waiting. They watched the Loyals out of the corners of their eyes, wondering when their switching pattern might dawn on them. Tense, waiting. "How about another game of backgammon?" one would ask. "Sure," another would answer. They would play with their shoulders hunched, their heads bent closely over the pieces as if their lives depended on a win. Tense, waiting.

Another week.

* * *

During the uneventful weeks, Elmer kept mostly to himself. He hadn't enough energy for socializing. He wasn't in the mood. He even kept his distance from Grace and Zach, despite their constant pleas for company. "Maybe later," he would tell them and slip off to whatever bedroom he claimed as his own that week. They would watch him go, their worried eyes on the back of his neat sweater as he hobbled away. But they never pursued him. They understood that something outside of their little clan, outside of the kitchens, outside of City B, outside of the present time, was eating away at the hunched, old man. They worried from a distance, but they always let him go.

Elmer would slip into his bedroom, click the lock into place, crawl into bed, and close his eyes. He would not sleep. Instead, he would think. He spent hours upon hours thinking during those empty weeks. Things were troubling him. Events from his past had somehow wended their way through the labyrinth of his mind and ended up, tangled and frayed, in the present. He attempted to detangle. He attempted to figure things out. He cursed the past for haunting him, for knotting up the creases in his brain.

His restlessness had started much like the restlessness of the other Hopefuls. He was excited and anxious. He waited impatiently for something to happen. When nothing did, he felt a void, a kind of strange emptiness. It seemed like a hollow pit had been dug into his head, like a deep well. His mind rushed to fill the void. Soon, his head was soggy with ancient memories and forgotten feelings. It started with a dream.

Elmer could feel the vague stirrings of the past rising in the back of his mind. He suppressed the stirrings. Slammed a door in their face when they came knocking. But the stirrings were strong. And the void wooed them with its hollow siren song, lured them into the abyss. "Fill me," it sang. "Fill me with your memories." The past burst through his closed door while he was asleep.

It began in church. Elmer knew it was the church from his childhood, but it wasn't the same. The wooden walls had been replaced with gold—shining, ornate, pure gold. It glittered immodestly as it caught the sun peaking through the tall, narrow windows. At the front of the church, the humble, square altar was now covered with gems and rhinestones, as if it had been covered with glue and dipped in a treasure chest. But Elmer could still see the rough-hewn oak underneath the veneer. It peaked shyly through the cracks of its elaborate covering. Behind the altar, a large portrait caught Elmer's eye. He studied it carefully. It was a woman—that much he could see—but her face was blurry and featureless. A long, blue veil flowed behind her like a waterfall and she seemed to be reaching out, stretching her arms towards the world beyond her frame. Instinctively, Elmer reached back towards her, answering her call for someone's hand.

A sound. Whirring. Then the creak of a door. Voices. Many voices buzzing behind him. Elmer turned. The aisles were conveyor belts. They slowly moved a gaggle of stiff church-goers towards the front of the room. The church-goers chatted happily amongst themselves, showing no sign of seeing the old man who stood awkwardly in the front. They wore their Sunday best—long dresses and suit coats, bow ties and giant, floppy hats. Elmer tried to look at their faces, but they were as featureless as the portrait behind the altar.

Eventually, the church-goers piled into the pews (they must have, anyway. Elmer didn't see it happen, but everyone was seated when the priest arrived). A burst of flames appeared behind the altar and a golden caged elevator rose, clattering out of the floor. The church-goers applauded. A man stepped out of the elevator and took a bow. The priest. Elmer gasped. It was the same man who led the crowd in their chant of "Judgment Day!" right before they covered him with thick, black dirt. But he looked different somehow. His bright green eyes were more beady. His face older. Bits of spittle clung to the corners of his mouth. The priest smiled. The golden walls reflected in his polished teeth.

"Today," he began, "we have the rare privilege, the rare *opportunity* to be in the presence of a sinner!"

The crowd gasped, a collective inhale that sucked the moisture from the room. Elmer licked his lips. He suddenly felt very small, like a young boy.

The priest continued. His voice was loud and echoey; it bounced off the lofty walls. "Today, we will teach that sinner about the value of *confession.* For, that is what all sinners must do. They must confess their sins to the Creator. They must offer up their black smudges so they may be cleansed, so they may be wiped clean. They *must* confess or they are doomed to be cast down into the fire! Cast down with the rest of their kind! Cast down with the filth! Do you not agree?"

"Yes!" they replied. Their voices were neither male nor female. Just sound. "We agree."

"Good. Shall we bring the sinner to the front? Shall we hear his confession? Shall we see if he is worthy of forgiveness?"

"Yes!" they replied in cadence. "Show us the sinner."

And Elmer was caged in the golden elevator—which had somehow moved to the front of the altar—and sat stonily on display for the church-goers, waiting for judgment. He wasn't sure how he got there, but he knew he was trapped. He knew it without rattling the bars or trying the door. He wasn't going anywhere. He quivered with fear and looked at the endless sea of blank faces.

"Your sinner!" the priest shouted, waving his hand at Elmer as if he had just said, "and now...your Brand. New. Car!" The crowd shrieked and hooted and stamped their feet. Elmer wasn't certain if they were still humans or if they had morphed into something different all together. His head started spinning.

"Now, sinner," the priest cooed, "confess."

"Confess!" the crowd shouted. "Confess, sinner! Confess!"

Elmer's eyes were wide and watery. He blinked them and tried to focus on the church-goers, but it was no use. They blended together in a mass of skin.

The crowd started chanting, "Confess, sinner! Confess! Confess, sinner! Confess!"

The priest smirked and was suddenly very close to Elmer's face, exhaling raw breath, eyes dancing playfully. "Yes, sinner," he whispered. "Confess." He held his right index finger towards the audience. Their mouths clamped shut. Silence filled the chambers.

"Our sinner has much to confess," the priest asserted, glaring at the caged Elmer. His mouth foamed white. "He has abandoned his Creator; he has abandoned His house. He has left his wife—his wife to whom he was sealed through God's hands. He has ignored the Sabbath day. He has befriended heathens. He has not been *Loyal.* He has *refused* to sign his last name in the guest book!"

"Boo!" the crowd shouted. "Down with the sinner!"

"AND," the priest thundered, "to top it all off, he has committed *Murder!*"

The word rang throughout the chambers of the church. It hit Elmer's ears with a metallic thud. "NO!" he protested, turning wildly towards the priest. The word filled the air like a persistent breeze, purring: *murrrder, murrrder, murrrder.* "No!" Elmer cried. "It was an accident! I never—" He searched for words. They didn't come. His tongue felt heavy in his mouth. His words stuck in his throat.

"Ha!" the priest shouted. "The sinner cannot defend himself! Even so, the grace of the Creator is great. Maybe he will forgive him yet. Sinner," he turned sharply towards Elmer, striking him violently on the back, "on your knees!"

"Confess, sinner! Confess! Confess, sinner! Confess!" the crowd chanted.

"Yes sinner!" the priest chimed in. "Confess!"

Elmer opened his mouth. He wanted to say something, anything. He wanted to defend himself. He wanted to cry out. He even wanted to confess. Nothing happened. His mouth opened. He tried to squeeze out words. Only a low hiss wheezed from his lungs. It sounded like a tire with a slow leak.

The priest laughed, high-pitched and forced. The crowd laughed too.

Elmer looked at them desperately, willing them to let him free, silently begging them to show mercy.

Again, the priest spoke. "If the sinner will not confess," he said, the corners of his mouth bubbling now, "then to the chamber he goes!"

Another animalistic uproar shook the crowd. They shrieked with glee and tossed their heads.

"To the chamber!" the priest repeated, pointing a stiff arm towards the floor.

The elevator creaked to life and began slowly descending into the floor.

"No!" Elmer tried to shout, emitting the same hiss.

The elevator continued, sinking down, down into the floor. Elmer looked up. He exhaled sharply; his eyes widened. Two gigantic hands, female, were placed on top of the elevator, pushing it down with mammoth force. Elmer tried to scream. His mouth flapped mutely. He looked past the hands, up the arms, and into the face of the enormous woman perched over him. The face stared blankly back, a blurry square of canvas. Arms stretched out of the painting and grasped the elevator. They still looked desperate and searching, as if reaching for a companion. Elmer wanted nothing to do with them anymore. He turned away.

The priest's voice returned to him, shouting above the din of the crowd, "To the chamber! To the chamber the sinner goes!"

Elmer looked down. The chamber. It loomed in front of him, a gigantic room filled with strange objects. He blinked. Suddenly, the room was a fitness center. The walls were lined with people, running, running, running on machines resembling hamster wheels. They didn't smile; they didn't stop. The machines whirred and hummed. They kept running and running. No destination, just movement.

The elevator stopped. Elmer looked up. The hands drifted away, back towards the painting. She was distant now, but somehow Elmer could still see her clearly. Her face. It had changed. It was no longer featureless, but wore the hollow, empty eyes of the girl in his former nightmares, the girl who was Irene and Daisy and Hilo all at the same time. He gazed up at her, trying to discern her identity, wondering what name to call her. But she defied classification. The lines of her face morphed and shifted like sand in a windy desert.

The elevator was on the floor now. It opened slowly. Outside, an empty hamster wheel stood, golden and shining, waiting for Elmer. "No!" he shouted, his voice returning with a burst of volume. "NO!" His arms and legs were shackled now. He found himself on a conveyor belt, moving closer and closer to the wheel. It rocked slightly back and forth, squeaking sharply. The belt moved. Elmer shut his eyes. He felt himself moving. Closer and closer to his chamber.

* * *

"Come on, Elmer. We're playing Hearts today. You love Hearts."

Elmer shook his head, "No, thank you. I'm feeling a little tired. You'd better go ahead without me."

Zach and Grace exchanged a look. Grace shrugged, "Suit yourself, Elm. You know where to find us."

"Yes, I know."

Elmer made his way to the fifth floor, found his room, locked the door, laid down on his back as usual. He stared at the ceiling. He sighed. The dream had invaded his sleep one week ago and it still lingered, as fresh and acute as when it occurred, in the front of his mind. It consumed his thoughts. On a typical day, Elmer usually spent half his time ignoring the dream, beating it back into submission and the other half his time confronting the dream, thinking about it, attempting to unravel its meaning. Now, he thought about it.

So many layers. So many layers of meaning. That priest. Pale and chilling. With beady eyes like the Bookkeepers. Green like Papa's. Like my own. Golden walls.

Shimmering like Abe's mosque. A thousand pounds of gold. Woman. That haunting woman in the portrait. Reaching out. Reaching out to me. For me? No. To me, I think.

He kicked off his shoes and crawled, fully clothed, under the covers. He brought the blanket up to his chin and closed his eyes. The image of a sea of people, dressed in their Sunday best, filled his head. They roared and stomped. They hooted and shrieked.

Like wild animals in a zoo. Like caged beasts… But I was the caged one in the end.

He smirked. *Good grief, Onyx and Cecelia and Craig would have a field day with this dream. What a mess.*

His mind drifted to a set of hands, pale and smooth, placed gracefully but firmly on the sides of the elevator. *Her featureless face. The face that continuously changed. Morphed. Peered out with strange eyes from the canvas. That face.*

He paused. His mind always lingered on her. Somehow, despite the countless symbols and curiosities in his dream, he always returned to her. She was the key. He just knew it. She was heart of the dream, the impetus *for* the dream. She was the one that haunted his thoughts, filled his mind. He had felt her presence before the dream—vague, but huge. Like oxygen in a room, she had coated his mind subtly, invisibly. He had ignored her in the past. Breathed in, breathed out, let the oxygen pass through his lungs, into his red blood cells. But now she had a form. She had manifested herself into a shape, a great and foreboding shape.

Elmer shuddered. *The women of my past. The women I've betrayed.*

It wasn't the first time this thought had passed through his mind. He thought of the torturous night at the Keys' home. He thought of the wild, hollow eyes of the young girl—the girl who attacked him over and over again. That was the first time she came to him in human form. He felt the chill of her cold eyes, saw the flash of the knife in her hands.

Again, he shuddered. *The women of my past. The women I've betrayed.*

She was bigger now, more commanding than the first girl with hollow eyes. She filled an entire wall. She had powerful hands that could crush him if they desired. And she refused to stay in her frame. She was much bigger; she would not be ignored.

"I'm sorry," Elmer whispered. "I'm so sorry." The blank eyes stared back.

He shook his head and focused his thoughts on the rest of the dream. He ran it through his mind, frame by frame, reliving it in its entirety. Together, they carried the overwhelming stench of the past, mixed obscenely with the present. *The past and the present collide in this dream. They are seamless. Ezekiel's Bookkeeper and Papa are married in the priest's body. The church of my childhood lined with Abe's golden walls. The caged elevator. The fitness center. The conveyor belt. The call to confess. Confess! That was the call of my childhood. I've tried to forget it, but I guess the guilt still lingers on.*

Elmer adjusted his blankets and closed his eyes even tighter. One line repeated itself over and over in his head. *The past and present collide. The past and present collide.*

He opened his eyes slowly. Subtle awareness dawned on him. *The images. The mix of past and present.* Elmer stared at a smudge on the ceiling. He felt an epiphany growing, coming to a head. "Yes," he whispered. "That's it. It seems so obvious now."

He kept his eyes focused on the smudge, wondering vaguely about its origins. "The past and the present collide. That's the theme of this dream. That's what it's trying to tell me. I am to make peace with the past." His confidence grew. His epiphany reached its climax. "I am to make peace with the past," he said a bit louder.

Elmer lowered his eyes. The message felt worn and familiar. He wondered if he knew it all along. He wondered if the dream was merely an expression of his subconscious, the culmination of separate thoughts and feelings he had attempted to suppress. They would not be suppressed. They had risen up like a tidal wave and flooded his world. The suppressed thoughts and feelings had taken on a life of their own, rebelled, shook him to the very core. Elmer marveled at their ferocity.

"Make peace with the past. Make peace with the past," he repeated. "And she—" he paused. The portrait of the woman with the blank face and the flowing veil appeared to him in his mind. She seemed so lonely, so sad and desperate for company. He smiled tenderly. "—she is the key." He felt confident in this assertion and he said it again, just to hear the words roll off his tongue, just to hear their truth. "She is the key."

He lay in bed a while longer, letting the dream imagery wash through his head as it pleased. *Now what? Where do I go from here? I have the what, but not the how. How do I make peace? How do I make it up to her? To them?* His mind went blank. He felt drained. Hollow.

Eventually, Elmer got up. He shook the legs of his pants and straightened his sweater. He breathed in deeply, breathed out. He picked up his cane and skipped out of the room, feeling lighter than he had in a week. He didn't have the how, but he did have the what. He knew he had to extend an olive branch to the past. He knew he had to make peace. The how would come later, he was certain. He lingered in front of his reflection in the hallway mirror, pondering.

Elmer, lad. Maybe you didn't interpret a dream after all. Maybe you've simply uncovered the hidden thoughts and feelings you've carefully tucked away and buried over the years. Maybe you're digging a little. Maybe you're starting to be honest with yourself.

He nodded at the reflection in the mirror. Honest with himself. He liked that thought. Elmer adjusted his glasses, gave himself a little wink, and continued down the hall. He wondered if the others were still playing Hearts.

Chapter 37

"Today is the day!" Abe's Bookkeeper proclaimed, an enormous grin poking through his beard. He looked across the crowded dining hall. Their faces turned towards his, enraptured. "Today is the day!" he repeated. "The unveiling. The revealing of a new improvement in Ibrahim Anbar's Soup Kitchen. I know you have seen the commotion in the gift shop this past week. You have witnessed the bustling around, the whirring of table saws and the pounding of hammers. You have wondered what all the fuss is about. Well," he paused, gauging his audience's reaction, "Today IS the day!"

Applause, somewhat tentative. They applauded because they were confident in the Bookkeeper, in his benevolence. He would not lead them astray. So they applauded.

"Brethren," the Bookkeeper continued, raising both hands to silence them, "you know as well as me the reason for such an improvement. You know why your beloved kitchen undergoes such changes, such enhancements. It is because Abe *understands.* Abe cares about you and your comfort. He is concerned about your happiness and wellbeing. Brethren," a dramatic pause, "Abe *loves* you."

Clapping hands, a few sniffles. They dabbed at their eyes with handkerchiefs. It was good to be loved.

"Because Abe loves you," the Bookkeeper went on, "he has decided to give you all a little treat. He has seen your *faithfulness.* He acknowledges your *loyalty* to this kitchen. And Abe is a firm believer in rewarding goodness. That is why," he paused and looked over his flock; he made a grand gesture to a plum-colored curtain on his right, "we are opening the *very* first Soup Kitchen Candy Shop!"

The curtain opened to the tinkle of light piano music. It was drowned by applause. A shimmering, metallic countertop faced the crowd, surrounded by bin after tub after jar of candy. Different colors and shapes. Tantalizing saccharine smells and alluring designs. They shrieked with excitement. Theirs was truly the superior soup kitchen. Theirs was the one, true leader, the *only* leader. And they were the chosen ones, the ones who would surely receive the Reward. It was obvious. Why would they ever stray?

The Bookkeeper grinned, smoothed one wispy, white eyebrow, and nodded curtly to a group of people in the back of the dining room. "The

Council," he thought. "They had doubted. They didn't believe that such a small thing as a candy shop would increase kitchen loyalty. Look at them now." He smirked. "They wear the sheepish expressions of children in dunce caps."

The Council members stood sullenly in the back, avoiding eye contact with the Bookkeeper. They didn't appreciate his self-satisfied grin, but in the end, he was right. There was no denying that. He understood the whims of the people, understood what motivated and charmed them. Something as simple as a candy shop—who would have thought?

The crowd continued applauding, craning their necks to have a look at the shining bins of candy. They were eager to sample them, to feel silky chocolate or tangy gumdrops in their mouths."Why?" they asked themselves, "Why would they ever stray?"

The Bookkeeper once again addressed the crowd. They fell silent. "Worthy allies," he said, "my heart gladdens at the sound of your applause, your *support.* And I'm sure our generous benefactor also appreciates your joy. Now, some of you are probably thinking to yourselves, 'Yes, this is a wonderful gift, but how am I to pay for such treats?' To you, I say worry not! Abe has already addressed your concerns. He is sensitive to your every need; he knows what is in your hearts. Our generous leader has asked me, once again, to be the ambassador of good news. He has asked me to tell you, brethren, that you will not pay a dime for your candy, not a single dime!"

The Bookkeeper smiled at their joyous faces; his toffee-colored skin tingled with elation.

"No," he continued, "instead of dollars, you will pay in deeds. For every show of loyalty to the kitchen, you will earn a token. For every day you stay in Abe's kitchen, for every friend you recruit to join us, a token will be yours. We will call this program Tokens for Treats and it will be grand! It will ensure that every resident is duly rewarded for his or her loyalty to this kitchen. Because Abe believes you should be rewarded. Because Abe believes you are worth it. I ask you, esteemed allies, is not your kitchen the best? Is not your kitchen the greatest?"

Through the raucous applause, one sound cut through the air—the sound of laughter. It cackled brazenly, rising and falling sharply and shocking the ears of everyone in the room. One by one, the audience became aware of the sound and turned towards its source. A hush fell over the crowd. The

Bookkeeper knitted his brows; his mouth pursed sourly. The moment had been ruined. The atmosphere of unabashed joy had suddenly turned rotten and cheap. "Who is the perpetrator," he wondered. "Who dares to desecrate my moment? Who dares to shit on my success?" He scanned the audience for the ruffian, the one who would surely be punished for their reckless interruption. His eyes settled on a small figure towards the back, bent and frail, clutching her sides and screeching with laughter.

"My!" she laughed, her soprano voice crackled slightly, revealing her age. She shook her head. "If that isn't the silliest thing I've ever heard! Woo!" She laughed and laughed, head back, shoulders shaking with each exhalation. The Bookkeeper's eyes narrowed.

"Pray, madam" he addressed her, his voice tense, "tell me what in heaven's name is the matter. What is the cause of this unseemly outburst? Please. Enlighten me."

"Woo!" the woman shouted again. "Enlighten you? You, the all-knowin' Bookkeeper? You need some enlightenin' eh?" She doubled over with laughter.

The Bookkeeper knotted his fists into tight balls. His mind raced, "If only she wasn't so damn old," he thought darkly. "I can't just call security. That would reflect poorly on Abe's Kitchen. No, this must be dealt with delicately." Again, he addressed the woman, the strain in his voice obvious, "Madam, it seems you have suffered a nervous breakdown. Our medical staff will be happy to assist you to the Wellness Center. Free of charge, of course. I will call them right away, madam, and I can assure you that you'll be treated with only the best of care." He picked up a small receiver and prepared to dial the medical staff, prepared to eliminate the threat. Again, the stooped woman interrupted.

"Nervous breakdown?" she hooted. "No, siree! I don't think so. I'm sound of mind, alright. Sound as they get. I was only laughin', I was. I was only laughin' at the spectacle b'fore me. Isn't it funny?" She placed her hands on her hips, steadying herself as her body once again shook with laughter.

"Stop that! Stop that I say!" the Bookkeeper was getting desperate. His dark eyes looked rabid. In the back of the dining hall, the Council smirked and shifted nervously. Part of them wanted to jump to the Bookkeeper's aid, to preserve the sanctity of the kitchen they supported. But a greater part of them was fed up and disgusted by the Bookkeeper and his power, so they sat back and watched him squirm.

A stray lock of steel-grey hair had fallen out of the old woman's bun and she licked a finger to plaster it back. She had stopped laughing. Now, she was staring down the Bookkeeper with the eyes of a tiger, menacing and fierce. "Stop that?" she said calmly. "I could say the same to you." The crowd was spellbound by the tiny, fiery woman. They couldn't take their eyes off her. She continued, "I could tell you to stop treatin' us like sheep. I could tell you to stop competing with E.B.'s Kitchen. I could tell you to cut the bullshit." A few people gasped; the Bookkeeper seethed, his body shaking like a volcano ready to explode. "Stop that? The nerve," the woman went on. "You're the one luring us with candy, like a pedophile in an unmarked van."

Nervous laughter. The Bookkeeper couldn't bear it any longer. He reached down and pushed a button on a small device on his side.

"Candy. Really?" she continued. "I've never witnessed anything so hilarious in m' life. I knew you all were desperate—always trying to claw yer way ahead—but I didn't think you'd pull a cheap stunt like this one. But honestly, thanks for the laugh. I haven't laughed that hard in—hey! Git off me! Git, I tell you! What's all this about? I can't speak m' mind? This is still a free country! A free country I tell you!"

"But not a free kitchen," the Bookkeeper thought darkly. "This kitchen is mine."

The two burly security men tugged on the woman's arms. "Come with me, ma'am. This way."

"NO!" she screamed. "I won't go!"

"Ma'am, we can do this the easy way or the hard way, now come on."

"No!" she said and threw a punch at one of their stomachs. It hit with a soft thud. She threw another and another, a thump-thump-thump of tiny fists. The man laughed.

"You're a feisty one, aren't you? Now come along." He stooped down to her level, wrapped one arm around her waist, and threw her—kicking and flailing—over his shoulder. She hung like a gunny sack, angrily pounding her tiny fists into his back. The guards shook their heads and ambled out of the room. Her screams could be heard echoing down the hall mixed with grunts of "Lemme go! Put me down, you brute! You've no right! No right at all!"

The crowd in the dining hall looked at each other nervously. They weren't sure what to think of the outburst or her words. They stood awkwardly, like children waiting to be dismissed from class. The Bookkeeper broke the silence, smiling at them a little too widely.

"Friends," he said in an overly cheery voice. They stared silently back. "Our medical staff will treat that poor woman well. She is clearly out of her head. Delusional. She cannot see the obvious truth that Abe loves us, that he would do anything for us. This candy shop is merely an example of his love. It is not the entirety. This is but a miniscule sampling of Abe's unending love for all of you. So, enjoy your treats. They are a gift and Abe feels you have earned them. They are your prize for loyalty. Come on! Step up to the counter! Sample some of the finest candy you've ever tasted—a gift from our benevolent leader. Come on! Don't be shy!"

The crowd hesitated. They were not much in the mood for candy anymore.

"Come. On." The Bookkeeper commanded.

They obeyed.

Dotted amongst the crowd, the Hopefuls watched the other residents jostle their way towards the candy counter. It had taken every ounce of their will power not to jump to the old woman's aid. They had watched helplessly and mutely as the goons hauled her away. They cringed with every cry of "Let me go," but kept their eyes focused straight ahead, mouths glued shut. The Bookkeeper had gone too far this time. He had overstepped his bounds. He had taken away one of their own—one of the Hopefuls—a frail, old woman who simply had the guts to speak out. Their anger bubbled beneath their skin. Yes, the Bookkeeper had gone too far. They had to do *something.* They were tired of sitting back, desperately willing the Loyals to notice their coordinated switches. Sunday. Tomorrow. The next switch. They would speak with the organizers then, let them know that the game was changing, let them know that lines had been crossed, decorum had been violated. Let them know they were ready for action. For war.

The Hopefuls nodded politely to each other as they reached the candy line. Their lips remained sealed, but their eyes burned. The Bookkeeper had messed with the wrong old woman.

* * *

Elmer was feeling better. He still thought about the dream, but he did not dwell on it. It didn't weigh on his mind and haunt his thoughts like it had during the first week. Now, he viewed it with mild detachment and occasionally reflected on the larger message it presented: make peace with the past.

Grace and Zach noticed a change right away. They breathed a sigh of relief and turned their attention towards the Hopefuls. They knew it was hard on them—almost four weeks worth of switches and little action. They saw them pacing nervously, biding their time until someone (anyone, absolutely anyone!) would take notice of their pattern and alert the Bookkeepers. It never happened. The Hopefuls sighed and continued to distract themselves.

Almost four weeks. Tomorrow they would make their fifth switch. Back to Abe's. Grace and Zach were also growing weary of the constant back and forth. Levi was growing irritable and put up a bigger and bigger fuss with each Sunday that came along. "Stop it, Levi," Grace would say in her even, calm voice. "Stop lying there on the floor. Time to get up and be a big boy. We're going to the other kitchen today. Won't that be fun? Now, come on. You don't have a choice, young man." Levi would wail and pound his fists into the ground and stick out his tongue. Before the last switch, he hid inside the library and Grace spent almost an hour tracking him down. She dreaded tomorrow. She braced herself for the inevitable tantrum. She shook her head. What kind of a mother was she? This was her revolution, not Levi's. She had forced it on him. Hot tears welled in her eyes and she quickly brushed them away. She wanted to quit, to give up and go far, far away with her son. It wasn't an option. So she steadied herself for another Sunday. Another switch.

* * *

"What in Heaven's name was that?" hissed the tall Councilman, his swarthy skin creased angrily and unattractively across his brow. He followed Abe's Bookkeeper down the moving sidewalk, step-stepping quickly behind him in order to keep up with his quick stride. "This is an embarrassment to us all! To the entire kitchen! You blundered this time, Bookkeeper. We all witnessed it. None of us are happy and I would *hope* you would want to keep your Council members—your greatest financial backers—happy." He dragged out the last word, forcing the Bookkeeper to cringe slightly and halt his step. The moving sidewalk whirred along.

"Listen, Mo," he snarled, "it's not my fault. You were there. How would *you* have handled the situation differently? She was openly challenging my authority, challenging this entire institution."

"She was a harmless old lady!" Mo retorted, looking down into the Bookkeeper's eyes. He stood at least a foot taller than the Bookkeeper and was twice as broad. Abe's Bookkeeper looked up into the dark brown eyes that glared irately into his. His lip trembled slightly, but his voice was even when he spoke.

"Harmless? Harmless!" he said. His voice sounded shrill and hysterical. His eyes rolled madly. "An outburst like that could set us back months! Months and months! Do you have *any* idea what it takes to build a loyal following like the one we have? Do you? Hmm?" He made an airy coughing noise in his throat that conveyed exactly *how* disgusted he was with the Councilman. "No," he sneered, "of course you don't. You haven't a clue how I do it, how I gain the unwavering loyalty of our residents. All you do is dump a pile of money at my feet and tell me to get to work. An indentured servant is all I am! A slave to the Council. You have no appreciation for what I do. None. And then you try to tell me I handled this situation incorrectly. Sir, you have *some* nerve." He grunted and crossed his arms, vaguely looking over the fitness center as they passed it by.

The Councilman dropped his voice. It exited his throat as an ominous rumble. "Did I hear you correctly, Bookkeeper? *All* we do is throw money at you? That's it? Perhaps it is *you* who do not appreciate what *we* do. You may be the voice of this kitchen. People may recognize you here, even revere you, but in the end what do you have? A trained army of vagabonds. We, on the other hand, control the community. We rally support for Abe's Kitchen. We run fundraisers, raise awareness for our deeds, build an outside support group that attends your lectures, that empties their pockets to uphold the good works of our kitchen. Our kitchen. Not Ezekiel Banks' Kitchen. Abe's Kitchen. You rely on us *just* as much as we rely on you. And let me tell you something, oh *esteemed* Bookkeeper. You are replaceable."

"Ungrateful bulbous rat!" the Bookkeeper screamed. His face flushed bright red beneath his beard. Beads of sweat stood out from his forehead. "You can't replace me! I'm the Bookkeeper. I've kept this position for years. I've been here since the founding of Abe's Kitchen. You can't just replace the Bookkeeper! I'm like gold to you!"

"I thought the Council was the currency and you were just the poor, pitiful servant. You're mincing words, Bookkeeper."

The Bookkeeper growled, but said nothing. He was out of breath and fuming. "How dare this cocky Councilman tell *me* what to do," he thought. "How dare this lout question the authority of the Bookkeeper. He's got some nerve."

"Bookkeeper," the Councilman sighed. He steadied his voice and attempted to sound civil, "we should not quarrel. When it comes right down to it, we depend on you and you on us. It is a symbiotic relationship that should be respected. Today has been hard on us all. Let's take the night off, mull this over, have a Council meeting tomorrow and discuss the whole thing. What do you say?"

The Bookkeeper knew the Councilman was extending an olive branch, that he was weary of arguing and wanted to make amends. He also sensed fear in the Councilman's eyes. He knew the Councilman was well aware of his value. He knew that he—the all-knowing, ever-wise Bookkeeper—could not simply be replaced according to the whims of the Council. The residents adored him. He was, after all, the mouth of Abe, was he not? No, the Councilman knew he should tread carefully. And the Bookkeeper knew he would continue to get whatever he wanted as long as he continued to prove his worth. He smiled to himself—a wet, sloppy smile, fortunately half-hidden under his white mustache and beard.

"Attendance is up, you know," he said casually to the Councilman. "Highest levels in years."

* * *

It was Sunday morning at Ezekiel Banks' Soup Kitchen and the Loyals were headed to chapel. Today's lecture was going to be a real treat, they had been told. They had caught wind of some happenings at Abe's, happenings that clearly demonstrated the superiority of E.B.'s Kitchen. As if they needed proof. They laughed and chatted as they strolled to the lecture. It was going to be a good one, they just knew it.

The Hopefuls watched them go. They too had heard the rumors of a small riot at Abe's. They ached for the details. They watched the clock and waited impatiently for their reunion with the other half of the Hopefuls' troop. Three minutes—three minutes—three minutes—three minutes. Grace decided to go last today. She sat in the dining room, calmly stroking Levi's hair, bribing him to be still with a cookie she had saved from yesterday's lunch. He munched; she sat, her eyes on the clock. Finally, her turn came and she moved gracefully towards the door, long skirt swishing around her, limbs moving like a dancer's. She threw a fetching smile at the young woman—a new face at Ezekiel's Kitchen—who guarded the guest book like a frightened terrier.

"Ma'am!" she wheezed, her fingers nervously entwined. "Don't forget to sign the book."

Grace nodded, reached out a smooth, thin arm and signed her name with an equally smooth, thin signature.

The girl watched her over thick-rimmed glasses. When Grace finished, the girl plucked the gold-encrusted pen out of her hand and tucked it into her pocket. "Can't lose this," she explained. "Not during my first week, anyway."

Grace smiled warmly at the girl, said nothing, and pushed her way through the heavy oak doors and into the daylight. The rest of the group waited. She sensed the tension among them, heard it in the nervous chatter and shifting of feet. They craved action, Grace knew. They hoped for thrilling news from Abe's. She didn't blame them. She also craved action, longed for a revolution. But she didn't get her hopes up. Why set oneself up for disappointment? At any rate, they would find out soon enough the details of what happened. Until then, she would focus on the sunshine, the friends at her side, and the three-year old on her hip. Those were the things that were real at that moment. They were the things that would remain, that would not falter through bad news, good news, or no news at all. She hugged Levi tighter. She felt lucky.

The group shifted nervously. They glanced down the sidewalk, waiting, waiting. Even after four weeks, this part of the switch always made them nervous. They had upheld their end of the plan, but what if the others did not? What if they had grown tired of the constant back and forth rigmarole? It was possible, you know. They had thought of jumping ship themselves, so why not the others? They watched and waited. Finally, someone spotted the partner clan of Hopefuls pacing down the sidewalk. They breathed a sigh of relief. As the group neared, however, they noticed something was amiss.

They weren't as chatty as usual. They weren't smiling. Instead, they looked wooden and grim. Silently, ominously, they approached their sister group and came to a halt. They stood awkwardly for a few moments, waiting for someone to speak. Finally, a spindly woman stepped forward, dark skin shining in the afternoon sun, golden necklaces clanking together. She cleared her throat.

"It's Eleanor," she said solemnly. "They took her away."

The Hopefuls murmured amongst themselves, concerned looks etched across their faces.

"It happened just yesterday at the grand opening of Abe's Candy Shop. She was too vocal. She said the whole thing was despicable—the way they were coercing us into loyalty through sweets. She said they should stop treating us like sheep, that they should stop bullshitting us. She went on quite a little tirade—even compared the Bookkeeper to a pedophile."

The laughter was strained. The woman continued her story.

"Anyway, they took her away after that. Two big thugs. One lifted her little body right onto his back like a sack of potatoes. She put up a good fight, that Eleanor. Kicking and screaming and raising hell. We were all proud of her."

The group from Abe's nodded, their lips tight together, their eyes trained to the ground.

"She hasn't been seen since," the tall woman whispered. A sob caught in her throat and she swallowed it down. "We think they've taken her away," she continued. "We think they've carted her off somewhere and dumped her. Can you imagine? A poor, helpless old woman like Eleanor?" Tears welled in her eyes and she turned to the nearest Hopeful on her right and threw her arms around his neck, sobbing into his tee-shirt. He patted her on the shoulder and returned the hug. They stared in silence for a moment, then—

"Un-fucking-believable!" It was Nathan, Elmer's first recruit. He stomped his foot irritably and tugged at his short, reddish beard. "How? How could they do this to a sweet, old lady like Eleanor? She was like a grandmother. And now she's in God-knows-where with nothing at all and no way out. I can NOT believe this shit! I just can't!"

"Nathan." Zach's bass voice rose over his. "Calm yourself. What happened is unfortunate—very unfortunate—but complaining won't help things. Eleanor is a smart woman. She lived on the street for years. I'm sure she will be able to survive on her own for a while. Besides, we're smart people; we can come up with a way to get Eleanor back, but we have to go about this business wisely. We have to continue to keep a low profile. Don't you see? Right now, we have an opportunity—an unprecedented opportunity. Abe's Kitchen has been caught in a moment of weakness. I say we capitalize on that. I say we raise a little hell!"

They cheered and Zach went on. "But we have to be delicate. We have to use the scalpel, not the cleaver. Eleanor's actions—as brash and careless as they were—created doubt in Abe's Kitchen. Everyone must have heard her accusations; they saw the way she was treated. A little fear and uncertainty *must* have been planted in their brains. They *must* have noted the brutality and force the Bookkeeper used to silence the complaints of an old woman. I'm sure it shook their beliefs...despite being bribed with this—what is it? A new candy shop?"

The group from Abe's nodded. Zach rolled his eyes. "Good grief, that *is* pathetic. Anyway, you see my point. The residents of Abe's have seen the ugly side of their beloved kitchen. It is up to us to keep that ugly side alive and apparent to them. Let's open their eyes. Let's give them reason to be outraged, to be discontent. I want to see them demanding change! I want to see rage so powerful that the Bookkeeper and his cronies will be forced to listen! Let's make it happen, Hopefuls! Let's do this!"

They cheered, dancing around in the noonday sun. "Yeah!" some of them cried. "Let's make this happen!" They talked excitedly amongst themselves, anxious to create some havoc, excited for action. Passersby would not have guessed they were the same group from fifteen minutes before—the group that had stood sullenly and grimly, on the brink of despair.

Zach, Grace, and Elmer watched them and breathed a sigh of relief. The fight wasn't over. They still had their soldiers. Zach squeezed Grace around the waist and cleared his throat loudly. Eventually, the crowd of Hopefuls hushed up and turned towards him, their faces eager and expectant.

"Now, I hope you all know this is going to take a lot of work. It isn't going to be easy to shake the Loyals from their stance. Remember, they are used to having Abe's back through thick and thin. They are used to calling people who criticize him 'infidels' and 'faithless.' We have our work cut out for us. We have to earn their trust, give them a reason to listen to us. I know we can do it."

Heads bobbed up and down in agreement.

"I have some ideas," Zach continued, "but I'm going to need your help. Twenty-three minds are certainly better than one." He stopped speaking for a moment, looked up at the friendly, cloudless sky. "It's a beautiful day. Why don't we push our schedule back an hour and spend some time out here brainstorming?"

They nodded in agreement.

"Excellent," said Zach. "There's a grassy spot over there with a couple of big oak trees for shade. I hope no one minds sitting on the ground—we haven't gone *that* soft yet, have we?"

They tittered. The kitchens may have spoiled them with gourmet meals and feather-soft beds, but it hadn't taken away their memories. Sitting on the ground would never seem all that bad compared to the trials of homelessness. It would never seem bad compared to begging for change or rooting around in trash bins or sleeping under cardboard. They smiled as they nestled into the grass. They felt good. They had never felt so free.

Grace approached the grass slowly, staring at her feet, thinking. They remembered their lives on the street, of course they remembered. But she knew they had changed. Maybe they hadn't gone soft yet. Maybe they could remember their raw toughness and face the streets once again, but why would they want to? Why would they want to go back to a life of pain and cold and hunger once they had tasted sweet freedom? Why would they choose suffering if they could help it? She thought of the day, not so long ago, when she was talking to Elmer and Zach after the Bookkeeper's lecture. She had compared herself to a wild animal who had forgotten how to hunt. "Well," she thought, "maybe I got it wrong. Maybe we really haven't forgotten how to hunt. Maybe we have just lost the will. Why hunt if your meat is served to you—marinated, grilled, and on a platter—each and every day? What's the point?"

"Grace!" Zach called. "I saved a spot for you over here. Come on!"

"Ok," she said quietly as she walked to his side. "Thank you." She sat down.

* * *

"I call this meeting to order!" bellowed the Bookkeeper. He sat in a high-backed chair in a circular room on the seventh floor. Ezekiel Banks' Council sat around the glass-topped table, wheeling softly back and forth in their office chairs or drinking decaf coffee or chatting quietly with their neighbors. "Order!" the Bookkeeper repeated, this time bringing a wooden gavel down onto the table with a loud rap. The chatted ceased. The Bookkeeper glared. "Good," he said. "Now, to business."

He looked around the room, taking in their faces. The usual crowd was here tonight, sitting in the same chairs as always, but a few new members had joined them this week. "Recruitment must be going well," the Bookkeeper mused. "Excellent." They stared at him with rapt attention, their heads cocked slightly, poised for optimal listening. The Bookkeeper stood up, his small frame dwarfed by the large chair behind him. The Council was reminded of a tiny prince trying out his father's royal throne. The Bookkeeper ran his beetle eyes around the room silently, building up to the moment when he would start his speech. He loved this dramatic pause, this calm before the storm. He inhaled slowly, watching their eyes take him in, watching them linger on the edges of their chairs, waiting for something to happen. The corner of his mouth twitched happily.

"Faithful friends," he began. The Council breathed normally again. "Welcome to tonight's meeting." He paused again, shorter this time. "I am so proud," he continued in a syrupy voice, "to witness such faith, such sense of purpose amongst you all. I really am." He smiled widely, like an old woman fawning over her cats. "You have aided our success in this fight, this mission, to be the *best* soup kitchen there is. Your unwavering loyalty and support has led us to have the most successful quarter ever. The books don't lie, friends. The books tell it exactly how it is. And how it is is grand, friends! Just grand!"

He beamed at the Council. They nodded and silently wondered who ever used the word "grand" anymore.

"Friends," the Bookkeeper went on, secretly disappointed they hadn't applauded. They were a tougher sell than the bums. "As most of you know, this meeting was called on special terms. We are not here tonight to wrack our brains over retaining more residents. We are not here to question the loyalty of our precious little vagrants. No. We know attendance is up. We know our street bums are loyal. The Pages for Points Program has been going swimmingly—better than anticipated—and we expect it to continue to hold weight for some time. No, friends. We are not gathered here tonight to scheme. We are gathered to celebrate! We have countless reasons to celebrate and embrace our position as the *superior* soup kitchen!"

They smirked and applauded politely. They didn't cheer and holler with wild abandon like the residents—they were Council members, after all. They were dignified and educated. They conducted themselves with the proper decorum of high society. Because that's what they were—the upper-middle class, the people who made decisions. They were the ones who sat at the front of the airplane. They were the ones who took piano and voice lessons. They owned townhouses with expensive artwork and billiard rooms and bedroom closets bigger than most people's living rooms. They had a designated person to attend to every part of their lives: their travels, their finances, their homes, their cars, their hair, their dogs' hair, their gardens, their fitness, their pools, their weddings, their deaths…No, they didn't cheer and holler.

"Not only are our numbers and retention outstanding at the moment," the Bookkeeper said, his chin jutted out, a cocky expression captured his face, "we have also caught wind of a leetle, itty-bitty incident that happened over at leetle Abe's Kitchen." He said the last part with a strange, mocking accent that caused the Council members to unleash a few silly giggles. The Bookkeeper leered at the crowd, terribly pleased he could illicit that kind of reaction from this particular group of people. They were eating out of the palm of his spindly, white hand.

"You may have heard about the incident I'm referring to—," he continued, the self-satisfied grin still plastered across his wrinkled face. "—the one where Abe's Bookkeeper ordered a batty, old woman to be sent away. I believe she was picked up by his goons—kicking and screaming I was told."

Again, the Council giggled. They couldn't help themselves. A few of them coughed or pretended to take a long drink of water in order to hide their giddiness. It wasn't proper, you know, to act so childish in a public setting.

The Bookkeeper paused, allowing the group to settle down and regain their rigid postures, their somber stares. He could still see the grins thinly masked behind straight-lined mouths. "This is proof, friends," he said, "that not only are we the best, our only competition is faltering. They are foolish and weak. They have grown careless. They will surely lose members due to this latest blunder and we will surely gain whatever they lose. Brace yourselves, friends. Brace yourselves for the Golden Age of Ezekiel Banks' Soup Kitchen. It is here!"

Cheers. The Bookkeeper couldn't believe it and neither could they. What had gotten into them? They were the Council. Separate from the animals that lived in the soup kitchen. Much more dignified. Yet here they were, leaping from their seats and applauding the Bookkeeper's speech with vigor and enthusiasm. What, oh what, had gotten into them? The Golden Age. That had to be it. They liked the sound of that very much. They liked the way it had rolled off the Bookkeeper's tongue—smoothly and naturally—as if it had always been, as if it was obvious that that was their kitchen's fate. A Golden Age. Of course they would prosper. Of course Ezekiel Banks' Kitchen would flourish and grow until the kitchen of Ibrahim Anbar would be nothing but a speck of dust in the wind, a crushed bug on the windshield. Golden Age. When they thought of it, they shivered. They were a part of it. They had supported the making of this masterpiece and now it was here, the Golden Age, and there would be no stopping them. They smirked to themselves. The cheering, the applause—it did, after all, make sense. They were on the cusp of a new era. If they couldn't celebrate now, when could they?

They cheered. The Bookkeeper nodded and bowed, his toes tingling with the excitement of the applause he had roused. He waited patiently for the commotion to die, for the last pair of hands to stop slapping together. He addressed the crowd again, "Allies," he said, raising a wine glass that had suddenly appeared by his elbow, "I would like to make a toast." The Council members grabbed a hold of the petite wine glasses that had materialized by their sides. "The servants are fast and efficient here," they thought to themselves. "That is quite pleasing."

The Bookkeeper kept his glass raised, ensured that all eyes were focused on him, and continued. "This is a toast to our benefactor, Mr. Ezekiel M. Banks, whose generosity and unparalleled intelligence has led to the creation of the world's greatest soup kitchen. If it were not for his constant supervision, his nimble mind, his deep understanding of the human condition, his admirable innovation, his greatness of spirit, *and* his steadfast loyalty, we would have no reason to celebrate today. He is worthy of all praise and accolades we bestow upon him. He is the maker, the beginning of our humble kitchen and he will support and sustain it for as long as he lives. So friends," he raised his glass a little higher, sloshing some of the deep cherry-colored liquid over the edge, "I ask you to please raise your glasses and join me in toasting the one and only, esteemed, magnificent, Ezekiel Banks!"

"Ezekiel Banks!" they chanted. They raised the glasses to their lips and drank deeply. The circular room rang with the timbre of their voices. By the time they wiped their lips and set their glasses on the table, rows of delicate hors d'oeuvres and tiny plates had been set before them. "Most pleasing," they thought as they filled their plates with the proper amount of food.

They set about talking and eating and taking tiny sips of wine. The atmosphere was light and snarky—just how they liked it. They half-paid attention to their neighbors as they prattled on about their children's soccer team and spouse's kidney problems. They remembered that the hedges needed trimming and the dog's fur was growing over his eyes; they made mental notes to call the gardener and the groomer tomorrow.

The Bookkeeper watched them with beady eyes narrowed in hawk-like observance. The Council liked to think of themselves as separate from the residents, a different breed. But they weren't so dissimilar. They were all willing to be persuaded, ready to believe. They all liked to think of themselves as members of a larger organism, an organism that is stronger and better than all other organisms. An organism that will win in the end. The Bookkeeper grinned and leaned back in his tall chair. He felt the crushed red velvet brush against his skin and he shivered a little. "They may be different animals," he thought, "but they all feed from the same trough."

* * *

The signs started to appear that Monday. Handwritten, tacked to the wall with tape, they shouted at passersby with big, bold letters. Hastily, unceremoniously, they were ripped down and hurled into trash bins. They reappeared with the same haste. This time, there were more of them. They littered the halls, the bathrooms, the fitness center. They were wedged between books at the library, deposited into video cases in the commons areas. They jumped out from around corners and behind closed doors. The residents were bombarded by the plain white paper and black ink signs.

Their minds raced and their skin itched as they thought about the messages scrawled across the paper. They were uncomfortable. They felt like they had entered a strange, hostile land. They were unsettling, those white-paper signs with black ink. Unsettling…

Dinner was served late on Monday; the staff was preoccupied with its mission of search and destroy. They hunted down every sign they could find, crumpled them up, tossed them away. Later, when they found the crumpled signs smoothed out and re-taped to the walls, they started shredding them. The sign-makers were efficient and wily. They replaced the shredded signs almost instantly and left the staff growling and grunting with frustration.

On Tuesday, security was on high alert. They patrolled the halls menacingly, seeking the gad flies that had invaded the kitchen and were nipping at its carcass. They would be caught, there was no doubt about that. And they would be punished. They combed the video cameras, attempting to pick out the rabble-rousers. They were terribly crafty, those rabble-rousers. You had to give them that. A herd of people would amble nonchalantly in front of the camera, leaving in their wake a string of signs. It was impossible to pin the blame on one person. Their actions were muddled and incoherent. They were like a great, rambling octopus who kept seven of its eight legs to itself while the other one was quietly wrecking havoc. It made security livid. They scratched their heads and hoped the trouble-makers would slip up soon. Wednesday would be the day; surely they would catch them then.

The residents spent three days alternately reading and avoiding the signs. They feared their messages, disagreed with their content. They suspected someone sinister was behind them and yet they were intrigued. They found it difficult to look away. With each passing day, they found themselves more uncertain with their beloved kitchen. They were nervous and jumpy. They didn't know who or what to believe. And the signs showed no mercy. They continued to plague them with hand-scrawled messages.

"NO MORE LECTURES. NO MORE MIND CONTROL."
"ABE'S KITCHEN: PROFITS BEFORE PEOPLE"
"ELEANOR WAS RIGHT!"
"DON'T BE SHEEP. THINK FOR YOURSELVES."
"STILL TRUST THE BOOKKEEPER?"

Some of the Loyals aided the staff in tearing down the signs. They patrolled the halls, glaring indiscriminately at everyone they encountered. No one could be trusted. They were all potential enemies—enemies of the Bookkeeper, enemies of Abe. And yet, the Loyals couldn't help but read the signs as they ripped them from the walls.

"HAVE YOU EVER SEEN ABE?"
"ABE'S KITCHEN: SPOON-FEEDING YOU MORE THAN SOUP."
"FACE THE FACTS—THE REWARD DOESN'T EXIST."
"BRING ELEANOR BACK!"
"DON'T TRUST THE BOOKKEEPER. (HE DOESN'T TRUST YOU)."

Elmer watched the chaos ensue. He smiled jovially at the Loyals as he passed them on the moving walkway in Abe's Kitchen. Things were happening. He was having a ball. The Loyals narrowed their eyes and pursed their lips as he passed. "Yes," they thought, "even a frail, old man cannot be trusted."

Elmer rode the moving sidewalk to the spa and wellness center. A Tai Chi class was in session, but it would finish in exactly two minutes and thirty seconds. He stepped off the sidewalk and glanced at the clock over the classroom door. Two minutes to four o'clock in the afternoon. Excellent timing. The ballroom dance class started immediately after Tai Chi and a queue of people waited impatiently outside the door, stretching, practicing their steps, making small talk. Elmer hovered by the door, pretending to read a yoga magazine. He kept his eyes straight ahead, not daring to glance at the young woman stretching her hamstring on his left or the bearded man stepping into the back of the queue on his right.

The clock ticked. The Tai Chi class came to a close. "Bye everyone," the instructor said in a serene voice. "Until next time." They piled out of the classroom, bumping elbows and gym bags, avoiding the mass of people waiting outside the door. This was the moment. Elmer tossed the magazine aside and sidled up to the herd of people exiting the room. Out of the corner of his eye, he saw the young woman and the bearded man join him. They all veered left, creating a block of humanity between the wellness center wall and the probing security camera that hung across the room. They walked as one organism, heel to toe, making it nearly impossible to tell where one human being ended and another began. When they reached the end of the wall, they scattered. Some jumped onto the conveyor belt sidewalk, some returned to the ballroom dancing class, some sat down in the nearby lounge chairs and began to thumb through the latest gossip magazines. The signs stared at them from the wellness center wall. Sign after sign. Bold, black letters on white paper. They smiled and went about their business, every now and again sneaking a glance towards their handiwork.

Elmer smiled as the moving sidewalk carried him to the dining room. Success. He would wait in his designated spot until he knew the details of the next sign posting. Lucinda would tell him. She was his messenger. Before the Hopefuls left their sunny spot on the grass and stepped back into their respective kitchens, they set up a system. The system consisted of a chain—a human chain—where one person would deliver a message to another person, that person would forward their message to the next person, and so on. The chain started with Zach and ended with Elmer. Everyone in between had an assigned person to whom they would deliver Zach's message. The messages were kept simple and to the point. The system worked beautifully.

The last message Elmer received was "Wellness Center, four o'clock." He nodded at Lucinda after she casually relayed the message. They then sat down at a table and played a quiet game of Backgammon. Quiet, but tense. Elmer could feel the muscles in his shoulders become taut with stress as he imagined the Hopefuls posting the next round of signs. He was a bundle nerves. He was part of a revolution, an uprising meant to challenge the status quo and strike down inequity. He felt proud.

The Backgammon game ended at a quarter to four. Elmer and Lucinda silently put it away and said their goodbyes. "So long, Lu," said Elmer. "I'll see you later." "So long, Elmer," she replied, blue eyes shining. "I'll beat you next time, I promise. You mark my words." They smiled at each other and Lucinda walked away towards the moving sidewalk, eyes towards the Wellness Center. Elmer adjusted his hip bones in his chair by the fireplace. He stared at the rows of games that lined the corner shelves. Row after row. He glanced at a clock. *Almost time.* He looked over his shoulder towards the moving sidewalk. Lucinda was out of sight. *Soon, soon.*

At seven minutes to four, he strolled across the dining room and onto the conveyor belt sidewalk. His hands quivered with excitement and he steadied them by grasping the railing with one, his cane with the other. He trained his eyes straight ahead towards the Wellness Center, towards the next round of signs. Finally they were doing something. Finally the Hopefuls were getting noticed. Elmer beamed. He stepped off the moving sidewalk and glanced at the clock over the classroom door. Two minutes to four o'clock in the afternoon. Excellent timing.

* * *

Elmer sat in the chair in the corner of the dining room. His designated spot. He pretended to eat a turkey and potato casserole, but his mouth wouldn't chew, his stomach grew tense and rejected the idea of food. Instead, he pushed the casserole around and around his plate, pausing every now and then to look at the clock overhead. *Maybe this is why Papa never owned a wristwatch. It's maddening to watch the seconds tick by, the hands slowly revolving to mark the passage of another minute.* He stabbed a piece of turkey and then buried it under a heap of potatoes. *When I was young, I was told it is a sin to waste food. But many things were sinful then.* He glanced back at the clock. Another revolution completed; another minute ticked by. *Almost five o'clock. Where is she?* He closed his eyes and tried to sleep. He heard the persistent tick-tick-tick of the clock. He cupped his hands over his ears and tried to focus his thoughts elsewhere. He took a slow swallow of water. He got up, stretched his legs, sat down. He toyed with the idea of going to the bathroom, but didn't want to risk missing his messenger. *Five-thirty. Where is she?* He played several games of solitaire. He eavesdropped on a conversation amongst several young residents at the table behind him. They whispered about the posters, asking each other what they thought of them, sharing their opinions in hushed tones. Elmer smiled. Things were happening. *Six o'clock. Good god, Lucinda. I hope nothing is the matter.* Six-thirty. Seven o'clock. Elmer gripped the arms of his chair, his knuckles turning white from the strain. *What is going on? Where are the others? I hope they're ok.* He thought of Grace, lovely Grace, with a presence like his Maggie, cradling little Levi in her arms. *What if they've sent them away? Oh god, oh god, oh god. I can't bear this…*

"Hello, Elmer." The low voice came from behind him and he quickly whirled around in his chair, nearly tumbling out of it.

"Zach! Thank god! What's happening? Is everything ok? Where are the others?"

"Don't worry, Elm. Everything will be fine. Just a small hiccup. Nothing unexpected. Come on, we're meeting in the library."

"Ok," said Elmer uneasily. He didn't like how Zach had skirted around his questions. A knot was growing in his stomach. "Ok," he repeated and followed Zach towards the moving sidewalk. They rode to the library in silence. Zach didn't offer any information and Elmer didn't ask for any. They stepped off the sidewalk and into the library. Tall shelves ringed them, displaying the multi-colored spines of books. Tables and over-stuffed chairs nestled themselves amongst the shelves and in the corners, creating hidden coves for those who wanted a bit of privacy, for those who needed an escape. Elmer gazed at the rows of books, at the elegant rolling ladders that clung to the shelves, daring him to climb. The libraries were his favorite spots in the kitchens. He felt safe inside their walls; he felt free to think, free to breathe.

Elmer followed Zach to the door of a small conference room on the far side of the library. He turned the handle and stepped through the frame. Frenzied voices filled the space. They mixed together and assaulted Elmer's ears with their clashing staccato rhythms. He walked into the room, seeking an empty chair. The voices halted; the barrage of sound ceased. Elmer and Zach sat down. At the head of the conference table, Grace balanced Levi on her knee. She nodded to Elmer and Zach as they came in and then turned to the rest of the Hopefuls seated around the conference table, their backs rigid, their eyes darting. "Let's get right to it, shall we?" she said, as soon as the hush had fallen over them.

Heads bobbed in agreement.

"Ok," she said. "For those of you who don't already know, Nathan has been taken away by security."

Elmer gasped. The rest remained mute. He realized they already knew, that Grace was passing on this information solely for his benefit. She was a wonderful, sweet person, that Grace.

"At the six o'clock sign posting," Grace continued, "only eight of the twelve Hopefuls showed up. It was not hard to figure out where the chain had been broken. It ended with Nathan. Lucinda tells us she saw security taking him away, marching him down the sidewalk at about a quarter to six."

Lucinda nodded gravely. Elmer was slightly miffed she hadn't passed this information along to him, but he also understood the panic she must have felt when Nathan passed her by. It must have been terrifying. Grace's voice cut through Elmer's thoughts, "At the moment, that is all we know. We are hopeful that Nathan is still within the walls of this building, but we can't be sure. We need to act quickly to guarantee his safety. We *need* to turn ourselves in."

"What? No!" someone shouted. The rest murmured angrily. "Turn ourselves in?" they said. "That's not what Nathan would have wanted."

"Ok, settle down," said Grace standing up. She handed Levi off to Zach so she could stand up and place both hands on her hips, visibly asserting her authority. "Listen. I'm open to other suggestions, but I've turned this over again and again in my head and I believe it is the only thing that makes sense. We don't want another Eleanor on our consciences, do we? We don't want them to take Nathan away and drop him off in a field somewhere, do we? I know I couldn't live with myself and I'm certain neither could any of you. Now, look. If we all turn ourselves in at the same time, what are they going to do? They can't banish us all. It would be too obvious. I think we wield the power here. I think we've got them between a rock and a hard place. If they throw us out, people will notice. They will see what happens to dissenters. They will note the treatment of anyone who disagrees with the kitchen. But if they keep us around, they will spend their days in fear, wondering what kind of shenanigans we will pull tomorrow. It's excellent, isn't it? We've got them. We've backed them into a corner. I'd like to see how they can weasel their way out of this one without meeting our demands."

The angry murmurings stopped as soon as she began speaking. They gazed at her in awe. They look around at themselves. It was true. This was happening. They, *they*, had the power now. Amazing.

"And another thing," Grace went on, "I don't think we should make the switch this Sunday. I think we should hold our ground and stay right here."

"Yes," they agreed. "Good idea. We're with you, Grace."

"Good," she answered. "One of us can check out of the kitchen, go to Ezekiel's, and relay the message. That person can also report on the progress the other Hopefuls are making over there. I'm curious to see if their Operation Eleanor went as planned."

They nodded. Elmer raised his hand.

"Yes, Elmer?" Grace said.

"I'll do it," he replied. "I'll check out of the kitchen and relay the message to the other Hopefuls."

"That would be wonderful," said Grace. "It's settled then. Alright," she looked across the room, taking in the excited features of the Hopefuls. "Let's turn ourselves in then."

A sharp knock on the door interrupted the meeting. "Open up!" a husky voice called. "Security!"

"Well, Grace" said Zach, shrugging and giving her a half-smile, "Looks like they're meeting us halfway this time."

"How generous of them," she replied. They chuckled and opened the door.

* * *

"How in the good Lord's name did this happen?" thundered Freddie Keys, his arms wobbling as he threw them into the air. "Just last week, we was toastin' our success, the dawn of our Golden Age. Now we're scramblin' to control the dirty bums from takin' us over! You've got some tough questions to answer, Bookkeeper."

"Yeah," said a chorus of voices behind him. The Council usually didn't let Keys speak. He was too undignified, too crass. He didn't understand the refined mannerisms and subtleties of the upper-middle class. He was new money. But he was money nonetheless. And he was wildly devout. They usually tolerated him, ignored him, and took his money. Today they allowed him to speak. It showed the Bookkeeper *exactly* what they thought of his authority, it showed him *exactly* how much respect they held for him. The Bookkeeper heard the message loud and clear.

"Sit down, Keys," the Bookkeeper growled, terribly annoyed. "I'll call on comments from the Council later."

"Later!" Keys exclaimed, eyes bulging over his sagging cheeks. "We've had enough of later. We want answers now! In't that right, Council? We want answers now!"

"Yes, now!" they said, pleased at the spectacle before them. Keys created wonderful entertainment when let loose at the proper time.

"Oh Jesus, Mary, and Joseph," the Ezekiel's Bookkeeper muttered. "What is there to tell? No one could have predicted this. It just sort of…happened. The bums went nuts. Nothing to explain."

"We heard that the vagrants have been plotting for weeks," said a shrill female voice from the back. "We heard that they've been switching kitchens every Sunday to show their disrespect for our facilities. Why Bookkeeper," she glared at him accusingly, "was this never addressed?"

The Bookkeeper sighed. So they had heard. His greeters had reported some fishy check-outs for the past few Sundays, but it seemed like useless paranoia at the time. After all, the numbers hadn't changed. Enrollment was steady. But after this week's riots, they had gone over the books once again. They found the pattern immediately. Every three minutes. The damn bums had checked out in three minute intervals every Sunday. The same ones returning the next Sunday. It was enraging. He hadn't bothered to look at their names in the past—why go through the trouble—but suddenly it was important to know exactly who had been fucking with them, who to punish.

"That," said the Bookkeeper, "was an unfortunate oversight."

"Unfortunate!" Keys shouted, his body jiggling with rage. "I'd say it's unfortunate. Bums makin' a mockery of our kitchen. Poor bookkeeping if I ever saw it, that's what it is."

The Bookkeeper drew himself up to his full, miniscule height. His bookkeeping had just been called into question—by Keys no less—and he took great offense to it. "Sir," he said, his voice calm and chilling, "be seated."

There was no room for argument, even Keys knew that. He sat down hastily, his great sides drooping sullenly over his chair. The Bookkeeper addressed the Council, maintaining the same icy tone.

"What has happened—is happening—at our kitchen is unfortunate. We can all agree on that. But bickering and placing blame will get us nowhere. We are in a moment of crisis. It doesn't pay to be divided at this time. Look, the bums have gotten out of hand. So what? It has happened before. We merely have to put them in their places. Subdue them. Make them sorry for ever dreaming to cross us. Do I make myself clear?"

They nodded stiffly. Damn this Bookkeeper. He still wielded power and they knew it. There would be no punishing him for his mistake, no putting him in his place. In the end, they needed him. They were loath to admit it, but it was true. They needed the Bookkeeper.

"Good," he continued, eyeing them carefully, scrutinizing every turn of their heads, every shift of their feet. "Then let's move on and discuss the situation at hand." He drummed his fingers together and collected his thoughts. "What we have at the moment is a band of deviants who are doing their best to stir the pot. They are not the norm and they know it. They are trying to rally the residents against us by pointing out our 'misdeeds' and 'shortcomings' with those damn signs. I'll admit, dropping them off the elevator was an excellent way to distribute them. Residents were shoving them in their pockets and stockpiling them in their bedrooms before our staff was even aware of the situation."

"I heard they formed them into paper airplanes and sent them sailing over the crowd during Tuesday's lecture!" called a wiry man in the back with dark, balding hair and a pencil-thin mustache.

The Bookkeeper rolled his eyes. He had hoped the Council would be less informed. "Yes. Yes, they did that too. And," he added, "some of them shouted 'For Eleanor!' as they did it, which leads me to believe that the little piss-ant lady over at Abe's was the inspiration for our troubles. It seems that some of these bums cannot distinguish between our great soup kitchen and the cheap imitation next door. Can you imagine?"

The Bookkeeper laughed, a great guffaw from his narrow belly. The Council laughed too, but it sounded strained.

The Bookkeeper took a gulp of water, stroked the hairs sprouting sparsely from his face, waited for the Council to resume their silence. He spoke again, this time softer, as if he was letting them in on a great secret. They leaned forward to catch his words. "The situation seems curious, does it not? Doesn't it seem curious that these self-righteous hobos have plagued *our* kitchen with their uprising. After all, the little piss-ant—this Eleanor broad—had her little outburst at *Abe's*, not here. Why, then, would we feel the brunt of the vagrants' wrath? Why would they unleash their anger on us? We have done nothing to incite their rage."

The Council murmured, their heads bobbing thoughtfully.

"The answer, friends, is simple. We are *not* alone in our troubles. Abe's, too, has suffered from the bum Eleanor's outburst. What we are witnessing here is just *one-half* of a two-front attack. The other half is being carried out at Abe's. I have it on good authority that the bums have employed precisely—well, almost precisely—the same methods of rebellion at our rival kitchen."

The news hit the Council like a sledge hammer to the back of a skull. They cried out in surprise. Panic and fear seized them by the throats. They started whispering to each other rapidly, their voices and hands quivering. A two-front attack? The bums were wrecking havoc in *both* soup kitchens? What the devil? Had they *actually* strategized? Had they *actually* taken the time to organize these raids? It was too coincidental. Yes, they must have organized. But how? When? How could they have missed it? What else were they plotting in those grimy little heads of theirs? Oh God, an army of bums—this is the stuff nightmares are made of. Oh God…

The Bookkeeper watched panic grip the Council and shake them to their very core. Finally, he had delivered to them a new piece of news. Finally, he was able to flaunt his superior knowledge and awareness. "He had sources," that bit of news told them. "He was informed." The Bookkeeper smirked at the Council, smirked at their stupid, jittery faces. Their eyes darted, their necks snapped towards one person, then another. "They look like little prairie dogs," he thought. "Little, stupid prairie dogs." It didn't surprise the Bookkeeper that the Council hadn't known about the parallel uprising at Abe's. Why would they? They had no friends, no contacts in Abe's Kitchen. They had no interest in keeping track of the goings-on in that place. No. Most of the time they tried their best to avoid their rival kitchen and anything associated with it. They turned up their noses, averted their eyes, told their children to look away as they strolled past the long, grey block building. Of course they hadn't heard about the riots at Abe's. They hadn't truly thought about the rival kitchen in years. They loathed it. They disparaged it. They were aware of their vast superiority and Reward-worthy ways. But they had never stepped inside Abe's Kitchen. They had never bothered to become acquainted with its members. Why go through the trouble? Why question the worth and goodness of one's own kitchen? That was sacrilege and they would have nothing to do with it. So they didn't question; they didn't wonder about Abe's; they didn't fraternize with Abe's people. Why do it? Why bother?

The Bookkeeper waved his hand; the Council settled down. They looked at him expectantly, their prairie dog eyes shaking slightly in their sockets.

"Yes friends," the Bookkeeper said in the tone of a doting father, "they are organized. Yes friends, it is worse than we feared. But I am not without hope. I do not believe the situation is out of our grasp. We do not, of course, like to run our kitchens by fear, but sometimes fear is the only way. Sometimes, we simply have to make an example out of the miscreants in order to uphold our honor, in order to show the others that their trouble-making will not be tolerated. I think," the Bookkeeper paused, tasting the drama in his silence, "the bums have underestimated us. I think they do not believe we will act. Oh-ho-ho, they are mistaken. We will act!"

They cheered.

"We will put them in their places!"

The cheering grew.

"And furthermore, we will quell these riots with more force, more efficiency than Abe's! We will strike such fear in the hearts of the vagrants that they will not dare cross us again! They will not dare!"

A roar of voices and clapping hands, people jumping to their feet.

"*That*, friends, is the Ezekiel Banks way. *That* is how we do things here. Efficiently. Strongly. Without hesitation. Now, who's with me?!"

The Council applauded louder, faster, applauded until their hands felt raw and numb. The Bookkeeper smiled. Such obedient, little prairie dogs. Such nice, little souls to work with. He sat down, rubbing his spindly fingers together menacingly. "The bums *will* pay for this," he thought. "There is no way around it. They'll be sorry for their sins, for their lack of loyalty, their abysmal lack of loyalty…"

Chapter 38

It was afternoon—around two-thirty or three o'clock, judging by the sun—and Elmer was walking southward. Clouds passed overhead, quickly, and moved on. They were light, cirrus clouds—mares' tails, as Papa used to call them. There would be rain in a couple of days, but for now there was sun. And it stared Elmer squarely in the face as he trod down the sidewalk.

It was Thursday and Elmer was walking through the day with only two hours of sleep under his belt. He had spent half the night with security—arguing, reasoning with them, refusing to sign this or that paper they shoved under his nose. "We've turned ourselves in," he had said. "Isn't that enough for now?" In the end, security didn't know what to do with them. They shoved the Hopefuls into one of the larger kitchen pantries and locked the door. Every once in a while, one of the guards would march in and threaten them, maybe kick one or two of them with a pointed boot, and then march out again. The Hopefuls endured the abuse silently, waiting until the guard left before they started spouting curses and insults. In between the interruptions, they also planned. They schemed of different ways to plead their case, to rally more support, to get Eleanor back. They talked and talked, sometimes in circles, sometimes repeating themselves for the thousandth time. They talked just to hear noise; they talked to distract themselves from their current situation. They talked until they were unceremoniously released.

The guards thrust open the pantry doors and flung them into the kitchen. A few Hopefuls crashed against the rack of pots and pans that hung from the ceiling. The guards snickered. "A'right!" One of them shouted. He was taller, meatier than the rest. He pointed at them with sausage fingers. "Time to go to yer rooms. That's orders. Get movin'. And don't even think about tryin' to leave this building. There'll be guards posted at yer doors. And the Bookkeeper wants an audience with you tomorrow night and if you know what's best for you, you'll be there. Six o'clock. Sharp! The Bookkeeper does not like to be kept waiting. Understood?"

"Perfectly, sir." It was Grace. Her voice was calm and even, tinged with the subtlest amount of sarcasm. "We wouldn't dream of leaving your lovely kitchen, now would we gang?" She looked towards the Hopefuls. They nodded nervously. "You see?" she turned her attention back to the guard in charge. "We will be perfectly well behaved."

"Hmph," the guard grunted. "We'll see about that. All right. To yer rooms now. And be quick about it!"

They scurried through the kitchen, past the dining room, and onto the moving sidewalk. Guards flanked them as they went. They passed a few people loitering in the dining hall and on the parallel moving sidewalk—strange for three in the morning—before they reached their rooms. They noticed the curious eyes, the prolonged stares and thought, "Good. Let them wonder. Let them see us like this—persecuted."

The guards deposited them roughly into their rooms and slammed the doors. Elmer felt the strained silence of the room, knew that anything that ruptured that wall of silence would be heard immediately by the guard. Every cough, every creaking floorboard. Elmer heard his guard outside the door. He shifted his feet; he cleared his throat. Elmer pulled the bed covers over his ears and attempted to sleep. Sleep refused to come. Every time he closed his eyes, he felt watched. Examined. Scrutinized under a microscope.

"Good god," Elmer thought. "What have we gotten ourselves into?"

Eventually, when the halls started to buzz with morning activity and his eyelids became too heavy to keep open, Elmer slept. But only for two hours. He awoke to the sound of tapping, of knuckles against wooden door. He sat up quickly and wished he hadn't. The blood rushed to his head and blinded him with vertigo.

"Whaddya want?" Elmer called sleepily.

"Uh. I uh—" the guard stuttered. "I was told to check and see if the old man is still alive. Well, uh, you appear to be, so…that's what I'll report."

"A most astute observation," Elmer replied bitterly and nestled his head back into the pillow. He tried to fall back asleep. He tried and tried, but his efforts were useless. Finally he got up to stretch his legs. He decided to go to breakfast; the guard followed. He sat down by the fireplace; the guard followed. He went to the spa; the guard followed. To the library; the guard followed. Elmer became increasingly annoyed with his lumbering shadow and decided to play the one trump card in his deck that might lose the big lug: his old man card.

"I need to take my medication!" Elmer shrieked, suddenly turning on the guard as he sat down for lunch. It was the first time Elmer had addressed the guard all day and it startled him so much that he became momentarily mute. "It is past noon and I need my medication!" Elmer whined, grasping his cane and shaking it accusingly at the oversized man. "Where's Grace? What is this? Cat got your tongue? I asked you a question—where's Grace?"

"Grace?" the man replied, finally finding his voice. "I have no idea who Grace is."

"You know, Grace," said Elmer, adding a little extra quaver to his voice. Just a typical old man throwing a tantrum. "She was with us last night. You surely noticed her—thin girl, dark skin, beautiful green eyes. Graaace." Elmer glared at the man.

"Oh, that Grace," said the man stupidly. "I guess I know the one you're talking 'bout."

"Good," said Elmer. "Now get her right away so I can take my medication. It's well past noon. I have to have it! I *need* to have it! I'll *die* otherwise. I'll die!"

"Ok, ok. Calm down," said the man, exasperated. He wasn't certain what to do, but he knew the old man was creating a scene and scenes were certainly frowned upon these days. "I'll get Grace and I'll be right back. You stay here. Stay put now. I'll go find her. Um—," he paused and scratched his head, "where do you s'pose she is?"

"How am *I* supposed to know, you nimrod?! I've been with you all day. I know as well as you, you hulking piece of meat! Now go get her! Now! I'm going to faint! Oh god, I'm going to faint!"

"Woah, ok. I'm goin', I'm goin'. I'll be right back, ok?" he swirled around and paced towards the moving sidewalk, his boots clicking with each rapid step. Elmer smiled wryly to himself. "Trump," he thought.

As soon as the man was out of sight, Elmer leapt to his feet and rushed towards the door. His hand was on the large, brass handle; he could feel the outside air whispering through the cracks.

"Wait!" said a voice, female and rough.

Elmer turned, saw a familiar prim woman in a velvet purple suit. "Yes?"

"The guest book."

Elmer sighed. "Oh yes. Right. Mustn't forget that." He snatched the pen from the greeter's hand, scrawled his name across the next empty line in the book, and once again headed towards the exit.

"Elmer H?" said the woman. "Hey, wait! You're one of the names on The List. Hey, stop!"

But Elmer was already out the door and hobbling as fast as he could down the sidewalk. He kept his eyes straight ahead, his gait steady. He knew the greeter wouldn't follow him. After all, what power did any of Abe's employees have outside the facility's walls? None, really. He was in the public arena now, free from the kitchen's regulations and statutes. He had taken a gamble with the greeter, but it had paid off. She knew exactly where the boundary of Abe's ended and outside jurisdiction began.

"Excellent," thought Elmer. "I am playing my cards well today." He faced the sun, felt the warmth on his cheeks.

Two-thirty, three o'clock. And it's Thursday. Less than a week ago, we were twittling our thumbs, looking for something to do. Less than a week ago, we were crying for action. We were bored and restless. We had no idea Abe's Kitchen would open a candy shop, that Eleanor would make a scene, that they would brutishly haul her away. We hadn't the faintest notion our paths would lead here—to heavy surveillance and an audience with the Bookkeeper. It's Thursday, it's Thursday. God, my head is spinning. Grace—all of them, really—they think we're winning, that we've got them by the tails, but do we? Do we really? Aren't they the formidable soup kitchens? Don't they own City B? And who are we? Tiny fleas on the back of a great beast.

Elmer was startled when his feet brought him to the door of Ezekiel's Kitchen. He hadn't thought about his route; he just walked. Somehow, they had carried him down the sidewalk, towards the sun and the seven-story kitchen, towards the other band of Hopefuls, towards the solid oak doors with the carved wooden sign dangling over it: E.B. Elmer looked at the letters framing the diagonal soup spoon. *Did Ezekiel ever simply want to feed the hungry? Or was there always an agenda?*

He heaved open one of the heavy doors and stepped inside. He found the greeter, signed the guest book. "No thanks, I'm fine without slippers." "Ok then, enjoy your stay." "Thanks." He walked past the entryway and into the dining hall.

Immediately, he sensed a change. The residents seemed tense, rigid. They didn't talk; they didn't laugh. They silently ate their sandwiches, their eyes darting occasionally around the room as if they were waiting for someone who was quite late. Elmer walked through the dining room and felt their fidgety eyes on his back. He reached the caged elevator and pressed the up button.

"Hey Elmer!"

He turned towards the husky female voice. "Oh, hello Charlene. Good to see you."

The woman nodded, her heavy faux-gold necklaces clinking together like a wind chime. "And you. We were hoping for some news from Abe's. How are things?"

Elmer looked at her a moment, studying her square jaw, her serious eyes. "Can I be honest with you?"

"Please."

"Ok." He sighed. "In my opinion, things aren't so good. They captured Nathan around six o'clock yesterday and the rest of us a few hours later. We had intended to turn ourselves in anyway—as an effort to protect Nathan, you know—but they beat us to it and shoved us into a pantry while they decided what to do with us. Now we each have a personal 'escort' following us around, monitoring our every move. Despite all this, the others believe—mostly due to Grace's encouragement—that we've got them right where we want them, that they wouldn't dare banish us for fear of retribution. I'm not so optimistic. Frankly, I think they're capable of all sorts of evil and we shouldn't underestimate them. Anyway," he paused, looked at the woman in front of him. Her necklaces hung still as leaned forward, taking in his every word. "That's our situation now. It's like an internment camp over there. Guards everywhere. I had to throw a bit of a tantrum in order to escape."

"Did you now? Good work."

"Thanks. I have to head back to Abe's in a bit—we all have an audience with the Bookkeeper tonight and I wouldn't miss it for the world—but first I wanted to let you all know we decided it would be best to stay put this coming Sunday. No switch. You know, come to think of it, we might not be able to switch anyway."

"Neither would we." She met Elmer's eyes and held his gaze for a few seconds. "Funny thing, Elmer—your kitchen sounds like a mirror image of ours right now. Last night, we were rounded up and tossed into the dance studio. They held us there for hours until one of the guards suddenly came in and told us to go to our rooms. They paired us off with the guards and they've been watching us ever since. There's my Goliath over there." She pointed to a man with a huge, shaggy head like a Grizzly Bear's. His great, hulking back rested against the wall about twenty feet away. He leaned forward and glared menacingly when they turned to look at him. Charlene waved mockingly.

The man grunted, "Hurry up, will ya! I don't have all day."

Charlene turned to Elmer. "He does," she said. "He does have all day. Anyway, we're not even allowed to speak to each other—the Hopefuls, that is. They won't let us. My guard was even wary of me speaking with you, but I convinced him that you had some questions about today's seminar in the library and I wanted to give you some more information. I mean, *really*. After all the protesting and rebelling I've done against this kitchen, does he *really* think I would know—or care—about some dumb seminar. Seriously. Oh well, I suppose they're not paid for their brains. Or their looks for that matter." She glanced over at the great, hulking man. "Speak of the devil, here comes my beastly guard now."

"What's all this about?" the guard demanded. "Haven't you told 'im all he needs ter know yet? Let's git a move on here!"

"Yes, yes, I've told him. But he would like it very much if we would escort him to the seminar. He's a little confused about which room it's in, see, and it's going to start in a few minutes and—"

"Oh-for-the-love-of-everything-holy, let's go! Come on, come on. Git in that elevator. I don't have all day."

Under Charlene's breath, "he does."

"What was that?"

"Nothing, nothing. Just saying thank you. Yes, thank you very much for escorting Elmer to the seminar."

The guard stared at her suspiciously for a moment. "Yer welcome. Now, move." He shoved them into the caged elevator and they started their ascent to the fourth floor. When they disembarked, they were greeted by a large sign in the shape of an arrow. The bold letters running across it read: "**Seminar.**"

"Yer tellin' me the old man couldn't figure out where ter go? You've got ter be kiddin' me."

"No, not kidding," Charlene replied. "He, uh," she lowered her voice to a whisper. "He can't read. Never learned how."

"Hey, I can—" Elmer started. Charlene jabbed him in the ribs.

"Oh," said the guard, his cheeks reddening a little, "Oh, I see. Alright, old man." He pointed to the sign and said in a painfully slow, painfully loud voice, "SEE THAT SIGN? It says SEM-I-NAR. The SEM-I-NAR is that way. OK?"

"OK!" Elmer shouted back and began muttering under his breath. Charlene suppressed a giggle.

They walked in silence through the library and to a small conference room in the back corner. In front of the door, a bulletin board was posted with the seminar's name and agenda. The guard gestured to the board, "THIS IS IT. This is the SEM-I-NAR."

"Ok, great," said Elmer flatly. He turned to Charlene and whispered, "Can you let the others know about our situation?" He glanced at the guard. "Somehow?"

"I'll find a way," she replied. "Paper airplanes are a surprisingly good way to distribute messages." She winked at him and turned to the guard. "Alright, skippy. I'm going to be late for my badminton tournament. Let's go."

"Now who-duh-ya think is giving orders to who? I'm the one in charge here!"

"Yeah, yeah," she replied and waved him off with a flick of her wrist. "See ya later, Elmer."

"Bye." Elmer watched them go, his meaty back juxtaposed awkwardly next to her slim frame. He shook his head and turned to go, but the name of the seminar caught his eye. He stared at it, entranced.

Really. Really? Who would have thought? But I really don't have time; must be going. Audience with the Bookkeeper in a couple of hours. But still. Still. I really shouldn't pass this up. What would Onyx say? Oh, alright. A few minutes, that's all. Why not.

He turned and walked into the conference room, closing the door behind him with a light click. The name of the seminar hovered over the agenda in hand-scrawled letters written in purple ink:

Are you a prophet of God? Interpreting your Heaven-sent dreams and visions.

With Ms. Patricia Snitly

Chapter 39

Elmer held his breath as he walked into the conference room. He slowly, softly closed the door behind him and turned towards the front of the conference room. It was empty. Empty, but expectant. The rows of chairs faced front, arranged in neat, perfectly spaced lines. Decorations—crepe paper and tapestries—hung from the walls, the ceiling, filling the blank white spaces with abstract shapes and color. Candles were perched on the front desk, emitting a sleepy, floral scent, their smoke curling lazily towards the ceiling. Ringed around the room were tiny throw pillows, each perched on top of a matching fuzzy blanket. Elmer took in the decorations, the candles, the tiny pink and orange and lime green throw pillows and shook his head. He was fairly certain this must be what a teenage girl's room would look like. He took another look around the vacant room, shrugged, and turned to leave. A pair of luminous, blue eyes hovered inches from his.

"Ahh!" he yelped and jumped backwards. "You scared the dickens out of me!"

"So sorry," said a smooth, feminine voice. It dripped into Elmer's ears like sap from maple trees. "I sometimes forget that not everyone is blessed with the same foresight as me. Please excuse my behavior and accept my most sincere apologies."

"It—" Elmer hesitated. He couldn't tell if her voice was mocking or strangely serious. Either way, it made him nervous. "It's fine. No big deal."

"But it is a 'big deal.' You are my pupil; you need to trust me. The first steps we take together are the most crucial, after all. Big deal. Or-deal. Deal or no deal. Do we have a deal?" She extended her hand out to Elmer. Tentatively, Elmer shook it, his head whirring slightly, his skin crawling from her honeyed voice.

"Ok then," she said, unaware of Elmer's sudden urge to vomit all over the cerulean throw pillow on his right. "Have a seat, pupil. Let us begin."

"I, uh—I really should be going. I think this was a mistake. Lots of things to do, really."

"There are no mistakes, pupil. Everything happens for a reason, according to the will of God. Let that be your first lesson. Now, sit down please. And grab a pillow-blanket set on your right there. Wonderful." She seated herself, cross-legged, on top of the desk at the front of the room.

Elmer chose a sunflower-yellow pillow and blanket and slunk into one of the chairs in the second row.

She shook her head, as if scolding a child, "Now, now, pupil. Why choose to be further away from the teacher than one needs to be? I think this chair will do nicely." She pointed to a seat inches away from her knee. Elmer hesitated, got up, and sat down in the chair. "Good, good. Now let us begin."

The woman who Elmer supposed was Ms. Patricia Snitly placed her hands, palms up, at her sides, closed her eyes, and began quietly humming to herself. Elmer stared. He was unsure what to do with himself, so he sat. And stared. The woman in front of him was in her mid-forties, short, with poofy blonde hair and large, flipped back bangs. She wore oversized, plastic earrings and bangles and a baggy t-shirt that hung off one shoulder. Elmer was reminded of the women that used to appear on television programs a couple of decades ago.

"Pupil!" the woman suddenly exclaimed, scrunching her face and eyeing Elmer out of one open eye. She looked very much like a fruity, blonde pirate. Elmer grimaced.

"Yes, ma'am?"

She opened the other eye and stared at him blankly for several seconds. Elmer felt his cheeks flush under her gaze. "Right," she said. "Right. We are doing it all wrong. All out of order. I should have consulted my angels on this. But no matter. It's not too late to start over. Do over. Over hill and dale. Over, under, upside-down."

Elmer's jaw hung open. He couldn't look away from the mass of hair, the neon-pink lipsticked mouth.

The woman glanced at Elmer with a start. She seemed to have forgotten for a moment that there was another person in the room. She noticed his slack-jawed expression. "What is it pupil? Why do you stare, so?"

"Just, um, your words. The phrases with 'over.' Sorry. It just didn't make sense."

"I happen to enjoy word play," she said indignantly. "But that's neither here nor there, nor there nor here. Now, where were we?"

"I think we were about to start over."

"Ah, yes. That. Let us start with names, shall we. I am Ms. Patricia Snitly, spiritually enlightened, handmaiden of the one and only God

Almighty, may His wisdom last forever. You can call me Ms. Patti. And you are?"

Elmer gaped. "Elmer," he muttered.

"Hmm. One does not hear of many people named Elmer anymore. Good, good. Now Elllmer," she held the "l" in his name like a purr. "Why have you come to me? Why have you sought the deep knowledge and wisdom of Ms. Patti, enlightened servant of God?"

"I guess I just stumbled upon your seminar. I was just passing through, you see and—"

"Nonsense!" Ms. Patti exclaimed, jumping up from her cross-legged position and kneeling on the desk. She pointed at Elmer. "Nothing—nothing, is an accident! Did you not feel the tug of God within you? Did he not guide your feet to my seminar today?"

Elmer thought for a moment about his feet leading him unbidden to places, as if they knew things he did not. He shook the thought from his head. "I—uh—I guess I've just had some strange dreams lately."

"Oh-ho! This leads us to the heart of the matter, does it not? This is what matters. The stuff locked in your brain matter. It eats you up—makes you madder and madder. Is that what's the matter?"

"I suppose," said Elmer tentatively, not quite sure what he was agreeing with.

"Of course it is," she replied. "You have been thinking about these dreams for some time, haven't you?"

"Well yes, I—"

"And you had a moment of elation, of relief, when you learned of my seminar, didn't you?"

"I suppose I—"

"And now you want to know if you are truly a prophet of God or just some ordinary bloke who happens to experience elaborate dreams."

"No, I never actually wondered if—"

"Well, let me tell you, pupil, nothing, I repeat, *nothing* is an accident."

Elmer nodded. He watched her hair bob up and down with each word, watched her large blue eyes wide and alert under their painted, equally blue lids.

"I have the answers for you, pupil," Ms. Patti whispered, leaning forward and staring, unblinkingly, in his face, like a makeup-sporting owl. "I have the answers," she said and sat back on the desk, crossing her legs once again and closing her eyes.

"First," she said, "we will practice breathing exercises. We will calm our minds, allow ourselves to connect with the Holy Spirit. Then, we will discuss the matter of your dreams. Now, follow me." She led him through several minutes of breathing exercises. Elmer followed, half-heartedly. He wondered what, exactly, he had gotten himself into. Finally, Ms. Patti opened one eye and squinted at him. "Pupil," she cooed, "are you ready?"

"Yes," said Elmer, because he couldn't think of what else to say.

"Excellent. Then let us begin."

Elmer wondered how many beginnings they would have. He looked around anxiously. No clock. No windows to gauge the sun. He fidgeted in his chair. "Say, Ms. Patti," he began, "I was wondering how long this might take. You see I—"

"You cannot rush the Holy Spirit!" Ms. Patti snapped, the sugar in her voice replaced by venom. "Now, let us begin."

Elmer sighed. "Ok."

"I sense that you have come to me regarding one dream in particular," Ms. Patti said, her eyes once again closed. "Is that correct?"

"Actually, I've had several strange dreams."

"Well choose one then!" she hissed. "My senses cannot be wrong. There is one dream in particular that is troubling you."

Elmer sighed. He thought of the church, of the green-eyed priest, of the blank-faced woman in the large picture frame. Of the golden walls and the caged elevator. Of the hamster-wheel cages beneath the church floor. He opened his mouth, hesitated, closed it again. "I—" he started. He chewed on his lip, pondering for a moment. A twinkle passed through his eyes.

"I'm on a great, black bird," he began, "and we're flying through the air."

Elmer hadn't meant to talk about his dream with the seven sages. He hadn't meant to describe the vast mountains, the plummeting bird, the cavern that led deep into the mountain's heart. He hadn't intended to relive the fear that coursed through his body when he sensed the great cat, felt her silently stalking him, saw her lithe body when she stepped serenely from the mouth of the cavern. But he did. The words poured out of his mouth as if they had been piled on the edge of his tongue, waiting to spill out. Word after word. He couldn't stop them. They flowed like a river: smoothly, naturally, unending. He wondered at himself as he continued to speak, watched the words as they sprang from his throat. They told the story of snakes writhing, of an old man dancing, remembering joy. They told the story of seven sets of eyes, seven thrones, seven colors, seven bodies appearing out of thin air, seven guiding voices. The words formed the story, rolled out the shape of it, tossed it lightly into the ears of Ms. Patricia Snitly. Eventually, the words ran dry and the story came to its natural conclusion. Elmer exhaled slowly and glanced at Ms. Patti for the first time since he began his tale.

He recoiled slightly when he saw her face, wide-eyed and distended, her jaw hanging loosely and her luminous, blue eyes bulging like a bullfrog. Beads of perspiration formed on her forehead and cheeks and dripped down her neck in orange, makeup-y streaks. He made a face and looked down at the sunshine-colored blanket on his lap.

"Well—uh, I guess that's it," he said to break the silence. He had not yet seen the woman in front of him at a loss for words and it vaguely troubled him.

"Indeed," said Ms. Patti, her voice small and distant. "Indeed."

"Ms. Patti? Is everything alright?"

"Hmm? Oh. Yes," she shook her head, the puffball hair bounced up and down together as one frothy organism. "Everything's just fine. Fine and dandy. I've paid all my fines. You look fine today. Where did you fine-d those glasses?"

"Um…I'm not sure. I've had them a while."

She crinkled her nose at him. "It was a rhetorical question."

"It was? But I thought—"

"Shut up, it was."

"Ok—"

"I can't believe you can be so thick when you have so much divine inspiration living inside that wrinkly little head of yours."

"Hey, now. No need for—"

"I mean, you are clearly a prophet of God, but I wonder if all the gears are chugging along as they should up there, if maybe there aren't a few screws loose in the machine, if you know what I mean."

Elmer stared at her in silence.

"At any rate, you have assuredly been receiving messages from our one and only Father, the God Almighty, Creator of Heaven and Earth, the All-Knowing, All-Seeing Divine Being. Him. There's no disputing it. That dream of yours was riddled with symbolism that points to Him. How you couldn't see *that*, I'll never know. It is fairly obvious. But, then again, many things are obvious to my finely tuned senses. So, I suppose you must be forgiven for your density. Yes, you must be forgiven for your foggy brain. Perhaps it will clear a bit with time, but you haven't got much of *that* left, now have you?"

Elmer glared, offended, at the woman chatting happily away and snarled, "Well, *miss*. Excuuuse me, but I was told that my dream is full of *other* symbols that do *not* represent 'Him.' The snakes, great cat, and bird represent the three levels of being—hell, earth, and heaven; the seven figures are the seven colors of the body's chakras, and—"

"Nonsense! Utter and complete nonsense! What sort of hippie, pagan, free-spirit scum fed you that garbage? Seven colors of the chak-what? What kind of made-up crap have you been swallowing? Just listen to Ms. Patti for a while and she'll set you straight. She'll use her acute awareness and reveal the dream's true symbols to you. My goodness, for being a prophet of God, you certainly are a useless one, aren't you? Now, let's begin."

Elmer cringed. *Another* beginning.

Ms. Patti leaned back, adjusted a flamingo-pink pillow under her bottom and breathed in deeply. "Yes," she murmured. "Yes, it is all very clear."

"What's very clear?"

"Silence! Do not interrupt while I am praying to the Holy Spirit."

Elmer was silent.

"Now, first of all," said Ms. Snitly in her overly sugary voice, "those colors. I don't care what you've been told by unbelievers, but those colors represent God's rainbow. Red, orange, yellow, green, blue, indigo, violet. The rainbow. God's covenant with man after he flooded earth. You do know the story I'm talking about, don't you?"

"Noah's ark," said Elmer, nodding. "Yeah, ok, but that doesn't explain the giant bird and the cat and—"

"One thing at a time!" Ms. Patti snapped. "Ok, so we have God's covenant in your dream. A very powerful symbol, indeed. But there is more." She looked at him mysteriously—or at least tried to look mysterious.

It seemed to Elmer that she was squinting at a very bright object after having just taken a bite of a lemon. She unpursed her lips and continued, "Let us talk about the animals in your vision. I have no doubt, no doubt at all that those are Biblical animals. *Think* about it, pupil. Simply use your noggin for one moment. Snakes, you say? I say Adam and Eve. Great cat? Daniel and the lion's den. Big, black bird? Eagle."

"Eagle?"

"Didn't you pay any attention in Sunday school?"

"Well, not much to be honest—"

"Will you *stop* answering questions that are meant to be rhetorical!" Ms. Patti nearly screamed. "You are *severely* cramping my style. I was on a roll with my interpretations and there you sit, all old and entitled, interrupting the Holy Spirit that is flowing through me. Good gracious, you're impossible."

Elmer blinked mutely at the woman. She continued rambling.

"So anyway, pupil. Your animals. The snakes clearly represent temptation and sin. They lured Eve to eat the apple, after all. And the great cat has to be one of Daniel's lions. One of the ones whose mouth he sealed shut when he was thrown into the den. That has to be right. I can't think of any other cats in the Bible. And your eagle…" she looked over at Elmer and shook her head. "People really do need to pay more attention in Sunday school. Your eagle most assuredly comes from the verse 'And he will raise you up on eagle's wings on the last day.' I think that comes from Proverbs. Or maybe Psalms. In any case, there you have it. Your animals explained." She sat, slightly out of breath and looking expectantly at Elmer.

He looked back, unsure if he was allowed to speak.

"Wellllll," said Ms. Patti testily. "What do you think of my divine interpretations thus far?"

Elmer thought about it for a moment. Maybe she was a little crazy. Maybe a little aggravating. Maybe eccentric and odd and sporting an out-of-date hairstyle. But what she was saying—some of it, at least—made sense. It really did. Elmer thought about the snakes, cat, and giant bird. He thought about the figures in their robes, creating a rainbow of colors. It all added up.

"Hmm," said Elmer. "I suppose that all makes sense."

"Suppose? *Suppose?* Well I never. Of course it makes sense. It not only makes sense, it is the God-given *truth*. If it was not the truth, it would not spring from my lips as it has. Now, don't give me anymore lip. Sit at the lip of your seat and listen up. There is more."

Ms. Patti spread a pink blanket across her lap and closed her eyes once more. "Yes," she mumbled. "There is a bit more. I thought so."

Elmer leaned forward, listening.

"Aha!" Ms. Patti shouted. Elmer nearly fell out of his seat. "Yes, that's right. Of course that's also a sign from God. Why didn't I catch it in the first place? Oh, brilliant. Thank you, Holy Spirit, for your guidance."

"What?" said Elmer anxiously. "What is it?"

"He is telling you to be more direct with Him, pupil."

Elmer looked at her quizzically. "What? How'd you figure—"

"You called out for him, didn't you? And he answered your prayer."

"I did? When did I—"

"Of course you did. You said the Lord's Prayer. Or at least some of it. You *do* know the Lord's Prayer, don't you?"

"Of course," Elmer said, remembering a time when he was forced to recite it every night before he fell asleep. He never understood the point. He always rushed through the prayer, the words tumbling out of his mouth in rapid succession so that he could get off his knees and go to bed. *That's not praying. That's speaking rapidly. I never thought about the words, never felt them.*

"Well then," said Ms. Patti, "then you know you said part of that prayer in your dream. Do you recall when?"

Elmer looked at her uncertainly. "Is this another rhetorical question?"

"Of course not!" Ms. Patti exclaimed, scoffing. "Just answer the question and stop being such a smarty."

"Ok, ok," Elmer replied hastily. He thought a moment. "Hmm," he said to himself, "I suppose that could sound like the Lord's Prayer. Interesting. I never thought of that."

"Speak up please. Don't mumble." Ms. Patti demanded.

"I said I never thought of that before," said Elmer. "The giant cat. I asked it to forgive me for trespassing. And the pit of snakes. When I didn't know what else to do, I asked to be delivered from their evil."

"Precisely," said Ms. Patti, casting a rare satisfied smile at her pupil. Elmer beamed. He wasn't sure why, but for some reason, it pleased him immensely to finally answer a question according to Ms. Patti's whims.

"And then God stopped the snakes. He pacified the cat. Just like He has removed so many perils for so many people throughout history." She looked up at the ceiling. "May His goodness endure forever." She sighed and then snapped her eyes towards Elmer, catching him off guard with their brilliant blue and making him jump a little.

"Now, pupil. We get to the meat of the matter. The purpose of our meeting. Where one road meets another." She looked at him silently for several, long moments. A grave look etched across her face in the furrowed brows, the straight-lined pink mouth. "Now," she spoke at last, "is when we determine the main message of the dream, the main purpose sent from God. And then you—only you—decide how to act. Then I will have carried you as far as I can, pupil. Then you will have to walk on your own two feet, think with your own, little brain." She frowned. "I *hope* that will not be a problem."

Elmer rolled his eyes slightly and shook his head. "No," he said, "That will not be a problem."

"Good," she said. "Then let us determine the main message." She wrapped the pink blanket around her shoulders, remained cross-legged, and once again closed her eyes. "Do it with me this time, pupil," she whispered. "Channel the divine guidance of the Holy Spirit."

Elmer hesitated, laid his sunflower-yellow blanket over his lap, and closed his eyes. He wasn't sure what he was listening for or to. He had no idea how one speaks to the Holy Spirit. But he closed his eyes anyway and felt oddly calm. He smelled the soft floral scent of the candles, felt the warmth of his blanket, and smiled as his body began to drift off to sleep.

"Pupil!" Ms. Patti's shout shook him out of his near slumber.

"Hrm? Yes?"

"I've got the message! Do you?"

"I, um. I'm not so sure. It's a bit fuzzy yet. Why don't you go first?"

Ms. Patti grunted disapprovingly and said, "Oh, alright." Under her breath, "Some prophet he'll make. Always the great lumps of human beings that are blessed with divinely-sent dreams. Aggravating, truly aggravating." She turned to Elmer and shook her head. "Ok, pupil. The message I'm channeling is this: Seek divine help and guidance to face your perils."

Elmer looked at her thoughtfully and nodded slightly.

"That is your message," Ms. Patti continued. "It is clear as day. Think about it. In your dream, you encounter several dangers—the diving bird, the stalking cat, the pit of snakes—and you cannot stop them on your own. You run from the cat, it catches up; you squirm around in the pit of snakes, they don't stop. The only way you are saved from your perils is by asking. And then help is sent. You are guided by seven God-sent figures—seven angels, really. This tells me, pupil, your troubles are too large to face on your own. Clearly, if the Lord Almighty is sending his angels to assist you, you have some real problems." She lowered her voice and grabbed a hold of Elmer's hand. For a moment, Elmer looked at his gnarled, veiny hand enclosed in her smooth one, noticing the different textures of their skin. Ms. Patti lowered her voice to a tender whisper, "You can't just run away from things, Elmer. And you can't face all your troubles on your own. You need help."

Still clutching Ms. Patti's hand, Elmer looked up into the blue eyes in front of him. It was the first time she had spoken his name.

"Oh pupil," she removed her hand and sat up; the fragile moment passed. "Pupil, pupil. The Almighty must really take a shine to you, despite your slowness. He's throwing all sorts of clues at you like a trail of bread crumbs and all you have to do is pick them up. So, pick them up, pupil. Pay attention to the signs. Ms. Patti won't always be around to deduce dream meanings for you. You must do it on your own. You must prophet-ize."

Elmer leaned back in his chair. His head felt thick and syrupy. It buzzed like a beehive.

"Pupil?"

"Mm? Oh. I, uh," he shook his head, looking at the blanket on his lap. "I think you have it wrong, Ms. Patti. Not the message. No. I think you're truly onto something there. Just the last part. The prophet part. I—uh. It's just that—"

"Spit it out, pupil."

"It's just that I don't *feel* like a prophet. I'm only an old man. I'm only Elmer."

"Pupil," said Ms. Patti sternly. "You are not *only* anything. Can you imagine if St. John or Matthew or Luke just shrugged and said 'I'm *only* me. Not going to amount to much. Might as well not even bother.' We would have never had the benefit of their divinely-inspired messages. We would have lost the words of God. Pupil, you have a responsibility. Embrace your prophet-ness. Live it."

Elmer didn't feel like arguing. He shrugged. "Ok, Ms. Patti. I'll do my best."

"Now, that's more like it. I can't wait to tell the Bookkeeper we have a new prophet in the fold. He will be tickled pink, he will. I bet he'll even—"

"Oh no!" gasped Elmer, sitting up straight. "The Bookkeeper! The time—what's the time?"

Ms. Patti glanced at the small, pink watch on her wrist. "It's ten to six. Have an audience with the Bookkeeper already do you? Splendid, splendid. And you were trying to trick me into thinking that you doubt your abilities. Pah! If you're confident enough to contact the Bookkeeper then—"

"No, no. Not *your* Bookkeeper, Abe's Bookkeeper. I'm running quite late. Sorry, but I have to run. So long, Ms. Patti. I appreciate your insight. It's been…interesting."

"What? *Abe's* Bookkeeper? Blasphemy! Traitorous blasphemy, that's what that is! You are *our* prophet, not Abe's. You came to us. You sought the divine teachings of Ms. Patti, faithful servant of God and the one true soup kitchen. You can't just run off to Abe's like a slimy, little rat! Hey, stop! Old man, I'm telling you to stop right there! Stop or you'll be sorry!"

As Elmer bolted through the door, he turned just enough to see the mad, blue eyes, the bouncing hair coming towards him. He scampered out of the room and into the library. He turned, hobbled down the nearest aisle, and pressed his body flat against the books. He heard the click of heels pass him and fade away. He breathed a sigh of relief and headed towards the elevator, towards the front door, and towards the rival soup kitchen. As he stepped into the evening air, he fought the urge to run off into the shadowy horizon, to disappear once and for all from City B and its dreadful kitchens. But he didn't. He stood his ground, forced his body to point northward, and began the agonizing march towards Abe's Kitchen. He wasn't going to run. He was tired of running.

Chapter 40

"I assume, infidels, you are aware of the crimes you have committed against our fine kitchen?" The Bookkeeper didn't wait for a response. "I assume," he continued, "you are aware of the trouble you caused, the panic, the misery you brought your fellow residents. It's quite shameful, really. Quite ungrateful. We have fed you, housed you, rehabilitated you, taken you in when no one else would, shown you nothing but love, and this—*this*—is how you repay us? Where is your honor? Where is your sense of gratitude? You speak of mind control; you speak of thinking for yourselves, but are you not guilty of the same crimes? Are you not attempting to sway the masses? To make them believe a certain way, think a certain way. To make them rebel. Pah. You are retched. Despicable. I can hardly bring myself to look at your traitorous, dirty faces. What you have done is unacceptable, sneaky, abominable and it will be dealt with in kind. Do I make myself clear?"

Stone faces stared back.

"Good. Then let's move on." Abe's Bookkeeper stretched his thin arms and adjusted the podium in front of him. He stared menacingly at the handful of faces in front of them. They fancied themselves rebels, representatives of the cause. They thought they had won the hearts of the people, that they possessed the upper hand. They were wrong. They possessed nothing. What could they offer the people? Food? Shelter? The finest amusements and entertainment? No. They couldn't offer a thing. Not a thing. They possessed nothing.

"Infidels," the Bookkeeper continued. "Perhaps you think I haven't the power, the tenacity, the gall to banish you all from this kitchen. Perhaps you think there will be an uprising on your behalf, that your fellow residents will rally around your cause and rise up and create the end of Abe's Soup Kitchen as we know it. Is that what you think? Do you *really* think you have power over this fine institution?" He lowered his voice to a shade above a whisper, "Do you really think you have power over *me*?"

The Hopefuls stared back, biting their lips, their eyes betraying the rage and disgust they felt towards the Bookkeeper.

"Infidels, you are sorely mistaken. You wield no power. You have not out-foxed me. You have merely put an unfortunate delay in my schedule, a mere crimp in my plans—"

The door at the entrance of the Bookkeeper's chamber—the door that led back to Abe's mosque—opened with a slow sqreeeee. All heads turned towards the sound. Two guards stepped through, framing an old man who barely came up to their shoulders. They dragged him through the door and closed it behind them, standing at attention and looking towards the Bookkeeper. The Hopefuls began muttering excitedly amongst themselves and waving towards the old man. The Bookkeeper rapped on his podium to silence them.

"What is the meaning of this?" the Bookkeeper snarled, annoyed his speech was interrupted.

"The old man, sir," answered one of the guards with peculiarly square features—back, shoulders, chin. "He's one of them."

"Ok, ok, bring him in then," said the Bookkeeper. "And why, pray tell, is he late?"

The squarish man shifted nervously in his boots. "He, uh—what I mean to say is, uh—"

"He got away," said another guard, stepping forward. His face was red and flustered. "He was under my watch and he scampered out the door while I was gettin' 'im his medicine. Never saw it comin.' He's a wily ol' thing, he is."

"I see," said the Bookkeeper in a low hiss. "Wily is he? And how, I must ask, did you get the 'wily' little creature back in our possession?"

"He, uh—" the square-jawed guard spoke again. "He just—came back. Signed in a couple o' minutes ago an' I grabbed him."

"I see," said the Bookkeeper again, narrowing his eyes towards the guards. "We," he said, pointing towards the great, hulking men, "will have a talk later. In the meantime, seat the old man with the rest of them. We don't want any more *mishaps* or *accidental* escapes, now do we?"

The guards nodded sheepishly and shoved their captive down the aisle. Elmer caught himself with his cane and squinted as he made his way through the dimly lit chamber towards his friends. The dingy room was nothing like the glittery mosque that lay outside and Elmer had difficulty adjusting to the sudden change in brightness. He hastily sat next to Zach on the end of a row of folding chairs. Zach smiled at Elmer and patted his hand. Elmer winked back.

"Now where was I?" said the Bookkeeper, looking sourly at the Hopefuls like they had just rolled around in fresh dog dung. "Ah, yes. That's it." The Bookkeeper cleared his throat and attempted to rekindle the original fire in his voice, "We were just about to discuss what to do with you."

Elmer steadied his labored breath—he had half-jogged from one kitchen to the other—and leaned forward to listen.

"Contrary to your beliefs," the Bookkeeper began, "I am not as stupid as you think. I will not banish you from Abe's kitchen, at least, not all at once." The Hopefuls listened closely, wondering what kind of twisted punishment the spidery man had concocted behind his heavy, white brows. "Instead," he continued, "I would like a show. A public apology. Individual testimonies decrying your deeds and vowing to behave from now on. Oh, yes. You will grovel; you will whine; you will beg for my forgiveness. And I—," the Bookkeeper drew himself up, straightened his shoulders. He seemed to be picturing the moment in his head. "I, in my endless mercy, will forgive you and embrace you and allow you to stay on and on. Yes. On and on and on, until whatever time you—or The Bestower—sees fit. And our loyal residents will see you—an example of disgrace and disloyalty—reformed and newly committed to the soup kitchen that has shown you boundless mercy. And their conviction and faith shall be renewed. They will believe like they have never believed before. They will bow down and worship the benevolence and goodness of Abe and his wonderful kitchen. This *will* happen, infidels. You cannot stop it."

"Not if we have anything to say about it!" Grace's voice cut through the egotism of the Bookkeeper. "We'll never testify for you. We'll never tell lies or bow down at your feet or do any of the disgusting things you described. People will know the truth about you, Bookkeeper. They'll know your words are not genuine, that you only see us as a number—as a way to keep the kitchen afloat, as a way to profit. They've always believed these things anyway. They've always known in their hearts that the kitchens are driven by ulterior motives, not kindness and concern for humanity—"

"Silence!" snapped the Bookkeeper, his dark eyes thinning to slits. "You *will* confess! You will apologize and grovel. There is no other way; faith must be restored. The residents will note the errors of your ways. They will acknowledge your sins and forgive you, just as I will forgive you. This *will* happen. You will confess willingly. Do you know why?" The Bookkeeper took the time to glare at each of the eleven faces, noting their stubborn jaws, their unblinking eyes. They were foolish, these infidels, foolish and small. Too small to be bothered by the likes of him. The Bookkeeper. The bearer of wisdom. The speaker of truth. Loved and adored. Revered. He straightened his back and became vaguely aware of his empty stomach. He wondered what the kitchen was serving for dinner tonight.

"Do you?" the Bookkeeper dropped his voice. It sounded like an unsheathed razor. "Do you know why you will confess willingly?" He waited a few seconds more, enjoying the echoey silence of the chamber. "Because you are soft. Because you care too deeply about your fellow conspirators. Because you loath the thought of watching one of your own—one of your fellow betrayers—die a slow, messy death in front of you tonight." The Bookkeeper turned suddenly and snapped his fingers at a female guard on his left. She nodded, her jaw sinking into the pouch of neck fat hanging under her face. With beefy hands, she reached up and pulled a gold, braided chord above her head. A curtain—a dusty maroon backdrop the Hopefuls had hardly noticed—slid from behind the stage on which the Bookkeeper stood and uncovered another room at the back of the chamber. An open-faced room. A tiny, damp-looking room. A room of seemingly singular purpose—to hold a prisoner.

The Hopefuls gasped. The Bookkeeper cackled with glee and watched their frightened faces, their desperate eyes. "No!" Grace cried. "No! Let him go! Let him go this instant!"

"Oh-ho!" the Bookkeeper said, his beard trembling slightly with excitement. "I think not. Why should I let him go—this traitor, this infidel. Why should I set him free? You have declared so adamantly, little lady, that you will not confess. That you will never kneel before my feet. Is that not what you said? Hmm?"

Grace stared at the thin-lipped mouth of the Bookkeeper and then back at Nathan. He was stripped down to his underwear, thin body standing, knees buckling from the weight of heavy chains. They were draped over his shoulders and across his bare stomach. They wound around his legs and down to the floor, falling off his calves like lazy snakes. Two chains dangled from the ceiling and captured his arms, which stuck out awkwardly at right angles to his body. He looked as if he wanted to fall over, to collapse onto the floor and let the steel links pile up on top of him—a cold, metallic blanket. Instead, he forced parched lips into a small smile, barely visible behind his sweat-matted red beard.

"It's ok, Grace," he whispered. "I'm ok."

Grace shook her head violently, tears stinging the backs of her eyes like a hundred trapped wasps. She looked at Nathan, pathetic and hanging in his chains. She looked at the hidden room, filled with strange, hard instruments and gleaming blades. They stared at her menacingly, mercilessly, from hooks on the walls. She shook her head again and shuddered at the same time, so that her body seemed seized with a momentary bout of epilepsy. "You bastard," she snarled, her stinging eyes focused on the Bookkeeper. A little louder, "You ugly, lousy bastard."

The Bookkeeper laughed, clutching his thin, hanging sides under his robe. "Ha! Such words. Such words from a little lady." His voice was patronizing and oddly shrill. The Hopefuls seethed. "Bastard or not, can you now see I have won? Can you see you are nothing, that you have nothing? Can you see my power? The extent of my reach? I have merely to lift my finger and your reckless little friend will lose his leg. Another finger, his arm. Another, his tongue." He wiggled his pointer to demonstrate. "*That* is the extent of my power. *That* is what you were up against when you started your silly campaign to debunk me and my glorious kitchen. I see your faces now. I can read their despair and regret. You were foolish, weren't you? Foolish to double-cross the Bookkeeper."

Abe's Bookkeeper rocked back and forth on his heels, pulling himself alternately towards and away from the podium. Elmer thought of a bearded, little monkey on a swing. The Bookkeeper grinned manically. "And now I have the upper hand. Me. The Bookkeeper. Oh, I'll admit you were clever enough. Were worthy adversaries for a time. You had our security half-mad trying to identify the culprits behind the sign-posting. But you slipped up, didn't you? All it took was one sloppy maneuver, one uncoordinated posting to reveal your friend here, to put his body directly in front of one of our cameras as he taped paper to wall. And BAM!" he thumped the podium with the flat of his right hand. "He was caught. One of *you* slipped up," his grin broadened to show uneven, brownish teeth. "One of you failed to cover your friend as he tacked up your propaganda. One of you. Which one?" His voice squeaked slightly, "Which one was sloppy? Which one was careless? Which one let down your friend here, allowed him to be seen, allowed him to be captured? Hmm?" The Bookkeeper laughed, enjoying himself immensely. "You'll never know, will you?" he sneered. "You'll never know which one *failed*."

The Bookkeeper allowed a too-long silence to pass. The Hopefuls stared guiltily at Nathan, at his thin naked body, at his outspread arms poised as if ready to be nailed to a cross. "And so," the Bookkeeper interrupted their thoughts, "you *will* confess and you will do so humbly and willingly. And in front of your peers. Oh, yes. Your confessions will be public. Any funny business and well…" he nodded towards two of the guards—one beefy and short, one tall and lean—and they strode mechanically towards the prison room. Without speaking, the tall guard selected a weapon off the wall—a long, gleaming blade that looked like a machete with a hook at the end. The beefy guard placed his broad hands on Nathan's shoulders and yanked them back so his flat chest became convex and vulnerable, like a desert dune in front of a sand storm. The tall guard stood to Nathan's left, raising his weapon slowly and theatrically so the audience in front of him had time to gasp, had time to watch the muscles in Nathan's chest grow taut and hard, had time to take in the gleam of the blade, the deadpan, emotionless face of the guard who held it. This scene had been rehearsed—it must have been. It was performed too effortlessly, too smoothly. The little ballerinas had practiced their pirouettes and grand-plies over and over until they were ready for opening night. Ready for the stage.

The Hopefuls watched in rapt horror. They had hoped the Bookkeeper was bluffing. They had hoped it was a big charade, that none of it was real, that they would open their eyes and the Bookkeeper's chamber and the hidden room and the thick-necked guards would all evaporate into the lost world of forgotten dreams. They now knew it was real. There was proof in the blood, in the humming blade as it sliced across Nathan's chest like a skate across ice. There was proof in his scream as it ripped out of his chest and spun across the chamber, filling it with the steely vibrations of expressed pain. The Hopefuls cringed and covered their eyes and drew in their breaths. They fought the urge to run to him, to cradle him in their arms and kiss his forehead and tell him everything would be ok. Everything.

Above the din of their whirring thoughts, the Bookkeeper laughed. It sounded thin and sparse, as if parts of the laugh became lodged in his wooly beard as it exited his mouth. "How now, infidels?" he squeaked, "How now?" He snapped his fingers towards the mismatched pair of guards. They silently exited the stage. "Not feeling so tough anymore, are you? Not feeling so rebellious." He sneered at the eleven bowed heads in front of him. They sat in silence, looking at their feet. "You will stand trial tomorrow," the Bookkeeper said, snapping into a business-like demeanor and abandoning his giddiness. The sudden change startled the Hopefuls; they looked up. "Starting at two o'clock. You will stand one at a time. I want all the residents to know the faces that betrayed our fine kitchen. I want them to see you weak and small, separated from the herd. And I *trust*," he let the word linger, "you will answer my questions appropriately." The Bookkeeper made a gesture with his head towards Nathan. He hung serenely in his chains. Blood oozed out of the long gash in his chest, slid past his genitals and legs and dripped, quietly on the floor below. Again, the Bookkeeper snapped his fingers and a slender figure, framed by guards, rushed forward, her hair bouncing behind her in a neat ponytail. The staff doctor fished around in her medical bag as the guards released their prize and roughly handcuffed his hands behind his back. The doctor seemed to find what she wanted and nodded to the guards. In reply, they marched Nathan out of the prison room, across the chamber, and through a narrow door on the side wall. The Hopefuls watched him disappear with despair. They felt scared and trapped. They wondered when the nightmare would end.

Before she faded into the darkness that waited beyond the doorframe, the staff doctor paused. She turned—just slightly, just her head and left shoulder—and looked at the friends of the prisoner, sitting small and helpless, in the center of the wide room. She gave them a small smile—really, more of a tightening of her lips—and gazed at their worried faces. Her eyes were tired and apologetic. They begged for forgiveness. The Hopefuls watched in wonder as the staff doctor stood before them at the door, showing them some small sign of life, showing them an ounce of humanity. They loved the doctor in that moment, appreciated her gesture. They felt the warm glimmer of hope burning somewhere deep inside them. It had not been extinguished. Not quite.

The doctor dropped her eyes and broke the spell. The Hopefuls blinked and adjusted themselves in their seats. How long had they been watching her? It must have been several years. The doctor breathed in, shook her head sadly, and melted through the mouth of the waiting door.

"Infidels," the Bookkeeper said. The Hopefuls turned to him, startled. They had forgotten he was still in the room. "I will dismiss you now. You are to return immediately to your bedrooms and stay there until tomorrow. Am I understood?" Silence. "Good. Any questions before you go?"

"Yes," said a voice, firm and clear, from the back.

The Bookkeeper looked startled. He gazed at the little, old man in front of him. The "wily" one who had run away that afternoon. "Yes," he said hastily, "what is it?"

Elmer looked at him squarely, his thin lips set in a firm line. "Will Abe be there?"

"I beg your pardon?" said the Bookkeeper quickly, leaning forward, thick brows knit.

"I asked if Abe will be there."

"Yes, yes, I heard you," replied the Bookkeeper, flustered. "Just a strange question, that's all."

"It's just," Elmer continued, "we would all very much like to meet him—the man behind the operation, the 'generous benefactor' you talk about so fondly. It would mean so much more if we could apologize to Abe directly."

The Bookkeeper scowled. "The old man is mocking me," he thought to himself. "He *dares* mock me after the demonstration of my absolute power. Hmph. He is trouble, that pale old man."

Elmer continued to stare at the Bookkeeper. The Bookkeeper stared back. Finally, he said, "Stupid old man, Ibrahim Anbar has much better things to do than watch the trial of some petty miscreants."

"Like what?" Elmer persisted.

"Like never-you-mind what!" the Bookkeeper shouted, annoyed. "At the trials, you will all apologize to me on Abe's behalf. That will be more than sufficient."

"Whatever you say," said Elmer. "You're the Bookkeeper."

"Damn right, I'm the Bookkeeper! And don't you forget it! Now, do you want me to bring your friend back in here for another round of punishment? Hmm? That's what I thought. Now shut up!"

Awkward silence ensued. The Bookkeeper fidgeted with his podium, attempting to regain his composure. Damn that old man. Damn that rotten, little old man! Finally, the Bookkeeper stomped over to the torture room, the room that held Nathan prisoner. He yanked a heavy, leather strap studded with metal spikes off the wall and shook it wildly at the Hopefuls. "I *said* you are all dismissed now. Go! Get out of my sight. And if I see any one of your dirty little faces outside your rooms, your friend gets a lashing with this! I will see to it personally. Now go!"

Silently, the Hopefuls stood up and sauntered out of the room. Their spirits hung low, like damp towels. But they were not destroyed yet. They still felt a tiny flicker of Hope and tried to kindle the flame as it licked at their hearts, attempting to catch. No, they were not destroyed yet.

Downtrodden, yes. Miserable, yes. But not destroyed.

They patted Elmer on the back as they walked to their rooms. Nothing was said, but he knew what their hands on his shoulders meant. They expressed the same gratitude he had felt towards the doctor as she paused in the doorway, silently apologizing on behalf of her kitchen, the kitchen that employed her and kept her fed. The kitchen that was much bigger than her. The kitchen that, in most ways, really wasn't so bad, was it?

* * *

That night, Elmer went to sleep. He went to sleep much like he had gone to sleep the night before his departure from Here or the night after the blaze tore apart the Modern Shamans' home or the night after he realized his Daisy would be plucked from his arms forever. He went to bed with a hazy sense of foreboding, a feeling that there was no reason for tomorrow, that the sun would decide it had better things to do than shine on another day.

Elmer rolled over with a sigh. His room had no windows, only a plain framed print of some purple flowers in a vase. Hotel art. Cheap and generic. Benign. His room was mostly dark, except for the sliver of light that squeezed its way through the cracks in the door. It was enough to reflect subtly off the glass that encased the boring flowers. "Ugh," thought Elmer as he stared crossly at the glare off the glass. *So canned, so fake. So frightfully boring. Nothing daring about them. Poorly drawn irises in a glass vase on a wooden table. Plain. A-dime-a-dozen. Just like my Irene.*

The thought startled him. His wife had been far from his thoughts lately, not even a glimmer in his mind. He wondered why she insisted on haunting him now, on this night. The night before his trial. The night when his mind should be focused on the present, on his current predicament and the fate of his friends. How dare she crop up now.

Elmer rolled over again, away from the flowers. He shut his eyes and tried to banish Irene from his thoughts, but she was persistent now. *Oh good grief. You always were pushy.* He thought of the girl from his dreams—the one who continued to grow, the one who began her life as a wild, hollow-eyed being and morphed into a blank-faced painting. A painting that reached towards him, gave up, pushed him down-down-down in his elevator cage. He shuddered. He felt the urge to apologize to the great painting.

I wish I could make you understand, Irene. But how could you? You were always content, always terribly pleased with your little life inside your little house in your little neighborhood with your little family. That is always how you thought—minisculely. Never caring about the world outside your tiny existence. How could you understand the storm in my head, the fire under my feet? How could you understand my need to escape, to discover myself, to get to the bottom of who I am and what my life is for? I am truly sorry for leaving you, but I was trapped. Suffocating. I needed to dig myself out.

He thought about the moon-faced woman in purple. *Dig myself out…*

Elmer took in his surroundings in the dim light. He smiled sarcastically. *Ironic, isn't it, Irene? I left my captivity in Here to become captive in another land, a different city. Maybe we're never truly free in life. Maybe we always must acquiesce to others' wills. Or our own selfish needs. But yet…*

He thought of himself huddled together with Grace and Zach, carefully going over their plans to reform the Kitchens.

…Maybe we're only as free as we decide to be. He thought of the long, flat fields of Here. He thought of the churches and the plain, practical buildings and years of pretending to fit in. He thought of his childhood, of running around barefoot in potato fields, kicking up clods of dirt as he ran.

Maybe I wasn't as trapped in Here as I thought. Maybe I was simply afraid to pursue my freedom.

Elmer looked at the light sneaking past the closed door. He listened to the creaking of a floorboard as the guard posted outside his room shifted from one heavy foot to the other.

Perhaps more than anything, freedom is a state of mind.

* * *

"Hello Bookkeeper."

"Hello Bookkeeper."

"I trust this day has found you well?"

"Oh yes. Quite well. And you?"

"Quite well."

"Excellent. Wonderful to hear."

"And how are things over at the kitchen of our esteemed Ibrahim Anbar?"

"I believe the situation is under control now. We used the young captive as an example to the miscreants. They were quite horrified, really. Boris and Tony did an excellent job with the torture—blade perfectly angled, standing back so all could see, just the right amount of blood. I think they got the message."

"Good. Good to hear."

"And you? How are the enemy-control methods working in Ezekiel's kitchen?"

"About the same, by the sound of it. We performed the same sort of theatrics. Our captive was a woman, put up quite a fight. But in the end she was pacified. The strap tends to break even the toughest shells."

"Yes. Assuredly, yes."

"Bookkeeper?"

"Hmm?"

"Nothing much. You seem a bit distant. Is something the matter?"

"Oh, do I seem distant? Hmm. I suppose I must. My thoughts were elsewhere, Bookkeeper. Forgive me."

"No harm done. Pray tell, where were your thoughts lingering?"

"Just over a troublesome old man, that's all. Probably nothing."

"Please. Indulge me."

"He asked if Abe was coming to the trials. He knew the answer perfectly well, of course. And this was after we employed the blade on his friend. Quite unnerving, his impudence."

"Quite. We can't have mindless infidels wrecking more havoc on our kitchens. Bookkeeper, you are right to worry. This is most troubling, indeed. Do you think he will behave at the trials tomorrow?"

"We can only hope, Bookkeeper. We can only hope."

"Perhaps we should *pray* about it!"

"Ha! Perhaps we should."

They laughed together for a moment, clapping each other on the shoulders and grinning. A streetlamp shone down the street, barely illuminating their spot in the park. They stood by a bench, not daring to sit. People might see. People might talk. Best to keep a low profile.

"Bookkeeper?"

"Mmm?"

"Were you worried this past week about the plight of our kitchens? Did you ever fear the repercussions of these trouble-makers' actions?"

"No, Bookkeeper. Not seriously, at least. Not when I reflected for a while. Just think—what do they have? Nothing, practically. And what do we have? Everything. Control, money, power. We own this town and the people in it. What can a group of rabble-rousers possibly do to our kitchens?"

"I suppose you're right. It's just—" Ezekiel's Bookkeeper paused for a moment and chewed on a his lip, smoothed his thin beard. "It's just that, they got so far. They reached out to so many residents, spread their message to so many people. None of the other rebels caused nearly so much of a fuss. It's just—it's unnerving, that's all."

"I understand your fear, Bookkeeper. But fear not. We will get rid of them yet. They think things will go back to normal after the trials. They think we will simply forget about their misdeeds, their *betrayal,* but they are wrong. We won't forget. Our memories are long and our grudges eternal. When things have settled down, we will make sure to eliminate the trouble-makers one-by-one until there is not one left. *That* is how we create harmony. *That* is how we maintain order."

"That *and* a little healthy rivalry between our two great kitchens."

They snickered a little, like twelve year-old girls at some inside joke.

"Yes of course, Bookkeeper. Where would we be without the rivalry? People thrive on it. They live for it. They suckle on it like so many little piglets at the sow's teat. Ah, the rivalry. It was a stroke of genius from the very beginning."

"Yes," said the Bookkeeper, nodding, a vague look in his eyes as he swam through past memories. "Yes, it was. How else to unite one's kitchen? Yes, the insignia is lovely. And of course there are the lectures. But nothing, not a thing, unites each kitchen like a common enemy. Thank you, Bookkeeper," he took his companion's hand into his darker one, "thank you for being that enemy."

The Bookkeeper tittered a little, cheeks flushed, and replied, "You're quite welcome, Bookkeeper. And I thank you as well."

That stood in silence for a moment, reflecting on their greatness, on the beautiful, soft power they cupped in the palms of their hands. It was lovely, this power. Just lovely.

"You know, Bookkeeper," said one of the thin-shouldered men, his voice cutting though the silent night air, "attendance has been quite strong this past month. Quite strong. About the best we've ever had."

"Oh really? That's wonderful, Bookkeeper. Just wonderful."

Chapter 41

The Friday trials were rich with smells. They permeated the dining hall and clambered into the nostrils of the fidgety, vast audience. A potpourri of clashing scents that made the onlookers feel nauseous and a little violent. They noticed the smells right away, locked them away in their memories, were reminded of them years later when similar scents invaded their olfactory systems. When the day was over, they tried to describe the trials to their peers, to the ones who weren't there. They found they could not. They found their descriptions falling cheap and flat as they spoke of the Bookkeeper and the row of twelve wrong-doers sitting huddled together at the front of the room and the narrow, wooden box in which they stood, one at a time, confessing their sins. They heard the descriptions leaving their mouths, knew their words formed some vague idea of what the trials were like, but realized they somehow failed to bring life to the setting. They had filmed the trials in color, but replayed them in black and white. They wondered how to rectify the true hue. The answer lay in the smells.

Bodies jostling, sweating, covering the room in a thick, human film. The walls lined with candles—purple and silver—emitting clouds of lilac and something foresty, piney. Clothing. Cheap cotton and denim in the front, fine leather and cashmere in the back. The scent of perfume—a couple dozen varieties—attempting to mask the natural scent of breathing skin and only succeeding, at best, as a distraction, a foreign body hovering around its host. The residents, crowded into folding chairs at the front of the dining hall, eyed suspiciously the townspeople and Council members in the back. They felt hedged in, trapped by the hovering perfume and the scent of cashmere sweaters. The townspeople gazed back sternly, daring the residents to take a chair from the back of the room—one of the purple-colored, cushioned chairs with ergonomic armrests. Just try it, they thought. Try to take one of our ergonomic chairs.

The trials began at a quarter after two, after the throng of watchers settled into their chairs and turned their heads expectantly towards the front, eagerly eying the makeshift stage, the wooden confession box, the elevated podium. They attempted to quiet the buzzing in their noses, to turn their attention fully on the scene in front of them. Their ears perked up at the click-clop sound of expensive shoes on hardwood. Abe's Bookkeeper emerged from the purple curtain that hung limply at the back of the stage. He burst through the curtain seams like a baby through his mother's birth canal: squinty-eyed and blinking, enthusiastically received by the waiting throng.

The audience applauded, the Bookkeeper bowed. It was a friendly world he had just entered. The Bookkeeper stood in front of the crowd; he smoothed his bushy beard, adjusted his robes. He was amongst friends, amongst allies. These were his residents. These were his townspeople and Council members. He loved them for loving him. The trials were won before they even began. What was the point? Of course the infidels hadn't changed things. Of course they hadn't permanently damaged the residents' loyalty. But the show must go on, he thought. The show must go on.

"Ahem," the Bookkeeper cleared his throat into his microphone. The audience silenced. "Welcome. Welcome everyone." His voice was grave, his face became stern, eyebrows knit. "We are here to address a serious matter, a serious breach in the harmony of our lovely kitchen. I think you all know the instances to which I am referring."

The audience nodded stiffly. Their faces mirrored the serious visage of the Bookkeeper.

"Of course you do. No need to discuss it in great detail. We all know that our wonderful kitchen has been invaded, *contaminated* with the heinous acts of a few individuals. These individuals, these poor lost souls, thought it would be *fun* to plague our fair kitchen with hateful propaganda, with vicious untruths."

The crowd grumbled angrily. It sounded like a giant heifer chewing her cud.

"Hateful, simply hateful acts!" the Bookkeeper exclaimed, tipping up on his toes, his beard bouncing slightly. "Inexcusable, vicious acts!"

"Grumble," said the crowd. "Grumble, grumble."

"It is sinful to lie, sinful to spread untruths! And yet—" the Bookkeeper rocked back on the soles of his feet. "And yet, we gather here today prepared to forgive these miscreants." He dropped his eyes and nodded at the floor in his best effort to appear humble. He hoped his self-satisfied smirk was hidden from the front rows. After a few moments of silence, the Bookkeeper straightened his mocking mouth, elevated his chin, and continued speaking. "We forgive because that is the spirit of Abe's Kitchen.

We do not hold grudges. We acknowledge the imperfection of man and are quick to give second chances. We only ask that the sinners admit their mistakes, confess their wrong-doings, and ask for the forgiveness that we so freely offer. Does that seem fair to all of you? Does that seem just?"

Heads nodded vigorously. The Bookkeeper wrestled with the musculature in his face. It insisted on grinning when common sense demanded a frown. He looked away for a moment, attempting to gain his composure. The audience noticed the movement and thought he was fighting back tears. Compassion and sympathy welled in their hearts. Poor Bookkeeper. Betrayed by members of his own flock. Disappointed in their actions. Ready to forgive and welcome them back to the fold. Poor, benevolent Bookkeeper.

The Bookkeeper got a hold of himself and once again faced the onlookers. A vein in his left temple ticked violently. "Friends," he said, "let us not delay any longer. Let us hear what the sinners have to say. Let us receive their words with open hearts. Let us begin."

He nodded towards a skinny, waist-coated man on his left. He bustled behind the curtain and emerged with a tall, thin man, his well-kempt dreadlocks reaching past his shoulders, his head held high, his light brown eyes proud and unafraid. The man was led to a high-backed chair inside a box with wooden railings. He sat down. The audience squirmed anxiously. They weren't quite sure what they expected—possibly someone smaller, someone less confident-looking, someone with shifty eyes and greasy clothing. The man in front of them didn't fit.

The Bookkeeper strode from the podium to the wooden box with his quick, elegant steps. He stood off to the side of the man so the audience could enjoy the benefit of seeing both sinner and forgiver play their parts in the scene in front of them. The Bookkeeper began, "State your name, please."

"Zacchaeus J. Hill."

"Age?"

"Thirty-four."

"Months at our fair soup kitchen?"

"Five."

"Good, good," the Bookkeeper paused before he jumped into the meat of his questioning. "And were you involved in the events of this past week?"

"Yes."

"Did you personally hang signs denouncing and smearing the good name of our kitchen?"

"Yes."

"Did you aid others in hanging the aforementioned signs?"

"Yes."

"Did you hang these signs with the goal of overthrowing or causing upheaval in our fair kitchen?"

"Yes."

"Did you hang these signs with malicious intent and a hateful heart?"

Zach swallowed. His lip quivered. He hesitated; the Bookkeeper leaned in towards him, fire in his eyes. "Y-yes," Zach answered finally. "Yes I did."

"Ok," breathed the Bookkeeper, relieved. "And do you admit your signs were full of lies, untruths, and far-fetched notions?"

"Yes."

"Are you sorry for the chaos you caused, the lies you spread, and the unrest you created?"

Again, Zach hesitated. The Bookkeeper repeated, snarling, "I say again, are you sorry for the chaos you caused, the lies you spread, and the unrest you created?"

Zach looked at the watchful eyes of the audience, the necks craned towards the stage. He bit his lip and closed his eyes. "Yes," he said. "I am sorry."

The Bookkeeper emitted a tiny squeak of glee. The audience members murmured amongst themselves. "And do you promise to never again spread falsehoods or perform other malicious acts against this kitchen?"

"Yes," Zach replied quietly, defeated.

The Bookkeeper didn't bother to hide his grin now. He peacocked around, his head bouncing in front of Zach's face, his eyes mad and luminous. "Do you promise to be a good and responsible member of our community, a role model for all, and a *loyal* resident?"

Zach looked away. "Yes."

The Bookkeeper giggled and clapped his hands together. "Good, good. Let us see if you have earned the forgiveness of the members of this kitchen." He strutted to the side of the wooden box and peered at the captive inside, his face leering and sarcastic. He gestured towards him like a tour guide at the zoo. "Friends!" he shouted. "I want you to listen closely to our reformed sinner now. He has something to say." He turned to Zach and muttered, "repeat after me."

"I, Zacchaeus J. Hill." "I, Zacchaeus J. Hill."

"Am sorry for my sins." "Am sorry for my sins."

"And for the chaos and disharmony I caused." "And for the chaos and disharmony I caused."

"To the esteemed residents of our fair kitchen." "To the esteemed residents of our fair kitchen."

"I know I am not worthy." "I know I am not worthy."

"Of mercy and forgiveness." "Of mercy and forgiveness."

"But I do implore." "But I do implore."

"The noble-hearted residents." "The noble-hearted residents."

"Of this fair kitchen." "Of this fair kitchen."

"To act in the spirit of our benefactor." "To act in the spirit of our benefactor."

"The praise-worthy, wise, generous, loving Ibrahim Anbar." "The praise-worthy, wise, generous, loving Ibrahim Anbar."

"And forgive my sins." "And forgive my sins."

"On his behalf." "On his behalf."

Zach's head hung limply; he had become a rag doll propped up in his seat. His eyes focused on nothing, just glazed across the floor. The Bookkeeper addressed the crowd.

"You have heard the words of the reformed sinner! You have heard his cry for forgiveness. You have heard him invoke the name of our great and glorious leader. I ask you now. Do you forgive him?"

"Yes," a few people murmured.

"I ask you now!" The Bookkeeper screamed, his arms flailing wildly. "DO YOU FORGIVE HIM?"

"YES!" they thundered in reply.

"Do you welcome him back to the fold?"

"YES!"

"Do you open your arms and your hearts to him?"

"YES!"

"Good, good," the Bookkeeper said. "Excellent." He turned abruptly towards Zach, holding his right hand tenderly, a glint in his eye. "Now kiss my ring."

Zach looked vaguely towards the little man, his face frozen and pale. He felt nauseous. He wanted to puke all over the prim leather shoes in front of him. He wanted to grab the Bookkeeper by the beard and bash his head into the floor again and again and again and again—

"Infidel," the Bookkeeper said in a voice so quiet Zach felt like it sprang from his own head. "Kiss. My. Ring."

Zach leaned forward.

"And kneel please."

He knelt. He bent his head forward towards the extended fist. His lips brushed the Bookkeeper's golden ring, felt the wiry hairs of his knuckle. He pulled away quickly, trying not to gag.

"Very good," the Bookkeeper grinned. He turned once again towards the man in the waist coat. "Next! Bring me the next one!"

The trials marched on. One-by-one. They sat down. Confessed. Repeated what was to be repeated. Hung their heads. Humbled themselves. Begged forgiveness. Kissed the glimmering, ruby-encrusted ring on the Bookkeeper's index finger. Were herded off to the side where they stood, shoulders touching, like cattle in an auction pen. With each confession, the Bookkeeper grew increasingly drunk. He swayed giddily and snickered. He gestured and grinned sloppily. The power intoxicated him, made him weak in the knees. He wanted more. More.

"Kiss the ring!" the Bookkeeper shrieked. "Kiss it! Kiss it!"

The audience chewed on their lips and looked away, ignoring the churning in their stomachs. They shouted louder, bellowed their support, hoped the noise would distract them from the nausea that bubbled in their guts.

Eleven reformed sinners stood across the stage in an even line. Spotlights beat down upon their hanging heads. The air around them was thick and greasy; they found it hard to breath. Behind the curtain, Elmer observed their silhouettes, followed the peaks and valleys of their rigid bodies. Soon he would be added to the topography.

The curtain was brushed aside. The waistcoated man slipped into the quiet world behind it. Here, there was little stimuli. There was not row after row of probing eyes and shouting mouths. The stench of bodies and cologne became as dim as the lights. Here, there was only one, miniscule man sitting in one, miniscule chair. The waistcoated man sighed. "Alright," he whispered. "You're up."

Elmer nodded and said nothing. He allowed the man to take him by the elbow and escort him onto the stage. Lights, voices, musk assaulted his senses and nearly knocked him flat. He leaned against his escort for support.

The Bookkeeper grinned. He watched the old man hobble stiffly to the boxed-in chair and sit down, his thin shoulders stooped and shaking slightly. Not so tough now, that wily old man. Not so tough anymore. The Bookkeeper pranced to his twelfth and final miscreant, like a hairy ballerina. The audience booed and mumbled; they shifted their weight and scratched; they whispered in hushed tones. The Bookkeeper leaned forward, so close Elmer could smell his stale, rotting breath. "Your name!" he shouted, his voice shooting down Elmer's ear canal and colliding with the drum.

Elmer shuddered from the force, touched his ear tenderly. He felt naked and violated.

"State your name."

Elmer swallowed, steadied his shoulders and his rapidly beating heart. He looked into the pits of eyes in front of him and cleared his throat.

"Elmer H."

* * *

Elmer awoke the morning of the trials with colors on his mind. He wasn't sure where they came from. As far as he knew, he slept hard and deep, his mind as black as a cave. But there they were. Red-orange-yellow-green-blue-indigo-violet. Swimming around. Carelessly invading his vision. Sometimes shapeless, sometimes smiling at him with brown or blue or multi-colored eyes. The seven sages.

"Hello," Elmer whispered softly, sitting up in bed. "You're back again I see."

"We never left," they responded or, at least, Elmer thought they responded. He couldn't be sure.

He stretched his arms upward, feeling a kiss of air from the cracks around the door. Striped rays of sunshine fell through the slats in the blinds and onto his lap. Elmer mused at the rays, thought about how they warmed his body. He turned his attention back to the colors.

"Never left? Seems to me you've made yourselves pretty scarce. There were many times I could have used your help."

"We never left; we never left," they insisted.

"Yeah?" he replied, anger creeping into his voice. "What about when Nathan was captured? Where were you then? Or when those brutish guards took Eleanor away? How about then? Hmm? Or how about every time a Loyal tries to pressure Grace into committing herself to one side or the other? Where were you then? You certainly weren't wiping away her tears."

"No," the crystalline voice of the moon-faced woman cut through the muddled hues, "but you were. You were there to wipe her tears."

Silence.

"And we were there helping *you*."

"Oh, right. So you were there, guiding my hand, telling me the right thing to say? You helped me pat her back? You helped me hold her hand?"

"Sometimes. But that was mostly you. We're always there, Elmer. We guide when necessary; we intervene rarely. Mostly, we support. You know, you've tapped into our guidance without knowing it. We've fed you strength and courage when you needed it. We've whispered words of advice when your heart was open to receiving them. Think about it for a moment, Elmer. Remember."

Elmer sat, his brows knit, thinking. Memories started creeping into his consciousness. Events. Instances. Times when he felt their presence, but never fully acknowledged it. Guidance, they said. Guidance is what they offered. Did they, then, guide him to Ms. Patti's seminar? Did they guide him during his recruitment of the Hopefuls? Did they prompt him to speak up during the audience with the Bookkeeper? Did they help him understand his dreams with the faceless women? Did they lead him away from the train station and back to the kitchens? Did they fortify him with courage and strength to help lead a rebellion?

Elmer looked up. The colors stared back at him, their bodies close, their brilliant robes swishing subtly. He got the impression they were floating, hovering somewhere inside the robes, their feet rejecting the ground.

"Thank you," he said. "For being there. For guiding me."

"You're welcome," replied the moon-faced woman. She absentmindedly picked at a sleeve of her long purple robe.

Elmer looked at her, frowning, thoughtful. "But why am I conscious of you now? Why did you suddenly leap back into my life after such a long absence?"

The woman looked up from her sleeve. "You tell us, Elmer. Why did you call for us?"

"Why did I—" Elmer paused. His brain wheels turned; a light came on. "That's it, isn't it? That's the answer to one of the riddles. You appear when I'm feeling lost. Helpless. That's why you first appeared, isn't it? In the strange mountainous land? That's why you led me to Roger? That's why you took shape and helped carry Hilo upstairs after the rock came through the window? I was feeling directionless during those times. Lost—yes, I think lost is the best word. And you guided."

"I suppose that sums it up well enough," this time the blue-robed man spoke, his basso voice mixing with the slanted sun rays and warming the room. "We're *always* guiding, remember? But sometimes you need a little more help than other times. You need to contextualize us. You need to harness raw emotion into human shapes. And so we appear."

"So you do," replied Elmer, his voice strangely distant. "So you do." He peered through a crack in the blinds and watched the day unfold itself like a lazy house dog. "I suppose it's obvious why you've materialized today. The trials."

"Hmm, yes. The trials," said the man in blue. He scratched a beard-covered cheek. "You have nothing to worry about, Elmer. Truly. Things will work out."

"Hmph," said Elmer, slightly peeved. "Is that the advice you wanted to give to me today? Things will work out? Of course they will. They'll work out exactly as the Bookkeeper wants them."

"Don't be so sure, Elmer," said the man, shrugging his broad shoulders. His voice was even and calm; it glided like butter on bread. "And no, that's not the advice we wanted to give you."

Elmer's cheeks turned crimson. He lowered his eyes. He was so jumpy lately, so nervous and high-strung. And now he was venting these emotions on his multi-colored friends, on the beings the Modern Shamans called his spirit guides. Perhaps it was crazy to talk to these beings—and even crazier to listen—but, despite everything, they comforted him. They gave him hope and made him feel secure, cared for…parented. Seven mothers and fathers.

Dispensing advice, holding his hand. He loved them, he realized with a shock. He truly loved them. It didn't matter if they were real or if they had hatched from his brain. He loved them.

"What advice then?" asked Elmer in a small voice.

"Simply to pay attention. Pay attention, Elmer. Observe. Listen. Solutions will come to you; you merely have to quiet your mind."

"Pay attention," Elmer repeated, his eyes trained on the sun-soaked maple tree outside his window. "Nothing too profound, but I suppose I need to be reminded of that from time to time. Pay attention. Alright, I'll do my best. Just for you—"

He turned back to the room. The seven figures were gone, leaving only a dusting of rainbow-colored light and a warm smell that reminded Elmer of frothed milk.

* * *

"And Elmer," the Bookkeeper sneered, "were you involved in the events of this past week?"

"Yes. Yes, I was." Elmer's gaze was unwavering. His eyes held the Bookkeeper's, firmly, relentlessly, as if he was grabbing him by the gonads.

"Did you personally hang signs denouncing and smearing the name of our fair kitchen?"

"Yes."

"Did you aid others in hanging these signs?"

"Yes, I did."

"Did you hang these signs with the aim of overthrowing or causing upheaval in this kitchen?"

"Yes."

"Did you hang these signs with malicious intent and a hateful heart?"

Elmer smiled. He imagined his grip tightening—squeezing, squeezing. "No."

* * *

"Gooood morning."

Grace looked at Elmer with dull eyes. "Someone's feeling chipper this morning."

Elmer shrugged and sat down. "I suppose. I just made up my mind not to let this place bother me, that's all."

"Hmph," Grace replied. "At least *you* weren't the one who promised the Hopefuls everything would be ok. At least *you* weren't the one who suggested we turn ourselves in."

"They caught us anyway, Gracie," said Zach. "Quit being so hard on yourself. No one blames you. No one feels any animosity."

Grace said nothing. She buried her face in her hands and looked away.

"There, there," said Elmer, patting her on the back. He remembered the words of his spirit guides. *We're always there, Elmer. We guide when necessary; we intervene rarely. Mostly, we support.* Now, it was his turn to support. "You're ok, Grace. You're ok."

Levi looked at his mother questioningly and started prying her fingers away from her face. "Mommy," he said. "Mommy. Mommy, what wrong? What wrong, Mommy?"

The hands lowered; the green eyes met. Gently, Grace wrapped her arms around the little boy and stroked his thick, curly hair. "Nothing, sweetie. Nothing's wrong. Everything is going to be just fine. Just fine." She rocked his little body back and forth, back and forth.

"Yes," Elmer said, "everything's going to be just fine. And Grace—," he waited for her to look at him, "Zach is right. Don't be so damn hard on yourself. We're all in this together and no one is blaming anyone else. Besides, can you imagine yourself sitting back and doing nothing while the kitchens slowly brain wash their residents? I don't think so. That's not the Grace I know. At least we gave it a shot, eh? At least we caused a little upheaval, some discomfort, right? I watched the faces of the residents after they read our signs."

"They were pretty nervous, weren't they?" Zach interjected.

"Nervous, yes," Elmer continued, "but mostly thoughtful. They looked awake, Grace. They were thinking for themselves for once. And you did that. *You.* You should be damn proud of yourself, that's what. Now, stop your moping."

There was a tone of finality in Elmer's voice that startled Grace and made her look at him curiously for several seconds. "Ok, Elm," she said. "I see your point. At least we tried, right?"

"That's right," he replied. "And it's not over yet."

Zach reached across the table and absentmindedly patted Levi's curls. He turned and addressed Elmer, "You know, you would have made a brilliant motivational speaker."

"Oh, psha," said Elmer. "I'm not so sure about that."

"No, really," said Zach. "You have been an inspiration to me. Truly."

Elmer blushed and looked away. "Well, thanks Zach. Not sure what I did, exactly, to earn that praise. But thanks."

"I think about when I first met you in the park, Elm," Zach continued. "You were this crotchety old man, bothered by everything, scared of everyone. And now you're sitting here amongst the poorest of the poor, patting our backs, lifting us up, fighting for us, *with* us. It's incredible. Elmer, you are incredible."

"Stop it, Zach. I'm not. I'm not incredible. I'm just an old man who got fed up with his old life and wanted to try something new. I'm nothing special. Just an old runaway."

"You're more than that to us," said Zach and squeezed the old man's hand. "Just look at you now. Sitting here like Jesus Christ amongst the tax collectors. That's who Levi and Zacchaeus were, you know. Tax collectors. The lowest rungs on the ladder. And now you sit between us—our friend."

"Now you're just being ridiculous, Zach," said Elmer, embarrassed.

"Am I?" said Zach. "I don't know. People listen to you, Elm. People adore you. Maybe you don't notice it, but I do. You are prophetic to them, a wise old oracle."

"Ok, ok," said Elmer hastily. "Let's not get carried away." The image of Ms. Patti suddenly cropped up in his head, her poofy hair framing the makeupped face, the luminous eyes. "Embrace your prophet-ness," she had said. "Live it."

What on earth. Why do they think I'm special? I'm just me. Just Elmer. Just a farm kid from the middle of nowhere. Don't they know that? Can't they see that?

"Think what you'd like, Elmer, but you're great to us. You're a teacher."

I'm just me; I'm just me. Goddammit! I'm just me. Why can't they see that? Isn't it obvious? Just a runaway; just an old man.

"You've helped us so much, Elm," Grace spoke up. "Always there, always dependable. Our rock."

If only they could glimpse my past life. If only they knew about the years of pretend living—of hollow actions and premeditated words. If only they knew about the wife I abandoned, the father I despised. If only. Prophetic? P-ha! I think not.

Grace wrapped an arm around his shoulder and squeezed. "Thanks for everything, Elm. Really. I was feeling pretty low this morning and you came around and changed that. Thank you."

But then again, maybe every prophet, every saint has felt the same way: 'Why me? Why have they chosen small, imperfect me?" Now, there's a thought.

"You're welcome," Elmer said.

Grace smiled at him. "Ok," she stretched and yawned. "I'm going to head back upstairs and take a nap. I didn't sleep very well last night."

"Sounds like a great plan," said Zach. "Elmer? You coming too?"

"Nah, you two go ahead. I was thinking about grabbing a cup of coffee."

"Ok, Elm," Zach clapped his hand on Elmer's back. "See you later."

"See you."

Grace and Zach strolled to the elevator, hand-in-hand. Elmer watched them go. They had such faith in him, such trust that he would live up to their expectations. He would try his best. He would do it for them. His friends.

Elmer strolled over to the coffee caddy and poured himself a cup of houseblend decaf. He emptied a packet of creamer into the cup, stirred, and watched the milk swirl into the mahogany brown, lightening it to the color of a dusty, dirt road. Movement on his right-hand side snapped him out of his trance. He turned. A woman—pale skin, short-cropped brunette hair, a little plump—scuttled across the room and over to a dining room table. He watched her sit down, spreading a newspaper, setting a glass of orange juice in front of her.

Had he imagined her stare? Or had she actually been watching him?

Elmer grabbed his cup of coffee and sat in one of the easy chairs by the fireplace. He stretched his legs and yawned. "Pay attention," the spirit guides had told him. "Listen. Quiet your mind." Elmer closed his eyes and felt hot liquid travel down his throat. He lowered the coffee cup from his lips and smiled. He was feeling pretty good, all told. He was feeling pretty good despite the pending trials, the uncertain future, the fact his personal guard was lurking around the dining room, assuring that he didn't run away once more. Pretty good for all that, he thought. Feeling pretty good.

Chair springs squeaked beside him, protesting the weight that had just settled itself on the seat. Elmer glanced at the chair. The woman—the plumpish brunette—was now seated beside him, perched nervously on the edge of the seat as if ready to bolt at any second. He stared at her curiously for a few seconds, then looked away. He shut his eyes again, attempted to follow the blue-robed man's advice and quiet his mind. His momentary peace was interrupted by a cough.

"Ahem-ahem," coughed the woman in the chair. "Ahem."

Annoyed, Elmer looked over at the woman. She stared back. "Can I help you?" he growled.

The woman remained wide-eyed and silent.

"Well?" said Elmer. "Whaddya want?"

"I—" started the woman nervously. Her voice sounded high-pitched and surprisingly child-like coming from a forty-something year-old mouth. "I—I mean—are you—are you Elmer H?"

Elmer hesitated. "Yes," he replied tersely. "Yes, I suppose I am. Now please, ma'am, what is it you want?"

She breathed in and out slowly. Elmer watched her full chest inflate and deflate under her maroon cardigan. "I thought so," she said. "I thought it was you."

"Well, it is. So, what of it?"

"I know you're one of the leaders in the rebellion here. I know you've helped arrange the sign-posting and all that."

"Ok…"

"I also know about the predicament you and your friends are in. I know you're being forced to stand trial today at two."

"Of course," said Elmer, "everyone knows that."

"Yes, well, not everyone knows that one of your number—the one called Nathan—had to get seventeen stitches to stop the blood from pouring out of his chest."

Elmer sat up. "How'd you—that is—how'd you know—"

"And not everyone," the woman continued, "knows about the Bookkeeper and his torture room. Or that he is forcing you all to stand trial against your will. Not everyone knows about the guards and how they locked you all up in a storage closet before they decided what to do with you. Not everyone knows all that."

"Well, clearly, clearly. But the question is, how do *you* know it? Who are you?"

"I'm Marta."

* * *

"No?" the Bookkeeper said, his eyes fiery, his mouth menacing. "Perhaps you didn't hear me correctly, reformed sinner. I asked you, 'Did you hang these signs with malicious intent and a hateful heart?'"

"I heard you just fine," said Elmer. "The answer is no. No, I did not hang these signs with malicious intent and a hateful heart. I hung them out of love. I hung them to set people free."

"Outrageous!" screamed the Bookkeeper. "All your cronies, your miscreant friends, admitted they hung these signs out of malice and hate. How are you an exception? How could you perform such a despicable act with pure intent? You sullied the good name of this kitchen! You drove our residents to fear and despair! You acted selfishly and cruelly! Now, I ask you again, did you hang these signs with malicious intent and a hateful heart?"

"No," said Elmer, louder this time, bolder. "I didn't." He sat up straighter, looked defiantly at the Bookkeeper. "You bully people around; you take them in when they're down on their luck; you force them to stay loyal to you. Of course they're going to be loyal! What choice do they have? You feed them, yes. You keep a roof over their heads. But mostly, you feed them rhetoric and keep a club over their heads. They are scared to step out of line. They are afraid to challenge. They worry that you will take it all away from them. And then, where would they be? Back where they started—in the street, hungry. Scared. But I'm telling you, they shouldn't have to choose. They shouldn't have to sacrifice their freedom for oatmeal in the morning and warm sheets at night. They shouldn't have to swallow the lessons you spoon-feed them. They are *people* for the love of god! They are people just like you and it's about time you started treating them as such. And I am *not* going to sit here and pretend to be sorry just because you've threatened my friends and me for protesting your *fucked-up* system! I am not! You can do what you want to me, but at least they know the truth now. At least your precious sheep know what a wolf you really are, what a hideous, disgusting—"

"That will be enough!" raged the Bookkeeper. "Enough out of you, old man! Lies, all lies! This one's as crazy as they come! I can't talk to such a lunatic. Guards! Guards, take him away now. Take him away until he decides to be honest with us. Pathetic, old man! Trying to strike fear in the hearts of my—our—residents. Pah! Simply pathetic. Don't believe a word he says! Off his rocker, that one. Completely insane. Guards! Hurry along, now. Take this one away; get him out of my sight. Guards!"

* * *

"Marta," Elmer repeated. "And how do you know what you know, Marta?"

"I happen to have a friend who works here. The staff doctor. She tells me all about the goings-on at this kitchen and what happens to those who step out of line."

Elmer recalled the staff doctor at the Bookkeeper's audience. He recalled the look on her face as she strode after Nathan and the guards. Human. She had looked human.

"I see," Elmer said. "And what are you doing here, Marta?"

"Trying to help."

"Yeah? You think you can?" Elmer attempted to keep the skepticism out of his voice, but, despite his efforts, it edged in anyway.

"Yes," said Marta, crossing her arms and looking slightly hurt, "I think I can."

"Marta," said Elmer soothingly, "I don't mean to offend you, but this is a pretty big fish to fry. You might not know what you're up against here. The Bookkeeper, Abe's Kitchen—well, they have vast resources, almost infinite power. I hear they control part of the town as well as the kitchen residents. Now Marta, certainly, we appreciate any help we can get, we really do, but this is beyond our control. We simply need to let the chips fall where they may and try to get out of the trials decently unscathed. That's the plan, anyway. We're all going to admit we were wrong and move on with our lives. We gave it our best shot, but the Bookkeeper won in the end. He won, Marta. That's it."

"That's not quite it," she replied. "Not as far as I'm concerned."

Elmer sighed. "I wish I was feeling as optimistic as you."

"But I'm telling you, I can help."

"Ok, Marta," said Elmer, slightly exasperated. "I just told you why the situation is hopeless. Maybe in the future you can help us get another rebellion together, but for now we're simply going to stand trial, ask forgiveness, and call it a day. Nothing else to do at this point."

"But there is," she insisted, her blue eyes shining above chubby cheeks. "I've talked it over with my doctor friend. She thinks I can help too."

"Well, that's nice, but—"

"She's confident I can make a difference. And I believe her Elmer, I really do."

Elmer nodded quietly and said nothing.

"In fact, she was the one who inspired me to go into the line of work that I'm in."

"Yeah?" said Elmer. "And what line of work might that be?"

Marta smiled. "Soup kitchens."

* * *

"Guards!" screamed the Bookkeeper again.

The guards hesitated, conflict stirring in their hearts. Another protester, another elderly soul to dispose of. Another person to gag, bind, throw in a trunk, haul to the woods. Another person to set free, like a rehabilitated bird. They weren't sure if they could stomach it again.

"Guards!"

Dirty work. They were always doing his dirty work.

"Guards!"

Dammit. What choice did they have?

Two mammoth men stepped forward; the Bookkeeper smiled thinly. They grabbed Elmer roughly by the shoulders. "Best to come quietly," one said in a low, rumbling voice.

"That," said Elmer, "isn't going to happen." He crossed his arms and stared straight ahead defiantly, his wispy white brows knit together. For a moment, the guards looked at the stubborn old man, a mix of admiration and exasperation in their eyes. The crowd watched silently, holding their breaths as the moment hung delicately in the air, like a falling leaf. They sensed they were witnessing something important, a turning point of sorts, as if this moment—like the leaf—marked a change in seasons. They leaned forward slightly.

"Wellll!" the Bookkeeper shouted. The leaf crashed to the ground.

"Right," said one of the guards. "Come with us. No fighting, please." He yanked Elmer by the elbow and forced him to stand.

"No," said Elmer, his voice dangerous. "I will not."

"Yes. You. Will," the guard replied, emphasizing each word with a tug on the old man's arm.

"No he WON'T!" came the reply. Dozens of eyes and necks and foreheads turned towards the voice. "He won't go with you! Not if I have anything to say about it."

"WHAT THE DEVIL!" shrieked the Bookkeeper. "Who the *hell* are you? What are you doing in *my* soup kitchen?"

"I'm Marta," said Marta firmly, standing as tall as her round, five-foot, three-inch frame would let her, "proud owner of Marta's Soup Kitchen and I'm here to collect my residents."

"Your residents? *Your* residents! Woman, you are mad. Get out of my kitchen. Now! Out with you. Out! Guards!"

The crowd watched with rapt attention. They cared very little about the outcome of this showdown. Mostly, they were pleased by the entertainment. Terribly pleased.

"I'm not leaving without my residents," Marta said loudly, calmly. "Elmer agreed to transfer kitchens this morning. See!" She held up a book, thick and leather-bound. "He signed my guest book!"

A few giggles from the crowd. The Bookkeeper's face turned the color of ripe strawberries.

"Outrageous!" he said. "You can't bind anyone to a kitchen with a stupid thing like a guest book!"

"Oh no?" said Marta, her eyes mocking. "Don't you?"

"Th-that's entirely different," the Bookkeeper stammered. "That's for record-keeping purposes only."

"As is mine," Marta replied. "And right now it says that I have one more resident than what I have. I must rectify the numbers, you know." She gave Elmer a little wink. The Bookkeeper seethed.

"Ridiculous, ma'am. Utter nonsense. Besides, the rest of them haven't signed it. You can't take *them*, now can you?"

"A slight problem I mean to address shortly. I did bring a pen, you know. And you haven't cut off their fingers yet, I see."

The Bookkeeper glared at her, his jaw hanging, throat restricted and gurgling.

"And I don't mean to take just them. I mean to take as many as I can, anyone who chooses to come. But first, let me be frank." She turned towards the crowd and addressed the watchful faces. "I don't have a big, fancy facility. I don't have tennis courts and a library. I don't have feather mattresses and deluxe sound systems. What I do have is food. Plain, old food. And a gym floor stocked with mats and sleeping bags. No one will be pampered with massages and seaweed wraps, but I can offer you camaraderie and a belly full of homemade food. You can come and go as you please, no hard feelings. I don't demand loyalty in exchange for my services. And I don't do lectures. Sorry. That's just not me. So, take it or leave it; the offer is on the table. Come sign my guest book if you wish to give my kitchen a try." She walked to the edge of the stage and set the book, open-faced, on the stage floor.

The Bookkeeper watched her nervously. Large beads of sweat stood out from his forehead and around his neck. He mopped them away and found his voice. "Woman," he said in a low, mocking tone, "you are insane. There are no other kitchens in this town besides Abe's and Ezekiel's. You are full of it. A fraud. Residents," he said, addressing the crowd, "listen not to this witch. She is trying to lead you astray. Remember your lectures. This is a test. A test from your evil rivals. Act accordingly, friends. Turn away from this sinner."

Marta furrowed her brow and drew in her lips. "A fraud, you say? An evil rival? Do you think they *actually* still believe you? Do you think they *actually* still swallow your rhetoric? They're smarter than that, Bookkeeper. And that's your biggest weakness, you know—underestimating your people."

"Don't listen, friends! She speaks lies, dirty untruths. Listen not! Listen not, I say!"

"Do whatever you'd like," Marta sighed, shrugging her shoulders. "I'm not here to sell anything. Come if you'd like. Stay if you'd like. It's completely up to *you*."

Silence engulfed the dining hall, thick as the potpourri of smells. The residents gazed, wide-eyed in wonder, looking first at the Bookkeeper, then at Marta, then back to the Bookkeeper. Their pupils bounced like ping-pong balls. Their brains whirred. Pleased, yes they were pleased. Entertained, yes.

But nervous as well. Nervous because they could feel themselves at the edge of a decision, looking down from the precipice and deciding whether to jump. Should they jump? Should they leap blindly off the edge. They weren't sure. So they watched and waited, entertained and pleased and nervous.

The Bookkeeper glared; he growled. He angrily picked at his white beard. "Sinners," he mumbled. His voice gathered strength. "Sinners!" he cried, looking over the cow-eyed audience. "We've a house full of sinners today!" A few assenting murmurs rose from the back. "It's despicable, utterly despicable." He shook his head. "Guards! Take her away!"

"So kind of you to offer me escortment, but I know the way, Bookkeeper," she gave a little wink that sent ripples of agitation through the Bookkeeper's thin frame. "Anyway, I have no reason to stay any longer. I'll be leaving now." She glanced around the room. "Who's coming with me?"

Her voice trailed off; the silence rose. Eyes glanced at each other, at her. The silence had a pulse. It drummed-drummed-drummed at their ears. After several seconds—or several years—the soft tap of shoes played above the beat of silence; the melody echoed across the stage. The audience looked up, spotted the source of the sound, watched mesmerized. The Bookkeeper also watched. He watched helplessly, not mesmerized. Nathan ignored the watchers and continued walking, tap—tap-tap, tap—tap-tap, to the edge of the stage, looking neither left nor right, his hazel eyes fixed on the squat woman in front of him. He paused for a moment, carefully lowered his body to the stage floor, and gingerly stepped down, clutching the front of his torso where the stitches tugged at his skin, attempting to keep him whole, but threatening to spring apart. His eyes never left Marta as he strode up to her, stopped, held out his hand.

"I'd like to sign the guest book please."

Marta grinned. "Here," she passed him a pen. He took it, turned, walked back to the stage where the book lay naked and inviting, its pages clean and white. With an exaggerated gesture he swooped down and signed his name in large, angled letters, crossing his "t" slowly and deliberately. The Bookkeeper grunted and flapped his arms a little, but said nothing. Nathan looked at him and smiled.

"I'd like to sign it too!" said another voice from the stage. Grace stood up, her son plastered to her side. "Pass me that pen, Nathan." The pen was passed, the book signed. Grace straightened up and walked over to Nathan's side. The Bookkeeper scarcely had time to glare his disapproval when several more voices rose from the stage.

"I'll sign it too, Marta." "And me!" "Count me in too!"

The Bookkeeper watched the dam burst, the humanity flow out. The Hopefuls, one-by-one, left the square wooden box on the stage and clustered around the guest book, grappling for the pen. They grinned unabashedly; they shot dirty looks at the Bookkeeper. "Gimme that pen!" they said. "Let me sign the damn book."

The crowd watched, less pleased. They no longer felt entertained. They felt pressured and awkward. They needed to make a choice. Bodies squirmed; eyes darted. A few people stood halfway and sat down again. Finally, one brave soul stood up, marched forward, reached for the pen.

Hoorahs and Yips came from the Hopefuls' throats. They clapped the resident on the back, ushered her into the cluster, congratulated her, smiled, shouted words of encouragement. Heartened, a few more residents stood up, made the journey across the sea of eyes, and docked by the guest book. "Sign it, sign it!" the Hopefuls shouted with gusto. "Sign the guest book!"

The dark eyes of the Bookkeeper brooded, analyzed, silently protested. He was rarely at a loss for words. His silent throat troubled him deeply. He watched anxiously, his eyes wide and unbelieving, his muscles taut and quivery. Finally, the gush of traitors slowed to a trickle. He breathed a sigh of relief. A couple dozen had left, but not all—not all by far. After all, attendance had been quite good lately. The kitchen was damaged, but not broken. The kitchen was wounded, but not dead. Another sigh. They would start anew. They would rebuild their kitchen with this group of supporters, this faithful group that refused the infidels' calls. They would be stronger than ever. The Bookkeeper clenched a fist—they would be stronger than ever.

After the signatures were captured and the din subsided, Marta turned once again to the Bookkeeper. "No hard feelings, Bookkeeper. I wish you well. Good luck." She scooped up the guest book and cradled it in the crook of her arm like an infant. With a wide turn, she faced the door and started marching, leading her troop in a straight, disciplined line to the front door. The remaining crowd watched, once again pleased and entertained. "Let them go," they thought. "Let them go with this crazy, little woman.

Let them be without their facials and hot tubs. They'll be back. And then we'll laugh hard, hard. They'll be back. They'll be back..."

At the end of the straight, disciplined line, hobbled an old man. First to sign the guest book, but last to leave, the old man leaned heavily on his cane as he walked. Another ending, another beginning. He wasn't quite sure where he was going or what he was leaving. But he didn't question. He simply walked—walked and leaned heavily on his cane. His muscles felt weak, barely capable of holding his bones in place. He walked in a straight line, placing one foot carefully in front of the other, as if balancing on a narrow tightrope. One-at-a-time, one-at-a-time. He couldn't feel the floor. He wondered if he was walking on clouds—a narrow band of clouds, or maybe a thin beam of white light. He liked that thought: walking on white light. White light that reflected colors, that sent oranges and greens and purples shooting through the air. He imagined every step he took squeezed more colors out of the thin beam of light. Step—cyans and ceruleans. Step—brick reds and tangerines. Step—midnight blues and forest greens. Step. Step. Step. Into thin, cloud-muffled sunlight. Beams from the air finding the beams under his feet. Colors dizzy and swirling. Unable to feel his toes. His three legs scramble to find the white-light tightrope. They cannot. They only find clouds. Elmer feels himself falling.

Grace reaches out and tries to catch him. Her fingertips brush his shoulder as he falls from Grace and lands in the waiting arms of Zach. Zach, short for Zacchaeus. Zacchaeus, the tax collector.

END OF PART II

-LIMBO-

Zach giggled and squeaked, flailing his little arms in the air. His mother tickled his belly, fingers scampering across mocha skin, laughing in cadence with her son. Sometimes she was happy. Times like these. Mostly, she survived.

Zach snorted and pawed his mother's hands away. The tickling ceased. Maggie collapsed with a sigh. She was back in The City. It was strange to be back in The City. It sucked at her energy, pulled her apart. And yet it propelled her, excited her, made her virgin-jittery. She didn't understand the back and forth tug of The City. But she let it happen, let it pull on her limbs like a stiff breeze rustling through branches. She dug in her roots and braced herself. Like a tree, never caught off guard.

* * *

Breeze rustled the grass, sent it dancing towards the north. Sun forced its way through cracks in clouds. Cars passed, left shoulder to left shoulder. City B hummed. Hummed like usual. Hummed in a quiet sort of way, a subdued sort of way. A few bicyclists churned pedals; lazy wheels spun. Clouds thickened. A few raindrops fell, staining sidewalks, saturating skin. Leaves rustled. They rustled in that quiet, smooth way, like a giant sigh, and then stopped. The old man knew it was going to storm.

* * *

The voluminous man shifted his weight and glared at the figure behind the podium. "Howcouldyouletsomethinglikethishappen?" he bellowed, words spilling over each other like the fleshy stomach that hung over his belt.

"Keys, sit down." The rational voice replied. "Let's calm down, everyone."

"We won't be calm, Bookkeeper. We won't be pacified. That woman barged in here, stole thirty of our residents, waltzed away. Calm! I'll show you calm!"

"Keys, sit down," the Bookkeeper repeated. He felt old, exhausted. World-weary and energy-zapped and dog-tired. Pronounced bags hung below his eyes, weighing down the lids. He imagined himself sprawled out on a beach somewhere, breeze playing across his pale face and thin grey beard, cool drink in hand, not a soul in sight. He breathed in deeply, the taste of sea-salted air tickled his tongue. "Let's everyone take a deep breath. Things aren't so bad."

"Not so bad! Not so bad? Thirty of our residents, Bookkeeper. *Thirty*. We can't just pick up thirty more tomorrow, you know."

"Keys, I said sit down," the Bookkeeper said sharply, trying his best to arrange his tired face in a menacing manner. "I'm telling you things aren't so bad. Yes, we lost thirty residents. Yes, that dog-faced woman barged into our soup kitchen—Ezekiel's Soup Kitchen—and ran off with our people. But I'm telling you, all is not lost. Look at it this way—our kitchen has been purified. Cleansed. We should be thanking this rogue kitchen operator, actually. She has separated the wheat from the chaff. We are left with the wheat. I suggest we make the most of the situation and bake bread."

The Council gazed at the Bookkeeper, awed. He was their leader. Eloquent of tongue. A vessel of unending wisdom and knowledge. How lucky they were. The Council nodded.

"Undoubtedly, we have some work ahead of us," the Bookkeeper continued. "We must restore the people's faith; we must cool the tempest before it causes any further damage. But I know we will emerge from the storm stronger, more united, dignified, and *loyal* than ever. We can do this. We are Ezekiel's Kitchen."

The Council murmured, their tempers mellowed. Why had they doubted?

"It's not going to be easy. That woman has shaken our kitchen to its very core, but I assume you are all up for the challenge. I assume you will put your shoulders to the wheel and push. Let us lead by example, friends. Let us show our residents the meaning of unity. Compassion. Faith. Let us be unwavering in our resolve. Let us start today. Now."

A few cheered. Their spirits lifted. The Bookkeeper was never without a plan, without a solution. He was the Bookkeeper. He knew. He knew everything. They trusted. They trusted their Bookkeeper.

* * *

Tack-tack-tack sounded the roofing nails, piercing the shingles. Cecelia thought of fish scales, row after row of delicate fish scales. She hammered lightly. Lightly but firmly. Roger looked at the shingles and thought of shingles. He pounded them fiercely. Every once in a while they looked at each other. Looked at each other and smiled. The house was bringing them closer together. Each nail, each two by four, each shingle pounded into place, knit their lives together a little bit more. This is Hilo's House, they said. This is hers. And they knew she agreed. They felt her presence there, felt her cool breeze as she glided past. It wasn't an angry breeze, just restless. So they built. They built on and on and on without end. They were tireless and fierce. They were determined to finish it. It, their project of love. Their project of respect and honor for their friend. Their friend whom they sorely missed. But then again, they missed the others as well. Craig-Kyle-Onyx-Ezzie-Maggie-Elmer. Elmer. Oh, Elmer. In some ways they missed him the most. Sweet man. So tragically lost in the world. They wondered what he was doing, where his feet tread these days. They wondered if he was happy. Or if he missed them in the same way they missed him. Tack-tack-tack. The roofing nails. Echoing through the neighborhood and down the street. Sometimes they wondered about the fire and how it started and if Onyx' accusations were correct. But the thought made them nervous and they continued connecting hammer to nail, pounding, pounding, arms growing stronger, skin darkening in the sun. Although your skin is already dark, Roger, Cecelia would say. Dark, dark, like a raven's feather. Not that dark, he would reply. More like a piece of cardboard. Not that light, she would laugh. Somewhere in between. They worked by themselves, hauling lumber, plugging in power tools. Shrugging off mistakes. Tearing off boards that didn't lay properly. Biting their tongues at times to stop angry words from flowing. Growing closer with every board laid, every nail pounded. Holding each other tight, tight at night, her creamy skin entwined with his somewhere-between-cardboard-and-raven-feathers skin. Talking little, saying much.

* * *

The old man walks. He feels a drop on the crown of his thin-haired head. Pat. He sees another drop on his shoe, feels another on his neck. Pit-pat. They quicken their paces. Another group stands on the sidewalk by E.B.'s Kitchen, shuffling around like nervous cattle. A greeting, a hail. That group joins their group like two rivers diverging. They walk on.

Where are they going? Only the round-faced woman knows.

They follow. Shoes pat-patting in time with the rain. Fast steps, quick steps. The old man keeps his head down instinctively. The heavens open up. Rain pours down down down. Slides down the old man's neck and dampens his back.

Wasn't there sunshine a few minutes ago? He thought there was. He couldn't be sure.

Pat-pat, the shoes. The old man can feel his feet now. They squish with each step. He hates the noise, but hates standing still even more. He must keep moving. Must keep up with the herd. His bones aches, joints and muscles and skin ache. He sneers at his human body, wrinkles his nose at the wooden prop that holds him up.

But there isn't much time to think. They must continue on. To where? Only the round-faced one knows. But they trust. And shoes go pat-pat-pat down the sidewalk and through the curtain of rain. The rain that slides down the old man's neck and dampens his back.

* * *

The Bookkeeper smiled weakly and left the podium. He walked past the Council, nodding, shaking hands, exchanging a few words. He walked out the door, down the hall, down the elevator, through the first floor, and out the entrance doors. The Bookkeeper was waiting.

"Hello, Bookkeeper."

"Hello, Bookkeeper."

"How was your Council meeting?"

"They were pacified eventually. I recited everything we talked about—a new sense of unity, separating the wheat from the chaff, cleansing. I think they bought it."

"Good. Very good. Of course they did. Of course they bought it. They're not really the ones we have to worry about, are they? They've already sunk their hearts, their finances, into our kitchens and they still want a return on their investment. They still want to believe they have some semblance of power."

"Hmph. That is what they think, isn't it? That they are betting on the winning side. That they will surely gain the Reward and that the other side will fail. That's it, isn't it? The goddamn Reward."

"Ha. Yes, that's it. A great invention, I must say. A beautiful creation of yours. Such a nice ring to it—the Reward. And so exquisitely vague."

"Yes," the Bookkeeper looked blankly into the dark. "Yes."

The Bookkeeper clapped a hand on the Bookkeeper's shoulder. "I have my Council meeting in a few minutes. I should return to Abe's."

"Funny, isn't it," the Bookkeeper said, his voice distant, thoughtful. "Both of our kitchens were invaded by that woman. She interrupted both our trials, ran off with dozens of our residents, and our Councils have no sense of their parallel lives. They have no idea that the same fate befell their rival kitchen. They don't know that they share the same burden, the same annoyance, as their rivals. And they'll probably never know. They'd rather die than communicate with someone from the other side. It's strange. They live in parallel universes—universes that never cross, but keep spinning, spinning, spinning in their own spheres. And they have no idea. No idea."

The Bookkeeper nodded. "Strange, yes. But that's the way we designed them, no? The design is working. We've manufactured perfection."

"Perfection," the Bookkeeper echoed. "Not quite."

"Ok, not quite. But close. Close enough to keep their universes spinning. Happily spinning."

The Bookkeeper nodded. "You should go, Bookkeeper, your Council awaits."

"Right you are, Bookkeeper."

They embraced for a moment, firm-armed and close, and then turned away, one Bookkeeper towards Ezekiel's Kitchen, one Bookkeeper towards Abe's, robes swishing softly as they walked.

* * *

Ezzie strode down the aisles of the greenhouse, observing, prodding, pinching at the plants. Flowers. Such useless vegetation. A veritable waste of space. But people loved them. They oohed and ahhed their way through Mabel's Greenhouse, past white and pink orchids, past ruby red roses and ivory lilies, past sunny Black-eyed Susans, past carnations, reaching out and caressing the petals. They dillied and dallied their way all the way to the other end of the greenhouse where the check-out—and Ezzie—stood. "I thought rose bushes were two-for-one," the old ladies with steel-grey salon curls would complain. They were always haggling over prices. "That was last week," Ezzie would answer. "Sorry." "Then I'm going to put one back," the old ladies would threaten. "Be my guest," Ezzie would shrug. What did it matter to her? Mabel might care, but she, on the other hand, couldn't give two shits about sales and moving inventory and special offers. She was there to look after the flowers and that's what she did.

The greenhouse was hot. Hot and stuffy. Ezzie rolled her eyes when groups of tittering, fluffy women pranced through the greenhouse saying, "Oh goodness, don't you have the best job on earth? What I wouldn't give to work in a greenhouse, tending flowers all day. It must be a like working in paradise. Your own Eden. How wonderful." Ezzie would wipe sweat off her forehead, adjust her gloves, and wordlessly get back to work. The women failed to notice her lack of enthusiasm.

The only break in the monotony, the only bright star in Ezzie's world, came every Friday at three o'clock. Ezzie worked nervously on Fridays, trimming plants that had just been trimmed, anxiously picking dead leaves off shrubs and absentmindedly tossing them on the ground. She glanced at the clock again and again and again and again. Now four hours to go, now two hours. She listened for the crunch of gravel, the purr of a minivan motor. She ran to the greenhouse entrance when she heard it, leaving trampled customers in her wake. Fridays were her best days. She saw Susan on Fridays.

* * *

They were out of the rain and into the shelter. Now what?

They were out of one kitchen and into another. Now what?

They owned the clothes on their backs and the shoes on their feet and not a thing more. Now what?

They had defied the system, caused chaos, bred distrust, sought revolution, stuck it to the man, created hope. Now what?

Now what? Now what? Now what? Now WHAT? W-H-A-T. What? What now?

They paced a lot that first night. Their bodies shifted in sleeping bags. Palms, feet sweaty. Eyes roaming, settling on each other.

They talked little that first night. Mouths dry, throats stuck. Mouths as dry as heads wet. Skin lubed, conversation not. Conversation jilted and stiff.

They slept little that first night. Pretending. Curled up on the gym floor. Bodies shifting, minds roving. Wondering.

Humming.

Questioning.

Asking now what, now what, nowwhatnowwhatnowwhat? What? Now?

Now What?

* * *

Three visitors came to Hilo's House after the last tack-tack-tack, the last coat of paint. The visitors had names. Cecelia greeted them by their names.

"Onyx! Craig! Kyle, darling! So happy you could make it. Come in! See what we've done. It's taken weeks and weeks, but we've done it. We've really done it. Come see. Come see!"

The three named visitors stepped through the door, gasped. They stood silently for a moment, just beyond the threshold, breathing shallowly and holding hands, fighting back tears. Finally, Onyx spoke.

"Cecelia. Roger. It's—I just don't know how you—it's—I mean—"

"Lovely," Kyle whispered. He squeezed Craig's hand a little tighter. "Just lovely."

"Yes," said Onyx, nodding. "Lovely." She looked into Cecelia's eyes, those blue-grey orbs. "Hilo would be proud."

Cecelia swallowed. "Glad you like it."

They spent the afternoon walking down hallways, up stairs, sliding their fingers along wooden banisters, admiring the craftsmanship of the new house. They felt the pulse of the fresh beams, throbbing beneath their fingertips. The house was an infant. New. Green. A bundle of nerves and life and energy, excited as a puppy. Onyx swore it was whispering to them, chattering away like a friendly, old aunt. They felt comfortable in the house. They felt at home.

"I'm not leaving," said Onyx firmly, crossing her arms and glaring first at Roger, then at Cecelia. "You're going to have to drag me away kicking and screaming because I am not leaving. I won't go back to my parent's house; I just won't. I'm crashing your little love nest Rog and Cec. You can't stop me."

Cecelia blushed. "Oh, Onyx. Of course you're welcome to stay. Do you think we built a five bedroom house for just us?"

"You and little yous," Onyx winked and Cecelia's blush deepened. Roger chuckled.

"Of course you can stay," he said. "That's the whole point. Reunite the Modern Shamans. Bring us back together. Continue growing and learning from each other. We were going to try to recruit *you*, but looks like that won't be necessary."

"It won't be necessary for us either," said Craig, stepping forward. "Kyle and I hate our new apartment. It smells like cat pee and the electrical system is a piece of work. Honestly, you can't plug in a toaster and a laptop at the same time without blowing a fuse. We'll put in our month's notice tomorrow."

"Oh Craig! Kyle!" Cecelia threw her arms around their necks, kissing first one and then the other cheek. "I was hoping you'd come! Now we have the beginnings of a household again, don't we? If we can just convince the others—"

"Don't get your hopes up, Cec," said Onyx quietly. "Maggie is in The City now. She's staying until she makes peace with her past. And Ezzie—well, Ezzie is near her granddaughter now and she's not likely to give up that spot, is she? I got a letter from her the other day (can you believe it? I always thought she couldn't stand me!) and she sounded sickeningly happy. I mean, nauseatingly, candy-sweet happy. She's even working in a greenhouse now, ol' Ez. Anyway, it won't happen. And then there's Elmer…"

Onyx' voice choked. She squeezed her eyelids together and opened them again with a sigh. "I think about that old geezer every day. He was really special, wasn't he? Like a prophet, almost. Or a wise old Jedi master. I wonder how he's doing in the big, wide world. I wonder if he's still teaching—or doing whatever he does. He doesn't quite teach, does he? He more just listens and understands. Oh, that Elmer. That Elmer. I carry him right here." She placed her hand on her chest, over her heart.

The others looked at her silently, eyes foggy, remembering.

"I wonder," Onyx continued, half to herself. "I wonder what on earth he's up to."

* * *

Elmer wondered what on earth he was up to. A permanent soup kitchen resident? A permanent bum? No. No, thanks. Not for him. Then what? A permanent helper-of-bums? That, maybe. But there were other things, weren't there? There were other cities and other lands. Other experiences and other people. His feet itched. He spent his days pacing. His hips hurt from sleeping on the gym floor and rolling back-and-forth, side-to-side. Dark, purple bruises boxed in his sides like bookends. It was time to leave.

* * *

Marta was happy. She hummed serenely to herself as she went about her day. She busied herself with laundry and cooking and cleaning and caring. She chatted and joked and giggled and listened and interacted in many other ways with the residents. They loved her. Their savior; their martyr. Their Martin Luther. Pinning up grievances against the establishment. Sticking it to the man.

When she walked by, they all vied for her attention, grappled to be near her. She was the local celebrity. They shook her hand, deluged her with praises. She nodded humbly, a little embarrassed by the whole thing, and went about her work. Humming, humming as she went.

* * *

This City. My City. The City.

Maggie stared out the window. Stared at fog-and-pollution-coated buildings. Grey. Vague grey giants poking brazenly out of the street. Sprouted out of concrete soil. Nurtured by iron and cement. She stared at moving cars, jostling for the road. Always moving, she thought. Always go-go-going. Bunching up, bumper to bumper, angrily pushing each other along. Engines turning over and over. Humming, buzzing, throbbing. The City.

This is my love song to The City, she thought. This is my heart beating in time with the engines. These are my legs spread over the skyscrapers, acquiescing to their block and brick and glass. I feel their textures inside me, within me. I shudder.

This is my love song to The City. Its churning, whirring madness. Its trash cans and alleyways. Its fullness and richness; its thousands of smells.

My love song. My love song to The City. I sing of interactions, of human skin brushing against human skin. Of colors. Of intoxication. Of creating nests in tiny cubbies, building lives twig by twig.

This is my City. My City. I see it through brown lenses; I see it with my wrinkled brain. I do not see your City. Your City is different than mine. Your City is different than hers or his. Or ours. Your City doesn't know the things my City knows; it doesn't feel the same, look the same, act the same. It doesn't understand The City in which I live. True, our feet tread the same sidewalks, navigate the same paths, but your footstep is different than mine. It doesn't fall in the same way, with the same rhythm. Not quite.

This is my City.

* * *

The Bookkeeper stretched and peeped around the curtain at his flock. They waited attentively, hands folded. Today's lecture was about the Reward.

"Ah, the Reward," the Bookkeeper had said to the Bookkeeper. "That ephemeral and delightful concept. We are wise to speak of it this week, I think. We need to give our residents a reason to keep believing. A reason for *faith*."

"Faith, yes. We have little to worry about with this bunch, I think. But it is always beneficial to remind them why they believe. The Reward. Their ticket to eternal happiness. No one quite knows what it is; everyone knows how to obtain it. Loyalty. Faith."

"Yes. It's beautiful. Yes."

"Our supporters have become more ardent, more fiercely loyal, you know. The exodus of their peers has brought them closer together. They have their *loyal* brothers and sisters by their sides now. None of the riffraff that's been floating around here lately. We should thank that little round woman, really. She's made our jobs easier in many ways."

"Ha, quite right, Bookkeeper. Quite right. The irony is hilarious, really. Oh well. We always win in the end, don't we?"

"Right you are, Bookkeeper. We always win in the end."

The Bookkeeper looked over his flock one last time, sucked in his stomach, straightened his shoulders, and marched to the waiting podium with a scowl on his face. The audience drew in their breaths and held them as he straightened his microphone, adjusted his sleeves. "Friends," he began, "all of our actions have consequences…"

* * *

Elmer didn't mind the plain meals and plainer décor. He didn't mind making small talk with Grace and Zach and the other homeless folk in the kitchen. Nor did he mind the daily chores—the scrubbing and the sweeping and the serving—that they all did on a daily basis. These things were not stressful. They were even vaguely relaxing. But Elmer was not in the mood to relax. He was in the mood for movement.

Grace sensed his anxiety, his restlessness. "Elmer," she said, "nothing is keeping you here. Not really."

"No?" he answered. "Not you and Zach and Levi?"

"Don't worry about us. I can tell you're not happy. And that doesn't make us happy."

Elmer bit his lip, nodded. *Not happy. She's right. I don't know what I am right now, but I know what I'm not. And what I'm not is happy.*

"Grace, Grace," said Elmer softly. "Am I such an open book?"

"To me you are," she replied with an equally low voice. "I can read you like my son." She pressed Levi to her hip. His curls nestled against her side. "Elmer," she said, looking into his emerald green eyes. "Do what you have to do. Listen to yourself. Listen to this." She reached over and patted his chest, right above his heart. Elmer swallowed and looked away.

"That's a lesson I've learned time and time again," he whispered. "And somehow I always manage to forget it." He looked up again, green staring into green. "Thanks for the reminder, Grace."

"Of course," she said and shifted her hand from his chest to his shoulder. They sat like that—Grace in the middle of the old man and the young man, the father-figure and the child—arms wrapped around each other, staring silently at nothing in particular, letting their thoughts ebb and flow. Eventually, Elmer's eye lids grew heavy and his muscles limp, he felt his body slip towards Grace as he teetered on the verge of sleep.

"Alllright," he yawned, stretching his arms towards the ceiling. "Time for bed."

They walked into the gym, found their sleeping bags, shuffled inside. Zach joined them shortly from the kitchen, wiping excess dish water from his hands onto his jeans. He smiled when he saw them and leaned down to kiss Grace on the cheek. She smiled in return.

"Elmer and I had a nice talk tonight," she said, looking squarely into his eyes.

Zach nodded gravely. He said nothing.

They arranged their sleeping bag-encased bodies on the floor so that their heads were nearly touching. A four-point star. Elmer sighed. He imagined his thoughts mingling with Grace's and Zach's and Levi's. Stewing around, mixing together in the center of the star. He liked that idea. Mixed-up thoughts, swirling around lazily, dipping in and out of the resting heads. Painting an intricate, multihued picture.

I suppose thoughts have colors. All the colors of the rainbow.

* * *

Nel Keys walked down the long hallway of her house. Bedrooms left and right, left and right. She ran her hand across each door she passed, feeling the wooden planks, thinking of the children inside. And the children who used to be inside. She paused. Looked up. Ran her hand across the wooden letters of the second-to-last door. I-R-E-N-E. Nel wondered how she was doing, her eldest child. She would be twenty-five now. No, twenty-six. Good God, how time flies. She hadn't seen her in years. Seven, eight years. Irene never liked City B. Or Ezekiel's Kitchen. Or her family. Irene was different, simply different. Nel had begged Freddie to keep her daughter's name on the door. One memento, one artifact bearing her name. That's all she asked. They weren't allowed to say her name. Freddie forbade it. But could they at least look at it from time to time? Could we at least keep it in writing, Nel had asked. Fine, Freddie gave in. But that's the line. The line has to be drawn somewhere. A sinner's a sinner, even if that sinner happens to be our daughter. Keep the name on the door. But that's the God. Damn. Line. You hear? She heard.

Nel's fingers lingered over the wooden letters. Hand-painted. Skillfully crafted. The work of their little artist. I-R-E-N-E. How was it that they gave up these letters for an E and a B? How was it they abandoned their daughter for the favor of a tiny, bearded man who pranced around in robes and salivated too much when he talked? How had that happened? How was this—this wooden placard—the only remaining footprint of their daughter's existence? Where had the other footprints gone? Washed away, she supposed. Dissolved, little by little, with the seasons. And this—she let her hand drop from the door—the only remaining footprint.

* * *

Friday. It was Friday. And almost Susan-time. Ezzie smiled and picked at the dirt under her fingernails. Maybe she would arrange the lilies one last time. Those were Susan's favorites, of course. Not carnations. No, certainly not those dreadful things. Lilies. The girl had good taste.

"Ma'am," a wispy woman with two matching barrettes—one on each side of her head—stepped up to the register. "Can you check the price of these chrysanthemums? It didn't seem to match the price that was listed in the Sunday paper."

Ezzie brusquely grabbed the scan gun and reached for the plastic pot containing the mystery-priced flowers. She paused. Gravel crunched, blue van rolled in, little girl jumped out. "Susan," Ezzie whispered.

Scan gun, flower pot fell to the ground. Black dirt jumped onto the barrette-woman's cream-colored slacks. Ezzie didn't hear the shouts or the scolding. She didn't notice the customers staring, watching her jog towards the door. All she heard were tiny footsteps on gravel; all she saw was her granddaughter. She crouched down, arms outstretched, and waited for the tiny body to throw herself around her grandmother's torso. The hug came and Ezzie returned it, arms wrapped around the young girl like a cocoon, reluctant to let her butterfly go.

* * *

Three o'clock a.m. and the old man stirs. He stretches. He wriggles slowly out of his sleeping bag like a caterpillar, inch-by-inch. The boy next to him shifts; he moans. The old man freezes. The moan stops. Breathe in, lungs expand. Breathe out, lungs deflate. Keep wriggling. Inch-by-inch-by-inch-by-inch-by-inch-by-inch-by-inch.

He's a stealthy jungle cat; he's a stalking wolf, moving silently towards his prey. His prey: the door. The door across the gym. He reaches the end of the bag and lets it slip past his feet. He gets up, stretches, feels the hair stand up on his skin. He's nervous, excited, anxious. His stomach is twisted into a tight, hard ball. He finds his shoes; he finds his duffel bag. Jungle cats don't have duffle bags. Oh well.

He sneaks towards the door, touches the handle, cracks it open slightly and feels the cool night air on his face. Pause. He can't do it. Not quite. He can't walk through the door. Something invisible, something invisible and strong, is pulling him back, pulling him back towards his sleeping bag. An unresolved matter, a guilt-soaked feeling. He tip-toes back to the now three-pronged star on the floor. He bends down where the heads meet. Green eyes stare at him from the dark. They glow as if they're producing their own light. Elmer jumps.

Grace smiles, sits up. Zach stirs, looks up. Levi follows suit. The three-pronged star has risen.

Elmer lowers his body until his hip-bones are seated in the center of the star. He puts his arms awkwardly at his sides, moves his mouth, tries to speak. But speaking isn't right, so he stays silent. Grace understands. She reaches for his thin body, encompasses it in her arms. Zach leans over and lends his arms as well. Levi gets up. He doesn't quite understand, but he knows this feeling. It's the feeling of joy mixed with sadness. It's the feeling of goodbye-good luck-I'll see you later. He spreads his arms as wide as they will go so he touches each adult, one-two-three.

They sit on the gym floor a while, letting emotions pass through and around their arms. Then Levi lets go. Then Zach. Then Grace. Elmer is sitting alone now. Bare, cold. He emerges from the middle of the little group, finds his strength, rises. Rises like the phoenix from the ash. A chick again, his whole life ahead of him. He strides for the door.

Part III: Tower I

Chapter 42

His first mission was to find her. He knew she was here somewhere—living, breathing, caring, protecting, healing, making peace. He knew she was walking sidewalks, smelling freshly baked bread, inhaling second-hand smoke. He knew that her long limbs stretch-stretched in the morning, hauled her body out of bed, reached for the coffee-maker.

Maggie.

Maggie the Wise. Maggie the Graceful. Maggie the Strong.

He felt her shadow stretched across brick-and-concrete buildings, stretched across café umbrellas and fire hydrants and the sides of taxis. He saw the imprint of her lips on tea cups, the whorls of her fingertips on discarded newspapers. Strands of her hair tumbled down sidewalks, making him turn, give chase, get lost in alleyways and fish markets.

He combed City C, street by street, borough by borough. Down streets named after trees and emotions and philanthropists. Down streets named after seasons and leaders and types of fruit and birds. Streets with endless numbers, numbers, numbers. Down Oak-Robin-Pleasant-King-Summer-Dale-Apple-Maple-Martin-Main-TwentyThird-FortySixth-TwelfthSouthwest-EightyNinthNorthEast. Hadn't he already searched Twenty-Seventh South and Maple? Or was that Twenty-Seventh North? Hadn't he already passed that café? The one with the bright blue umbrellas? Or had they been green?

The city of There had been difficult, overwhelming, stressful. But it didn't hold a candle to City C, *The* City. Elmer wondered what would have happened if his first stop had been The City. Most likely an instantaneous heart attack. Open up the train doors and BOOM! Dead! Killed by the wave of stress that sprang out of nowhere—ninja-like—jumped down his throat and nunchucked his aorta.

But no. He had a decent transition from There to City A to City B, meeting "those people," the "others," "them" along the way, learning about them and from them, accepting them as human life, embracing their struggles, loving them. Now, as he navigated City C, the city everyone called "The," he was less afraid of those people/others/them. He didn't balk at piercings and green hair and ripped fishnet stockings. He smiled at the waitress with the half-shaved head and Gemini tattoo across her chest and tipped her well. She was friendly, a good conversationalist, and was working her way through business school. And she had a slightly impish smile that reminded him of Onyx. He slid her some cash, wished her luck, and was on his way—back to hunt. Back to the streets filled not with others, but human beings. Living, feeling human beings whose lungs expanded and contracted like his.

At night he slept in the kitchens. They were everywhere in City C. In churches, old warehouses, private homes, gymnasiums. He searched for the corruption he had found—felt—in City B and breathed a sigh of relief when he didn't find it. He chatted with the residents, made friends, avoided the ruffians and drug-dealers, and moved on, always dipping into his duffel bag at the end of his stay, retrieving a five or ten, and slipping the bill into the hand of a new-found friend.

He paced through The City for nearly a month. Up and down and up and down and up and down streets. There was a favorite coffee shop, a favorite restaurant, a favorite soup kitchen. Every once in a while, he treated himself to a hotel room. But he never really enjoyed his stays, never really got over the vanilla-washed rooms and sameness, sameness, sameness. Same tiny bottles of shampoo, same starchy white towels, same hospital corners at the ends of the double beds, same ice machine, coffee maker, iron, hair dryer, same foreign housekeepers and white upper management, same chlorine-saturated pool, same wallpaper, same Bible in the nightstand, same feelings of falseness and make-believe. He fought the urge to rip away the beige wallpaper with his fingernails and paint the walls with his hands. He cringed at the generic houseinthecountryside wall-art. He lined up the tiny toiletry bottles (shampoo-conditioner-lotion) and knocked them over with a flick. He undid the hospital corners and mussed up his bed until it looked like a giant, fluffy maroon-and-beige nest. In the morning, he would check out, resolving to stay out of hotels and in the kitchens. Resolving to never set foot in another hotel for as long as he lived. Inevitably, he would forget. The memories of sameness and sterility would fade. The longing for a comfortable bed and air conditioning and television would return. He would fight the urge for a while and then—in the true way of human beings—give in.

Elmer cursed himself and his short memory. Cursed his memory as he handed the front desk clerk a wad of bills, got his room key, punched the elevator button, stepped down the hall, slid the card in the slot, opened the door, and immediately thought Oh Shit. Oh Shit, here I am again. Damn my short memory.

Summer was growing old and weary. It drooped and wilted. It turned brown and dull. As brown as the spots on Elmer's hands and arms. As brown as his well-worn loafers. Summer had had its run. It had thrived, prospered, exalted, sang, sweated, pole-danced, skipped, lounged, whispered, caressed, and…expired. With a quiet breath, it extinguished and Autumn rose to take its place. So the cycles go, so the seasons. Circles within circles. Repeating, twirling, spinning. Never ending. Circles and circles and circles.

Elmer noticed the circles, vaguely. He felt Summer's dying breath, felt Autumn's quivering life. Leaves rattled nervously, preparing to submit to their new master. Autumn. Like so many Autumns Elmer had known. Cool, crisp, foreboding. Marking the place between Summer and Winter. Promising colors and the sound of dry leaves underfoot. Elmer shivered when he thought of that sound. He loved it. It reminded him of home. Home with forest-ringed fields and oak, maple, birch trees. Leaves to rake and jump in. Dead leaves. Dead leaves making way for new leaves. So the cycle goes.

Elmer looked up. He found himself in a park. Not a large park, just a small neighborhood park that was home to one basketball court, one swing set, and one box of sand. And trees. In the center, a giant elm stood, limbs outstretched, desperately competing with the sky-scratching buildings of City C. Elmer walked towards it and placed his hand on its rough bark. "Hello, elm," he said softly. "I wonder how old you are. Surely older than me." Elmer kept his eyes trained upward, watching the branches sway and sway, observing how they tapered off away from the trunk and grew more dense and intricate, all twigs and leaves. "I have been around for seventy-nine of your cycles, tree," Elmer said. "I have been on this earth while you have shed and regained your leaves seventy-nine times. And now," he smiled warmly at the canopy, "we finally get to meet. Elm to elm."

He let his hand linger for several more minutes, breathing in and out deeply, slowly. Watching, watching. His mind grew quiet, his breath soft.

After a while longer, Elmer sighed, removed his hand from the tree, turned and walked away. "Enough searching for the day," he thought. "Enough."

* * *

Elmer had a favorite soup shop named Karmedic Relief. Maggie had a favorite soup shop named Karmedic Relief. Elmer went there whenever he could, whenever he was in the area. Maggie went there whenever she could, whenever she was in the area. The owner of Karmedic Relief was Napoleon, a rotund, jowly Sicilian man with a propensity for making too many jokes and over-explaining them. Elmer and Maggie thoroughly enjoyed him. "Do you get it?" he would say, over and over, a hundred times each day. "The name of my restaurant, do you get it? Kar-mee-dik Relief. Like Karma and Comedic Relief put together. And like medic, medicine. Because soup is the best nurturer for the soul, I always say. And," he would add, "there are several books that would agree with me." Then he would wink—he winked in abundance—and serve up a generous helping of soup, always splashing some over the edges. "Which is no problem," he would explain, "that's what the bread's for. Sop up the excess, I always say. Don't let any of that soup go to waste. There was plenty of blood, sweat, and tears that went into making that soup. Those are the secret ingredients." He would wink again and send Elmer/Maggie on his/her way with the steaming bowl of soup and perhaps a sandwich on the side. Maggie's favorite soup was the squash purée. Elmer's favorite, chicken dumpling. It reminded him of home.

As Karmedic Relief would have it, Maggie and Elmer met in their favorite soup shop by bumping into each other, quite literally.

"Yowch! Son-of-a! Watch where you're going, sir!"

"Just getting more napkins. Sorry! There was no one there second ago. I—"

Pause. Recognition. Smiles.

"Elmer?"

"Maggie?"

"Jesus, Elmer, how are you!"

"Great, just great. Better now. Wow, I can't believe I ran into you here. Come here often?"

"All the time, actually. I live right down the street."

"No! Really? Well, I'll be. I thought I saw the back of your head disappear into that apartment complex down the way, but I always seem to be seeing the back of your head these days. It's made for some awkward moments, let me tell you. Running down the street hollering 'Maggie, Maggie' at the top of my lungs and then realizing it's not you. Story of my life these days."

"Elmer, don't tell me you've been looking for me this whole time. Good grief! How long have you been here?"

"A few weeks, maybe a month. I guess I've lost track."

"What? A *month*? Elmer, what the *hell* have you been doing for a month?"

"Searching for you mostly. Getting to know your City C. It's such a strange place, Maggie. Miles and miles of nothing but concrete and bricks. But it has a soul too, you know. I understand that now. I've felt it in the strangest places."

"Yes," said Maggie, nodding, "I know what you mean. But, Elmer, seriously. *Where* have you been staying this whole time?"

"In soup kitchens, mostly. Hotels on occasion. But hotels are so lonely and vapid when you're by yourself, you know. I usually prefer the kitchens."

"Am I hearing you correctly? You? Elmer? You're staying at soup kitchens. In The City. With gobs of dirty, homeless men and single black mothers with their hungry brood. Is that right?"

"Single black mothers like you?"

She tossed him a crooked smile and rolled her eyes. "Touché, Elmer. Touché."

"Yes, I'm staying at the kitchens here. That's what I did in City B as well, although those kitchens were quite a bit different than these. Fewer libraries and luxury spas in the ones here. But really, they're not so bad. Sure, you'll get a few people with mental illnesses, a few rabble-rousers. Sure, you need to watch your possessions like a hawk because there are a lot of sticky fingers around. But honestly, Maggie, most people are like you and me. Most people are just plain old down on their luck. Besides, who's going to harm a skinny, old coot like me?"

Maggie shook her head. "You never cease to amaze me, my friend." She brought a spoonful of squash purée to her mouth and swallowed it down slowly, then ran her tongue along her lips, licking the remnants of flavor. She liked to eat her soup this way: slowly, a bite at a time, savoring the complexity of flavor that melded into the solid-liquid thing in her mouth. "It sounds like you've been through a lot since I last saw you. We have some catching up to do. Sorry Elmer—I'm not allowing you to stay in some soup kitchen tonight. Tonight, you're staying in my apartment and you're going to tell me about all the adventures you've been having since City A. I'm curious to hear about these—what are they?—luxury spas in soup kitchens. Who ever heard of such a thing?"

"You don't know the half of it."

* * *

The City doesn't sleep. It whirs on and on and on and on, people going, cars moving, cars stuck, on and on. The sun never sets; the skies are always bright with neon rays, flooding eyes, giving people nervous ticks—they haven't slept for days and days. They've lost track of time—day and night blurred together and they forget which side of the blur means awake and which side means sleep. So they wake and sleep indiscriminately, walking down sidewalks illuminated by a thousand false suns. Sleeping in windowless concrete rooms. And The City spins, on and on.

The City doesn't sleep. And neither do Elmer and Maggie. They talk and talk as the neon suns shine on pale faces, buzzing monotonously. At night, Maggie sometimes thinks about that buzz, waiting at a bus stop or walking back from her favorite diner. It's not an irritated buzz, she's decided. It sounds more bored than irritated. Or lonely, even. Why so lonely, City lights? Don't you shine on thousands upon thousands?

Elmer and Maggie talk all night and into the morning. They barely notice the hazy morning sun replace the false ones. Coffee is brewed. No thanks, says Elmer. He had better get some rest—not so young as he used to be. Rest sounds nice, says Maggie, but there's work to do at the coffee shop and Zach to take care of. Right, Zach. How is he, asks Elmer. Look and see for yourself, she replies.

Zach scurries into the room, rubbing his eyes, hair tousled from sleep. Elmer smiles. He has grown so much in such a short time. Zach reaches his mother's leg and throws his arms around it. She smiles, stoops down to stroke his hair.

"Look who's here, Zach," she whispers.

Zach turns shyly, spots Elmer, and gives a tiny joyful yelp. He pitter-patters across the room to the old man and hugs him around the waist. Startled, Elmer pats the boy on the head.

"Well, he's more active then he used to be, isn't he? Nice to see you too, Zach."

* * *

"I'm still making peace with my City C," Maggie said the next afternoon. "It's a long process, you know. Lots of City to make peace with."

"No denying that," Elmer replied, stepping over a pine cone. They were strolling through a large park, headed for a brightly-colored playground on the other side. The playground curved and twisted in reds, purples, and sunny yellows, standing out boldly against the soft greens of the park. Elmer was getting used to such juxtapositions in The City. They cropped up everywhere: horses plodding down Main Street, old women in leopard-print leggings and motorcycle leather, men with huge arms and chests walking tiny white dogs in pink velvet jackets. These were things a citizen of Here would never see. These were things better left to the circus. In Here, everything and everybody had a place and you had damn-well better stick to your place or there would be hell to pay. The few who did choose to step a toe outside the box were chastised and ridiculed and rarely stayed. Not so in The City. The City was a breeding ground for originality and strangeness, so much so that eventually all the originality and strangeness seemed tired and overdone. The abnormal quickly became normal and it was difficult to shock anyone anymore. Even Elmer—Elmer, with his decades upon decades of Here-living—was slowly growing accustomed to the oddities of The City.

Maggie kept by Elmer's side, walking slowly, stifling her long legs from achieving their full stride. Zach trotted ahead of them and paused every once in a while, waited for them to catch up, and then took off again. Elmer could tell he was anxious to get to his slide-and-swing-set-filled mecca, but he didn't whine or complain. He just trotted and paused, trotted and paused until they finally arrived at their destination. With a sigh, Elmer seated himself on a nearby bench. Maggie joined him and gave him a pat on his knobby knee. Her eyes absentmindedly watched Zach as he ferreted around in the sandbox, picking up fistfuls of sand and moving them to a large pile in the center. "You know, Elmer," she said, "I waited three weeks before I contacted my mother to let her know I was back in The City. Three weeks. What a coward, right? But we didn't exactly part on the best of terms."

Maggie stayed silent for a while, watching Zach move sand from here to there, here to there. "She didn't approve of me joining the army. But—"

she paused and gave Elmer a sideways glance, "She approved even less of my behavior before the army. I had some friends who weren't…the most reputable characters, you might say. Nothing too terrible—just some drugs and petty thievery—but it made my mother crazy. Here she was, a single mother working two jobs, attempting to raise a daughter who was constantly mad at her because she was never around. And when she was around, it was always goddamn grammar and spelling and history lessons because she didn't think my school was challenging me enough. The younger Maggie *hated* those lessons. I spent so little time with my mother that the *last* thing I wanted to do was study subjunctive verbs and gerunds when we were together. But my mother insisted and *I* insisted on pulling away and brooding. I was annoyed that I didn't have a father or siblings *and* I was stuck with a mother who never wanted to go to the movies or shopping, but would rather spend all afternoon reading about Ferdinand and Isabella."

Elmer watched her dark eyes as she spoke. They didn't seem to look outward at all, but inward, focusing on something deep inside her chest cavity. "Of course, now I see the sense in all of it," Maggie continued. "She wanted the very best for me and that meant plowing forward with my studies despite my protests. That meant coming home after work and refusing to put her feet up and sit in front of the television. There was a daughter to educate, after all, and that couldn't wait. Television could."

"And that, Elmer, is why I waited three weeks before calling my mother. I've been ashamed and embarrassed by my former life for a long, long time, but I'm so goddamn stubborn. I hate admitting when I'm wrong, so you can imagine how difficult it was for me to own up to the fact that I was wrong in many ways for many years. A whole era of wrongness." She chewed on her lip and squeezed Elmer's hand. "And," she said, her voice softening, sounding worn and thin, even tired, "I wasn't sure what she would think about him." She gestured with a nod of her head towards her tiny son, who was now attempting to build something—a castle, maybe, or a house—with the sand he piled up.

"Zach?" said Elmer, puzzled. "Why wouldn't she love him? Why should she judge you for having him? Wasn't she also a single mother?"

"Yes and no," said Maggie, feeling suddenly heavy and dull, like a can of grey paint. "My mother and father were married when they had me. My mother wouldn't have it any other way. But my father never really liked being tied down. He would roam the streets and sometimes be gone for days on end, mixing himself with drugs and women, forgetting his family for a while, enjoying his freedom. At the time, I only had a vague idea of what was happening. I would see my mother's worried face watching out the window as she nervously washed the dishes or folded my clothes. She was a cleaning fiend when my father was gone, always keeping her hands busy so that they wouldn't clench up in angry fists and start pounding the walls. I would tread cautiously around her during those times, but I knew I *really* had to be careful when my father returned. That's when the angry words and fists flew; that's when the poison was unleashed. I would hide in my bedroom under the covers until the words morphed into sobs and they both lay in each other's arms, weeping, my father promising he would never do it again. Never, ever. And he wouldn't…until the next time. And the next. And the next. His little hiatuses grew longer and longer and longer until one time he simply didn't come back. He left us wondering and watching and cleaning like fiends and did—not—come—back."

Elmer watched Maggie's face. She told the story with little emotion or emphasis, as if she was releasing words from her throat that happened to be trapped there for a while. It was like watching air escape from a balloon. Elmer hesitated, then asked the question that had been pressing on his mind. "Well, what about your story?" he asked. "It can't be as bad as all that. What about Zach's dad? He couldn't have been any worse?" He hesitated again, "Right?"

"No, no, he was fantastic!" she moaned. "He was everything anyone could have wanted from a man—honest, loyal, affectionate. We met during our first week of basic training and instantly fell for each other. We saw quite a bit of each other over the next few years and stole every moment we could to be alone in each other's arms. When he found out I was pregnant, he was ecstatic, just thrilled. He started talking about raising a family together. White picket fences and all. I got scared. I didn't feel ready for that kind of life. The first chance I got, I sent in my notice and left the army—and him—for good. I didn't even say goodbye."

She shook her head as if brushing off a pesky fly. "You see, Elmer," she said sadly, "I was the bad guy. I was the one who ran away without explanation. I was my father." She closed her eyes and continued shaking her head, banishing the fly that kept nipping at her thoughts.

Elmer sat silently for a moment, searching for the right words to say. He patted her hand. "There, there. Don't be so hard on yourself."

"I'm an awful person, just awful," Maggie continued. "I denied my little boy a father and I left the only person I ever loved. I'm awful, just awful. I don't blame my mother for being disappointed. I don't blame her at all."

"Well, I'm not disappointed," said Elmer firmly. "When I see you, I see an intelligent, young lady with a good head on her shoulders and a darling little boy who—excuse the language—loves the *shit* out of her. And Maggie—," he gently pulled her chin towards his face so their eyes were level, "I understand the need to run away sometimes."

She swallowed and nodded, holding their eye contact.

"And who knows," he continued, "maybe you'll find him again when the time is right and you can build a life together—with or without the picket fence."

She smiled slightly and said, "Thanks, Elmer. Really, thank you. You're the best, you know that?"

Elmer winked. "So I've been told."

* * *

How many panes of glass are in The City? Five million? Five hundred million? Five million trillion? How many pairs of eyes are looking through the panes of glass? Looking into the world outside, watching and observing, judging, scrutinizing, wishing they could join. How many pairs of eyes are looking in? Spying, peeping.

How many factories manufactured the glass? Where are they? How did the glass travel from factory to City? Over bodies of water and fields and forests? Through the thick of cities and languages? Carried on trucks and ships and the backs of human beings?

How many hands touched the glass? Smeared whorls and rings on its surface. How many insects crawled across it? How many birds ran into it? Surprised and concussed, confused by the clear mass that sprang out of thin air. They only wanted to fly into the nice room.

Elmer wondered about these things as he walked through The City. These and a thousand other things. Or maybe a million. Or a thousand million. Who's to say?

* * *

After Zach grew bored of sand-walled castles and red-purple-yellow equipment, they left the park. Maggie looped one hand in the crook of Elmer's arm and the other held Zach's tiny fingers. They walked in chronological order: young, middle, old. As they marched forward, Elmer mused that they were behaving exactly how his life behaved—marching forward, peeling back days, months, years with insistent footsteps. They pressed onward, silently, until they reached the apartment complex.

"Here we are," Maggie said. Her words made her realize that none had been spoken since the park.

Elmer jolted into un-silence with a start. "Erm, yes. So we are, so we are."

They rode the elevator to the sixteenth floor and continued speaking—small talk—in order to climb out of the crevices in their heads, the spaces between brain wrinkles where they had nestled, munching on the matter around them and forgetting the world outside. Now they were out—naked and vulnerable, still wishing they could reside in their head spaces—and they did their best to clothe themselves with word after word.

"—and that's why autumn is my favorite season in The City," Maggie explained.

"I see," said Elmer. "The parks, yes, the bustling people in their light jackets, the foggy breath. I can see why you love autumn. Grand, just grand. Yes, autumn will be lovely in The City."

"It's just around the corner, you know. The trees told me. You can learn a lot from trees, you know."

"So you've told me."

"I suppose I have."

They reached the apartment door and clambered inside, feeling sufficiently extroverted and talkative now, their private thoughts once again locked away. Elmer kicked off his shoes and made his way towards the wide, cottony couch. Zach followed him and settled down next to his elbow. Maggie smiled.

"He really has taken a shine to you."

"He's a good boy," Elmer replied, patting Zach on the knee, "just like his mother."

Maggie blushed and walked over to the couch. "Say, are you two hungry? I was thinking about heading down to Karmic Relief and picking up some soup and sandwiches. Chicken dumpling, Elm?"

"That sounds fine, Maggie. Just fine."

"And me too!" came a voice from the next room. Elmer sprang to his feet, elbowing Zach and almost knocking him to the floor. Zach yelped and scrambled further back onto the couch.

"What in heaven's name—" Elmer started.

"Oh right!" said Maggie, slapping hand to forehead. I forgot that my roommates were coming back today.

"Roommates?"

"Well, yes. I met them at the little coffee shop where I work. Really great people. Besides, do you know how expensive The City is Elmer? It's just ridiculous."

"Couldn't agree more, lil' lady," said the voice again, this time accompanied by a body emerging from the back room. "Rental rates keep on goin' up and up and it's all us poor folks can do to keep from goin' down. Isn't that right, Tilda?"

"Sure thing," another voice answered, trailing behind the first figure like a shadow. "It's us against the man…whoever that is."

"I'm sure I've plumb lost track," the first voice guffawed.

The two roommates stepped into the living room and stood side-by-side, smiling across the room at Elmer.

He gasped. "YOU! You? Here? What on earth? I mean—it can't—I just—I...I need to sit down." Elmer swung his hips onto the couch and sat staring straight ahead, wide-eyed and unblinking, refusing to make eye contact with Maggie when she kneeled beside him.

"Elmer?" she whispered, her voice thin and concerned. "What's going on? What's the matter? Do you know Matthew and Matilda from somewhere? Have you met?"

"He seems mighty familiar," Matthew called from across the room, "but I don't s'pose we've met before. And Lord a'mighty—," he walked around the couch and looked into the old man's frozen face, "I don't think I've ever had such an effect on people, even an old codger like this 'un."

Elmer looked at him, reddened, tried to speak. "I—sorry—it's just that, I know you. Yes, I know you. There's no mistaking it."

Matilda stepped to Matthew's side, her round face scrunched up in curiosity. "Me too? Or just Matthew?"

"Oh yes, you too. Of course you too. You're Marta from the soup kitchen. Marta's Kitchen. The one who helped us get out of the bind with the Bookkeeper? Good grief, you have to remember. And you—" he turned to Matthew and shivered, "—you're supposed to be dead. At least—at least that's what I thought."

Elmer looked nervously from Matilda to Matthew, back to Matilda, back to Matthew. Matilda and Matthew looked at each other and burst out laughing.

"Woohee!" Matthew rasped in his cigarette-scratchy voice. "You really had me goin' there fer a minute. Did Maggie put ya up to this? She's a rascal, that 'un. Dead! Ha! Never heard anything like it in mah life. You had me goin' for a minute there, ol' man."

"You sure did," Matilda chimed in, her round cheeks puckered above a huge grin. "Calling me 'Marta' instead of Matilda. I tell you. You're funny, old man. Pretty darn funny."

Elmer blinked and stared at the two clones in front of him. Exact replicas of Levi and Marta. *Whatintheloveofeverythingthatisholy? What is going on here? I can't be mistaken. They are the same; I know it! Down to the missing teeth on Levi and the cropped, brown hair on Marta. Or Matthew and Matilda. Or whoever they claim to be. Either I'm crazy or—*

"I swear I'm not crazy," said Elmer. "And I'm not joking either. I know you two."

They—Maggie, Matthew, Matilda—scrutinized the face in front of them. There was no glimmer of humor in the taut mouth, no sign of sarcasm in the wide, green eyes. Just seriousness mingled with a touch of fear. Their smiles faded.

"Elmer, you can't be serious?" Maggie hesitated. "Right?"

"Dead serious."

"That's what I was afraid of," she replied. "Well, there has to be some explanation for this."

"Course there is," Matthew chuckled, "He's plumb outta his knocker, I'm afraid. You know, I haven't heard *anythin'* so ridiculous in quite some time. Knows me, does he? But I'm dead as a doornail? Well, I'm standing right here, ain't I? I don't feel very dead at the moment."

"That's enough, Matthew," said Maggie quietly, ominously.

Matthew hesitated, opened his mouth to say something, looked at Maggie again, and closed it. "Oh, all right. He seems harmless enough anyway."

"He is," said Maggie sternly. "And what's more, he's our guest and as such he should be subjected to the utmost respect and hospitality, don't you agree?"

Matthew nodded and Matilda said, "Yes, Maggie. We didn't mean to offend. Of course we agree."

"Good. Then I suggest everyone shut up about the whole thing and let's get us some food. I'm starving. Now, who's with me?"

Nods all around.

"Excellent. I'll run down to Karmedic Relief and pick us up some soup and sandwiches. And seriously guys, I don't want to hear another peep about all this for the rest of the night. Is that clear?"

* * *

The City sparkled that morning; it was a morning covered in dew. Cold dew. Not the soggy, friendly dew of summertime and spring, but the sharp, icy dew of autumn that has no scent, only clarity. The dew covered windshields and blades of grass. It covered cardboard boxes in the southside allies that, in turn, covered people. The people under the boxes wondered why they stayed. Life is easier, they've heard, in the south where food grows on orange and peach trees and the sun is rarely shy or moody. Here, you never know what the sun will do, what his temperament will be. Maybe if they knew about the Solstice festival they would practice it too. Maybe they would bang drums and utter chants in an attempt to placate their shining overlord. Maybe.

But they don't, so they continue complaining and shivering as the cold, cold dew soaks their boxes and their lashes become glued together with frozen tears. "This is our home," they say. "It will take more than a little icy dew to drive us away."

And so they stay and sometimes complain and sometimes dream of peach trees and orange trees. But mostly, they just stay.

This is the morning when Elmer woke up with a mouth full of words. This is the morning after the night of silence, the night when Maggie forbade them to talk about the one thing they ached to talk about. They sat in silence, noshing on soup and sandwiches, eyes skirting eyes, lips busy chewing, lips not busy forming words. Elmer felt words, explanations, pleas, lectures, sermons, phrases, quips, paragraphs jumping into his mouth, but he swallowed them down with dumplings and broth, excused himself, and went to bed. Which is why Elmer woke up with a mouth full of words.

He brushed his teeth violently, trying to shake them loose from amongst his gums and the top of his tongue, but they insisted on staying and he found himself pacing around the house until he heard voices—one low and gravely, the other high-pitched and sing-song—and burst into the living room to find them seated next to each other on the couch, the bum and the martyr, their heads leaning forward over morning coffee. The Thub-Tub noise of Elmer's feet and the door startled them away from their brews and they stared, looking up as the old man wheezed and puffed, waiting for him to explain the motivation behind his intrusion and worked-up state.

Elmer placed one hand over his pounding chest and steadied his quivering legs. "Yes?" said Matthew flatly.

"Are you ok, Elmer?" asked Matilda.

"Yes, fine," Elmer managed between breaths. "Just—need—to—talk." He looked at Matilda. "Mind if I sit down?"

"Not at all."

They shimmied to the right-hand side of the couch; Elmer lowered himself down. The couch was floral and rather squishy and Elmer's thighs sank several inches into the cushions, like two sticks in a marshmallow. Once he was situated, Elmer turned to his right. Matilda waited expectantly, her eyes fixed on the elderly man like a dog biding her time for morsels. Matthew, on the other hand, kept his eyes trained straight ahead, crossed his arms, and scowled at nothing in particular.

Elmer cleared his throat. "Ahem. Well, I uh…I thought I would start out by saying that I feel like we all got started on the wrong foot."

"I'd say," Matthew muttered. "I didn't expect to meet a crazy person under my roof when I woke up yesterday morning."

"Matthew!" Matilda scolded. "For the love of god, cut it out! And besides, it's not *your* roof. It's *ours*. This is a friend of Maggie's and deserves to be treated with a little more respect than what you're offering at the moment."

Matilda's tone singed the air and caused Matthew's already ruddy cheeks to redden even more. He hung his head slightly and said, "Sheesh, Tilda. I didn't mean anything by it. But he *is* the one that's acting all funny around us."

"I don't blame you for thinking I'm crazy," Elmer said. "I've questioned my sanity more than once this year. But please believe me, I know what I'm saying—I've seen you before. Now, this has been gnawing at me all night, so will you kindly hear me out? I want to share part of my story with you."

"Oh alright," sighed Matthew. "Talk away. I'd like to hear more about this dead guy who I'm supposed to be."

Matilda gave him an exasperated elbow in the ribs and turned to Elmer. "Please, Elmer. It looks like you have quite a bit to get off your chest. Please, tell us your story."

"Ok," said Elmer. He breathed in deeply and let out a long sigh. By the end of the sigh, he was on a train headed west, chug-a-chugging past fields and forests, his thoughts full of wonder and fear, anticipating his next steps (his next life?) in There. And then he was dreaming. And then waking up. He glossed over the dream, but highlighted the feats of the two unlikely heroes in the park—the two bums, the ones who shared their names with Biblical tax collectors. They had watched over him—the old, feeble stranger—as he slept, offered him protection and comfort, guarded his few possessions. He had been thankless. He had cringed at their dirty hair and mud-smeared skin and fled.

"I regret my actions in There. I was a big snob. I felt young and naïve, despite my age. It seems like I have lived several lives since then. In fact," Elmer paused and pondered this thought, "that's the best way I can describe my journey: several short, potent lives."

Matilda nodded, understanding. Matthew didn't say anything.

Elmer continued his tale, skipping from There to City A, breezing through his time with the Modern Shamans and neglecting to mention the death of his friend/diamond in the rough/runaway/Hilo. Onto City B. Onto the part where Marta enters the story. Matthew cocked one ear to the side when Elmer described the spas and cashmere bathrobes and dining quarters of the soup kitchens. He let out a grunt of disapproval when Elmer introduced them to the Bookkeeper and his infamous lectures.

"If that ain't the sickest thing I've heard," he muttered. "That's some Big Brother, mind-control shit, that is."

Elmer nodded and gave him a grim smile. "It was an eerie place, no doubt. But fortunately, there were some residents who were just as fed up with the connivings of the soup kitchens as we were." Elmer relived the soup kitchen rebellion. He described the Hopefuls and their plans—subtle and unnoticed at first, but then more flashy and ostentatious. He described the amoebic mass of humans that would ooze down hallways, pinning up flyers—a seamless organism that couldn't be picked apart and identified by the eyes behind the security cameras. He recounted the eventual slip-up; told how one of their number was caught, held hostage, forced to stand in front of the rest of them as the Bookkeeper's goons slashed him across the chest and spilt his ripe-cherry blood down his thighs and over the chains that bound him. Matilda gasped and cringed. Matthew clenched his fists and muttered, "The nerve. The nerve of some people. Disgustin'."

"I know," said Elmer, looking first at Matilda, then at Matthew. "It's vile, isn't it? But don't worry—this is where our dear Marta comes in. Our martyr. Sticking it to the man with her alternative kitchen. I met Marta right before the public trials, when I was feeling fairly low and heavy-hearted. I spotted a woman staring at me from across the room. She had this short, cropped hair and, well—" he looked into Matilda's light blue eyes. "She looked just like you. And I mean just—like—you."

Matilda didn't say anything, but turned slightly crimson. Elmer gave her hand a small squeeze and continued. He wrapped up his tale with the trials and Marta's speech and the small exodus to her safe haven—her bare-bones, simple soup kitchen. "I didn't stay long," he said. "My feet became itchy and I knew it was time to move on. I knew I was finally ready for City C, ready for *The* City. So, here I am." He looked at his audience. "Now you know my story. You have free license to judge my level of sanity."

Matthew and Matilda remained silent for a while, studying their shoes. Then, Matthew sprang to his feet and stepped in front of the elderly story teller. He grasped Elmer's hand and looked into his eyes. "I'm so sorry!" he howled. "Elmer, can you ever forgive me? You aren't crazy. 'n fact, you're a great man. A man who's been through a lot. It's as if you've been on a quest of sorts or mission or—"

"Spirit journey," Matilda finished.

"Good gawd, you're right! Elmer, you *have* been on a spirit journey this year. Just think of everything you've experienced. It's as if you're on the fast track towards Enlightenment. Like the Awakened Ones!"

Matilda stared, wide-eyed at the nearly bald head to her left. She looked as if Awe had run over her face and left tire tracks. "You're right, Matthew," she whispered. "Just like the Awakened Ones."

"I haven't the foggiest idea about what you people are yammering about," Elmer spoke up. "I'm just telling you what happened. The facts, pure and simple. I don't know about this 'Awakened Ones' business, but at least you don't think I'm loony anymore—"

"Loony! Good gravy, no!" exclaimed Matthew. "Elmer, you're marvelous. And you know, I believe every word of your story. Every last word. It's strange; I feel like I actually *was* a part of all the action. Like it was in my head all along—like a spider web you can't see unless dew or dust collect on its threads and reveal all its intricate weavings. You provided the dust, I guess. I'm tellin' you Elmer, I feel like I was there."

He looked at Matthew's eager eyes, his scruffy chin and tan, weather-beaten skin. "You were. For some of it, at least."

Matthew didn't respond for a moment. "Maybe I was, Elm. Maybe I was. I feel like human beings have many parts—many different facets—and maybe it's not so far-fetched to think part of me has been trailin' your footsteps. Or maybe people are interconnected in ways we just don't understand. And maybe part of you has been hauntin' me and I just haven't paid attention."

"Woaaah," said Matilda.

Elmer smiled. *Elm. Matthew called me Elm.*

"But seriously, man. This is some heavy shit you're packin' with you to The City. Some real heavy shit. I think you need to take yo'self straight to Tower I, if you ask me."

"Did someone say Tower I?" Maggie's voice preceded her into the living room. She walked lazily through the doorjamb, one thoroughbred leg after the other.

"Yes, ma'am. I was just tellin' our friend Elmer here that he needs to take himself directly to Tower I to get evaluated. I'm sure they'd all have a field day with him. Say, that's a pretty interesting tale he's got there, now isn't it Mags?"

Maggie winked at Elmer. "Told you he's not crazy, didn't I?"

"Yeah, yeah, rub it in, Mags. Right as usual."

"Sorry, Maggie," said Matilda sheepishly. "We didn't mean to doubt your friend. But you have to admit, at first he seemed to be a few horses short of a polo team."

Maggie laughed. "Well, sure. I don't suppose many people introduce themselves by saying, 'Hello, you remind me of a dead guy I used to know.' But then again, not many people are quite like Elmer. He's a special one, he is."

"Oh stop it, Maggie," said Elmer, waving an embarrassed hand towards her. "I'm nothing special. I'm just old. Old enough to stop caring about what other people think and start living my own life. Shoulda done it a long time ago, as a matter of fact. A long time ago. I never had the gumption to do it. Never had a rebellious streak in me quite like yours."

"You're a bit more than a rebel, if you ask me, Elm."

"Yeah, you're a master!" squealed Matilda.

Elmer's face fell. "I'm no such thing," he muttered. "And I wish people would stop saying I am."

Maggie studied his face: green eyes drooping, mouth sagging in a frown, brows knit. "You've been told that a few times, haven't you Elm? That you're something more than average? That there's something special about you?"

Elmer raised his bright greens so that they met her luminous browns. Her eyes matched the tone of the rest of her face: stern and serious. Elmer sat up straighter, cocked an ear forward.

"Maybe Elmer," Maggie continued, "it's time to listen. Maybe it's time to go to Tower I."

Chapter 43

Irene is dead. She had to die. No way around it, mortal as she is.

Her children buried her. Not literally, each with a shovel, but close enough. They paid the hands that bore the shovels. They paid the hands that built her box—rectangular, pine, and five foot six plus four inches on either end. They watched as she was lowered into the hole, the hole they paid the shovel-bearing men to dig. You don't have to watch, someone said. You can go home now. That's ok, they answered. We'll stay.

The ceremony was over; the flowers were placed in her hands and alongside her body and in front of the casket. The family and friends arrived, mourned, ate, went home. They would move on with their lives, for they were still living. But the children felt slightly dead. That feeling would eventually pass. Like a bad case of the flu. But right then, it was present and miserable and painful and raw. They turned away from the interred body and let themselves feel that way—slightly dead.

It wasn't hard to lay their father to rest. Easy, in fact. How does one mourn air? One minute he was there, the next he was gone. By the time they wrapped their heads around his Houdini vanishing act, mourning time was over. They didn't artificially prolong it. They moved on.

But with their mother it was different. She was there. She was around. They watched her wither and fade and eventually die. It was appropriate to grieve. It was appropriate to weep. They knew their mother was dead. They witnessed her decline. They felt her life slip into the great unknown and leave its flesh and blood shell behind. It was real. Her death was real. Not so with their father. His disappearance, his note, his maybe/maybe not death was full of riddles and masks.

How does one mourn air?

One does not mourn air. One finds it silly to do so.

The children left the graveyard with that feeling, that slightly dead feeling hanging off their bodies like a broken toenail. A secret part of them was relieved to have this feeling, happy almost. To them, it meant something was there and now it is not. Someone was living and now they are dead. Point A to Point B. Logical. Sensible. Their father's "death" was neither logical nor sensible. He wasn't buried in the ground like a proper dead parent. Why couldn't he just behave? He spent seventy-eight years of his life doing just that: behaving. Why step out of line now? What was the point? At age seventy-eight, what was the goddamn point?

At least their mother died correctly. At least they knew where her dead body lay, rotting, creating fertilizer for the grass next to her tombstone. At least her death was tangible. They could mourn tangible.

How does one mourn air?

* * *

"What on earth is this Tower I? And is it 'Eye,' as in 'Look me in the eye?' Or 'I' as in 'I see you?'"

"Both, in a way," said Matilda, smiling mysterious.

"Don't be an ass, Tilda," said Matthew. "It's 'I' like 'me.' It's 'I' like '*I* want you, Elmer, to go to the goddamn Tower to get evaluated."

"And *who's* the ass?" retorted Matilda.

"Hey, hey," Maggie cut in. "Why don't we at least *try* to be a little civil around our guest."

"It's fine, it's fine." Elmer smiled. "I just had the most wonderful flashback to the house of the Modern Shamans. Do you keep in touch with Onyx and Cecelia, Maggie?"

Maggie smiled. "Why do you ask?"

* * *

The Tower is tall, but so are the buildings around it.

The Tower is grey, but no greyer than its neighbors.

The Tower looms, but blocks out the appropriate amount of sun.

The Tower is made of steel and cement, but sways slightly in a strong wind.

The Tower is vertical, watching, alert, but it isn't alive.

Not alive in the usual sense, at least.

The Tower is tall, but so are the buildings around it.

* * *

Elmer must have walked by it several dozen times during his traipses around The City. The Tower. Tower I. He never noticed it. It was nestled between larger, more imposing buildings that mercilessly shoved it to the back of the stage as they shook their boas, flashed their stilettos, seduced the audience with boldness and charm. As they walked past Tower I's showy neighbors, Matthew shot them a dirty look. Elmer understood.

They turned and marched down the long walkway leading to The Tower and Elmer sensed a change, a visceral feeling that something was different. For some reason, the tiny hairs on the back of his neck stood on end. As they neared the door, Maggie held out an arm that gently caught Elmer by the chest.

"Listen," she whispered. "Just listen for a few seconds."

They stood in silence, straining their ears. Nothing. No sound of engines grinding, shoes clip-clopping, bicycles ringing their bells. No sound of horns or voices or children crying or music blaring. Only pure, clean silence.

"That's it," Elmer murmured. "The silence. It's eerie."

"I thought so too when Tilda and Matthew brought me here the first time," Maggie replied, letting down her hand and continuing towards the door. "But then I decided it's only eerie if you want it to be." Elmer followed her, paying attention to the air, to the thick silence that enveloped them like fog on a river. He imagined himself swimming through the air and doggy-paddling up to the waiting door. It didn't seem farfetched.

They reached the door—walking, unfortunately, as normal people are likely to do on sidewalks—and stepped inside. A subtle breeze tickled their cheeks and danced into their nostrils. Elmer smelled the soft essence of lavender, mingled with Jasmine and a pungent, citrus-like scent he could not identify. He breathed in deeply, inhaling the aromatic breeze into his lungs for a moment and then releasing it.

"We're here," Matilda whispered. "Tower I."

Elmer glanced at his surroundings. Every chair and table in the waiting area seemed carefully selected and placed. Each picture was hung with a purpose. Each floor mat had a reason for lying where it lay. There was no excess or fluff on the first floor of Tower I. Everything was minimalistic. Minimalistic and tasteful. The only indulgent bit of the first floor was a small garden in the far right-hand corner of the wide space. Elmer spotted it from across the room and began walking towards it, lured by the taste of fresh oxygen and the sound of bubbling water.

"Elmer, where are you going?" asked Matthew. "The reception desk is right here."

"I'll just be a minute," Elmer called over his shoulder and strode on, leaving the three roommates staring after him. Matilda started towards him, but Maggie held up a hand and said, "Wait, Tilda. Let him be. We have some time, anyhow." Matilda nodded and watched the small, hunched back disappear behind a juniper bush.

Elmer breathed in; he breathed out. He touched the leaves of a tiny bonsai tree. He poked his cane into the little koi pond in the middle of the garden, making ripples and startling the fat orange fish. He found a plain wooden bench and sat down. From his vantage point, he could easily take in the entire garden. He looked around and marveled at its order. *Neat and tidy. Everything in its place and a place specifically for each thing. Nothing superfluous or gaudy. Just enough.*

Though the garden was by no means enormous, it managed to accommodate a couple dozen species of shrubs and flowers, the koi pond, several large mossy rocks, and a small expanse of sand that had been raked into whorls and waves by someone's careful hand. A narrow path wended its way around the garden in a kind of irregular circle: no end, no beginning. Elmer's eyes followed the path, then jumped to the raked sand. He attempted to find a starting point in the pattern, but the artist left no hint of where the design might begin or end. It curved, arced, twisted and made his eyes spin round and round the sand like hamsters in a wheel. The sand just like the path: no end, no beginning.

Elmer lost himself in the patterned dust and nearly fell out of his seat when someone sidled next to him and said in a cheery, high-pitched voice, "Well, hello there! You must be Elmer."

"Gah!" said Elmer.

"Oh my. Sorry to startle you dear! Your friends said I might find you here. I'm the receptionist, you see. I suppose I should have known you would lose yourself in the Meditation Garden. People tend to do that. Quite common really. I mean—uh, Elmer? Are you ok, sir?"

Elmer's face had turned ghostly white; his eyes were wide and frozen. "I, well I—" he stammered. He continued to stare at the woman by his side. "Ms. Patti?" he managed in a meek voice. "You're *here*?"

"Ms. Patti?" said the woman, wrinkling her forehead that lay under a mass of fluffy hair. "Oh no, dear. You must have me confused for someone else. I'm Peggi. Peggi with an 'i,' that is." She tittered. "And only a few people call me *Ms.* Peggi."

Elmer held an expression much like the koi fish in the pond next to him: wide-eyed with flapping lips.

"Honestly dear, I don't know what's gotten into you."

"Sorry. Sorry." Elmer swallowed. "It's just—it's just you look just like her." He took in the large, plastic hoop earrings, the makeup-encrusted blue eyes, the shockingly-pink lipstick. "You don't by any chance have a sister, do you?"

Again, Peggi tittered. "Oh no, sir. Just me, I'm afraid. Now, let's bring you over to the front desk and get you registered for today, shall we?"

Elmer nodded mutely and followed the mass of bouncing, blonde hair to the center of the room, where a low, sleek desk stood waiting. Maggie, Matthew, and Matilda sat on one side in three matching chairs. They smiled as Elmer approached. He nodded and sat down next to them in an identical, straight-backed chair. Peggi ran her hand across the dark, polished wood of the desk and seated herself across from the quartet.

"Now," she said, all business, titters and silly grins tossed aside. "You are here for an assessment, is that correct, Elmer?"

"So I'm told."

"Good. We have an opening in the Orange Room on the fourth floor. One of our teachers will be waiting for you. All we ask is that you go in with an open heart and mind and let the teacher do the rest. Is that clear, Elmer?"

"Yes."

"Good. Sign here then." She slid a single piece of paper across the desk. Elmer read the two lines in a few seconds, shrugged, and scrawled his name across the bottom. Matilda read over his shoulder.

I, the undersigned, agree to receive an official assessment from one (1) certified teacher in Tower I. I agree to accept the results as best I can and not use them for destructive purposes or selfish personal gain.

"Peggi," Matilda said, "I never had to sign a release form when I got my first assessment."

"Times have changed a bit, Matilda. Unfortunately. We had a few people a couple years back use their new knowledge as an excuse to fall into despair and start a life of crime. They were told they had made little progress on their path towards Nirvana so they decided that bettering this life was a waste of time. Might as well toss it to the wind and worry about improving themselves in the next life. Foolish, really. I wouldn't be surprised if they came back as toads next time around. Anyhow…"

Elmer stared, but didn't say anything. He mentally added this conversation to the list of unusual/uncomfortable/strange interactions he had experienced in the last year. He shrugged once more and stared at his feet to keep from chuckling.

"Anyhow, that's neither here nor there," smiled Peggi. "I'm sure you have nothing to worry about, Elmer."

"I'm sure."

"Excellent. Then, let me escort you to the elevator. Your friends can wait for you in the garden."

The group of four arose, shuffled their feet uncomfortably.

"Ok then," said Matthew. "Go get 'em, Elm."

"It'll be fine, Elmer, really," said Matilda.

"Sure thing, old friend," added Maggie softly. "You'll do great."

"Friends," said Elmer firmly, "I'm not worried. I'm old and beyond the point of self-destruction. Now, will you please go get some fresh air in the garden? I think you all need it."

"Look at Elmer bein' all bossy," Matthew grinned impishly. Elmer couldn't help staring at the gaps between the man's teeth—one in the upper row, one in the lower—lined up diagonally in his mouth, just like Levi's. They were the same down to their unfortunate oral hygiene.

"Uh, yes," said Elmer, tugging his eyes away from the man's spare-toothed grin. "Yes, must be going." He turned and followed Peggi to the elevator.

"Up we go!" she chortled, her fluorescent lipstick framing a Cheshire cat smile. "Fourth floor."

Elmer silently examined the many rows of buttons inside the elevator. Thirty-one. Each button a slightly different color. Peggi punched the orange one and the doors slid shut. Up, up they went for precisely six seconds. Ding. Doors opened and they stepped out. Elmer squinted his eyes for a moment, adjusting to the brightly painted, tangerine-colored walls.

Like the first floor, the fourth floor was large and open, with only a few separate rooms partitioned off from the main area. It was tidy and plain. A few plants hugged the walls, a few pictures adorned them. The floor housed several straw mats in neat rows and a smattering of low tables surrounded by cushions. It looked like the perfect room for a five-year old to build cushion forts, take a nap on the mats, and use the low tables for tea time with stuffed animals. Elmer grinned at the thought.

"This way," said Peggi and they walked slowly to the center of the room. Elmer became aware of the wump-thump of his clumsy shoes and the click-tick of Peggi's heels. They walked towards the center of the room, where a slightly elevated, squarish platform rose at their feet. In the middle of the platform, a man in long, orange robes sat on an equally orange cushion facing them, back straight, legs crossed, eyes closed, mouth relaxed. The man sighed deeply, slowly opened his eyes, and met Elmer's gaze.

Elmer froze.

* * *

The Meditation Garden in Tower I had rarely been so tension-filled. Maggie, Matthew, and Matilda avoided each other's eyes as they talked about small things—the lovely koi pond, the delicious tea Peggi had brewed for them, the sand garden. They chatted absent-mindedly, their thoughts drifting towards Elmer and his assessment in the Orange Room. Their hearts pounded heavily, their palms sweated and slipped as they brought their teacups to their lips.

"Did you notice the cherry tree?" asked Matilda.

"Lovely," said Matthew and wondered why he felt inclined to use such an insipid word as "lovely."

"Yes," said Maggie distantly. "It is. I've always enjoyed cherries."

"I agree," said Matilda. "Delicious little things."

"A wonderful fruit, really. Just lovely," said Matthew.

* * *

He had noticed the patterns before. The ironic similarities, the eerie parallels. He had observed the congruent character traits and the identical names, acknowledged them, taken them with a grain of salt. He wondered about the similarities, had fleeting thoughts about the unusual trends, dismissed his half-formed thoughts as poppycock. But the patterns continued. They grew stronger and more obvious and he had no choice but to recognize them and call them out. Something was amiss and he had known it for a while now.

The people he met this year cycled through his life, following him from City to City, manifesting themselves in different forms. It couldn't be coincidence anymore. It simply could not. Too many similarities. Too many parallels and similar habits and goddamn identical names. They submerged and reappeared further down the river of his consciousness. Like fucking dolphins, trailing his boat and clicking their tongues in mockery. Because if it wasn't mockery, then what was it?

He wasn't sure. But he did know one thing: they were the same. Or similar. Or something. Or maybe he was a crazy old man with a thin grasp on the world, walking on an even thinner tightrope between life and death. But no, it had to be! The City confirmed it. First there was Matthew, then Matilda, then Peggi, and now this. It had to be!

The more he thought about it, the more it made sense. Pieces clicking into place, patterns arising, symmetry appearing between City A, B, C, There. Zach and Roger, for instance. Hadn't Zach the bum and Roger the trumpet-player been cut from the same cloth? They mirrored each other, Roger and Zach, down to their dreadlocks and musical inclinations. And Maggie and Grace. There's another pair, yes? The two lovely, calm, mahogany-skinned, honey-tongued, single mothers. With the same child, of course. Zach/Levi. Levi/Zach. Shy and bright, lots of potential, in love with their mothers. The children bearing the same names as the street bums. Levi/Zach, the names of tax collectors. How could this be?

And Matthew and Levi. Both scruffy, foul-smelling, and grimy-mouthed with surprising souls behind their plain, brown eyes. The same man reincarnated in a different time, a different City. And Matilda and Marta. Identical voices and hair and light blue eyes. Both quietly determined to do good. Both with their faith in humanity intact.

And don't forget Ms. Patti/Ms. Peggi. With an "i" for the love of god! With a fucking "i." The same. Exactly the same, down to the poofy hair and obnoxious lipstick. *If Peggi starts up with any nutty wordplay, I'll lose my shit. I swear, I'll lose it.*

So many patterns and symmetry and repeat characters. So many parallel lives and parallel names. What, in the name of all that is holy, is going on? What is going on! Am I going nuts or is this some elaborate cosmic joke? Tell me. Goddamn it, tell me!

"No really, please tell me what is going on here."

"In due time," said the man in orange. "Peggi, leave us please."

* * *

The woman in indigo folded her hands and sat back on her cushioned chair. She stared off for a while, a vaguely amused look on her face, as her eyes took in nothing in particular. She absentmindedly stroked her now-thick, now-thin hair and twisted the end with each stroke. Stroke, twist. Stroke, twist. Constant, like a metronome. After several long minutes, she lowered her hand and her eyes, locking gazes with the man in front of her.

"Everyone reincarnates. Everyone who's not enlightened, you see. The goal is to be enlightened, to be Awake, to escape the pain and suffering of this world, to escape the agony of rebirth. But most people never learn to escape. They cling to their material bodies and the endless, painful cycle of birth-death-birth-death, thousands upon thousands of births, thousands upon thousands of deaths. Few escaping. Few striving for and obtaining the ultimate goal: Enlightenment.

But student, don't think of rebirth as an entirely new life. You're not starting from scratch. Lessons you've learned, progress you've made—those things stay with you. You're not quite the same from life to life—perhaps not even the same gender—but then again you are the same. Somewhat, that is. Somewhat the same." The woman in indigo moistened her lips with her tongue, tugged on her hair again. "Think of rebirth like passing a flame from candle to candle. The fire isn't the same from one wick to another, but its qualities remain constant. The qualities are residual. You have built one life from another, which was built from another, which was built from another. Residual qualities—that's the key concept here. *Residual.* Is that clear?"

The man nodded.

* * *

"In due time? When is due time?" Elmer asked after he watched Peggi's face disappear behind the elevator door, heard the swoosh of the metal box as it descended on its cables.

"That, my friend, is up to you."

"Well, I think due time is right about now," Elmer snapped, balling his fists.

"It's not quite that simple, Elmer. I could give you an explanation now, but it would only float on your consciousness, like a leaf on water. I'd rather you *truly* understand things; I'd rather the explanation sink in like a rock, not a leaf."

Elmer's fists relaxed. When he spoke, his voice sounded resigned and sullen. "Ok. I'll wait then. But I must say, I'm getting a little anxious. All this repetition. All these people with similar attributes and tendencies and names. It's getting out of hand. I keep waiting to wake up and find myself in bed in Here."

"Wake up," the man in orange smiled. "Now there's a phrase with meaning."

* * *

"To be Awake is the goal," the woman in indigo explained. "Most people sleepwalk through this world, through their lives, zombified by society, drunk on the populous kool-aid, drained of purpose and vision. Few are Awake. Few even realize they're asleep. We drink society's poisons—ignorance, aversion, and desire—and cling to our temporary bodies like velcro to cheap sneakers. Do not cling, my dear student."

The student nodded.

Your material body is temporary. It means little. Besides, your body is not truly your own. It is interconnected with birds and pine trees and human beings and tomatoes and leopard frogs and honeybee larva and lilies. It is a vessel that carries you, not vice versa. You own your body; it shouldn't own you. Too many people fall victim to the whims of their human body. They become obsessed with it and captivated by it. They are burdened by its heavy emotional tides.

This is one of the last lessons you need to embrace, student. You need to let go of the emotions that have plagued your body. You need to become free of the suffering attached to such emotions. Only then can you be truly liberated. Only then can you be an Awakened One.

* * *

Elmer gazed at the man in orange. He took in his beetle-colored eyes, the wisp of a beard, the pale skin, the skinny arms poking out from wide sleeves. The man's face was wrinkled and worn. He wore a serene expression—one that radiated kindness and a sense of peace. It was because of this expression that Elmer barely recognized the man. But there could be no mistaking it.

"Bookkeeper?" ventured Elmer after several long seconds of silence. "Can I at least ask why you are here?"

The corners of the man's mouth turned up slightly. "Bookkeeper, you say? I'm sorry. I am not familiar with that title. I can tell you this, however. I am here, Elmer, because you wanted me here. I am here because I fit into your world; I fit into Tower I."

"Then you are not the Bookkeeper?"

"I'm afraid not."

"You're sure? You're sure you're not Ezekiel's Bookkeeper? Ezekiel Banks. The Bookkeeper with slightly lighter skin and thinner beard."

"No."

"Then what shall I call you?"

"Names aren't so important, Elmer. Temporary names for temporary bodies. But if it means that much to you, you can call me Roger if you'd like."

"Roger?" *Another repetition, another parallel.*

"Yes, Roger."

"Ok," said Elmer hesitantly. He wanted to scream. He wanted to flee. He wanted to leap upon the platform that rose in front of him and throttle the skinny, beady-eyed man. But then again, he didn't. He didn't actually want to do any of these things because, although the man in orange looked and sounded an awful lot like the Bookkeeper, he most certainly was not. His entire essence was different. This man was peaceful, benevolent, honest, simple, true. He was comprised of a lengthy list of adjectives that the Bookkeeper was not and never could be. The man in front of him felt more like a teacher, more like a wise grandfather or a…

"Spirit guide," Elmer whispered. "You—sir—Roger, that is—you remind me of them. Maybe it's your eyes. I'm not sure. But by golly—," he paused and once again assessed the scrawny man in front of him, "you're even wearing their robes. The orange robes. You're wearing them."

Roger laughed. It sounded like water. "Elmer, I always wear these robes. Now, you're talking in circles around me and I'm struggling to keep up. I may be intuitive, but your brain is whirring a mile a minute, my friend. Please sit down." Roger gestured towards a low, salmon-colored cushion on his left-hand side. Elmer couldn't think of a reason to protest, so he slowly stepped onto the platform and lowered himself onto the cushion. It sank slightly under his weight, but remained surprisingly firm and comfortable. The cushion butted up to a bright orange pillar and Elmer rested his back against it and let out a long, deep sigh.

"Excellent, Elmer," said Roger. "Release your tension. You've built up too much of it during your lifetime. Can I offer you a glass of water? No? Ok, then. Let's get to it, shall we? Let's start the assessment."

* * *

Downstairs, Peggi offered Matthew, Maggie, and Matilda another round of tea, saying that jasmine is her absolute favorite and doesn't the cherry tree smell divine and isn't that little old Elmer just a doll and don't look so grim there's no need to worry about the assessment it'll be just fine. The Ems nodded and said they agreed with her. Everything would be just fine. Yes, they should stop looking grim. And my, that cherry tree is truly wonderful, isn't it?

Peggi smiled and tittered, as she does best, and scampered off to perform her clerical duties behind the low, dark-wood desk. The three Ems stared after her and breathed a sigh of relief when she had gone. Nice lady, they agreed, but much too overpowering. She has a thing or two to learn about personal boundaries, they decided. And a thing or two to learn about enjoying silence. Yes, that's for sure, they agreed. That's for sure.

They sat in the garden, unspeaking, unmoving. Not enjoying the silence at all.

* * *

The man in orange rose from his flat cushion and walked a few paces towards Elmer. He paused before the salmon-colored cushion and crouched down before the old man so their eyes lined up and their wrinkles nearly touched. Elmer jumped slightly as the man-who-wasn't-the-Bookkeeper reached out his hands and cradled the back of Elmer's head. The man in orange exhaled slowly, the fog of his breath drifting across the skin of Elmer's cheeks and across his mouth. His breath was light and lemony and Elmer found himself more curious than repulsed. The man in orange breathed in, took a step back, and lowered himself to the ground, folding his legs almost instinctively into a cross-legged lotus position. The small, dark-brown eyes studied the man before him, scrutinized the thinning hair, the bright green eyes, the stooped shoulders, the worn cardigan. He sat silently for several minutes, staring unblinkingly ahead. Elmer grew uncomfortable with the eyes, the corpse-still body, and looked away, embarrassed by his examination. He hoped it would end soon. He hoped the man in orange would (sooner, rather than later) find what he was looking for. He did.

"Elmer," the man in orange finally said.

Elmer jerked to attention. He had been staring off to his left in the vague direction of a vivid painting depicting a man cradled by a many-headed serpent. "Mmm. Yes?"

"Elmer, Elmer," the man repeated the old man's name. "Things have not been easy for you, have they?"

Elmer stared at the man in orange—at Roger—unsure of what to say.

"I sense a blackness right here," Roger reached out a spindly arm and touched the left side of Elmer's chest. "Something is weighing you down. There is a stone in your heart and it's making it impossible for you to achieve Enlightenment. And if my senses are correct, I believe it stems from your childhood and—" he paused, removed his hand, settled back into the lotus position. "And I believe it has something to do with a woman. Or maybe several."

Elmer stared again, unsure of what to say. He opened his mouth to speak, but Roger snapped a finger to his lips and said, "Hush, Elmer. No need to speak right now. Just listen. Listen to me; listen to yourself. Ok?"

Elmer nodded.

"Ok. Good." Roger leaned back and paused, poised as if he was resting against an invisible wall. When he spoke again, his voice sounded as if it was coming from a deep cavern somewhere in the hollow of his chest. "Elmer," he said. It was not a call of attention to the old man; it was simply a statement. Elmer. The man in orange tasted the name between his teeth, as if he was sampling a new flavor of gum. "Elmer," he repeated. "You are close, my friend, oh so close. You have collected many life lessons along the way. You have harvested many teachings along your journey. But you are not there yet, not quite."

Elmer watched the man in front of him. The Bookkeeper or Roger or whoever he was. He continued to lean back against his invisible support and spoke to Elmer with his eyes closed and his voice springing from someplace deep within his body—somewhere tucked behind his stomach, along the base of his backbone. Elmer listened as the man uttered his name again.

"Elmer, you have learned many things in your recent lives. Many more than most people learn in a thousand lifetimes. You have followed most of the necessary steps towards Enlightenment: you left the distractions of home, recognized the illusions in your surroundings, triumphed over the three poisons, embraced spiritually-rich companions, practiced selflessness…" Roger paused, pressed his eyelids closed a little bit harder, and continued. "But it is not enough."

He opened his eyes and looked at the elderly man sitting calmly across from him, hands folded across his lap. "Elmer," he chewed on the name, "you have trod a long ways down the path of Enlightenment, but it is this," he pointed to his own chest, right above the beating organism within it; he paused and felt the pulsations drumming through his fingers, "that is holding you back." He nodded towards the old man. "It is your depth of emotion, your attachment to people and things and sentiments that is obstructing your obtainment of the ultimate goal. That," he said, "is something you will have to work on, but you won't be working on it with me."

"No?" said Elmer. He realized he hadn't spoken in some time.

"No, Elmer. Not with me. This is a project for the thirtieth floor, I believe. The indigo floor. Indigo—the color of spiritual attainment, self-mastery, and wisdom. Indigo—the color associated with your third-eye, your higher conscious. It is on the indigo floor where you will learn to release your pent-up emotions. It is where you will learn to practice emptiness." His dark, irisless eyes pierced Elmer's. "I believe, Elmer, you know what I mean by emptying one's emotions. I believe you have experienced this at one time."

Elmer nodded. He remembered his life in Here, a life that was not his own, a life filled with perfectly mechanized, finely-tuned actions. He remembered the storm that brewed in his head over those years—the storm that grew in strength and size, the storm that beat against his head, nearly concussing him with its power. And he remembered the day he left Here, the day the storm ripped out of his brain and went spinning into the world. At the time, he wondered what would fill the gaping hole it left behind. He didn't think about that anymore. Life happened. Life and people and spirit guides and dreams filled the hole; he didn't bother with dwelling on the storm's absence.

"The storm may be gone, Elmer," the man in orange said, "but its ripples remain."

Elmer nodded. He was getting used to nodding. Somehow, Roger knew. He knew about the storm, about his journey, about the depths of his emotions. He knew that emotional ripples coursed through his veins and across his memory, stirring the pools that harbored his dead father and his lost love and the people he had wronged. Damn those ripples.

"It is on the indigo floor, Elmer, that those ripples will be stilled."

Elmer nodded.

Chapter 44

"You're studying on the *indigo* floor?" Matilda squeaked, shaking her tiny fists in mock rage. "Not fair, Elm! I've been studying in Tower I for four years and I'm still on the sunflower-yellow floor. I've only moved up two floors! From light-yellow to sunflower. Not *even* fair."

Elmer shrugged, "I don't know a thing about it. All I know is that I'll be starting my studies on the indigo floor next week. I'm not so sure I understand the whole system, but the Bookkeeper told me to go to the indigo floor, so that's what I'll do."

"Bookkeeper?" asked Matthew.

"Well, Roger, I suppose. That's his actual name. But he looks just like that blasted Bookkeeper from Ezekiel's Soup Kitchen in City B. Gave me the shivers at first."

"Roger?" asked Maggie.

"I know it, Maggie. Another Roger in my life. I'm starting to feel like Alice in the rabbit hole. I'm wondering when the madness will end."

"Things have a purpose, Elmer. Everything in life has a purpose."

"Spoken like a true forest-green student," Matthew teased. "I'm stuck way down on the burnt orange floor. But no hard feelin's, Elm. I'm happy fer ya, I really am." Matthew clapped Elmer briefly on the back. Elmer smiled.

They walked back to the apartment, females in front, males trailing behind. The sun shone through gaps in the buildings, fighting its way between the long shadows of City C. It had been a long afternoon for all four of them and they dragged their feet slightly as they made the trek from Tower I to Apartment. Elmer hummed slightly as he walked. He wasn't certain why he felt so dizzy with excitement, but something about Tower I had lightened his mood and made him feel more grounded, more confident in himself, and more excited about life. He was on a new adventure in a new city and he felt good.

"Tower I has certainly helped me, Elmer," Maggie said over her shoulder. "When I came back to The City after my long absence, I felt more than a little directionless. Fortunately, I had my wonderful friends," she gave Matthew and Matilda each a wink, "and my friends had Tower I."

"If anyone can actually *have* Tower I, that is," said Matthew. "In a way, I feel like Tower I is its own entity—a living, breathing structure that just happens to house us. Silly, I know."

"Not at all," Elmer responded quietly. "I think Maggie would agree with you on that, as well."

Maggie nodded silently, remembering the house of the Modern Shamans, remembering its happily creaking boards, its emotion-saturated wood. And then remembering its agonized screams on the night of its death. Maggie shook the thought from her head. "Let's take a right here, all," she said. "I have to pick up my little boy from daycare."

They nodded and turned, walking the two blocks to the daycare. They walked in silence, thinking about the nature of homes and places. Eventually, they arrived at their destination and the group waited outside as Maggie eagerly pushed open the swinging door of the daycare and scampered inside. Immediately, her mind switched away from smoky lungs and burning timbers to her son, her joy, her rock, her reason. Her reason for everything. As little Zach ran into her waiting arms she thought, "Someday I'll make it to the indigo floor. Someday I'll be as wise as dear Elmer. I'll do it for me; I'll do it for my son."

Maggie swung Zach into the waiting harness on her back and stepped out the door and back onto the sidewalk. She gave her son's toe a squeeze, joined her friends, and continued her march towards home. Matilda trotted by her side, making funny faces at Zach and attempting to keep up with Maggie's long stride; Matthew chatted amiably with Elmer, describing a prime fishing spot located "not too far from the ol' City, jus' a half hour bus ride, give or take." Elmer nodded as Matthew spoke, daydreaming of another time filled with fishing poles and bare feet.

Maggie smiled at her friends as the sun sank lower in the sky and the buildings' shadows grew. In that moment, everything was right in the world.

* * *

It was nighttime and Tower I slept. The City hummed; The City whirred, but Tower I slept. Breathing in and out, quiet and unaware of the outside whirring and humming. Tower I slept. It slept because Elmer slept. It slept because Maggie slept. It slept because Matthew and Matilda and little Zach slept. Tower I is more sensible than the rest of The City. It needs its rest just like the rest of us.

People walked The City's streets, not resting. They prowled and capered and snuck their way from one block to another, down Maple-Elm-Oak streets, down King-Duchess-Princeton streets, down streets named after birds. The people walked and sometimes, when they approached a certain part of The City, a certain part of The City comprised mostly of gigantic, sixty, seventy, eighty-floor buildings, they paused. They paused because a hush fell between the behemoths. A silence tickled at their brains and calmed their emotions. They could feel the silence stretching its tentacles from a certain building tucked behind the sixty, seventy, eighty-floor buildings. A building about half the size of the others (thirty floors, maybe?). It called to some part of their being, some part of their human fabric that needed rest, that craved it and cried out for it. The half-sized tower answered their call.

The night-walkers paused for a while. They momentarily halted their prowling and capering and sneaking and felt their stomachs settle and their bones relax. They breathed in; they breathed out, in cadence with Tower I. And then they moved forward, back into the whirring, humming night. Because it is ridiculous to stand still and commune with a building.

* * *

This Week died and Next Week rose up to take its place. It was time to go to Tower I; it was time to make the trek to the indigo floor. The next step in Elmer's journey lay in Next Week and Next Week was finally here. Elmer ate breakfast with the three Ems and a Zee, silently probing his oatmeal with a spoon, bringing it slowly to his mouth, and chewing for much longer than anyone ever needs to chew oatmeal. Tower I. It had been in his thoughts all week and now the day—the hour even—was finally here.

Matilda prattled on and on as Elmer's oatmeal slowly diminished. She talked about her childhood in the suburbs of The City, how she was never exposed to homelessness and disease and poverty and people of different races, sizes, creeds. Usually, Elmer would have found such talk to be interesting and enlightening. Usually, he would have empathized with her ignorance. Today, however, there were other things on his mind.

It is on the indigo floor that those ripples will be stilled. That's what he said, the man in orange. Roger. That's what he promised: the emptying of emotions. That's my aim, I suppose. To free myself from the emotional bonds of the past. What a task that will be…

"Elmer," Maggie's voice cut through his thoughts, "are you done with your oatmeal?"

"Hrm? Oh, yes. Thank you. Yes, I'm done."

"Your thoughts were elsewhere, Elmer. They have been elsewhere for days now."

"My thoughts? Well, yes. I suppose you're right. No hiding anything from you, Maggie. My thoughts have been wandering down the street lately, about a mile and a half to the south."

"Tower I?"

"Tower I."

"I assumed so. Elmer, there's nothing to worry about. You'll be there with a teacher—a yogi, if you want to call him that—and he will help you. He will guide you through your troubles. In fact, you'll probably receive quite a bit of personal attention since I doubt many people make it to the indigo floor. Most of us are spread out in the lower floors. Very few make it into the blues and purples."

"So I've been told. Can't quite understand it, myself. I'm the most ordinary fellow there is."

Maggie shook her head and looked down at the dishes she was washing. "That's the most extraordinary part, Elmer. You don't realize the gifts you have. You don't understand your power. You have something within you that draws people to you, that makes them comfortable enough to open up and bare their souls."

"It was never that way in Here."

"Then things have changed. You've changed. Elmer, you're not in Here anymore."

Elmer nodded and swallowed down the rest of his orange juice. "Must be off," he said, grabbing his cane. "Can't keep Tower I waiting."

"Good luck to ya, Elm," said Matthew, giving him a slight smile. "I know you'll do great."

"Good luck, Elmer," called Matilda. "We'll be thinking of you."

"Great, that's great, thanks," he muttered and rushed out the door. One elevator ride and a few paces later, he was on the sidewalk, breathing in the musk of The City and smiling into the warm sun that shone over head. "Two o'clock," he said to himself and strode down the sidewalk.

At precisely two twenty-eight, Elmer pushed open the humble entry door of Tower I and entered the hush of the first floor. The garden smiled at him; Peggi smiled at him. The garden stayed in its corner; Peggi rushed across the room to meet him.

"Elmer, Elmer, Elmer," she sang, "so good of you to be on time. How was the walk here? Are you very tired? Can I offer you a glass of water? No? Ok, then. Let's be off. The indigo floor is ready for you. Ready and waiting." They walked to the elevator, Peggi slid in a key card, and the elevator door glided open. They got in, shared the time between the first floor and the thirtieth floor, and stopped. The elevator creaked slightly as it leveled itself. They disembarked.

Blackness. That's what greeted Elmer's eyes as they blinked and strained and dilated in an attempt to see. "Just over there," he heard Peggi mutter as she gave his shoulders a little push. Keep walking straight ahead; that's where you'll find her. Before Elmer could reply, he heard the click of heels, the rub of the elevator door, a ding, and Peggi was gone. He stared after her for several seconds, shrugged, and began walking in the direction in which he had been shoved. The wide room was seemingly empty—not a stitch of furniture or a painting or a rug that Elmer could see—except for the square pillars that rose in two rows, splitting the room into thirds. Elmer's footsteps echoed as he crossed the lonely room, calling into the blank space, like lost lambs bleating for their shepherd.

"Hello," he called. "Hello, hello, 'ello, 'lo," the room answered.

"Anyone there?"

"There, err, err, rr."

"Hmph. I thought they were expecting me," Elmer mumbled and kept walking. His palms were slippery now, betraying his jittery nerves. They slipped and slid on his cane and he gripped it tightly as he moved forward into the darkness. Suddenly, straight ahead between two distant pillars, a light snapped on. "Oh, praise be," thought Elmer and moved towards it, the veins popping out of his right hand as he continuing to squeeze his wooden cane.

As Elmer moved forward, he saw there was, indeed, furniture in the room, but it was minimalistic and plain and butted up snuggly against the far wall. It consisted of two chairs—one thin and tall-backed, the other squat and low, with a cushion covering its seat. On the tall-backed chair, her head posed rigidly on her swan neck, her eyes staring unblinking ahead of her, sat—

"The dream girl!" Elmer gasped. He stared, eyes and lips frozen wide in terror at the hollow-eyed woman in front of him and let out a breathy scream that sounded exactly like a small dog whose tail has been stomped on. "I—you—I must be going. This must be a mistake. I'm dreaming, that's all." Elmer turned to leave, his cane gliding wetly under his palm.

"This is no dream, Elmer," a low, even voice called at his back. Elmer paused. "And it's anything but a mistake," the voice continued. "Things have a purpose, Elmer. Everything in life has a purpose."

"Things have a purpose," Elmer repeated slowly, turning around to face the dream woman. "Maggie. Maggie said that exact line the other day."

"Maggie is a wise woman, Elmer. You are prudent to count her as one of your friends." The woman's eyes shown at Elmer. They were dark, dark grey. Dull, empty pits. They made Elmer's spine tingle and a trail of sweat trickle down his back. He feared this woman. To his very core, he feared her.

"Don't be afraid, Elmer," the woman said. "Come, sit down."

Elmer trembled as he made his way towards the squat, cushioned seat. He kept one eye on the dream woman as he lowered himself into the chair, adjusted the thin cushions.

"That's right, Elmer," her voice was familiar, soothing almost. If he simply used his ears instead of his eyes, he might be ok. He might resist fleeing. His discipline flagged. He raised his eyes.

The woman smiled at Elmer or, at least, he thought she was smiling. Her lips curled up at the sides, but her eyes remained dark and bottomless. For a moment—briefly and inexplicably—Elmer thought of Irene. The woman shifted her thin body within the long, indigo robes that draped off her shoulders. "You don't have to be afraid of me, you know. I'm here to help you, Elmer."

"I—I'm not afraid," said Elmer.

The woman raised one eyebrow, "As you say."

Elmer tried to look away. He tried to shut his eyes; he tried to keep her blank stare at bay, but even behind his eyelids he saw her face—the dull, coin-like eyes, the features that reminded him of Irene and Hilo and Daisy all at once. It was a face full of guilt. It was a face difficult to look upon.

"There is a reason you were placed on the indigo floor, Elmer," she said, ignoring his quivering jaw, his trembling hand. "You are close. You are close to perfecting your soul. You have drained much of the poison out of your being, but you haven't drained it all. There are still some demons to battle. And that's where I come in."

"You're one of the demons?" Elmer ventured a guess.

The woman scoffed, tossing her thick blonde—no, thin brunette—hair over her shoulder. "Not quite. I am a teacher. Your teacher. The one you dreamed up a long, long time ago."

"I did?"

"Yes, you did."

Elmer stared at the woman—her constantly morphing hair, her changing jaw line, the young—now old—glow of her cheeks, her high forehead. He found it hard to believe that he would create a teacher like her. But then again, stranger things had happened. He shrugged (as he found himself doing often this past year) and met the woman's eyes/pits. "Ok then," he said softly. "I'm ready to learn."

"Good. That's the spirit. Now, the first thing we're going to do is address that black stone in your heart. My heavens, it's awful! So black and hideous."

Elmer looked at the woman's hollow sockets and raised an eyebrow, but kept his mouth tightly closed.

"You are lugging around too many emotions, my dear student."

"So the man in orange told me."

"He told you correctly. We need to extract the heavy feelings weighing down your heart—and your soul—and banish them into the ether."

"I can't help it if I feel things deeply," said Elmer sullenly. "It's just who I am."

"No, no, no!" the woman screamed. Elmer jumped. "Get rid of that notion right now. Detach yourself from the 'I.' You are nobody. You must end your greed for existence. There is no independent existence. We dwell in an interdependent state, inextricably attached to others."

"Ok…it's just that I had kind of a rough time of things in the past. I mean, my childhood was no cake walk and my life in Here was one, big lie and it's just a *little* hard to forget all that and dump all my memories and emotions into the ground and bury them and—"

"Elmer!" she snapped. "Did you not hear a word I said? Get out of your head for once. You think too damn much sometimes—"

"—Never been accused of that before—"

"You have to let all those things go. They matter not. They should pass through your heart and mind like clouds. The mind is a fickle thing. It fluctuates and sways like branches in the wind. It is your job to control those branches. It is your job to cease the wind. Can you do that?"

"I think so."

"I'm not wasting my time on 'I think so.'"

"Ok, ok. Yes. Yes, I can do that."

"That's better. Now, let's get to it. We've already wasted too much time and that stone in your heart won't chip away by itself. I think it's time you tell me about her."

"Her?"

"The woman from your childhood."

Chapter 45

Once there was a young boy named Elmer who had a very close friend. Her name was Daisy. Ever since Daisy saved young Elmer from a fight with the schoolyard bullies, they became inseparable. At first, Daisy thought of herself as Elmer's protector. His guardian. His wild card against a stacked deck. But then she simply thought of herself as his friend. Elmer was tickled pink.

At first, he was nervous around Daisy. He stumbled on his words and stared at his feet in order to avoid staring at her hair. Fortunately, she was a forgiving playmate and talked at her new friend instead of with him until he eventually decided to hold up his own end of the conversation. One time, early in their friendship, Elmer asked Daisy, "Why are you playing with me today? Why don't you go over there and play with your girlfriends? They've been asking about you." Daisy sighed and rolled her eyes.

"Truthfully," she said, "I find girls frightfully dull. All they talk about are dolls and marriage and other girls' hair. We have pretend tea parties and play house. I'm so sick of it, I could puke." Daisy crossed her arms and wrinkled her nose. Elmer fought the urge to jump up and kiss her on the cheek. "Besides," Daisy continued, "I have three older brothers and I'm used to boys things. I feel lost in girlie land." She laughed. Elmer laughed.

"So," said Elmer, growing more pleased with his friend by the minute, "do you like playing catch?"

"Catch? Yes. Yes, of course. Two of my brothers play baseball and they taught me everything they know."

"How about riding horses. Do you like riding horses?"

"Yes, I do. Lovely creatures."

"And fishing," Elmer asked, "do you like to fish?"

"I do enjoy fishing," Daisy replied. "Although I haven't done it much and I rarely catch a thing."

"It's all in the technique," said Elmer, "and the location, of course. And I happen to have a secret fishing spot."

"You do, Elmer? You do? I want to go. Oh, can I please?"

"Of course you can. But school will be out next week. How will I see you?"

"You can come to my house anytime. I live right down the street from the schoolhouse. Down that way." She pointed to the east. "It's a big house with oak trees in the front. Number three-oh-one. You can't miss it."

"Ok. Will your family mind if you go fishing with me?"

"Mind? Of course not. My daddy's gone at the bank all day and he doesn't give two shits about what I do."

"What about your mom?"

"She died a long time ago when I was little."

"Oh. I'm sorry, Daisy."

"Don't be. I don't remember her at all. It's been just my dad and my brothers for as long as I can remember."

"Your brothers can come too if they want," said Elmer, suddenly nervous at the thought of spending all that time alone with Daisy. What if she didn't like fishing with him? What if he couldn't keep up a conversation? What if she got bored and decided to find a new playmate?

"Meh. I'll ask, but I doubt they'll want to hang out with 'baby sister' and her friend. Regardless, it'll be lots of fun, won't it Elmer? We'll catch buckets of fish, won't we?"

"I can't promise buckets, but I can promise you we'll catch some. The brook trout are pretty active this time of year."

"Oh goody, Elm! I can't wait."

Elmer grinned from ear to ear. No one had called him Elm before.

* * *

After their first glorious summer together, Daisy and Elmer were closer than ever. They spent almost every day together—fishing, running in the hay fields, playing kick the can with Daisy's brothers. They absorbed the summer sun and each other's laughter. Eventually, they had trouble picturing themselves without the other. They grew with each other and within each other, unconsciously intertwined. Their friendship ebbed and flowed as they aged. Sometimes, they grew apart and found new friends and hobbies, but they always returned to each other.

Elmer's love for Daisy grew with the years, nurtured by smiles and shared dreams and the gorgeous blonde hair that he never got over. At first he was content with her friendship, grateful for each moment they shared together, but eventually he grew restless. He worried that he would be forever stuck in a platonic friendship, that he had gained a fishing buddy, a confidante, but not a lover. Daisy would sometimes divulge her little crushes to Elmer, confessing that she thought this or that boy was "a real looker" or "a true gentleman" and Elmer would bite his tongue, nod, and feel a bit of his heart crumble away like feta cheese. He longed to tell her how he felt, but he worried that such a confession would send her running to the hills. So he kept silent, biting his tongue and nodding.

Papa never liked Daisy. He hated the idea of his son fraternizing with the banker's daughter. He forbade Elmer to spend time with "that rich little tart," but Elmer refused. No matter how many tongue lashings and belt beatings Papa doled out, Elmer stood his ground. This was one battle that he would not lose. And that was that. Elmer's mother noticed the tenderness in little Elmer's eyes when he spoke of Daisy. She saw the tenderness turn to steel when he stood up to Papa. She knew the men in her life were dangerously close to murdering one another and she decided to intervene. When Elmer was twelve, she pulled Papa aside and convinced him to soften his stance on Daisy. Their conversation lasted several hours and Elmer never knew what was said, but from that time onward, Papa looked the other way when Elmer scurried off to meet Daisy. He stopped speaking about the matter and, consequently, nearly stopped speaking to Elmer altogether. The beatings and harsh words lessened, but the fire behind Papa's eyes did not. It smoldered wickedly, fed on hatred for his oldest son, a son that had always been a disappointment to him, a son that was not cut from the same, sturdy cloth as him. Head always in the clouds. Friends with that little girlie-girl. Always focused on his studies and reading and other such nonsense. Sometimes he wondered if the boy was actually his.

Elmer could sense the fire behind Papa's eyes, but he did his best to appease him and tip-toed delicately around his temper so the fire would not leap into life. He worked hard, did his chores, kissed his mother on the cheek before he scampered off quietly to meet his friend. Sometimes, there were long stretches when he couldn't see Daisy at all. If it was planting season or if the potatoes were suffering from a blight or if it was harvest time, Elmer stayed home for weeks at a time, slogging through the back-wrenching, raw-handed work. He worked furiously during these times, putting in long hours and laboring like an ox in order to finish the work as quickly as possible. A couple of times, Daisy made the mistake of trekking to the Heartland household to check on her friend. Each time, Elmer's mother had to step between her hot-tempered husband and the lippy girl in order to stop him from lashing her with his belt. Elmer knew better than to intervene. That would only serve to fuel Papa's rage. Somehow, his mother was able to cast a magic spell on the man and he would let Daisy go, unscathed, back to her life in house three-oh-one. Daisy always went grudgingly. She hated losing any battle, especially one that might cause her friend harm. But Elmer knew how to deal with his Papa's wrath; he had dealt with it his entire life. Besides, he appreciated these small gestures from his friend. He appreciated feeling cared for. Loved, even.

During the summer of his sixteenth year, Elmer decided to tell Daisy how he truly felt about her. It was a ballsy move and he felt like puking every time he thought about it, but it had to be done. He didn't think he could stand another summer of fishing and frolicking without the truth being known. It wasn't fair to him; it wasn't fair to her. He began reciting the moment in his head, churning around the various outcomes and phrases and rebuttals that might crop up until he felt somewhat confident about his speech. Then he waited. He waited for the perfect day—a not-too-hot-not-too-cool, sunny, light-breezy day. He and Daisy walked from her house in Here to the cool creek that ran through his family's farm. They talked casually, feeling the whisper of wind across their faces, sweating slightly from the rays of friendly sunshine. Elmer had the entire afternoon off, a bucket full of earthworms, and a heart full of poetry. The creek was amiable that day, bubbling and gurgling happily to itself, and Elmer and Daisy listened to its quiet music as they dipped their fishing lines in the water and waited for the trout to bite.

"Daisy," said Elmer after several minutes of silence.

"Yes?"

"There's something I've been meaning to tell you." Elmer plowed ahead through his speech without thinking. It tumbled out of his mouth in one long breath, like a single shoe lace pulled out of a boot. He confessed his admiration of her, told her he harbored feelings for her since the first day he saw her sitting in Miss Anne's classroom, long blonde hair rippling down her back. He admitted he had wanted to say something for a while—years actually—but never quite worked up the courage because he was afraid he'd lose her.

"God, I hope I won't lose you." Elmer paused. "Will I?"

Daisy sat in silence for several seconds, letting the meat of Elmer's words settle in her stomach. Elmer's palms were damp with sweat and he hastily wiped them on the grass at his side. He looked into Daisy's dark brown eyes, mutely begging her to say something. When she spoke, her voice was even and calm. "Don't be silly, Elmer. Of course you won't lose me."

Elmer breathed out, long and slow.

"I just want to know what on earth took so long."

"What's that?"

"Really, Elmer. Did you think I didn't know? Did you think I didn't have some inkling about how you feel? I've known for quite some time now, but I decided to let you tell me in your own way. Well, it's about damn time."

"You—you've known for quite some time?"

"Yes, Elmer."

"Oh. I see." He thought to himself for a moment. "Well, at least you're not repulsed by the idea. At least we can still be friends, right? I mean, despite my fancying you, we can still remain friends?"

"I don't think so, Elmer."

"Oh. You don't? Ok, then. Very well. I understand, I think—"

"Good grief. Do I have to do everything myself in this relationship?" Daisy dropped her fishing pole, turned to Elmer, cradled the back of his head, and planted a long, wet kiss on his mouth. Elmer held his lips in a stiff pucker, too surprised to actually kiss back.

"Oh," he managed to say after several stunned seconds. "I see."

"Come on, Elmer," Daisy said. "The fish aren't biting here. Let's go down river a ways."

Elmer nodded, picked up his bucket of earthworms and his fishing rod, and followed the fleet feet of his beloved down river. He watched the sun glint off of her yellow hair as she nimbly picked her way along the rocky river bank. Elmer smiled. He loved her more than ever.

* * *

Elmer and Daisy enjoyed the greatest summer of their lives that year. They remained best friends and life continued as usual, with the exception of some kissing and touching added to their list of activities. They spent every free minute together and Elmer would return home late at night, starry-eyed and light-headed. Elmer's mother noticed the change in him almost immediately. She saw his secretive smiles, his far-off looks. She attempted to hide his tardiness from Papa; she attempted to straighten out poorly-performed chores, but eventually Papa smelled a rat.

"That dumbass, good-fer-nothin' son of mine came in late again last night, didn't he? I heard the door swing closed 'round midnight, I did! He's been spending more time with that banker's daughter, hasn't he? Hasn't he?"

"I'm not sure, dear. Are you certain you heard the door last night? It could have been the wind. There was a storm brewing, I think."

"Oh, I'm sure. And you would do well to quit coverin' up his tracks fer him. I saw you sweeping out the barn the other day. We both know that was Elmer's task. God damn duty-shirker. Lazy bumpkin that takes everything he has for granted."

"*That* lazy bumpkin is our son."

"Is he now? Maybe he's yours, but he's no son of mine."

"Papa!"

"Now, don't you 'Papa' me! I'm going to teach that boy a lesson. Now outta my way!"

The belt lashings didn't stop Elmer, even though they were unleashed with the fury of a man rabid with rage. The welts on Elmer's arms and legs and back only made him grit his teeth and stay away longer. Sometimes, he even stayed at the banker's house—the house of Daisy's father. He was always embarrassed when he stayed with Daisy. Her father would grudgingly lend him pajamas and point to the couch. Elmer obeyed meekly, tossing and turning as he attempted to sleep on the too-short piece of furniture. Daisy's father was never thrilled when Elmer stayed over, but he understood why it had to be. He looked at the red, blistering welts on Elmer's shoulders and wrists, shrugged, pointed to the couch, went to bed. He knew why it had to be. He knew the boy was in love and he would stop at nothing to see his daughter. He had a love like that once—once several years ago. She had hair like freshly cut hay. Yes, he understood.

Summer ended and fall began. Back to the classroom and Miss Anne and row after row of gossipy children. It wasn't long before the entire schoolhouse caught wind of Elmer and Daisy's love affair. It was the talk of the school for several weeks, the boys whispering taunts into Elmer's ear, the girls asking Daisy if Elmer was a good kisser. The couple was grateful when the hubbub died down and they could concentrate on each other rather than the classroom whispers. The year marched on and the cold winds of winter picked up.

At first, Papa thought it was nothing. Just a cold, he said. Nothing to fuss over. A good night's sleep would cure it. But a good night's sleep didn't cure it. If anything, Papa became more tired—tired and feverish. He had trouble focusing on his tasks and his head pounded like the pistons in a two-hundred ton locomotive. He ran to the outhouse constantly, looking pale and worn whenever he came back, as if he had been fighting some great battle against his body and wasn't sure of the victor. "Get some rest," his wife told him. "I'll call a doctor." "You'll do know such thing!" he roared in reply. "No doctor. And I'm working these fields until I drop."

He did drop. Elmer found him collapsed in the north potato field, face up, eyes closed, wheezing and gasping for breath. He half-dragged, half-carried him back to the house. Papa cried all the way, talking nonsense and struggling for his breath. Elmer listened to his Papa's sobs and felt sorry for the man for the first time in his life. Elmer tucked him into bed, poured him a glass of water and ran out the door to the stable. He tossed a saddle onto one of the draught horses, cinched it, threw on a bridle, and was out the stable doors, galloping across the fields to Doc Myrtle's home.

"The doctor is out," Doc Myrtle's wife informed Elmer. "He's delivering a baby for the tailor's wife in town." Elmer leapt back onto the horse; the hooves thundered on. He found Doc Myrtle at the kitchen sink of the tailor's house, washing his hands and his instruments with soap. "What is the meaning of this?" demanded the tailor. "What is it, boy?" asked the doctor.

"Papa—my Papa—it's bad—real bad—collapsed in the field—can hardly breath—fever—please—please help Doc—please."

"Ok Elmer, ok. You ride on ahead and I'll be there in a minute. Just wrapping up some things here."

"Oh thank you, Doc, thank you. And Doc, can you please hurry?"

The doctor looked at the boy in front of him, covered in dirt from the potato fields and gasping for breath. "I will."

"Thanks, Doc. See you there."

"See you."

The doctor's medicine tamed the illness, offered temporary relief. Over the next several days, with the aid of an assortment of powders, pills, and constant care, Papa's fever was reduced and he came back into his head once again. But he didn't get well. Not quite. A rash spread all over his body, causing him to itch and squirm. And the chills and hallucinations remained, flaring up whenever they pleased. "I've done everything I can," the doctor informed them. "He had been suffering from typhoid fever for days—a week even—before I was summoned. There have most likely been complications—kidney failure, perhaps—and you should think about getting his affairs in order."

Elmer watched Papa deteriorate before his eyes. He watched his great, hulking arms become atrophied and saggy. He watched his cheeks sink in. He watched the raging fire in his vivid green eyes fade into a pile of smoldering, smoking ash. Elmer shivered when he saw him; he was the ghost of the father he used to have. He was no longer real.

Papa spoke very little after hearing Doc Myrtle's prognosis. He stared a lot. Stared at the ceiling and at the walls, weak and shivery, willing himself to die. His family watched over him in shifts, holding his hand, stroking his fever-soaked hair. One Monday morning in November when Elmer was keeping watch over his father, Papa stirred and looked over at his son, eyes clear and lucid, mouth set in a firm, straight line. "Fetch your mother, boy," he said. "I need to talk to her. It's about time I do what Doc said and get my affairs in order."

"Yes, sir."

Elmer's mother sat on the edge of Papa's bed for over an hour as they discussed his final wishes. For the most part, Papa spoke and his wife sat quietly, passively agreeing with everything he said. However, when she stepped out of the room, her cheeks were pale and her mouth was grim. "What's wrong?" Elmer asked. "Nothing," she replied quickly. "Run to town, Elmer, and get our family lawyer. We need to draw up a will." "Yes, ma'am."

The lawyer arrived with neatly-pressed trousers, a leather brief-case, and his pencil-thin mustache. He wrinkled his nose at the Heartland's tiny, clapboard farmhouse and gingerly, daintily walked up the stairs to Papa's room. "Hello sir," he said dryly, sitting down and resting the briefcase on his long, skinny thighs. "Let's begin."

Papa must have smelled the putrid sting of Death's breath blowing down his back, because it wasn't twelve hours after the will was drawn up that he drew his last mouthful of air and expired. In death, he looked small. Small and serene. Elmer had trouble picturing this feeble man whipping him with criticisms and the leather of his belt. In death, he was merely Papa—a father and husband, the dead patriarch of the Heartland family. Elmer stroked his father's limp hair, kissed his hollow cheek. He felt tears building up in his eyes and he hastily rubbed them away. He was the man of the house now. No time for crying.

After the sparsely-attended funeral, the widow Heartland and her five children walked down the street to their lawyer's office. They formed a dark black cloud on the sunny sidewalk and passersby gave them an extra-wide berth so they could avoid the solemn procession of mourners. They didn't want such a grim group to dampen their spirits, especially on such a lovely November day. So they stepped aside and the dark cloud passed, floating by woefully and silently as if tugged along by a fat, oppressive wind. The group arrived at the lawyer's office and stepped inside. The town of Here breathed a little easier.

The lanky lawyer sniffed at the downtrodden family over his pencil mustache as they filed into his office. He ignored them for a full five minutes as he shuffled through papers, sipped his herbal tea, smoothed the hairs of an errant eyebrow. Finally, he looked up, as if surprised to have company, and jumped straight into business.

"You're here for the reading of the will, I assume."

They nodded.

"Have a seat." There were only two seats in the office. The lawyer snickered to himself as he watched the widow claim one and the herd of children clamber for the other. "Now, let's begin shall we?"

They nodded.

The lawyer rushed through the will quickly. There wasn't much to it. The house was to be left in the care of his wife. His quarter horses were bequeathed to his daughters. His hunting rifle and ammunition was left to his youngest son. Elmer listened while all of Papa's worldly possessions were divided amongst his younger siblings. It didn't surprise him much, but he couldn't help feeling a little disappointed.

"And to Elmer Heartland," the lawyer read. Elmer's ears perked up; he raised his sullen eyes and looked at the thin-faced man behind the desk. "My eldest son, I bequeath the Heartland farm, including all potato fields, hay fields, farming equipment, outbuildings, the team of Percherons, the dairy cows, and the milking equipment..."

Elmer's mouth hung open. He hadn't expected the family farm; his father knew how much he hated it. He was flattered and disgusted at the same time. Papa had entrusted him with his most precious possession, but had he done it out of love...or spite?

"On the condition," the lawyer continued; Elmer leaned forward, "that he court and wed Ms. Irene Gorsheim, daughter of Nathaniel Gorsheim, owner and operator of Gorsheim Dairy Farm, within one year of my death. If the aforementioned condition is not met within one year of my death, the farm and all its accessories will instead be bequeathed to my second eldest son, William Heartland."

The lawyer stopped speaking and looked up. Elmer looked down. His cheeks burned with rage; his thoughts spun like a top. He felt something akin to a tiny tornado whirling around the edifices of his brain. In that moment (though he didn't realize it at the time), the storm began—spinning, spinning, spinning, whirring and buzzing, raging and fighting—and did not let up for over sixty years.

"The will has been read," the lawyer said. "Please sign here," he pointed to the bottom of the will, "to indicate that you have heard and understand the conditions of the will."

Heard, yes. Understand, no. That bloody, stinking bastard!

Widow Heartland signed first, then the children. Elmer signed last, in large angry letters, dribbling ink down the side of the sheet. The lawyer wrinkled his nose at the impudent boy. "That is that, then," he said, sneering at the family disapprovingly. "Any questions? Good. I must be off. Meeting to attend. You can see yourselves out, can't you? Very good. So long." He snatched up his briefcase, breezed past the family, and strode down the street towards the corner tavern. The Heartland family stared after him for a moment, then quietly gathered their things and walked, slowly and arthritically, towards home.

* * *

Elmer avoided Daisy for several days. He dropped out of school (there was the farm to attend to, of course) and stayed, resolutely, within the Heartland property lines. He didn't speak to anyone in his family, except to growl at them to milk the cows or muck out the horse stalls. He behaved much like Papa, stomping around angrily, striking fear in those around him. He didn't care. Let them be afraid of him; he was lord of the household now.

One night, Elmer's mother softly knocked on his bedroom door and asked to come in. "Mmm," he muttered and opened the door. Elmer shared the room with his brothers and they were already asleep, strings of drool dangling from their open mouths.

"Come downstairs for a minute, Elmer. We need to talk."

"Why should I bother?" Elmer sneered. "There is nothing to say."

"Yes, Elmer, there is. Now come along."

He followed her grudgingly down the stairs and to the kitchen table. They sat down across from each other, his eyes turned away, hers resolutely fixed on her son. "Elmer," she began, "I know this is hard on you. I am aware of the pain you're going through right now—running the farm, giving up your banker's daughter—but this is the only way, son. You have to understand that. Papa didn't hate you, he truly didn't, but he could never stand that banker's daughter, that…Daisy. And he wanted to put an end to it, once and for all. But Elmer, you have to understand—"

"There's nothing to understand!"

"Yes there is! Now listen, please!"

Elmer's mouth clamped shut; he sat rigidly across from her, his emotions brewing and bubbling under his skin.

"Elmer, this is for the best. I know you don't think so, but believe me, it is. For one thing, the banker would never let his daughter marry some lowly potato farmer's son. You may have fooled yourself into thinking he would consent, but you've always known deep down that it wouldn't be so. Besides, Daisy is rather a delicate thing, isn't she? Better to have a sturdy girl like young Irene at your side when you're working a farm." She paused and tugged on a thread dangling from her sleeve.

"And secondly, you should feel honored to inherit this farm. Your father worked hard to put it together, to make it run like clockwork, to make it successful. It is a privilege to inherit your father's dream and you should be grateful. Your Papa may have been a hateful man at times, but he wasn't full of hate when he decided to grant you the farm. He simply thought it would give you a chance to live up to your potential, to be the farmer he always hoped you would be. He thought of your inheritance as a gift, not a prank. For the love of God, Elmer, he's not that cruel."

"Yes he is," Elmer said quietly. "I hate farming. Always have. Did he think that would change when he kicked the bucket? Mmm? No, he didn't. He wanted to torture me. He wanted his ghost to haunt me for the rest of my life."

"Elmer, he knew that you weren't enamored with farming, but he hoped that you would *grow* to love it. Or tolerate it, at the very least. I can assure you, he only had your well-being in mind."

"My well-being? *My* well-being? Is that what he thought when he added the clause about marrying the Gorsheim girl in his will? Was he thinking about *my* well-being?"

"Yes, as a matter of fact! I already told you, son, it is no good courting the banker's daughter. Society will never have it."

"Then we'll run away together."

"You'll do no such thing! I know you, Elmer. You aren't the type to run away. Your place is here. Your place is in Here."

"But mother, I love her! I don't know a thing about the Gorsheim girl, except that she has great, hulking thighs."

"Well, you'd better learn to love those thighs, Elmer, because it has already been arranged. Papa and Nathaniel Gorsheim have been talking about this match for years. It will happen. You have no choice in the matter. And you'll inherit not only Papa's potato farm, but also Gorsheim Dairy as part of the bargain."

"I don't want a fucking dairy farm! And I don't want Papa's farm either! I want Daisy and that's it. Is that too much to ask? Is it?"

"Watch your tongue, young man! Yes, it is too much to ask. We need to keep this family together. We need to run this goddamn potato farm and work our hands to the bones because that is all we have. If you want to be a self-serving brat, you can run away with your beloved Daisy. All the best to you. But if you want to remain a part of this family, you will get your act together and marry the fat-thighed Gorsheim girl and that is that!"

Elmer glared at his mother. He felt the storm rising in his head, whipping around his limbic cortex and inundating him with a flood of rage. It wasn't fair! None of it was fair! He didn't want to marry the Gorsheim girl; he didn't want to inherit a dairy farm; he didn't want to leave the love of his life in order to appease his family. But he saw no way out. He thought of his brothers and sisters, his well-meaning mother and saw no way out. He was trapped.

His mother looked at him from across the table, her eyes round and pleading. She stretched out a thin hand and cupped it over Elmer's. "Elmer, please try to understand," she whispered. "This isn't the end of things. This is only the beginning."

"I'm selling the farm as soon as my sisters are grown and out of the house," he growled.

"You can do that if you want, Elmer. It's your farm."

"And I won't ever love the Gorsheim girl."

"You might not, Elmer. That's completely up to you."

"And I'm going to spend as much time with Daisy as I can before the year is up."

His mother paused, sighed, spoke. "Ok, Elmer. But be careful. Don't sink yourself any deeper into that relationship than you already have. Instead, you should try to dig yourself out."

Dig yourself out. What a curious thing to say.

"Yes, mother. I'll try."

"You're a good son, Elmer. A very good son. I'm proud of you."

Elmer nodded.

* * *

Daisy didn't take the news well. When Elmer told her about Papa's death and his will and the particular clause regarding Irene Gorsheim, she leapt to her feet screaming, "Where does that Gorsheim whore live? I'll kill her myself and that'll be the end of it! I'll stab her with a kitchen knife!"

"Daisy, Daisy, shh," said Elmer, grabbing her around the waist and forcing her to sit down once again. "Calm down, love," he said cradling her in his arms. "There is nothing we can do about. It has already been decided. It's for the good of my family that I stay at home and work the farm now. You wouldn't hurt her anyway, would you?"

"Well, no," said Daisy between sobs, "but I would, Elmer. I would if it meant keeping you."

Elmer bit his lip. "I'm sure you would, Daisy, but I'm afraid it's decided now. Besides, your father would never approve of you running away to live with me on the farm. You're meant to marry a businessman, someone who is successful and rich, not a potato farmer."

"I don't care what my father thinks! I want you, Elmer. I want you!" Once again, she sprang to her feet. This time, Elmer didn't have a chance to calm her down. She took off, running furiously in the direction of her house, bits of thin November snow flying behind her feet. Elmer chased after her for a few feet yelling, "Daisy, stop! Daisy, let's talk about this! Daisy!" But he gave up quickly. There was no stopping that girl if she was determined to do something and right now she was determined to run away.

Elmer trudged home, away from the icy river and the giant oak tree they had been sitting beneath. His tears froze to eyelashes, creating tiny crystals below and above his eyes. When he arrived home, he spoke to no one and marched straight into his room and climbed into bed, his wet clothing still clinging to his skin. Perhaps things would be better in the morning.

* * *

It took several months and constant urging from his mother before Elmer brought himself to begin courting Irene. Nathaniel Gorsheim was pleased as punch and bought his daughter a number of new dresses, all of which reminded Elmer of gooey, pastel frosting on an overly plump cake. He grudgingly brought Irene to the cinema and the soda shop and all the typical date locales frequented by the teenagers of Here. He never brought her fishing.

By this time, Daisy had come to terms with her fate. She and Elmer were once again on speaking terms and they did their best to act normally and keep their conversations civil. Every once in a while, they were painfully aware of the unfair cards life had dealt them and they spent time moping or crying on each other's shoulders, wishing things could be different. But things weren't different and most of the time they held their heads high and accepted the cold fact that they would not end up together.

Elmer spent as much time with Daisy as he could, but once he started dating Irene in mid-March, things became even more complicated than they were before…mainly because Irene enjoyed being paraded around. She was not used to much male attention and relished the fact that she suddenly had a handsome young escort to take her to the movies. She talked loudly and brazenly about Elmer in the Here public schoolhouse, giggling with the other girls about his muscled shoulders and his beautiful green eyes. Because of Irene's shameless flaunting, Daisy not only heard about Elmer every day in school, she also frequently saw the pair of them in town, arm-in-arm, walking to the candy shop or the hamburger shack. Whenever they saw each other, Elmer would avert his eyes and shuffle Irene into the nearest shop. Daisy was more than a little miffed whenever this occurred and sometimes refused to speak with Elmer for days. Elmer panicked whenever this happened because he wanted to spend all the time he could with Daisy before November and dating Irene was already draining what little time he had.

Fortunately, summer rolled around, school was let out, and Daisy was no longer forced to listen to Irene's brags. However, it was also planting season and the fields could not wait. Elmer explained to Daisy that he would have to work from sun-up to sun-down for a couple of weeks and might have scant opportunity to see her. Daisy crossed her arms, pursed her lips, and didn't say a word. The next day, she showed up at his doorstep at 4:30 a.m., wearing overalls and holding a shovel.

Elmer laughed when he saw her, gave her a giant hug, and said he never saw anything so adorable in his entire life. She flicked her long, golden braid over her back, frowned, and said, "I'm not adorable; I'm serious."

"Ok," said Elmer. "You're serious. Now, come grab some breakfast. You'll need a good meal in you before we start working the fields. It's going to be a long, sweaty day."

Elmer's mother watched from across the room, a disapproving look in her eye, but kept her mouth shut. He was her son, but he was also the man of the household and was doing a damn fine job of running things since his father died. "Besides," she thought, "that prissy thing won't last two hours."

Daisy lasted well over two hours. She lasted twelve days. She helped turn the soil, add the fertilizer, pick out weeds, chop up the remnants of last year's potatoes, plant the useful remnants—the ones with tendrils growing out of their eyes, water the new plants, scare off the hungry ravens and cowbirds. Within a week, her skin was bronzed and chapped and her hands grew calloused.

"You're getting to be a regular farm girl, Daisy," Elmer commented.

Daisy smiled. "And I don't have to have a wide ass and tree-trunk thighs to do it."

Elmer poked her. "Yeah, yeah. Rub it in."

"Rub this in!" she shouted and threw a clod of black dirt at his chest.

"Hey! Just because you're a girl, doesn't mean I won't get you back," Elmer said, hurling a dirt chunk at her face. She ducked and ran at him, grabbing him around the waist and tackling him to the ground. They lay in the dark soil, laughing hysterically, dirt clinging to their clothing and shoes and smeared across their skin.

"Why don't we call it a day, Daisy? We've worked hard today and the potatoes can wait."

"Fine by me."

They gathered some fishing equipment and scurried down to the river, hand-in-hand. When they reached the rocky banks, they immediately stripped off their clothes and dove into the frigid water. "Whoo!" called Elmer. "Pretty nippy for June."

"You're telling me," Daisy replied, hugging her body. "But at least I feel clean for the first time in days."

They floated in the river for several minutes, letting the water cleanse their skin and hair. When their fingers turned wrinkly and they began to shiver, they emerged from their chilly bath and lay down in a nearby patch of grass to dry off. They lay side-by-side, letting the sun dry their bodies. Suddenly, Daisy scrambled to her feet.

"Let's dance, Elmer! I feel like dancing!"

"Wha? Dancing? I don't know, Daisy. I'm feeling pretty comfortable here in the grass. Maybe some other time."

"No! Not some other time. Now! We don't have many 'other times' left. Come on, Elmer! Please."

"Oh, alright. If it means that much to you."

"It does, Elm," she said, tugging on his hand. "It really does."

They danced under the late afternoon sun, holding each other's hands, spinning in circles until they were dizzy, singing silly songs as they moved. Their troubles and cares evaporated, like the river water from their bodies. Elmer forgot about Irene and the potato farm and Papa's death and the unfairness of the world. All his energy was focused on her—the beautiful, stunning, perfect woman in front of him. After a while, he pulled her hand towards him and she fell into his arms. They tumbled backwards into the soft grass and lay, panting and smiling, in each other's embrace. Elmer brushed the golden hair away from her face and whispered, "I love you, Daisy. I love you and nothing can change that—not time, not people."

"Elmer, I love you too. But you can't promise that won't change. We're young. Who knows what the years will bring."

"I don't care. I'll always love you. Always."

Daisy smiled, locking her deep brown eyes with his green ones and planting a long, fiery kiss on his mouth. He kissed her back and wrapped his fingers around her hair, tugging gently. Soon they found themselves entwined, bodies dancing to the same rhythm, melting into the other's soul like rain into the parched ground. They danced well together.

That November, Elmer married Irene Gorsheim. It was a happy day for many people and Elmer knew that. He put on a brave face, laughed and smiled, pretended to be the happiest man on earth while tiny worms of misery ate at his raw heart. When he took Irene back to the farmhouse and carried her over the threshold, she laughed and giggled and declared that she loved the little house and had never been happier.

"Don't get used to it," Elmer said. "I plan on selling it as soon as my sisters are grown."

"Oh, Elmer. You're too funny!" Irene tittered. "Now, why don't you give me a tour? Such a lovely little place. And Elmer—"

"Yes?"

"My father asked me to invite you to his Lions Club meeting this Wednesday. He says it is a great place to meet new people and establish rapport with the local boys. Whaddya say Elmer?"

"Ok."

"Great! I'll tell Father you'll be happy to go. Oh Elmer! Aren't you just tickled that we're married. You and me. We're starting a brand new chapter of our lives right now. A brand new chapter! And we'll be together forever. Isn't it exciting Elmer? Isn't it?"

Chapter 46

The woman in indigo stared blankly at Elmer over her pointed nose. The hollow eyes didn't blink. "What happened to Daisy?" she asked matter-of-factly in her low-octave tone.

"I didn't see much of her after I married Irene," said Elmer. "She moved from Here with her betrothed."

"Her betrothed?"

"Yes. Some guy from down south who was friends with her father's cousin. Wealthy guy. Big chin and a little potbelly. That's about all I know about him. Not even sure of his name." Elmer paused and stared vacantly into the dimly-lit room. "You know, that's the most tragic part of the whole thing. I didn't get to see Daisy grow old with me. In my mind, she'll always be seventeen. It makes me wonder and agonize about the other sixty years she has lived."

"And this distresses you." It wasn't a question.

Elmer nodded. "Very much. She was—and still is, I suppose—the love of my life."

"You need to get your head out of your childhood, Elmer. It's no use."

"I know that, but—"

"I don't mean to be harsh, but that's the way it is. You can't dwell on the past. Remember what I said earlier? Let these things roll through you like clouds. Clouds exist at one point or another and then they do not. They dissipate. This should be the key teaching that you take with you from this lesson. We are made weak and irrational by our emotions. Practice emptiness, Elmer. Practice control over your feelings."

"Does that mean erasing Daisy from my memory, because I am *not* about to do that."

"I see you still feel quite strongly about this woman," the indigo lady commented, "and after hearing your story I understand why. But no Elmer, you do not have to erase her from your memory. You should, however, dull that memory a little. A dull knife is still a knife. It simply does not cut."

Elmer was quiet for several seconds. "Tell me what I need to do."

* * *

Maggie was quiet while Elmer was gone. She held Zach and absentmindedly washed dishes and thought. Mostly she thought. She thought of Zach's father and lost love and a wasted opportunity that would probably never crop up again. The teachers in Tower I told her to forget these things. They told her time and again to detach herself from her human body, to drain herself of useless emotions like anguish and fear and elation. "Easier said than done," she thought bitterly.

Maggie was quiet while Elmer was gone. She wondered if she had steered the old man in the right direction or if she had only aided in muddling his already confused mind a bit more. Before Elmer came into her life, she hadn't thought much about elderly folks. She hadn't cared much about them. She barely acknowledged their existence on the bus or in coffee shops or hobbling across the street. These were vacant people with problems no greater than "What, oh what, shall I feed Mr. Whiskers tonight? The tuna or the chicken-flavored cat food?" or "Denise hasn't called in weeks. I must check up on that girl." That was all the elderly cared about. Their cats and their negligent children. They figured out life a long time ago. They stopped growing and changing. They became stagnant human beings, wandering about in knobbly sweaters and slacks they had purchased several decades ago.

When Elmer came into Maggie's life—abruptly and beautifully—she immediately changed her mind about the elderly. He was so vulnerable, so human. He was awkward and uncomfortable. He was an excellent listener and didn't prattle on about his Yorkshire terrier or his seven grandchildren. Elmer revealed to her a hidden side of the elderly. He revealed to her that the elderly are human beings—living, breathing, feeling, sensitive, self-conscious, growing, changing, dynamic human beings. The revelation made her relax slightly, made her less nervous about growing old.

Maggie hoped the thirtieth floor—the indigo-colored one—wouldn't drain Elmer of his three-dimensionality. She hoped he wouldn't come out of it dull, blank, colorless, free of all emotions. But that's what Tower I taught, didn't it? That's what it preached. It advised emptiness; it promoted blank slates. That's the only way to Enlightenment, isn't it? To free ourselves of all the nonsensical emotions we lug around each day. To recognize the frailty and impermanence of our human bodies and float off into the ether with the other enlightened souls.

Maggie was quiet while Elmer was gone. She baked bread (she never baked bread), kneading the dough forcefully on the countertop. Knead, knead, knead. Pounding her fists into the dough, flipping it over, grinding the meat of her palms into the fleshy concoction. Zach watched her from his place on the couch. He wondered what was wrong. She never baked bread. And she was being unusually quiet while Elmer was gone.

* * *

The City is a breathing thing. It inhales people's lives, sucks them into its sooty lungs, and spits them out into the street, slightly used and a good deal unhealthier than when they came. The City relies on its oxygen. It relies on people scuttling around and causing mischief. It relies on the mischief-enders, the bringers of order, the law of the land. It depends on the makers, the craftsmen, the creators of buildings and baklava and paintings and cappuccinos and sidewalks and auto parts and cigarette ads. It also depends on those who use, who feed off of the makers, the craftsmen, the creators. It depends on those who live in the buildings, who consume the baklava, who buy the paintings, who slurp down the cappuccinos, who roam the sidewalks, who install the auto parts, who glance at the cigarette ads. The City depends on this balance. It relies on the great inhale and exhale of life. It keeps breathing because of the endless cycles of life and death that exist within it.

The City may be greedy. The City may be heartless. But it serves a purpose; it has a function. It exists because the givers and the takers exist. It exists because the creators and the consumers exist. It exists because the makers of mischief and the makers of order exist. The City could not exist without these facets swimming through its concrete veins, filling the marrow of its steel bones. It could not exist without the pulsating, mad rhythm that the life within it provides. And the life within it could not survive without The City. The life within suckles at The City's teat and burps into its fermented air. The City and the life within it live symbiotically, encouraging each other like jaded lovers trying to get each other off.

* * *

"How was yer first lesson, Elm?" Matthew asked through a mouthful of homemade sourdough bread. "Was it e'rything you thought it might be?"

"It was…something," Elmer said, carefully smoothing a knifeful of strawberry jam over his bread. He took a sip of coffee, rubbed some sleep from his eyes. "My teacher was a woman in long indigo robes. She looked just like a woman who appeared to me in a couple of dreams. Very odd."

"A dream-woman, eh?" Matthew snickered. "She must be a looker then, am I right?" He gave Elmer a sly sideways smile.

Elmer sputtered his mouthful of coffee. "Good god, no! Certainly not. She is more like a demon than a lady. Great hollow eyes. Features that keep changing. First she has long, golden hair and a petite nose, then she has straggly brown hair and thin cheeks. It's damn eerie, that's what it is."

Maggie listened as she poured herself a glass of orange juice. "But did she teach you any valuable lessons, Elmer? Did she help guide you in any way?"

"She did. No denying that, I suppose. But it was mostly me who talked during our lesson. She wanted to know about my childhood love and so I told her. I talked and talked and talked some more until my throat was raw and my head was pounding. Then she imparted some advice."

"Can we hear the story?" Matilda spoke up. "It sounds so romantic, Elm!"

"Mmm. Maybe some other time. I'm not really up for marathon story time at the moment."

"Oh, alright," Matilda said, a little crestfallen.

"You were saying, Elmer?" Maggie prodded. "The advice she imparted?"

"Right, right. She told me I have too many emotions bungled up inside me and I have to let them out. I'm supposed to practice being empty, stilling my mind."

"I see," said Maggie quietly.

"Hey, that's kind of what I'm working on in the burnt orange floor," Matthew chimed in. "We've been practicing meditation. Lots of people on that floor have lived troubled lives, you know, so we have to work on calmin' the ol' nerves."

"Have you?" Elmer asked.

"Beg yer pardon?"

"Have you led a troubled life?" Elmer wondered why he had asked the question. Somehow it had formed in his mind and shot out of his mouth before he could control it.

"S'pose I have, Elm. S'pose I have. Life is not especially kind to orphans."

"I know it," said Elmer. "I have met a few." He thought of Cecelia and her life in Mrs. Terwilliger's Foster Care and Berry Patch. He remembered her warm smile, her patience, her limitless kindness. He thought of the way she sat at the piano—back straight, arms flowing with the music—as she played Clementi. He wondered if there was something deep inside him, deep in the recesses of his bowels, that led him to troubled people like Matthew and Cecelia. Or maybe they were led to him.

"My assignment this week," said Matthew, shoving another piece of bread into his mouth and chewing while he spoke, "is to go to a quiet place and work on breathing. Like, steadyin' the rhythm of my heart and controllin' my breath and all that shit. Would you want to come with me, Elmer? It might help you to release some pent-up emotions. Ya never know…"

"Sure, Matthew. That would be fine."

* * *

For the next several weeks, Elmer observed The City with new eyes. He actively drank in the sights and smells, but tried his best not to respond to them. He practiced neutrality, detachment. He challenged himself to traipse into the harshest areas of The City, note them, walk away. He thought of clouds and how they pass overhead and disappear. He thought of flowers and how they bloom in the summer and then wither away. He thought of his own life—his short-lived, heart-wrenching youth—and how it had slipped away like silk off a dandelion. He thought of these things and the impermanence of them and applied this lens to The City. It was all impermanent, wasn't it? Trees and pavement and the hotdog vendor. It was no use getting attached to them. They would change and shrivel up and fade and die. He decided this outlook wasn't morbid. Really, it wasn't. It was practical. Practical and necessary. This was the only way to achieve Enlightenment, the indigo woman had told him. To leave one's physical body and focus oneself on matters beyond the petty concerns of average man is to obtain the ultimate awareness. To become Awake.

Elmer desired to wake up. He wanted to know Enlightenment. He wanted to be free of all the emotional baggage he had lugged around for years. This was the way. He was treading down the path and approaching his destination little by little. He could see it; he could smell it. It overpowered all the other sights and sounds of The City. It possessed him.

Usually, Elmer walked The City streets by himself. He preferred it that way. It was easier to concentrate on his body, on each emotion that passed through his brain. If he was alone, it was easier to acknowledge those emotions, grab them by the hair, throw them out the door. He preferred working alone, but sometimes he didn't have a choice. Matilda or Matthew or Maggie would insist on joining him on the cold pavement of The City. They would see him heading for the door and call, "Wait a minute Elmer! Let me grab my scarf and I'll be right with you. Don't want you out there all by yourself."

"No really," Elmer would say, "I'm fine on my own."

"I don't believe you, Elm. Those City streets are mighty lonely."

"Alright," Elmer would concede. "Let's get going then."

When Elmer walked with others, it was much more difficult to become empty, to become a neutral vessel, a carrying case for his soul. His friends were distracting. They insisted on chatting and giggling and patting him on the back. They made it difficult to feel nothing at all. He caught himself bouncing between pleasure and annoyance as he alternately enjoyed and then despised his friends' company. "They are holding me back, he thought. I have to do this on my own."

When Elmer was able to get away from the Ems, he would stay away for a long time. Hours—days, sometimes—would pass and he would dwell in solitude in a city of thousands. He stayed in homeless shelters at night and paced the sidewalks during the day. Eventually, he would grow weary and cold and return to his friends. They welcomed him with anxious eyes and voices. "Where have you been, Elmer? Not back to the shelters again? We've been worried about you."

Sometimes Matthew would not talk to Elmer for days after his return from the street. He took the old man's absence personally and wondered what he did to push Elmer away from them. These long bouts of silence were tough on Elmer and he was forced to concentrate hard in order to ignore them. Thankfully, Matthew always came around and things would feel normal in the house of the Ems for a while…until Elmer decided his concentration was flagging and it was time to leave again.

* * *

Three long weeks had passed since Elmer's first visit to the woman in indigo and he was due for another session. He picked his way through a litter-strewn ally—a shortcut to Tower I—and successfully ignored three homeless men sleeping on top of flattened cardboard boxes. A month ago, Elmer would have felt sorry for the bums. A year ago, he would have felt disgust. At the moment, he felt nothing. He simply stepped by them and continued walking through the ally. Elmer was pleased with his progress, pleased with the fact that he was somewhat able to separate himself from the emotional, physical world. He then recognized the pleasure he felt and attempted to push it out of his mind. By the time he reached the tower doors, he more or less succeeded.

Peggi grinned as he stepped through the swinging doors and into the entrance hall. Today she wore a frilly, lime green blouse with white polka dots littered across it. "Hellllllo Elmer!" she sang as she walked towards him. "You're looking in rare form today! Ready for your session on the thirtieth floor? Mmm, excellent. Let's not waste any time then. To the elevator!" She pranced ahead and Elmer followed her, shaking his head and smiling quietly to himself. He had trouble imagining Peggi achieving a state free of emotion.

The room was just as dark as before. Elmer crept ahead, feeling prickles on the back of his neck and along his spine. His forehead glistened with sweat as he moved into the darkness.

No! I'm in control. I control my emotions! No fear. No fear or sorrow or nervousness. Come on, Elmer. Get it together.

A light flicked on across the room and once again Elmer walked towards it. His heart beat rapidly as he began to make out the figure of the indigo woman sitting on her tall, thin chair. As he drew closer, he became increasingly irritated by the fear his body betrayed. Why couldn't he keep it together in her presence? Why did she make him want to fall to his knees and weep? Or curl into an embryonic ball until she disappeared? Good grief, he was irritated and he knew that was no way to start a lesson.

"Elmer," the woman said flatly.

"Hello there," Elmer replied, refusing to meet the empty sockets that were carved deep into the skull behind her feminine face.

"You have been practicing self-control, I see. You have been working on detaching yourself from the faux world of sentiments and squalor. You are becoming Awake."

"I have," said Elmer, "but how did you know? I'm afraid I'm not doing very well at the moment. My emotions seem to have flooded back in one giant wave."

"Not to worry, Elmer. I can already sense an improvement. You are more in tune with your emotions. You can tap into them easily and you can let them go with almost the same amount of ease. The reason your neglected emotions have come crawling back at the moment is because I remind you of someone. I remind you of someone from one of your lives who affected you deeply. Am I right?"

"Well yes, multiple someones, actually."

"True, but we've already exercised the ghost of your former lover. What remains?"

Elmer thought for a moment. He pictured the thin, brown hair, the shy smile. He pictured the small features of her face and her brown, shining eyes. "Hilo," he whispered.

"Yes," said the woman in indigo. "Her." She studied Elmer's face for a while. "Elmer," she said after several seconds, her voice becoming softer, more motherly. "I think it's time you tell me about the fire."

"No," he replied quickly. "I won't." He looked away, away from that awful face that hung above him, taunting him with its changing features, teasing him with identical stringy hair, thin nose, high cheeks. "I—," he choked down a sob, "I can't."

"Elmer," the woman replied sternly, "take a seat." It wasn't an option. Elmer sat down reluctantly in the squat chair situated across from her.

"Now," she said. "Tell me about the fire. It is time. And I won't take no for an answer."

Elmer took a deep breath and when he released it he fired off a string of words, one after the other, shooting rapidly out of his mouth like ammo from a MAC-10. "Good god I'm so sorry it was all my fault and I should never have let her go back I should never have cried out for my painting but it was so fresh and new and lovely and sentimental and Roger made it for me personally as a gift a truly heart-felt lovely present and it meant so much to me all the dancing colors it reminded me of the seven and I just didn't want it burned to bits so I cried out for it and now Hilo is dead and it's all my fault all my goddamn fault. Shit!"

He sat huddled in the chair, panting, clutching his cane as if it was trying to run away from his gunshot words.

"I see," the woman in indigo said. Her voice was calm and unbothered, even slightly bored. Her eyes bore into Elmer with their usual cold detachment. "So you've learned something from this incident, I take it?"

Elmer didn't meet her eyes. He didn't hear her voice. He remained panting and quivering until the indigo-clad woman raised herself from her chair, stepped over to the old man, and lay one thin-boned hand upon his shoulder. Elmer shot up in his chair, eyes wide with terror, mouth gaping. He wasn't sure what to do. She was so close. So damn close! Her face was inches away, the eye pits staring into his. He could faintly make out her thin, rattling breath and smell her cool, damp skin. Then she turned and slid back into her chair as if nothing had happened.

"Are you listening now, Elmer?" she asked. "Are you still open to learning—healing?"

"Yes," Elmer squeaked and balled up his knuckly fingers into two arthritic fists. "I am."

"Good," she said. "Now tell me, Elmer, what did you learn from the fire?"

"I don't know. That my friends are precious to me?"

"Wrong!" the woman snarled. "You learned about the uselessness of emotions. You learned how attachment to earthly things can only lead to pain. You were attached to the girl; you loved her and cared about her. You were attached to the painting. It was a gift; it was heavy with sentimental value. Both were taken from you. Both were plucked from this earth with a fiery hand and turned into ash. You've heard the phrase 'ashes to ashes, dust to dust,' Elmer?"

"Yes. From the Bible."

"Indeed. It's one of the more insightful passages in it. It reads, 'By the sweat of your brow you will eat your food until you return to the ground, since from it you were taken; for dust you are and to dust you will return.' That is the temporary nature of things, Elmer. Our bodies are on loan—just fleshy, compacted dust—and when we die, to dust we will return."

"I understand," said Elmer softly, "but I still feel terrible."

"Don't," the woman in indigo said coldly. "She'll probably live a better life next time around. After all, she too has learned a valuable lesson about the danger of emotions. She'll most likely carry that with her into her next life."

"Next life?" said Elmer. "You're saying she's going to be reborn?"

The woman stared at Elmer for four long seconds. It seemed like four long minutes. When she finally spoke her tongue was sharp and knifelike. "Elmer, that's nearly the point of all our exercises."

"I thought the point was to achieve Enlightenment, to be Awake."

"And," she said, "to end rebirth. Rebirth is a painful, traumatic process and it is best to avoid it at all costs. The only way to avoid rebirth, however, is to become Enlightened. That is what we're working towards, Elmer. We are working towards perfection. We are striving to eliminate all the hurt, pain, suffering, scars, trauma, distress, disease from your being. These are things you have accumulated along the way—life to life—adding experience upon experience."

Elmer sat quietly for a moment, soaking in this new information. "I have had many lives, haven't I?" he asked.

"Oh yes, Elmer. Many lives. And when one becomes close to Enlightenment, one begins to remember those past lives."

"Remember…"

"Yes, Elmer. You begin to remember. Which is why you probably remember your separate lives in Here, There, City A, City B. That is probably why the details have begun to blend together."

Dawning passed over Elmer's face. He was too stunned to move, too stunned to blink. He stared at the wall behind the tall, skinny chair. Finally, his lips formed words.

"Holy shit."

* * *

Maggie picked up the phone, put it down again. She twirled her hair around her finger, paced nervously, wiped the kitchen counter for the third time that morning. Zach watched her, his tiny brow knit, his deep eyes troubled.

"Mommy?" he asked.

"Yes, baby?"

"What's wrong?"

Damn, the kid was perceptive. "Nothing, sweet pea. Are you getting ready for the park? Remember I said we're going this morning before Mommy heads to work."

"I don't wanna go to the park."

"No? Ok then, mister. Suit yourself." Maggie sidestepped to the phone again. She knew his number by heart. She had looked it up as soon as she returned to The City with the intention of calling him when she got a spare minute. She had been keeping busy in The City—working, caring for Zach, attempting to figure out her place in this complex, bewildering world. But she had had spare minutes—several, in fact—and she had chosen to do things like clean the counter three times.

Zach stretched out on the couch and pounded his little fists into the pillow. Punch-punch-punch-punch-punch.

"Zach!" Maggie exclaimed, surprised by the sudden outburst from her usually mellow, reasonable son. "What's gotten into you?" But she knew very well what had gotten into him. She had been pacing around for days now, frantically scrubbing tiles and dusting shelves. She was acting exactly as her mother used to act when her father disappeared: nervous, twitchy, out of her head. That nervousness was powerful. It affected everyone nearby and cast a dark shadow on the household. She kicked herself for perpetuating that shadow, but she couldn't help it. Things were not right. The harmony in their household was quickly deteriorating and she wondered if it was partially her fault. There was tension every time Elmer disappeared and took to the streets. Matthew felt betrayed; Matilda became mopey; Maggie tried to not think about her deadbeat father. Then, Elmer would return and things would feel somewhat right for a while, but only somewhat. They were more on edge now, never truly relaxed. They couldn't be sure what the old man—their friend—would do next.

Maggie sat down in the beige, cotton armchair and closed her eyes. Immediately, she pictured Tower I, nestled in between the behemoths, quietly lending help and consolation to those who needed it, those who sought it. Or did it have its own selfish desires, the Tower that seemed so alive and human? Did helping others help it? Surely, all the teachers within the Tower benefitted from their students. Surely, they earned Enlightenment credits by helping poor souls in need. Maybe it was all one, gigantic selfish game.

She pondered this notion and refused to believe it entirely. After all, Tower I had aided Matthew, a troubled street urchin with not a penny to his name. It had helped him gain confidence and a more positive outlook on life. But then again, he was at the base of the Tower, where things were less complicated. At the base, one had only to concentrate on things such as proper breathing and calming one's body through certain stretches and poses. As one climbed the Tower, things became more abstract.

Maggie sighed deeply and opened her eyes. Zach was sound asleep, his body stretched out, his miniature fists still clenched. He was the only thing that made sense to her at the moment. He was her Tower base. It was probably time. Or past time, she thought wryly. She picked her long body off the armchair, stretched, drank a glass of water, and dialed Zach's dad.

* * *

Elmer tried to pay attention as the woman in indigo spoke at him. She spoke about cycles and improving oneself and learning new lessons. Mostly, it was a blur.

"But student," she said.

"Yes," he replied, attempting to focus.

"Don't think of rebirth as an entirely new life. You're not starting from scratch, you see. Lessons you've learned, progress you've made—those things stay with you. You're not quite the same from life to life—perhaps not even the same gender—but then again you are the same. Somewhat, that is. Somewhat the same." The woman in indigo moistened her lips with her tongue, tugged on her hair.

"So some of the things I've learned stayed with me?" he asked skeptically. "How does that work?"

"Think of rebirth like passing a flame from candle to candle. The fire isn't the same from one wick to another, but its qualities remain constant. The qualities are residual. You have built one life from another, which was built from another, which was built from another. Residual qualities—that's the key concept here. *Residual.* Is that clear?"

Elmer nodded. "But there are a few things I don't understand," he said. "You say that I've lived a new life in each City, but what about the other people I've met along the way? Some of the same people appear in different Cities. Or sometimes they bear the same names or characteristics. What's happening with them? Are they following me from life to life?"

"Some may very well be, Elmer. Souls tend to travel from life to life in groups. They are more comfortable that way. So yes, it is possible that some of the people you've met have died and then came back to join you in a different time and space."

"But what about my childhood? I didn't have a childhood before City B, for example. I showed up as an old man."

"You didn't have a childhood that you remember, at least," the woman said, a tiny smirk on her face. "You won't remember *everything* from your past lives. Just bits and pieces."

Elmer thought about this for a while, staring at a milky cobweb in the corner. The spider clung to her web, patiently waiting for a careless insect, not giving a shit about reincarnation or past lives. "No," said Elmer after a few minutes. "I don't think any of that is true. I don't think people's souls are following me from place to place. They are *exactly* the same from one life to the next. How do you explain that?"

"They've made the same mistakes, then," the woman said with a shrug. "They haven't grown or improved themselves enough to escape their current state."

Elmer shook his head. "I don't know."

"Remember what I said about residual effects, Elmer?"

"Yes, I do."

"Well, you create your own reality. And how do you create that reality? From your experiences. Your *residual* experiences. Now, it's possible that Maggie in City C is very different from Maggie in City A. It's possible that Peggi is nothing like Ms. Patti and Matthew isn't actually the spitting image of Levi, the park bum. You've projected *your* ideas onto those people. You have assigned them an identity in your own little brain and made that identity reality."

"Hmm, I don't know—"

"Just like you've created me. Think about it, Elmer."

He thought about it.

"I am the culmination of your most personal realities."

Elmer lowered his gaze, turned his head. "The women I've betrayed."

"If that's what you believe, then so it is," said the woman cryptically.

Elmer brought his hands to the sides of his head and pressed them against his skull as if he was trying to let loose a particularly nasty headache.

He held his hands in this way for several seconds as his brain spun and his thoughts whirred. Finally, slowly, he dropped his hands and looked up. "Woman in indigo," he began and then halted. "Actually," he said sheepishly, "I don't know how to address you. I've never asked."

"Teacher will do."

"Teacher, then." He swallowed. "What does all this mean? How does this knowledge help me on my path towards Enlightenment?"

"It doesn't. It's simply background knowledge about how the whole thing works—the cycles of life, the interdependence of souls. The only reason we're talking about all this right now is because you asked."

"I'm a little sorry I did."

"Don't be. It's good for you to know these things." The woman in indigo twirled her hair and thought for a while. "Student," she said. "Last time we met, I sent you home with an assignment to empty yourself of emotions, to free yourself from their burden. In light of where the lesson has gone today, I am going to give you a new assignment revolving around the past."

"The past," Elmer echoed faintly.

"Yes, the past. You have a lot of past to sift through, but I believe most of your pain resides in what you believe to be your current lifetime. I want you to think about the individual people—or identities, if you will—that have caused you grief or anguish: Papa, Irene, Daisy, Hilo, etc. I want you to imagine yourself holding a conversation with each of these people and I want you to make peace with them."

"So," said Elmer skeptically, "you want me to have imaginary conversations with people who haunt me from the past. I don't see how that will solve anything."

"With that kind of attitude it certainly won't!" snapped the woman, her eyeless pits growing wide and her now short hair standing on end. "How many times do I have to remind you, Elmer? Everything is in your head. This life, that life. This person, that person. Me, you. It's all in your head. You see, you perceive exactly what you want to see and perceive. Now, if you truly wish to have a conversation with your dead father or former lover or whoever, you *will* have one, and that is that."

"Yes, teacher," Elmer whispered. "I will."

* * *

Elmer didn't go home that night. Or the night after that. Or the night after that. He needed time to think. He needed time alone. "Solitude is important," the woman in indigo had said. "Solitude helps you remember who you are, frees you from distractions, allows your mind to flow more easily." "Ok," he had said and left with a strange feeling in his stomach.

That feeling still lingered as he bunked down for the night in a homeless shelter about a mile east of Tower I. The apartment of Maggie/ Matilda/Matthew lay to the west. He climbed under a grey sheet and a mustard colored blanket and pulled the covers up to his chin. Perhaps being alone was necessary; perhaps it was the only way to walk on the path towards Enlightenment, but Elmer didn't like it one bit. It reminded him of his life in Here, when the fabric of his being was as fake and ethereal as marshmallow fluff and he spent his days surrounded by solitude. The wife, the job, the friends in the Lions Club were all flimsy constructions that never actually lent him companionship. And now Here he was again, miserable and alone.

Teacher knows what she is doing. Despite my doubts and reservations, I can feel her wisdom. If she says this is the only way to Enlightenment, then by golly it's the only way. I wasn't sent to the Indigo Floor for nothing, you know. Everything has a purpose, right? That's what Maggie said. That's what Teacher said. I think they know. I think they must know…

Elmer tried to sleep that night, but he couldn't help picturing the three Ems, bundled up in sweaters to combat the cold, cooking stew or pineapple curry or green bean casserole. He pictured their smiles, their warm faces, and soon he was surrounded by a thousand smiles, a thousand warm faces. He saw Onyx and Cecelia, Roger and Ezzie, Kyle and Craig, Zach and Grace, Hilo (oh, my little Hilo), Maggie, little Zach, little Levi, big Levi, Daisy (seventeen and lovely, of course), the seven sages in their rainbow colored robes…

Whatever happened to the sages? Where have they been during my time in The City. They have been strangely absent. I haven't felt their presence in some time now. Odd. Quite odd. And a bit disconcerting.

Elmer pictured the smiling faces and then reached up into image, saw his hand appear amongst the faces, and swatted them away. The faces dissipated; the smiles faded. Elmer was alone once again. He shivered. "Oh well," he thought. "It's better this way." He wasn't convinced, but that's what he told himself over and over again as he fell asleep.

It's better this way. It's better this way. It's better this way. It's better this way.

He drifted off and woke in the early morning to the sound of bodies rustling and sausage frying. He shook off the images from last night and sat up, stretching his spine and arms upward. Time to start the day. Not a moment to lose. He wasn't getting any younger and Enlightenment was not about to wait around. He leapt to his feet, scarfed down some breakfast, and hit the road.

His feet led him to a park. It was the same park that held the gigantic elm tree, that lent him a moment of solace. "Good job feet," he thought. It was a warm day for late fall and he didn't mind the slight nip at his cheeks as he sat down on one of the swings in the playground. He swung back and forth for a while, listening to the wind and the creaking of the chains that held him. Then he started to talk.

"Irene," he began. "Irene, are you there?" he paused a moment, listening to the empty echoes in his ears. "I've been a terrible husband, a truly rotten sorry excuse for a husband. It was never fair to you. You didn't do anything to deserve such terrible treatment. It was all me, my dear. All of it. You pretended not to notice, but deep down I'm sure you knew…"

"I forgive you, Elmer," he heard Irene's distant whisper. "I forgive you."

"You do? That's wonderful. Because truly, Irene, I was never any good at being a father. You practically raised our two children on your own and you did a damn fine job at it. Sorry I didn't notice at the time. I was too busy being miserable. And I'm sorry I was a terrible listener. You probably shared your hopes, dreams, ambitions with me, but I was too self-absorbed to notice. God, I was a prick! I don't know how you're able to forgive me right now, but I'm so thankful you are, Irene. So thankful…"

Elmer talked on and on like this for hours. He continued conversing with Irene, apologizing, begging her forgiveness. She didn't say much, but seemed understanding and rational, taking his discretions in stride and not betraying any strong emotions.

Next, he talked to Hilo. He expressed his admiration and love. He said he was proud of her for coming out of her shell, said he thought of her like a daughter. "Could she forgive him?" he asked. It was all his fault for cutting her beautiful life short. It was all his fault for placing too much value in a painting. "Yes," she said in her small voice. "Of course I forgive you, Elm, because there is nothing to forgive. You are my guide. The wise Old Turtle." "Oh thank you," he said. "Thank you, thank you."

He didn't know whether the voices came from his head or if they floated to him through time and space on the back of the wind. He didn't care. They were comforting and he trusted them. He kept talking.

Next, he addressed Daisy. Their conversation was short. He felt as if he had exercised her spirit enough in the past few months. The only thing left to say was, "Sorry, Daisy. Sorry for not having a strong enough backbone to stand up to Papa and Nathaniel Gorsheim and confounded social expectations. Sorry for not trusting my love to the bitter end. I love you, Daisy."

"Yes, Elmer. I know."

"And I'll always love you."

"I know."

He saved the toughest ghost for last: Papa. He swung back and forth on the park swing, lost in his head trance, listening to his father's voice echo in the caverns of his brain. This conversation was different. He did a lot less talking and a lot more listening.

"Elmer," Papa began.

"Yes, Papa?"

"I know we haven't always seen eye-to-eye—"

Elmer scoffed. He wrinkled his nose and turned away from the voice.

"Ok, so we never saw eye-to-eye. I was a terrible father at times. I pushed you too hard. I lashed you too hard. I said some things I regret. I was perpetually disappointed by the fact that you didn't want to be a farmer and—," he sighed in Elmer's ear, a mournful sigh that felt like dust blowing out of an ancient fan, "I was never afraid to let you know my disappointment."

Elmer swung back and forth on the swing, eyes shut, ears open.

"Despite what your mother said," Papa continued, "I knew exactly what I was doing when I forbade you to marry the banker's daughter."

"Daisy," Elmer growled. He felt like a teenager again—acrimonious and hostile. He crossed his arms and stuck out his lip.

"Daisy," Papa whispered, voice humble. "I hated the idea of you becoming 'city folk.' I hated the idea of you inheriting wealth you didn't work for. I had to earn my money, honest and true, and I wanted you to do the same."

"Hmph," said Elmer.

"The match with the Gorsheim girl was perfect in my mind. It would ground you, get you back down to earth and into the soil again. I didn't think about the emotional repercussions. I didn't think about your wellbeing. I did, however, hope you would grow into your role. I hoped you would learn to find happiness. Looking back, I was clearly in the wrong. I was selfish and cruel. Can you ever forgive me, Elmer?"

"Hmph," said Elmer once again. He had never heard Papa apologize for anything and he wasn't sure what to make of it. He sounded sincere; he sounded full of regret. He didn't sound a thing like Papa.

"Elmer," Papa continued. He hesitated. "Son."

Elmer felt the sting of tears strike at his eyes.

"No one is perfect. People inflict pain and act cruelly and make mistakes. You have spoken to many ghosts today. You have confronted your past discretions and made peace with them. Please, Elmer, look into your heart. Do you have a sliver of the same forgiveness they granted you? Just a sliver. That's all I ask. Can you at least grant me a sliver?"

Elmer was silent for several minutes. He listened to the swing's chain creeee—creak as he swung back and forth, shifting his weight subtly to propel his hanging seat. His thoughts climbed the chain like vines, twisting upward and drowning out sound and light. He hung onto the vines and swung softly, aware of Papa's gentle inhale-exhale in his ear.

"Papa?" said Elmer at last.

"Yes?"

"I've decided that I do not grant you a sliver of my forgiveness."

"Oh," said Papa, crestfallen. "I see. It was worth a try. I hope you now realize I never intended to harm you. I never meant to—"

"I do not grant you a sliver of forgiveness because I am granting you the whole thing. Papa, you are entirely and absolutely forgiven. I don't want to hold onto my grudges for a second longer. They have only served to putrefy and curdle my soul. I don't need that any more. I don't want it. I'm ready to let go. After several decades—or several lives, if what Teacher says is true—I am finally ready to forgive."

A sob choked Papa's throat. He coughed it away and whispered in Elmer's ear, "Thank you, son. From the bottom of my heart, thank you. You always were a good boy."

Elmer bit his lip, holding back the tears. "Thanks Papa," he replied quietly. Elmer waited, listening. Nothing. Papa's voice had vanished; his presence melted away. Elmer felt a new hollowness overcome him. He exhaled deeply, imagined his breath boring into the soil beneath his hanging feet. Papa haunted him no more.

* * *

On the way back to the Ems' apartment, Elmer felt light and happy. His feet barely touched the sidewalk as he floated home like an elated ghost. The air was crisp and nourished his lungs. Cafés, restaurants, office buildings seemed less grey and more colorful, showing off their rich textures and materials, boasting their exoticism. Elmer reached out and touched the sides of buildings and tree trunks and street signs that he passed. He saw The City through a clean lens. By the time he reached the apartment, his heart was so full he was afraid it might violently burst across the sidewalk.

Elmer skipped up the stairs, foregoing the elevator, and felt the suppleness of his limbs, the lifeblood in his veins. Perhaps Teacher would not approve of the afternoon's emotion-laden journey, but at the moment he cared not a lick. All he knew was that he was finally free of his nagging, ugly, cannonball-heavy demons and that felt good. There. He said it. It *felt* good. And Teacher could shove it. Restricting his emotions could wait for another day.

"Knock-knock-knock," went Elmer's fist against the apartment door.

"Who is it?" Maggie called.

"Me. Elmer!" Elmer replied.

The door swung open and Maggie stood before the beaming old man, her face hovering a good six inches above his. "Hello there, Elmer," she said. Her voice was strange, almost muffled.

Elmer swallowed. His sunny mood instantly darkened. "Look, Maggie. I'm sorry for traipsing around like I have. I have been struggling lately—struggling with myself. I'm sure you understand. It's just that…I couldn't concentrate here in the apartment and…good grief, you must think I'm a right old ass."

"You could have called," she said tersely. His cheeks reddened. "And you could have checked in with us every once in a while." They turned a darker hue. "And you know Elmer, you're not obligated to live here. We didn't lock chains around your ankles." His cheeks were melting from their heat.

"I'm sorry, Maggie," he said sheepishly. "It won't happen again. I got a lot of things sorted out today and I don't think I'll need as much alone time from now on."

"Well, it's none of my concern anyway," Maggie said with a sigh, turning away. "I'm going away."

"What? You're *what* Maggie? Why?"

"Hey vagabond," Matthew's gruff voice called from the living room, "why don't *you* tell me why she's leaving. You know *all* about abandonin' the people who care about you."

"Matthew!" Matilda scolded. "Shut up about it, will you? Why don't you just be grateful that Elmer is back."

"Hard ter be grateful when he doesn't give a rat's arse about us, isn't it, Tilda?"

"Now, now!" Matilda said. "That's enough. We all just need to calm down and be reasonable. Besides, Maggie isn't leaving us forever, now are you Maggie?"

Maggie shrugged, stooped to pick up a few clothes that had been strewn across the kitchen table, folded them, and packed them. "I honestly don't know Tilda," she said finally. "It all depends on how things go. I mean, it's been a while. I haven't seen him in years."

"Maggie?" Elmer called to her, feeling significantly more sheepish and insignificant than he had a few minutes ago. "Can you tell me what this is about? Where are you going? It looks like you're packing for more than a few days."

"That's because I don't know how long I'm going to stay and I—"

"That's because she's going to stay permanently!" Matthew interjected.

"Damn it, Matthew!" Matilda let out a rare curse. "Quit interrupting people, quit feeling sorry for yourself, and for the love of god, quit making people feel like horse shit for every decision they make that doesn't win your approval. Just stop it!"

Matthew shut up, but continued to mope. "Well, that's a little better," Matilda said wryly. "As you were saying, Maggie?"

"Right," said Maggie, folding up a sky blue t-shirt and placing it carefully in her bag. "Elmer, I'm leaving with Zach tomorrow. We're going to meet his father. We have a lot of catching up to do, so we're going to stay for the week, maybe longer if it works out."

Elmer tried to summon up happiness for Maggie. He attempted to smile when he said, "Well, that's great, Mags," but he could not. He wasn't sure if he was drained from the day's activities or if he had simply learned to shut off his emotions towards other people lately. Whatever the case, he felt nothing—just hollow and echoey like a seashell—and it made him more than a little disconcerted.

* * *

Winter crept up on The City like a panther, its movements slow and discreet, its piercing eyes fixed on its prey. It circled The City, flicking its tail occasionally, its spine rigid and spring-loaded, ready to shoot forward when the moment was right. The residents of The City could feel Winter's presence and it made them nervous. They tugged their collars up around their chins, pulled their hats down low, and walked hastily down sidewalks, doing their best to ignore the bite of wind that nipped at their ears and the backs of their necks and the tips of their noses.

The people did their best to avoid Winter. They scampered quickly from building to building, zig-zagging away from its chill, attempting to evade its icy claws. Winter laughed as it circled the jittery people. It laughed as it caught them with one swoop of its giant paw, enveloping them in arctic air. The people shivered as Winter toyed with them, catching them by the leg and releasing them, catching and releasing, teasing them with bursts of freedom in which they saw the sun, felt its heat, remembered the warmth of summer and early fall, smelled the deliciousness of fresh grass and sweaty, salty skin. They would run, run, run away from the clutches of Winter, letting their memories go wild with the heat of summer, but Winter would inevitably catch them again and their fragile, rose-bud hopes would shrivel and fall.

Eventually, Winter will grow tired of teasing. Eventually, it will dig its claws into the flesh of its prey and devour it whole. But for now, it is catching and releasing, catching and releasing. The people of The City grow weary of its game. Dark circles hang below their eyes; their skin dries up and peels off. Winter should just get it over with, they think. It should catch them and swallow them and embrace them in its frigid arms. It should just fucking get it over with. Damn Winter. Damn catlike Winter. It never fails to put them on edge with its infernal teasing.

When Winter circles The City, the people get nervous.

* * *

"Student, a change has overcome you."

Elmer sat in Tower I, legs crossed on the seat of his broad chair, neck rigid, eyes facing the thing in front of him.

"It's tangible," the teacher continued. "You have shaken the shackles of the past; you have released yourself of its burdens. You are closer than ever to achieving the ultimate goal—to achieving Enlightenment."

Elmer sat stone-faced, silent. Several weeks had passed since his last encounter with Maggie, Matthew, and Matilda. After Maggie moved out, the apartment seemed corpselike, the air rotting and stewing around them. Matthew walked around in a huff, cursing under his breath, rambling on about everyone abandoning him. Matilda kept deathly quiet, her chubby cheeks pallid, her mouth sealed tightly and frowning. Elmer couldn't stand it. There was no way to shake off worthless emotions in such a place. After only a day, he left once more, returning to the streets and the soup kitchens, leading his life like an old, solitary wolf. The whispers of past lives and experiences crept into his ears every once in a while, but he shook them away like raindrops off an umbrella. He stayed disciplined and focused and by the time his next appointment in Tower I rolled around, he felt almost nothing at all.

"Your Nirvana is near and there is little I can teach you anymore. You have learned the value of solitude; you recognize the foolishness of excessive emotions. In your recent lives, you have learned to overcome the three poisons: ignorance, aversion, desire. Student, you have been through much in your past lives. You have met many people and learned many lessons. You have experienced different ways of living, different outlooks on worship. The hour of Enlightenment is near, but—," she paused and squinted the holes where her eyes might have been. "I sense there is some *thing*, some sentiment, holding you back."

Elmer said nothing, continued to stare.

"Yes, there is something. It seems—," her eye pits bore into his body, dissecting his soul, "there is something bothering you, something that has been nagging at your thoughts for quite some time. What is it? Please speak freely, student. We need to clear all noxious air before you truly arrive at your destination, before you Awaken. Come now. Speak."

The request was not optional. Elmer opened his mouth, closed it, thought a moment, and obeyed.

"I will speak, teacher," he said. He sat a little straighter, cleared his throat. "At the beginning of my journey," he began, "after I rejected my faux existence in Here and banished the nagging storm from my brain, I had a vision. Or a dream, perhaps. I was dropped into a strange mountainous place by a giant black bird. In this place, there was a gigantic cavern, carved into the side of one of the mountains and supported by enormous pillars. I stepped inside and discovered that each pillar was etched with carvings of different shapes and themes—no two carvings alike. I remember a lamb, a plow, a skull, a turtle; there seemed to be no rhyme or reason to the things. As I was examining the carvings, I heard footsteps and became aware of a giant cat stalking me from the shadows. I ran away from the beast (as quickly as I could, given my arthritis) and emerged into the sunlight, only to trip into a pit of ugly, writhing snakes..."

As Elmer described his vision, the woman in indigo sat rigidly in her seat, hands squeezing the arms of her chair, fingernails digging into its wood.

"And these seven robed figures," Elmer concluded, "these 'spirit guides,' as some people have called them, continued to stay with me from City to City, helping me when needed, offering advice and guidance, comforting me during difficult stretches. They became a fixture during my journey—a constant—and now they simply aren't here. They seem to have vanished as completely as my emotions. It's strange. They were always nice to have around in the Cities and now a part of me seems, well, empty..."

"Hmph," the indigo-clad woman grunted. "So you miss your playmates, do you?" Her voice was annoyed and icy. Elmer shivered, then rejected the fear that temporarily gripped him.

"Well, they're not so much playmates, are they? But yes, I suppose I do miss them. I don't know, Teacher. It's just curious, that's all. They show up abruptly and leave just as abruptly and I guess I want to know what it all means. Others have offered their interpretations of my dream and the purpose of the seven, but I want to know what you think of the whole thing."

"I think it is one gigantic test, that's what I think."

"You do?"

"Yes, I do. Here are these seven robed figures, clearly mocking Tower I and its noble teachings, leading you to believe that it is ok to dance around like a madman and get caught up in joy and friendships. Since the physical body is but a temporary casing for our souls, it is useless to obsess oneself with such trivialities. I think the seven little imps have been trying to lead you astray. Well, it didn't work, did it? You're here now, aren't you? Not roaming around the countryside with the seven false prophets, a tune on your lips and your head in the clouds."

"I never thought of them like that. They always seemed so genuine and kind and comforting—"

"Evil is skilled at disguising itself. But fear not, the dream is not without its merits. You learned the uselessness of fear and anxiety when you fell into the snake pit. As soon as you stopped struggling, as soon as you gave yourself up completely, the snakes desisted, the giant cat slept, and you were free. That was when you began to feel joy—uncontrollable joy. As you are well aware, it is ill-advised to be consumed by emotions in the physical realm. However, I think we can learn something from the dancing colors and your boundless happiness. That, student, is a mere fraction of the feeling you will experience once you are Enlightened. Every moment will be euphoric, blissful. The boundaries of the finite self will melt away and you will be aware, awake, conscious."

Elmer was silent for a few moments, then said, "What about the other parts of the dream? What about the giant bird and the cat and the pillars? Others have said that those things have profound meanings and that I should pay attention to them—"

"Others are wrong," Teacher snapped. "The bird and the snakes and the mountains are all physical entities. They are distractions. They are tied into emotions and superstitions that weak-minded people carry around with them in order to avoid truly thinking."

"I see," said Elmer, recognizing an emotion much like disappointment cropping up in the back of his head and quickly ushering it away.

"On a different note," the woman continued. "As much as I disagree with the sappy sentiments of your 'seven sages,' I do agree with one thing the moon-faced woman expressed. You need to dig yourself out in order to succeed. You need to peel away the layers, dig-dig-dig away the excesses and frivolities of this earthly plane and rise above it. I don't know if your moon-faced lady understood all the implications of her words, but regardless, it is good advice to follow."

The woman in indigo shifted in her seat and stared at the small-framed man before her. When she spoke again her voice was stern and severe. "Student," she said, "it is best you forget about these seven robed beings. As I mentioned before, they are more of a nuisance than a help. They ape the wise teachers of Tower I and provide little substantial guidance. Forget about them, student. Banish them from your mind."

"As you say," Elmer said quietly.

"Good. We are finished then."

"Finished?"

"Yes, finished. I have taught you enough. The rest is up to you. Go into The City, Elmer. Be amongst it. Avoid its poisons. Think. Ponder. Reject silly sentiments and physical pleasures. Return to the Tower when you are ready."

"How do I know when I'll be ready?"

"You'll know, student. Like a mother about to give birth, you'll know."

"As you say, Teacher."

Chapter 47

The icy edge of Winter's claw scraped the back of Maggie's neck as she hustled down the street. She felt it travel beneath her upturned collar and down her long spine, as smooth as scissors cutting wrapping paper. She shivered and clutched Zach a little closer. "Not far," she whispered to her son and to herself. "Not far now." The child made not a peep and the pair continued down the familiar sidewalk of The City.

Maggie kept her head bent and eyes lowered as she walked, avoiding the punishing wind that swept along the pavement and between buildings. She knew this route by feel, not by sight. Her feet knew exactly when to turn, when to stop for a red light. If her sight ever failed, she would have no trouble maneuvering these three square miles. This is where she grew up, her stomping grounds; this was home.

She cut sharply to the left and felt the blast of wind whipping through the alleyway. "It's a shortcut, Zach. We'll be there soon. Not to worry, son." Zach remained silent. At the end of the alley, they veered right, crossed the street, and arrived. "Good God," Maggie muttered, "they still haven't replaced this damn creaky door. Still the same tired green paint flaking off the heavy steel doors—prison doors, I always thought. Don't you agree, Zach? And the same tenants too, judging by the list. Hmm, let's see."

Maggie found the number, two-oh-one, and stabbed the little white buzzer next to it with her pointer finger. She waited for a few seconds, grew impatient, tried again.

"For the love of God, Maggie!" a voice called through the speaker. "Give an old woman a break. Not as quick as I once was, you know."

You're not *that* old, Mom," Maggie answered. "Now, open up, will you?"

"A little please wouldn't hurt," the voice replied.

"Oh, for Pete's sake," Maggie murmured, rolling her eyes. "Ok, Mom. Please. Please can you buzz us inside? It's freezing out here."

The door buzzed in reply and Maggie shoved it open with her shoulder. It gave an irritated groan as it swung open lethargically, as if Maggie had just awoken it from a long, deep nap. She stepped past the steel bars, flung the door shut, and scampered up the stairs. Her mother was waiting for her when she reached the second floor.

"My Maggie," she said, her arms opened wide, a grin plastered across her face. "I've missed you, Maggie-Mae. And you too, my handsome little grandson. How are you Zachy? Give Grandma a kiss." She placed her cheek close to Zach's lips and he puckered slightly against it. "There we are. That's a good boy. Oh Maggie, you've been back for so long and you've only visited once! You're really awful at keeping in touch, my dear. Just awful."

"You're not much better, yourself," Maggie winked at the woman in front of her. "You could come and visit Zach and me you know. You're not *that* far away."

"Far enough, dear. I don't get around as well as I used to. Anyhow, let's not stand here squabbling while the others wait. Come in, dear, come in. Take your coat off and relax a little."

Maggie followed her mother down the hall and to apartment number two-oh-one. "She's here!" Maggie's mother proclaimed as they stepped through the doorway and into the warmth of the living room. Amongst the familiar photographs and furniture, two smiling faces greeted the trio. Matilda rushed forward first and flung her stubby arms around Maggie and Zach.

"Oh Mags, Mags! It's so good to see you. Things haven't been the same without your smiling face around. We've both missed you so much."

"She speaks nothin' but the truth," Matthew chimed in, stepping forward and giving Maggie and Zach a rough hug. "The place has been a tomb, what with you disappearin' and Elmer takin' off to Lord knows where. Been right depressin', that's what it's been. In fact, they almost demoted me from burnt orange to cherry in Tower I. Said I wasn't makin' any progress lately. But how can I when people are leavin' left and right, 'specially people I care 'bout so much. But dammit Maggie, that's enough 'bout me. How've you been?"

"I've been good, Matthew. Really good."

"Well," Maggie's mother chimed in. "You've been *well*, my dear."

"Right. I've been well. But what's this about Elmer? What do you mean he took off?"

"I mean just what I said," Matthew replied. "He plumb took off. Haven't seen him in weeks. Must of high-tailed it out of town."

"Elmer wouldn't do that."

"No?" Matthew said skeptically. "I've heard some of his stories. Seems like he has trouble sticking in one place for too long. Isn't that so?"

Maggie didn't reply, but shook her head brusquely, shaking away the image of her friend—the frail, old man with the bright green eyes and warm smile. She wasn't sure what to make of his disappearance, but hoped he was doing well in the world.

"Maggie, won't you sit down?" her mother asked. Maggie sat.

"Mom, thank you for inviting my friends here," Maggie said, glancing at Matilda and Matthew and smiling. "It means a lot to me."

"Well, it means a lot to me too," she replied, reaching out a long arm and stroking her daughter's cheek. Their matching deep brown eyes met. "I'm so proud of you, dear."

Maggie smiled. "Thanks, Mom. And thank you, Tilda and Matthew. I'm so happy you could make it to my engagement party."

"Of course dear!" Matilda smiled underneath her shining blue eyes. "We wouldn't miss it for the world."

"Mommy!" Zach spoke up for the first time since they arrived. "Where are the others?"

"What others, love?"

"The others, Mommy." His tone was serious and slightly anxious. He wrung his hands as he spoke. "The other *friends*. I want to see them too."

"I'm not sure what you're talking about, Zach. All our friends are here…besides Elmer, I suppose."

"No. No they're not. They're all missing." Tears started to well up in his eyes. "All of them."

"Zach honey—"

"Maggie," Maggie's mother interjected, her voice quiet and serious. "How on earth did he know?"

"Know what?"

"I was going to keep this a surprise. I'm really not sure how he knew. Strange really. Seems that your boy has a gift."

"Mother, will you please explain what is going on?" Maggie demanded.

"Yes dear, of course. Like I was saying, I was going to keep this a surprise, but now that the cat's out of the bag—"

The buzzer for the outside door interrupted her sentence. Maggie's mom answered it. A voice—a woman's—blared through the intercom. "God-damn, Jesus Christ, son-of-a-bitch, it's cold out here! Let us inside, will you.

My fingers are frozen to the bone. Good gravy, Maggie, why would you leave City A for a fucking freezing hellhole such as this? Sheesh!"

"Ezzie?" Maggie said, incredulous. "Ezzie, is that you?"

"Damn straight it's me," Ezzie replied. "But it will only be the wide-eyed, frozen corpse of Ezzie before long if you don't open the goddamn door."

Maggie laughed and buzzed open the door. "Man alive, she hasn't changed one bit! Mom, how on earth did you find her?"

"Them, you mean." Maggie's mother replied. "And it wasn't too hard. After I tracked down your old house in City A, the current tenants told me where to find Ezzie and everyone else. Seems that half of them are still living together in City A. I never quite understood the appeal of communal living, but to each his own, I suppose. From what you've told me about the place you seemed happy there at the time. Isn't that right, Maggie? Maggie?"

Maggie was standing by the door, holding it open, as she stared, slack-jawed at the people pouring inside. Craig, Kyle, Onyx, Cecelia, Roger, Ezzie jostled through the doorjamb, jabbering and teasing as they made their way inside. Tears coated her eyes and fell down her cheeks as they all clambered towards her, stretching their arms around her and each other as they all piled in for a collective hug.

"This is amazing!" Maggie cried, squeezing Roger's shoulder. "I can't believe you're all here! I must be dreaming. Someone pinch me, please!"

"You're not dreaming, Maggie girl," Kyle said. "We all heard about your engagement to Zach's dad and we decided to road trip it across the country. It took four long days, but we're finally here!"

"Four days! You all are crazy! But I wouldn't have it any other way. And Cecelia, good god, what is this!"

"I've been meaning to tell you, Maggie," Cecelia said softly. "Roger and I are due in March."

Maggie gently placed a hand on Cecelia's pregnant belly. "Congratulations to you both," she said. "This is fantastic news. I'm so overwhelmed right now! We have so much to celebrate. Come in, come in. Make yourselves at home. This is Matilda and Matthew, by the way. They are my friends and roommates here in The City."

"Welcome," Matilda said to the group.

"Pleased to meet you all," said Matthew.

"Matthew's upbringing is similar to yours, Cecelia," Maggie said, turning towards her friend. "You've both been through some rough times."

"Orphan too, eh?" asked Matthew.

"Indeed," said Cecelia. "No matter what you do in life, it's always a part of who you are, isn't it?"

"Ain't that the damn truth," said Matthew. "I'm pleased to meet your acquaintance, Ms. Cecelia. Won't you sit down?"

"Yes, all of you come and sit down," Maggie's mother spoke up. "We have drinks in the fridge, sandwiches and snacks on the table there. Here, let me take your coat miss."

"Miss? For the love of the goddess, don't call me miss!" Onyx said. "That reminds me too much of my parents' servants, which reminds me of my parents, which reminds me of their hideous house. These guys all know what I'm talking about. Better to not think about that awful house unless you absolutely have to. Ugly-ass thing."

"Sorry, young lady."

"Nah, don't worry about it. It's Onyx, by the way."

The group settled into the living room and began noshing on the sandwiches, fruit salad, and tuna noodle casserole that Maggie's mother had prepared. They smiled and laughed, swapping stories and grins. Maggie was so happy, she could feel herself glowing. After a while, talk inevitably turned to Elmer.

"So, that old bastard was *here* Maggie?" Ezzie said. "In The City? Jesus, that little old man gets around more than a five-dollar hooker."

"You don't know the half of it," Maggie replied. "He's had quite a few adventures since you've seen him. I thought The City would be a good change for him. I thought I could help him stave off the confusion we've seen him experience." She swallowed and turned away. "But I think I might have done more harm than good."

"What do you mean, Mags?" asked Onyx. "Is Old Turtle in trouble?"

"He might be," she said quietly. "You see, there's this tower. It's called Tower I. And it helps people reach Nirvana."

"The tower does?" Onyx asked incredulously. "That's ridiculous."

"Not the Tower exactly," Maggie said, "although sometimes I feel like the Tower is as alive as you and I. No, what I'm talking about are the guides inside the Tower."

"Like the guides in Elmer's vision?" asked Cecelia.

"Sort of," said Maggie. "Although, I've been getting an uneasy feeling about the guides lately. On the lower levels they're fine. For instance, Matthew is on the burnt orange floor and is learning how to breathe properly and calm his restless mind. Obviously, these are worthy practices. But once you get to the upper levels, things get a little more…abstract."

"Abstract?" asked Onyx, her voice slightly edgy. "In what way?"

"Elmer has been meeting with a strange woman on the indigo floor," said Maggie. "She has been telling him to reject all emotions and all ties to the physical world. This is the only way, according to her, to reach Nirvana. He has taken those lessons to heart and has been practicing rejecting his emotions and those around him. He's changed."

"Damn right he's changed!" Matthew spoke up. "He's turned into an old, callous bastard, that's what! Leaves whenever he pleases. Doesn't bother thinkin' about our well-being. He's as distant as the Milky Way, he is, and it's annoying as hell!"

"Right, Matthew," Maggie said quietly. "I agree."

"Well then, someone needs to stop him," Onyx said matter-of-factly. "We just have to sequester the old man and put him in his place."

"I don't know if it's that simple, Ons," said Maggie. "He's already deep into his lessons. That woman seems to have worked some magic on our Elm."

"Of course it's that simple," said Onyx, jumping to her feet and shaking her right fist in the air. "Where do you suppose the old bugger is? Let's go get him!"

"I haven't the faintest idea, Ons. He could be anywhere in The City. When I met him, he had been wandering around for nearly a month, sleeping in homeless shelters and soup kitchens. Who knows where he's gotten to."

"The City may be big," Onyx said, looking Maggie in the eye, "but it's not big enough to hide a little, old hobbling man for too long. Let's go find him, guys!"

"Ok, Onyx," Ezzie spoke up. "Let's go find him. But seriously, can't it wait until tomorrow? It's cold as fuck out there right now."

"And Elmer's in it," said Onyx defiantly. "Or he's in some nasty-ass homeless shelter. I don't know about the rest of you, but I'm going to go look for him *right now* whether I get any help or not."

Onyx glared at the room and they stared sheepishly back. Ezzie was the first to cave under her accusing eyes. "Oh alright, little spitfire. I'll go with you."

"That's the spirit! Now, who else?"

One-by-one the Modern Shamans rose to their feet and nodded at Onyx. Matilda and Matthew remained seated.

"What about you?" Onyx asked them. "You're friends with Elmer too, aren't you?"

"I don't know," said Matilda quietly. "I kind of like Tower I. I'm not so sure he needs to be rescued from it."

"Tilda," said Maggie, her eyes understanding and warm, "Tower I is like any center of faith. It performs great feats, but it's not perfect. It does well with some things and fails miserably at others. It comforts some people and makes others feel awkward or disconcerted. It speaks the truth and tells awful lies in the same breath. Tower I is fantastic on the surface, don't get me wrong. It preaches love and understanding. It emphasizes a sense of respect for yourself and nurtures your personal wellbeing. It also promotes a simple lifestyle and detachment from the excesses of the modern world. All of these things are what drew me to Tower I, but once I grew closer to the top of the tower, once I observed Elmer immerse himself deeper into its guts, I realized that Tower I is just as flawed as any religious institution. It is as flawed as the dueling soup kitchens Elmer discovered in City B or the mindless, artificial order of Here. And do you know why it is flawed, Tilda?"

"Why?" she asked timidly.

"Because you didn't invent it. It's not *yours*."

"It's not mine?"

"No. It's not yours or mine or anybody's. It belongs to someone else. Someone else created its structure. Someone else built its walls. It claims to know the way to Nirvana. It claims to be able to shoot you up there in an elevator. It's wrong. There is no neat, tidy way to Nirvana. There are many paths. Some are long; some are short. Some are straight; some are windy. We cannot account for others' twists and turns and divots in their paths towards Nirvana because we are not them. We don't walk down their path; we don't live in their shoes. Sure, Tower I might work for some people. It may provide the exact formula and structure some people need in order to better themselves throughout their existence. But that's rare. Most people need to figure it out for themselves."

Matilda sat silently, looking thoughtfully at Maggie. The rest of the room joined her in silence. Finally, Onyx spoke up.

"Are you done preaching from your soapbox, Mags?" she teased.

Maggie laughed. "Yes, Ons. I'm done."

"Good. Because my head is starting to hurt from thinking too goddamn much."

"What you said makes sense," said Tilda, barely above a whisper. "I enjoy the Tower, Maggie. I enjoy its teachings and its comfort, but I think you're right. I should be a little more wary of its formulaic approach from now on. And as for Elmer," she rose to her feet and locked eyes with Onyx, "I will help you find our friend."

Cheers and applause erupted from the Modern Shamans. Matthew also leapt to his feet proclaiming, "Yeah. Let's find that old geezer! He may think he can get away from us, but we'll show him! We're not giving up that easily."

"Woo-hoo!" said Onyx.

"Fab!" said Kyle.

"Let's get going," said Ezzie, "it's already afternoon and I don't want to be out and about looking for his old ass after dark."

They gathered their things, thanked Maggie's mother for the lovely engagement lunch, hugged Zach goodbye, and rushed out the door. They weren't sure where they were going or how long it would take, but they weren't worried. They had faith on their sides. Not faith in the Tower or the saint of lost objects or the Andean heaven-bird, but faith in themselves and faith in their love for their friend. And that faith they could trust.

Chapter 48

Elmer hadn't eaten in five days. He nervously paced through The City, mumbling to himself, occasionally scoffing at his scruffy reflection in shop windows and the mirrors of parked cars. He tried not to judge his grungy appearance; he tried not to feel anything. But it was hard. Flecks of wounded pride and loneliness floated on the surface of his consciousness, mingled with sprinkles of doubt and a hint of misery. He brushed them away and continued to pace.

Pace and rest, rest and pace. That is how he spent his time these days. His head wasn't his own. It floated off somewhere, vaguely aware of his restless body below. He tried to tether his thoughts; attempted to pin down his meditations, but they refused to be fettered. Instead, they floated and bounced, all helium and ether.

Elmer hadn't eaten in five days. The smell of food made him nauseous, made his stomach turn. He visited soup kitchens and shelters for one reason alone: to avoid the bitter cold. He didn't visit them for their meals. When dinner was inevitably served, he averted his eyes when others ate; he couldn't stand their awful chewing, the smacking of their lips, the saliva-filled mouths. Eventually, he would stumble to his feet, exasperated, and rush out the door into the frosty world, ranting as he went. The other homeless folks watched him leave, shook their heads, muttered that it was a shame there were so many crazies amongst them lately. More and more all the time, it seemed. Must be the drugs. Must be the increase in demand and the decrease in price. Shame, real shame.

Elmer thought about the shelters as he walked. Why couldn't the tenants just leave him alone? Why must they hassle him and start meaningless conversations and break his fragile concentration? Couldn't they see he was busy? Couldn't they see he was nearing Enlightenment? That he had only one floor to go? That he was steps away from the ultimate goal?

No, they don't understand me. Why should they? They are nowhere near the indigo level. Nowhere near the burnt orange level, probably. They are poor pathetic souls and I would feel sorry for them if that would get me anywhere. Instead, I must concentrate. I must forget them and remember my purpose. I must plow ahead. I must fast. I must reject all physical pleasures and yearnings and tethers. Enlightenment. I can almost taste it.

Elmer walked; Elmer thought. His mind bobbled around his body and his thoughts bobbled with it. The woman in indigo—Teacher—had told him he would know when he was ready for Nirvana, that he would know when he stood on the precipice of Enlightenment. "Like a mother about to give birth," she had said, "you'll know."

Well, he didn't know. He wasn't sure of his body, his thoughts, his impulses, let alone the moment of Awakening. He walked through the streets lost, troubled, beating away nagging emotions. He was pregnant with doubt.

I only have to trust. Elmer repeated the phrase over and over in his mind. *I only have to trust. Teacher knows best. She knows. I only have to trust.* He turned down an alleyway and stepped over some rusty tin cans and a small pile of puke.

I only have to trust. I only have to trust. Teacher's advice has never failed. She has led me this far, hasn't she? Didn't she instruct me to confront my demons? Didn't I make peace with the past because of her? I have learned so many things from her guidance. I have learned to let go of useless emotional baggage. I have learned to be free of the ghosts of my past, to rid myself of their burden. I have learned to step forward and onward and upward; I have learned to reach towards Enlightenment. I only have to trust. I only have to trust. I only have to trust. I only have to trust.

Elmer reached the end of the alley and turned right. Instantly, his feet hit ice, he lost his balance, and he fell face-forward into a bank of hard, icy snow. His body was fatigued and waif-like. He could hardly move his arms underneath his body in order to pick himself up. He stood and touched his forehead gingerly. A smear of blood stained his fingers as he drew them away. He needed to get inside; he needed to find some shelter. His fingers were frozen and numb. He could barely feel his toes. He needed to rest.

He glanced around him. Directly above him, a sign sprouted out of the air. A bright, comforting sign. He sighed and stepped inside. Warm air rushed around him; the smell of fresh bread and soup stung his nostrils and he did his best to calm his heaving gut. The round and robust shape of Napoleon greeted him with a wink and a smile and said in an equally round and robust voice "Ha-llo, Mr. Elmer. I 'aven't seen you in Karmedic Relief in a long, long time, my friend! One 'ot chicken dumpling soup coming right up!"

"Not today, Napoleon," Elmer muttered. "Not hungry. I just need to rest."

"Elmer, pardon the phrase, but you look like a dog's shit, my friend."

"I suppose I do," he wiped the fresh blood off his forehead and looked down at his shoes, embarrassed. "Look, Napoleon," he said, still staring at his feet, "just make me a green tea, will you? Thank you, sir. That would be great."

Elmer took his tea and sat down in a booth at the far end of the restaurant. There were few patrons today. Most people bunked down in their homes, bundled up and thankful they weren't outside in the biting air of Winter. Elmer sighed as the warm liquid made its way down his esophagus and into his starving belly. The tea felt marvelous and somehow made his head and body feel more like a single entity. His mind relaxed; his shoulders slouched. He leaned forward. His head seemed to be expanding with its new-found warmth. Slowly, Elmer let himself sink towards the tabletop, down, down, until his forehead rested flatly against its smooth, wooden finish. In an instant, he was asleep, snoring contently to himself, lost in a flurry of dreams.

* * *

At first, Elmer was walking. He walked in a blank world with only a bright, golden path that unfurled at his feet with every step he took. His gait was as easy as his breath and he hummed to himself as he strolled. "Hum-dee-dum," Elmer said. "Humm, humm." He walked smoothly along the path, cane-free, light as a feather, barely touching the golden path. Suddenly, his muscles tensed. He heard something.

A low buzz sounded in his ears, vibrating along his body. He paused and listened. From somewhere straight ahead the noise emanated from the pitch black. The buzzing grew louder, more pronounced. It sounded like a swarm of bees closing in on his face. He ducked, braced himself for the impact.

Swoosh!

Something flew past his face.

Swish-swoosh!

Two more things.

Swish-swoosh! Zoom, buzz! Sssss!

Elmer held up his hands against the onslaught of things that raced past his body. It took him several seconds to realize that the flying objects were colors. Great streaks of colors. They moved past him with lighting speed, as easily as a river past a pebble. Soon, the colors overtook the blackness of Elmer's dream world and he found himself overwhelmed by hues of amber and indigo, pale peach and tangerine, red and chartreuse, eggplant and lavender, forest green and pink. The colors swirled; they mixed and danced like the fat snowflakes that fell on The City. He squinted against their bombardment, attempting to make sense of the different shades and shapes that pummeled his consciousness. He stood, perplexed and overwhelmed amongst the violent colors as they breezed by his sides, whisked past his ears. Eventually, he had enough.

Dream-Elmer shut his eyes, breathed in, breathed out, felt the rush of colors subside to a quiet trickle, felt his body become less defensive and more relaxed. When he finally dared to open his eyes, he found that the colors had compacted. They had molded together, wrapped around each other, blended. They had melted into seven colors, each one rising before him like pillars of light, shooting upwards and shimmering in a manner reminiscent of aurora borealis. Elmer stood in awe as he watched the colors flicker, watched them pulsate within their column, itching to burst forth once again and stream past his face. But the colors did not burst. Instead, they calmed and smoothed themselves into the shapes of seven familiar robed figures.

"The seven," Elmer whispered. "You're here. I—," he swallowed, ashamed of his sudden wash of emotions, "I haven't seen you in a long time. It was before The City I believe."

The man in blue stepped forward. "Yes and no, Elmer," he said, his deep voice like plum-colored velvet. "We haven't interacted, but we've always been here. You haven't acknowledged us, but we've acknowledged you."

Elmer's cheeks flushed. "Sorry," he said bashfully. He felt like a small child again, taking a scolding from Miss Anne. "It's just that—I mean—I've been...busy."

"Yes, we know," said the man in blue. "We've seen."

"Oh." Elmer shifted nervously from one foot to the other. "It's nothing personal, it's just that I'm trying to obtain Enlightenment—"

"And we're getting in the way," the moon-faced woman finished, stepping forward, her violet robes swishing around her as she moved. "Isn't that right, Elmer?"

Elmer lowered his eyes, chewed on his lip. "I don't know. That is, I suppose you're right. But, at first I was just busy—finding Maggie and all. Then, I was so focused on my tasks—emptying my emotions, making peace with the past, and so on. Then, I told Teacher about all of you and—well—yes, I guess I was told to forget about you." He continued looking at the ground. "I don't like saying this—believe me, I don't—but this is the way of things. I have to focus on Enlightenment. I have to ask you to leave."

"Elmer," the woman in violet said, her voice more kind and understanding than Elmer had ever heard it. He melted a little under that voice. "We are your spirit guides. We are your guardians. We're not leaving without a fight."

"My guardians..." Elmer repeated to himself. "My guardians; my spirit guides. I thought so. That's what the Modern Shamans told me all along. And that's what I felt in my gut. But I've never heard you admit it. I've never heard *you* articulate your role until now."

"That is because it wasn't necessary until now," a new voice spoke up. Elmer locked eyes with the startling yellow pupils of the part-bird/part-man guardian. Elmer stared into the piercing eyes as the creature continued, "We have never been in greater need of your trust. You are on the precipice, human. A choice is to be made soon and we are doing everything in our collective power to ensure you make the right one."

"How do you know what is right for me?" Elmer said indignantly. "You've been holding me back, keeping me from success. That's what Teacher told me. She said you are false prophets who take pleasure in mocking the teachings of Tower I. She said you have been leading me astray with your talk of joy and your silly dancing. Because of you, I rediscovered joy, re-embraced useless emotions. They were dead inside me. For years and years, I didn't feel a glimmer of joy or disappointment or elation. I just existed." He paused for a breath; his stomach and chest heaved. "Yes, I was discontent with my life in Here. Yes, I needed to escape. But I didn't need to jump from one extreme to another. I didn't have to start frolicking and acting like a fool. I didn't have to associate myself with emotion-laden friends like the Modern Shamans (you led me to them, you know). No good came of it. No progress. It set me back. I might have already achieved Enlightenment by now if it wasn't for your misguidance. That's what Teacher says and that's what I believe now and there's nothing you can say that will change my mind. Nothing."

Elmer's speech ended with a long and cavernous silence, during which he crossed his arms and glared at nothing in particular. The beginnings of tears glimmered in his eyes and he blinked them away, irritated.

"Oh Elmer, Elmer," the moon-faced woman spoke again. "What has it done to you? What have you become?"

"I don't know what you're talking about," Elmer retorted, his voice still angry, but cracking slightly under its tough exterior.

"The Tower," the woman answered. "What has it done to you?"

"I think The Tower is quite nice," Elmer replied. "It has helped me in my journey. It has given me some direction in life, shown me a goal, pointed me down the right path."

"The Tower isn't all bad," she replied, her voice still kind, still empathetic. "Much like Abe's Soup Kitchen isn't all bad."

"Don't be absurd," Elmer scowled.

"Listen to me for a minute, Elmer," the woman commanded, a stern edge creeping into her tone. "Listen. Tower I is a fixture in your journey. It is a religious institution. It is built upon beliefs and sustained by beliefs. It is an opinion. You have been presented with an array of fixtures during your journey and you have reacted strongly to each of them. You have not reacted the same way twice."

"I don't quite understand—"

"Just listen, Elmer. Please listen." The woman cleared her throat, straightened her shoulders, continued. "Your journey may seem muddled, but if you ponder it for a moment, it is as clear as glass. You have experienced three religions. First, the House of the Modern Shamans. Second, the Dueling Soup Kitchens. Third, Tower I. You enjoyed the House of the Modern Shamans, but never quite met its level of mysticism. You loved the people you met, but you felt like a bit of an outsider, like there was something else out there for you and you were right. There was. Two somethings."

Elmer gazed at the violet-robed woman as she spoke. Her words wove around him like an intricate tapestry.

"When you arrived in City B, when you encountered your second set of religious institutions, you were repulsed by them. You loathed the Dueling Kitchens because they reminded you too much of Here. They embodied the monotheistic rigidity that you had come to despise. You sensed the false intentions, the leaders' thirst for control. You heard the hypocrisy in the Bookkeepers' voices as they preached both boundless love and bitter rivalry. You reacted with fear, anger, and rebellion. And then," she cleared her throat a second time, "you moved on to City C."

"And here you are, Elmer. The third religious experience. You have embraced the teachings of Tower I and practice them with maniacal devotion. You believe you've stumbled upon the answer. You believe that after floating around agnostically in Here, journeying through Cities A through C, you have finally arrived. This is the conclusion, is it not? This is why you began your journey. You were seeking an answer and you've found it, haven't you? You've found the purpose of life. It resides within yourself, doesn't it? The great 'I.' Isn't Tower I just another way of saying Tower Me? Think Elmer. Have you really hit the correct answer? Does your journey really end here? Are you ready to quit?"

Elmer didn't respond, but looked thoughtful and a little scared as he gazed towards the woman in violet. Uncertainty gnawed at his mind as he reflected on what she had said. Finally, he spoke, carefully and quietly. "I don't know," he said. "I don't know if I've hit the correct answer. I hope I have. But in reality, I don't know. I don't even know if there is an answer."

"Very good, Elmer," the blue-robed man spoke up again. "There isn't an answer. And that's what makes life so beautiful. One can never truly figure it out. What is its purpose? What is our final aim? When do we reach the end point? Elmer, there isn't an end point. There is only growing and changing and being."

Elmer shook his head, attempting to sort his conflicting thoughts, trying to clear his addled brain. He wanted to believe the robed figures in front of him; he wanted to trust in their wisdom, but Teacher had warned him against them. And Teacher had been right about a lot of things so far. He could feel his blood begin to boil; his fists clenched up tightly. "But there is a purpose!" he cried. "I mustn't lose sight of it! It's the thirty-first floor. It's Enlightenment!"

"And you think everything will end there?" the man in blue questioned. "On the thirty-first floor, all things will come to an end? Then what? What does the end look like, Elmer?"

"I don't know!" he screamed. "I've never been there! How should I know? I only have to have faith, that's all. I only have to believe and Enlightenment will be mine."

"That's a little selfish, don't you think," the woman in violet cut in, "wanting Enlightenment all for yourself."

Elmer scoffed. "Psha. Selfish? No. It most certainly isn't. It's a noble aim. Anyway," he sneered at the seven before him, "you'd all be out of a job if everyone was Enlightened. Not a lot of guiding to do if that was the case. Isn't that right?"

The seven looked at Elmer mutely. Their expressions didn't change; their eyes gazed straight ahead.

"Maybe it's you who are selfish," Elmer continued. "Maybe you don't want me to succeed because you want me to remain an imperfect being. You want someone to toy with. You don't want to lose your titles as guardians or sages. Am I right?" he said, accusingly. "Am I?"

The seven didn't speak for several seconds. Elmer could sense a heaviness about them. They seemed downtrodden, sad. Their eyes remained fixed on the small-framed man in front of them, a mix of pity and distress emanating from their looks. The woman in green—the one with the long, grey braid and ever-changing irises—brought a gnarled hand to her leathery face and wiped away four, fat tears.

"It's ok," the violet guardian said to her, gliding towards the woman in green and breaking the continuity of the rainbow colors. Now, purple stood next to green, patting her back and comforting her, wiping away her tears. "It's ok," Violet repeated. "We haven't lost him yet."

Elmer watched the scene and attempted to steel his heart. He turned away, focused his thoughts. Finally, he said, "So you are afraid of losing me? As I suspected. You have been using me for your own personal gains."

"She's not crying for herself!" the violet guardian snapped, her eyes becoming much less comforting and much more dangerous. "She's crying for you. She's afraid you're going to make a grave mistake. She's afraid you're not following your heart, that you've forgotten how to be you. Please remember, Elmer. Remember how to be you!"

Elmer swallowed and looked away, muttering. A flash of guilt passed through his body. His body. He had spent the past several weeks denying the ownership of his body. "On this earth," Teacher had said, "we become slaves to our physical bodies. We often forget the bigger picture and acquiesce to the needs of our hungry shell. Give this up, Elmer. Reject your body. It is not yours, anyway. It is part of the collective, part of everyone and everything. Shed your body like a snake sheds its skin and step into the light. That is the only way to become Awake."

Elmer looked at his hands. They were weather-beaten and worn; they looked like road maps. These hands. These hands had held dusty potatoes and door knobs and the bodies of his newborn children. They had held slippery brook trout and Irene's thighs and tickets for the train. He loved his hands. He loved the way they worked, the way they held a fillet knife as it glided under the flesh of a fish. He loved how his hands carried things—useful things—from point A to point B, how they drove a car, how they held his cane, how they wiped away tears that gathered in his eyes, how they interlocked with others' hands, how they dressed him in the morning, how they undressed him in the evening, how they brought spoons and forks to his waiting mouth, how they ran themselves across his mostly bald head, how they reached towards others when he needed help…

Usually Elmer took his hands for granted, but at this moment he was grateful for their presence. They provided comfort and stability. They were something he could depend on. Elmer thought of Papa and how his life revolved around the use of his hands—whether wrapped around the stalk of a potato plant or the leather of his belt. Yes, Teacher called for him to reject his physical body. Yes, he could see the sense in that. But for the time being, all he wanted to do was admire and thank his hands. Rejecting his physical body could wait for just a while.

"Elmer."

He stirred from his trance.

"I'm begging you, Elmer," the woman in violet picked up where she left off, as if no time had passed, as if he hadn't spent a decade looking at the lines and contours of his hands, "don't forget who you are. Remember. This has been a long and arduous journey, but I think it has led you to some sort of understanding, some sort of peace. I believe that through the ebbs and flows, you have uncovered *you*. You have dug yourself out and are on the edge of something great. Don't leap the wrong way, Elmer. Don't forget your roots. Don't forget who you are."

Elmer absorbed her words and suddenly felt exhausted. "Mind if I sit down?" he mumbled as he began to slide to the ground.

"Careful there, Elm," cautioned the man in blue as Elmer attempted to seat himself. "Take it slow."

The red-robed lady rushed to his side. She smiled at him—a small, closed-lipped smile—and grabbed his arm. He felt warmth course from her fingertips and into his bloodstream, filling him with vibrancy. His heart began to swell with emotions and he made no attempt to shake them off. Slowly, the woman in red helped to lower him to the ground, where he arranged his legs in a cross-legged lotus pose, sighed, and said, "Thank you. That's much better."

"Elmer," the violet spirit guide/sage/guardian spoke to him once again. "Let me set the record straight on one thing."

"Ok," he said, looking at her questioningly, trying to sort out the stew of thoughts and emotions that were bubbling away in his conscious.

"We don't disagree entirely with your Teacher's advice. We understand the benefits of controlling one's emotions and avoiding physical temptations and pursuing a higher kind of thinking. We agree with these concepts to some degree. We do not, however, agree with the kind of all-or-nothing approach that your Teacher is promoting. We do not believe individuals can or should follow a cookie-cutter method to reach a final goal. Furthermore, we don't believe in a uniformed 'final goal.' Nirvana is fine for some people, but others would rather not get there at all. Others are perfectly happy in the physical plane."

"But the world is full of pain and suffering," Elmer retorted. "Who would want to be stuck in that forever?"

"Those who can see the good through the bad," the man in blue cut in. "Those who wish to do the best they can and act as a positive influence for others. Those are the people who reject Enlightenment and choose a physical existence. They are the ones who still believe, the ones who cling to any kernel of hope the world offers. Who are we to judge their decision? Are they less worthy than those who choose Enlightenment?"

Elmer bit his lip and wrinkled his brow. He remained silent for almost a minute as he pondered the guardians' words. Finally he said, "So you would support my decision either way? You wouldn't judge me for choosing Enlightenment over a physical existence? Or vice versa?"

"No, Elmer," said the rumble of the blue guardian's voice. "We wouldn't judge. You are free to choose either way."

"But you would clearly prefer that I remain in the physical world, isn't that right? You want to remain my guardians, don't you? After all, you actively promote emotions and friendships."

"We do," said the soft voice of the woman in violet. "We don't believe all emotions are a bad thing Elmer. They make you feel; they make you human. We understand the concept of emptiness, but we don't actively promote it."

"Because you'd be out of a job?"

"Because we find it difficult to tell an old man who hasn't experienced joy in years to stop dancing."

Elmer swallowed. He suddenly felt very small, miniscule, dwarf-like next to the seven pillars of color before him. He knew it was his turn to speak, but he couldn't. Instead, he stared at the robed figures and silently begged any of them to speak. Finally, one did.

"We have said all we need to say, Elmer," boomed the man in blue. "We will leave you now; we will leave you to make your decision."

Elmer swallowed again, nodded.

"It's up to you now, friend," the man said. "The world is at your fingertips. All you have to do is grab it." He smiled; his teeth shone through his nest of a beard.

"Good luck, Elmer," the moon-faced woman said. "We have faith in you, but that's not enough, you know. You have to have faith in yourself." With a smile and a quick wink, she folded herself into her robes, disappearing behind the fabric like a flower closing at nighttime. Startled, Elmer watched the other guardians do the same. When they were all encapsulated within their billowing robes, the violet-colored guardian shot forward, zipping past Elmer's ear and into the blackness behind him. He squeaked and hopped to the side. A streak of indigo buzzed past his right hip, nearly knocking him backwards. Then blue. Then green. Then yellow-orange-red. All the robed sages rocketed past him and disappeared into the abyss.

After red whipped past Elmer's cheek, causing him to bring his hand to his face to ensure flesh was still attached to bone, he turned around and stared after the streaks of colors. Even though he could no longer see their hues, he could still feel their presence, still sense their warm eyes watching him. He sighed. The time had come. The thirty-first floor was waiting.

Elmer stood in his dream world and felt the golden path once again rise at his feet. This time, it branched into two different directions—one to the left, one to the right. Elmer wondered for a moment how much his decision would affect others, how many people had placed bets on left and how many had placed bets on right. Then, the moment passed and he stepped forward. He decided he didn't care about what other people thought. He was choosing for himself now. He was forming his own destiny.

He stepped right.

Chapter 49

"Elmer," a voice whispered out of the blackness. "Elmer, come on now. Elmer!"

Elmer groaned and walked towards the voice. His surroundings became lighter; he could see the outlines of shapes and colors.

"Elmer, wake up now. Elmer, come on."

His eyes blinked open. Napoleon hovered over him, shaking his shoulder, smelling of broth and butter. Elmer rubbed his bleary eyes, held his throbbing forehead.

"My god, Mr. Elmer," Napoleon said. "You 'ave been out for four hours. I wanted to make sure you are ok."

"Four hours?" Elmer gawked at the man. "Incredible." He shook his head and looked at the half-finished green tea in front of him. Bits and pieces of his dream came surging back to him, flooding his brain, consuming his thoughts. He remembered his interactions with the robed guardians, remembered their words of advice. A sting of urgency nipped him in the back and he jumped forward.

"Napoleon," he said hastily, "what time is it?"

"Quarter past five, my friend. Not to worry, the soup shop is still open a while longer if you want to stay. It looks like you're in need of rest, my friend. Please relax, 'ave yourself a bowl of soup. It's on the 'ouse."

"No thank you, Napoleon. That's very generous of you, but I need to go. Now."

"What is happening Elmer, my friend? Is everything alright?"

"Yes, yes. Everything's fine. There's no time to explain though. An explanation would take all day anyway." He slid out of the booth and turned to go. He paused. "Thank you, Napoleon," he said.

"For what? I didn't do a thing, my friend."

"But you did," Elmer replied. "You gave me refuge while a storm was passing through my head."

"A storm? What kind of a storm?"

"A color storm," said Elmer, rushing out the door and into the frosty evening.

Napoleon stared after him, shook his head, got out the dish rag tucked behind his belt, and began wiping tables with slow, thoughtful strokes.

* * *

The City hummed like a lethargic furnace under Winter's chill. It kept going, it kept spinning and whirring, but at a slower tempo, a lazier beat. It watched its citizens with disinterest as they hustled from storefront to storefront, from work to home, from restaurant to movie theater. Always hustling now. Never stopping to enjoy the air on their faces. Always rushing away from ice and wind and cold.

The City watched the brave few take to the sidewalks and defy the cold. It watched them keep their chins down and their feet quick. It watched their eyes tear up from the wind, watched tiny icicles form on their lashes. It watched as an old man appeared amongst them, leaving the warmth of a soup kitchen and heading west. It was still early, but the sun was already sinking heavily in the sky, like an overripe fruit preparing to fall. The man looked at the sun, zipped up his coat, lowered his head, and walked. He didn't walk as quickly as most of the citizens of The City, but his pace was steady, his footsteps were sure, and it didn't take long for him to reach his destination—a modest tower in an area known for its towers, a tiny tower amongst behemoths.

The man turned and faced the tower, letting his shadow fall long and lanky by his side. He breathed in, breathed out, marched towards the doors and pushed them open. The City watched him with an air of indifference, shrugged, and resumed its lethargic whirring. There were more old men and more towers and more wintry evenings ahead and there was no use dwelling on this one.

* * *

Elmer breathed a sigh of relief as the heavy doors of Tower I heaved open under his push. He wasn't sure how late the tower stayed open and he didn't want to miss his opportunity. This was his window. There was no other time but now.

As he rushed inside, the warm air and the tangy scent of citrus met him head on. He felt his skin thaw, watched the snow on his shoes melt and leave footprint-shaped puddles behind him. He walked up to the dark, wooden desk. Peggi was leaning back in her office chair, her head lolling to one side, snoring peacefully.

"Peggi," Elmer whispered. "Peggi!"

"Hrm? Huh?" Peggi answered, coming to. "Wha? Elmer? What are you doing here?"

"I came to visit the thirty-first floor. Can you take me there?"

"The thirty-first floor? Well I suppose, but that floor is by appointment only. I'd have to check the book and—" she ran her finger down the rows of her planner. "That's odd," Peggi said, looking at Elmer through puzzled eyes, "it says 'thirty-first floor expecting guest, 5:37 p.m.' Well, that must be you, Elmer. It is 5:35 p.m. at the moment. Ok, come along."

"Thank you," Elmer said and followed the poof of hair—slightly squished in the back from resting against her chair—to the elevator. She slid her card, pushed the button, and the elevator door dinged as it opened.

"Are you usually here this late?" Elmer asked as they stepped inside. "Only on Wednesdays," she replied. "Wednesdays are my late days. You're lucky you chose to visit today."

"I'm not sure if I believe in luck anymore," said Elmer quietly to himself.

They rode the elevator to the top of the Tower, the box stopped, the doors slid open, and they stood staring into a small, white room. Peggi suddenly reached out and snatched Elmer's hand. "Elmer," she whispered, "good luck in there. Not many people make it this far, you know. I'm not even allowed to go into the room."

"You're not?"

"Oh, no. I wouldn't dare. Anyhow, good luck to you, Elmer. It's been a pleasure getting to know you, a real pleasure."

"Thanks Peggi," said Elmer, unsure of how to feel or what to say. "The pleasure was all mine."

She gave Elmer a small, sad smile, squeezed his hand, and ushered him out the door. "Through there, Elmer," she pointed to another door in front of them. "Again, best of luck."

Elmer stepped out of the elevator and turned around. He watched Peggi's face disappear behind the steel doors, heard the gears grind as the box descended Tower I. He shuddered and turned towards the plain, white door. There was only one thing to do.

He walked across the room in three strides and reached for the door knob. A cacophony of whispers and hisses flowed into his ears. He jumped back, startled. The whispers stopped. Cautiously, he reached for the door knob a second time. As his skin brushed the handle, the humming voices once again jumped into his ears. He shut his eyes and grabbed a hold of the knob. The jabber crescendoed until all he could hear was a loud, muddled roar. Elmer closed his lids tighter, clamped down on the handle, turned it, slammed it open.

The voices ceased. For a moment, the room around him echoed with their memories, but then fell deathly silent. Elmer opened his eyes.

His corneas were struck so violently with the brightness of the room, that he stumbled backwards against the wall and stood, panting, against it, eyes tightly shut. Eventually, he opened his lids once more, this time slowly, and braced himself for a second assault against his senses. The second blow wasn't nearly as bad as the first, but he still struggled to keep his eyes open, blinking against the bright, white light, finding no refuge in the equally bright walls. He thought that this is what living inside a glacier must feel like.

He squinted and began to make sense of his surroundings. He was in a large, blank room with no furniture, no pictures, no life to speak of. He reached his hand towards the nearest wall and trailed his fingers along it as he walked. The wall was smooth and silk-like under his touch. He thought of water and clouds and Daisy's skin. It took him four minutes to walk to the other end of the room. When he got there, he turned the corner, squinted ahead, saw more white nothingness. He paused. "Hey!" he called. "Hey-yy-yyy!" the room echoed back. "Hey, hello! Anyone in here? Anyone at all? I'm here to obtain Enlightenment. Hi!"

Elmer wondered for a moment if this *was* Enlightenment—pure white walls, blank and silky. No one, nothing to distract him. "Kind of underwhelming," he thought. "I thought there would at least be some nice oak trees or a river or something." He stepped forward again.

A voice sailed above him and blanketed the room with its tenor pitch. Elmer jumped. "In Enlightenment, human, you won't need rivers or trees. You'll be filled with a feeling so profound, so blissful, that everything else will pale in comparison. That feeling is enough. That feeling has the power to sustain you forever."

Elmer swallowed. His throat felt dry and sandpaper-scratchy. The hand gripping his cane was shaking and he leaned against the wall to steady himself. He looked around, seeking the source of the high, airy voice, but saw nobody. "I see," he said in a small voice. "And can I ask, who are you sir? And where are you? Maybe it's the light, but I see no one else in the room."

"You can control the level of brightness, you know," the voice answered. "This is your reality, human."

"I see," said Elmer once again. "In that case, I'd like the light much softer then." As if his words triggered a dimmer switch, the intensity of the white room dropped several notches and Elmer could see without having to blink and squint. He sighed. "Oh thank you, much better."

"Don't thank me," said the voice. "Thank yourself. This is the thirty-first floor, after all. You didn't get here through my designs; you got here through hard work, dedication, and focus."

"And who are you?" Elmer insisted. "I don't mean to pry—"

"No, no. Quite alright. I should have introduced myself right away. I am white light, human. I am the source of life and growth. I am both the culmination of every color and the lack thereof. I am what remains. I am what is left when everything else falls away."

"You are what remains?"

"Yes, human. When you peel away layer after layer of material human existence, you are left with only one thing: inner light. And that is where you stand today, student, on the razor's edge of existence, on the cusp between humanity and divinity. Are you ready to leap? Are you ready to be Awake?"

Elmer felt his mind spin, felt his body become limp like a rag. He continued to lean against the wall. "And after I leap," he said, "then what? What's next for me?"

"Student," the voice scoffed, "after you leap you will not be concerned with this ridiculous 'I' and 'me.' You will not be concerned with time or space or entertainment. You will simply be. Your inner white light will become part of a great halo of white light and you will exist above consciousness, above human physicality. It is a state of pure ecstasy, of infinite orgasm, of delicious escape from your painful, earthly chains. Are you not excited for this release, human? Are you not excited for your union with the halo of light?"

Elmer gripped his cane with a slippery hand. A small trickle of sweat ran down his left temple and he wiped it away with an equally wet palm. "Yes," he said, "I am excited."

"Good," said the voice, thin and shrill. "Because you must surrender yourself fully to the light when you make the leap. You must desire to be a part of it with every fiber of your being. Otherwise, it will reject you. It will eat you up and spit you out, shred you like light passing through a prism. And that," said the voice, "is something you do not want to happen."

Elmer gulped. "I suppose not," he whispered.

"Certainly not," said the voice. "No one wants pieces of their soul flung across the universe. It is nearly impossible to gather them up and stitch them back together again. Nearly impossible."

The voice let its words ring through the air as Elmer cowered under them. *Am I ready? Is this really what I want? To be part of a great halo of white light?*

"Now is the time," the voice continued, "to decide. Now is the time," it crescendoed sharply, "to put your earthly ties behind you. Now is the time TO LEAP!"

The words pierced the air, cutting into Elmer's ears like a steel blade. They echoed throughout the room, reverberating off the walls like bullets. Elmer hugged his body closely. Eventually, the ringing words concentrated themselves in the middle of the room and began boring down, down, down, with tornadic force. A hole opened in the floor. It reached out wider and wider, growing until it spread itself throughout the entire space, leaving a two-foot wide ledge running around the room. Elmer teetered on the edge, hugging the wall above the gaping space.

"Look, human!" the voice shrieked. "Look into your destiny!"

Elmer gulped and stuck his neck out cautiously, peering over the edge. A gust of wind blasted his face and threaded itself into his ears, his nostrils, his open mouth. It tasted bitter and slightly metallic. Below him, the immense pit looked up at him menacingly. Menacingly and colorfully. It was painted with every color of the rainbow and morphed from icy blues at the top into flaming reds at the bottom. In between, stretched greens-yellows-oranges. Elmer peered down the hole and counted the bands of colors. "Twenty-eight, twenty-nine, thirty…" He stepped back. "My god," he said, "You've split open the Tower."

"After Enlightenment," said the voice, "the Tower will not matter. The 'I' will not matter. They will be left behind like a discarded cocoon. Are you ready, human? The indigo teacher says you are. She says you have steeled your concentration, rejected emotions, embraced solitude, avoided the poisons of the physical world. She says you have made peace with your past so that you may live in the present. She says all of these things, but what do you say, human? Does she have it right? Are you ready to leap? Are you ready to be Awake?"

Elmer stared at the massive tunnel that lay inches before his feet. He thought of Matthew and Tilda and Maggie and their struggles to climb through the colors, to reach the pinnacle. Would they really want to reach the top if they knew what came next? Would they take the leap?

"It is the time, human," the voice spoke again. "Time to gather your faith and take the plunge. Time to exist in a state of superconsciousness and awareness, part of the Enlightened collective."

Elmer closed his eyes. His thoughts zipped down the tunnel, plunging like a boulder down the thirty-one floors, and out the door into the streets of The City. From there, it dodged traffic and pedestrians, zig-zagging down alleyways and along causeways, racing to City B. In City B, it dashed past the kitchens, past the maniacal grins of the Bookkeepers, past Freddie Keys' Bible Lot, and down the highway out of town. Pow! He was in City A, flying past beige houses and playgrounds, past rain and mud, past a wooden house crying out in agony as it burned to the ground. And There. Past hookers and street bums, past stale-smelling hotel rooms, past the train station. Bam! The roads widen, the people thin out, fields rise up in place of buildings, and he's Here. Elmer's mind screeched to a halt and looked around.

He was on the outskirts of Here, in farm country. The air was still and not a ripple of sound disturbed it. A hill rose at his bare feet and he climbed it, his legs powerful and young, his lungs pumping fresh air in and out. At the crest of the hill, a forest sprang before him and in front of that forest, rushing quickly and clearly, was a river. Elmer yelped and ran towards it, grinning wildly as he went. His clothes melted away, his arms shot forward, and with one mighty leap he dove into the chilly water. He swam back and forth for a few seconds, appreciating the elasticity of his muscles and joints. He heard a sound from the shoreline and stopped swimming mid-stroke. He looked towards the riverbank. A head popped out from behind the bushes and gave him a sly wink.

"Wha? Daisy? Is that really you?"

"Guilty," she said, picking her way towards the edge of the river.

"Come on in, Daisy!" Elmer called. "The water's wonderful."

In one movement, Daisy shucked off her dress, flung it aside, and dove into the water beside him. He reached towards her, wrapped her body in his arms, and said, "Good to see you old friend. Really good to see you."

"Is it good to see us too?" a voice called from the riverbank.

Elmer's eyes darted towards shore and towards the speaker. They were greeted with the sight of dark, bobbed hair and an impish grin. "Onyx!" Elmer cried. "You're here too? Hello, hello! Come in if you want. It feels great."

"I hoped you would ask," she said, still grinning. "But unlike you jaybirds, I came prepared." She tossed her clothes aside to reveal a black and white striped bathing suit. "I think the rest of them came prepared too," she said, leaping into the river.

"The rest of them?" Elmer said.

"Yes, the rest of us," a gruff voice replied. Ezzie stepped to the edge of the water, followed by Craig, Kyle, Roger, Cecelia, Maggie, and little Zach. "Thought you could get rid of us, didn't you Elmer? Thought you could run off to The City and leap from some tower and forget about life on this messed up little planet, didn't you?"

"I never wanted to get rid of you," Elmer protested. "I just needed to find my way; I needed to figure some things out."

"And have you figured them out?" asked Ezzie, wading into the water.

Elmer didn't answer. Water rushed up to his naked body, passed by it, and continued its journey downstream. Elmer wished his thoughts flowed as easily and as clearly as that water. He took a deep breath, ducked his head underwater, and listened to the humming in his submerged ears as he attempted to sort his thoughts. When he broke through the surface of the water, more faces and bodies had joined the already large gathering at the river. Matthew and Tilda were talking animatedly to Zach, Grace, and Martha as little Levi watched the other Levi cast a fishing line into the river, downstream of the crowd. Next to them, Irene sat on the shoreline with their children, serenely watching the water. She waved when Elmer looked her way. He waved back. From behind the crowd on the shoreline, Elmer spotted a pair of bodies moving slowly towards him. They worked their way through the gathering of people and to the water's edge.

"Hello, Old Turtle," said Hilo quietly. "It's good to see you again."

"Hilo!" Elmer swam towards the riverbank, hardly believing his eyes. "My sweet, sweet girl. You're here too? This is the best day of my life."

Hilo smiled.

"And Papa," Elmer said, turning towards his father, "it's good to see you too." He extended a hand. "Truly good to see you."

"Good to see you too, son."

"I don't know what to make of this," said Elmer, "but it is positively wonderful." He grinned and gazed down the river at the gathering of his friends and family. He had rarely seen anything quite as beautiful as the scene around him. As he was soaking it all in, a glimmer downstream caught his eye. He swam towards it, skirting around his friends and moving towards a slight bend in the river. When he reached the bend, the glimmer grew stronger and he discovered a rainbow of colors skirting across the water's surface. Cherry reds chased after sunshine yellows and greens danced with blues. The colors ducked and dodged each other, as if playing tag. Elmer could feel the joy emanating from them. They made him want to dance.

"Hello again, guardians" said Elmer to the colors. "It's good to see you too."

The colors shimmered in reply.

"Elmer!" a voice called from upstream. "Elmer, it's time!"

"What?" he replied, turning around, seeking the source of the voice. "Time for what?"

"Elmer!" the voice cried once again. "Elmer, it's time! Elmer!"

Elmer's eyes snapped open and he discovered himself once again in the white room, the gaping pit in front of him, his feet inches from the ledge. The shrill voice called to him. "Elmer!" it howled. "The time is now. Face the pit, human, and jump! Go! Do! The time is now. The time is now!"

Elmer braced himself against the wall, reflecting upon his vision. His thoughts twisted and turned in all directions. He had no idea they were so acrobatic. Elmer once again leaned forward, looked down the wide-mouthed hole, and said quietly, "No."

The wind from the tunnel stilled; the voice stopped shrieking. An eerie silence cloaked the white room. Elmer quivered as he clung to the wall. Finally, the voice spoke in a high, menacing whisper.

"What do you mean, *no*?" it hissed.

Elmer held his chin up high, stared into the white air defiantly. "I mean just that. No. No, I don't want to jump. No, I don't want to obtain Enlightenment. N-O. No."

"Aaaaaaaaaaaaaarrrrrrrrrggg!" the voice screamed. The walls shook with its vibration. Elmer squashed his body against the wall and began edging his way backwards. "No one says no to Enlightenment!" the voice cried. "No one!"

"That's not true," Elmer said, willing every fiber in his body to stay steady as he skirted around the corner of the room and started edging towards the door. "I am saying no."

"You're crazy!" the voice accused, whipping around his thin shoulders and between his ankles. "This is the ultimate goal, the ultimate desire. This is what humans work towards; this is the whole point of bettering oneself—to achieve Enlightenment."

"I disagree." Elmer's voice was stronger now. He spoke loudly at the voice as his feet shuffled along the precarious ledge. "Everyone is different. Everyone follows a different path. What's right for one person may not be right for another. Who are you to say? Who are you to dictate others' destinies? Maybe some people want to spend the rest of eternity caught up in some magical ring of white light, but not me. I'd rather live on earth in the confusing, frustrating, tragic, beautiful, imperfect physical plane. I'd rather be amongst flawed human beings with problems to fix. I'd rather be helping those human beings than floating above them. That's my ultimate goal. That's my ultimate desire. Not some abstract existence in the ether, but a gritty, sometimes painful, sometimes wonderful existence on earth. So keep your orgasmic white-light halo—I choose the world. I choose the dirt and the trees and the water. I choose tragic loves and beautiful friendships. That's my choice. I will not leap."

The voice rose up again, this time screaming like a train whistle—shrill and eardrum-shattering. Elmer staggered on the ledge for a moment, his balance thrown by the awful, demonic noise. He leaned backwards with all the force he could muster and fell against the wall. "Stupid human!" the voice screeched. "Do you know what you're doing? You are rejecting the ultimate release! You are turning your back on progress. People would *kill* to be in your shoes at this moment. They would *kill* to have this opportunity."

"They can have it!" Elmer shouted back, sliding along the wall quickly now, willing his feet towards the small, white door.

"Insubordinate lout!" the voice continued to scream. "This is *the* ultimate goal and you are rejecting it. Don't you realize, there is only one way in life—the way of the Tower, the progression towards Nirvana!"

"There is NOT one way!" Elmer cried. "You're all the same, aren't you? High and mighty, touting your superior beliefs. You're just like the dueling soup kitchens, you know that? So sure yours is the only way. You're just like the town of Here—formulaic, precise, certain there is only one way to do things. Well, I reject that notion!" Elmer shook his fist at the white walls. "I reject the idea that my path—or anybody else's—is as straight as an elevator shaft. It's not, damn it! It's windy and crooked and full of hills and ruts and mud. It's twisty and rocky and…you know something? It never ends! It keeps going and going and there is no end point. I'll be on my path forever and I don't mind one bit."

"You will LEAP!" the voice howled, blowing against Elmer's right arm and causing him to topple sideways. His foot dangled over the edge of the thirty-story hole, his face once again felt the sting of wind from the tunnel. He scooted back, desperately hugging his body against the wall.

"I will not leap," he said as he crawled towards the door. He looked straight ahead; the door stood facing him, silent and stoic. He had only to reach the end of the wall, turn the corner, slide another eight feet along the wall, and he would reach it. He balled up his fists and glared at his destination. The door gazed mildly back.

"You will leap! You will LEAP!" the voice insisted, tugging at his ankles, dragging him towards the pit.

Elmer felt his arm wrench sideways—the arm that was clutching his cane. He watched as the voice forced the cane outwards, perpendicular to his body, hovering over the hole in the floor. His body started to inch towards the edge.

"NO!" Elmer shouted and released the cane's handle. He watched it leap from his hand and spiral down, down the tunnel beneath him. Wind whipped around Elmer's body and he could feel himself sliding towards the edge of the cliff, felt himself hanging in the moment before freefall. Elmer shut his eyes.

The river darted into his mind and peace enveloped him. He swam lazily, treading against the current, watching his friends downriver, splashing and laughing. A breeze played softly across his face. He smiled and started swimming faster. The water was cool and clear; it felt like heaven. He brought his arms alternately over his head and stroke-stroke-stroked against the current. He felt his body propel, felt the water pass beneath him. His legs were strong and supple; they had no use for a cane. As Elmer swam, he became aware of another presence and glanced, startled, over his shoulder. On either side of him, an array of colors skipped and leaped through the water, like a school of rainbow trout. He smiled wider, swam faster, felt strengthened by the colors flanking his sides. He reached up.

Elmer opened his eyes and saw the door handle above him, jutting obscenely into the white room. The voice seemed distant now, like a muted trumpet, crying "Leap! Leap! Leap! Leap! Leap!" Elmer stretched his arm, reached the handle, and grasped it. He thought of his muscular legs, cutting through the water, forcing his body against its flow. He stood.

Wind tugged at his arms, his legs, his torso, ripped at his clothes. It snaked behind him, grabbed hold of his waist, yanked him towards the edge. He resisted, planting his feet firmly on the floor. His legs felt strong and powerful; he knew the multi-colored guardians were at his side. Before he turned towards the door, before he twisted its handle, he stood and faced the white room defiantly, head tall, eyes steady. He breathed in and shouted out, "It's *my* path, damn it! MY PATH!"

Elmer twisted the handle and hurled his weight at the door. It flew open and he felt his body propelled forward into the waiting arms of the Modern Shamans.

Chapter 50

The day was cold; The City was bored. It watched the people scurry like spiders to a kill. They didn't enjoy their journeys that day; they were only concerned about their destinations. They were only concerned about the comfort of their homes, the thawing of their skin. One group emerged from a shabby apartment building, turned down the street, scattered in different directions, calling out someone's name. There were eight or nine of them, running like madmen, desperately combing alleys and restaurants, poking their heads into hotels and soup kitchens, checking every public area they could think of—parks, libraries, restrooms, museums—for some sign of some person.

The City watched them with vague amusement. It wondered who they were seeking and whether or not he or she was alive or dead. The eight or nine individuals kept up their frantic searching for several hours. Finally, they converged in front of a restaurant, a soup and sandwich shop. They huddled together, waving their arms animatedly, pointing and shouting. After a few minutes, the huddle disbanded and they took off running westward.

The City followed their bobbing heads as they made their way towards a modest tower in an area known for its towers, a tiny tower amongst behemoths.

* * *

It was Roger who caught the full brunt of Elmer's force. He barely had time to think as the old man's body rocketed out the white door and into his arms, nearly knocking him to the floor. The rest of the group stood behind Roger, bracing themselves, acting as a large, soft basket to catch the men hurling towards them. Both Roger and Elmer landed against the outstretched arms with a flat *whump*. The white door slammed behind him and melted into the wall, leaving smooth white plaster, without so much as a crease.

The Modern Shamans, Tilda, and Matthew watched the door melt into the wall, shook the vision from their heads, and turned their attention to their friend. Elmer lay, gasping and wheezing on the floor, looking up at the friendly faces surrounding him.

"It's—it's—you," he gasped. "What on earth are you doing here? Am I—asleep? Or…dead? How—how is this possible?"

"Shh, Old Turtle. Just relax," said Onyx, cradling his head. "We came to The City for Maggie's engagement party. She told us you were in trouble. We've been looking for you for the better part of the afternoon."

"Ma—Maggie," he stammered, still catching his breath. "You knew? You knew I was in trouble?"

"I had a feeling," she replied quietly.

"Oh my friends, my friends," Elmer muttered. "Maggie engaged. Congratu…lations…" His body went limp for a moment, his eyes closed.

"No!" cried Ezzie, leaping upon Elmer's body. She grabbed him by the shoulders and shook roughly. "Elmer, hang in there! Let's get you out of here."

Elmer's eyes opened lazily. "Hrm?" he said. "Oh yes. Let us go, please. I'm feeling weak. Quite weak, in fact. Yes…" his voice trailed off.

"Good goddess!" shrieked Onyx. "Let's get him the fuck out of here. Come on, let's go! I've got his shoulders if someone else can get his legs. Thanks, Kyle. Ok, let's walk to the elevator. Come on people! Move, move, move!"

They shuffled to the elevator, Kyle supporting Elmer's legs, Cecelia helping with his torso, Onyx at his shoulders. Elmer's eyelids fluttered. He murmured semi-coherently about colors, violet-indigo-blue-green-yellow-orange-red, going down, down, down. "I won't leap," he said. "Won't leap, your way, not mine, not my path, not my white light, won't do it, won't leap."

"What on earth is he rambling about?" said Ezzie. "What went on in there?" She turned to Roger. "Hey, do you still have the elevator key that you wrestled off that funny-looking receptionist? Good. Slide it please. Elmer needs to get the hell out of here."

Roger slid the card and Matthew held the elevator door as the group jostled to get inside. They set Elmer gently on the floor and squished together—all nine of them—around his restless body. The elevator door glided shut, someone punched a button, and the box began to fall. It descended rapidly, pushing the group against the walls, and as quickly as it started, it stopped. The friends breathed a sigh of relief and stepped out of the box. They were greeted by a sputtering and rather miffed-looking Peggi.

"Ruffians!" she shouted accusingly. "Thieves! I'll have you know I already called the police and they are on their way as we speak. Did you think you would actually get away with breaking into the Tower and forcing your way to the thirty-first floor without an appointment? Not on my watch!"

"Peggi," Elmer said weakly, his eyes barely open. "These are my friends. They came to rescue me."

"Rescue you?" Peggi squealed incredulously. "Rescue you? From the thirty-first floor? From the place of infinite happiness and peace?"

"It's not so, Peggi," Elmer breathed. "It's horrible. It's all endless white light and floating in the cosmos. I'd rather be here on earth—here with my friends." He smiled palely at Onyx, who was still holding his shoulders. "I would rather finish my life on earth and start the next one here as well." He winked at Onyx. Her eyes filled with tears.

"Oh, Elm!" she cried. "We want you here with us too! That may sound selfish, but just think of all the lives you've affected, all the people you've helped. Hilo for sure. And me."

"Me too," said Roger quietly, his large brown eyes fixed on the old man's face.

"And me," said Ezzie, reaching out and squeezing his hand.

"And me," said Craig, said Kyle, said Cecelia. "Me too," said Matthew and Maggie and Matilda.

Elmer looked at the faces of his friends, staring at him intently. He began to laugh. "Woo-wee! You all have a flare for the dramatic, don't you? Acting like you'll never see me again or something."

They started to chuckle, tentatively at first. Then it escalated, the tension broke, and soon they were laughing loudly and clutching their sides. Onyx, Cecelia, and Kyle struggled to hold onto their friend as they laughed and laughed and laughed until their bellies hurt and their arms were sore from holding his weight.

When the laughter died down, Elmer looked at his friends and smiled. "That's better," he said. "Now, if you don't mind, I'd like to be taken to the garden."

"I'm not sure that's such a—" Peggi started. She glanced at Elmer's face, serene and stoic, the face of wisdom. "Oh fine," she muttered. "Take him to the garden. I'll call the police and tell them not to come. But I'm only giving you fifteen minutes, ok? Then I'm heading home. It's been a day, I tell you. It's been a day."

They carried their friend to the garden in the corner of the first floor. Elmer felt the strength of a half dozen arms supporting him. He closed his eyes. He imagined himself being carried by the current of a friendly stream. When he opened his eyes again, he was lying on his back on a long, wooden bench, a few feet away from the little koi pond. He rolled his head to one side and watched the plump fish swimming in idle circles, round and round, no real destination in mind.

"Friends," Elmer whispered. Nine bodies stepped towards the bench, knelt by his side, leaned over him, held his hands. "Friends," he said again. It felt good to rest; it felt good to lie down and listen to the gurgling water and feel the presence of his companions. He looked up at them again and was pleased to see that Hilo, Papa, Daisy, and Irene had joined the group. "Excellent," he said. "You're here."

"Yes, Elmer," Cecelia whispered. "We're here for you."

"Yes, yes," Elmer muttered. "And they are too."

Cecelia looked puzzled, but continued to stroke his hand saying, "Yes, Elmer. We're all here."

"Not all," said Elmer, nearly inaudibly. "But most." He looked at the koi pond, watched one fish dart away from another. His eyes wandered to the path beyond the koi pond, the short garden path, the path that wove its way around the shrubs and rocks, no beginning, no end. He exhaled. Rest would be nice. His bones were so tired. His body ached. Yes, it would be nice to rest.

"Look at that path," he said, his voice gaining strength and clarity. They looked. "No end, no beginning. Only being."

They nodded. They understood.

"That is the lesson," he said, his voice fading once again. "Be. Just be." He looked up at their faces, they blurred together like a kaleidoscope. "It's funny, isn't it?" he said, smirking. "Seventy-nine years and I've only just discovered how to fit into my skin. Maybe I'll get it right a little earlier the next time around."

Elmer turned his head once again towards the koi pond. He sighed deeply and let his tension melt away. He imagined it leaving his body, collecting in the air, and floating away like a cloud over the horizon. As his eyelids closed, he noticed how they felt like feathers, light and airy. He sighed again. Through his lashes, he noticed bits of color leaping off the pond, subtle at first, but growing in intensity. Red to violet, the colors dashed and skated, weaving a lullaby with their movement, singing him to sleep.

As he drifted away, a smile crept onto Elmer's face. He was ready to join them. He was ready to dance.

END OF PART III

-LIMBO-

"I can certainly see a resemblance," Onyx laughed. "Both bald, wrinkly, and overly-emotional."

"You should talk, Ons," said Ezzie. "You're the one who always gets her panties in a bunch when things aren't going the way lil' Onyx wants them." She grinned slyly, "Or should I say lil' *Beatrice*."

"Oh you evil woman! I will skin you alive!" She pounced on Ezzie, laughing, seizing her in a headlock.

"See! See!" Ezzie giggled. "You call Elmer overly-emotional? What about this, hmm?"

"Cut it out, you two," Cecelia called. "You're going to wake him."

"Right, right," said Onyx. "*Then* we'd witness 'overly-emotional,' alright. I've never seen anyone cry so much from being woken up from his sleep, except maybe Kyle."

"Oh shut it, Ons," Kyle laughed. "You're the queen of morning grumpiness and you know it."

"Yeah, yeah," Roger cut in. "You're all comedians, I know, but seriously guys, little Elmer is right in the middle of his afternoon nap. You know how things will go for the rest of the day if he doesn't get a full two hours of sleep—no fun for anyone, especially Cecelia and me."

"He's got a point," said Onyx, shuffling towards the crib at the end of the room. "Sleep tight, little Elm," she whispered. "Don't let the gay bug bite!"

Ezzie and Kyle chased after her as Onyx scampered, laughing, from the room. Roger shook his head, gave Cecelia's hand a little squeeze, and followed the sound of laughter out the door. Cecelia lingered behind and crept silently to the edge of the crib. She gazed down at her son. "Elmer," she whispered, smiling. "Elmer, my little Elmer." She touched him lightly, stroked his thin hair. "I love you, little man, but you need to hurry up and get big. You need to grow up so Mommy can take you swimming and fishing and tell you stories about your namesake. Promise you'll grow quickly? Alright, I'm sure you will. Sleep well, little one." Cecelia flicked off the light and left the room.

In the dark of the bedroom, little Elmer woke up. He stretched and yawned, opening his green eyes slightly. He didn't know much, but he knew he was safe Here—in this crib, in this house, in his mother's and father's arms, surrounded by caring faces and voices. Love covered him like a blanket. He knew he was safe; he knew he was home. He rolled over and fell back asleep.

Coming soon from Kate Leibfried:

Ten Thousand Lines
A dystopian novel inspired by the lyrics of Ben Cooper

Cover Design by Jacob Riggle

17287897R00286

Made in the USA
Lexington, KY
03 September 2012